PRAISE FOR

Delta Belles

"In a world of cotton-candy religiosity, where sweetness is valued over substance, Penelope Stokes is a bright beacon. Her stories touch the heart, engage the brain, and expand the spirit."

—Philip Gulley,
author of the *Harmony* series

"Sing me a song of enduring friendship, of women bound deeply to each other. Sing me a song of hope and survival, of loss and disappointment, of forgiveness and a sweet reunion. Sing me a song I will treasure. Sing me *Delta Belles*."

—Lynne Hinton,
author of *The Arms of God* and *Hope Springs*

OTHER BOOKS BY THE AUTHOR

Circle of Grace

Delta Belles

Penelope J. Stokes

BROADWAY BOOKS

New York

PUBLISHED BY BROADWAY BOOKS

A hardcover edition of this book was originally published in 2006 by Doubleday.

Published in the United States by Broadway Books, an imprint of The Doubleday Broadway Publishing Group, a division of Random House, Inc., New York.
www.broadwaybooks.com

BROADWAY BOOKS and its logo, a letter B bisected on the diagonal, are trademarks of Random House, Inc.

Book design by Lisa Sloane

Library of Congress Cataloging-in-Publication Data
Stokes, Penelope J.
Delta Belles / Penelope Stokes.
p. cm.
ISBN 978-0-7679-2125-1
1. Female friendship—Fiction. 2. Women college students—Fiction.
3. Class reunions—Fiction. 4. Widows—Fiction. 5. Lesbians—Fiction.
6. Coming out (Sexual orientation)—Fiction. I. Title.
PS3569.T6219D45 2006
813'.54—dc22
2005054761

PRINTED IN THE UNITED STATES OF AMERICA

1 3 5 7 9 10 8 6 4 2

First Paperback Edition

To the memory of Frances and Sue,
mentors who inspired me,
believed in me,
challenged me,
and tuned me to hear the singing in the stars.

Your spirit lives on
and will never be forgotten.

Music, when soft voices die,

Vibrates in the memory . . .

—PERCY BYSSHE SHELLEY, 1821

PART I

INVITATION

The sweetest word
upon the tongue
is
"Come."

Come back to where
you once belonged,
back to those who
knew you,
loved you,
believed the best of you.

Row, if your ship has sailed;
Swim, if all your bridges have been burned;
Fly, if the chasm seems too wide or deep—
But come.

ONE

Delta Alone

Decatur, Georgia
September 1994

"Rankin!"

Delta Ballou sat bolt upright in bed, shaking and sweating, the familiar sickening panic washing over her. Something had roused her—a noise. She inhaled deeply, trying to regulate her breathing, trying to shush the pounding of her heart.

Delta might not be alone in the world, but still she felt it—every day, every waking moment. Especially every night, before sleep overtook her, lying there in the dark with his side of the bed cold and untouched. She always stayed up too late these days, dragging herself reluctantly to a few hours of fitful sleep, only to awaken groggy the next morning and discover that it hadn't been a terrible nightmare, after all. That her husband really was dead. That she was, at the age of forty-seven, a widow.

She had been annoyed with Rankin the morning of his death, exasperated over some real or imagined slight—she couldn't remember now what it was. Something minor, no doubt, something utterly unimportant in the cosmic scheme of things. But at the time it had seemed sufficient cause to snub him, to refuse to kiss him properly as he went out the door.

As usual, he had not taken offense at her irritability. Instead he gave a benign laugh, kissed her cheek as she turned away, and told her he loved her. His civility only exacerbated her peevish mood, and she had railed at him for ten full minutes after he was gone.

Strange how the qualities that distinguished her husband as a minister were the very things that aggravated the hell out of her. He was so . . . *good.* Generous, understanding, compassionate in the face of anger and opposition. Gracious amid stress, poised to listen to anyone who needed him.

Delta, on the other hand, "did not bear fools gladly."

Or at all, her husband jokingly amended.

It was true. When she and Rankin had met and fallen in love, she had shared his passion for peace and justice, had taken his hand and sung "We Shall Overcome" with a soul-deep conviction that change was just beyond the horizon. But he had a serenity about him that she had never managed to achieve, a patience with human shortcomings and failures.

By all accounts, Rankin Ballou had been an extraordinary man. In both his work and his life he blended spirituality with social conscience, weathering criticism over his stands on equal rights and fair housing and a multitude of other injustices. His persuasiveness and passion made a difference in people's lives. He spoke the truth. He protected the weak. He lived by what he believed, died by it.

Died with God's name on his lips. The very thought of it infuriated her. . . .

"Delta?" Cassie's voice came to her, low and anxious, through the bedroom door. "I heard you yell. Are you all right?"

Delta looked at the clock. It was ten till seven. The sun had barely risen, and beyond the slatted blinds she could see the faint rose-hued wash of dawn.

She pushed the flame of anger down, banked it against the back wall of her chest. She held still, not breathing, hoping her sister would go away. She hadn't wanted to leave the parsonage she had occupied for almost twenty years and finally made her own. Hadn't wanted to crowd her belongings into her little sister's garage and live in this travesty of a guest room, decorated in blood red and mildew green as if designed by one of Satan's more flamboyant henchmen. But she hadn't any choice. Other people's lives went on, even if hers had stopped. Her daughter, Sugar, had gone off to college. The new pastor had arrived, moved his family in, and begun the process of trying to fill Rankin's shoes.

"It's only temporary, Delta," Cassie had said. "Until you're ready to find a place of your own." And Delta had thought, *You're damned right it's temporary.*

That had been five months ago. Five months of fitting herself into the busy lives of her younger sister and her brother-in-law, Russell, and her six-year-old niece, her namesake Deborah, whom Russ called Mouse.

"Delta, I'm coming in."

The door opened a crack, and Cassie's head appeared at an angle, as if detached from her body. She edged into the room, followed by Mouse in footed flannel pajamas and the golden retriever Grand-Nanny, two generations removed from the original

Nanny, who had belonged to Delta and Rankin when Sugar was just a baby. Mouse crawled onto the bed and snuggled up next to Delta. The dog jumped up and laid her chin across Delta's feet.

With the warm little body crowded up against her side, Delta's anguish and rage flared up again. She thought of Sugar, now eighteen and beginning a life of her own. Rankin would never experience the joy of seeing his girl become a woman, get married. He would never hold his grandchildren, would never—

He knows, a faint voice inside her whispered. *He sees.*

Delta shoved the assurance away. The promise of heaven, of another life, gave her no comfort. Time healed nothing. God's presence was an illusion. She wanted Rankin back. Here. Now.

"We're going out to breakfast, Aunt Delt," Mouse said, butting her head against Delta's shoulder. "And to the Disney Store. You come too."

Delta regarded the child, who had Russell's olive skin and brownish hair, but Cassie's narrow chin and startling blue eyes. Objectively speaking, her nickname fit her perfectly, but Delta wasn't about to admit that to Russ. "I don't know," she hedged, then tweaked Mouse's nose. "Don't you have to go to school? Doesn't your mom have to go to work?"

Mouse giggled. "It's *Saturday,* Aunt Delt."

"Ah," Delta said. "I forgot."

Cassie ran a hand through her short-cropped blonde hair, sighed, and fixed Delta with a come-on-snap-out-of-it look. "Come with us, Delta. It'll be fun. We'll do some shopping, maybe catch a matinee. You know—" She grinned at her daughter. "Girls' day out. Just the three of us."

"I don't know," Delta repeated.

"Suit yourself. It'll be an hour or so before we leave, in case you change your mind. Russell's got a golf date. There's chicken salad for lunch if you want it." She glanced at her watch and motioned to Mouse. "Let's go, honey."

Mouse gave Delta a pleading look and slid off the bed.

The door shut behind them, and Delta looked down to see her hands gripping the blanket as if daring someone to drag her out of bed and back into life.

Delta sat at the small desk in the guest room and sorted through the mail Cassie had brought to her. There wasn't much. Junk mail—ads, unsolicited catalogs, mostly.

For a moment she fingered the large bulky envelope from Publishers Clearing House. *You may have already won ten million dollars.*

Delta snorted. What could she possibly do with ten million dollars, besides pay half of it to a government she didn't trust and set up a college fund for grandchildren who hadn't yet been born? What did normal people do? Take an around-the-world cruise? Buy a gas-guzzling SUV? Accumulate stocks, houses, boats, diamonds?

None of that appealed to her knee-jerk sense of justice. It was hard to break a habit ingrained by twenty-five years of standing up against power systems that encouraged personal greed and oppressed the little people. Hard to forget that it was all woven of one fabric—big business, racism, sexism, poverty, warmongering. From the early days in college, when she and her friends had sung at voter registration rallies, she had gone on to marry a man of deep social conscience and embraced other issues—fair housing, food banks, help for the homeless, environmental concerns, human rights, women's rights, domestic abuse.

Rankin called it "walking the way of Jesus."

Theoretically, it sounded good, noble, the right thing to do. But did the outcome have to be so damnably predictable?

She sighed, ran a hand through her hair, and kept on sorting. There was a newsletter from the Human Rights Campaign and a renewal notice from the ACLU, both in Rankin's name and forwarded from the parsonage. She really ought to notify them of Rankin's death and the change of address, but every time she thought about him, she felt the phantom pain of the severed limb, nerves hanging loose from the joint so that the least current of moving air brought fresh excruciation. Every time she wrote *deceased* next to his name, a little more of her own soul died.

She was forty-seven years old. What was she supposed to do now? Start over? Become the merry widow, begin dating, kick up her heels? She had her master's degree, of course, and most of the coursework toward her Ph.D. She had taught some lit classes off and on over the years. But most of her energy and attention had been taken up with the church.

She hadn't resented it, not then. Not consciously. But she sure as hell resented it now.

"God," she groaned into the empty, silent house.

Not a prayer. Not a supplication. She wanted nothing to do with God, with the church, with the expectations of sacrificial living. She had sacrificed enough, thank you very much. She was done.

One final piece of mail caught her eye. A manila envelope on the bottom of the stack, addressed to *Delta Fox Ballou* in a loopy, flourishing handwriting. It had been sent to the parsonage and forwarded on.

She considered the logo in the upper left hand corner: a large scrolling *W*, with *Mississippi College for Women* superimposed across the middle, and below, in smaller print, *Alumnae Office*.

Probably a plea for money, Delta thought. She received mailings from the college every six months or so and a thick four-color newsletter once a year. As always, it would go in the trash largely unread, but she pried up the flap nevertheless and took out the sheaf of papers inside.

Twenty-Fifth Anniversary Homecoming, the header of the first page read. *Class of 1969.* Delta let out a short laugh, which even to her own ears sounded mirthless and empty, the rustle of a sudden wind over dead leaves. She was about to toss the whole thing on the junk mail pile when a handwritten note at the bottom of the page arrested her attention.

Please come, the note said in that same loopy style. *Please say yes.*

Delta sat back in her chair and scrutinized the cover page more carefully.

Dear Delta,

Our twenty-fifth reunion is coming up soon, and even though we haven't seen each other in ages, I can't seem to get you out of my mind. I'm on the Alumnae Board this year, and part of my job is to contact people about the reunion and anniversary banquet.

I remember our time at the W and how the Delta Belles made those years so special. Surely you recall those wonderful concerts, how everyone loved the group and the music and the . . . well, the life *those songs represented.*

And so I am writing with a request. I think it would be wonderful to get the Delta Belles back together to play for the anniversary banquet. It wouldn't have to be anything elaborate or formal. A few familiar tunes, just for old times' sake.

Enclosed you'll find plans for the weekend, which is scheduled for the third weekend in October. Hope to see you there.

There was an address somewhere in Tennessee, two phone numbers. And then the handwritten postscript. *Please come. Please say yes.* The letter was signed *Tabitha Austin Black.*

"Well, I'll be darned," Delta muttered. "Tabby."

Tabitha Austin's face swam up from the depths and hovered before her like a relentless ghost. By now she was probably dumpy and showing her age like everybody else, but Delta's memory insisted on the younger version. In her mind's eye, Tabby was still fresh and beautiful, with long lustrous red hair and that ubiquitous effervescent smile.

Yes, she remembered Tabby. She remembered the Delta Belles. But it didn't matter. The answer was unequivocally no. The Delta Belles were dead. Exhuming them was completely out of the question.

She fingered the edge of the letter and formulated a polite but resolute response to Tabby in her mind: *It was sweet of you to ask, but I couldn't possibly . . .*

With the internal refusal came a wave of relief, a lifting of tension Delta hadn't even known was there. That was settled. She'd send a letter this afternoon and be done with it. She pushed the reunion information and Tabby's letter off to one side of the desk and stared out the window.

But despite her best intentions, the ghosts rose up to haunt her. . . .

TWO

Harvest Fest

Freshman year
Autumn 1965

October came shyly to Mississippi, a virgin bride to the wedding bed, clad in golden silks and rustling sky-blue satin. One tree on front campus, however, had no patience for a slow and sinuous fall. There, near the tall iron fence that surrounded the college, a hundred-year-old ginkgo spread its massive branches overhead and shook its amber, fan-shaped leaves in a seductive dance, a teasing preview of the annual shedding ritual.

Chinese legend held that the ginkgo dropped all its leaves in a single autumn night, baring itself to the onslaught of winter with a bold striptease. According to the accompanying college lore, any girl who stood under the tree by moonlight and caught a ginkgo leaf in flight would find the love of her life before the ancient tree reclaimed its modesty and reclothed itself in spring.

Delta had little tolerance for legends and lore and voodoo spells contrived to trap a man. If she had been looking for a husband, she would have gone to Emory and hooked up with a med student who had both money and prospects. She wanted an education, and for that purpose, Mississippi College for Women was the best the South had to offer.

Still, the college lived and breathed such traditions. The Kissing Rock at the front gate had been worn smooth by the oblations of generations of students—virtuous young women who kept their lips primly closed and their tongues to themselves when saying good night to a gentleman caller but were eager enough to press their open mouths against the top of a mossy old boulder. It struck Delta as ironic that otherwise intelligent women could be so terrified of remaining "spinsters." But intelligent or not, when the ginkgo began discarding its leaves, every student in every dormitory was expected to drop whatever she was doing and bolt to the tree.

It was a glorious Saturday afternoon. On her way back to the dorm from the library, Delta ambled toward front campus and gazed up at the ginkgo tree. The leaves had gone from green to pale yellow. It wouldn't be long until shedding day, and even though she secretly ridiculed the legend and didn't give a second thought to meeting Mr. Right, any tradition that allowed for a midnight bonfire and the chance to be out after hours was just fine with her.

This afternoon the wide shaded space under the tree was crowded with folding tables and chairs. A cardboard poster thumb-tacked to the tree trunk read:

MCW Harvest Fest, October 29–30, 1965

The girl sitting behind one of the tables looked vaguely familiar to Delta. She tossed her hair—long and red and lustrous, as if it too had undergone an autumnal metamorphosis. The crown of her head shone copper in the dappled sunlight. "Hey," she said. "Want to sign up?"

"Hey," Delta responded automatically. She looked down at the clipboard the girl held out. "Sign up for what?"

The redhead pointed to another poster, this one affixed to the front of the table with wide strips of masking tape. "The Harvest Fest Talent Extravaganza. It's a W tradition, the last weekend of October. Today's the final day to register."

"This is like a big Halloween bash, right?"

The girl tilted her head. "We don't do Halloween at the W. It's *Harvest Fest.*"

Delta gazed down the line at the signs attached to other tables:

DECORATIONS. REFRESHMENTS.
HARVEST FAIR. FLAG FOOTBALL.

"Flag football? At a women's college?"

"Oh, yes." The redhead nodded enthusiastically. "Friday night is the talent show. Saturday night there's a street dance. During the day on Saturday there are all kinds of games—three-legged races, that kind of thing. The sophomores put on a fair with contests and prizes, and the athletic department sponsors junior-senior flag football. Mostly for the P.E. majors, though. It can get pretty rough." She peered up at Delta. "You're a freshman?"

Delta nodded.

"Me too." She held out a hand. "I'm Tabitha Austin, from Jackson. Tabby, to my friends."

Tabby, Delta thought. Perfect. The girl almost purred.

She knew of Tabitha Austin, of course, although they'd never met. Everyone had heard about Tabby—wealthy, smart, and immensely popular, she was already involved in a dozen campus organizations and was a shoo-in for freshman class president. The golden child. The perfect W girl.

"And you are?"

Delta realized she was staring and gave herself a little shake. "Deborah Fox, from Stone Mountain, Georgia. People call me Delta."

"You live in Castlebury Hall, right?" Tabby said with a laugh. "I heard what some of your cronies did to you last weekend. Wish I had seen it."

"It wasn't a pretty sight."

"A friend of mine told me they lathered up your sheets pretty well. Used two cans of shaving cream."

Delta nodded. "I had been up until one in the morning, down in the common room writing a paper, and I was exhausted. Believe me, when I slid into bed and felt that stuff all over my sheets, I was not amused." She chuckled. "I made them clean it all up, but not before we'd had a shaving cream fight and made so much noise the house mother came up and gave us five reps each."

"Five reprimands? For a shaving cream fight?"

"Not for the fight. For waking her up at that hour." Delta grinned. "My revenge is coming. Don't know what I'm going to do just yet, but I'll think of something. We'll probably all get campused."

Tabby smiled broadly. "Sounds like you've had quite a welcome to the W."

"Yeah." Delta shifted from one leg to another. "So, if you're a freshman, how come you know so much about what's going on?"

"Third generation. My mother and my grandmother are both alumnae. Also two aunts, three cousins, and my older sister."

Tabby leaned across the table. "Getting involved—that's the key to making your college years memorable," she said, putting a hand to her heart. "The W is rich in heritage and tradition—"

Tabby's well-rehearsed tribute was interrupted by the appearance of an upperclassman who bent over the table and scrutinized the list for the Talent Extravaganza. "Where's the football sign-up?"

"Down at the end."

"Great." She straightened up and smiled. "Don't miss the game. We're going to kick some senior butt this year."

Delta watched as the woman made her way down the line.

"So, do you want to sign up for an act in the talent show?" Tabby repeated. "It's going to be loads of fun. Last chance."

Delta started to refuse, and then an idea dropped into her head. A perfectly brilliant, evil idea.

"You bet I do," she said. "Let me have that clipboard."

"You did *what*?" Rae Dawn DuChamp sat cross-legged on the bed with a thick American history book open on her lap.

"You heard me." Delta looked across the room with satisfaction. Lined up on the bed were the girls she already thought of as her best friends, the three coconspirators in the shaving cream incident: Rae Dawn, dark-eyed and olive-skinned, with her low sexy voice and exotic New Orleans ways; and the small towheaded Cantrell twins from North Carolina, Lauren and Lacy.

"You signed the three of us up for the Harvest Fest talent show?" Lauren said.

"Without our knowledge or permission?" Lacy's voice cracked like an adolescent boy's, screeching to a panicked crescendo on the final word.

Delta nodded vehemently. "Yes, I did."

"Forget it," Lacy said. "We'll go back on Monday and take our names off the list."

"Too late. Today was the last day to sign up. By Monday the list will be at the printer's. If you renege now, everybody will know you chickened out."

"But we have no talent!"

"Speak for yourself," said Rae Dawn in her low, husky voice. "I've been playing piano since I was twelve years old."

Lauren turned to Rae Dawn. "You play the piano? I thought you were an elementary ed major. Why didn't you—"

"It doesn't matter," Lacy protested, talking over her sister as if she'd been doing it all her life—which she probably had. "We'll make fools of ourselves!"

"Exactly." Delta grinned. It was a wickedly ingenious idea, to put them up onstage with guitars and straight blonde wigs, looking like clones of Mary Travers. They would bring the house down simply because they were so *bad*. "And in case you're curious, you're billed as the Delta Belles All-Girl Folk Band. Call it payback, for the Burma-Shave incident."

For a minute no one moved. Then Rae Dawn responded. "I think it sounds like a hoot," she said. "Let's go for it."

They all stared at her as if she'd lost her mind, but no one objected. Not even Lacy.

"On one condition," Rae Dawn continued. She pointed a long brown finger in Delta's direction. "The Delta Belles will be a *quartet*, not a trio. If we're going to make idiots of ourselves in front of the whole school, you're going to be onstage too."

"Oh, no—" Delta began, but any misgivings she might have expressed were drowned out by the laughter of the others and by the pillow that sailed across the room into her face.

"ALL RIGHT," DELTA SAID the next evening as the four of them waited for the doors of the dining hall to open for supper. "I've been thinking about this, and we need a plan."

The crowd around them jostled and pushed, edging them nearer to the entry. Meals at the college were all home-cooked and served family-style in an elegant antebellum hall, with work-study students as servers. The logic, Delta thought, was to teach them to behave as proper young ladies—chandeliers overhead, napkins in laps, elbows off the table, quiet conversation with the table monitors serving from the left, removing from the right (or vice versa—she could never quite remember). But the result proved far different from the intent. When the dinner whistle blew and the doors opened, there was a wild stampede for tables, pigs to the trough. The servers were so eager to get their jobs done and get out of the kitchen that they'd take your plate out from under your nose if you didn't hold onto it with one hand for the duration of the meal.

Sunday suppers tended to be sparsely attended, so there wasn't the usual crush tonight. Sunday dinner, at twelve thirty after church got out, was another matter altogether. It was an elaborate affair. By college mandate, all the students dressed up—skirts, heels, and hose—whether they had attended services or not. There were white tablecloths and linen napkins and lots of visitors, and the tables were decked with fried chicken and homemade yeast rolls and four or five kinds of vegetables. Where most college students faced the Freshman Ten—those inevitable ten pounds that appeared like magic during their first semester away from home—W girls had to contend with the Freshman Twenty. Or Thirty.

The six o'clock whistle blew, and the crowd moved forward as the doors opened. Delta led them toward a table on the left side of the hall, behind one of the high Corinthian columns.

"Good," she said when everyone was settled and grace had been sung. "We've got the table to ourselves. Now, about my plan—"

Delta was interrupted twice more as their server arrived, first bringing iced tea and then setting steaming bowls of vegetables and platters of cornbread and sliced ham in the middle of the table.

"Your plan for what?" Rae Dawn asked as she helped herself to fried okra and collard greens and passed the bowls on.

"For the Delta Belles, of course. For our act."

Lacy scowled. "Since when did this become an *act*?" she asked, spearing a chunk of ham and sandwiching it inside a triangular wedge of cornbread. "It was just a joke, right?"

"Well, it kind of started out as a joke," Delta said. "But since you're determined to make me do it too, we're going to do it right."

Lauren raised her eyebrows. "If you've got a plan, Delta, let's hear it."

"Can I leave?" Lacy asked irritably, rising from her seat.

Lauren glared at her. "Sit down." Lacy sat. "All right, out with it. What's your problem?"

Lacy shrugged. "I don't know. I just don't like the idea of . . . of being laughed at."

"Who's laughing at you?" Rae Dawn motioned toward Lauren to pass her the butter.

"Well, nobody . . . yet," Lacy hedged. "But if we do this talent show thing, we're going to be the laughingstock of the whole school."

"And why is that?" Delta asked calmly.

"Because when she was in kindergarten," Lauren volunteered, "she was asked to sing in a Thanksgiving pageant, forgot the words, then peed in her pants and had to be carried dripping offstage."

Lacy shot her twin a venomous look. "Will you shut up? You don't have to tell everything you know."

Delta leaned forward, grinning. "Is that true, Lace? You peed in your pants onstage?"

"I was five years old," Lacy said between gritted teeth.

"Yeah," Lauren jibed. "But you never set foot on a stage again, did you? Come on, admit it. You don't want to do this talent show because you can still feel that warm pee running down your leg—"

"For God's sake, can you quit talking about pee?" Rae Dawn snapped. "I'm trying to eat here." She lifted her fork and sniffed at the collards.

"I don't want to do this talent show *because we've got no talent!*" Lacy slammed a fist against the table, rattling the ice in her glass. "I devoutly wish we'd never even thought of that shaving cream." She looked around at the others. "Don't you get it? She's out for revenge, just to make us look like fools. And now you're all acting as if this is some great career opportunity. As if—as if we're not going to be booed off the stage and totally humiliated."

Delta sat with her chin in her hand, waiting for Lacy's tirade to wind down.

"Okay," she said when Lacy fell silent. "First of all, this is a college talent show, not the Met. Second, there are going to be lots of stupid acts designed simply to make the audience laugh."

Lacy glared at her darkly.

"And third, we are *not* going to be one of those acts."

Lauren picked a corner off her cornbread, shredded it to bits between her fingers, and smiled slyly. "Lacy's teaching herself to play the guitar."

Lacy exploded. "Lauren, what kind of sister are you? Why'd you tell them? Whose side are you on, anyway?"

"We're all on the same side," Delta said as Lauren gave Lacy a shut-up-and-listen look. She turned to Rae Dawn. "You play the piano, right?"

"Right."

"So you know music." Delta smiled triumphantly. "Lacy can play the guitar, and you can teach us—chords, harmonies, stuff like that."

"In less than three weeks?" Rae Dawn shook her head.

"Haven't you seen *The Sound of Music*?" Delta rushed on. "You know: 'Do, a deer, a fe-male deer; Re, a drop of golden sun.' It's easy. If Julie Andrews could teach seven kids in three minutes, you can teach us in three weeks."

"I don't know, Delta."

"Come on, Rae. It'll be fun. A challenge."

"Hold it!" Lacy was boiling now; Delta could see the fury building in her eyes. "No one's bothered to ask, but I am *not* going to play the guitar in front of a thousand people. I'm just starting to learn; I only know a few chords. I—"

"Folk music only *uses* a few chords, Lacy. It's simple." Rae Dawn chewed her lower lip. "Let's see. We could do 'Blowin' in the Wind'—that's easy, and everybody knows it. And then for an encore—"

"Encore?" Lacy jerked an arm convulsively, and the remains of her cornbread sandwich shot off her plate onto the center of the table. Lauren smiled sweetly, retrieved the cornbread, and set it back on her sister's plate.

"We'll have to practice a lot." Rae Dawn went on, ignoring Lacy's outburst. "I'll track down some sheet music and book a rehearsal room in the music department. I use their pianos all the time." She pulled an appointment book out of her bag and jotted down a note to herself. "All in favor of Delta's idea?" she said.

Three hands went up. Lacy sat frowning with her arms crossed and her elbow in the butter dish.

"Then it's settled. Rae Dawn, let us know when we start practice."

"Isn't *anyone* listening to me?" Lacy demanded.

"Oh, lighten up, Lace," Lauren said. "We're all in this, and you're going to have fun, whether you like it or not."

THREE

Old Friends

Decatur, Georgia
September 1994

Delta had fully intended to craft a polite response, send her regrets, and inform Tabitha Austin that she would not be attending the reunion. Or at the very least promise to think about it and then call back and tell her no.

It was a ploy she had often used as a pastor's wife, when someone wanted to volunteer her for a job she didn't want to do. Most of the time she didn't need to think about it—or, in religious terms, *pray* about it—but inexorable personalities could, on occasion, be mollified by this semblance of consideration.

Delta, however, made the mistake of telling her sister about Tabby's invitation.

"Well, you should do it, of course," Cassie said with a determined nod. "It sounds like a great idea, getting the old group together. I remember how much fun you all had. And you haven't seen them in ages. Go visit them, Delta. Go for it."

"Visit them?" Delta balked. "Don't you mean call them? Write to them?"

Cassie sat down on the bed next to Delta. "If you really want to reconnect with these friends of yours, you need to do it in person."

"You're assuming this is a good idea, reuniting the Delta Belles." Delta shook her head. "I don't know, Cass. It sounds like a lot of effort. Makes me feel overwhelmed just thinking about it."

"What else do you have to do? Since Rankin's death you've been holed up here like some sort of hermit. Remind me again where they are."

"Lauren and Lacy are in Durham and Hillsborough. Rae Dawn's in New Orleans."

"Give me their addresses. I'll get online and plan a route for you." Cassie got to her feet. "You can pack. Clean clothes are in the basket in the laundry room."

"What, you mean go *now*? I can't just drop everything and go off on a road trip."

Cassie sat down again. "Drop what, Sis? Exactly what is it you're going to miss so desperately if you take a few days to go visit your friends? Besides, you need some time away."

An icy chill crept into Delta's gut, an inner paralysis that came all too frequently since Rankin's death. "I can't do this."

Cassie tilted her head and looked intently at Delta. "Well, then, call them at least. Ask them if they're going to the reunion. Spend a little time catching up with them. You can manage that, can't you?"

"I suppose," Delta said reluctantly.

THAT EVENING AFTER DINNER, Delta sat in her room with her address book in one hand and the telephone in the other, battling with a nagging suspicion that she had been hoodwinked by her little sister.

Cassie hadn't believed for a minute that Delta would jump up and go visit her old friends at such short notice. But given the choice between a road trip and a telephone call—

Delta exhaled a sigh and flipped through the address book. Lauren lived in Durham, North Carolina, and her sister Lacy in Hillsborough, only a few miles apart. The last time she had seen them had been five or six years ago, when she and Rankin had driven from Asheville to Raleigh for a church conference, and the dinner they had shared had seemed strained and uncomfortable. Afterward, Rankin had questioned her about the twins.

"What's going on with those two?" he asked. "I thought they had a pretty good relationship in college."

"They did. I mean, they had the typical sibling rivalries and picked at each other sometimes, but mostly it was all in fun. We laughed a lot." Delta shrugged. "Something happened during our last year, though. Lacy had been dating this guy named Trip Jenkins, and then later on, after graduation, we found out he had married Lauren."

"Ouch," Rankin said. "That's got to hurt."

"I'm sure it did. But Lacy and Lauren were far too close to let that get in the way of their relationship."

Now, thinking about the twins, Delta wondered. That night at dinner, they had all skated around the issue as if on wafer-thin ice. Lacy had become a high school history teacher and seemed to love her work, but she had never married. Lauren had raised a son—a handsome boy if the pictures were any indication. He would be grown now, in his twenties. Lauren might even be a grandmother by now.

Delta turned forward a few pages from the *C*'s to the *D*'s and found Rae Dawn DuChamp's number. New Orleans, on Dauphine Street in the Quarter.

Only once since graduation had Delta managed to get together with Rae Dawn. Three years into their marriage Rankin had accepted a call to a new church in Asheville, and during a two-week hiatus between pastoral duties, they had taken a few days to drive down to the Big Easy.

She remembered Rae Dawn just as she had been in college—dark and exotic-looking, with a deep smoky voice and a musical laugh. Delta and Rankin had sat in the club and listened to Rae sing, and at the memory a bittersweet longing rose up in Delta. She hadn't realized until this moment how much she missed Rae Dawn and how much her friendship had meant.

Over the years they had written only sporadically—Christmas cards, mostly, a hasty note now and then. Much as Delta hated to admit it, Cassie was right. It would do her good to talk to her old friends again.

She picked up the receiver and dialed Rae Dawn's number. It rang six times before anyone picked up.

"Maison Dauphine," a male voice answered.

"Oh—" Delta stammered. "I may have the wrong number. I was trying to reach Rae Dawn DuChamp."

The man on the other end hesitated, and Delta heard noises in the background—a vacuum cleaner running, she thought, and the clinking of glassware. "Uh—yes," he said at last, "this is the correct number. But I'm afraid she isn't available at the moment. May I take a message?"

Delta paused, thinking. "I suppose so, if you don't mind. Do you have a pen?"

"Yep," the man said. "Whenever you're ready."

"Please tell her that Delta Ballou called. Delta *Fox* Ballou."

"B-a-l-l-o-u? As in *Cat Ballou*?"

"That's right. Area code 404—" She gave him Cassie's number. "Tell her I'm in Atlanta. Decatur, actually. Emory University area."

"Atlanta," he repeated.

"Right. Do you know when she might be available?"

She heard a mumbling, as if he had put his hand over the mouthpiece and was consulting with someone else.

"I'm not sure, but I'll give her the message and have her get back to you."

"Okay, thanks," Delta said, and, with a sense of disappointment that left her unaccountably bereft, she hung up the phone.

FOUR

Bourbon Street Dreams

Rae Dawn took the cocktail napkin from Nate the bartender and leaned her elbows on the shiny mahogany surface of Maison Dauphine's bar. Behind Nate she could see her own reflection in the lighted mirror, and she stared forlornly at the image.

"Who is she?" Nate asked, gazing down at the name and number on the paper napkin.

"An old friend," Rae said. "From college. My best friend, to be more precise."

"And you didn't want to talk to her?"

Rae Dawn shook her head. "I don't want to talk to anyone right now." She gave him a narrow glance, and he raised both hands in surrender.

"Okay, I get the message." He retrieved a clean towel from under the bar and began polishing glasses.

"Could you get me a Diet Coke, please?" Rae asked.

"Coming right up." Nate filled a glass with ice, poured the soft drink with a flourish, and set it in front of her.

"Thanks." Rae looked at him, the familiar boyish face, the

blond curly hair, the soft downy beard he had been growing for two months now. Nate had been with her for years at Maison Dauphine—not just an employee, but a friend. A good friend. He didn't deserve to be on the receiving end of her depression. "Sorry I snapped your head off."

Nate grinned and twisted his head first to the right, then the left. "Still attached. No problem." His blue eyes softened as he gazed at her. "I understand."

"You're a good man, Nate," she said as she moved off toward a table near the front windows.

"Yes, I am," he called to her retreating back. "And don't you forget it."

Rae Dawn installed herself at the corner table, sipped at her Diet Coke, and fingered the cocktail napkin. Nate *didn't* understand. It wasn't that Rae didn't want to talk to Delta; she simply couldn't bring herself to do it at the moment. Like everything else in her life, even a simple telephone call felt completely insurmountable to her. She would have to make conversation. She would have to explain.

Besides, she'd lay odds on the fact that Delta was calling about the twenty-fifth anniversary bash, to ask if she was interested in coming. She'd probably gotten an identical letter from Tabitha Austin, suggesting a reunion show of the Delta Belles.

Rae would have to call her back, of course. But not now.

Nate appeared at her elbow and put a bowl of fresh popcorn on the table, then silently slipped back to the bar. Rae Dawn stared out the window at tourists passing by on the sidewalk, at old Mrs. Beaulieu upstairs across the street, shaking her rugs over the wrought iron railing of her balcony. Her husband had died last year, and Mrs. B had grown frailer and thinner every day since his death, until now she looked like a naked baby bird with parchment-thin skin and clawlike hands. Rae Dawn wondered how much longer the old dear would last, having to climb those stairs to her apartment.

Rae ate a handful of popcorn and sipped at her drink, crumpling Delta's telephone number into a ball in her fist. So many losses. And yet so many gifts, too, as Mrs. B would undoubtedly remind her. *You only feel the pain if you've felt the love.*

She smoothed out the napkin and stared at Delta's name, scrawled in blue ballpoint in Nate's distinctive handwriting.

Even the name took her back. Back to the autumn of her freshman year. Back to the place where her life—where the gifts—had truly begun.

Freshman year
Autumn 1965

Most of the rehearsal rooms in the music building were dark and quiet this early in the morning, but the front doors were unlocked. Rae Dawn slipped inside and stood in the echoing marble foyer. At a distance she heard a *click-click* of footsteps, the creak of a door, the hollow *thunk* of a lock being turned, and then the faint, haunting sounds of scales from a clarinet.

She leaned against one of the massive columns in the entryway and closed her eyes. Music—any kind of music—carried her to a different place, a better place than where she'd come from. A clean, green, sunlit place caressed by fresh breezes and the scent of hidden blooms.

Music, for Rae Dawn, generated a kind of homesickness of the soul, a bittersweet longing, a faint hope on the horizon.

Not that she'd ever had much hope. Not until two months ago, when she came to college, anyway.

The clarinetist had segued from scales into some bluesy,

improvisational runs—easy on the ear, hard on the heart. An old Louis Armstrong tune: *Do you know what it means to miss New Orleans. . . .*

The song reminded Rae Dawn of home, and she felt tears prick behind her closed eyelids.

Home. She always claimed the Big Easy as home, and maybe it was, at least on some mystical, soul-deep level. New Orleans reached out to her, with its French flavors and its sensuous, gutsy music. Every good thing that filled her senses, every creative impulse that nurtured her spirit, had been birthed between Canal and Esplanade on the cobbled streets of the Vieux Carre. The soulful piano tunes that lingered like smoke on the air above Bourbon Street. The gray stone towers of St. Louis Cathedral and the bright, optimistic artists' canvases that lined the wrought-iron fence around Jackson Square. The rich crispy smell of fried oyster po'boys from Acme Oyster House on Iberville. The scent of strong chicory-laced coffee and fresh warm beignets at Café Du Monde.

The truth was, Rae Dawn had always *wished* New Orleans was her home. Not Picayune, Mississippi, thirty miles northeast of the magic. Not a broken-down Airstream trailer at the dead end of a rutted, sandy track that bordered a tributary of the Pearl River called Hobo Creek.

At thirteen, she had made her first solitary journey to New Orleans, accepting a ride from a gregarious trucker who never questioned—at least out loud—her far-fetched story about going to visit her estranged birth mother. After that one trip, she was hooked. Every school holiday and most weekends she managed to hitch a ride or scrounge up money for the bus. Anything to get back to the place where she belonged. She never questioned the risks, never felt in danger. The Quarter was a womb, not a threat. It fed and nurtured her, birthed her into a life marked by music and beauty and hope. As long as she roamed those familiar streets, she could forget all about her real life and become the person she was destined to be. The dirty brown water of Hobo Creek might run in her blood, but the heart that pumped it was pure New Orleans.

And then, every time, came the moment of leaving. . . .

It was like dying over and over again. Forever, it seemed, she had been trying to flee Picayune permanently, to escape the Airstream and her father's drunken rages and her mother's deadening inertia. She dreamed about making New Orleans her real home, living there, being part of its blood and breath, adding her harmony to the music in the air. But she had no money, no education, no skills.

Thus, when the grant offer from MCW came—not the piano scholarship she longed for, but a "resident need subsidy," what Rae Dawn called "the poverty package"—she took it and was grateful.

It wasn't New Orleans, but it wasn't Picayune, either. . . .

The front doors opened with a creak and a bang, startling Rae Dawn out of her reverie. She jumped and turned to see Dr. Manfred Gottlieb, head of the Music Department, standing backlit by the morning sun.

"*Guten Morgen,*" he said with a little bow. The professor was tall and thin. His wild graying hair stood up at all angles, and he reminded Rae Dawn of pictures she had seen of Albert Einstein. He was dressed in a starched white shirt and a worn brown tweed cardigan with suede patches on the elbows. His eyes were a soft gray-blue, and his smile revealed a dimple in his right cheek. He looked very old, but other things besides the passing of years could age a person.

Against her will, Rae Dawn's eyes jerked toward his forearm, where the sleeve of his sweater covered any evidence. Rumor had it that twenty years ago Gottlieb had been liberated from a Nazi death camp—Dachau, Buchenwald, Rae Dawn couldn't remember the details. She had seen the professor in the halls and around campus, but mostly at a distance, never close up. She wasn't quite certain what she expected of a survivor of a concentration camp—an expression of blank emptiness, perhaps, or else an unquenchable fury. But Manfred Gottlieb's face, now gazing into hers, held only kindness, interest, and a tinge of mild amusement.

"You are one of my students?" he asked in a quiet voice, his head tilted to one side.

"I—ah, no," Rae said. "I'm just—just coming in to use one of the pianos."

"I see. Unfortunately, there are no pianos out here in the hallway."

"N-no," she stammered. "I know. I was . . . thinking."

He wiggled his eyebrows at her—a high arch, up and then down again. "Thinking, this is a good thing. People should engage in it more often, I suspect."

Rae Dawn chuckled. "You're probably right. Except that what I was doing was more like daydreaming. Woolgathering."

"Ah. And yet such wool can keep the heart warm on a cold winter night, no?"

It was a lovely thought—and indeed, Rae Dawn's dreams of New Orleans did have a warming effect when life seemed cold and barren. She smiled at him. "I'd better go practice."

He inclined his head. "And I have lessons to prepare."

She moved off down the hall, but Gottlieb spoke again. "Pardon me. Your name?"

"DuChamp," she said, turning to face him once again. "Rae Dawn DuChamp." She uttered the name in the French way, although her father and his father and all the Picayune DuChamps before them pronounced it *champ,* like the winner of a boxing match or a racehorse itching to run.

"A pleasure to meet you, Miss DuChamp," Gottlieb said, and turned toward his office.

When he was gone, Rae Dawn made her way down the dim-lit corridor and into one of the practice rooms. The space was barely large enough for a baby grand and a bench, but the ceiling was fifteen feet high, and a frosted glass window diffused the morning sun and cast a cheerful yellow glow across the walls.

The sunlight on her back warmed her as she sat down and flexed her fingers—warmed her almost as much as Manfred Gottlieb's respectful words and gracious smile. Only one person in Rae Dawn's life had ever affirmed her desire to become a musician—Teresa Cheever, a seventh-grade teacher who had discovered her pounding away at the ancient, battered, out-of-tune Everett upright in the school auditorium. Rae had a gift, Mrs. Cheever said, a gift that ought to be developed. Whatever she heard, she could instantly reproduce from memory. But she had no understanding. No foundation.

Until Mrs. Cheever came along, Rae had no idea how to read the mysterious runes of a music score—she simply played by ear, by instinct. Like a starving refugee, she devoured everything the teacher put in front of her—fingering techniques, form, dynamics, music theory. She learned to read with unbelievable speed and accuracy, and soon experimented with composing music. By the time she entered high school, she had begun work on her own sonata.

The DuChamp family had no piano, of course. The only instrument Rae Dawn ever got her hands on was the school's old Everett, and she had to wait until late afternoon, when everyone was gone, to get in any practice time at all. But whenever she sat at the keyboard, everything else disappeared—the trailer, the fear, the abuse, the stench of whiskey that hung about her father, the haunted expression in her mother's eyes.

Over the years other teachers had written her off simply because she was poor and the only child of the town's most notorious drunk. Her mother never had an encouraging word to say about life in general or her daughter in particular; she spent the bulk of her days sitting at the small built-in kitchen table in the Airstream, chain-smoking and tracing patterns in the Formica with a blunt fingernail. And Daddy—when he was there, which wasn't often—entertained himself either by yelling at the two of them or by parking himself in a rusted metal lawn chair and firing shotgun pellets into the eroded bank of Hobo Creek.

No one cared much about a ragged, introverted child caught in a web of crushing poverty and neglect. No one except Teresa Cheever.

Mrs. Cheever had saved her. Mrs. Cheever and the music.

The woman taught Rae Dawn everything she knew, encouraged her, believed in her. But in the end, she readily admitted that Rae Dawn's genius far outstripped her own abilities as a tutor. Rae needed another mentor, someone with advanced education and abilities.

Given her background and financial situation, however, Rae knew that wasn't likely to happen. She was on her own, and had to make do with what she knew.

She ran some scales to limber up her touch, then began to recreate the tune the clarinetist had put into her mind. The music transported her, and she moved easily through three or four familiar pieces—torch songs, mostly, from Billie Holiday, Lena Horne, Sarah Vaughan. She played by ear, by heart, feeling the riffs in her soul.

Rae Dawn loved all kinds of music, but mostly she loved jazz. Loved the freedom of it, the way she could experiment with it to make it her own. Just for fun, she had reinvented some of Bach's inventions, taken classical pieces and fiddled with them to bring them into the twentieth century. And now, as the music took her over, she simply let herself go and began to pour out her soul into music of her own creation.

At last, when she had played herself far away from Picayune and the Airstream trailer and Hobo Creek, back into the embrace of the French Quarter, Rae Dawn stopped for a moment and rifled through her bag. She had found some rudimentary melody sheets and chord charts for the folk songs the newly formed Delta Belles would be singing at the talent show. Not exactly her kind of music, nor an auspicious beginning to a career in performance, but it would be a chance to find out how well she could do in front of a large crowd.

Within five minutes, she was bored out of her skull and wondering why she'd ever agreed to such an insane idea. Folk music, the way most people played it, was infuriatingly simple. Three or four chords, always in major keys like G or C. Rae Dawn experimented a little with the accompaniment for "Blowin' in the Wind" and came up with a version that was recognizable but infused with her own particular style.

She jotted down a few chord changes and made notations for an improvisational bridge between the second and third verses. No reason a song like this should be insipid and predictable, even if eighty percent of people under the age of forty could play it passably well on the guitar.

Another thirty minutes passed, and by the time the warning whistle blew for nine o'clock classes, Rae Dawn was confident that she would be able to give the Delta Belles some good options for their debut at the Talent Extravaganza.

She felt oddly satisfied. This was what she'd always dreamed of doing—not simply playing for herself and Mrs. Cheever in an empty school auditorium, but performing before an audience, drawing them into the world she had created, making the music her own.

A light knock sounded on the door. Rae Dawn stowed her music in her bag and prepared to clear out to allow someone else into the practice room. But when she opened the door, she found a weathered face and a shock of gray hair.

"Dr.—Dr. Gottlieb!" she stammered. "Were you—have you—how long have you been out here?"

"Long enough," he said. "Do you happen to be free at four o'clock this afternoon?"

"I—ah, yes," she said, scrambling to think of her schedule. "I have practice with my friends at four thirty. For the talent show."

"Then meet me in my office at four, if you please," he said. "I believe there are some things we should discuss."

And without another word, he turned on his heel and moved noiselessly back down the hallway, as if gliding on a song.

AT FOUR O'CLOCK, Rae Dawn stood outside Manfred Gottlieb's office door. Her stomach squirmed, and her brain spun out imaginary scenarios, most of which centered around being banned from the practice rooms, told that she had no right to think of herself as a musician.

She raised a tentative hand and rapped lightly. Through the frosted glass window, she could see a shadowy form rise and move toward her.

The door swung open. "Miss DuChamp, come in please," Dr. Gottlieb said, giving a slight bow and a wave of his hand. "Punctuality is one of your virtues, I see."

Rae Dawn looked at him. The starched white shirt was limp and a little rumpled, and his tie was slightly askew. The tweed cardigan he had worn earlier that morning now draped casually across the back of his desk chair. He seemed more approachable, somehow. More human.

She entered the office—a spacious room with high ceilings, scarred wood floors, and an ornate chair rail that ran the perimeter of the walls. Or rather, it would have been spacious, had it not been cluttered with books and papers on every available surface.

The professor's desk sat squarely in the center of the office, flanked by overflowing bookcases and tall filing cabinets. In an alcove to one side stood an ancient baby grand piano, finished in mahogany and piled with stacks of staff paper and spiral-bound music scores.

Dr. Gottlieb scooped an armload of books from a battered leather chair in front of his desk and nodded for her to sit. He dumped the pile on the corner of his desk, where it teetered precariously. Rae Dawn kept a wary eye on the heavy volumes, expecting them to fall at any moment. Dr. Gottlieb, completely unconcerned, went behind the desk and sank into his office chair.

"Now, Miss DuChamp," he said, tenting his long fingers together, "let us have a talk about your career."

"My career," she repeated stupidly.

"Precisely." He ignored the obvious—that she sounded like an ill-trained parrot—and continued. "This morning you informed me that you are not a music major, is that correct?"

Rae Dawn nodded. "Yes, sir."

"And why is that?"

"Excuse me?"

"Why are you not a music major?"

"Well, I . . . I guess because—" She shrugged and lifted her hands in surrender.

"Because some foolish, ignorant pragmatist in your past—some so-called teacher, perhaps, or a parent—informed you that music is not a viable option for making money and fulfilling the American Dream? That smart people position themselves to have a regular paycheck coming in, a house in the suburbs, a white picket fence, a color television set?"

He paused and ran his hands through his hair, making it stand up even more wildly. "Forgive my bluntness, Miss DuChamp. My own life experience has led me to value that which nurtures the soul above all else. Beauty, art, poetry, music . . ."

At the words *life experience,* Rae Dawn's mind jerked to images of emaciated bodies from the concentration camps, and she shuddered. She barely heard his next words: "For me, of course, music is the primary passion. And from what I heard this morning, for you as well."

She stared at him. "You think I have *talent*?"

Dr. Gottlieb raised an eyebrow. "You are, shall we say, unfinished. Rough, like unsculpted marble. But talent? Yes. A fire in the belly. A hunger in the spirit. I hear these things. I see them in your eyes." He leaned forward. "This is your first year in college?"

"Yes, sir. I'm a freshman."

"And yet you say, quite decisively, that you are not a music major."

"Yes."

"So you have settled on something else, even so early in your education?" He tugged at one ear. "May I ask what you have determined to be your life direction?"

Rae Dawn ducked her head. "Elementary education."

He cleared his throat. "Because there are jobs available to you when you graduate."

It was not a question, and Rae Dawn did not answer. She

kept her eyes fixed on the unsteady pile of books on the corner of Gottlieb's desk. Something in her gut told her that everything in her life was about to tumble.

All she had ever wanted to do was live in New Orleans and make music. But growing up in an Airstream trailer on the banks of Hobo Creek had skewed her values. Teaching might not make her rich, but it wouldn't keep her poor either. As much as she loved music, it was—as Dr. Gottlieb himself had admitted—a calling that destined her to financial instability.

He was still gazing at her from under his bushy white eyebrows.

"I could—" she began hesitantly, avoiding his gaze. "I could *teach* music."

"You could." He nodded. "Bringing music to children is a noble profession. But not for you." He leaned back in his chair and closed his eyes, as if considering a monumental decision. "I will train you, if you would be willing."

Rae Dawn blinked, and for a moment her heart soared. "*Willing*? Of course I would be willing." Then she came back to herself. Lessons cost money, money her scholarship did not provide. The momentary flame of hope guttered and died, and the dream went out of her on a sigh. "I can't, Dr. Gottlieb. I wish I could, but I can't."

"And why not?"

Memories flashed across her mind—all the times she had come home to find that once again Daddy had blown the welfare check on liquor and shotgun shells. The week after Christmas in third grade, when Julie McKenzie identified Rae Dawn's new red wool coat as a castoff her mother had given to the Goodwill. The winter they had lived on nothing but sweet potatoes stored in an ammo box under the trailer and a few tough, stringy rabbits her father shot in the woods near the creek.

But she wasn't about to tell Gottlieb any of this. She had escaped. She was barely getting by on her stipend, but she still had her pride.

"Pride nourishes the ego but does not feed the soul." He said the words softly, as if he'd read her mind.

Rae Dawn looked up and, to her dismay, a tear slid down her cheek. The professor did not turn away, but continued to gaze at her, his blue-gray eyes shining.

"Your family is poor?"

He uttered the word boldly and without apology, and it pierced her like a blade. The sharp edge of poverty was usually tempered by euphemism: families had *financial challenges* or just needed time *to get on their feet.* No one used real words like *destitute* or *indigent* or *impoverished.*

Dr. Gottlieb's honesty broke loose something inside Rae Dawn. She swiped the tear away with one hand and stared him down. "Yes," she said fiercely. "We're poor. Dirt poor. My father is an alcoholic. My mother's useless. I grew up wearing clothes other people had thrown away. I'm in college now only because I received a resident need stipend."

Admitting the truth brought an unexpected sense of liberation. She exhaled a pent-up breath and ventured a tentative smile.

He crossed his arms and smiled back. "Yes. The poverty package."

Rae Dawn felt laughter welling up inside her. "Dr. Gottlieb, I have never met anyone quite like you. You make me feel . . . I don't know. Accepted."

He unbuttoned his cuff, rolled up his sleeve, and held his arm out toward her. The inside of his forearm bore a hazy, bluish tattoo, a string of numbers. "How old do you think I am?" he asked.

She hesitated, not wanting to offend him. On appearance alone, she would have guessed seventy, perhaps more. But his spirit seemed younger than that, and his step lighter. Besides, he wouldn't likely be teaching if he were that old.

"Sixty?" she offered.

"You are kind," he responded with a smile. He rolled his sleeve down and rebuttoned the cuff. "I will be fifty-two in January."

Rae Dawn tried not to let the shock register on her face, but she felt a hot flush creep up her neck.

"I was not yet thirty when the Nazis came," he went on. "We lived in Berlin, and my family was well off—wealthy, by many people's standards. My father was an art dealer, and my mother a pianist and composer. On the train to Auschwitz, I worried most about what would become of our beautiful piano, and my father's art collection." He shrugged. "But when the ovens began to belch out smoke and people were being murdered, twenty thousand or more a day, material things no longer mattered."

His eyes took on a faraway look, as if calling up memories Rae Dawn didn't even want to imagine. "I do not often talk about those terrible days," he said. "But I felt it imperative that you should understand. I have known abundance, and I have known deprivation. There is no shame in either." A slight tremor went through him, and he shook his head. "What matters is life. What matters is holding fast to the dreams and values that fill your heart, even when others try to rip them away from you. What matters is hope."

Rae Dawn had no answer for this, and so she kept silent.

"You are a musician," Dr. Gottlieb went on. "It is in your soul. To deny it would be death to your spirit and would rob the world of beauty we so desperately need. And so I repeat my offer: I will teach you, if you are willing."

This time Rae Dawn understood. He was offering to teach her for free.

He rose from his chair. "Come by tomorrow, and we will set a schedule for your lessons."

"Thank you so much," she said as she walked with him to the door. "I don't know how to express my gratitude—for your offer, for your faith in me. For everything."

He held the office door open for her and reached to shake her hand. "I am grateful too. For the opportunity to hear and create music. For the honor of teaching a student such as yourself. For the grace and the joy of being alive."

Rae Dawn left Dr. Gottlieb's office and walked down the hall into the echoing foyer of the music building. She felt as if she had just stepped out of a dream—or into one. For the second time in her life, someone believed in her. Someone who could teach her, mentor her. Someone who could help her find her voice, the music of her soul.

She would not tell anyone, of course, what Gottlieb had revealed of his horrific past. It was his story to tell, if and when he chose to share it. But she knew, or thought she knew, why he had opened those painful memories to her. It was a link between them, a connection. He understood suffering and poverty and did not bow to shame.

She would learn much from him, this man who had survived such terrors and still found hope and wonder in the world.

FIVE

The Twin Factor

Hillsborough, North Carolina
September 1994

Lacy Cantrell stood in the center of her living room, looked around, and sighed. Having a spotless house was a great feeling; actually *doing* the cleaning was a royal pain in the butt.

Still, fall was upon her. School had already started, and she hadn't yet finished her spring cleaning. Yesterday she had discovered a bit of old tinsel from last year's Christmas tree in Hormel's litter box. Where he'd found it she had no idea, but she was pretty sure that sparkly things in the cat's poop couldn't be healthy.

"You could help, you big lazy lug," she said.

The cat, an enormous cinnamon-colored brindle with a snow-white belly, lay sprawled across the sofa taking her in with his inscrutable green gaze. He twitched his tail but made no reply.

Lacy laughed and sat down beside him. When she began

rubbing his ears, he responded with a rumbling purr and closed his eyes in ecstasy. He had come to her as a kitten three years ago—simply showed up on her doorstep one Saturday morning when she was cooking sausage, and demanded to be let in. She complied, and as soon as her back was turned he filched her breakfast off the kitchen table and wolfed it down, then dragged the empty sausage wrapper out of the trash can and wore it on his head like a hat. Clearly, the beast had chosen his own name.

Despite his penchant for stealing food, however—a habit Lacy had never been able to break—Hormel turned out to be a most loving and noble animal. Fastidiously clean, he never made messes except when she inadvertently left the lid off the kitchen garbage, and his loyalty and affection rivaled that of the most devoted dog. He followed her everywhere, waited in the window when it was time for her to come home from school, slept at the foot of her bed, and gave unerringly accurate advice about the character of her friends. Hormel was wise beyond his years. If he didn't like you, you didn't stand a chance.

Lacy gave the cat a kiss on the top of his furry head and went back to the onerous job of cleaning the hardwood floors and washing the baseboards. As she worked, her mind drifted to yesterday's mail, which still lay on the coffee table. To the invitation to her college reunion. To the answering machine message from Delta Ballou. And to the past—inexorably, to the past.

Everyone had gathered in Practice Room C for the first rehearsal of the Delta Belles—everyone except Lauren, who was always late. "All right, Lacy," Rae Dawn said, "come over here and let's tune your guitar." She plunked out an E, and Lacy fiddled with the tuner peg until the first string more or less approximated the sound of the piano. "Up, up," Rae Dawn said. "That's it."

They continued tuning until Rae Dawn seemed satisfied. "Okay, now." She pointed at the sheet music. "We're going to start with 'Blowin' in the Wind.' Here are your chords, up here above the staff. It's pretty simple—just C, F, and G."

Lacy strummed the guitar and hummed under her breath as Rae Dawn played slowly through the accompaniment. "Now, when we get to here"—she pointed—"I'll play an interlude on the piano before we go into the next verse."

She ran through the segue. By this time Delta had come to stand next to the piano. "That sounds great, Rae," she said.

"I worked on it a little bit earlier this morning," Rae Dawn said. "You think the interlude's all right? I can tweak it some more."

"You *wrote* that?"

"Yeah, well, it's kind of instinctive. This song is so familiar to everybody, always sung the same way. I just wanted to give it a little something extra."

Delta put a hand on Rae Dawn's shoulder. "Well, there goes *my* plan."

Rae Dawn turned around. "What plan?"

"The plan to have you all get up onstage and make fools of yourselves. This is going to be good. Really good."

"Don't get your hopes up," Lacy said gloomily. "You haven't heard me sing yet."

Fifteen minutes into the rehearsal, Lauren finally did show up. Perhaps it was the dramatist in her. She did love to make an entrance. All their lives, Lauren had been upstaging Lacy, grabbing the spotlight for herself—walking first, talking in sentences while Lacy still struggled with "Mama" and "Daddy" and "no."

Lauren was the one who garnered most of the attention, sometimes angelic and adorable, sometimes petulant and demanding, in opposition to Lacy's steady, compliant, docile nature.

Now Lauren's late arrival interrupted what might have been a pretty good first run-through.

Lacy rolled her eyes and bit her tongue to keep from saying something rude, but clearly Lauren got the unspoken message, because she shot a glare at her twin and said, "Don't start with me, Lacy. I'm late because I was *doing something for all of us.*"

She held up an enormous bag so full it bulged at the seams.

"Right," Lacy said, not even trying to curb her sarcasm. "Shopping. For the group."

Lauren propped the bag on the seat of an empty chair. "That's exactly what I was doing." She dug around and came up with something that looked suspiciously like a rug made from dead ferrets. "Here."

She tossed it toward Delta, who shrank back and let it fall to the floor. "Jeez, Lauren," Delta said, poking it with her toe. "What is that thing?"

"It's a vest." She pulled three more out of the sack, in various fur patterns, and passed them around. "I've been thinking about wardrobe," she said. "We want to be folky, right? I thought we could wear black pants and black turtlenecks and these vests."

"I don't want to wear this," Rae Dawn protested. "Dead animals creep me out."

"They're fake fur," Lauren said, as if this answered all their objections. "And then I found *these*—" With a flourish she extracted something yellowish and stringy from the bag. "Ta-da!"

"Wigs?" Delta began to laugh.

Lauren shrugged. "Well, we ought to be blonde, right?"

"We're *already* blonde," Lacy said.

"Of course you and I are blonde," Lauren shot back. "But we

don't have long hair. Rae Dawn's a brunette, and Delta's hair is blonde, but not light enough."

"Light enough for what?"

"For the Mary Travers look, of course." Lauren gazed around as if expecting applause.

"*You* be Mary," Lacy said, eyeing the wig with distaste. "I'd rather wear a beard and be Peter. Rae Dawn's tall and thin; she can be Paul."

Delta chuckled. "What about me?"

"Matthew, Mark, Luke, or John," Lacy suggested. "Take your pick."

Everybody laughed. Lauren was clearly not happy about being upstaged by her twin sister. She stuffed the wig back into the bag. "Fine."

"Ah, come on, Lauren," Delta said, sidling over to her. "We're just kidding. Where'd you get all this stuff, anyway?"

"At the thrift store downtown. The vests cost five bucks apiece. The wigs were only two." She put on a wig and one of the vests and modeled for them.

Amid general laughter and hoots of approval, a thought occurred to Lacy, an idea that infuriated her. Where had her sister come up with money to buy these costumes? Since she had spent every cent of her monthly allowance on new loafers, Lacy suspected Lauren had probably embezzled the funds from the stash Lacy kept hidden in the dorm room.

"Lauren," she began in a threatening tone, "where'd you get the money?"

Her twin turned, and the identical face took on a guilty expression all too familiar to Lacy. "I, uh—"

"You stole my allowance to buy this crap, didn't you?"

"Well, I—I sort of *borrowed* it."

Delta intervened. "Hold on, let's not have a war here." She

put a restraining hand on Lacy's shoulder. "She was just trying to help out, Lace."

Lacy narrowed her eyes, shooting Lauren an I'll-get-you-for-this look, but said nothing.

"I think we can all pitch in to pay for the wigs and vests," Delta went on in a calming voice. "You'll get your money back, Lacy."

"That's not the point—"

"The point is," Rae said in a determined voice, "whatever we wear, we've still got to *sing*. Can we get back to rehearsal, please?" She heaved an exaggerated sigh. "If we don't get this right, *I'll* be the one peeing onstage."

As the memories came, Lacy found herself fighting back tears. Despite herself, she missed the camaraderie of those days, missed her old college friends, missed her sister most of all.

Growing up, she had longed for an identity of her own. Being a twin could be complicated. Lacy recalled how captivated she had been in Psych 101 when the professor first introduced her to Maslow's hierarchy of human need. She had latched onto the concept, clung to it like a drowning woman to a life raft. *Self-actualization.* That was what she wanted. To be not someone else's mirror image, but her own person, a unique, fully self-actualized human being. . . .

An image from their teenage years rose in her mind, what Lacy thought of as *the burger ritual.* It happened every time: Lacy would remove the pickles from her cheeseburger, setting aside each slice one by one, and one by one Lauren would pick them up and eat them. It was the same with salads; Lacy took the tomatoes off Lauren's greens and gave her all the croutons. They never asked, never discussed it; they did it automatically, in fluid movements as if a single person just happened to inhabit two bodies.

Lacy cringed at the thought. That was the way most people perceived twins, after all. Because they shared the same DNA, the same physical appearance and stature and coloring, folks assumed that they shared a mind too, and a personality. Teachers and friends, sometimes even family members, were forever mixing them up, and although occasionally in junior high and high school they had used that confusion to advantage, Lacy had always loathed the idea of being mistaken for her sister.

She wasn't quite sure why. Lauren was more outgoing, better at sports, and generally more popular. Lacy, the studious, serious one, was included in her sister's circle of friends, but always as an afterthought, a tagalong. All her life Lacy had longed for one thing, her single wish every time she blew out candles on their shared birthday cake: *She wanted to be different.* Even before she was old enough to articulate it, she wanted it so badly that she took drastic measures to distinguish herself from her twin. Like cutting all her hair down to the scalp during Christmas break of second grade.

Now they were grown, and Lacy realized—at least theoretically—that she no longer had to compete with Lauren in order to be a self-actualized individual.

Unfortunately self-actualization had its downside too. The bond had been stretched beyond its limits, the connection severed. At forty-six, Lacy Cantrell was her own person.

But her emancipation had cost more than she bargained for.

SIX

The Other Sister

Durham, North Carolina
September 1994

Water poured down the eaves and ran in gushing streams out the gutters into the backyard. From the screened porch that overlooked the lawn, Lauren could barely hear the chiming of the mantel clock underneath the steady thrumming of the rain.

Midnight.

The air was chilly and damp, and she shivered, pulling her robe more closely around her shoulders. She ought to be in bed, but she couldn't sleep. For an hour she had tossed restlessly before deciding to get up again. Now she sipped at a steaming mug of tea and read Tabby Austin's letter for the third time.

Neither the letter nor the invitation to the reunion had affected Lauren as much as Delta's voice mail message. She had sounded depressed, empty, her voice flat and emotionless. Delta hadn't pressured Lauren to agree to Tabby's wild notion of getting the Belles back together again—in fact, Lauren had gotten the impression that Delta didn't really want to do it either. Nevertheless, the very idea of reuniting their old singing group brought up a wave of nostalgia and longing in her, a yearning that would not let her go.

And despite her attempts to push the realization away, she knew that her wakeful restlessness wasn't only about the group, but about her sister.

Lacy. Her mirror image, her second self. Her womb-mate.

She could hardly believe how far they had drifted since college, when they stood onstage and sang together, laughed together, lived together. How much they had lost over the years.

One of those old folk songs surfaced in Lauren's mind—Peter, Paul, and Mary's version of a childhood ditty: *Rain, rain, go away, come again some other day. . . .*

But the storm did not diminish. Mist seeped through the screens and gathered on her cheeks, and on the rhythm of the pounding rain, the music took her back.

BACKSTAGE AT COLTRANE AUDITORIUM was pure bedlam. Half the students, it seemed, had cooked up some kind of act for the Talent Extravaganza, and the other half were out in the audience, stomping their feet and yelling for the show to begin.

Lynn Stanton, leader of a group called the Pillowcase People, had her crew all dressed and ready to go on. The group wore pillowcases pulled down to their knees, painted with enormous faces so that the girls all looked as if they were giant heads with little stick legs and no arms at all. Presumably they had eye slits somewhere near the top, but evidently they couldn't see a thing, because they kept thrashing into people and tripping over equipment.

Lauren caught a glimpse of Tabitha Austin dashing around

with a clipboard, making sure all the acts knew what to do. Tabby glanced over and waved and then, looking frazzled and dazed, went to break up an altercation between a ballet dancer and one of the pillowcases who had just stomped on her toe.

"Come on," Rae Dawn said, gripping Lauren under the elbow. "Let's go back here and collect ourselves."

Lauren followed Rae to a dim back corner near the emergency exit, where Lacy was doing a last-minute tuning. She and Delta were wearing the outrageous straight blonde wigs Lauren had bought, but by majority vote they had dispensed with the ferret vests and were all clad in black pants and black turtlenecks.

"All right," Rae said as she tucked her dark hair up under the wig, "are we ready?"

For a moment no one spoke. Then, as if on cue, everyone turned and looked at Lacy, who seemed very pale and was breathing more heavily than usual.

"What?" she demanded. "Yeah, I'm okay. What are we singing again?"

An expression of horror rippled through the group. Lauren was about to say something when Lacy poked her in the ribs and started to laugh. "Just kidding."

"Don't *do* that!" Lauren said. "We're all nervous enough as it is." She folded her arms and regarded her sister. "Did you go to the bathroom?"

"Let's focus, all right?" Rae Dawn interrupted. "We start with 'Blowin' in the Wind.' Do you want to go ahead and do 'If I Had a Hammer,' or wait to see if they want an encore?"

"I think we should wait," Delta said. "I'll check with Tabby and let her know we've got a second song if she wants us to do it, and if there's time."

"Okay then. Delta will give us the sign if we're going to do the second one."

"Of course we'll end up doing it," Delta said. "They're going to love us."

"Ha!" Lacy jibed. "And you started out thinking this would be a big joke."

"It *will* be a joke if we don't get onstage," Rae said. She pointed to the wings, where Tabby was frantically motioning to them and holding up two fingers. "We've got two minutes. Let's go."

For just an instant, when they first stepped out onto the stage, Lauren thought that *she*, not Lacy, might be the one to pee in her pants tonight. The auditorium was packed all the way up to the balcony. Halfway across the platform, she froze in her tracks. Her feet had turned to stone, and her knees were about to give way. She looked out into the audience, and faces swam before her eyes, an enormous sea of them, undulating like a wave.

When the audience caught sight of the long blonde wigs, they began to laugh and point and applaud. Lights glared, and from somewhere above her emanated an earsplitting squeal, feedback from one of the microphones.

Then out of the darkness a calming hand touched her shoulder, and Rae Dawn's low voice spoke into her ear. "Relax. It'll be fun. If you get nervous, just look around at me."

Miraculously, Lauren was able to move again. She followed Rae to center stage and took her place at the mike farthest from the piano. Lacy moved in opposite her, while Delta claimed the remaining microphone, closest to Rae Dawn. Rae nodded, and Lacy jumped in on the second bar of the introduction.

It was amazing. The microphones, the speakers, the acoustics in the auditorium swelled their voices. After three weeks of practice in the rehearsal rooms, Lauren knew they had the notes and the blend right. But she had never in her life imagined this . . . this *sound.* This enormous, confident, harmonious *sound.*

Everyone else seemed surprised too. Delta and Lacy wore dazed, stunned expressions, and at one point during Rae Dawn's segue, Lauren turned around and mouthed, *Is this us?* And they all laughed, right out loud, because it was so much *fun.*

Then, almost before she realized what had happened, Lauren heard it: a surging noise, the sound of wooden auditorium seats clattering. The crowd was on its feet, applauding, cheering, whistling. Rae Dawn stood up at the piano, and the rest of them stepped from behind the mikes, waving and nodding. Tabby, shrouded in the near dark of stage right, stepped forward, gave them a thumbs-up, and made a rolling motion with her hand.

"She wants the encore!" Delta hissed over the noise of the crowd. Rae sat down again, adjusted her mike, flexed her fingers, and launched into "If I Had a Hammer."

This time no one in the auditorium bothered sitting down. They clapped and swayed and nodded their heads in time to the music. Lacy pounded away at the guitar, and Lauren could barely sing because her grin kept getting in the way. The music sailed and swirled around and through her—Rae Dawn's gorgeous deep alto, Delta's clear lead.

As the song lifted and soared, Lauren's heart lifted with it. By the time they came to the last verse, she was flying.

The words echoed in the hall: *Justice. Freedom. Love.* The crowd roared its approval.

Lauren grabbed her sister's hand, took a bow, and grinned. "Damn," she said as the applause washed over them, "that was *fun!*" And perhaps for the first time in her life, Lauren Cantrell felt herself totally set free.

If only I could know that freedom again, Lauren thought as the rain continued to pour from the dark sky.

But she was forty-six years old. It was too late to change. Too many years had gone by, too much pain. Too much water had passed under the bridge.

Or perhaps the bridge had been washed out altogether.

PART 2

The Golden Years

Like amber leaves upon a branch,
the hopeful gilded dreams of youth
shimmer in the sunlight,
tempting, out of reach,
yet never out of mind.

Ah, we were true believers then,
convinced our dreams
were weightless
and would
never
fall.

SEVEN

At the Goose

Sophomore year
Autumn 1966

For generations the college grill had been known as the Gray Goose, a reference to certain ceramic figurines that had decorated the tables back in the early 1900s, long before the current café had been so much as a glimmer in an architect's eye. Here and there a few goose remnants remained, such as the goose-shaped clock on the wall and an enclosed patio with the outline of a goose stamped in the paving stones.

At a wrought-iron table on the outdoor terrace, Delta Fox pushed aside her textbooks—English lit, *Crafting the Short Story, Intro to Social Work.* Last year had been core courses mostly. Now, as a sophomore, she was finally getting into subjects that really interested her. Especially literature and creative writing.

At last the heat of September had spent itself and given way to cooler weather and glorious autumn colors. This was Delta's favorite season, the time of year that always stirred a restless energy in her. A leather-bound journal—a gift from Cassie last Christmas—lay on top of her books, and she picked it up and flipped through it. Only a month and a half into creative writing, and already the journal was crammed with notes—descriptions of characters, snatches of dialogue, titles, fragments of ideas. Even an opening scene for the short story that was due in two weeks. Delta had no delusions of becoming a writer, but she was thoroughly enjoying the process. Creative writing was her favorite class.

She closed the journal and settled herself in the afternoon sunshine to read through her mail. The process took a while, since people kept coming to the back windows of the grill, knocking and waving to get her attention. She waved back but did not invite any of them to join her.

Delta took a sip of iced tea. The first letter, thinner and rather crumpled looking, was from her longtime boyfriend, Ben Rutledge, in Atlanta. An architectural engineering student at Georgia Tech, Ben wasn't much of a writer, and his letter would undoubtedly be short and to the point, a hastily scribbled note, a memo: *When are you coming home?* Or, *Everything's fine here. I miss you. Will call Friday at 7:30.*

The second letter, postmarked Stone Mountain, Georgia—a thick, heavy, legal-size envelope with extra postage—was addressed in her mother's handwriting, old-fashioned and flowy. From the heft of it, it probably included pictures drawn by her six-year-old sister Cassie, who worshiped Delta.

Delta's father called her *Daddy's Little Afterthought.*

She laid her mother's letter aside and opened Ben's. As Delta had expected, it was one page, printed neatly in the angular, precise hand of a future architect.

Hey, cute thing—

Had dinner with your folks on Sunday. Your dad took me out to the park to see the progress on the Big Rock. He appears to think it's a matter of Southern pride to follow every move of the torch, and can't seem to remember I'm a Yankee at heart.

Classes are going well. My Architectural Design prof, Dr. Butts, says he thinks I have a lot of promise. More potential than if my name was "Butts," that's for sure.

Will call on Friday eve, usual time. Try to come home for a weekend soon, OK?

Love,
Ben

Delta reread the letter and smiled. Ben was right: Delta's father still had trouble realizing that Ben wasn't really a southern boy. He had moved with his parents from Vermont to Atlanta during junior high, and by then his liberal northern turn of mind was already firmly entrenched. It was one reason among many that Delta adored him. He was different, and unafraid. He didn't own a single firearm, didn't drive a pickup truck, didn't fall in line and salute the Confederate flag like most of the boys she had grown up with. He kept his own unshakable opinions. And yet he indulged Daddy in his fascination with the Stone Mountain carving.

Since 1928 the six-hundred-foot granite dome that gave the town its name had sat untouched, its unfinished carving a mute testimony to the faded glory of the old South. A year ago work had finally resumed on the project, an enormous bas-relief of that Holy Trinity of the Confederacy—Robert E. Lee, Stonewall Jackson, and Jefferson Davis. Delta's father was ecstatic. To anyone who would stand still long enough to listen, he rhapsodized about the magnificence of the sculpture, prophesying that one day the Stone Mountain park would be a world-class attraction, drawing people from all over the world. He went out to the park at least once a week, rain or shine, to check on the progress, as if he were personally responsible for the completion of the sculpture. And whenever Ben was around, Daddy would drag him out there to oversee the work as well.

Neither Ben nor Delta could understand the obsession. Stone Mountain was a nice little town with a picturesque main street and a laid-back atmosphere that contrasted sharply with the tension and haste of Atlanta proper. But, as Ben often pointed out, the mountain itself wasn't a mountain at all—just a huge slab of granite sticking up out of nowhere, with none of the charm or peacefulness of the Green Mountains of Vermont or the Blue Ridge Mountains three hours north of Atlanta. Besides that, the sculpture, though massive, wasn't exactly Mount Rushmore. Thus, while everyone around them oohed and aahed over the carving and its historical significance, Delta and Ben privately shook their heads in amazement and dismay.

This was the 1960s, for God's sake. The War Between the States had been over for a century, and in case nobody in Georgia had noticed, the South had *lost.* Atlanta, once burned to rubble, had in the past hundred years risen from its ashes to become a thriving, diverse, cosmopolitan city. Last summer President Johnson signed the Civil Rights Act into law. The future was Coke and Delta Airlines and Martin Luther King, not *Gone With the Wind* and the KKK and Lester Maddox.

Delta did not, of course, voice these opinions aloud. Her parents, though good people and not overtly racist, seemed apprehensive and confused by the changes that were rapidly coming to the deep South. They had difficulty moving beyond their nostalgia for the simpler, more placid days gone by, and the knowledge that their eldest daughter supported such a revolution would have troubled them even more.

Delta sighed, set aside Ben's letter, and opened the one from her mother.

Dear DeeDee . . .

Delta cringed. She despised this nickname her mother had imposed on her before she had the vocabulary to protest. It brought up memories of scratchy pink crinolines and uncomfortable black patent shoes, and the hideous perm she had endured when she was six and about to enter first grade. Daddy was the one who had first called her Delta.

She pushed her irritation aside and read on:

Dear DeeDee,

Hope all is going well with you there at college. We are all right. Cassie is (as we knew she would be) far beyond any of her little friends in first grade. While they're learning to sing the alphabet and can barely manage "See Jane run," she sits in a corner and reads everything she can get her hands on. I swear she goes through about a dozen books a week.

I worry for her. She doesn't seem to be adjusting well to being with the other children. The teacher says she's bossy sometimes, and other times withdrawn. I wonder if we ought to let skip ahead, except that she's so small. People see her and think she's four years old, and then she opens her mouth and sounds like she's thirty. Last week she complained about having to participate in a reading circle. "The stories are just so juvenile," she said. "I wouldn't mind school so much if it wasn't so infernally boring."

Where does she get this stuff?

Anyway, I've included some pictures she drew for you and a story she wrote. She still thinks she ought to be at college with you, and occasionally I suspect she might be right.

Daddy says to tell you that the carving is coming along nicely. They're using something called thermo-torches to slice away the stone. Your father made friends with Roy Faulkner, who's the new chief carver, and Roy took him up on the mountain to show him how the torches work.

Ben came for dinner on Sunday. He's so nice and intelligent and considerate, even if he does have some strange ideas for a southern boy. And he's really sweet on you. I think you could do worse than marrying an architect.

Write soon and come home when you can. We all miss you.

Much love,
Mama, Daddy, & Cassie

All three names were signed in Mama's handwriting. After the two pages of Mama's letter came three heavy sheets torn from a sketchbook. Cassie's crayon drawings showed a good deal of artistic promise, Delta thought. First a landscape scene of a brown and white horse running through a meadow, with a giant rock in the background. Then a rendering of Stone Mountain's main street, again with the granite slab hovering overhead. And finally—a tribute to Daddy, no doubt—a close-up rendering of the monument itself, with a half-carved head dominating the foreground.

Delta wondered what a psychiatrist would make of these drawings. She could just see Sigmund Freud scratching his beard: *Ja, but what is the psychic oppression symbolized by the colossal boulder hanging over her head?*

The last few pages had been ripped from a first-grader's writing tablet, wide double lines with a dotted line in the middle. In a careful, childish hand, Cassie had filled these sheets with a story that made Delta laugh—the tale of a young and beautiful princess, captive in a high tower on a massive stone outcropping. But when the handsome prince climbs up to the tower window to rescue her, he finds his true love surrounded by tall stacks of books. The princess refuses to leave with him because she hasn't yet finished the one she is currently reading.

It was the last sentence that cracked Delta up: *"Go away and learn your alphabet," the Princess told him. "And don't come back until you've got something interesting to say."*

"What's so funny?"

Delta looked up, startled, to see a flash of wispy light brown hair backlit by the sun. She hadn't heard anyone come out onto the terrace. It was Dr. Suzanne Hart, her creative writing professor, holding a white ceramic mug in one hand and several books in the other.

"Am I interrupting?"

Delta stood up abruptly. "No, it's fine. Let me clear some space." She moved the letters to one side to give Dr. Hart room on the table for her books.

"Do you want something? Coffee?"

Delta had already resumed her seat, and now she found herself craning her neck to look at Dr. Hart. The woman was in her forties, perhaps, but seemed younger. She had a round, girlish face with just a hint of crow's feet. Delta knew from experience that those hazel eyes could go steely and stern in class, but at the moment they seemed open and welcoming. Dr. Hart was smiling, anticipating an answer to her question. Suddenly Delta realized the incongruity of the scene—herself seated, her professor standing there like a waitress poised to take her order.

She jumped to her feet. "Yes, coffee would be great. But I can—"

"Stay put," Dr. Hart said amiably. "I'll get it. You want cream or sugar?"

Delta sank awkwardly back into her chair. "Saccharine, if they've got it. No cream. Ah, thanks."

"You want me to take that in?" She pointed at the plastic glass that held the remains of Delta's watery iced tea.

"That'd be great."

Dr. Hart took the glass and her own coffee cup and returned in a moment with two steaming mugs, several paper napkins, a spoon, and a small bottle of liquid sweetener. "It's getting a little chilly out here."

"It's autumn, all right." Delta shook a couple of drops of the sweetener into her cup, stirred it, and glanced at her watch.

"Do you have to be somewhere?" Dr. Hart asked as she settled herself across the table from Delta.

"Not until four thirty. I have a rehearsal. For the—uh, for the Delta Belles." Delta felt herself flush. "It's kind of a singing group, informal, really. Folk music. We got started as an act for the Harvest Fest last year, and it just snowballed from there. Now we're being asked to sing other places, and—" She sputtered to a stop. How embarrassing was this, to be talking with a professor about a stupid talent show?

Dr. Hart grinned. "I remember. You were the highlight of the show. You and Lynn Stanton's Pillowcase People, that is. From the sublime to the ridiculous, I suppose. Lynn's act is so dumb it's funny. Your group is really good."

Delta gaped at her. "Thanks."

"So, what were you laughing at when I came up?" the professor asked. "It seemed pretty hilarious, whatever it was."

"My little sister Cassie," Delta said. "She sent me drawings and a story she wrote." She showed Dr. Hart the pictures, then gave her a brief synopsis of the princess's tale and read her the last line.

"Sounds like you're not the only one in the family with creative talent. How old did you say she is?"

"Six. Just started first grade—which is, in her words, *infernally boring*."

"She sounds smart."

"Maybe too smart for her own good. She learned to read before she was four."

Dr. Hart sipped at her coffee and looked at Cassie's pictures again. "She's six, and you're—what, nineteen? That's quite an age difference. How is that for you, being a big sister?"

Delta grinned and ducked her head. "I have to admit, at first I wasn't thrilled about it. I was thirteen when she came along, and accustomed to being an only child. Besides, when you're thirteen, you pretty much feel different all the time—you know, out of step with the rest of the world, uncomfortable in your own skin."

Dr. Hart raised an eyebrow. "I can't imagine. You're attractive and intelligent—and, unless I miss my guess, popular."

"Think newborn colt, all legs and eyes, then add braces, and you'll get the picture. I was a test model for some alien species."

The professor smiled. "I suppose we all feel that way in adolescence."

"Then, as if your typical teenage angst weren't enough, add a new baby sister to the mix. I felt as if I were walking around wearing a sign that said, 'My parents still have sex,' and believe me, that's the last thing a thirteen-year-old wants to advertise."

Dr. Hart laughed. "But clearly you dealt with it and have a good relationship with her."

"Yes, I do—now," Delta said. "As a teenager I complained about babysitting for free, but for the most part I liked being a big sister. I grew up. And now I can't imagine life without her." She took another sip of coffee, shook in two more drops of sweetener, and chanced a surreptitious glance at the professor. "Did you mean that, about me having creative talent?"

"Relax, Delta," Dr. Hart said. "This isn't an inquisition, it's a coffee break. And yes, I did mean it. You're doing very well in my class. Creative writing is about creative thinking, and I like the way you think."

"Really?"

"Really. In fact, that's why I stopped by today. Frankie and I would like to have a talk with you."

"Frankie?"

"Frances Bowen. She teaches Shakespeare and Renaissance Poetry, among other things. She's—" Hart paused for a moment. "My housemate."

"I haven't met her yet."

"Trust me, you will. You'll either love her or hate her, but however you feel about her, you'll learn a lot in her classes." The professor chuckled. "Compared to her, I'm a pushover."

"Ah," Delta faltered, not knowing quite what to say, "I'll look forward to it."

"Anyway," Dr. Hart went on, "Frankie and I have been talking about you, and we believe you'd make a good English major. Have you declared a major yet?"

"Actually, I haven't. But I've thought about English," Delta said, a little less intimidated. "Lit was always my favorite class in high school, and I do like to write."

"Great. Come to dinner Wednesday, and we'll talk."

"Dinner? At your house?" Delta fought it but couldn't keep the panicked tone out of her voice.

Dr. Hart gathered up her books. "Right."

"Wednesday," Delta repeated.

"Six o'clock. I'll give you directions. It's walking distance from campus."

"All right," Delta said. "Thanks for the invitation."

Dr. Hart drained the last of her coffee and stood up. "It's not the lion's den, you know." She gave a little laugh. "Well, to be perfectly honest Frankie *does* roar a little, I'll admit, but she rarely bites. And she's one hell of a cook. You won't be sorry you came."

EIGHT

Flint and Steel

Delta stood on the tree-lined street in the gathering dusk and pulled her jacket more closely around her. A few tired leaves let go in a gust of wind and swirled around her feet.

She checked the address Dr. Hart had given her. This was it: a cozy-looking brick Arts and Crafts cottage that sat back from the street with an enormous maple tree arching overhead. The maple hadn't shed yet, and its crimson leaves caught the last glow of sunset and blazed in fiery radiance against the purple sky. Above the maple, one star winked on—Venus, she thought, low in the southwest.

Nervously Delta checked her watch. Five-fifty-seven. Was she dressed all right? She had chosen bell-bottom jeans and a sweater—casual, but not too scruffy. She didn't want to look like an unwashed hippie or a disrespectful teenager.

Okay, she thought, *no more stalling.* Exhaling heavily, she opened the gate, latched it behind her, and went to ring the bell.

Immediately all hell broke loose. From behind the closed door Delta heard a wild scrabbling sound, deranged barking, a crash, a curse. At last the door opened on a harried-looking Dr. Hart clutching the collars of two enormous poodles—one black, one white.

"Sit," she commanded.

Delta looked frantically around for something to sit on.

"Not *you,*" Hart amended. "You come in. I hope to God you like dogs."

The poodles had stopped barking and, much to Delta's amazement, were perched on their haunches gazing eagerly at her, their tongues lolling. She had never seen a standard poodle up close before and had always derided the miniature variety as pampered little furballs. These were *real* dogs, muscular and alert, surveying her with intelligent, perceptive eyes.

"Sure, I love dogs," she said, stepping across the threshold and extending a hand for the animals to sniff.

"Meet Bilbo and Frodo, then," the professor said. "Frodo's the black one."

"Hello, boys." Delta got down on one knee and petted each of them in turn.

"Beasts," Dr. Hart muttered. "Well, come on back to the kitchen. Frankie's cooking. Hope you like Chinese."

Only once had Delta seen her writing professor outside the classroom, and now she looked small and unimposing in faded jeans and a navy pullover sweater, with her hair tied up in a ponytail.

Dr. Bowen, hovering over a wok in the kitchen, was also clad in blue jeans, and wore a denim work shirt. Delta hadn't had her for a class yet, but the woman had a reputation for being an excellent professor, hard as nails and extremely demanding. Up close, she reminded Delta a little of Hawthorne's Great Stone Face, with intense, deep-set eyes divided by a permanent frown line, uncompromising features, and short, thick, salt-and-pepper hair.

"Frankie, this is Delta Fox," Dr. Hart said.

She looked up and smiled briefly. "Frances Bowen," she said, wiping a hand on her jeans and extending it in Delta's direction. "We're having egg rolls and crab Rangoon and Cantonese chicken with mushrooms. Oh, and there's sweet and sour soup on the stove." She turned to the dogs, who had come to stand on either side of her. "No begging," she said in a quiet but authoritative voice. "Out of the kitchen and into your beds."

The two poodles gazed up at her with an utterly crestfallen expression, then went to the breakfast room and lay down on two enormous pillows situated under the windows.

"They're very obedient," Delta said.

"Discipline is a gift to intelligent minds," Bowen said. She arched an eyebrow in Delta's direction. "Remember that when you get into my class."

DR. HART HAD BEEN RIGHT. Dr. Bowen was, in Hart's words, "one hell of a cook." Dinner was exquisite, especially the crab Rangoon, which turned out to be delicate, crispy wonton shells filled with cream cheese and crab. Delta had never used chopsticks before, and it took her a while to get the hang of it, but once she mastered the technique, she found the Cantonese chicken to be equally good.

Even more interesting than the dinner, however, was the discussion around the table. Dr. Hart mentioned the Delta Belles and folk music, and from there the conversation segued to protest rallies and civil rights and the state of the nation. It took Frankie Bowen all of ten minutes to get wound up and going strong.

"Anyone who's not outraged," she said, "isn't paying attention. It's 1966, for God's sake. The Civil Rights Act and the

Voting Rights Act have both been passed, but how many black students do we have here at the W? Two? Three? How many high schools in this state are still segregated? How many people are hindered from registering to vote, or required to take literacy tests or pay poll taxes? We might as well be living in *1866*, for all the difference it's made."

"Frankie—" Dr. Hart said, reaching a hand in her direction.

"Don't shush me," Dr. Bowen said, glaring at her. "Somebody needs to speak the truth. King said, 'Injustice anywhere is a threat to justice everywhere.' If we don't stand up for other people's rights, it'll be *our* rights that are taken away next."

Dr. Hart listened patiently until Dr. Bowen's rant wound down and then said, "Well, that was, ah, *impassioned*."

Dr. Bowen turned and gave a little nod. "Thank you. I'm glad you enjoyed it."

Delta suppressed a chuckle. Dr. Bowen might have a reputation for being forged of steel, but Delta liked her. Most professors lived in the academic netherworld, not bothering with anything that did not relate directly to their areas of expertise. Dr. Bowen was intelligent and articulate and passionate about issues that went well beyond the range of Renaissance literature. She was real. Her friendship with Suzanne Hart was real. Clearly they cared about each other, but they challenged each other too. Like flint on steel, sparks flew and fire was born.

Now that fire rose up inside her, a compelling voice, and for the first time she had a name to put to it: a sense of calling. It felt like driving on a country road with all the windows down, like standing at the ocean at sunrise.

Like leaving home and coming home all at the same time.

NINE

Rae Dawn's Revelation

Sophomore year
Spring 1967

Alone in her dorm room, Rae Dawn sat staring at her philosophy textbook. She had read the page in front of her three times already, and not a single word of it had registered.

She sank back in her desk chair and looked out over front campus, dappled in light and shadow as moonlight shone through the trees. Across the quad, porch lamps illuminated the wide veranda of the music building. Two students sat on the top step, talking and laughing, and over their voices she could hear the sounds of a piano drifting on the night air. A rectangle of yellow light pooled on the grass outside Manfred Gottlieb's office window.

Philosophy didn't concern her in the least. Oh, she would study it dutifully and would no doubt do well in the class—she had always compensated for her background by being a good student, and those habits were hard to break. But philosophy was a requirement for the education program, and the idea of teaching had fled to the farthest recesses of her mind.

She was now an officially declared music major. She was being taught by Manfred Gottlieb. Nothing else mattered.

She gazed down at the golden rectangle of the professor's window and felt a glow rising up in her, as if the light were a fire that warmed her through to the core. A complicated counterpoint echoed inside her head—a score the professor himself had recently composed and had played for her in his office after her lesson yesterday. A piece of such immense power and emotion that it seemed to swirl within her very soul, filling her like helium, inspiring her and lifting her beyond herself. She couldn't get it out of her mind.

Nor could she rid herself of the nagging voice that told her she had been untruthful with her friends.

Every time she left a lesson with Dr. Gottlieb, Rae Dawn was flying, exultant, empowered as if nothing could touch her. But whenever she thought about her deception, she felt twisted, wrung out, and hung to dry.

With Lauren and Lacy—even with Delta, her closest friend—Rae had kept her secrets. No one except Gottlieb knew about her background, about her parents or the Airstream or growing up on Hobo Creek. Not even about the nature of her scholarship. They all thought she was from New Orleans. They teased her about being exotic and mysterious, and she played along, content to keep them in the dark. On holidays, when she had no choice but to go back to Picayune, she returned to school as soon as possible and spoke to no one about her family.

But she couldn't keep up the charade forever. She couldn't share with them her excitement about Gottlieb's lessons or her change of major or her hope for the future unless they knew the rest. And besides, she was weary of the facade.

She had determined to do it at dinner tonight. But then Tabitha Austin appeared at their table, and Rae Dawn clammed up. She wasn't about to confess all with Tabby hanging on every word.

Rae sighed and raked her hands through her hair. People like Tabby inevitably set her nerves on edge. Rich, beautiful, popular people who seemed utterly convinced that the world owed them everything.

Delta Fox was popular, of course. And pretty. And if not rich, at least well off enough not to have to worry about things like tuition and clothes and books. But Delta was different. She wasn't caught up in herself. She was . . . *real.* Authentic.

That was the word Dr. Gottlieb had used today when they were discussing principles of creativity. "For a composition to live," he said, "it must be *authentic.* It must rise from the very depths of the soul. It may emanate from agony or joy, from struggle or victory. At its best, it comes from all of these, reflecting the breadth and depth of human experience. But whatever else it is, it must be transparent, vulnerable, holding nothing back." He had looked into her eyes with his cloud-blue gaze. "If the composer hides in darkness, the light will not shine through the music."

Now Rae Dawn looked again at the light streaming from the professor's window and made her decision. She snapped the philosophy book shut, slipped on her loafers, and went out into the night.

"May I come in?" Rae asked when Dr. Gottlieb answered her knock.

He stood aside. "By all means."

"I'm sorry to come so late. I saw your office light on, and—"

Gottlieb shrugged. "The hour is of no consequence. I am a night bird."

Rae Dawn smiled. "Night *owl*."

"Ah." The professor gave a little self-deprecating laugh. "I would think that after twenty years my English would be better. But your idioms escape me at times."

Rae entered the office and seated herself in the leather chair across from his desk. "I've been thinking about what you said. About authenticity. Transparency."

He nodded and motioned for her to continue.

Despite her earlier determination, a shudder of nervous tension ran through her. "This isn't really about music, Professor," she said apologetically. "I probably shouldn't be taking up your time."

"I am here for you no matter what you wish to speak about," Dr. Gottlieb said. "Surely we are more than professor and student by now." He laid a hand on his chest. "For my part, I think of you as the daughter I never had. The child of my heart." He smiled. "Besides, for a musician, everything is about music. Life is music. Music is life."

At his words, a radiant warmth shot through Rae Dawn's veins. He was so kind, so accepting. So . . . fatherly. She'd never had a father—not a real one, anyway, and with a shock of recognition she realized that she had grown to think of him that way too.

"All right. Well, you see, I haven't told my friends the truth about myself. About Picayune. About my family and background. I've been rationalizing it, telling myself it doesn't matter. But then you said what you did about hiding in darkness and not letting the light shine through the music—"

Dr. Gottlieb twined his fingers together and inclined his head. "And . . . ?"

"And I need to tell them, don't I? I need to be honest. I can't be authentic in my music if I'm not authentic about myself. Otherwise I'm just blowing smoke out my—" She stopped abruptly and felt heat rise into her face.

"Smoke out your ass?" he finished with just the hint of a smile. "That is the correct phrase, yes?"

"Yes."

"I must admit I do not understand that one very well. I have never personally seen this smoke from the buttocks, and believe it to be a physical impossibility. But then there are many things I have not yet experienced."

Rae Dawn laughed, and her tension dissipated a little. "Anyway, I want to tell them the truth. I really do. But—"

"But you are afraid of how they might respond," the professor finished.

She nodded.

"You fear they might not wish to be your friends any longer if they knew the secrets you have been hiding from them?"

"I don't know," Rae said miserably. "I can't really believe they'd reject me because of my background. But they might not be too happy that I've kept it from them for so long."

"And yet—" He made a rolling motion with his hand.

"And yet I have no real choice."

The professor raised an eyebrow. "We always have choices, child. As long as we live, we choose. You can choose to be honest or not. They can choose to accept you or not. You are responsible not for their reactions, but for your own integrity." He tilted his head. "Besides, how do we ever know that we are fully loved unless we are fully known?"

RAE HAD INTENDED to return to the dorm, gather her nerve, and then go down to Delta's room to talk. But while she was still pacing, trying to formulate the right words, the door opened and Delta came in.

"Hey," she said, plopping down on Rae Dawn's bed. "This is such a great space. I'm jealous." She looked around. "Where's your roommate?"

"Gone." Rae shrugged. "She transferred to Rowan Hall to room with a friend, and the Student Affairs office never got around to assigning anyone else. I lucked out."

"I can't imagine why anyone would move out of Castlebury into Rowan," Delta said. "Those dorms on back campus are like rabbit warrens. Small rooms, with high little windows and concrete block walls. Reminds me of jail."

"Like you've ever been in jail." Rae Dawn forced a laugh. "I prefer being on front campus too. It's so peaceful. We may not have private baths or elevators, and sometimes going up three flights of stairs is a pain, but it's a fair trade-off."

Delta wandered over and peered out the window. "I love these tower rooms. Nice view. You've even got a balcony up here." She pointed to a small glass-paneled door angled across a corner of the room.

"Yeah, but I have to keep the door closed. A small colony of bats has taken up residence in the eaves."

Delta shuddered and moved away from the corner.

The superficial talk dissipated like fog, and an uncomfortable silence settled over the room. Delta continued to pace.

"Okay, what's up?" Rae Dawn said at last.

Delta looked at her. "That's exactly what I was about to ask you. You've been acting strange lately."

"Strange?"

"I'm your best friend—at least I think I am. But lately I don't feel as if I know what's going on with you. And you were really rude to Tabby Austin at dinner tonight."

"Rude? How was I rude? I was very restrained, if you ask me. Didn't say a word to her."

"Exactly. You ignored her completely, as if she wasn't even there. It's not like you, Rae Dawn. Something's bothering you."

Rae let out a sigh. This wasn't going the way she had planned, not at all. "Yeah," she said, "something *is* bothering me. But I'm not about to spill my guts in front of Miss Priss."

"What do you have against her? She's a perfectly nice girl."

"Right. She's perfect." Rae Dawn flexed her shoulders and twisted her neck, trying to release the tension. "Want to know the truth? It's *because* she's so perfect. She makes me feel—I don't know. Different. Inferior."

The word was out before Rae could call it back. She felt a tingling chill creep up her spine.

"Inferior?" Delta repeated. "How could you possibly feel inferior? You're smart, you're talented—"

"I've *always* felt inferior," Rae Dawn said, cutting her off. "And it's not a figment of my imagination, Delta. You don't know what it was like, growing up the way I did. You have no idea."

Delta leaned forward, and when she spoke her voice was quiet, entreating. "So tell me."

The compassion, the openness in her voice took Rae Dawn by surprise. No wonder Delta was so popular, so welcome anywhere she went. It wasn't because of her looks or her personality. It was because she cared.

Tears stung Rae's eyes, and she swallowed against the rising emotion. Then the floodgates opened. She propped her elbows on her knees and looked directly into Delta's eyes. "When I was a little girl—" She paused.

"In New Orleans," Delta supplied.

"No, not in New Orleans." Rae Dawn sighed. "New Orleans

is a fantasy, a dream wish. I was born and raised thirty miles northeast, outside of Picayune, Mississippi."

"But you told us—"

"I made it up, all that stuff about New Orleans. I mean, the places I told you about are real enough. I spent a lot of time there as a teenager. But I never lived there, even though I desperately wanted to. To live *anywhere,* actually, other than Picayune." She took in a ragged breath and went on, describing the broken-down trailer, the experience of living on Hobo Creek, her father's drunken rages, her mother's apathy.

"So anytime I could hitch a ride, I'd escape to New Orleans. I'd hang around the Quarter, listen to the music. Sometimes tourists would take pity on me and give me a little money. All I dreamed of was being able to live in New Orleans and play the piano. And then out of the blue I got a scholarship to come here." She paused. "A resident need stipend."

Delta looked puzzled.

"It's a grant for state residents who have no way of paying for college otherwise," Rae Dawn explained. "Reserved for the most desperately poor." She shook her head. "And I almost didn't get that, because I had a hell of a time just convincing my parents to sign the application papers. They didn't think I needed to go to college. I suppose they expected me to work at Winnie's Washeteria and take care of them for the rest of my life."

The memory of the trailer, and her parents, and the moldy, fishy smell of Hobo Creek caused Rae Dawn to cringe. "I'd had enough of being teased and taunted, of being yelled at or rejected—or worse, invisible. I got on a Greyhound and left it all behind, and once I've graduated I'm never going back there. Never."

"You were laughed at because you were poor?"

"Because I was poor and dirty. Because I wore clothes from

the Goodwill. Because my daddy was a drunk and my mama was a zombie. You name it."

"And the worst offenders," Delta ventured, "were little clones of Tabitha Austin. Rich, pretty, privileged."

A stab of remorse caused Rae Dawn to flinch. "I guess so."

Delta smiled. "Or little clones of me."

"Not you," Rae protested. "You're not like that. You're different. You understand. You care."

"But how would you know I cared if you didn't give me a chance?"

Rae Dawn looked up. Delta was gazing at her, and there was no hint of condemnation in her expression. Just a softness that spoke of empathy and affection.

"What makes me different from Tabby?" she asked.

"Well . . . I *know* you."

"Right." Delta nodded. "So let us know *you*. Tell us what's going on in your life."

"As a matter of fact, there's a good deal going on," Rae said. "But I should tell Lauren and Lacy too."

ON THE WAY DOWNSTAIRS to round up the twins, Delta considered the implications of Rae Dawn's revelation. She couldn't even imagine what it was like to be that poor, to grow up ashamed of your own parents, to hate going home.

Delta had never considered her parents rich, by any stretch of the imagination. Solidly middle class, with a split-level house, two cars in the driveway, and two children, the Foxes represented the consummate small-town family.

Mama seemed bored once in a while, now that Delta was looking at her family from the outside, with a dispassionate eye. Occasionally Daddy was grouchy if business was in a slump. But nobody got drunk or yelled or cursed, and everybody always had clean clothes and plenty to eat and lots of books and a television to watch Ed Sullivan.

Delta had never known deprivation or hunger or isolation. Never been teased or bullied. There had never been a question of whether she could or would go to college, or whether there would be money enough for tuition. If she lived to be a hundred, she would never truly understand the kind of upbringing and family life Rae Dawn had endured.

She paused outside the twins' open door and then entered without knocking. Lauren sat at the desk painting her fingernails a violent, ghoulish shade of red, and Lacy sprawled across one of the beds practicing her guitar.

Both of them looked up.

"Hey," Lauren said. Lacy waved and went back to strumming.

"Can the two of you come upstairs for a minute?"

"Give me a sec," Lauren said. "I'm almost done." She held up a hand. "Like it?"

"Ah, sure." Delta winked at Lacy. "It's kind of the color of vampire blood."

Lauren blew on her fingernails and capped the polish, then stood up. "Exactly the look I was going for. Lady Dracula."

RAE DAWN TRIED TO SUPPRESS the writhing in her stomach as she sat facing Delta and the twins lined up sideways on her bed, shoulder to shoulder. The image of a firing squad came to mind, but she pushed it aside. She'd already told Delta the bad part, which had turned out not to be so bad after all. But now she had to repeat everything for Lauren and Lacy, and the stiff formality of the situation made her even more anxious.

She blew out a breath. "Okay, here's the deal," she said. "I, ah—" She paused. This hadn't been quite so difficult in the context of the conversation about Tabitha Austin. But just to blurt it out, cold turkey, while Lauren and Lacy sat there eyeing her with curious expressions . . . well, she hadn't the faintest idea how to get started.

"Do you want me to summarize our earlier conversation?" Delta offered.

A surge of gratitude flowed over Rae Dawn. "Please. If you don't mind."

"All right." Delta adjusted her position on the bed so she could make eye contact with the twins. "It's like this—we all thought Rae was from New Orleans, but she isn't. She's from Picayune, Mississippi, and she grew up really poor, and she's here on a need scholarship, and she didn't want to tell us about it because she was ashamed." She said all of this very quickly, then turned back toward Rae.

Stunned, Rae Dawn gaped at Delta. She hadn't been prepared for such a blunt, truncated narrative of her past. And yet it seemed easier, somehow, to hear it in such a matter-of-fact tone, without any drama.

"What, you're embarrassed about your family?" Lauren asked.

"Yes." Rae Dawn nodded. "My father is an alcoholic. A drunk. My mother pretty much checked out of life years ago, except she still keeps on breathing. I was raised in a broken-down trailer and never knew where my next meal was coming from. It was—" She paused. "Bad."

"And you were self-conscious about telling us?"

"Yes. No." Rae frowned. "Not self-conscious. Mortified. Humiliated."

"What a load of rubbish," Lauren said. "For God's sake, girl, we don't give a damn about your family."

"Well, yes, we do," Lacy broke in. "We give a damn about how it has affected you and hurt you. But it doesn't matter where you came from. It matters who you are."

Relief rolled over Rae Dawn, a cleansing, healing wave. She began to tell them the whole story, even parts Delta hadn't heard. Her visceral response to music, the longing to play and write and be somebody. Her love of New Orleans, details of her furtive visits as a teenager, her fantasies about being part of the music scene in the Quarter. Her ultimate escape from Picayune via the scholarship offered to her. The way she had resigned herself to becoming a teacher instead of a musician because it gave her security, a means of supporting herself.

And then, finally, she came to the best part. The miracle. She told them about Manfred Gottlieb listening outside the practice room and asking her to come to his office.

"I don't know how he knew about me," Rae Dawn said, "but it was like he had an inside track on my life. He *understood.*"

She judiciously omitted the part about *why* he understood. She wouldn't feed the rumors about him or betray his confidence.

"Anyway," Rae Dawn concluded, "he's been giving me lessons. Teaching me—for *free.*" She beamed at them. "He believes I have real talent, both as a professional musician and as a composer. And he's helping me."

Hoots and whistles and applause filled the little tower room as Rae Dawn's friends celebrated with her. They hugged her and laughed and talked over one another. At last a serious-looking brunette stomped down the hall and stood in the doorway staring at them until they all shut up.

"Sorry," Rae said, glancing at the clock on her bedside table. "I didn't know it was so late." It was after eleven, and ten o'clock was the start of quiet time in the dorm. They were lucky the house mother hadn't heard them.

"Never mind about that," the girl said. "I'm just passing the word. There's a moon tonight, and the ginkgo is shedding!"

With a whoop and a holler, the four of them trooped down the stairs and out into a beautiful October night. Someone had built a bonfire in the fire pit on front campus. "Dean of Students has brought s'mores!" a tall upperclassman informed them as she dashed by on her way to the tree.

Together they ambled over to the ginkgo tree and watched as the yellow, fan-shaped leaves cascaded down in lazy spirals. All around them, girls were jostling and jumping to grab a leaf before it touched the ground.

"Catch it!" Lauren called to Lacy. "You'll find the love of your life before next spring!"

"Do you believe this stuff?" Delta asked Rae.

Rae Dawn shrugged and held up both hands in an attitude of surrender. A single ginkgo leaf drifted into her palm and lay there quivering like a golden butterfly.

"Not really," she said. "But I'll keep it anyway."

Delta snatched a falling leaf from the air and stuffed it into the pocket of her pajama top. "Come on, everybody," she said as she grabbed each of the twins by an arm. "Let's go get some s'mores before they're all gone."

Out of the corner of her eye, Rae caught a glimpse of burnished copper illuminated by the moonlight. She turned. Tabitha Austin was standing under the ginkgo alone, with a single leaf caught in her hair.

Gently Rae Dawn pulled it out and handed it to her. "This is yours, I believe." She hesitated. "Why don't you come on over and have s'mores with us?"

After a moment's indecision, Tabby nodded. "All right," she said in a tentative voice. "I—ah, I've been meaning to tell you. I really enjoy your music—with the Delta Belles and all. You're so gifted—on the piano, I mean. And your voice. You could be a star."

"Thanks." Rae Dawn smiled, and she felt something warm and accepting break open inside her. For the first time in her life, she didn't feel ashamed to be standing next to the likes of Tabitha Austin.

TEN

The Promise of the Ginkgo Tree

Senior year
February 1969

In the empty parking lot behind the maintenance building, Lacy sat in the back seat of a 1964 Chevy Corvair convertible making out with Trip Jenkins. The top was up, but a weak spot in the roof dripped rain onto her neck, and her shoulder blade pressed painfully into the edge of the seat.

She struggled to a more comfortable position and pulled away slightly. The windows were fogging up. A raindrop slithered down her spine, causing her to shiver.

"What's wrong?" Trip asked. He shifted his long legs, but there wasn't enough room, and his knees knocked hard into the back of the driver's seat. "Ow." He grinned and raked a hand through his already disheveled hair. "Not the best venue for getting hot and heavy, I guess."

"It's all right. I have to go soon anyway." Lacy peered at her watch. "Dinner's in fifteen minutes."

Trip heaved himself up a little and retucked his shirt while Lacy regarded him. The ginkgo tree had taken its own sweet time, but it had finally come through. This was the love of her life, the man of her dreams. She was certain of it, even though they'd only been dating for six weeks.

He was a senior at State, twenty-five miles due west of the W. Drop-dead gorgeous and smart to boot. A pre-law student who bore a striking resemblance to Richard Chamberlain, with his lean muscled body, ash blond hair, and boyish smile.

And except for a fluke, a twist of fate or magic or miracle, Lacy never would have met him.

"LACY, YOU'VE *got* to go," Lauren said. "I've borrowed Delta's car, but she wouldn't let me take it unless I promised you'd come too, in case I had a little too much to drink. Steve's expecting me. We haven't seen each other since last year."

"Last year was two weeks ago," Lacy said.

"A technicality." Lauren let out an exaggerated sigh. "We went out on December 18, and then he went to his parents' for Christmas and we went home to Hillsborough and I haven't seen him since."

"You talk on the phone every damn day."

"It's not the same, and you know it." Lauren hesitated. "Well, maybe you don't know it, but—"

Thus, with much wheedling and begging, Lauren dragged an unwilling Lacy over to State to attend a fraternity New Year's party where she was meeting her current boyfriend, Steve Treadwell. The moment they crossed the threshold into the frat house Lauren predictably disappeared, leaving Lacy to fend for herself.

The noise in the house was deafening. From some unseen stereo, the Beatles were belting out "Back in the USSR." Couples were dancing, spilling beer, making out; the crowd was so dense you could barely walk across a room without getting caught up in the surge of bodies. Lacy accepted a beer in a plastic cup from a guy in a maroon football jersey and found an overstuffed armchair in a corner. For twenty minutes she sat there, watching the action and feeling desperately out of place and furious at her twin. She was just about to go track down Lauren, get Delta's keys, and leave her sister to find her own way home when someone sidled up to her and perched on the arm of her chair.

"Hey," he said. "I'm Trip Jenkins, and I'd like to know how such an adorable girl can look so thoroughly miserable." He took her hand, led her to a quiet room off the back of the frat house, and shut the door. It was a library of sorts, with books lining the walls, comfortable sofas and chairs, and gas logs burning in the fireplace.

Trip was the perfect gentleman. For the next three hours, while his frat brothers were groping their dates in various dark alcoves of the house, the two of them talked, ate junk food, and drank about a gallon of Coke.

Trip, amazingly enough, was not involved with anyone else, nor was he a sociopath or a mama's boy. He had, as it turned out, been dating a girl who had graduated early and gone on to Harvard Law, but they had broken up three months before.

"The long-distance thing was just too difficult," he admitted. "I've been accepted to Ole Miss, Duke, and Emory, so whatever law school I end up at, we'd still be separated. We finally realized that it wasn't going to work. It was a mutual decision." He grinned sheepishly. "Besides, I'm not so sure it's a good idea to have two lawyers in the house. Makes for a lot of arguments."

"Well then, I'd better leave now," Lacy said. "I'm in pre-law too."

He flushed a bright pink. "I'm sorry. I didn't mean—"

"Just kidding. I'm actually a secondary ed major. History and social science. I just started my practice teaching." She winked at him, and he grinned back.

Lacy had dated a number of boys during her years at the W—mostly guys Lauren lined up for her, double dates, a lot of first dates that didn't go anywhere. But always, when Lauren was around, Lacy felt like an also-ran, a second choice. When the two of them double dated, she could see her own date's eyes drifting toward Lauren, who perpetually held the center of attention. Finally Lacy quit going out with Lauren and her boyfriends altogether, and turned her concentration to her studies.

And now here she was, in a frat house of all places, having a wonderful conversation with a man who didn't even know her twin sister existed.

"Listen," he said finally, "it's after midnight, and I really don't want to end this, but I have a study group early tomorrow morning."

"On Saturday?"

"Yeah." He shrugged. "Can we go out sometime—on a real date, I mean?"

"Of course," Lacy said immediately, then cursed herself as he looked away. Now she had done it. She had sounded too eager, and guys hated that.

He chewed on his lower lip for a minute, then gazed directly into her eyes. "I don't want to sound too eager or anything, but I also don't want to play games. I like you, Lacy—a lot. I want to see you again. So just tell me and put me out of my misery, okay? How long do I need to wait before I call you?"

"Have you got a pen?"

"Let me look." He dug in his pocket and came up with one. "Give me your hand."

He extended his left hand, and she wrote the dorm telephone number across his palm. "Call me before you wash this off," she said. "If you wait more than two days, I'll know your personal hygiene isn't up to par, and we'll be history before we ever get started."

He put an arm around her and walked her into the living room, where the party was beginning to wind down. "Do you need me to take you home?"

"No, I came with—" She paused. "I've got a ride. Let's just say good night here, all right?"

He leaned down and kissed her—a kiss much more chaste than Lacy would have liked, but very gentle and sweet. "Tomorrow. We'll talk tomorrow."

"WHERE'D YOU GO?" Trip said, running a finger lightly across the nape of her neck.

"Oh, sorry." Lacy smiled. "I was just thinking about the first time we met."

"That horrible fraternity party." Trip grimaced. "To tell you the truth, I can't stand living in the frat house. If it weren't for my dad, I'd never have pledged at all."

"The party was pretty awful," she agreed. "But it turned out just fine for me."

"For both of us." He leaned forward. "Anything you regret about that night?"

"Well, maybe one thing."

Trip's eyebrows arched up into his hairline. "What's that?"

"The kiss."

"I shouldn't have kissed you?"

"No." She chuckled. "It was the *way* you kissed me. So . . . restrained."

"I was *trying* to be considerate. We'd only just met."

"Yes, but I was already crazy about you. I wanted you to kiss me and never stop. I went home worried that you might not be any good at it, and kissing is *very* important to me."

He gathered her into his arms and kissed her again. Rain drummed on the cloth roof of the Corvair in time with the pounding in her veins.

"I guess we've got that kissing thing taken care of," he whispered.

"I guess."

"So," he said, leaning closer, "when do you think we might—" He paused. "You know."

Lacy's stomach began to writhe. This wasn't the first time he had asked. She loved him, she really did, and there was no question that she was physically attracted to him. But the idea of sex—not just petting, but going all the way—was foreign territory for her, and a little scary. What if she didn't like it—or worse, if he didn't like doing it with *her*? What if she got pregnant? What if, afterward, he didn't want her any more?

Overhead, a shrill whistle sounded, an eardrum-splitting noise, given that they were sitting directly under it.

"What the hell is that?" Trip yelled over the shriek.

"The warning whistle for dinner," Lacy said when the racket had subsided. "Five minutes till they close the doors." She grinned at him. "It doesn't sound that loud from elsewhere on campus."

He opened the door, pushed the seat forward, and moved to the front behind the wheel. "I'll drive you up there."

Lacy climbed over into the front seat as well. Two minutes later she kissed him good-bye, ducked out of the car, and ran through the rain into the dining hall.

"Where have you been?" Lauren demanded before Lacy even had a chance to sit down. "You're all wet."

"Yeah, well, it's raining outside, isn't it?" Lacy ran her fingers through her dripping hair, removed her raincoat, and slung it across the back of the chair.

"So, where *have* you been?" Lauren repeated.

"What Lauren means," Delta interpreted, "is that we tried to find you and were a little worried about you."

Lacy began to laugh. "What Lauren *means,*" she corrected, "is that she's pissed off at me for *not informing her of my every move.*" She finished the sentence in a hiss, through gritted teeth, and shot a mocking scowl at her twin.

"Actually, we were *all* wondering, when you didn't show up for practice this afternoon," said Rae Dawn. "We were going to work on a couple of new songs for the senior banquet, remember? Simon and Garfunkel's 'Sound of Silence' and 'Flowers Never Bend with the Rainfall.' "

Lacy slapped a palm to her forehead. "Damn! I forgot. I'm sorry, I really am." She looked around the table. "What else have I forgotten? We don't have a gig this weekend, do we?"

"No." Delta shook her head. "There's an antiwar protest at the courthouse on Saturday afternoon, and I'm going, but we're not scheduled to sing or anything."

"That's a relief," Lacy said. "I don't usually lose track of things like that. I guess my mind is somewhere else."

Lauren leaned in and gave her sister a rakish look. "Don't think we don't know where your mind *is* these days," she said. "Button your blouse, Lace; you look like a tramp."

Lacy's stomach lurched, and her fingers went instinctively to the front of her blouse. All the buttons were firmly in place.

"Gotcha!" Lauren gloated. "Now, are you going to tell us about this secret love of yours?"

"Details, please," Delta added. "You've been keeping him under wraps for over a month. All we know about him is his name and the fact that he's a senior at State."

"And *handsome*," Lauren added. "He's in Steve's fraternity, but even I haven't met him yet."

"Well . . ." Lacy thought about it for a minute. She had her reasons for keeping quiet about Trip, and yet maintaining her privacy had its drawbacks. It had been hard not to tell them; she was in love, and she wanted to shout it from the roof of the administration building. She wanted them to be happy with her, to share her joy. And as much as she hated to admit it, she wanted their approval.

"All right," she said at last. "As you know, his name is Trip Jenkins, and—"

"What kind of a weird name is that? Trip?" Delta asked.

Lacy raised an eyebrow. "No stranger than *Delta*, I'd say. Especially when you live in Stone Mountain." Everybody laughed. "His real name is Thomas—Thomas Edward Jenkins III. He was named after his father and grandfather, but three Toms in a family was pretty hard to negotiate. Thus, Trip."

"Oh, like in *triple*," Delta said.

"Exactly. He's a senior at State—an honor student, I might add—and he'll be going to law school in the fall."

"Where's he going?"

Lacy shrugged. "He's been accepted at Ole Miss, Duke, and Emory. Personally, I'm hoping for Duke."

"Is Duke close to home?" Rae Dawn asked. "I don't know North Carolina geography very well."

"Hillsborough to Durham? It's practically in our backyard,"

Lauren answered. "Ten or twelve miles, maybe." She narrowed her eyes at Lacy. "You're thinking marriage, aren't you?"

Lacy felt herself flush. "Well, he hasn't asked me yet, if that's what you mean. But yes, I think it's getting pretty serious."

Rae Dawn looked skeptical. "How long have you been dating this guy? A month?"

"Almost two months," Lacy said. "Well . . . six and a half weeks. But you know, don't you? When it's right, you just . . . *know*." Rae opened her mouth to protest, but Lacy rushed on. "That doesn't mean we'd get married right away. I could live at home for a while, try to get a teaching job while he starts law school."

"Aren't you getting a little ahead of yourself?" Delta asked. "It's customary to get engaged before you get married."

"And to introduce your intended to your *family*," Lauren chimed in.

"And to your *friends*," Rae Dawn added.

"All right, already!" Lacy laughed. "I suppose you're right. It is time you met him. And just for the record, Lauren, I'll invite him to come to North Carolina during spring break."

"Great," Lauren said. "Maybe I'll ask Steve to come too. Now, when do we get to meet the wonder boy?"

"How about Sunday dinner?" Lacy narrowed her eyes and looked around the table. "That way you'll already be dressed up so I won't have to make excuses for you."

They all seemed to think this was a good idea, and Lacy went back to her catalog of all Trip's wonderful features. She was gushing, she knew, but she couldn't seem to help herself. Once the floodgate had been lifted, everything she was holding inside rushed to get out. It was pure glory, telling them about the man she loved, having her feelings for him confirmed over and over again in her heart.

One little tooth of nagging doubt chiseled away at her gut, but she couldn't identify it, nor could she make it go away. One small torque of uncertainty, a nervous flutter in her stomach.

Ridiculous. He *was* the right one; she was sure of it. Trip loved her, and she loved him. They were perfect for each other. And nothing—*nothing*—could ever change that.

ELEVEN

The Green-Eyed Monster

After dinner Lacy had run off through the pouring rain to meet with her student teacher group in the library, and for once Lauren was glad to have the room to herself. Delta was crunching a deadline on one of Dr. Bowen's innumerable lit papers, and Rae Dawn, as usual, was practicing in the music building. A couple of girls from the other end of the floor had invited her to come down to their room and study with them, but Lauren had made an excuse about a project due the next morning.

There was no project. Lauren and her fellow elementary ed students were scheduled to be at the local kindergarten tomorrow, and she didn't exactly have to prepare to do ABCs and teeth-brushing. She simply did not want to be with people tonight. She spread a towel across the top of the door—the W's dorm symbol for "Do Not Disturb"—and shut herself in.

Normally Lauren would do almost anything to avoid being alone. From the cradle she had been with Lace, with her family, with dozens of other friends. Since puberty she had been surrounded by boys who clamored for her attention. Always there had been laughter and joking and endless activity, a manic white noise that kept her from having to think too much.

But tonight she *needed* to think. Needed to figure out the source of this burning in her gut, this heavy weight that lay over her like a shroud.

Lauren had little experience with self-examination, and she hardly knew where to start. She knew only that the feeling had begun over dinner, as her twin sister had talked—finally—about Trip Jenkins, about the newfound wonder of their love.

The cynic in her was tempted to blow off her sister's joy as so much naïveté. Lacy had always been an innocent. She had never been in an intimate relationship, didn't have a clue what love was about. Lauren could have told her a thing or two about men, about how they used that four-letter word to lure a girl on until they succeeded in coercing her into acting on the three-letter word that consumed their every waking moment.

Not that Lauren didn't like sex. She had lost her virginity on prom night her senior year in high school, with a bony basketball star named Phil Putnam. He had been an inefficient, groping, selfish lover—most high school boys were, she supposed—and she clearly recalled the sensation of revulsion and disbelief when she caught her first glimpse of his penis. The experience had been . . . well, not exactly electrifying. But once that ship had sailed, there was no turning back.

After Phil, Lauren had known a succession of boys, even a few who might be counted as men—not hundreds, of course, but several. Enough to realize that for the male of the species, sex was the end goal of all things romantic.

The pattern rarely varied: a few walks in the park, a few dinners, a few movies, all of which inevitably led to a dark car in some isolated make-out spot, where kissing and petting led to panting arousal and eventually to an uncomfortable, half-clothed coupling in a back seat littered with hamburger wrappers and beer cans. And afterward, when the dinners and movies and long walks had vanished into the mist, the guy became either possessive or indifferent, leaving nothing but the sex as common ground between them.

A few of Lauren's boyfriends had been more skilled than Phil Putnam and had managed, even in less than ideal surroundings, to awaken her to her own pleasures. But she had discovered that pleasure itself could be disturbing when her mind and heart did not follow where her body was going. On one or two occasions, she could actually recall looking down to see some oaf sucking on her breast, fumbling to get his hand between her legs, while she reacted with little more than mild surprise. She was, for all intents and purposes, somewhere else—planning a midterm project or making a list of Christmas presents she needed to buy.

Her current steady, Steve Treadwell, was by far the best of them, the most attentive, the nicest, the least demanding. But even with Steve, Lauren had never felt for a man what her virginal sister obviously felt for Trip Jenkins.

Lacy actually *knew* Trip, it seemed. Knew how he thought and felt about things like politics and religion and the state of the world. Understood his passions and dreams, why he wanted to become a lawyer, what he hoped to accomplish with his life. According to Lacy, they talked. They cared about each other. Their relationship was based on more, much more, than the convergence of body parts.

And Lauren was jealous.

When the word darted into her mind unbidden, she tried first to ignore it and then to bat it away. But it kept swooping back, a bold blue jay harassing a prowling cat. Vaguely she recalled something from sophomore lit, some Shakespeare play, she thought, where a character referred to jealousy as a big green monster.

Never in her life had Lauren been jealous of Lacy. Why should she? For twenty-one years Lauren had been the one in the spotlight, garnering all the attention. Lauren was the one who had the boyfriends, the popularity, the good looks—

Her mental processes squealed to a halt. Wait a minute. How could she possibly believe she was prettier than Lacy, when they were twins? These days Lacy kept her hair short, but other than the haircut, the two of them were virtually identical: same facial features, same eyes, lips, teeth. Even the same figure, down to the half-inch.

And yet, Lauren realized, she had *always* felt that way; she had just never admitted it to herself. All these years she had felt superior to Lacy—had *needed* to feel superior.

Now she was on the outside looking in. Lacy had Trip, and she had . . . Steve. Lacy had love and passion and joy and excitement, while Lauren had—

Sex.

Good sex, sometimes. But nothing to build a future on.

The bitter taste of bile rose up in her throat. She went and leaned against the window, where raindrops pelted like rubber bullets across the frozen glass.

A shiver overtook her. But even as she stood there trembling, Lauren could not deny the truth: The chill came not from the February storm, but from an icy emptiness deep in her own soul.

TWELVE

Something More Than Music

Rae Dawn sat slumped over the piano in Rehearsal Room A, shivering from the rain that had soaked her on the way to the Music Hall. For the past hour she had been playing frenetically, trying to escape the writhing in her stomach, the throbbing in her head. But it was no good.

All during dinner, while Lacy had been extolling the virtues of her new love, Rae Dawn had managed to keep a cheerful face plastered on, had even forced herself to ask a few questions and pretend to be happy for Lacy.

And Rae *was* happy for her. Truly she was, deep down.

She was just not happy for herself.

None of it made any sense, these conflicting feelings that assaulted her. She had what she wanted, didn't she? She had a wonderful mentor in Dr. Gottlieb. She had prospects and possibilities for after graduation. The professor even had a contact in New Orleans, someone who owned a jazz club and might be willing to give her a chance. She was passionate about her music, loved what she was doing. Why then did she have this insane, unpredictable response to Lacy's good news?

Immediately after dinner, she had sequestered herself in the rehearsal room, as she always did when she was upset or confused or had something she needed to figure out. Music soothed her soul, set her mind free, enabled her to get to the deepest, most hidden emotions of her heart.

But this time, what came to the surface when she played only served to intensify her agony. Every tender ballad, every hot jazz riff, every plaintive love song reminded her of the adoration in Lacy's voice when she talked about Trip, the light in her face, the fire in her eyes. The sensations crashed in upon her, a clashing dissonance, a cacophony of desire and self-contempt.

She played until her fingers grew numb, trying to outrun the emotions. But she hadn't succeeded. The feelings followed her, terrified her, a rabid dog snarling at her heels.

She was jealous. Jealous of Lacy Cantrell.

She had known jealousy before, of course. As a child she had envied those around her whose lives were easy. Kids who had relatively normal parents, a decent home, enough to eat, new clothes rather than hand-me-downs. She had felt the gut-twisting burn, had understood, when she had finally read *Othello*, why Iago called jealousy "the green-eyed monster which doth mock the meat it feeds on."

But she had never been jealous of a *friend*. Never envied the good fortune of someone she had grown to love. And certainly never thought herself capable of being jealous because Lacy had finally, deservedly, fallen in love.

It simply wasn't possible.

After all she had endured growing up—her father's liquor-induced rages, her mother's gaping emptiness—the last thing in the world she wanted was to marry some man and risk living out the rest of her days as a stranger to herself, ripped to pieces by the shards of her own shattered dreams.

She had her music. She had a future.

But suddenly, unexpectedly, it wasn't enough.

The truth overwhelmed her, and she sat rooted to the piano bench, sobbing, her tears dripping onto the keys. How long she stayed that way, she did not know, but at last her weeping subsided, and her mind began to drift.

She thought of Delta's major professors, Dr. Bowen and Dr. Hart. She had spent a bit of time with them now and then, when the Delta Belles had sung for voter registration rallies and civil rights protests. She had even been invited for dinner at their house a time or two.

They had never done anything inappropriate in her presence, had barely even touched. But nevertheless, Rae Dawn saw it. The love between them. The commitment. The *connection.* A connection that, because of society's prejudices, had been and would continue to be unspoken, unacknowledged.

The injustice of it sliced through her like a hot knife.

For a long time, she had been dimly aware of a truth lurking deep beneath the surface of her consciousness. A dragon, a subterranean beast waiting for the moment it would strike. But she had kept it leashed, suppressed it, escaped it through her music. Now the dragon reared its head again, and she could feel it stirring within her.

Yes, she was jealous. But not because she wanted what Lacy had. She was jealous because Lacy had the freedom to speak it, to let the world know how she felt and what she hoped for.

Rae Dawn's desire was different, and yet the same. She wanted to be a professional musician, certainly, but she wanted more than that too.

A life, a love. A house and two dogs and a leisurely late

breakfast of waffles and scrambled eggs on a Saturday morning. A piano in the bay window and someone to listen when she played.

The awareness writhed within her, a truth she could never declare the way Lacy Cantrell had declared her love for Trip Jenkins.

Because that *someone,* in her imagination, was not a husband but a partner.

Not a man but a woman.

THIRTEEN

Springtime in Stone Mountain

Spring Break
March 1969

Delta stepped out of the car and stretched. At the end of the driveway, twin forsythia bushes draped their yellow skirts across the lawn. Up next to the house, azaleas stooped under a load of blossoms—pale pink, magenta, and snowy white. Fragrant blue and yellow hyacinths lined the sidewalk. On a single breath she inhaled the scent of new grass and pine trees and daffodils.

It was spring. She was home.

She barely had time to exhale, however, before the front door slammed open and a small towheaded missile launched through the door and rocketed toward her.

"Delta! Delta! You're *here*! You're finally here!"

Cassie gave a flying leap and hurtled into her arms, knocking her back on her heels. Delta staggered, recovered herself, dropped her purse. Then, laughing, she embraced her little sister, swung her around, and set her back on the ground.

"You're getting so big!" she marveled, though it wasn't really true. Cassie had always been compact and petite, and although she had grown a little, she was still very small. Over her sister's bony shoulder she caught a glimpse of her mother and father standing on the front stoop. Mama had a handkerchief in one hand and was pulling distractedly at one frayed corner. Daddy's eyes looked empty and tired. In that unguarded moment, Delta saw something she knew instinctively she wasn't meant to see. But she couldn't quite articulate what it was.

Then her mother was bustling down the steps, pasting on a smile. "Well, come on in, DeeDee," she said while Cassie danced in wild circles around her sister. "Cassie, where are your shoes?"

Cassie shrugged. "Look, Delta, I can do a cartwheel." She flung herself onto the grass, all elbows and knees, flipped over, and landed on her skinny little butt.

"That's enough, Cassie," Mama said, a bit more sternly this time. "Get inside and put on your shoes—it's not summer *yet.* Delta can watch you perform later."

Reluctantly, Cassie obeyed. Delta followed her father as he went to the car and extracted her suitcase from the trunk.

"Car running all right?"

Delta smiled. It was such a dad thing to say. "Yes, Daddy. It's running just fine. I love it."

"Can't beat a Ford. I'll change the oil and rotate the tires while you're here. Maybe do a tune-up, too." He stroked the rear fender. "Needs washing."

He had bought the used car for her the summer between her sophomore and junior years—a silver '63 Falcon convertible with a black top and matching leather interior. The leather got hot in the summer, but otherwise the little car was a great ride.

Daddy claimed to have purchased it in self-defense, so he wouldn't have to make the trip to and from the college every spring and fall. But Delta knew better. He had fallen in love with the Falcon and wouldn't dare buy it for himself.

He was still standing there, holding her suitcase in one hand and fondling the fender with the other.

"Want to take it for a spin, Daddy?"

He shook his head but didn't smile the way Delta had expected him to. "Your mama would kill me. Let's go inside. Maybe later the two of us can take a drive out to the park to see the carving. There's something I need to talk to you about."

Delta frowned. "Is something wrong, Daddy? Mama's not sick, is she? She looks a little—I don't know. Worn out. Worried."

"Later," he said. Then he hefted her suitcase and headed toward the house.

Dinner that first evening home turned out to be a boisterous, chaotic affair with no time for real conversation. Mama had cooked all of Delta's favorite foods—pot roast with potatoes and carrots, creamed baby peas, and, for dessert, a homemade buttermilk pound cake with sliced strawberries.

She had also invited Ben Rutledge, who was on spring break as well but had stayed in Atlanta once he found out Delta was coming home. Besides, Ben never turned down an opportunity to feast on Mama's cooking. According to the bits and pieces of conversation that swirled around the table, it appeared he came to dinner at least once a week.

Since the moment she had arrived, Delta had known something wasn't quite right. Now her antennae were up, and she began to see things that as a child growing up in this house she had never noticed. The way her parents didn't really talk, or even look at one another, but used Cassie—and even Ben—as a kind of buffer between them. Her mind cast back to the pre-Cassie years, when it was just the three of them in the house. Mama cooked and cleaned and did whatever else mothers did. Daddy got up every morning and went to work, came home and watched the news, ate dinner and fell asleep in front of the television. Mama knitted. Beyond that, they had few other interests, and none in common.

Had they been doing this all their lives, passing back and forth like two flashlight beams in a darkened room, and she had never noticed?

"Tell my daughter about the progress on Lee's horse, Ben," Daddy said. "She thinks I'm totally obsessed—"

"Have some more potatoes," Mama said. "I know you like them. Why, last time you were here—"

"Ben and Delta, sit-tin' in a tree, k-i-s-s—"

"Cassie! None of that!" Mama reprimanded. "You'll embarrass your sister."

Cassie's bright eyes darted from Delta to Ben and back again. "Ben, what are you going to do when you get out of college?" she asked with a teasing note in her voice.

Ben leaned across the table and tousled her hair. "You know perfectly well what I'm going to do, Squirt," he said. "We've talked about this a hundred times. I'm studying to be an architect. I'll design houses, maybe, or skyscrapers or bridges."

Cassie pounced. "So when you and Delta get *married*, you'll build her a house and you'll live together and spend all your time hugging and kissing and—"

"Cassandra Elizabeth Fox!" Mama snapped. "Unless you want to be sent to your room right this very minute—"

The little girl drew herself up and gazed placidly at her mother. "All right, Mama, if you're determined to stand in the way of my education. . . ."

Ben let out a howl of laughter. "How old are you, Cass? Thirty?"

"Eight and three-quarters," she said. "But I'm very advanced for my age."

Everyone was too full for dessert right away, so after dinner Delta and Ben went out onto the covered patio and sat in the porch swing that hung suspended from the beams. Now and then Delta could see Cassie peering out at them through the blinds.

Ben put an arm around her and pushed his foot against the paving stones to get the swing moving. "They all expect it, you know."

Delta leaned against him and looked across the back yard at the rising moon. "Expect what?"

"For us to get married, of course. Cassie's just repeating what she's heard."

"Cassie," Delta said, "makes things up just fine without anyone's help."

Ben chuckled. "Quite true."

Delta gazed into his eyes. He was so sweet, and she was so content in his presence. Ben Rutledge was like an old pair of jeans that had been washed a thousand times. A perfect fit. Familiar, soft, and comfortable.

The metaphor continued to spin out in her mind. Preshrunk. Faded. Predictable.

Her mind shifted to Lacy Cantrell's romance with Trip Jenkins. She recalled with vivid clarity the spark in Lacy's eyes when she finally broke her silence and told them about Trip. The passion. The anticipation. The goose-bump, fire-in-the-veins, mice-in-the-stomach thrill that Delta knew she would never, ever have with Ben.

Still, he was a good man. Solid. Reliable. Already part of the family. As Mama had pointed out, she could do a lot worse.

ON WEDNESDAY, five days into spring break, Delta was out in the backyard, playing Wiffle ball with Cassie. Delta was getting pretty adept at making the perforated plastic ball curve and dip, which frustrated Cassie to no end. The kid was accustomed to doing things right, and a strike rather than a home run was simply not acceptable.

Finally she threw down the bat in exasperation, ran to the patio, and flung herself into the swing. Delta followed, sweaty and breathless.

"That was fun." She pulled the rubber band out of her hair and rearranged her ponytail.

"For you, maybe." Cassie crossed her arms and scowled in the direction of the back fence.

"Ah, c'mon, don't be a spoilsport. It *was* fun. Admit it."

Delta poked at her ribs and began to tickle her. "Okay, I give," Cassie said at last. She leaned against her sister and heaved an exaggerated sigh. "I just hate to lose."

"Lose?" Delta repeated. "There's no winning or losing in Wiffle ball. Hell, it's not the world series."

Cassie's eyes grew wide. "You *swore*."

"Oh. Yeah, well, I apologize. I guess shouldn't have said *hell* in front of you."

"I don't care about that," Cassie said with an impatient shake of her head. "Can you teach me to do it?"

"Teach you to swear?" Delta laughed. "Honey, it's not something you have to be taught. You just pick it up. *When you're older.*"

"Other kids at school do it, and they're my age."

Delta regarded her sister, taking in the disheveled blonde hair, the round blue eyes, the heart-shaped little face, already tanned though spring had just begun. At five, Cassie had possessed the appearance of a three-year-old and the vocabulary of a high school junior. Now, at almost nine, she looked to be six or seven at most, and although she was the smartest kid in her class, she undoubtedly got teased at school for being so diminutive. It probably didn't help any that she had skipped third grade.

"Listen," Delta said, pulling Cassie onto her lap and putting her arms around her, "you don't have to swear to be accepted. You don't have to pretend to be tough. You're intelligent and gifted and beautiful. Just be yourself."

Cassie picked at a loose thread on the hem of her shorts. "I'm not beautiful. *You're* beautiful."

Delta suppressed a smile, noting that her little sister did not challenge the notion that she was intelligent or gifted. "When I was your age, or maybe a tad older, I had a mouthful of metal and pimples and knobby knees."

"Did not!" Cassie objected, but she seemed heartened by this bit of news.

"Did so. Go look at Mama's photograph albums. I was hideous."

The child squirmed her bony butt in Delta's lap until she was sitting more or less upright. "Like the ugly duckling growing into a swan," she mused. "Okay, maybe I do have a chance. The genetic combinations seemed to work pretty well in your case."

Delta gazed at her. "What do you know about genetic combinations?"

"I know plenty," Cassie declared. "I've been reading all about it. Genes are carried in the DNA, and the combination of genes from your mother and father determine what you'll look like, talents and abilities you'll have, maybe even personality. Did you know that it's impossible for two blue-eyed parents to have a brown-eyed child? Blue is recessive—that's Mama, she's got two blue chromosomes. Daddy has brown eyes, which is dominant, but he must have a blue chromosome, because I came out with blue eyes instead of brown, like yours. Do you realize there's a one in four chance . . ."

She went on that way, talking at about a hundred facts per minute, until some synapse in her brain jolted her onto a different track.

"So, are you and Ben going to get married?"

"Shit," Delta muttered.

Cassie perked up. "Ooh, that's a good one. I should write it down."

"Forget I said it. Listen, Cassie, whatever you might have overheard, Ben and I have been friends since junior high. *Friends.* That's all, at least for now. Maybe he's the right one, and maybe he's not. I don't even know if I want to marry *anyone.* Maybe I—" Delta stopped short. Cassie was biting her lower lip, and her wide eyes glittered with unshed tears. "What's the matter, Cass?"

"How do you know for sure?" she said in a gritty whisper. "How do you *know* who's the right one? The one who will stay forever?"

Delta narrowed her eyes. "What's this about?"

The tears welled up and brimmed over. "You'd better ask Mama and Daddy," she said. "I'm not supposed to tell."

BUT DELTA DIDN'T HAVE a chance to ask. That evening her father didn't come home from work—a meeting, Mama said, although the exact nature of the appointment remained undisclosed. The three of them ate a silent meal of leftover fried chicken at the kitchen table, and her mother's distracted, snappish mood precluded conversation.

At eleven Delta was reading in her bedroom at the front of the house when her father's car drove up. She heard footsteps on the porch, the creak of the front door opening, the squeaking protest of the loose floorboard on the stairs. Then the rasp of their bedroom door closing, and voices.

If Daddy had intended to be quiet so as not to wake Mama, he evidently had not been successful. Delta could hear her mother's muffled voice through the wall, although she couldn't make out the words. The groan of the bedsprings followed by two dull thuds—Daddy sitting down to take off his shoes, Delta guessed. Muted steps down the hall, a toilet flushing, water running. Then the shutting of the door again, and more conversation.

Most of what they said Delta couldn't make out. The words were garbled, hushed, although a time or two a voice would be raised, and she caught snatches of sentences—something about *your own daughters in the house* and *not my decision.* Mama's voice, when Delta could hear it, sounded angry, and Daddy's simply weary and resigned. Within a few minutes she heard the click of a lamp being turned off, then silence.

On Thursday morning Delta awoke at quarter to nine, stumbled sleepily down to the kitchen in her pajamas and slippers, and found both her parents sitting at the table drinking coffee. The instant she saw them, she was wide awake with a churning of acid in her stomach. Her father, punctual as a Swiss watch, invariably left for the insurance office at eight thirty, and her mother always cooked breakfast for him before he went. But this morning there was no sign of breakfast anywhere—not even toast, or those little white powdered doughnuts Daddy liked.

"What's wrong?" Delta said. "Did somebody die? Where's Cass?" She dropped into a chair.

"Cassie's at school." Mama set a mug of coffee in front of her and pushed the sugar bowl in her direction. "Your father has something he needs to talk to you about." She resumed her seat and stirred her coffee so manically that Delta was sure the cup would shatter.

She looked at her father. He had his head down and was busy turning a spoon over and over in his hands.

"Your mother and I have decided—" he began

"No," Mama interrupted, a tone of warning in her voice.

"All right." He sighed and ran a hand through his thinning hair. "I don't know how to say this that will make it sound any better."

"Just say it," Mama snapped. "Tell the truth, for once in your life."

He took off his thick glasses and rubbed the bridge of his nose, pressing a thumb and forefinger into the oval indentations where the glasses sat. "I'm in love with another woman," he blurted out. "And I've asked your mother for a divorce."

Time pitched and shuddered backward, ground to a halt, then began to move forward again, in slow motion. On a screen in the back of her mind, images flashed across Delta's consciousness. Her father in his chair. Her mother at the stove or at the sink or sitting in the rocker knitting. The boredom in Mama's eyes. Daddy's bald spot, spreading wider every year.

Then, without warning, another image presented itself—a picture of Daddy with his arm around a woman who was not her mother, his head thrown back, laughing as he had not laughed in all the years she had known him.

She should have had a hundred questions, a thousand. But only one pushed its way to the forefront of her mind: *Why hadn't this happened sooner?* Twenty-five years they had been married, and suddenly Delta realized that most of those years had been unhappy for both of them. Caught in the quicksand of familiarity, they had gone on slogging in place, hardly aware that they were sinking until Daddy had caught hold of a branch Mama couldn't reach.

As the awareness overtook her, one of Dr. Bowen's favorite aphorisms came to Delta's mind: *A rut is a grave with the ends kicked out.*

Mama was crying quietly now, leaning her whole body away from Daddy, refusing to meet his eyes. Just briefly, Delta wondered what she had to cry about. Surely she was relieved. Surely a sense of liberation was mixed in there with the anger and betrayal and, quite possibly, shame.

"What will you do?" she asked, the question addressed to nobody in particular.

"Your mother will stay here in Stone Mountain," Daddy said. "The house is paid for, and I'll take care of basic expenses. I've sold the agency to my partner. Caroline and I will move into Atlanta and start over. I'll be close enough to see Cassie, and far enough away to—" He paused. "This is a small town. There's no sense putting your mother through any more embarrassment than necessary."

Delta stared at him. "Caroline? Caroline Lawler, your secretary?"

Her father nodded.

Delta let this pass without comment. She doubted it was necessary to point out the stereotype—a middle-aged man falling in love with a secretary fifteen years his junior. She supposed the red sports car would come next.

But despite this cynical turn of mind, Delta knew in her heart that it wasn't just a midlife crisis. It was a moment of truth two decades in the making.

After her father's revelation, all Delta wanted was to get away. Instead she waited around all day Thursday, holed up in her room trying to avoid her parents. When Cassie finally got home from school Delta sat with her through the difficult and emotional conversation, took her out for pizza, cuddled with her until she finally went to sleep. On Friday she packed her bags and left Stone Mountain shortly after noon.

Now Delta gripped the wheel and aimed her car due west, out of Atlanta and across the state line into Alabama.

Cassie would be all right, Delta thought. The girl had amazing inner resources, a grit and determination no one would guess from looking at her. She was a fighter. A survivor.

Her mind drifted toward her parents. Twenty-five years. A quarter of a century. All those days and nights without any real connection.

"My parents are getting a divorce," Delta said aloud, trying to make herself connect with some emotion, some grief—something. But all she could feel about their breakup was a sense of inevitability. How, she wondered, had two people so ill suited for each other ever gotten married in the first place?

Delta tried to remember the wedding photos her mother kept in a small, yellowed album in a box under the bed. April 1944. V-E Day was still a year away, but her father had stayed home, classified 4-F because of his abysmal eyesight. Mama stood thin and pale in a tea-length dress with a matching pillbox hat, Daddy in a shiny-looking suit with a rose in his lapel. They had both been smiling at the camera, she recalled. Had they been madly in love at the beginning? Had they met at the altar and said their vows with absolute certainty that their relationship would last forever, that their life together was and would continue to be perfect, exactly as they had envisioned it?

And what *was* the perfect relationship, anyway?

Another image crept into her mind, superimposed upon the picture of her parents. An image of herself and Ben. A weight pressed down on her chest.

This wasn't what she wanted for her life. Of course she wanted security and safety and steadiness. But she also wanted fireworks and candlelight and insanity, challenge and intensity and growth.

Delta focused on the mental reflection of his lean, familiar face. A pang of regret shot through her.

She wouldn't marry Ben Rutledge. Not now, probably not ever. When she got married, if she ever did, what she wanted was a relationship that engaged all of her—heart, soul, mind, and body. Not an inevitability but a choice. A partnership. A love that would never grow stale or boring.

And God help her, she'd rather be single her whole life long than to settle for anything less.

FOURTEEN

Judas

Hillsborough, North Carolina
March 1969

Spring break had been pure agony for Lauren. All week she had stood to one side while Lacy and Trip reveled in the attention that washed over them like a fountain. Mother fawned over him, feeding him, laughing at his jokes. Dad welcomed him home like the Prodigal, the long-lost son, and barbecued the fatted calf—or the ribs, at least—to celebrate his coming.

Steve Treadwell had not made the trip. Lauren had fabricated a reason, some reading he had to catch up on—an excuse that caused Trip to raise his eyebrows in skepticism. The truth was, Lauren didn't *want* Steve with her. Two days before they were scheduled to leave for North Carolina she had ended their relationship, telling him in vague ramblings and nonspecific clichés that she was sorry but it just wasn't going to work out between them.

If she were honest with herself—a practice woefully unsuited to Lauren's temperament—she would have to admit that poor Steve suffered terribly by comparison. He was a nice enough guy, she supposed. Easy on the eyes, and a hell of a lot more considerate than most of the boys she had dated, slept with, and then rejected. He liked her, certainly, and she had no problem with being physically attracted to him.

But once she saw Lacy and Trip together, her spirits plummeted. Every time she looked at Steve, she was forcibly reminded of what she'd never have with him. What she'd never have, she feared, with anyone.

Precisely what it was, this connection that Lacy and Trip had between them, Lauren was not certain. But she was determined to find out, even if her heart broke in the process.

Her chance came on Thursday, two days before they planned to leave to go back to school. Mother had determined to take her girls shopping, and although the M word had not been spoken a single time during the entire week, Lauren sensed that the clothes-buying spree was for Lacy's benefit, a kind of pre-engagement trousseau, a celebration of the celebration to come.

Trip had decided that, instead of following the women around and carrying their packages, he would take a drive over to Duke and scope out the college. Sometime during the early part of the week, the decision had been made that he would attend law school there. Duke University, like the W , was on spring break this week, but he hoped he'd at least be able to get a tour and meet the dean.

"You know," Lauren said casually as she walked with her mother and sister out to the driveway, "I think I'll pass on the shopping trip."

Both mouths gaped open. Never once in anyone's memory had Lauren missed the opportunity to model clothes for an entire store full of admirers.

"Trip's not familiar with Duke's campus," she hurried on. "I thought maybe I'd ride over there with him and show him around. We haven't had any time to get to know each other." She caught Lacy's frown and averted her eyes quickly. "If it's all right with you, Lace. He *is* likely to be my brother-in-law, after all." She gave her sister a wide, innocent smile.

Before Lacy could respond, Mother jumped in. "Why, I think that's very considerate, Lauren. Don't you, honey?" She peered at Lacy, whose face had hardened into an inscrutable mask. "We'll bring you a surprise." She ushered Lacy into the car, slid in behind the wheel, and waved as they headed off.

IT WAS A SUNNY SPRING DAY, and at Lauren's insistence, Trip put the top down on the Corvair. Her long hair swirled around her face as they drove. The front bucket seat, she noted, was much more comfortable than the cramped rear where she had ridden all the way from Mississippi, and she stretched her legs and leaned back with a sigh.

Trip almost ran off the road staring at her.

"Whoops!" She leaned forward and guided the car back onto the pavement, grinning at him. "Strange, isn't it?"

"What's strange?" His face had turned a brilliant pink, as if he'd been out on the beach all day.

"Dating a twin. You wouldn't be the first guy who felt it."

His eyes veered back to her. "Lacy didn't tell me. I didn't know it until that day I came to Sunday dinner."

Lauren nodded. "Sometimes she prefers to keep me out of the picture."

"It's eerie," he said. "It's like I'm looking at Lacy, and yet it's not Lacy. Except for the hair, you're exactly alike."

She gave a low purring laugh. "Well, not . . . *exactly*." She winked at him, and he blushed again.

The Duke campus was a magical place in springtime—or any time of year, for that matter. A few students loitered about here and there, but for the most part Lauren and Trip had the place to themselves. Once they had driven around for a bit, Trip decided not to bother touring the law school. Instead, like children playing hooky, they walked around the grounds and lounged on the grass, talking under the shadow of the imposing brick and stone buildings.

He told her about how he met Lacy and how they had hit it off immediately, about his enthusiasm for the law, about his passion for Van Gogh and his love of the blues. He laughed a lot and seemed to grow comfortable with Lauren, but didn't ask her much about her own life and plans for the future. After a while Lauren began to feel as if she were standing in for her sister, as if he were talking to Lacy by proxy.

Trip was clearly mesmerized by the beauty of the campus—the expanses of green lawn and blossoming trees, the gargoyles that leered down at them from rooftops, the magnificent gothic chapel with its central tower rising two hundred feet into the sky. At last they entered the Duke Gardens, which lay spread out as the centerpiece of campus, fifty acres of emerald velvet adorned with ponds and fountains, shaded walks and sun-drenched bridges, blooming things in a hundred hues of sapphire, topaz, ruby, and amethyst.

Midweek, in the middle of the day, in the middle of spring break, the gardens were nearly deserted. They walked and gazed and said little to one another, stopping as if by mutual consent to toss pennies from a bridge and make a secret wish. "I've seen Ole Miss," Trip said at last, "and I've seen Emory, both of which are nice enough. But if I had ever seen this campus, I can't imagine I would have applied anywhere else."

He turned to face her, and the pure dazed joy in his expression made Lauren's heart lurch. In that instant, she knew—if she had ever doubted—why Lacy loved him, and why Lauren herself would never be able to settle for the likes of Steve Treadwell.

They walked some more; she stumbled; he took her hand to steady her and somehow never let go. Lauren wondered if his mind had lost track of which twin he was with—it had happened before. But at this moment she didn't care. She didn't care about anything except the sensation of her hand in his, the soft blue lake of his eyes.

"Let's go sit awhile," she suggested, and led him off the path into a dappled grove. Here the springy ground was soft and cool, with dogwood blooms fluttering like tiny fairy wings overhead. A secluded spot, invisible to anyone who might be walking in the gardens.

Trip dropped down onto the moss-covered bank, lay back, and closed his eyes. Above them birds sang and a breeze stirred the branches. The hush was hypnotic, restful, a lullaby. Within a minute or two his breath grew even and shallow, and he slept.

Lauren's gaze roved over him. He had a swimmer's body, muscled but not bulky, sculpted features with blondish hair swept back from the temples. A wide, untroubled brow, and tiny indentations on either side of his mouth, the hint of dimples around his smile. A man in wakefulness, a boy at rest.

He stirred in his sleep. She reached out a finger and stroked the side of his cheek, lightly touching the smooth skin above the line where he shaved. He gave a little moan of pleasure.

Carefully, so as not to wake him, she stretched out next to him, laid her head into the crook of his out-flung arm, and nestled against him. Her fingers continued to trace the contours of his face, down his jaw line, across his chin. She wet a forefinger on the underside of her own lip and ran it gently, the barest kiss of a touch, across his mouth.

She heard the little intake of breath, saw his tongue come out and run across his lower lip. A lightning flash shot through her. She had to touch him—*had* to. She eased his shirttail out of his jeans and moved a hand lightly up his chest, feeling his nipples harden under the caress.

Lauren was on fire now, pulsing with desire. He felt it too, even in the hazy world of sleep. She could see his arousal, and it inflamed her all the more.

His eyes snapped open, wide and darkly dilated. "What are you doing?"

"Giving you what Lacy can't—or won't." She gazed at him. "Don't tell me you don't want it."

He bit his lip but said nothing.

"I know my prude of a sister," she went on. "She's given you this—" She kissed him, fluttering her tongue inside his parted lips. "And maybe even this—" She took his hand and slid it inside her blouse. "But never this—" She guided his hand down between her thighs and pressed her legs together.

Trip let out a groan. "I can't do this."

"You can," she countered, her voice husky with emotion. "You want to." She pushed closer to him. "My sister is in love with the notion of being in love," she whispered. "She has no idea what it's all about. But I know. I can give you what you want."

She shifted a leg over him, felt him stiffen, felt her own craving ignite even further. He was still murmuring "No, no," as he arched toward her. His mouth closed over hers, his tongue probing, his hands reaching for her. Locked in his arms now, she rolled over onto her back, bringing him with her.

His hand went inside her blouse, inside her bra, around her breast. He writhed against her, as if desperate to get closer, closer. Her body responded to his movements, the sensuous dance of passion driving them on, propelling them toward the point of no return.

"God, no," he breathed as his hands touched bare flesh. He pulled her nearer, caressing her, impelling her hunger with lips and fingers and tongue. A fumbled moment with zippers and underwear, and then—

She'd had sex before, plenty of times. But it had never been like this. This joyous ache, this exquisite pain, this soaring, this flying . . .

A dazzling light, a pounding crescendo like nothing she had ever known. Her breath caught in her throat, and she let it out in a burst. "Ah!"

Trip's eyes snapped open. "Yes!" he cried, then shuddered and collapsed in Lauren's arms.

If Lauren had thought watching Trip and Lacy together made her jealous before, it was nothing compared to the way she felt now. The last two days of break she could barely stand to see them together. Trip turned out to be the consummate actor, smiling and laughing and pretending everything was normal, but casting sidelong glances at Lauren every chance he got.

Lustful glances, or regretful ones? Lauren hadn't been sure until Friday, when they were packing Trip's car. They had decided to leave a day early and break up the long drive with an overnight stop at a motel along the way. Lauren was already entertaining fantasies of sneaking out of her and Lacy's room and into Trip's.

Alone in the garage, he had pressed her up against the side of the car and kissed her, one eye on the garage door and one hand sliding down inside her shorts.

"We'll have to be careful," he warned, his deft fingers stroking her. "Lacy can never know."

How they would manage to keep such a thing hidden, Lauren had no idea. But at the time, distracted by his caress, she had merely nodded.

Shortly after they got on the road, it began to rain—a dull gray drizzle that suited Lauren's mood perfectly. Lacy sat in the front seat, fawning over Trip, laughing at his jokes, holding his hand on top of the gearshift.

Trip Jenkins was everything Lauren had always longed for, everything her other boyfriends were not. And even while she burned with resentment toward Lacy, she clutched the precious secret to her breast. *She* was the one Trip wanted. The one he had made love to. She had won.

All during the drive, she replayed it in her mind. The way his eyelashes lay in dark feathers across his cheeks. The way his lips and tongue moved against hers. The sensation of his hands on her flesh, his weight pressing down upon her, the tenderness, the virility. The explosion of intensity and power at the moment of climax.

The feelings rushed into her on a warm wind, remembered passion giving way to fresh fire. She ought to feel remorse, Lauren thought. She'd had sex with her sister's boyfriend and was planning to do it again at the first opportunity. But all she could think of was Trip. The way he looked at her, the way he touched her.

She drew her knees up to her chest and huddled uncomfortably in the back seat as the leak in the convertible's roof dripped water on her head. But even the thrumming of the rain could not stem the tide of her desire.

FIFTEEN

Facing the Dragon

Rae Dawn lay across the bed in her dorm room and stared at the tree outside her window. The spring green leaves stirred on a breath, cutting the light into lace and spreading it in moving patterns across her pillow.

She had not even considered leaving the college for spring break. The mere idea of returning to Picayune, even for a day or two, was unthinkable. Everything she owned was here, everything she was. Delta and Lacy and Lauren were her family. And Dr. Gottlieb, of course. This was home.

Rae missed her friends and would be glad for their return, but she had needed this week alone, this time to think.

Since that cataclysmic moment, that flash of jealousy over Lacy and Trip and the insight that followed, her entire world had changed. She had—finally—admitted the truth to herself, and there was no going back.

All her life Rae Dawn had assumed she felt different, an outsider, because her family was poor, because she wore hand-me-down clothes, because her father was a notorious drunk. But that had been only part of the reason. There was more.

Far more.

The hard lessons of childhood experience had taught her not to get too close to people, not to allow herself too much hope. She had never dated much, never been particularly interested in boys. She had watched from the sidelines as girls her age underwent the sea change of puberty and became obsessed with the idea of love and sex and (eventually) marriage. They talked about it constantly—not to Rae, certainly, but to each other. In the hallway and at lunch and in the locker rooms as they dressed for gym. Who had kissed whom. How far this girl or that one was willing to go—first base, second base, all the way. The baseball metaphor always seemed a bit odd to Rae Dawn, and it took her a long time to figure out what the bases represented. But every time she overheard such conversations, she felt a nervous flitting in her stomach, that you-don't-fit feeling that had become so familiar to her.

One experience stood out in Rae's mind, a long-ago memory now marked in her mind with a flapping red flag. She had been in junior high—eighth grade, she thought, fourteen or so. Everyone was in the dressing room after P.E., and a girl named Maria Curtis, an extroverted life-of-the-party type, was holding center stage. "Look, everybody!" she called. "I'm preg-nant!"

Minimally dressed in bra and panties and half slip, Maria had pulled the elastic of her slip up over her breasts and thrust out her belly so that she looked as if she were wearing a maternity dress.

Rae stared at her, curious. All the other girls were crowding around, imitating her, chattering like squirrels about how they all couldn't wait to be in love, to be married, have babies. About what they would do with—or to—the boys who were smart enough to choose them. As far as Rae was concerned, they might as well have been speaking Swahili. She couldn't identify with a word they were saying.

Then Maria's best friend, Kate Killian, stepped into the little drama, adopting the part of a man. She swaggered up to Maria and put an arm around her. "Oh, baby," Kate said in a low, growling voice, "you make me so hot." With that, Kate yanked Maria into a mimicry of a passionate embrace, ground her pelvis lustfully into Maria's, and kissed her full on the lips.

In that moment the world stopped dead. Everyone else was laughing, clapping, cheering the performance. Rae Dawn stood rooted to the spot, breathless. Something warm and fizzy moved through her veins, spreading into her chest and down into her crotch, and she gave an involuntary gasp. The sight of two girls kissing, even in mocking play, roused a response in her that had never been awakened by all the constant talk of boys and body parts and fumbling experimental sex.

She should have known, Rae thought. Should have realized. All her childhood crushes had been on women teachers, all her adolescent longings centered around having a girlfriend. A best friend, she had rationalized at the time. But now she knew better. Not just a best friend. A *girlfriend.*

How many nights during those teenage years had she lain on the sofa bed in the cramped living room of the Airstream, listening to make sure her parents were asleep, sinking into a half dream with her hand under her nightgown, fondling herself until she thought she'd go mad with a desire she didn't understand? How many times had she dreamed of someone falling in love with her, taking her away from Picayune and Hobo Creek and the perpetual depression that was her life? And when the fantasies came—those romantic scenarios of being swept away, kissed, touched, made love to, adored—the person who aroused her and loved her, who took her hand and led her into their new life was . . . a woman.

Rae had known nothing about lesbian sex back then, not even enough to fantasize about. To tell the truth, she didn't understand much more as a senior in college. Now that she was exploring the past more objectively, she did admit to occasional attractions, but the self-protection she had learned so well in her early years had served to keep her from pursuing any of them.

This was an aspect of sexuality that no one ever talked about, except in obscene jokes punctuated by nasty words like *fag* and *dyke.* And if she *had* talked about it, she supposed that most people—even her best friends—would likely tell her that since she'd never acted on those feelings, she couldn't possibly be . . . that way.

But as little as she comprehended about the matter, Rae Dawn was certain of one thing: It wasn't exclusively about sex, any more than being straight was only about who you slept with. It was about connection, about love and romance and attraction and how you felt on the inside. It was about being yourself and being accepted for who you were.

Rae had never known true acceptance until she had come to college, and her friendships with Lacy and Lauren and Delta—especially Delta—had made life worth living for the first time. She had to tell them, had to be honest with them. Yet she worried how they might take it. This wasn't just a confession that she was poor and hadn't really grown up in New Orleans. Would she lose the only friends she had ever known? Would they be concerned that she might be attracted to one of them, an attraction that could not be reciprocated?

She sighed and sat up on the bed. Well, she'd just have to deal with that when it came. In the meantime, she knew—or thought she knew—two people who could help her work this out.

Frankie Bowen and Suzanne Hart.

"To tell the truth," Dr. Bowen said when Rae Dawn had finished telling her story, "we wondered when you might be coming to see us." She grinned over at Dr. Hart, who was throwing a tennis ball for Bilbo and Frodo.

Rae gazed out over the lawn as Frodo came loping back to the patio carrying a ball lopsidedly in his mouth. Against the far wall a pink dogwood tree bloomed, and beds of irises and daffodils blossomed purple and yellow in a sunny bed in the corner. It was a peaceful place. A safe place.

"You knew?" she asked. "How? I wasn't even sure, until recently."

Dr. Hart shrugged, took the slobbery ball, and tossed it into the yard again. "We get a sense about these things," she said. "But we would never have asked. It's not our place to pry. Still, it might help you to know that you're not the first student who has come to us with a similar tale."

Rae Dawn took a sip of her iced tea and reached down to pet Bilbo, who had abandoned the game and now sat next to her with his curly muzzle propped on her knee. "I don't know quite what to do with all this," she admitted. "I haven't met anyone. I'm not in love."

"But you'd like to be." Dr. Hart reached over and squeezed Dr. Bowen's hand, and they both smiled.

"Well, sure." Rae Dawn felt herself blush. "But people never talk about this stuff. How am I supposed to find the right person? Nobody wears a sign."

Dr. Bowen chuckled. "Some do. But knowing you, I doubt if you'd hit it off with any of them."

"There are places more open and accepting," Dr. Hart interjected. "California, New York." She pointed a finger in Rae Dawn's direction. "New Orleans. You're going back to New Orleans after graduation?"

"Yes. At least I'm going to try."

"Good place, New Orleans. We have a couple of friends down there who might be able to introduce you around."

"That would be great." Rae fell silent for a minute. "What's it like, being . . ." She paused. "Being a lesbian couple?"

Lesbian. Rae Dawn was pretty sure it was the first time she had ever said the word aloud, and it felt good. Rebellious. Liberating. Just hearing the word roll off her own tongue gave her the sensation of stepping out of a dank, moldy basement into sunlight and fresh air.

"It's absolutely wonderful, when you've found the right person," Dr. Bowen said. "But it can also be hard to live with the rejection and condemnation. Critics talk about the moral issues—you know, that it's a choice against nature and against God. Absurd. This *is* nature. No one would choose to be part of a maligned and censured minority."

"Still," Dr. Hart added, "once you *have* found the right person, you wouldn't go back even if you could." She shrugged. "Sometimes it's just frustrating, feeling as if you have to live a secret, to hide the most important relationship in your life in order to keep your job or protect your safety."

"I don't know how the two of you do it," Rae said. "I mean, you've been together how long? Ten years?"

Dr. Bowen rolled her eyes. "Fifteen. Suze was twenty-five and a first-year instructor when we met. I was thirty-six, an associate professor." She chuckled. "I robbed the cradle, I suppose."

Dr. Hart laughed. "Or I robbed the grave."

"And you've never been able to name your relationship publicly."

Dr. Hart shook her head. "As long as we're not obvious about it, everything's fine. People know, but they don't want to *know,* if you get my drift. Frankie and I just go about our business, and folks perceive us as two old spinster teachers sharing our living expenses."

"God, that must be hard."

"In some ways it is," Dr. Bowen agreed. "But we have supportive people in our lives. And we try to be careful. It would only take one phone call to bring the whole house of cards crashing in on us."

SIXTEEN

Woman on the Wind

The morning after her conversation with Dr. Bowen and Dr. Hart, Rae Dawn awoke to a chilling fear that she had made a terrible mistake. Three times she picked up the telephone to call them, to beg them not to tell anyone what she had said, to convince them—or herself—that it couldn't possibly be true.

After all, she'd never had any kind of sexual relationship with another woman. Delta Fox was her best friend, the person Rae loved most in the world, and she wasn't physically attracted to Delta. Not much, anyway.

Besides, you couldn't be a lesbian unless you had actually *done* something, could you? She'd never even kissed a girl.

For hours—alone in her dorm, walking across campus, working on her senior composition in the rehearsal room—she carried on the internal debate. How could she deny what she felt? But how could it be true when she had never acted on those feelings? This argument, she now realized, had been going on inside her for years. All her life, or at least since puberty, she had been trying to figure it out. Trying to ignore it. Trying to learn to live with the anxiety that bubbled like molten lava in the subterranean crevices of her heart.

And yet in a deeper place beyond her fear, the reality was there, inside her. Even the word *lesbian* conjured up images in Rae Dawn's mind of soft, willing body parts—small attentive breasts and warm liquid caresses, the electrifying newness of skin on skin, the curve of a thigh, the arch of a back . . .

And the liberation—no, the *resurrection*—that had come when she had finally said, "Yes. This is who I am."

She could suppress the feelings, dismiss the longings. She could live celibate for the rest of her life, stay safe, never let anyone get close enough to be a danger. But she could not deny the fresh air that had rushed into her lungs in that instant, the sun that had blazed down upon her light-starved soul. The tomb had cracked opened and could not be sealed again.

"This is who I am," she repeated to herself. "Come hell or high water, whatever the cost, this is who I am."

MUCH TO RAE DAWN'S SURPRISE and pleasure, Delta arrived back at school just before dinner on Friday evening. The dining hall was practically empty, and the two of them sat at a table alone while Delta told Rae what had happened with her parents.

"I am so sorry," Rae said. "Divorce is awful, no matter what the circumstances. But believe me, I can understand when you say you wonder why your parents ever got married in the first place. My folks are the same way, only I doubt they will ever split. They're too stuck in their ways. They'll just go on tormenting one another until one of them dies."

"It's weird," Delta said. "I don't feel any of the things I'm supposed to feel. I just keep thinking that maybe now Daddy will be happy and maybe Mama can find a way to recover her dreams again."

"What dreams are those?" Rae asked.

Delta shrugged. "I have no idea."

"And how's your little sister taking it? She's pretty young to have to deal with this."

"Cassie will be fine," Delta said in a voice that sounded to Rae like wishful thinking. "She's smart, and she's tough. She'll adjust." She exhaled heavily. "So, what have you been doing with yourself this week? Working on your senior composition, I suppose."

Rae hesitated. She had planned to wait until she had a better grip on things herself, but suddenly she wanted to tell Delta everything. She was hopeful that Delta, given her love for her two major professors, would be supportive and accepting. But no matter what the outcome, Rae wanted to pour it all out in a rush and get it over with, like pulling an abscessed tooth. Her stomach twitched and heaved with the risk of telling, and yet she felt a fluttering of anticipation too.

Rae's mind had drifted. Delta was frowning at her.

"Are you going to answer my question?" Delta said. "I asked about your senior composition."

"Oh." Rae Dawn dragged her attention back to the present. "It's going very well; I think Gottlieb will be pleased. I've decided to call it 'Woman on the Wind.' "

"That's a fabulous title. I can't wait to hear it."

"I'm still tweaking it, but I'll play it for you later, if you like," Rae said.

They were done with dinner. Rae Dawn pushed her plate back and steeled herself to launch into her disclosure. But she never got a single word out.

Delta jumped up from the table and jerked her by the hand. "What's wrong with right now?" she said. "Come on, Rae. I want to hear your masterpiece."

THE MUSIC BUILDING was deserted, so they took one of the larger practice rooms. Delta perched on a stool while Rae Dawn settled herself at the piano. She couldn't decide if she was disappointed or relieved to have been given a reprieve from the confessional.

She shifted on the bench and fiddled with the score. "As I said, it still needs some revision."

Delta rolled her eyes. "Always the perfectionist. Just let me hear it, please."

Rae Dawn began to play, a minor-key, bluesy piece reminiscent of the old slave songs. Soulful enough to make you weep, the melody wound around them like a living vine, a tether forged of tears and heartbreak. Something within the music strained against its bonds, seeking release. And then, just as the agony became unbearable, there was a breath—a flash of light, a flutter of wings, a wind high in the trees. Like new life erupting from the womb, the notes burst forth into glorious movement, streaking skyward, plummeting toward earth again, soaring on the currents of the song.

The music was ecstasy, indeed, mounting up from earthbound bondage to climb the currents of the wind. Rae Dawn played on, her head thrown back and her eyes closed as the harmony rose toward a climax of the soul so deep and powerful that it ended, for both pianist and listener, with a breathless tremor.

The final notes drifted into silence. Rae Dawn sat at the keyboard for a moment, then opened her eyes.

Delta's face was streaked with the silver tracks of tears. Her mouth hung slightly open, and she had both hands clenched in her lap. Neither of them spoke.

Then Delta seemed to come awake. "Wow," she said.

Rae Dawn put her hands to her cheeks and could feel the heat emanating from her skin. Unaccountably, she felt exposed, embarrassed, as if she had been glimpsed naked.

"That was amazing," Delta went on. "It was—" She hesitated. "Pure poetry. It reminds me of Hopkins's poem 'The Windhover'—the bird darting and falling, rising and swinging." She closed her eyes and tried to call up the poem from her memory: "His riding/ Of the rolling level underneath him steady air, and striding/ High there, how he rung upon the rein of a wimpling wing/ In his ecstasy!"

Rae smiled and ducked her head. "Coming from you, that's high praise."

"It was incredible, Rae. I've never heard any piece of music that moved me so profoundly." Delta leaned forward. "I want you to talk to me about how it happened. What goes on inside your soul that enables you to write something like that?"

Rae Dawn gathered up the music and sat for a moment, her hands absently caressing the score. This was her invitation, her open door. She wouldn't get a better chance than this. "Let's go to the Goose and get some coffee," she said. "I'll try to explain—about the music, and about a lot of other things."

THEY WALKED IN SILENCE. It was a glorious evening, the stillness broken only by invisible birds twittering in the rustling trees overhead. The Goose was uninhabited except for Mary Jo, the wiry, blank-faced woman who worked behind the counter. She filled their order—two cups of coffee and two slices of coconut custard pie—and then went back to reading her paperback novel.

They settled themselves in a corner booth near the glass wall that looked out onto the patio. Rae Dawn, facing the window, could see her own reflection in the glass as clearly as if she were looking into a mirror. She lowered her eyes and busied herself with the pie.

Delta took a sip of coffee. "So tell me," she said, "where does genius like that come from?"

"Genius?" Rae Dawn shook her head. "I wouldn't call it genius."

"I would." Delta smiled. "You're going to say I don't know much about music, and that's true, but I know plenty about poetry. 'Woman on the Wind' is a poem, the kind of poem that evokes deep and significant images in the listener. Don't be modest, Rae. It's genius. It's artistry. It's a gift."

Rae took a bite of her pie and pushed the plate back from the edge of the table. It was delicious, but her stomach swarmed with fluttering wings. Maybe she could finish it later, afterward.

"What images?" she asked Delta, trying to buy time while her mind scrambled for some semblance of order. She had thought she was prepared for this, but now that the moment was upon her, her brain had gone to mush. "What images does the music evoke in you?"

Delta bit on the tines of her fork while she considered her answer. "Well, in the beginning, the minor-key part, I felt weighed down, trapped. In chains, perhaps, but less like forged metal chains than natural chains, if you know what I mean. Like heavy vines growing and wrapping around my limbs. I felt as if gravity had increased, pulling me downward toward the earth."

Rae nodded. "Go on."

"And then something—I don't quite know what it was—

broke free. The sun came out. The air was fresh and clean, the way it is after a rainstorm. And I began to fly. Not just released from gravity, but soaring, dancing in the air, chasing the clouds and darting toward the heavens. It was liberating, powerful. It was—" she paused. " 'Woman on the Wind.' "

Rae Dawn smiled. This was exactly the response she had hoped for, exactly the reaction she had experienced when writing the music—and when coming to grips with the truth about herself. "What about the ending?"

"Whew," Delta said. "I can still feel it. It was like—" She shook her head. "This is going to sound strange, I know, because I'm not religious and I don't usually talk about God stuff. But it was like being present at the moment of creation. Like making love to God and the universe."

Rae felt tears sting at her eyes. "Thank you."

"No, I should be the one thanking *you*," Delta said. She tapped her fork rhythmically on the table top. "I'm fascinated with the imaginative process, with what goes on in an artist's mind and heart during a moment of creativity. Is it just instinct, or can you articulate where it came from?"

"I can try." Rae Dawn had the sensation of standing on a cliff edge, the precipice of now or never. "You know my background, know what my childhood was like," she began. "I always felt different, ostracized."

"Because of your parents and your living situation. Because you didn't fit." Delta nodded. "That experience is reflected in the minor-key section at the beginning, feeling trapped and held down."

"Yes. But it has to do with more, much more, than just growing up poor and isolated. It has to do with—" Rae Dawn felt her resolve weakening. "Well, it's a little hard to explain."

Delta leaned forward, her expression intense. "Something happened to you during spring break, Rae. A change. A transformation. I see it in your eyes. I felt it in your music. Trust me to understand. Tell me."

"All right." Rae Dawn took a deep breath, peered over the ledge, and leaped. She told Delta about the dark flame of jealousy that had overcome her concerning Lacy's relationship with Trip, about that visceral memory from junior high when Kate Killian kissed Maria Curtis, about her conversation with Frankie Bowen and Suzanne Hart and her self-examination during spring break.

"I suppose I've known subconsciously since eighth grade or so," she finished, "although I couldn't admit it, not even to myself. Maybe I felt I was different enough already and didn't have the courage to add anything else to the mix. But I can't deny it any longer. I have to accept myself, even if other people don't accept me."

"And when you finally did name it and accept it," Delta said, "you experienced a miraculous burst of wonder and freedom and lightness and joy, all of which poured out into your score—that soaring, leaping dance of passion and intimacy."

The tightly wound spring inside Rae's chest let go, and a flood of love and gratitude flowed into her. "You understand," she whispered.

"Well—" Delta shrugged. "I can't really comprehend what it means, since I have never experienced those particular feelings. But I think I do understand about breaking free, about taking the risk to be true to yourself no matter what the cost."

"I—I wasn't sure you would," Rae said quietly. "The first time we heard the rumors about Bowen and Hart, back during our freshman year, I got the impression you weren't quite certain what you thought about the idea."

"I'm an English major, for God's sake," Delta shot back with a mocking scowl. "I spend most of my time with those two, and I'm neither stupid nor naive. Besides, I think we've *all* grown up since then." She tilted her head. "Well, maybe not Lauren, but the rest of us, anyway."

Their laughter drew the attention of Mary Jo, who left her post behind the counter and brought them a refill of coffee. "You two okay?" she said, narrowing her eyes at them as if she were certain they'd been drinking. "Black coffee, that's the ticket. Lots of it."

She moved away, muttering to herself. When they had finally regained their composure, Delta pushed Rae Dawn's plate back across the table. "Eat your pie," she said. "Everything's going to be fine."

SEVENTEEN

THE OUTING

But everything wasn't fine. On Saturday afternoon, all hell broke loose.

By the time Rae Dawn got to the quad in front of the administration building, it was packed with people, many of them carrying signs and yelling. She made her way across the grass, scanning faces as she ran. At last she spotted Delta near the front of the building. She threaded her way through the press of bodies until she reached her, flushed and panting.

"What's going on?" she shouted above the clamor.

Delta turned. She looked haggard and worn, and her eyes held an expression bordering on panic. "It's Bowen and Hart," she said. "Apparently someone called the academic dean and complained about them. The Board of Trustees is having a special meeting right now, to decide whether to fire them or not."

"Fire them?" Rae repeated. "For what?"

"For being gay, I guess," Delta said. Her eyes were red-rimmed with tears. "They're the best teachers this college has ever had."

The bottom dropped out of Rae Dawn's stomach. "Shit," she muttered. "They can't get fired."

"No? Look around."

Rae Dawn looked. The quad seemed to be divided straight down the middle by an invisible barrier about ten yards across. On the opposite side of the fountain stood a group of people, mostly adults, holding up hand-lettered posters.

PARENTS AGAINST IMMORALITY

one of the signs read. And another,

GOD HATES DIKES AND FAGOTS

"Jeez," Delta breathed. "You'd think they'd learn to spell, anyway."

Despite herself, Rae let out a chuckle. "Thanks, Delta. I needed that." She peered into the crowd. "Who are these people, anyway?"

"I don't know," Delta said. "Some are townspeople, I think. Most of them are parents—I recognize a few of them. Over there on the right, the tall woman with auburn hair and the man in the Ole Miss jacket? Those are the Austins."

"Tabitha's parents?"

"Yep."

"I should have known. Tabby looks just like her mother."

Nearby a group of students milled about, carrying counter-protest signs that read

LIBERTY AND JUSTICE FOR ALL

Some of the faculty were there as well, looking nervous and angry.

"Seems like the professors have a good many supporters, though," Rae said.

"Yeah, but the other guys are louder."

"How did this all come about? Bowen and Hart never did

anything to hurt anyone. Who on earth would call the administration?"

Delta sighed. "I don't know."

"I do." The voice came from behind them, and both Delta and Rae turned. It was Tabby Austin, looking even more miserable than Rae felt. "It was all a mistake," she said. "A huge, awful, terrible mistake."

Rae took Tabby's elbow and steered her to the edge of the crowd where the noise wasn't so deafening. "Who told?"

"I did."

"What?" Rae, still holding Tabby's arm, gripped harder and shook her a little.

"Like I said, it was a mistake," Tabby wailed. "Somebody—I don't know who—called my dad. He's given a ton of money to the college over the years, and there are a lot of alumnae in our family—"

"Yeah, we know all that," Rae snapped. "Five generations or something, dating back to the Civil War. Get on with it."

"Apparently a rumor was going around, some student who had told her parents she was a lesbian. She said she had talked with a couple of professors who helped her come to an acceptance of herself. Everybody got all riled up, like they had recruited her or something, and then my father said he was determined to find out who they were and put a stop to it, and that he had the clout to do it. I said I didn't know why it had to be such a big hairy deal, when they were just nice, normal people—"

"You didn't."

"Well, yeah. I never dreamed it would come to this—"

"So what happened then?"

"My parents made me tell them—" Tabby choked and began to sob. "And then my father called the dean and the president, and—"

"And here we are." Rae Dawn rolled her eyes. "I swear, Tabby, if Bowen and Hart are fired, I will have your head on a plate. Count on it."

Rae had vanished with Tabby, but Delta hadn't moved. She stood on the front edge of the crowd, her eyes scanning the opposition. In the center of the quad between the two groups stood a fountain, a square marble base with a bronze likeness of a woman, reaching upward toward the heavens. Water fell around her like tears, and on the ledge of the base were inscribed words from Tennyson's poem "Ulysses": *'Tis not too late to seek a newer world . . . To strive, to seek, to find, and not to yield.*

A newer world. Delta sighed. If memory served, Tennyson published "Ulysses" in the 1840s. Evidently the new birth was a long time coming. She felt the labor pains in her own soul every time the Delta Belles sang, every time she faced down racists at voter registrations, every time she read a hateful picket sign. Where was the hope for a newer world when malice still reared its head at anyone who was deemed different?

The crowd across the way had resumed its chant: "*Fire the queers, fire the queers.*"

"They won't be fired," a voice at her elbow said. "They've got tenure."

She turned to look. Beside her stood a man in blue jeans and a brown suede shirt—not tall, but well built and modestly attractive. He seemed vaguely familiar to Delta, but she couldn't place where she had seen him. He had shaggy brown hair and a beard, and his eyes, also brown, brimmed with confidence and an expression she could only define as joy. A hippie. A flower child. He grinned at her. "You're Delta Fox, aren't you?"

"Yes, but I—" She hesitated. "Have we met?"

He extended a hand. "Rankin Ballou. Our paths have crossed. I've heard your group sing on several occasions."

Awareness flared in Delta's mind, a light bulb coming on. "Right. You've been at a couple of the voting rallies."

"And the antiwar demonstrations, and the civil rights sit-in over at the courthouse. I'm surprised we haven't been formally introduced before now."

She regarded him with interest. His gaze was warm and entreating, and she felt immediately drawn to him. He was older than she—late twenties, thirty, perhaps—but wore no wedding ring . . .

Delta jerked herself back to reality. She was here to support her major professors, for pity's sake, not to get a date. Besides, she had just broken up with Ben Rutledge and vowed not to get involved with anyone else, at least for a long, long time.

"How do you know they won't get fired? Tenure can be overturned."

"True. But the chairman of the trustees is a—let's just say a close acquaintance of mine. He says the charges won't stick. There's no evidence of any wrongdoing, any inappropriate behavior or undue influence on students, and although I suppose they could be dismissed for moral turpitude, a handful of distraught parents won't be enough to turn the tide."

"Looks like more than a handful to me." Her eyes drifted to the crowd across the way.

Rankin smiled again. "Hatred always seems to shout louder than love," he said. "But love will win in the end."

It was an odd thing to say. "Do you really believe that?"

"I do," he answered. "And so do you, deep down. I've seen you in action. You're far too passionate about justice and truth not to have hope."

Delta felt herself at a distinct disadvantage. He seemed to

know her so well, seemed to look right down into the depths of her heart. Her first instinct was to be obstinate, to tell him he didn't know what the hell he was talking about. But he was right about the hope, and even though Delta had a stubborn streak, she recognized the truth when she heard it.

"I hear you'll be hanging around after graduation," he said, "starting your master's program. How would you feel about having dinner with me next week, getting to know each other better?"

As soon as the words were out of his mouth, Delta realized she had been praying he'd ask. Well, maybe not praying, exactly, but wishing. Wanting.

"Sure," she said casually, as if it didn't matter one way or the other. "Why not?"

It was a minor deception, downplaying her enthusiasm, but in the face of his openness it felt like betrayal. "I'd like that very much," she amended.

"Good. I'll call you."

"Don't you need my number?" Delta asked.

"I've got it," he said. "But I should give you mine in case you need to get in touch." He fished in his pocket and handed her a small card. "And now, if you'll excuse me, I have something I need to do."

Delta watched him move toward the front of the crowd, then glanced down at the business card.

FIRST COMMUNITY CHURCH
REV. RANKIN BALLOU, PASTOR

"Holy shit," Delta muttered. "I've got a date with a *preacher*."

═══

But he was like no preacher she had ever heard. He mounted the steps of the administration building two at a time, and when he turned back toward the quad, a rippling murmur ran through the crowd. The shouting and jeering died, and on both sides of the invisible barrier, all eyes turned toward him.

"Some among us," Rankin began, "would have us believe that God hates those who are different from the majority. That people who do not live the way we live or love the way we love are an abomination." His voice rang with confidence and authority across the green, and his eyes rested on the group to his right with an expression not of hatred or contempt, but of compassion. "We are afraid, and in our fear we strike out at those who threaten the beliefs we hold dear.

"Fear expresses itself in words and deeds of hatred," he continued. "Ugly, embittered words like *dyke* and *faggot*." He lifted his eyes. "*Dyke*, by the way, is spelled with a *y*, and *faggot* with two *g*'s." A titter began to thread its way through the crowd. "Just for future reference," he said. "You might want to correct your sign before the next protest."

The laughter increased, and whoever was carrying the poster in question put it down. Rankin's gaze swung around toward the left, and he caught Delta's eye and gave a solemn nod.

"I am sometimes ashamed of being a Christian," he went on, "because of what Christians have done to the name. I am sometimes ashamed of being a minister because of how ministers have abused their power. I am sometimes ashamed of claiming the Bible as my sacred text because of how it has been misused to hurt millions of people.

"But it remains my sacred text," Rankin declared, "because the voices of hatred and hostility do not tell the story of who God is."

The crowd had fallen silent now, mesmerized. No one moved or spoke. Delta felt a presence at her side and turned to see Rae Dawn standing next to her, with Tabby Austin in tow.

Rae, still furious with Tabby, pushed in beside Delta. She refused to stand next to the traitor who, in her utter stupidity, had shot her mouth off and caused this commotion in the first place. But it didn't take long for Rae to forget her irritation. Peace emanated from the man who was speaking, a peace that had to do with his inner spirit as well as his words.

"Who is this guy?" she murmured to Delta.

"His name is Rankin Ballou, and he's the minister at"—she glanced down at the card she was holding—"First Community Church."

"Jeez," Rae breathed. "I've never heard of a preacher who would stand up for gay folks. That's the kind of church I might actually want to go to."

"I've seen him around at protests and rallies," Delta whispered. "He's very involved in social causes. But I never met him until today."

Rankin Ballou was speaking again, his words gaining momentum, rolling over his listeners like the waters of righteousness.

"God's voice," he said, "is not the voice of violence and malice. God's voice is the voice of love.

"The voice of love is heard in the words of Martin Luther King, Jr., who declared, 'Injustice anywhere is a threat to justice everywhere.'

"The voice of love is heard in the words of a Holocaust survivor, who wrote, 'Thou shalt not be a victim. Thou shalt not be a perpetrator. Above all, thou shalt not be a bystander.'

"And the voice of love is heard in the words of Jesus of Nazareth, who proclaimed, 'Let the one who is without sin cast the first stone.' "

The silence deepened. "Jesus was not a bystander. Not only did he speak with the voice of love, he lived by the law of love. He ate with sinners, drew outcasts into his circle of friends, embraced those whom society called unclean. He touched. He healed. He forgave. In the end he died for it, but while he lived, he lived the best example of the love of God the world has ever seen. An example not of hatred and exclusion, but of acceptance and affirmation."

Rankin's eyes roamed over the assembled multitude. "Who will cast the first stone?" He looked into the eyes of one person, and then the next. "Who among us is so pure of heart and so perfect in love as to dare to judge another? Who among us is so righteous as to condemn another's love, when God's own name is Love? Who will cast the first stone?"

His voice had grown quiet now, but the crowd had no difficulty hearing him. "Who will cast the first stone?" he repeated.

A murmur ran through the knot of those gathered on the opposite side of the green. Some of them were shaking their heads, and a few threw angry glances in the minister's direction. But many were shifting, walking away. The knot unraveled, and Rankin Ballou stood there in silence, unflinching, as most of them returned to their cars and drove away.

Rae Dawn watched as the protesters on the other side of the quad dispersed. A breath of hope blew into her soul. Hope for Frankie Bowen and Suzanne Hart. Hope for herself. Hope for the future.

And then she saw him. In the back of the crowd, almost hidden at this angle by the tall bronze fountain. A thin, wiry figure with a shock of unruly white hair.

"How could you?" Rae Dawn demanded. "How could you advocate the dismissal of two of your own colleagues? How could you betray them like that? How could you stand there on the side of bigotry and injustice? You, of all people!"

Dr. Gottlieb sank down into his leather office chair and ran his hands over his face. "Why me, of all people?" he asked in a weary voice.

"Because you were *there.* You survived. You saw it firsthand, the result of blind hatred and inequality."

"This is not the same."

Rae towered over him, and he seemed to shrink. "Tell me why it is not the same. Why is it evil for Jews to be persecuted and ostracized and murdered, but it is not evil to do the same to any other group?"

Gottlieb managed a wan smile. It seemed a monumental effort. "You are like a daughter to me, Rae Dawn. God's gift to an old man's heart. When I look at you, when I hear your music, hear your laugh, I can almost believe you have been given to me as a gift, a reparation for those years behind the barbed-wire fences. I would willingly throw my body between you and the Nazis' rifles, between you and the gas and the ovens. But you are young. Young and innocent and impressionable. Do not be angry with me. You do not understand the ways of the world."

"I understand a hell of a lot more than you give me credit for," she snapped.

"Perhaps. Perhaps not. Trust me, this issue of homosexuality—it is different."

"You haven't answered my question. *Why* is it different?"

A momentary fire blazed in his eyes, and his jaw clenched. "Because I could not *choose* no longer to be a Jew."

The words, clipped and precise, beat a staccato rhythm against her eardrums. She wanted to respect him, to love him. But the implications of his position burned like acid in her gut. "And they could choose not to be gay?"

He stood suddenly, slamming his hands down flat on the top of his desk. "I saw them there, in the camps, those pink triangles!" he shouted. "They defied the laws of God and human nature, and they were punished. They *chose* their fate!"

"So it's their fault that they died?" She held his eyes and would not look away. "Or is it God's fault?"

All the fire went out of him and he sagged into his chair like a deflated balloon. "They chose," he repeated stubbornly.

"They did not choose," she whispered.

"And how are you so certain, daughter of my heart?" he said in a cracked and shaky voice.

Rae Dawn leaned on the edge of the desk and gazed down at him. Her answer would hurt and confuse him, but she spoke the truth anyway.

"Because *I* would have worn a pink triangle," she said, "and *I* did not choose."

PART 3

Losing Touch

Frozen, captured in the dark,
we take an arbitrary step,
squint our eyes and strain our ears
but cannot see or hear
what lies beyond,
shrouded by fog and shadows.

And so we stumble forward,
oblivious to how one small diversion
veers us toward a different path,
or how one voice
can lure us to our doom
or to our calling.

EIGHTEEN

Woman on the Wire

New Orleans
September 1994

Upstairs, in the spacious apartment on Dauphine Street, the memory returned to Rae Dawn in such vivid clarity and detail that it might have been a movie reel spinning out inside her head. That day in his office, when they had argued, had been the last time she had seen Manfred Gottlieb alive—really alive, anyway.

They had both gone through the motions until graduation, speaking with caution and restraint when they had to speak, keeping silent and avoiding one another when they didn't. Rae had completed the final revisions of "Woman on the Wind" and played it at her senior recital to a rousing ovation. She had sat through the mind-numbing commencement speeches, received her diploma and the music department's coveted composition award, played one last concert with the Delta Belles at the graduation banquet—events that should have been highlights, and yet her recollections of them were grainy and faded. In those final weeks between her confrontation with Gottlieb and her departure from the college, Rae had apparently been on autopilot.

Still, Gottlieb had been true to his word. He had contacted an old friend from New Orleans, the owner of a small club called Maison Dauphine. The man hired Rae Dawn, sight unseen, on the strength of Gottlieb's word alone.

"Manny said I wouldn't be sorry for doing this," Chase Coulter said the first time Rae met him. "Don't make a liar out of him."

"Manny?" Rae almost laughed, then caught herself. She had never heard anyone refer to Gottlieb with a nickname, and the idea that he'd be friends with a man like Chase Coulter was almost beyond belief. Chase was a beefy, red-faced tough guy who looked more like a bouncer than an owner. Rae suspected he probably still did double duty during Mardi Gras and on weekends. "How did you two meet?"

Chase ducked his head. "My unit, we were the guys who went in to liberate the camps in Germany," he said in a low, choked voice. "Jesus, what a mess. Bodies piled up everywhere. People caged like rats." He cleared his throat. "Anyway, Manny was there, all skin and bones and looking like he was a hundred years old, but alive. Once we secured the camp, we took the survivors into the officers' quarters to get them some food. There was a piano in there. Everyone else was chowing down, but Manny, he went over to the piano and started to play. In a daze, almost. Like he had been starving for music."

"Yes," Rae said. "That's exactly how he'd put it, I bet."

"I liked him," Chase went on. "Gave him my address and told him to look me up after the war. When he came to the States, well—" He shrugged. "You go through something like that, you become friends for life."

That had been more than twenty years ago, and never once

had Rae Dawn given Chase Coulter reason to regret his decision to hire her. From backup pianist, she had gradually moved up to headliner, with her photograph posted out front on Dauphine Street. Word spread, and customers had flocked in droves to hear her sultry, smoky renditions of the old blues and jazz pieces, love songs, torch songs. Eventually she had begun to work her own compositions into the act, attracting the attention of talent agents and music publishers. Contracts followed, and gold albums, and concert tours. Rae Dawn had become the new Billie Holiday, and everybody adored her.

Still, she never forgot her beginnings. Wherever she went, her heart drew her back. Back to New Orleans. Back to Maison Dauphine, to Nate the bartender, to Chuck Coulter, Chase's son, who now managed the place since his father's death, to the fans who jostled in the street trying to get in. Back to the place she called home.

Rae crossed the wide living room of her apartment to the old mahogany baby grand that sat in the front window. She sat down at the keyboard and played a few runs, only to be interrupted by a voice drifting in the open window.

"Helloooo?"

Rae went to the wrought-iron balcony that faced the street and looked out. On the other side, Mrs. Beaulieu stood at her own balcony, waving a shaking hand. "Hellooo," she called again. "I'm so glad you're home, Rae."

"Do you need something, Mrs. B?" Rae shouted back. "Is everything all right?"

"Oh no, dear, I'm fine. Just fine. I was just wondering. . . ."

Here it comes, Rae thought. Mrs. B was a grand old lady, and Rae loved her company. But since her husband's death, she had been seeking Rae out more and more. Of course she was lonely. Of course she needed someone to talk to. But—

Rae was about to make up an excuse to get herself off the hook when Mrs. Beaulieu spoke again. "I was just sitting here thinking," she said, "and then I heard you at the piano. Would you—could you," she stammered, running a claw through her thin white hair. "Would you mind very much playing that song for me? The one I like so much? It was our song, Robert's and mine. . . ."

She drifted away again, back into her apartment, and Rae Dawn could see her through the open window as she sank into her chair and began to rock.

Rae knew without question what song Mrs. B wanted to hear. The song she had refused to play since—

She sighed. What difference did it make now? It was just a song. A favor for a sweet, sad, grieving old lady.

Rae barely got through the first line of "Come Rain or Come Shine" before her voice cracked. The tears came. And with the tears the memories she desperately wanted to suppress, memories dragged to the surface by Delta's telephone call. Memories of a certain December, nearly five years after she had first come to sing at Maison Dauphine. . . .

Christmas 1973

Rae Dawn aimed her eight-year-old Honda into the December darkness and sped toward Picayune, a reluctant missile launched northward against her will. The night was black and chilled, the waning quarter moon already set over the Crescent City, but now that she was outside the range of the city's pink glow, she could make out a spangle of stars overhead. Just north of Bayou Sauvage, she crossed the eastern tip of Lake Pontchartrain. To her left, on the surface of the dark lake, she could see the distant dance of glimmering lights—not stars, but artificial lights, human lights. And on the shore, reflected in the placid waters, a Christmas tree strung with red and green and gold.

On the radio, Bing Crosby was crooning "I'll Be Home for Christmas." With a grunt of disgust Rae Dawn snapped it off and was plunged immediately into a claustrophobic silence, broken only by the Doppler whine of the occasional car whizzing by and the thud of her tires on expansion cracks in the pavement.

Rae hated Christmas. She ought to love it, given the increase in business for Maison Dauphine and the resulting increase in her own meager revenues. New Orleans was a favorite holiday destination, and from Thanksgiving to New Year's the Quarter was alive with twinkling lights and festive music, concerts and plays and laughter and costumed carolers in the streets. Not to mention money—the *ching* of the cash registers, the tips pressed down, shaken together, and running over in the large brandy snifter on top of her piano.

But Christmas also meant that she got endless requests for those sappy Christmas songs, the ones about love and family and how wonderful it is to be home again. Never mind that most of the folks who asked for these tunes weren't home at all, but rather drowning their loneliness in a French Quarter bar, waxing nostalgic about Christmas past and inventing memories out of pure imagination.

Never in her life had Rae Dawn experienced the kind of Christmas portrayed in the songs or depicted on Christmas cards. Even as a child—*especially* as a child—she had not known the tantalizing excitement of an interminable Christmas Eve waiting for Santa Claus, or the thrill of colorfully wrapped presents under a glittering tree, or the warmth of friends and family gathered around a table groaning with the weight of the Christmas feast.

No, Christmas at Hobo Creek had been nothing like the photos in the advertisements. No tree, no stocking, no presents—unless you counted the new underwear from the Dollar Store or a secondhand coat or sweater from Goodwill. Once, years ago, Rae Dawn had taken it upon herself to try to make the Airstream a little more festive. She had found a couple of strings of old multicolored Christmas lights in the dumpster and, by switching bulbs, had gotten one string to work. The flame-shaped bulbs looped across the front of the trailer did make the place a bit more cheerful, until her father came home drunk and used the lights for target practice.

After that, Rae gave up on Christmas entirely.

Besides, what kind of Christmas would she have even if she had the desire to celebrate? She lived alone, played at the club every night. Karen and Charlene, who owned the tiny apartment she had rented for the past five years, were kind to her and always invited her when they threw a party, but most of the time she politely declined. Spare time, what little there was of it, she gave to writing music.

Rae had never deliberately determined not to have a social life. Sometimes she wished she could meet someone and fall in love, have a real home and a family—that old dream she cherished back in college. But real life got in the way. Taking the stage at Maison Dauphine from ten till two six nights a week tended to eliminate the possibility of dating. And without a partner, a lover, or even close friends to share it with, the holiday season had little meaning beyond the opportunity to work harder and make a few extra bucks.

Her drive to Picayune tonight, certainly, had nothing to do with celebrating the season. A nurse had called from the hospital shortly before midnight, just as Rae was about to begin her second set. Her mother had suffered a heart attack, a bad one, and had been taken to the emergency room. She was stabilized for the time being, but there was no assurance she would make it.

Rae's emotions as she sped along the deserted road vacillated between sorrow and relief. Sorrow for her mother, that her life had been so empty, so totally bereft of love or friendship or any sort of meaning or purpose. And relief for herself, that once Mama was gone she could finally and forever leave Picayune behind her.

Daddy had died two years ago—wrapped his pickup truck around a telephone pole and never felt a thing. At the funeral Mama had barely spoken to her daughter, and not once did she turn to her for comfort or consolation. Rae had dutifully made the requisite arrangements, stood beside her mother at the graveside, and then, confronted with her own uselessness, had quickly gone away again. Mama had stayed put in the Airstream on the banks of Hobo Creek.

Rae hadn't set foot in Picayune since the day they put Daddy in the ground. But she could imagine how things had been since her father's death. Her mother still sitting at the table in the kitchen, smoking and staring into space and tracing patterns in the Formica with a broken fingernail. She could envision the place disintegrating around Mama, the trailer covered with kudzu and gradually being absorbed into the wildness.

A stab of regret shot through her. What a rotten daughter she had been, thinking only of her own needs, the compulsion to extricate herself from the past and its oppressive memories. She had gone straight to New Orleans after graduation, without giving more than a passing thought to Picayune or Hobo Creek or the Airstream that hunkered on its red clay banks. She had made it. She had escaped.

But now, picturing Mama alone in the Airstream, Rae wondered: How was her life that different from her mother's? She sang her songs, wrote her music, played three sets a night, and went home to an empty apartment at two o'clock in the morning. What had she accomplished, really? She had realized her dream, only to discover that a dream fulfilled, when there is no one to share it, can be every bit as empty as no dream at all.

THE BLINDING WHITE LIGHTS of the hospital emergency room loomed up before her. Rae dashed in through the sliding doors, dazed and disoriented by the brightness after the dark womb of the car.

This was a small-town hospital, and at this hour the place was nearly deserted. One old man with a grizzled beard dozed in a chair in the corner. Behind a high counter two nurses in green scrubs talked in quiet voices, their heads bent over a patient's chart.

"Lorna DuChamp," Rae Dawn demanded, raising her voice to get the nurses' attention. "Where is she?"

One of the nurses came over to the counter and checked a list. "DuChamp. Yes. She was brought in a couple of hours ago. Room 104, down the hall to the left."

Rae took off down the corridor, rounded the corner, and stopped short. The door bearing the number 104 stood ajar, and from within she could hear ominous sounds—beeps and clicks and a kind of wheezing noise.

She pushed the door open and went inside.

Mama lay motionless on the bed, covered with a pale green sheet and connected by a maze of tubes and wires to an array of monitors. On one side of the bed stood a young woman in a white lab coat—about her own age or a little older, Rae guessed. She had short reddish brown hair and tanned freckled skin, and her eyes, when she lifted her head to look at Rae, were an arresting shade somewhere between hazel and light brown, and very kind.

"You must be Rae Dawn," the woman said, leaving the bedside to come to her. "I'm Noel Ridley, your mother's doctor. We spoke on the phone."

Rae couldn't quit staring at her. The hair, the complexion, the eyes, all combined to give her the look of a young lioness, fiercely protective but with no hint of violence or aggression.

"*Y-you* called?" she stammered. "I thought—I thought it was a nurse."

"An easy mistake to make," the doctor said. She refrained, Rae Dawn noticed, from commenting on the stereotype that assumed a woman to be a nurse rather than a doctor. "I wanted to do it myself," she said simply. "We're all so fond of Lorna."

Rae frowned. "You *know* my mother?"

"Well, yes, of course." Dr. Ridley nodded. "Picayune is a small town. Everyone knows her. She has many friends here."

Rae opened her mouth to respond but could think of nothing to say, so she shut it again. "How is she?" she asked at last.

Dr. Ridley shook her head. "Not good, I'm afraid. It was a massive heart attack, and although we thought at first she might pull through it, she took a downhill turn about twenty minutes ago. Apparently she threw a clot. She's in a coma. The respirator is keeping her alive, but—"

"But she won't come out of it."

"No. I'm sorry."

Rae Dawn exhaled a deep, ragged breath, and felt the warm weight of the doctor's hand on her arm.

"Things are pretty quiet around here at the moment," she said. "Why don't we go down to the cafeteria and get some coffee and talk?"

"All right." Rae cast a glance at her mother. "Give me just a minute."

"Take your time. I'll meet you there." She smiled. "Left at the nurses' station, then all the way down the hall at the end."

When the doctor was gone, Rae went to the bedside and took her mother's hand. Her skin, rough and reddened, was cool to the touch—not cold as death, but not warm with life either. It seemed to Rae Dawn that Mama was hovering someplace between the two worlds, waiting for release, and it was clear she couldn't come back to this one even if she wanted to.

Rae gazed down at her mother's face. Years of stress and misery and despair had ravaged her, cutting deep lines into her cheeks and brow. And yet now, here, in this waiting place, her skin had smoothed so that the wrinkles appeared as tiny hairline scars instead. She looked . . . peaceful. Almost pretty. The way she might have looked had her life taken a different direction.

Rae Dawn brushed an errant hair back from her forehead and again that knife-edge of remorse sliced into her. "I'm sorry, Mama," she whispered. "Sorry for everything."

She couldn't remember the last time she had kissed her mother, but Rae kissed her now, her lips lingering on the soft cheek, a single tear running down to salt the kiss. "I'll be back soon," she promised. "And then this will all be over."

RAE DAWN FOUND Dr. Ridley in the cafeteria at a corner table next to the window. She took the seat opposite and focused her eyes on the doctor's graceful, freckled fingers as they wrapped themselves around a white ceramic mug of steaming coffee.

"It's regular," the doctor said, pointing at the carafe that sat on the table between them. "When I'm on nights I prefer the caffeine. If you want decaf, it's available."

"This is fine." Rae poured herself a cup and took a sip. It was strong but not bitter, and tasted faintly of the chicory blend she had become accustomed to in New Orleans. "Tell me about my mother."

The lioness lifted her eyes and held Rae Dawn's gaze. "The patient, or the woman?"

Rae bit her lip. "Dr. Ridley, I can only imagine what you think of me. I haven't been a very good daughter."

"Noel," she corrected. "Please, call me Noel. It's funny, I know—especially at Christmastime. I keep hearing my name on the radio." She drained her cup and pushed it to the center of the table. "Your mother," she said, "was very proud of you."

"Excuse me, but how do you know her?" Rae interrupted. "She's lived in this town for years and never, to my knowledge, had a single friend. She spent her life—" She stopped. No. The way they had lived—the crushing poverty, the isolation, her father's drunken rages—none of it was this doctor's business, however kind and compassionate she seemed.

"She spent her life in that dismal trailer?" Noel Ridley finished the sentence, then nodded. "Yes, I know all about it. About your father too. About the way you grew up."

"How . . . ?"

"Lorna told me," she said simply.

Rae felt heat rising into her face, and she put her hands to her cheeks.

"There's no need to be embarrassed," the doctor said. "I'm very clear on your family's situation, Rae Dawn. How you were raised. What your father was like. How your mother buried herself out there, purely out of shame."

"So what changed?"

Noel shrugged. "Your father died. And your mother came alive. You didn't know, I suppose, that she volunteered here at the hospital. That she spent Tuesday afternoons reading to children in the library. That she went to church."

"Church?"

"Yes, she was very faithful. Our paths crossed there too. As I said, she was very proud of you. Talked about you all the time—what a gifted musician you are. How you write your own music and have built a career for yourself at the club—Maison Dauphine, isn't it? How do you think I found you?"

Rae shook her head. "I didn't—"

"Listen," the doctor said. "In situations like this, when a parent dies without the chance to say good-bye, the emotion it most often brings up in survivors is anger. Self-recrimination. I knew your mother fairly well, and I feel I know you too. Don't beat yourself up, Rae Dawn. Your mother understood why you had to separate yourself from this place. She was proud of you. Proud of who you are. Proud you got away."

Rae heard the words but didn't quite believe them. "How can you be so sure?"

"Because she told me. Her only regret for you was that you hadn't yet found love. She said she always hoped you'd meet the woman of your dreams and—"

"Hold on," Rae interrupted. "Did you say the *woman* of my dreams?"

"Yes, that's exactly what I said."

"But she didn't—"

"She *did* know. We talked about it." Noel chuckled. "In fact, she thought the two of us might be a good match."

Shocked to the core by the revelation of her mother's uncanny insight, Rae Dawn almost missed this last sentence. "Excuse me?"

"She wanted to introduce us," Noel repeated. "Unfortunately, she never had the opportunity—until now." She stood up and extended a hand in Rae Dawn's direction. "If you're ready, I think it's time to go and say good-bye."

IT WAS A LITTLE after three A.M. when Lorna DuChamp slipped quietly from this life to the next. She never woke. Rae stood holding her hand while Noel shut down the respirator and removed the tubes.

"Thank you, Mama," she whispered. "Thank you for setting me free. I'm glad you found your own sort of freedom in the end."

And then she was gone with nothing, not even a breath, to mark her passage to the other side. Just a gradual cooling of the flesh, a softening of the lines of her face.

At the end Noel came and stood beside Rae Dawn with one arm around her shoulders. The warmth of her nearness felt right, somehow—familiar and alive and comforting.

"We need to take the body," she said in a quiet voice.

Rae nodded. Her mother's organs would be harvested—heart, liver, and kidneys—to give life to nameless others waiting for transplants. What remained would be cremated. It was Rae's decision, and she made it without hesitation. She would not have her mother buried alongside the man who had made her life a living hell.

"That's it, I guess." Rae Dawn sighed when the orderlies had left with the body.

"What will you do now?" Noel asked.

"Go back to New Orleans, I suppose." Rae shrugged. "I suppose I do need to go out to the trailer, but I really don't ever want to see the place again."

"My shift ended at two. I'll go with you if you like."

"You've done enough already. This is not a doctor's duty."

"I didn't offer as a doctor."

Rae Dawn looked into the tawny eyes and found them filled with a strange luminosity, burning like liquid gold. She felt quite suddenly as if she could drown in those eyes, as if they were drawing her home. And then, just as quickly, she realized what vulnerability her own gaze must be revealing, and she tried to break the link.

But Noel did not look away. "Let's go," she said softly.

THE TRACK LEADING from the main road to the trailer was black as midnight, overgrown and muddy. The headlights of Noel's car revealed deep ruts in the earth, fresh grooves made by some heavy vehicle. The ambulance, Rae Dawn supposed.

The closer they got, the more violently her stomach churned. Her hands were trembling, and she clenched them in her lap. All the old memories flooded over her—the hungry, miserable days, the terrifying nights punctuated by her father's rampaging drunkenness and the deafening crack of his shotgun. The resigned emptiness of her mother's face.

Everything looked so much smaller than it did in recollections from her childhood. The rusted Airstream, illuminated in the headlights, tilted oddly to one side, crouched in its nest of kudzu like some strange and frightened forest creature, its curved haunches riddled with buckshot. Behind and to the right, the shadow of a dilapidated shed, barely larger than an outhouse, leaned precariously toward the bank of Hobo Creek. The air was permeated with the stench of decay—rotted wood, leaves gone to mulch, stagnant water. Rae Dawn's interior atmosphere, too, smelled of deterioration, despair, and shame.

"It's all right," Noel's low voice murmured behind her.

The door to the trailer stood half open, and on shaking legs

Rae climbed the rusted metal stairs, stepped inside, and turned on the lights. Here, too, the world she remembered had shrunk. The cramped living room where she slept, the meager kitchen with its scarred Formica table, the narrow passageway that led to a tiny bath and a single bedroom barely wide enough to lie down in. Something scuttled along a baseboard.

A wave of nausea gripped her, and for an instant she was sure she was going to retch. She reached for the edge of the table and felt Noel's strong warm hand supporting her instead. "It's all right," she repeated. "Take it easy."

Rae Dawn sank onto one of the vinyl kitchen chairs and took several deep breaths.

"You okay?" Noel asked.

Rae nodded. "I just—I can't believe—" She squeezed her eyes shut and slammed a fist down on the table. "How could my father do this to us? He was supposed to love us, to protect us—"

"Get it out," Noel urged. "All the anger, all the pain. Don't let it poison you any longer."

The penetrating compassion in her voice, the innate understanding, nearly undid Rae Dawn altogether. She began to cry—deep, racking sobs. She put her shaking hands up to her face. "I've got to pull myself together."

"No, you don't," Noel countered. "Not on my account. Your mother told me everything, Rae. I know how bad it was."

"I hated him," Rae said. The admission felt strangely liberating, cleansing, like the first good breath she had taken since she set foot in the trailer again. "I *hated* him! I *still* hate him." All the rage she had suppressed throughout her childhood came roaring back. She stood up, tipping the chair over with the force of her movement, and with two steps she was standing in the living room. "This place! This terrible, filthy, shitty place!" She careened through the confined rooms, tearing down the ragged curtains, kicking over a chair, pounding her fist into the lumpy sofa cushions. "He sucked all the life out of everything he touched. My mother, me. That's where I slept," she said, pointing toward the sagging, mildewed couch. "I didn't have a room of my own, dammit, didn't even have a space of my own. Even if we were poor, we didn't have to live like this. He had a pension; there was a little money coming in. But every last dime went to liquor. I can still smell it—his precious whiskey, his stinking vomit in the rug."

She lifted her head, caught her reflection in the dirty glass window, and turned, suddenly shamed by her outburst. "I ought to forgive him, I suppose."

"There's a time for forgiveness," Noel said in a firm, quiet voice. "But right now, at this moment, what do *you* want, Rae Dawn? What do *you* need?"

Rae wheeled around. In that instant, as she looked into Noel Ridley's eyes, she saw what she had been looking for all her life. A kindred spirit. Someone who, even though she hadn't lived it, instinctively understood.

"Matches," she said. "I need matches. I want to burn this hellhole to the ground!"

Noel pointed toward the stove. On the back ledge sat a large box of wooden kitchen matches, the kind Mama used to light the propane burners.

"Take the car up to the road," Rae Dawn said. "I'll be there in a minute."

Above them, over the dark country road, a million stars gleamed against the blackness. Rae stood on the gravel, shoulder to shoulder with Noel Ridley, and watched as her childhood home went up in flames.

At first it was just a glimmer of yellow light in the living room window, as if someone had lit a lamp to welcome in a stranger. Then the sofa caught, soaked as it was with old kerosene from the shed, and the fire worked its way through the kitchen to the mattress on the bedroom floor.

Now the whole place was ablaze, a bonfire at a pep rally, a giant Yule log roaring in the grate. Yellow and orange flames leaped and danced, candle-shaped, like hands clasped in prayer. The ceiling gave way and fell in. Sparks flew skyward, mingling their gold with the silver stars overhead.

It was, for Rae Dawn, a moment of complete release. As the fire raged and spread, engulfing the Airstream in a matter of seconds, some chrysalis in her own soul cracked open. All the years of suppressed fury and shame rose and left her, propelled toward heaven on the rising flames.

Music threaded through her mind, a score she had written for her final performance project in college. The minor-key oppression of a burdened soul. The turn, the movement upward, the change to a lifting, soaring flight. "Woman on the Wind," she had called it, but until this instant she had not fathomed all its varied meanings. What new life would rise from the ashes she did not know, only that her spirit, at last, was free.

Rae Dawn's eyes never left the trailer, but she felt the doctor's hand reach for hers and drew strength from its warmth.

"Now *that,*" Noel said softly, "is what I call a Christmas celebration."

NINETEEN

Come Rain or Come Shine

New Orleans
February 1974

Maison Dauphine, jammed to the rafters, seemed to close in on Rae Dawn as she took the stage for her second set of the evening. Friday nights the club was always packed, but when the audience consisted mostly of regulars she knew by sight if not by name, the place didn't feel so claustrophobic. On this Friday before Mardi Gras, however, with a wild and rowdy mob of out-of-town revelers, she found her nerves on edge.

The lights came up, diffused by a haze of blue smoke. At the bar, a group of guys in LSU jerseys, clearly drunk, were causing some commotion. Rae glanced to the edge of the stage, where Arlen Crocker, Chase's army buddy and head of Maison Dauphine's security, stood with his arms crossed over his massive chest. She caught his eye and nodded in the direction of the troublemakers.

Mardi Gras might well be called the biggest bash on earth,

but it was also the most dangerous time to be in New Orleans. Large quantities of alcohol did not mix well with thousands of anonymous partygoers shedding their inhibitions in the streets. Bar fights were common, and a broken beer bottle served as well as a shiv for a murder weapon.

Arlen moved toward the bar and positioned himself close to the college boys. The crowd quieted a little, and Rae Dawn launched into an arrangement of "Come Rain or Come Shine."

"Hey, baby!" one of the boys yelled. "Take it off, why don't you? Come on, show us some tits!"

Rae kept on singing. This was the downside of the career she loved so much. The regulars at Maison Dauphine showed respect. They listened when she sang and filled her tip jar when she remembered their favorite tunes. Even the habitual drunks fell into a stupor quietly, without interrupting the show.

The LSU boys were wound-up, ugly drunks. Over the music and the low buzz of conversation, they shouted obscenities and made lewd suggestions about their own personal endowments and what they could do to make Rae Dawn happy.

She chuckled to herself. These dogs were definitely barking up the wrong tree.

"Tits!" the leader of the pack yelled again, and his cohorts took up the chant: "Tits! Tits! Tits!"

Then it happened. The alpha dog lunged off his bar stool and made for the stage, evidently intent on helping Rae Dawn undress. He shoved several other patrons aside, spilling drinks. Someone threw a punch, and all hell broke loose.

Arlen was on top of the situation and jerked the college boy into a choke hold long before he reached the stage. But his intervention, though effective, came just a little too late. By the time he and his other bouncers had corralled the troublemakers and shown them the door, the floor was covered with shattered glass and blood was flowing. One man had been hit in the head with a bottle and clearly needed stitches.

"Stand aside; I'm a doctor," came an authoritative voice from the shadows.

The crowd parted like the Red Sea before Moses' staff, and out of the darkness stepped a diminutive woman with red-blonde hair and the tawny eyes of a lioness.

Noel Ridley knelt before the injured man, examined his wound, and staunched the bleeding with a bar towel. "You're going to be all right," she assured him, "but you need to get that cut sewn up. Did anyone call an ambulance?"

The bartender nodded, and as if on cue, flashing lights appeared outside the doorway of the club. Two paramedics came in and took the guy away to have his head stitched. Cops hustled the college boys into a couple of squad cars and carted them off to the drunk tank.

The rest of the crowd, much subdued, went back to their beer while the bartender began sweeping up the broken glass.

Rae, however, did not return to her piano. She stood on the edge of the low stage and watched, entranced, as Noel got to her feet and turned in her direction.

Suddenly Maison Dauphine didn't seem claustrophobic at all. For Rae Dawn, there was no one in the club but Noel. The woman had an aura about her, an unearthly gilded brightness. As if in slow motion she turned and smiled, radiating that light in Rae's direction.

This, Rae Dawn thought, *is it.*

To be perfectly honest, she wasn't at all sure what "it" was, only that Noel's presence—in the room, in her life—changed everything.

Since New Year's, Noel had been coming to New Orleans almost every week on her days off. They had taken in a few of the quieter clubs, listening to other singers, but mostly they sat in Café Du Monde drinking coffee and eating beignets, strolled among the artists in Jackson Square, bought po'boys, picnicked along the river.

They talked about Rae Dawn's music and Noel's medicine. Healing was not a job, Noel said, it was a calling. It was art and poetry, prayer and worship, heart and soul. It was the place where she felt most connected to God and herself and the universe.

The strands of their conversations coiled and twisted inside Rae Dawn, a haunting motif, diverse notes weaving together into impossibly beautiful harmonies. The differences between them were every bit as lovely as the similarities, an ethereal inner melody that caught her heart and held her fast.

Noel came, and she went. Her coming brought a measure of peace and well-being unlike anything Rae had ever known; her going left that golden glow behind like a benediction. Expectation lit Rae Dawn's days as she waited, and when Noel departed no emptiness remained in her wake, only a contented fulfillment and a sharpened sense of glad surprise.

But Rae Dawn had not known that Noel was coming tonight, and her unexpected appearance sent a palpable flash of longing through her veins. With her eyes fixed on Noel's, she stepped back to the mike. "I'm going to take a break and regroup after our little melee. But don't worry, I'll be back."

"How about finishing the song, at least?" someone suggested.

Rae Dawn's brain had turned to mush. She couldn't for the life of her think what song she had been singing when the fight broke out. Then it came to her, and with a self-deprecating smile she sat down at the piano. "Just this one," she agreed. "And more later."

Noel sank down into a chair in front of the stage. Her amber eyes shone, illuminated from within. Rae Dawn couldn't have looked away even if she had tried.

Rae began to sing. The words flowed through her veins, reborn, newly alive, words about a love that was high as a mountain, deep as a river. A love like no other. A love that would last forever. How many times had she sung this song? Hundreds? Thousands, even?

And yet she had never sung it at all until this moment, this night.

BACKSTAGE, IN THE TEN-BY-TEN CLOSET that had been made over into Rae Dawn's dressing room, the two of them clung together as if they'd never let go.

"What *happened* out there?" Noel said, searching Rae's eyes.

"I don't know." Rae Dawn shook her head. "When I saw you, sort of materializing out of the darkness, it was like a vision. A dream. Like all the pieces fell into place."

Noel collapsed into the single chair that nearly filled one side of the room and pulled Rae Dawn down onto the padded arm. "I have to be back tomorrow, but I needed to come. Needed to talk to you. It's all right, then, my just showing up like this?"

"All right?" Rae began to laugh. "What do you mean, 'all right'? It's *wonderful*."

A look of relief passed over Noel's face. "That's good to hear. Because—" She hesitated. "What would you think about me taking a job here?"

Rae Dawn stared at her. "What are you talking about?"

"An old friend of mine from med school is opening a practice. A twenty-four-hour clinic for low-income families. He's invited me to join him."

"In New Orleans?"

"Yes." Noel nodded. "But our patients will mostly be single mothers and their kids. I won't be making much."

"So what?" Rae said. "You'll be here, and that's what counts."

Noel's expression changed—subtly, but Rae Dawn saw it. "There's one other thing we have to talk about."

Rae slid off the arm of the chair and sat on the rug at Noel's feet. "Okay, shoot."

"I want us to be together."

Rae Dawn frowned. "We *are* together."

"No, I mean, *really* together." Noel ran a hand over her face. "I don't know how to say this. There's no language for it. We can't be, well, married. Not technically. Not officially. But that's what I want. A commitment. For life."

Rae stared at her as this bit of information sank in. For a minute she said nothing. Then the humor of the situation overcame her. "Damn, honey, if that's a proposal you really need to work on it. Sounds more like a criminal conviction than a romance."

Tears welled up in Noel's eyes and she looked away.

"Whoa!" Rae said. "Hold on. I was just kidding. I didn't mean to hurt your feelings." She reached up and pulled Noel out of the chair and into her arms. "There is nothing I want more," she whispered, "than to be with you forever. I want you with me—here, now, all the time. We fit. We complement each other. Like melody and harmony." Rae kissed her on the eyelids and tasted the salty tears on her tongue. "When I saw you come into the club tonight, I thought, 'This is it.' I wasn't quite sure what that meant, but now I know."

She glanced down at her wristwatch. "It's time for my last set. Come listen to me sing."

Noel got to her feet. "If you sing anything else the way you did 'Come Rain or Come Shine,' I'm going to have difficulty restraining myself." She arched her eyebrows. "You *were* singing it to me, weren't you?"

"What do you think?" Rae finished touching up her makeup and held out a hand. "Let's go."

"Wait," Noel said. "I forgot to tell you something."

Rae opened the door to the stage, and the noise nearly knocked them over. She had to shout to be heard. "What did you forget to say?"

In that instant the house lights went down and the noise in the club subsided. "I'm in love with you!" Noel yelled into the sudden quiet.

In the darkness someone let out a piercing whistle.

"I'm in love with you too," Rae Dawn whispered, and kissed her.

WITH BILLIE HOLIDAY PLAYING on the stereo, Rae Dawn moved swiftly around the apartment, clearing out drawers and closets, purging, filling black plastic garbage bags with things she didn't really need and shouldn't have kept all these years. Housecleaning wasn't her favorite activity by a long shot, but today she worked with a fervor born of love.

They had talked until dawn and then, after two hours of sleep, Noel had left to return to Picayune. But everything was decided. It would take her some time—several weeks, probably—to tie up loose ends and get moved. Still, Rae Dawn was determined to be ready. Eventually, once Noel got settled in her new practice, they would look for a larger place together, maybe even a small house. But in the meantime, they would share this apartment.

She swept the dust bunnies out from under the bed, then straightened up and regarded the bedroom with a critical eye. The apartment, though quite sufficient for one, seemed to draw in and constrict upon itself when she considered how it might work for two. The closets were inadequate, the kitchen outdated, the bathroom barely large enough to turn around in without putting one foot in the tub. But the living room was light and spacious and would easily accommodate Noel's furniture, which was far superior to the hodgepodge of secondhand stuff Rae Dawn had collected over the years.

She wished, just briefly, that they could afford the apartment over Maison Dauphine. It was an expansive place, with two bedrooms, a terrace that extended over the back garden, and a wrought-iron balcony that faced toward the river and offered a view of the spires of St. Louis Cathedral four blocks away. Unfortunately, it was far out of their league. Noel's new practice wouldn't bring in a great deal of money, and Rae had long ago resigned herself to the reality of what kind of income a musician made. It was a nice dream, but that's all it would ever be.

Still, it didn't matter. They would be together.

Together. The very word caused Rae's heart to swoop and soar. Never in her life had she felt this way, as if the world itself rejoiced. Never had she known that anything other than music could bring this sense of wholeness, of well-being.

For years she had sung the love songs that had propelled her career forward, had watched the way couples in the audience held hands and gazed into one another's eyes when she sang. Somehow she had infused into those songs a passion and desire that came from a well of longing deep within her. But now for the first time she realized that the images in those songs were not mere metaphors. Skies really *were* bluer, stars closer, the moon brighter. All creation moved together in a windswept dance of celebration. Life really *did* begin when you fell in love.

At last Rae Dawn understood. She had awakened from a dream to find that the dream had come true. The dream of loving and being loved. The dream of Noel Ridley.

TWENTY

Ecstasy and Agony

New Orleans
February 1979

"Are you planning to sleep all day?"

Rae Dawn opened her eyes to see Noel standing over her with a tray. She struggled to a sitting position, and Noel placed the tray on her lap. Waffles and scrambled eggs, steaming strong coffee, fresh orange juice.

"Good morning," Rae mumbled.

"Never mind morning," Noel said with a laugh. "It's almost afternoon, and I don't want to waste our entire anniversary." She sat on the edge of the bed and leaned forward expectantly.

Rae put a hand to her mouth. "Trust me, you don't want to kiss me until I've brushed my teeth." She shifted the tray, pulled on a robe, and dashed to the bathroom. When she returned, Noel had arranged the pillows against the headboard and settled the breakfast tray between them.

"So, what would you like to do with our day?" Noel forked up a slice of waffle.

"I'd like to *celebrate.*" Rae sipped at her coffee and smiled. "Dance in the streets and throw confetti in Jackson Square."

"I know exactly how you feel." Noel grinned. "Five years. The best five years of my life."

AT NOON THE FOLLOWING MONDAY Rae Dawn sat in Chase Coulter's office with the door closed. She stared at him, not believing what she was hearing.

"You expect me to do *what?*" she demanded.

Chase's jaw flinched convulsively beneath the flesh of his cheek. "I'm sorry, Rae. I'd be the first to argue that you should be able to live however you want. But you've got to consider your career."

Rae frowned. "What are you talking about?"

"I'm talking about you, Rae, and your doctor girlfriend."

"My life with Noel is nobody's business, Chase. Besides, this is New Orleans, not Podunk, Iowa."

Chase slammed a palm down on the desk. "You have to listen to me, Rae Dawn. Why do you think people line up every night to get in here?" He gritted his teeth and pointed at the door. "Because of *you.* Because of your music. Love songs, torch songs, jazz, blues. Look at you. You're steamy, you're sexy. You're gorgeous and mysterious and fascinating."

"No, I'm not. I'm just—me."

"Well, *just you* is what they're buying. The men want you and the women want to *be* you. And if word gets out about you and Noel—" Chase shook his head. "Nobody's going to come hear you sing if they know you're belting out love songs to another woman."

"So you're saying that I'm public property and don't have the right to be in love? That I'm supposed to hide my relationship with Noel?"

"I'm saying you can't bring your private life into the public eye, especially when it would ruin your career—and mine, if you get my drift."

Rae could hardly believe this. Chase Coulter *knew* Noel, for pity's sake. He liked her, thought she was cute and funny and smart. And now he was talking about her as if she were some kind of one-night stand, a minor employee in an all-girl escort service.

She tried to reason with him. "Chase, what's changed? Noel has been living with me for five years now. She moved here to be with me, took a new job for me. She has an established practice, and—"

"I know," he interrupted. "She's a saint. She's Mother Teresa. But she talks too much."

Rae frowned. "What do you mean?"

Chase sighed. "This guy came in yesterday afternoon looking for a job. Said he had been to the clinic and his doctor had told him that her partner was the headliner here and we were advertising for another bartender."

"So what?"

"So if your girlfriend is talking that freely about the two of you—"

Rae Dawn shook her head. "Chase, this is ridiculous. The Quarter is a very diverse and accepting place. This is my life—"

"And it's my club. Besides, we're not just talking about the Quarter. We're talking about the *country,* Rae. Middle America. White-bread heterosexuals. Two talent agents and a scout for Arista Records are coming to hear you on Friday night. You're going national, and I'd bet my ass you're going to be big. This is your chance. I suggest you think long and hard about whether you really want a future as a singer."

"So," Noel said over dinner that night, "the bottom line is, your boss wants you to hide who you are. Who *we* are."

Vividly Rae recalled—though it had been ten years ago—the scene on the quad at college, when furious protesters had carried signs reading *God Hates Dikes and Fagots* and chanted, "Fire the queers, fire the queers." She would never forget her last conversation with Dr. Gottlieb, who had been both mentor and father to her. The angry words they had exchanged still burned in her memory, the expression on his face when he told her "You do not understand the ways of the world."

Perhaps he was right. For a long time—five years before Noel, and five incredible years with her—Rae Dawn had lived in the insular bubble of the French Quarter, a universe unto itself where the unusual was commonplace. Even during the Civil Rights Movement, when people were being attacked by police dogs and set on with fire hoses, interracial couples in the Quarter barely merited the lift of an eyebrow. Gay Mardi Gras krewes had been taking part in the Carnival celebrations since the late fifties and early sixties. New Orleans was a progressive Mecca surrounded on all sides by the battlements of conservatism.

Now Rae Dawn's career was about to break out, but apparently that meant catering to a less liberal fan base. As Chase had put it, nobody wanted to be confronted with the truth that their favorite sexy torch singer was "belting out love songs to another woman."

Still, there were always compromises to be made. For anyone in the entertainment business, a larger public meant less privacy. It was part of the price you paid for success.

Rae just hoped the price wouldn't be too high.

Noel reached out and took her hand. "Is this what you want?" she asked. "Record deals, tours, national exposure?"

Exposure. The word sliced across Rae's nerves like a scalpel. The truth was, she was afraid of failure but equally terrified of success. What if she took the risk and couldn't make it in the big leagues? What if she did make it, and it changed her life forever?

"I don't know what I want," Rae said. "This is the chance I've worked for all my life, but—"

"Then let's just take it one step at a time," Noel said. "Meet the agents. Sing for the scout. We'll see what happens from there."

WHAT HAPPENED FROM THERE Rae Dawn didn't like to think about.

An agent by the name of William Tyce. A contract from Arista Records. An album, entitled simply *Dawn,* with a corresponding name change to Dawn DuChante and a sultry close-up of Rae's "new look." Interminable months on the road in a tour bus, opening for Aretha Franklin and other stars of the Arista firmament.

The first year Rae thought she'd go crazy. She missed home, missed Noel. Static, furtive conversations on the telephone didn't begin to make up for long talks on a rainy afternoon or cuddling on the couch on Saturday morning.

And the worst of it, in Rae Dawn's mind, was the fact that she couldn't tell anyone. All the musicians on the tour complained openly about the difficulty of separation. They filled the empty hours with conversations about their husbands and wives and lovers. They all raced for the telephones whenever the bus stopped and never gave a second thought to being overheard saying "I love you."

Everyone had left someone behind to chase the dream; it was the common bond that held them together. All of them except Rae Dawn.

"You're lucky, girl," one of Aretha's backup singers once told her. "It's easier when you're single with nobody to worry 'bout but yourself." And always the assumption, always the assurance: "Focus on the music, baby. Time enough for love later on. You'll have your pick of men."

They all called her Dawn. They didn't even know her name.

The second year, two days before Christmas, Rae came home and fell exhausted and weeping into Noel's arms, ready to give it all up.

The third year, a call came from her agent, Will Tyce.

"The album's finally making its way up the charts," Tyce told her excitedly, as if presenting her with some magnificent gift. "Slowly, but it's getting enough attention that Arista wants another one as soon as you can get to New York to record it. We're going to book concerts all across the country to promote it. And we're sending down a photographer for some new publicity shots. This is it, Dawn. You're an overnight success."

An "overnight success" that took years to achieve.

And so it continued—another two years of painful separation and silence. Concert audiences loved her. For a while the album sales held their peak, and money poured in like water. But money couldn't stop the drift. Money couldn't fill the awkward pauses during those late-night calls when both of them were too exhausted to talk. Money couldn't buy back what they seemed to be losing.

On the telephone from Boston, Rae negotiated a deal with

Chase Coulter to buy out Maison Dauphine, which included the large apartment upstairs. On the telephone from Minneapolis, she and Noel decided what furniture to take to the new place and what they should buy. On the telephone from Seattle, she listened helplessly while Noel cried. On the telephone from Dallas, Rae cried while Noel listened.

And then the final straw: a Grammy nomination for Best Female R&B Vocal Performance. "Okay, here's the plan," Will Tyce said, taking charge as usual. "We'll get you a fabulous dress—black sequins, low cut in front. A great diamond necklace, the works. I'll take care of everything. February 26, in L.A. And you'll be going with—"

"Hold it," Rae Dawn said. "I'm taking Noel."

"No, you're not."

Rae's breath came in shallow gasps. "Will, this is what I've worked for, what Noel and I have both sacrificed for. She deserves to be there."

"Right. I'll get her a seat in the balcony. But you will not appear in public with her. Understood?"

Rae Dawn caved. Noel stayed home. And then, on the red carpet going in for the awards show, the unthinkable happened. Rae's escort—Arista's newest discovery, a handsome, arrogant jerk by the name of Brian Hearn—pulled her into a hip-crushing embrace, french-kissed her, and announced their engagement to the crowd. Brian, almost ten years younger than Rae, was a flaming queen who put on a macho act for the fans. Now he swaggered at her side, half-drunk already, and leered at her while one hand groped her butt.

Rae didn't win the Grammy, but the pictures, predictably, made the next day's papers. The tongue-thrust, the ass-fondling, all of it. National television. *Entertainment Tonight*. Front page of the tabloids.

The flight from Los Angeles to New Orleans was the longest of Rae Dawn's life. When she arrived, Noel was already packed.

"I can't take this anymore," she said, choking back tears. "The travel, the separation, the deception." She threw one of the tabloids down on the coffee table and pointed at the photo of Rae being groped by Brian Hearn. "You *kissed* him!"

"I didn't kiss him. He kissed me." Rae Dawn knew, even as she said it, that it sounded like a blatant rationalization. "Besides, we both know he's gay."

"It doesn't matter," Noel said. "All of this makes me feel—" She groped for words. "Cheap. Invalidated. Either I'm your partner, or I'm not. I didn't sign on for a part-time marriage. Or a secret one."

Noel let her gaze drift around the spacious apartment above the club, and Rae's eyes followed. The place was beautiful, but it didn't feel like home. Rae Dawn hadn't been here often enough to make it home.

They should have stood together on the balcony looking out toward the cathedral, watching the morning mist rise off the river. They should have eaten breakfast on the terrace overlooking the back garden. They should have built a fire and made popcorn and snuggled up to watch old movies on a rainy winter's night. They should have had a dog.

"I'll quit," Rae said as desperation and misery welled up in her. "I'll quit it all—the touring, the appearances, the record deals. We've still got Maison Dauphine."

"*You've* got Maison Dauphine," Noel corrected. "I've got a job waiting back at the hospital in Picayune."

"Please," Rae said. "I love you."

"I love you too," Noel whispered. "I'll always love you."

Then she was gone. A week before Carnival. A week before their tenth anniversary.

New Orleans
September 1994

Rae got up from the piano and went to the front balcony. Through the windows of Mrs. B's apartment, she could see that the old woman had fallen asleep, her chair rocking a little and her head lolling to one side. Dreaming, no doubt, of her Robert, of the half-century of love they had shared together. Of the children she had borne and lost—one to a car wreck and one to breast cancer.

How sad it is, Rae thought, *to outlive everyone you've loved. . . .*

Her mind lurched from Mrs. B's life to her own, to the people she had loved and lost. Her mother, whom she'd never really had the chance to know before the heart attack took her. Dr. Gottlieb, who had been both mentor and surrogate father until the issue of her sexual orientation had divided them. And Noel Ridley, not dead, but vanished from her life for nearly ten years.

She had friends, she supposed. Nate the bartender, Chuck Coulter the general manager of Maison Dauphine. Some of the younger musicians who took the stage and sang to the crowds downstairs, and then moved on as their careers shifted into high gear or fizzled out from lack of talent. But they all had families—or, in the case of the performers, an obsession for success that obscured everything else. They cared about Rae, they liked her, but with none of them did she really belong.

All she had now was the club. The insane schedule of tours and concerts and recording contracts was long since behind her. There had been no third album, no more tours or Grammy nominations. The few people who remembered Dawn DuChante thought of her as something of a legend, which in the music business translated to *has-been.*

But Rae Dawn didn't really care. Other artists now performed her songs, making her a quiet, behind-the-scenes success. Money would never be an issue—the profits from Maison Dauphine and residuals from her own albums and copyrights would be sufficient to keep Rae and a small country afloat for decades to come. What mattered to her—what depressed her whenever she allowed herself to think about it—was that she was forty-seven years old and alone.

Even after all these years, precious few artists took the risk to come out. A handful of singers. A few actors here and there. Most, Rae Dawn suspected, got shoved into the mold, coerced into masquerading as straight or losing all hope of a career.

She wandered over to the stereo and picked out an album by a little known but magnificently talented young blues singer, Suede, then loaded the disc and sank down on the sofa.

Suede was singing "No Regrets," but Rae had plenty of them. She regretted not having the backbone to stand up to her agent, her studio, to the music industry itself. She regretted the pretense, the deception, the tidal wave of expectation that had swept her and Noel apart. But most of all, she regretted her own lapse of character. She should have been stronger, more determined, more honest.

She had started out that way, with Gottlieb, anyway. She had tried to explain to him that being gay was not a choice, any more than you choose to be blue-eyed or left-handed. You could learn to walk in heels; you could wear contacts; you could train yourself to be ambidextrous, but you couldn't alter what you were born with.

All you could do was accept it and live into it with integrity.

It was a commendable theory. But it had taken Rae Dawn a long time to get there.

And the turning point, oddly enough, had come through Gottlieb himself.

Rae Dawn walked back to the baby grand piano in the front window and touched its yellowed ivory keys. Dr. Gottlieb's piano, that familiar, battered old instrument with the glorious voice. He had willed it to her when he died. One sunny September afternoon in 1988 it had arrived in a truck, accompanied by two moving men and a sealed letter from the executor of his will.

With shaking hands she opened a small carved box to one side of the piano, smoothed out the letter, and read it for the hundredth time:

Dear Rae Dawn,

This letter comes too late, even though I have written it a thousand times already in my mind. I always hoped that, before I died, I would have the opportunity to see you again and ask your forgiveness face to face. But that is not to be. I have waited too long.

Over the years I have followed your musical career with the pride of a father whose gifts have been handed down to his daughter. Still, I have let my stubbornness and arrogance get in the way of accepting you and loving you for who you are. Forgive me if you can. I wanted you to be different. I wanted you to be like me.

Now, too late I fear, I see that you are exactly like me. You refuse to give in, refuse to be broken. Refuse to give heed to the voices of prejudice and bigotry—even mine.

When I told you that I would fling myself before the Nazi rifles or go to the ovens to protect you, I imagined myself to be noble and self-sacrificing. I did not want to believe myself to be like my captors, those evil, arrogant men who sought to purge the world of diversity. But the end of one's life brings a terrible clarity of vision, a merciless mirror that forces us to see ourselves as we are, not as we wish to be.

I thought I had learned the lessons of captivity, the stripping away of all that is unimportant to bring us to the essential truths of life. But one essential truth I never faced: Love comes to us as a gift and must be honored and received with grace.

I trust that by now you have found someone to share your life with. Love her, and keep on loving. Let nothing come between you. Honor her above all else. And be true to yourself, no matter the cost.

Your father, your friend—
Manfred Gottlieb

The irony pierced Rae's soul like a blade.

She had, finally, thrown off the disguises imposed upon her by others, had at last looked the music world in the eye and said "This is who I am—take it or leave it." A few gigs were canceled, a few fans wrote nasty letters expressing their outrage and disappointment. But for the most part the world kept spinning and the royalties kept coming and other singers kept asking to record her original songs.

The world kept spinning. But it was a world without the woman she loved.

possibly that of a young, perhaps a nurse [illegible]
wrong, not as we wish to be.

[illegible] I had let the blade [illegible] against [illegible]
[illegible] to bring us to the [illegible] But [illegible]
[illegible] [illegible] [illegible]
[illegible] of grace.

[illegible] [illegible] [illegible]
[illegible] [illegible] ground between [illegible]
[illegible] [illegible]

Your [illegible]

Marty [illegible]

The story pierced the soul like a blade.

She had [illegible] of the [illegible]
by others [illegible] the [illegible] and [illegible]
[illegible] who [illegible] [illegible]
[illegible] [illegible] [illegible] and [illegible]
[illegible] for the most part [illegible] and
[illegible] [illegible] [illegible]
[illegible] original [illegible]

The world [illegible] but it [illegible] without [illegible]
[illegible]

PART 4

Shame and Blame

Caught in the silver web,
we flail and thrash,
but struggle brings no liberty,
only a tighter cord around the heart,
a binding of the soul
that cuts off light and air,
hope, and the promise
of tomorrow.

Be still.
Let go.
Stop fighting.
For the way out
is not out
but through.

TWENTY-ONE

The Thinking Pool

Durham, North Carolina
June 1969

There was no church wedding, no father walking her down the aisle. No flowers or reception or twin sister as her maid of honor. Just a hurried civil ceremony before Irving Neazle, Justice of the Peace.

"Do you take this woman to be your lawfully wedded wife?" the decrepit old judge yelled.

"I do," Trip murmured.

"Eh? What's that?" The old man put his hand to his ear.

"I *do*," Trip repeated, a little louder.

The judge narrowed his eyes at Trip. "Speak up, young man! Do you want to marry this girl, or don't you?"

"I DO!" Trip shouted.

Finally satisfied, Judge Neazle nodded beneficently and turned to Lauren. "Do you take this man to be your lawfully wedded husband?"

"I do."

The judge continued to stare at her, waiting.

"I DO!" she yelled at the top of her lungs.

"Well, that's better," the withered old justice said, patting Lauren on the arm. "I like to see a girl who's enthusiastic about getting married." He turned toward Trip. "You could take a lesson or two from her, young fella."

It would have been funny... if either of them had been happy about the wedding. But Lauren felt shame wash over her as she was forced to shout aloud what she had held in secret for so long.

As soon as the deed was accomplished, they fled the judge's office, ducking the barrage of good wishes and marital advice the old man flung after them at the top of his lungs. They dashed down the steps and hurled themselves into Trip's Corvair.

"Now what?" Lauren panted.

Trip shrugged. "I don't know. What do most couples do?"

Lauren leveled a glance at him. "The honeymoon."

"Oh yeah. Seems sort of... anticlimactic," Trip said.

In the end they drove around Durham for a while, picked up a bucket of chicken and a six-pack of beer, and found a cheap motel. After a few minutes of perfunctory sex, they lay in separate beds and stared at the television until they fell asleep. The next morning they bought coffee and doughnuts and a newspaper, and by noon they had rented a small furnished apartment in the basement of a widow's house a few blocks from Duke University.

The decor was horrible, and the stench was even worse. Cat urine and mouse droppings and mildew. The smattering of sunlight filtering in through high dirty windows did little to make the apartment less dingy. Still, it was affordable, and Lauren, who had never done any more housework than was absolutely necessary, found herself looking forward to making the place their home. The work would be her payback, penance for her betrayal of Lacy.

But as the weeks passed, she discovered that the immediate gratification of a clean toilet or a freshly scrubbed kitchen floor could do nothing to remove the taint of guilt and shame. She had thought it would go away, once she and Trip were honest about their relationship, once they were married. But the marriage was a sham, and she knew it. For the first time in years, she recalled her childhood Sunday school lessons and understood why Judas had gone out and hanged himself.

It wasn't that she regretted marrying Trip. They'd had no choice, really. But it was the *way* she had married him—the haste, the vain attempts at explanation, the expression on Lacy's face when they had finally told her.

At first it had been a game, a competition with her sister that Lauren won hands down. Experience had been on her side, after all. She knew what Trip Jenkins really wanted and how to give it to him. Poor Lacy was depending on charm and personality and emotional connection. All Lauren had to do was throw out the bait and reel him in. No contest.

After that bittersweet seduction during spring break, Trip continued to see Lacy—to let her down easy, he claimed. But he also met secretly with Lauren every chance he got. There was something intensely stimulating about the forbiddenness of their liaisons, and the sex was, frankly, incredible. The back seat of Trip's Corvair turned out to be horribly cramped and uncomfortable, and since neither of them could afford a motel room, they got very creative. A blanket in the woods behind the college maintenance building. The fourth-floor stacks in the library. Occasionally, on weekends when most of the fraternity brothers were out of town, they sneaked into Trip's frat house. Once they did it in the laundry room of Lauren and Lacy's dorm—an experience a bit too nerve-wracking for Lauren, although Trip seemed to find the danger arousing.

Gradually an unsettling realization formulated itself in Lauren's mind—the awareness that her relationship with Trip was turning out to be just like her relationship with Steve Treadwell and the others who had gone before him. Mostly about sex, with little else to attract them. All the things she had been so jealous of in Lacy's relationship with Trip—the emotional intimacy, the sense of knowing one another, the communication—seemed to be missing.

And something else was missing too. Her period. She couldn't recall when it was supposed to come in March. By April she was paying attention. By May, with graduation fast approaching, she was sure.

And so the confrontation with Lacy, the hurry-up wedding, the miserable apartment, the scrambling to make ends meet. And the boiling in her gut that never seemed to subside.

All that first summer Trip worked on a construction site to support them. By the time law school started in September, with Lauren's last trimester drawing near, they moved to a better apartment, a place with south-facing windows and a second tiny bedroom for the baby.

But they weren't talking. They weren't having sex. Trip seemed morose and distant much of the time. Maybe he was just tired. Maybe he was being sensitive to her "condition." Maybe he didn't find her attractive, with her bulging abdomen and heavy breasts. Lauren tried to push the constant worry to the back of her mind. It was going to be all right. Somehow it would work out.

And then, in December, with Trip's constitutional law final looming the next morning, her water broke at three in the morning.

Trip had come to bed less than an hour ago, but he was sound asleep. She reached over to wake him, and a memory raked through her. For a moment she watched him just as she had watched him that spring day nine months ago, the first time they . . .

The first contraction hit her hard, and Trip, startled awake at the sound of her cry, sat bolt upright, dazed and confused.

"Is something wrong with the baby? Should I take you to the hospital?"

"No. Yes," she croaked between gasps. "It's time."

The next few minutes were utter chaos. Trip hopped around the apartment trying to pull on his jeans with one hand and brush his teeth with the other, while Lauren put back on the only clothes that still fit her. As she waddled toward the front door Trip found his lost keys by stepping on them with his bare foot. "Damn!" he yelled, and Lauren, despite herself, laughed.

It was like an episode of the *Dick Van Dyke Show*. Just as Trip helped her into the car, she remembered the suitcase sitting in the hall closet, the one she had packed diligently a month ago, just in case. He ran back in to get it and returned carrying his old bowling ball bag. She didn't bother to tell him.

As they pulled out of the parking lot, another contraction hit, and Trip slammed on the brakes in response.

"Just *go!*" she said through gritted teeth.

"Is the baby all right?" he demanded.

"The baby's fine. But *you* won't be unless you get me to the hospital now!"

Trip apparently knew better than to argue with a woman in labor. He ran seven stop lights and broke every speed limit getting her to the hospital.

They needn't have hurried. By the time they got her admitted into the hospital, the contractions had slowed down. At seven thirty, assured by the OB nurse that first babies take a long time coming, Trip left the hospital and went to take his exam.

Throughout the early hours of labor, Lauren lay alone in the hospital room crying, but not from the physical pain. She had never felt so alone in her life. She didn't blame Trip for leaving—law schools didn't reschedule exams for everyday events like babies being born. But her mother wasn't here to assure her that everything would be all right. Her father wasn't here to pace the waiting room. Her sister wasn't here to hold her hand.

And Trip had asked, "Is the baby all right?" Not "Are you all right?"

She wasn't all right. She had never been less all right in her life.

As the contractions quickened and strengthened, Lauren prayed with every breath that Trip would love this baby and that, in loving his child, he could find a way to love her too. But four hours later, when the doctor laid the infant in her arms, she gazed down at his innocent face and knew she was lost. He was not fair and blond like herself, like Trip, but olive-skinned with a thick mass of dark hair.

Like Steve Treadwell.

"His name?" the nurse asked, her pen poised over the birth certificate.

"Thomas," Lauren choked out. "Thomas Edward Jenkins IV."

"Why didn't you tell me?" Trip shouted. "You *lied* to me!"

At least he had waited to confront her. When Trip had arrived at the hospital, bleary-eyed and disheveled from his exam, she was still clutching the bundle and sobbing. He took the baby from her, kissed the red and wrinkled forehead, and uttered not a single word about the obvious truth that his infant namesake, whom they called Teddy, was not his biological son.

But now that they were home, the anger that had been building for days could no longer be contained.

"You intentionally deceived me, tricked me into marrying you, lying to me—"

"I didn't lie," Lauren repeated with an edge of desperation in her voice. "Not deliberately, anyway. I thought he was your baby, Trip, I really did. I had broken it off with Steve the week before spring break, but—"

"I should have guessed." Trip ran a shaking hand through his hair. "Steve always bragged to everyone about his conquests. But when you got pregnant, it never even entered my mind that the child was his."

"Me neither," Lauren mumbled.

"I mean, if I'd known . . ." His voice trailed off.

"If you'd known, you'd have done what?" Lauren shouted. "You'd have dumped me and married my sister, after all? You'd have pretended this never happened? Or you'd have kept meeting me in secret, screwing me behind everyone's back?"

Her yelling woke the baby in the next room, and the child began to cry. "I didn't lie," Lauren repeated over the squalling. "I didn't know. Not until . . ."

She went to retrieve the baby and sank wearily into the rocking chair her mother had bought for them. Trip flung himself onto the sagging sofa. Lauren lifted her T-shirt, exposed a breast, and began feeding the infant. Little Teddy made soft sucking sounds as he nursed.

Lauren looked up at Trip, who appeared to deflate before her eyes. It seemed as if his anger had been the only thing keeping him upright and moving, and once it drained out of him, he was left looking empty and tired. He stared at the baby for a long time. Neither of them spoke.

When Teddy finished nursing, Trip took him from his mother's arms and cuddled him close. The baby stirred in his sleep and smacked his tiny lips.

"Are you going to tell Steve?" he asked quietly.

Lauren blinked at him. "And what? Ask him for child support? Divorce you and demand that he marry me? Not a chance." She bit her lip. "What are *you* going to do?"

Trip stared at the baby in his arms. "I'm going to do what I promised," he said at last. "I'm going to finish law school, get my degree, support my family. I'm going to be this little boy's daddy."

He had kept that promise, and then some.

Trip Jenkins turned out to be a wonderful man who adored his son. He taught the boy to throw a football, to ride a bike, to stand up to bullies, to be kind to the kids in school whom everyone else teased. He adored being a dad. But he was not Ted's father.

That knowledge, however, never stopped Trip from loving him—loving with fierce depth and frightening power. And now the boy was growing up to be smart and generous and handsome, even at the awkward, gangly age of fourteen. Ted might have inherited Steve Treadwell's looks, but his character was the result of nurture rather than nature.

Lauren looked out the window at her husband's back as he sat on the park bench at the edge of the koi pond. Rain was falling, pocking the surface of the dark waters, but he didn't seem to care.

Trip had built the pond himself. It was eight feet across,

crafted of stone in an irregular kidney shape, with a small waterfall that rushed over the rocks and aerated the pool. A couple of water lilies floated on the surface, and beneath them, in the dim cold greenness, three lazy koi perpetually eased back and forth. Papa Bear, the largest of the three, was a Showa Sanke, red and black and white with a pattern just above his dorsal fin that looked like the state of Florida. The other two were dubbed, predictably, Mama Bear and Baby Bear.

Whenever Trip needed to work things out, he retreated to the waterfall pond, to the silent fish. Lauren watched him now, hunched over, oblivious to the rain.

What was he doing out there? What was he thinking?

She wondered. But she had learned not to ask questions.

Especially if she wasn't sure she'd like the answers.

TWENTY-TWO

The Ties That Bind

Hillsborough, North Carolina
June 1969

The bus left Hillsborough at midnight, heading west. For an hour or more, Lacy sat next to the window staring into the darkness. Every now and then a car would pass, its headlights glaring into her eyes and making her squint. But for the most part, all she could see was her own reflection, the dim image of a pale, tear-streaked face, a shaken young woman fleeing for her life.

She had no idea where she was going, only that she had to get away. As far away from North Carolina as possible. As far away from *them.*

Mother and Daddy had tried to reason with her. It didn't make sense, just to take off for parts unknown when she had a job waiting for her at Hillsborough High. What would she do? How would she live? Why couldn't she just accept what had happened and go on with her life, find someone else? They weren't condoning what Lauren had done, certainly, but she *was* Lacy's sister. And family was family, no matter what.

But Lacy was adamant. She was determined to leave, and nothing they could say or do would stop her. In the end, Daddy had given her some money to tide her over and Mother had stood crying in the depot as the bus pulled out.

The thrumming of the tires against pavement lulled her, and for a while she slept with her head leaning against the glass. When she awoke, the seat next to her was occupied.

"Where are you going?" the woman asked when Lacy turned in her direction.

At first Lacy didn't answer. She didn't want a seatmate, didn't want to have to talk to anyone. And yet this woman, who looked to be a few years older than Lacy, had a kind face.

"I have no idea," Lacy answered candidly. "I'm not exactly going *to* anywhere; it's more like I'm going *from*." Tears welled up in her eyes and she turned her head back toward the window.

The woman laid a hand on her arm—the lightest of touches, a brief warmth—and then took it away. They sat in silence for a while as Lacy cried. When Lacy began rummaging in her bag for another tissue, the woman handed her one with a soft smile. "I'm Alison Rowe, by the way."

"Thanks," Lacy muttered. "Lacy Cantrell." She sighed and resigned herself to small talk. She looked down at the woman's hand, which bore a small diamond solitaire and a gold band. "What about you? Where are you headed?"

"Home to Kansas City."

"Is your husband there?" Alison glanced up with a startled expression, and Lacy pointed. "I noticed your rings."

"My husband is . . . dead." Alison bit her lip. "He was stationed at Fort Bragg before he was called up to Vietnam." She exhaled heavily. "There didn't seem to be any point in staying after. . . ."

"I'm—I'm really sorry," Lacy managed. "When did this happen?"

"A couple of months ago. I had to pack up the house and sell everything."

Something was bothering Lacy, and it took a minute or two to put her finger on what it was. "If you came from Fort Bragg, you were on the bus when I got on."

Alison nodded. "I was sitting a few rows back. I saw you crying. Looked like you might use some companionship." She appraised Lacy in the dim light. "You're very young to be setting off cross country by yourself with no destination in mind."

Lacy hadn't thought she wanted company, but clearly Alison Rowe was a woman who knew how to listen. And once the floodgates were opened a crack, everything came flowing out.

All through the night they talked. Alison told Lacy about her husband, Richard, who had, the army reluctantly told her, been killed by friendly fire. About growing up in Missouri. About her family—a mother, brother, and two sisters—in Kansas City. Lacy told Alison about Lauren and Trip, about her plans to marry Trip and teach at Hillsborough High School after graduation. About her sister's betrayal. About her anger and bitterness, and the need to get as far away as possible, to put the whole thing behind her forever.

To Lacy's surprise, it helped a little just to be able to talk about her pain. Alison understood suffering. And there was no risk in telling her the whole sordid mess. Once this bus ride was over, she'd never see the woman again.

But Alison had other ideas.

"Why don't you come to Kansas City with me?" she said as they ate breakfast at a small depot somewhere in Tennessee. "My brother is on the school board; he can probably get you a job. You can stay with me at my mom's house until you can afford a place of your own."

It was an extravagantly generous offer, and before she realized quite what she was doing, Lacy said yes. What difference did it make, anyway, where she ended up—as long as it was far away from her sister and her ex-fiancé and the memory of their treachery and deception?

IT TOOK A LONG TIME for Lacy to emerge from the emotional wreckage of Lauren and Trip's betrayal. Like the victim of some natural disaster—earthquake, fire, flood—she wandered about in a fog, aimless, bracing herself for the aftershocks, for another explosion or a second rush of rising water.

She went on with life, certainly. She got her master's degree and established herself as a popular teacher at the high school where Alison taught literature. She dated a variety of eligible men, had even come close to being engaged once or twice. On the surface, anyway, she got along pretty well.

Years passed—two years. Five years. Ten. Twelve.

And in all that time she'd had no contact with her sister. She had kept in touch with her mother and father, of course, had written letters and talked to them on the telephone occasionally, but it was easier to keep things superficial when she didn't have to see them face to face.

Only once had she visited—in Christmas of 1982, when Mama had called to tell her that Lauren and Trip were spending the holidays in Dallas with Trip's parents. And the moment she set foot over the threshold of her childhood home, she knew coming back to Hillsborough had been a mistake.

A huge one.

On the mantel in the living room stood several framed photographs. Lauren holding an infant in her arms. Lauren and Trip with a dark-haired three-year-old at a birthday party. Trip with the same boy, a few years older, carrying fishing poles and holding up a large brook trout. School photos of the child as he grew, the metamorphosis of baby to toddler to disheveled boy to gangly preteen.

Lacy felt a numbness creep into her chest, and on wooden legs she made her way over to the photographs. "This is Ted, I assume," she managed to say. She peered at the picture of Lauren with the baby. Her own mirror image stared back at her. This should have been her photo. Her baby. Her life.

Somehow she forced herself through three days of torture. It was obvious her parents were attempting to be sensitive, but no matter how hard they tried, they couldn't keep from talking about their grandson—what a bright boy he was, how well mannered and considerate. What wonderful parents Lauren and Trip were.

By the time Lacy got on the plane back to Kansas City, her nerves were shredded raw. She tried to sleep on the flight, but every time she closed her eyes she saw that picture of Lauren holding the infant Ted in her arms.

Alison met her at the gate and followed her down to baggage claim. "So, how was it?"

"Don't ask." Lacy dragged her suitcase off the carousel. "Can we go get something to eat? I'm starving."

They drove through a light snow to the Fireside Grille, a restaurant that specialized in steaks and burgers. Lacy ordered a prime rib sandwich on crusty French bread, but once the order arrived she found herself unable to eat.

"Come on, tell me," Alison urged. "What happened?"

Lacy grimaced. "You know, I thought I was done with it—the Lauren and Trip thing. But the minute I set foot in that house, it all came back. Mom had photographs of my nephew all over the house. There was one of Lauren and the baby—you know, the typical Madonna and child thing, with this ethereal light around the edges. I looked at it and thought—" She lifted her shoulders. "Well, I don't know what I thought."

"You thought it ought to be you," Alison said.

"Yeah, I guess I did." Lacy tried in vain to eat a bite of her sandwich, just to postpone this discussion.

Alison waved a french fry in Lacy's direction. "Jealous?"

"I don't know. Maybe." Lacy shrugged. "Alison, what the hell is wrong with me? I have a good life, don't I? I've got friends, I've got a great job. I thought I was over this."

"Of course you're not over it," Alison said. "How could you be over it when you've never dealt with it?"

Lacy felt her stomach lurch. "What do you mean, I've never dealt with it? I've spent the past thirteen years—"

"You haven't been *dealing* with it," Alison corrected. "You've been *suppressing* it. You were running away when we met, and you're still running." She leaned forward. "Lace, I'm your best friend. We tell each other the truth. Why did you say no when Hank asked you to marry him?"

"Well," Lacy hedged, "it just didn't feel right."

"And Rob?"

"He wasn't the one."

"He wasn't Trip Jenkins, you mean."

"I didn't say that."

"You didn't have to. You've lived here for years, Lacy. How many of your friends even know you have a twin sister, much less how she betrayed you?"

"I don't know."

"Well, I do. None of them—except for me, and fortunately for you I know how to keep my mouth shut."

"What's your point?"

"My point is that you haven't dealt with your pain and anger over Trip and Lauren. You've just shoved it under the surface. And you can't risk letting anyone too close because they might find out what's down there."

The arrow found its mark, and Lacy winced. "When we met on that bus you were so tender and compassionate. What happened to that woman? How did you become so damned direct?"

"I became friends with you," Alison retorted with a grin. "And I got a lot of counseling. It's called tough love, Lace. Get used to it."

"So what do you suggest I do?" Lacy asked reluctantly.

Alison took a pen from her purse and wrote a telephone number on a paper napkin. "Call this number. It's my grief counselor. She can help."

"I don't need a grief counselor," Lacy protested. "Nobody's died."

Alison raised an eyebrow. "Just call her, will you?"

DR. MAMIE WITHERSPOON, a squat, maternal woman in her late fifties, looked more like someone's grandma than a therapist. But Lacy soon discovered how utterly deceiving looks could be.

Mamie took no bull from anyone, and she could spot a lie—or even a slanted half-truth—quicker than a robin could snap up a fat earthworm. She had a birdlike way of jerking her head and fixing Lacy with those bright, beady eyes.

"Thirteen years," she said when Lacy had finished the short

version of her story. "And in all that time, you've never had contact with your sister or her husband or your nephew."

"No," Lacy mumbled. "Like I said, I've put all that behind me."

"Have you now?"

"Yes. I've made a new life for myself. I've become a self-actualized individual."

Mamie adjusted her wire-rimmed glasses and smiled. "Self-actualized?"

Lacy nodded. "When I was in undergraduate psych years ago, we studied Maslow's hierarchy. I remember it very clearly, because as a twin, I had never felt a sense of individuality. I wanted to discover myself, to be fully self-actualized, differentiated."

"And so you cut yourself off."

Lacy frowned at the counselor. "Haven't you been listening? I didn't cut *myself* off. I was the injured party here."

"The victim."

"Well, yes, if you put it that way. But I haven't let it control my life. I've moved on."

The bright bird-eyes fixed on her as if she were a particularly juicy worm. "It's hard to move on when you're dragging your baggage behind you."

Lacy tried to dismiss the image, but she felt the truth of it nevertheless—the weight of the past, holding her back, hindering each stumbling step toward the future.

"It's not that big a deal," she muttered.

"On the contrary," Mamie said. "It's an enormous deal. Your fiancé was unfaithful to you. Your sister betrayed you. She stole the life you thought you deserved. That's enough to supply rage and bitterness for a lifetime."

"I'm not angry," Lacy protested, but even as she spoke the words, she knew it was a lie.

"Have you ever read *Lord of the Rings*?" Mamie asked.

The non sequitur jerked Lacy to attention. "A long time ago. But what does that have to do with—?"

"Remember Gollum? He finds the sacred ring and claims it, calling it 'my precious.' Even though it is destroying him, he clings to it, will do anything to get it back when it's taken from him."

"All right," Lacy said hesitantly.

Mamie tilted her head. "We all have a 'precious,' an obsession that well may destroy us, and yet we cherish it, hold onto it at any cost."

"And my obsession, my 'precious,' is—?"

Mamie glanced at the clock. "Our time is up. Shall we make another appointment for you?"

Lacy stared at her. "You're just going to leave me like this, without an answer?"

"You have the answer within you," Mamie said. "You merely have to find it for yourself."

LACY SPENT EIGHT MONTHS with Mamie Witherspoon, searching for the answers that lay within her own soul. It was hard work, emotionally grueling and mentally exhausting. But gradually she felt the baggage slip away a piece at a time, until there was only one issue left that bogged her down.

Forgiveness.

Mamie raised the subject. Lacy resisted.

Mamie raised the subject again. Lacy balked.

Alison raised the subject. Lacy told her to mind her own damned business.

Alison simply lifted her left eyebrow at Lacy in that annoying, I-know-you-better-than-you-know-yourself look. Lacy tossed her wadded-up napkin across the dinner table and grinned when it hit Alison directly on the forehead.

"Listen," Lacy said, "I've worked hard to face the truth about myself." She ticked off each item on her fingers. "I've dealt with the anger and the jealousy. I no longer feel like a victim. I've accepted the fact of Lauren and Trip's relationship, and I see that it might not have been the best thing in the long run if I had married him instead. I've become aware of my tendency to withdraw to avoid getting hurt again, and I've started letting people get closer. But forgive Lauren and Trip? Let bygones be bygones? Forget what they've done to me? There's no way."

Alison cocked her head and looked at Lacy. "Who said anything about bygones? Who said anything about forgetting?"

"Well, that's what forgiveness means, doesn't it? Letting stuff go, reconciling relationships, forgetting what someone else has done to you. Having everything go back to the way it used to be. Besides, Lauren and Trip haven't *asked* for forgiveness. They haven't said they were sorry for what they did."

"And the government hasn't apologized for causing the death of my husband," Alison replied softly. "That's irrelevant."

Lacy leaned forward in her chair. "Apologies are irrelevant? Taking responsibility is irrelevant?"

"Whether or not someone has apologized is irrelevant to our need to forgive." She took a deep breath and a large drink of tea before she continued. "Forgiveness is not absolution, Lacy. Forgiveness is the process of liberating ourselves from the web of pain others have imposed upon us. Forgiveness is about freedom, Lace. *Your* freedom. You forgive for your own sake, so that you no longer have to be controlled by what that person has done to you. You let it go, abandon any pretense of having power over the situation. You control your own life, because you certainly can't control anyone else's."

"I don't know how to do that."

"Ask Mamie" was all Alison would say in reply.

LACY DIDN'T LIKE THE FEELING that her counselor and her best friend were tag-teaming her, but she also knew they were right. She was tired of the anger, the hate. It took her a couple of months, but she finally asked Mamie how she could begin to forgive.

"You've already begun," Mamie replied with a smile. "Think of a spider's web. You're all wrapped up in pain and heartbreak and self-imposed exile. Then you come to and realize you're caught. You have to do something, and thrashing around only makes the bondage worse. So one thread at a time, you cut yourself free. You face the truth. You give up being a victim. You accept reality. One thread at a time, until you can move and breathe again. The last thread that binds your freedom is unforgiveness. You need to understand that forgiveness is a process and doesn't always look like what it is."

Mamie smiled, and her beady eyes almost disappeared. "If I might be permitted a personal anecdote—"

Lacy waved a hand. "By all means."

"I had a difficult relationship with my mother when I was growing up. She was very domineering and demanding, always had to have things perfect. And I wasn't perfect. I was plain and fat, and although I overcompensated by being intelligent and creative, that was never enough for her. I always felt put down, demanded. Then one day, pretty much out of the blue, I came to a decision. I was thirty-eight years old, had a Ph.D. and a growing counseling practice, and I still felt like that fat ugly child who couldn't please her mother. So I said—out loud, to myself, 'I don't give a damn what she thinks of me.' "

Lacy grinned. "If that's your example of forgiveness—"

"But it was, don't you see? I declared my independence from her opinion. And gradually, as that truth took hold in my life, I was able to forgive her, to realize that at her age she wasn't likely to change. I could either accept her as she was, or I could live under the cloud of her disapproval for the rest of my life. I couldn't choose my feelings, but I could choose whether or not I let her perceptions control me."

"And so with my sister—"

Mamie nodded encouragingly. "Go on."

"I can choose to forgive her not to set *her* free, but to free *myself* from the rage and bitterness that have controlled me."

"And what would that look like in practical terms?"

Lacy bit her lip. "I would be able to face Lauren and Trip and have some kind of relationship with them. I could be an aunt to the nephew I've never met. I could go home without feeling tense and self-protective." She paused. "And what happens then?"

"Then," Mamie said, "your time with me will come to an end."

THE END CAME SOONER than Lacy had expected. Just before Thanksgiving break, she received a frantic call from her mother.

Daddy had suffered a stroke. A bad one. Mama needed help and support.

The principal hired a substitute to finish out the semester and administer exams. Reluctantly Lacy tendered a midterm resignation.

It was time to go home.

TWENTY-THREE

Family Christmas

Hillsborough, North Carolina
November 1983

When she pulled her fully loaded VW bug up in front of the house two days after Thanksgiving, Trip and Lauren were there to meet her, accompanied by a dark-haired intense young man who turned out to be her nephew.

Lauren stepped forward and gave her an awkward hug. "Welcome home, Lace," she said with a grave formality. "You, ah, remember Trip. This is our son, Ted. He's just about to turn fourteen."

He looked older than the pictures she had seen at her parents' house, but when he smiled, she could see the little boy in him. He hesitated, then gave her an awkward, one-armed hug. "I'm glad to meet you, Aunt Lacy. Finally."

Lacy regarded him. There was something unusual about him, something she couldn't quite articulate. Then it dawned on her.

Both Lauren and Trip were blond and fair. Her nephew had dark curly hair, olive-toned skin. And brown eyes.

This might be Lauren's son, but he definitely wasn't Trip's.

She glanced over at Trip, who was standing apart from them. He said nothing, but Lacy felt his eyes on her, as if he were trying to communicate without words. The awareness of his attention was unsettling.

"I sold everything I couldn't pack into the car," she said. "There's a big trunk in the back seat, a couple of suitcases, and up front there are six boxes of books." She moved to open the front hood, and her hand brushed Trip's as he reached out to grab the handle. Lacy pulled back as if she had touched a live wire, and after that she supervised the retrieval of the luggage from a safer distance.

Lauren looked . . . different. Lacy hadn't seen her since graduation, and although this woman standing next to her was readily recognizable as a sister, the twinness had succumbed to time in a way Lacy would have thought impossible. It was like gazing into a magic mirror and seeing ten years into the future.

She seemed tired. Weary. Worn out. She was only thirty-six, but fine crow's feet already fanned out from the corners of her eyes. She had gained weight, about fifteen or twenty pounds, Lacy gauged. Enough to make her look saggy and bloated. Her hair had been bleached several shades lighter than her natural blonde. Its texture looked coarse and brittle, and the color did not complement her skin tone.

Trip, on the other hand, was every bit as handsome as he had been the day they met. Heavier, certainly, but he carried it well and in the right places. Once he smiled tentatively in her direction, flashing a dimple at the corner of his mouth. She remembered the eyes, lake-blue and liquid. How could she have forgotten the dimple?

"I hope you like the house," Lauren was saying, pointing to the little brick place sitting back a ways from the street. "It was the best we could find this close to Mom and Dad. We rounded up some furniture for you—just temporarily, of course, until you can get what you want."

"I'm sure it will be fine," Lacy muttered absently.

"Dad's still in the hospital. They say they're going to release him tomorrow. I told Mother I could manage things, but she insisted on calling you. I guess I should thank you for coming."

"It's okay," Lacy said. "I wanted to come."

It wasn't the whole truth, of course. She had returned out of duty, out of family responsibility, when the very last thing she wanted was to be thrust into an uncomfortable truce with Lauren. But it had been her choice. No one had pressured her.

"After we unload, we had planned to go to the hospital and see Dad, and then go to our house and have turkey sandwiches." She paused. "But we put some Thanksgiving leftovers in your fridge, just in case you were too tired."

Lacy pounced on this excuse like a terrier on a rat. "It *was* a very long drive," she said. "Two days on the road has left me exhausted. I think I'll unpack and rest up a little, then go to see Dad later this evening."

Lauren didn't protest. She, too, seemed relieved. "All right. I'll tell the folks you'll come by later."

And then, with perfunctory hugs all around, they were gone.

It didn't feel like home yet, this tiny rental house with its two small bedrooms and a pink tile bath that harked back to the fifties. But it was on a side street within walking distance of the house she had grown up in—close enough to her parents to be helpful and, she hoped, far enough away to maintain a semblance of independence.

Lacy had a little money saved up, enough to make the move and keep her in groceries for a few months. The principal at Hillsborough High, thrilled to be getting such an experienced teacher, had promised her a position come September.

She missed Kansas City. Missed Alison. Missed the snow at Christmas. But coming home had been the right decision. Daddy was making progress, thanks to the exercises and speech therapy. On the days when the physical therapist didn't come, Lacy went over and made him do the painful stretches.

And she was doing some stretching of her own.

November burned itself out in a blaze of red and yellow leaves. The air grew cold, and the Carolina sky arched a brilliant blue above. Although still unable to walk on his own, Lacy's father seemed to be improving, and he insisted on having them all for Christmas.

This was what Lacy had been dreading. For a few weeks she had been able to negotiate a little two-step around Lauren and Trip, avoiding them whenever possible and being formally courteous when circumstances forced her into their presence. But there would be no escaping them at a family Christmas.

She arrived first on Christmas morning, resolutely determined to make the best of it. But the moment she stepped across the threshold, memories assaulted her on a wave of familiar scents. Turkey roasting in the oven, spiced pumpkin, yeast rolls. Her mind lurched and spun out a collage of old home movies with herself and Lauren in the starring roles. The twins in identical green velvet dresses, singing carols at the piano. The twins with their first bicycles. The twins in long white robes and halos, Mama's little angels.

She dumped the corn and broccoli casserole on the kitchen counter and took her packages to the tree. Arranging them gave her a moment to collect herself, to push back the tears.

She barely had time to paste on a smile, however, when the door opened and Trip came in on a blast of cold air. Lacy rocked back on her heels and looked up at him, pleasantly disheveled, his cheeks flushed pink from the wind.

"Merry Christmas," he said, his voice low and tentative.

Before she could respond, Lauren and Ted pushed in after him, their arms full of brightly wrapped packages. "Gramma!" Ted called. "We're here!"

Lacy's mother came out of the kitchen wiping her hands on her apron. "Come on in," she said. "I was just taking out the last of the pies. Pumpkin, of course—Teddy's favorite." She glanced at Lacy. "Where'd you get off to?" she asked. "I was talking to you, and then I turned around and you were gone."

"Putting presents under the tree," Lacy muttered. As she moved to get up, Trip held out a hand to help her. Their fingers touched and their eyes met. The bottom dropped out of Lacy's stomach. "I'll—I'll come help," she said, pushing her mother back toward the kitchen.

"There's nothing to do right now," Mama said. "The turkey's got another hour to go, and the dressing has to bake. Let's all sit down."

Ted looked around. "Where's Grampa?"

"He's holed up in the bedroom, wrapping my gift." She laughed. "Always did put it off till the last minute. Why don't you go help him, Teddy? Don't know how he figured on doing it himself, with only one good hand."

Ted went off in search of his grandfather while the adults

moved into the living room. Lauren and Trip sat on the couch, and Lacy took the chair adjacent to them. Lauren reached out for Trip's hand. His head whipped toward her, and she smiled at him.

"So," Lauren said when they were settled. "We haven't had a chance to catch up since Dad got home from the hospital. Tell us about Kansas City, Lace."

The next hour or so they filled with small talk—Lacy's teaching, her friendship with Alison Rowe, the story of Alison's husband being killed in Vietnam. Lauren told family stories, mostly about Ted. And Trip, reluctantly dragged into the conversation, related a few tales about his law practice and odd clients he had represented. "One woman," he said, "wanted to sue her husband for having an affair. She didn't want to divorce him, just to get control of all their finances—" He broke off suddenly and flushed as Lauren pinched the soft flesh between his thumb and forefinger.

By the time dinner was ready, they had exhausted the supply of readily available superficialities. Conversation around the table centered mostly on the food—why fresh turkey tasted so much better than frozen, what recipe Lacy used for her corn casserole. Lacy watched as her mother cut her father's food into manageable bites. Although it pained her to see her father's helplessness with a knife and fork, she found herself warmed by the obvious love between the two of them. Her mother did not seem the least bit repulsed by the drooping muscles on one side of her husband's face or his inability to feed himself without dribbling. On the contrary, she gazed at him with conspicuous adoration, as if he were the handsomest, most vital man on the face of the earth.

She thought Lauren had noticed too, but she kept her eyes averted from her sister and Trip.

At last the uncomfortable meal was over. Lacy volunteered to do the dishes and for a blessed thirty minutes had the kitchen to herself. But when the call came to open presents, she had no choice but to rejoin the family in the living room.

"Teddy's going to play Santa Claus," her mother announced when Lacy had settled herself on the rug at her father's feet.

The tradition hadn't changed since childhood. Each present was delivered individually, and everyone watched while it was opened, uttering oohs and ahhs of approval. Lacy had bought generic gifts—a silk scarf for Lauren, a pair of gloves for Trip, a regulation NFL football for Ted. This last gift was a big hit, as was Ted's for her—a paperweight of bright red marble, in the shape of an apple with a bronze stem and leaf attached.

"Oh, Ted, it's beautiful," she said quite honestly as she held it up. "You couldn't have gotten me anything I'd like more."

Her nephew, rather pleased with himself, grinned and turned almost as red as the apple's shiny surface. "I picked it out myself."

"Well, thank you." She went to him and gave him a kiss on the cheek.

By midafternoon, after a second slice of pie, everyone was full and sleepy, and Lacy felt she could make her exit without offending anyone. She gathered up her gifts, said good-bye to the family, and headed for the door.

Ted caught up with her on the porch. "I'm glad you're back, Aunt Lacy," he murmured self-consciously as he hugged her. "I hope you'll stay."

THROUGH THE WINDOW over the sink Lauren could see out into the backyard all the way to the koi pond, where once again Trip sat motionless in a slant of winter sunshine with his head bowed and his hands clasped between his knees.

In this attitude of absolute stillness, he could have been praying, could have been a saint in meditation. He looked a bit like Rodin's sculpture of *The Thinker*—clothed, of course, and less muscular, but equally lost in the depths of his soul. Perhaps this was her husband's version of prayer, watching the fish gliding under the dark water, listening to his own breath and heartbeat.

She wondered what he heard inside himself in moments like this. Did he, like Lauren herself, question how they got to this point in their lives? Did he regret, as she did, the convolution of guilt and duty and good intentions that had left them, fifteen years down the road, stuck in an unhappy partnership and bound by promises that should never have been made?

Those years had changed Lauren more than she could have imagined. She felt old and wrung out, depleted. And now Lacy was back, still young and slim and looking like she had when they were in college.

Trip had noticed. Lauren could see it in his eyes, feel it in the tension that gripped him every time he came within a dozen yards of her sister. Well, if that was what he wanted—what Lacy wanted—she wouldn't fight this time.

The game was over. She was too tired to play again.

Besides, she had won once, and look where it had gotten her.

TWENTY-FOUR

Epiphany

January 1984

It didn't take long to clean a house as small as Lacy's. She had already vacuumed twice and now was dusting everything for the second time. She couldn't seem to sit still for more than a minute.

Nerves. It was just nerves.

She went to the pantry and stowed the dust rag. Wiped down the kitchen counter again. Paced around the tiny living room, fluffing up the sofa pillows.

A blustery January rain beat against the windows. In an attempt to dispel the chill and gloom, Lacy bent to turn on the gas logs in the small fireplace, and when she stood up again she found herself staring into the mirror over the mantel. The person who stared back at her was no woman at all, but an agitated schoolgirl anticipating a first date. She looked young and frightened and out of control.

"Get a grip," she muttered to herself.

But no grip was forthcoming. She glanced at the clock. In thirty minutes he would be here, assuming he was as punctual as he used to be. Half an hour, and Lacy would be sitting face to face—alone—with the only man she had ever loved, the man who fifteen years ago had jilted her in favor of her twin.

On the mantel in front of her stood the last of the Christmas decorations, a small crèche consisting of Mary and Joseph, the Baby Jesus in the manger, two sheep, a shepherd, and a single Wise Man riding on his camel. The set had belonged to their family. She and Lauren used to take turns—one reading from the Bible and the other walking the figurines into place as the familiar story was told. They had fought about it every year, Lauren always insisting that it was her turn to move the pieces. For several years the argument had escalated, resulting in the loss of one shepherd and two Wise Men, until their mother started putting a note into the box each year before stowing it away with the rest of the decorations.

In her haste to pack up the tree and ornaments, Lacy had forgotten the ceramic figures, and now she picked up the Wise Man and considered him.

Where, she wondered, did wisdom come from? Was it written in the stars, or upon the human heart? Was it simply knowledge, an understanding that had its source in human experience? Or more than that, the gift of some higher power? Lacy didn't know, although at this moment she desperately wished she could find the wellspring and tap into it. With Trip arriving in thirty minutes, she could use all the help she could get.

A determined rapping on the front door startled her, and the figurine slipped from her fingers and crashed to the hearth below. It cracked cleanly in two, just at the saddle where the Wise Man joined his camel. Flustered, she bent down and scooped up the pieces.

He was early. *Very* early. Lacy took a deep breath and exhaled in a vain attempt to still the pounding of her heart, then went to the door and opened it.

Lacy's knees nearly gave way beneath her. It wasn't Trip.

For a moment she stared at her twin, uncomprehending. Again she marveled at the differences between them, at the haggard circles under Lauren's eyes, at her brittle, too-blonde hair.

Instinctively Lacy reached up to touch her own hair and realized she still held the Wise Man and his camel in her hands.

"May I come in?" Lauren said at last. Her voice sounded brittle as well, as if it too had been overbleached.

Lacy's eyes darted to the clock.

"I won't take much of your time."

Lacy nodded and stepped aside as her sister passed through the narrow foyer and went on into the living room.

"The house looks nice," she said. "Cozy."

"What are you doing here, Lauren?" The question came out more snappish than Lacy had intended, but she had neither the time nor the patience for games or small talk.

"I'm here to . . ." Lauren shrugged and sat down on the couch. "I don't know. To see you, I guess. To talk to you."

"Why now?"

"Trip's left me."

Lacy pretended this was news to her. "Really?"

"Really. He stuck it out fifteen years, so maybe I should be grateful. But losing him is . . . well, let's just say it's the first time I understand what I put you through. I didn't take the time to understand before. Too busy trying to hold things together, I guess. Now I know how awful it feels to be abandoned, to be alone."

"No kidding." Lacy crossed her arms.

Lauren raked her hands through her hair. "Look, Lace, I'm

not doing this very well. I've made so many mistakes and let them go on far too long. Trip's leaving woke me up a little. I can't change what's happened between us. Believe me, if I could, I would. But you're my sister. That should count for something."

"It should have."

"What do you want from me?" Lauren said with an edge of panic in her voice. "What can I do to make things better?"

Suddenly exhausted, Lacy sank into the armchair next to the sofa. Without realizing it, she had been gripping the two halves of the broken figurine, and the sharp edges had cut into her palms. She laid the pieces on the coffee table next to Ted's marble apple and surveyed the pinpricks of blood.

"The truth," she said. "I want the truth."

"All right." Lauren squeezed her eyes shut. "It happened that spring break, when Trip came home with you. We made love."

"You made love," Lacy repeated mechanically.

"I seduced him," Lauren amended. "I was jealous, and unaccustomed to coming in second. It was stupid. A moment of sheer madness."

"But you had what's-his-name. Why on earth would you be jealous?"

Lauren shook her head impatiently. "What I had with Steve Treadwell was nothing compared to what you had with Trip. Steve never loved me, and I never loved him. We hung out together, had fun, had sex. But as soon as I saw you and Trip together, I knew that I had settled for a whole lot less than I really wanted."

"So you decided to go after Trip."

"Not consciously. It just—"

"Don't say it," Lacy warned. "Don't say it just happened."

Lauren sighed. "You're right. I *made* it happen. I don't know why. I felt terrible about it afterward."

"And yet you got married."

"He did it out of guilt, out of some perverted sense of honor. There was the baby to consider—"

"Ah yes, the baby." Lacy didn't comment on her nephew's questionable parentage. She wanted to see if Lauren would come clean with that piece of the story as well.

"As it turned out, Ted wasn't Trip's child," Lauren admitted, much to her own credit. "But I didn't know that at the time. I thought he was Trip's; we both did. It only became obvious . . . afterward. And by that time it was too late." She picked at a loose thread on the arm of her sweater. "Trip thought he was doing the right thing."

"And now?"

"Now I think Trip is trying to get his life back. I don't blame him, really. He never loved me. It was always you, Lace."

Lacy felt a peculiar sort of trembling in her stomach. "He said that?"

"He didn't have to."

A strange metamorphosis had been taking place while Lacy listened to Lauren's confession. Time dropped away from her sister's face, a rewinding of the years. Lacy could see—almost—the mirror image of herself, as she had seen it since childhood. Their shared life, mangled by circumstance, certainly, and shadowed by pain, but still bound with cords that could not be broken. Her sister. Her twin.

Lauren got to her feet. "I need to go."

Lacy opened her mouth to speak and then shut it again. Forgiveness, Mamie Witherspoon had said, was both a decision and a process. A chasm created over fifteen years couldn't be bridged in a single moment, but the reconstruction could begin. Here. Now.

But the moment passed. Lauren did not ask forgiveness, and Lacy did not offer it. Instead, she stood and followed Lauren to the door. One final question churned within her, hovering there, demanding an answer. "Do you—do you love him?"

Lauren ducked her head, but not quickly enough. Lacy could see the tears that had sprung instantly to her eyes.

"Yes," she said after a moment. "I didn't realize how much until he left, until I was faced with the prospect of losing him forever. But yes, I do love him. More than I ever imagined."

Trip, when he arrived, looked soft and eager—the old Trip, her Trip, the one who had made her feel loved and special.

The sensation was intoxicating. Lacy's eyes drank him in, the first oasis in a long and lonely desert. She wanted to take his hand and run away with him, to make a mad dash toward a future she had long ago given up on. This time he would be completely hers, heart and soul. She wanted him to quit talking and simply hold her.

But he would not shut up.

Trip, like Lauren, obviously felt the need to unburden himself, to confess and seek absolution—or, at the very least, amnesty—for the sins of the past. The guilty never realize, she mused, what baggage they transfer to the innocent because of their own need for relief.

Still, she listened as he rambled on, circling around his shame like a vulture homing in on its prey. His was much the same story as Lauren's—one mistake compounded by a lifetime of others. But his tale differed from his wife's by two notable exceptions. For one thing, Trip did not lay blame on Lauren for seducing him. Nor did he mention the fact that Ted was not his son.

These omissions caused Lacy's heart to swell with pride and love. Trip Jenkins was, despite all that had happened, an honorable and ethical man who did not shift responsibility or try to weasel out of his own guilt.

"I am sorry, Lacy," he concluded. "Sorry I let my hormones get out of control. Sorry I hurt you. Sorry for so many things."

Lacy regarded him, letting her eyes roam over his handsome features. He was more mature now, but still intensely attractive, and she found herself having difficulty focusing on what he was saying.

She could see it in his eyes, read it in his body language, the way he leaned toward her. All she had to do was say yes, and her dreams would come true.

Better late than never.

"I kept thinking that if I just tried hard enough, I could make it work," he went on. "I had made this mess, and I had to deal with it. And I wanted to be a good father to Ted. But with each year, each month, each day that passes, I feel more and more trapped." He paused and looked at her intently. "Lacy, do you know anything about koi?"

She frowned. "The fish?"

Trip nodded. "We have three of them in a pond I built in the backyard. It's a beautiful pond, a shady glen with a rock waterfall and a couple of lily pads. I spend a lot of time there; it's my only place of solitude."

"It sounds nice."

"It is." He exhaled heavily. "Anyway, koi will only get as big as their surroundings will allow. They'll stop growing if their pond is too small. And that's me. For years I have been swimming in claustrophobic circles, trapped in silent misery, trying to atone for my sins. I want out. I want to be free."

Lacy's heart raced as she heard his confession. Her dreams

would come true, after all. And what sweet revenge, for him to leave Lauren and come to her. She could almost taste it. . . .

But Trip wasn't finished. "I never stopped thinking about you, Lacy. Look at you—you're exactly the same. It's amazing. You haven't changed a bit since we were in college. It's like these years never happened."

The dream spinning out in her mind snapped to an abrupt halt and fell to earth.

She hadn't changed since college, he said. In his mind, she had simply been waiting for him, caught in time and unable to move. Holding the torch aloft, keeping the flame alive. Praying someday he'd return.

And perhaps he was right. Maybe that's what she had done. The thought sickened her, but she tried to face it squarely, honestly. She recalled the angry years, and more recently, the empty ones.

"I'm not asking for an answer," he said. "Or any kind of commitment. I just want to know if we can go back to where we used to be. Start over, try again. Have a second chance."

The words echoed inside Lacy's skull. Her eyes drifted to the coffee table, where the broken pieces of the ceramic crèche figure lay side by side with Ted's marble apple.

Metaphors, Alison would say. The forbidden fruit. The camel. The Wise Man.

What was the proverb about the camel with its nose in the tent?

Already the beast had pushed its way in. The sweet flavor of revenge, the seductive idea of returning to the love that had captured her heart so many years ago.

The broken Wise Man, lying on his side, gazed into the distant beyond. Toward the stars. Toward an unknown future.

Go back, Trip had said. Start over. But there was no going

back. She was not the same person she had been in college. She was older now and, she hoped, wiser. Wise enough to realize . . .

That he didn't love her. What he loved was the image of her, the memory of the girl she had once been.

There was no way to recapture the past. It was a beautiful illusion, but it wasn't real. He didn't love her. And she didn't love him.

The truth broke over her like a bright and liquid light. Lauren was real. Ted was real. The rest was smoke and mirrors, a mirage, a distorted reflection. At the end was a cliff and a deadly fall.

She looked at him again and saw him as he was. And once more she asked the question that demanded to be answered:

"Do you love my sister?"

Silence. He cleared his throat, pressed his hands against his knees, shrugged. "She doesn't love me. And how could we love each other when you were always there?"

Lacy smiled. Trip was a good man. A good father. He would be a good husband too, given the chance. "She does love you. So does Ted."

At the mention of his son's name, Trip's countenance changed. She could see the agony there, the raw longing. He didn't want a divorce or a different life. He simply wanted to be free.

"Go home to your wife and son," she said quietly. "You made the right choice. You married the right twin."

He held her gaze for a moment, staring into her eyes as though wishing to see something that belied her words. Then, without uttering a sound, he made his exit, shutting the door behind him.

After he left she sat there for a long time, crying a little but not turning away from the pain.

Dusk was falling. She had not yet turned on the lamps, and in the flickering glow of the gas fire the shattered Wise Man still lay on his side on the table, gazing into the distant beyond.

Toward the stars.

Toward an unknown future.

TWENTY-FIVE

Labor Day

September 1984

Lauren stood at the kitchen window and looked out into the backyard, where a slow gray drizzle soaked the lawn and ran in rivulets along the edges of the grass. What was Trip doing out there in the rain? For fifteen minutes he had been sitting on the bench next to the koi pond, getting drenched, just staring into the water.

After breakfast Ted had flung himself from the table and stomped upstairs to his room. Lauren could hear the steady *thump thump* as he tossed a tennis ball against the wall. Poor kid. He had been looking forward to the annual Labor Day baseball barbecue put on by Trip's office. Lauren suspected—although Ted would never confirm her suspicion—that he had a crush on the teenage daughter of one of Trip's colleagues, an adorable little redhead named Ainslee Long.

Ainslee attended a private school. Ted never got to see her except at office functions like the barbecue. Now the event had been canceled because of the rain, and Ted had lost his chance to impress his girl by knocking a home run out of the park.

She could, of course, invite the Longs over for dinner, but then Ted might feel as if he'd been set up, and the results could be disastrous.

Lauren sighed. Parents always thought the worst was over when their babies finally learned to sleep through the night, express their feelings in words, and use the potty on their own. They had no idea, when they lamented the sleep deprivation that came with infancy, that teenage romantic angst would try their patience to new limits.

She wondered what it would be like next year, or the next. Anxiety about drugs and alcohol and smoking, no doubt. Uncomfortable sessions about sex and condoms and deadly diseases and respect for the girls he dated. Late-night discussions with Trip about how to handle the most recent crisis. Constant worry every time Ted took the car.

But at least she wouldn't be in it alone.

Nine months ago Trip had left her, and then, like a miracle, he had come back.

Ted had assumed his dad was off on a business trip, and Lauren had chosen not to tell him any different. Five days later, when Trip returned, it was no big deal. The boy never knew how close he had come to losing his father for good.

No one knew, except Trip and Lauren. And Lacy, of course.

Lauren hadn't spoken with Lacy since that day in January. Whenever the two of them were together with the family, they feigned politeness and avoided any genuine conversation. Lauren longed for a real reconciliation with her sister, yet she wasn't in a position to press the issue. She believed, though he had never admitted it, that Trip had visited Lacy too during his five-day absence from hearth and home. When he returned, he said not the first word about what he had been doing—he simply unpacked his suitcase and merged back into the family.

But since that moment, everything had changed. Whatever Lacy said to him had made a difference. And what Lacy had said to Lauren had changed everything.

Do you love him? she had asked.

For the first time in years, Lauren had been forced to consider the question, and her answer brought her face to face with reality. Up until that point she couldn't have articulated any realistic definition of love. She had always thought love equaled heat, passion, sexual desire and fulfillment. But it had to be more than that. Commitment, focus, oneness. And yet not only oneness. Twoness was important as well, an identity both within and apart from the relationship.

Lauren's understanding of love still was not as clear as she'd like it to be. And yet she knew she loved Trip. Living without him seemed utterly unthinkable.

A week after his return, he had come to her with the news that he had scheduled an appointment with a family therapist and asked, politely and formally, if she would be willing to go with him.

She went. At first it was sheer hell, rehashing the past, dredging up old sins from the murky recesses of her soul and displaying them in the harsh light of objective scrutiny. Seduction and lies, betrayal and denial—all of it came out, including the truth about Ted's paternity. Everything seemed so much worse when you said it out loud. But admitting the truth resulted in a strange kind of catharsis too, a lifting of the weight that had pressed in upon her for all these years.

Trip's love for Ted, as it turned out, became the glue that held them together during the dark months of counseling. Just as

Lauren couldn't imagine living without Trip, Trip couldn't imagine abandoning Ted.

"I married her because it was the right thing to do," he had told the counselor one day. "And I don't regret it. I fell in love."

At the words, Lauren's heart leaped into her throat. And then he went on.

"I hadn't counted on falling in love with such a small, wailing, demanding little bundle of human potential," he said. "But the minute I took that baby in my arms, I fell in love with him."

The revelation shredded her ego, and in that moment any hope she had harbored crashed into shards at her feet. Trip was honest, at least. He didn't pretend to love his wife, but he did love his son.

"The problem is, love for my son isn't enough anymore," he continued. "I'm tired of feeling trapped."

Gradually, as the bitter truth emerged and they faced it head-on, therapy began to take an upward turn. The path through purgatory began to lead them toward the surface, away from the sulfurous hell that burned below. Silence gave way to a little laughter. They watched movies, played games, bonded, became a family as they had never been before.

Things were better. More normal. And yet a bittersweet longing swelled in her as her own love deepened. At night she wept silently in the darkness, soaking her pillow with remorse.

Nine months they had been in weekly therapy sessions, and in all that time he had never touched her. Not even the occasional dispassionate sex that had marked their marriage for years. Through it all Lauren had watched Trip, as she watched out the window now. Waiting. Searching for a sign.

What she saw, instead, was a flurry of activity. Trip suddenly stood up and strode to the shed. He returned with a net, a shovel, a length of black plastic liner, and a huge corrugated tub. He filled the tub with water, and then, after transferring the three koi to the tub, he began to dig.

Lauren sloshed through the puddles into the far corner of the backyard. "What are you doing?"

Trip looked up. He was drenched to the skin and covered with mud, but he had a look of utter delight on his face. "I'm enlarging the pond," he said, as if this should be perfectly obvious.

"I can see that. Why?"

"Because they don't have enough room to grow." He pointed at the tub, where the temporarily transplanted koi hovered as if in suspended animation.

The back door slammed and Ted came loping across the waterlogged grass. "What'cha doing?"

"He's enlarging the pond," Lauren answered.

"Yeah, I know. But why?"

Lauren shrugged. "He says the fish don't have room to grow."

Ted dug the toe of his sneaker into the mud. "You're nuts, Dad, you know that?"

Trip leaned on his shovel and grinned. "Probably. So, do you two want to help, or do you want to just stand there and criticize?"

Ted grinned back. "I figured I'd just criticize."

Lauren wasn't quite certain who threw the first fistful, only that within five minutes all three of them were splattered with mud and laughing hysterically. She wiped the goo out of her face and chanced a glance at Trip. He was gazing at her as if he'd never laid eyes on her before, as if she were the most beautiful woman he had ever seen.

She walked to the shed and came back with two more shovels, one of which she pushed into Ted's hands. She raked her mud-caked hair back and placed one foot on the lip of her shovel.

"You want a bigger pond?" she said. "We'll give you a bigger pond. Let's dig."

IT WAS THE LIGHTEST OF TOUCHES, a tentative caress on her shoulder. Even before his fingers brushed her, she felt his warmth at her back, edging nearer. "Are you awake?" he whispered.

"No, I'm sound asleep," she responded, and he chuckled.

"That was fun today," he said. "Digging the pond and all."

She turned over, and his arms went around her. "It *was* fun. I'm still not certain I quite understand it, but—"

"I'm not sure I can explain it either," he said. "I just know it's time to put the past behind us and move forward."

Lauren shifted in his arms and peered at his face, illuminated faintly by the streetlamp outside their bedroom window. "What does that mean, put the past behind us?"

He let out a breath. "It means I've been holding out on you. Refusing to forgive. I want to let it go, all of it, and start fresh. Can we do that?"

"You're willing to forgive me?"

Trip tightened his hold on her. "I should have forgiven you a long time ago. Can you forgive *me,* for being such an ass?"

"What have you been an ass about?" she murmured

His muscles tensed, and his face went cold in the blue of the streetlight. "When I left in January, I went to see Lacy. I asked her to take me back."

Lauren exhaled sharply. "I know."

"You *know*? How—"

"I should say, I suspected as much."

"But you never said anything."

"I figured you'd tell me when it was the right time. I went to see her too. Tried to reconcile with her. It didn't work."

He was silent for a moment or two. Then: "What did she say?"

Lauren hesitated. "She asked me if I loved you."

"What answer did you give?"

"I said—" Lauren paused.

"I hope you said yes," he murmured. "Because she told *me* I had married the right twin."

"My sister," Lauren whispered, "is a very wise woman."

She nestled in his arms, and for the first time in years she felt safe. The last of the secrets had been told.

In the vague drowsiness that comes just before sleep, she thought she heard him whisper that he loved her. And then she surrendered to a dream of a wide lake fed by a waterfall, with enormous koi swimming in its clear green depths.

PART 5

Mercy

One voice
can lure us to our doom
or to our calling.

Let those who have
eyes to see
and ears to hear
watch
and listen,
perceive, interpret, understand—

For no one ever tells us
that doom can serve
as well as call
to lead us home.

TWENTY-SIX

The Road Less Traveled

Decatur, Georgia
September 1994

For two weeks Delta had wandered around Cassie's house aimlessly, plagued by an empty churning in her gut. Rae Dawn had never returned her call, nor had she received any response from the answering machine messages she had left for Lauren and Lacy.

"Are you sad, Aunt Delt?" Mouse asked one night.

Delta looked up from the novel she had been pretending to read and surveyed her small niece, who lay facedown on the rug working word puzzles from a book Delta had bought her. The child reminded her so much of Cassie at that age—not her looks, but her intelligence, her quickness, her razor-sharp evaluations of her world and the people in it.

Delta hedged. "Why do you ask?"

Mouse shoved the puzzle book aside and sat up. "For one thing," she said, "you don't smile and laugh as much anymore."

"I'll try to do better."

Mouse frowned. "It's not about pretending. It's about really *getting* better on the inside."

Delta laid her own book aside. "Come here, honey."

The child scrambled up and settled herself on Delta's lap.

"You remember your uncle Rankin, don't you?"

Mouse nodded solemnly. "I'm losing my picture of what he looked like, but I remember him. *He* laughed a lot."

A knot twisted tight in Delta's throat. "Yes, he did. He was my husband, you know, and my best friend. I loved him very much. And I was very sad when he died."

"I know." The little girl gave Delta a worried look. "Mom and I talked about it before you came to live with us. She told me about dying, and how people react to it when someone they love a lot gets dead. But . . ." She hesitated. "I heard her tell Daddy that you have eight out of ten."

Delta peered down at the child. "Eight out of ten what?"

Mouse furrowed her brow in thought. "Eight out of ten symptoms of chemical depression."

"Do you mean *clinical* depression?"

She bit her lip. "I think so. Is that like a tropical depression? I heard about that on the Weather Channel."

Delta stifled a laugh. "What's a six-year-old doing watching the weather channel?"

"I'm *seven,* Aunt Delt," Mouse said, looking offended. "And the Weather Channel is very interesting. You should try it sometime."

"I'll do that." Delta tightened her arms around the little girl's warm body. "Now, don't worry about the depression. I'll talk to your mom about it."

"Promise?"

Delta gazed down into the eager, trusting little face. "I promise."

Just as they were finishing their conversation, Cassie came in from the kitchen. "What are we promising? Or is it a secret?"

Delta gave Mouse a kiss on the top of the head and sent her back to her word puzzles. "We were talking about depression. About how I apparently have eight of the ten symptoms." She let out an exasperated sigh. "Look, Cass, I know you're a therapist, but—"

"But what?" Cassie sat down on the sofa next to Delta. "I'm sorry my daughter overheard a conversation I had with her dad. But I can't just ignore this, Sis. I'm worried about you." She narrowed her eyes. "Did you ever call those friends of yours—the ones in the singing group?"

"I tried a couple of weeks ago. Left messages on the machine for Lauren and Lacy, and talked to some guy at Rae Dawn's club. I gave him the number, but she never called back." She shrugged. "End of story."

"You're not going to try again? This reunion would do you good, you know."

"Really?" Delta said, making no effort to keep the sarcasm out of her voice. "It would do me good to tell old friends about Rankin's death over and over like a gruesome video loop on the nightly news. To pretend I'm over it, that everything's back to normal. Whatever *normal* is."

"You could use a change of scenery, not to mention the support of those friends," Cassie insisted. "Besides, the telling makes it real."

"It's plenty real to me," Delta shot back. Having a therapist in the family wasn't all it was cracked up to be. She looked over at Mouse, who had abandoned her puzzles and was staring at both of them with wide, knowing eyes. "Let's not talk about this anymore," she said. "Trust me, I'm fine."

But the following morning, after another restless night interrupted by dark dreams, she knew she wasn't fine, even if she wasn't about to admit it to her little sister.

She had to do something. Had to pull herself out of this.

Maybe Cass was right—not about the reunion, but about getting out of the house, getting a change of perspective. Russell was at work, as was Cassie, and Mouse wouldn't be home from school until three. She could have the whole day to herself, outdoors in the sunshine, if she wanted.

Delta scrawled a note to Cassie and posted it on the fridge, then took her battered old journal and left the house.

The shaded sidewalks near Emory University were a perfect place to walk. The day was warm and bright, but not hot. The sky had cleared and the humidity had dropped. Leaves were beginning to change. Already she could feel a hint of fall in the air.

Autumn was her favorite season. The beginning of the academic year. A new start. A time of change and renewal. And although Delta herself didn't feel particularly renewed, she was at least able to appreciate the break from another stifling, sweltering Atlanta summer.

She wasn't paying much attention to where her footsteps were leading her until she looked up and found herself on campus, near Cannon Chapel. Bishops Hall, which housed Candler School of Theology, lay across an expanse of brick courtyard to the left, and to the right, Pitts Theological Library fronted on the grassy quadrangle.

She skirted the library and found an empty bench facing the quad. A few students loitered here and there, talking and laughing. Two young men in jeans threw a Frisbee back and forth across the sidewalk. A few yards away on the grass, four girls lounged together drinking Starbucks from tall cups.

College campuses always evoked nostalgia in her, but today more than usual. Delta dug in her bag searching for her journal and a pen, all the while trying to stifle the wave of longing that had washed over her.

After a moment's searching she found the journal, pulled it out of the bag, and ran her hands over it. The cover was a rich saddle-brown cowhide, worn smooth and soft by more than twenty years of use and rather dog-eared at the corners. It had been a gift from Cassie the Christmas of Delta's freshman year in college, when she was eighteen and her little sister was only five. Cassie had picked it out herself, she told Delta proudly. And it was perfect—beautiful, durable, and infinitely practical, a standard five-by-eight cover that over the years had housed dozens of refillable notebooks.

Delta's fingers caressed the velvety surface. All she had to do was touch the journal, inhale its rich leathery scent, and her mind kicked into overdrive. She never knew what would come out of her when this Pavlovian response overtook her, but anything would be preferable to the inertia that had seized her of late.

She opened to a blank page and wrote the date in the upper left-hand corner. But before she could go any further, something arrested her attention. A stiff, yellowed page, folded and stuck between the notebook filler and the cover.

Delta pulled it out and unfolded it. It was a page torn from a sketch pad, a crayon drawing of a small-town main street, with a towering gray slab looming overhead. And in a careful, childish hand at the bottom: Cassandra Fox, Age 6.

In a split second all the pieces converged upon her: the campus. The quad. The journal. Cassie's picture. That first dinner with Bowen and Hart, and the discussions that followed.

Countless hours of conversation—about politics, about God and religion (Dr. Bowen firmly denied that these two were necessarily connected), about civil rights and human rights and the state of the world. About the war in Vietnam, about literature and writing, about beauty and truth and Delta's future. Discussions in the back corner booth of the Goose, lubricated by gallons of black coffee. Arguments over egg foo yung at their house with the dogs lying at her heels, or slapdash suppers of a thrown-together rice and beef dish Dr. Hart called "hamburger mess." Even the occasional jaunt to the Bavarian Steak House out on the highway, for planning sessions over rare steak and cheap wine and fried crab claw appetizers.

So many discussions that Delta had long ago lost count.

But she never lost track of the *effect* of those conversations.

In ways she could only begin to articulate, Frankie Bowen and Suzanne Hart had helped Delta to discover herself. Because of them she had become an English major, and on an academic level, they had introduced her to the intricacies of great literary minds of the past: Shakespeare, Milton, Spenser, Herbert, Blake, Wordsworth. They had encouraged her to find her own voice in writing and to be meticulous about research. They had even pulled some strings to get her a work study job as their office assistant.

But even more important, they had taught her how to *think*. How to exhume the universal truths in fiction and poetry and drama, and to make connections between those writings and her own twentieth-century soul.

In the same way that Dr. Gottlieb had taken Rae Dawn under his wing, guided her, and become a kind of surrogate father for her, Dr. Hart and Dr. Bowen had become Delta's mentors. They had given her a vision for the kind of difference she could make in her own students' lives when *she* became a professor.

She remembered it all: the challenge, the passion, the fire. The sense of coming home to herself.

It had simply been too long since flint had struck steel.

All around the Emory quad, doors flung open and students poured out, clustering in groups and heading toward the food court down the hill behind Cannon Chapel. Delta glanced at her watch. It was nearly noon, and her stomach rumbled.

She stowed her journal in her bag, walked down to the Park Bench Tavern, and ordered a Philly cheese steak sandwich, fries, and a Diet Coke. The place thrummed with activity—a gaggle of undergraduate girls laughing and chattering, a table full of divinity students arguing theology. While she waited for her lunch, Delta sipped her drink and absorbed the atmosphere by osmosis.

This was where she belonged—on a college campus, teaching these eager, open young minds how to think for themselves, how to dig out their own truth from the great literature of their heritage. And yet, despite the influence of Frankie Bowen and Suzanne Hart, despite the love of learning that had carried her through her master's degree and beyond, despite the dreams she had once cherished, this wasn't where she had ended up.

She had ended up as a minister's wife.

A poem surfaced in her mind, one she had chosen so long ago for her final American lit paper: Robert Frost's "The Road Not Taken."

The poem had haunted her, day and night, as she was writing, as she was making decisions she never dreamed would change the course of her entire life. Subconsciously, she understood. This was her story—perhaps everyone's story. Two roads. A fork. A choice. No turning back.

Where would her path have led, Delta wondered, if she had finished her doctorate? If she had become a college professor?

If she hadn't married Rankin Ballou?

MAY 1969

After spring break, graduation seemed to speed ever closer with the velocity of a steam locomotive on a downhill run. Delta could hardly believe that within a week, final exams would be over and the friends with whom she had spent the past four years would be scattering to the winds.

Although the day was warm and sunny, front campus was shaded from the afternoon heat, and a slight breeze stirred the damp hair on her forehead. Delta sat at the top of the steps leading to the Music Hall and settled herself to wait. A few more rehearsals, one last gig at the graduation banquet, and the Delta Belles would be history.

A current of memory swirled over her, catching her heart in the eddies. Delta herself would not be leaving the college, of course. Much to her relief, her major professors had not been dismissed. The tumult over Dr. Bowen and Dr. Hart had subsided, and her plans to stay on for her master's degree remained intact.

But everything else was changing—indeed, had already begun to change.

The chasm that separated Rae and Dr. Gottlieb persisted. They seemed to maintain a distant civility, but the warmth between them had cooled. Delta felt the loss too, for the music professor had been a great supporter of the Delta Belles. True to his word, however, Gottlieb had lobbied an old friend on Rae Dawn's behalf. She now had a part-time job lined up—as a backup pianist at a club in her beloved New Orleans—and had arranged to rent a small apartment owned by friends of Drs. Bowen and Hart.

Trip still had not popped the question, but Lacy had won the coveted teaching position at Hillsborough High School and would be living with her parents while he got settled in law school. Lauren, in typical Lauren fashion, was waiting until the eleventh hour to decide what to do after commencement. She blamed the procrastination on the fact that she'd had a stomach flu on and off for weeks, but everybody knew she was predisposed to be indecisive. Lauren would land on her feet, Delta was certain. She always did.

At home in Stone Mountain, Daddy had moved out and settled into an apartment in Atlanta with Caroline Lawler, leaving Mama and Cassie to rattle around the house like pinballs careening off the banks. Cassie phoned at least twice a week begging her to come home, and Ben Rutledge had called several times since spring break, wanting to get back together.

Delta felt sorry for Ben. She missed him, and a time or two was tempted to rekindle their relationship and see where it might lead. But every time she circled around the idea, her mind kept calling up images of her parents, divorced after more than twenty years of mind-numbing boredom, and she realized that pity was no basis for a lasting marriage. He would eventually realize that the breakup was as much to his benefit as to hers. They would be friends again. And in the meantime, as much as her heart ached for the impending finale to her college days and for the strange, awkward balancing act that her family represented, she had something else to occupy her attention.

A dinner date with Rankin Ballou.

Delta rummaged in her closet for something modest—preferably black. Her bed was already piled with rejects, and she still hadn't found anything appropriate to wear. "Rae, don't just stand there—help me. Get me out of this."

Rae Dawn laughed. "You don't want to get out of it, and you know it."

"This date's already been postponed twice," Delta muttered. "I should have taken it as an omen. He's a minister, for God's sake."

"Well, you're not exactly a wild child," Rae countered.

"Yeah, but what if I slip and swear in his presence, or do something that offends him? What if he isn't interested in me at all? Maybe I'm some sort of project—a challenge. Maybe he only wants to lure me in and then corner me with the truth, get me saved or something."

The questions—particularly the ones about faith and God and religion—nagged at Delta. She believed in God in a vague, disjointed way—God in nature, in the universe, in beauty and creativity. But when pressed to accept a label, she called herself an agnostic. Years ago, as a young teen, she had abandoned the church and had never felt a need to return. And yet now here she was, dressing to go out to dinner with a *preacher*!

"So how come this date got postponed twice?" Rae asked. "Weren't you supposed to go out with him the week after spring break?"

Delta shrugged. "He had some kind of emergency—somebody in the hospital, I think. That was the first time. The second was—well, I forget." She searched under the bed for her black shoes. "I've actually picked up the phone three times this week to cancel. But what reason could I possibly give?"

"You could tell him Satan called with a better offer."

Delta pulled her head out from under the bed and scowled at Rae Dawn. "Very funny." She slipped into her shoes and twirled in front of the mirror. "How do I look?"

"A little bit like the Salvation Army lady."

"Perfect." Delta grabbed her purse and headed for the door.

"I MADE RESERVATIONS at the Boathouse," Rankin said as he held the passenger door open for her. "Steaks, seafood, that kind of thing. Hope it's all right."

He was wearing khakis, a pale blue denim shirt, and a burgundy tie. Very handsome, Delta thought. He had even trimmed his hair and beard.

She hoisted herself into the seat of the Volkswagen van, which turned out to be quite a challenge in three-inch heels. She could have used a stepstool—or a crane. "Sounds lovely," she panted when at last she was settled. "Is it on a lake?"

"Not exactly. It's a renovated warehouse, and to be perfectly honest, I don't think there's a lake—or a boat—within a hundred miles of the place." He laughed. "But I do believe there's a really big pothole in the parking lot."

"So, what's with the van?" Delta asked as they drove. "A holdover from your hippie days?"

He craned his neck and grinned at her. "What makes you think I was a hippie?"

"First impressions when I met you at the protest," she said. "You know, long hair, beard, jeans. Now the van. And—" She tilted her head. "Your ear is pierced. I can see the hole."

"Very observant. I did spend some time in San Francisco—in fact, I went to seminary in Berkeley—Pacific School of Religion. The van comes in handy for carting youth groups around. As for the pierced ear—" He shrugged and flushed pink. "The beard is enough of a stretch for my parishioners. I don't think I'll challenge them with an earring just yet."

They arrived at the restaurant and were ushered to a small table in a corner, away from the traffic flow. On the drive over in the van, Delta had felt relatively comfortable with him. But now that they were sitting face to face, all her misgivings came rushing back. She barricaded herself behind the menu and came out only after the waiter had taken their orders and pried the leather-bound folder from her grip. Suddenly she felt naked, exposed, vulnerable.

If Rankin was aware of her discomfort, he gave no indication. He smiled at her, his eyes warmed by the candlelight. "Nice restaurant," he said. "I've never been here before. I'll have to remember to thank Frankie."

Delta stared at him. "Frankie?" she repeated stupidly. "You mean Dr. Bowen?"

"Yes. She recommended this place."

"You *know* her?"

"Of course I do. I was at the protest when they wanted to fire her and Suze, remember?"

"Well, yes, I remember. I just thought that was—I don't know, part of the job."

Rankin grinned. "You haven't been to church in a while, have you?"

Delta felt her neck grow warm. "Not exactly. Why do you ask?"

"Because most pastors wouldn't consider advocating for gay rights as part of the job."

The waiter arrived with a bottle of Chardonnay and presented it to Rankin for his inspection.

"You ordered wine?" Delta asked. She had been so absorbed in hiding behind the menu that she hadn't noticed.

"Is there a problem? White with shrimp, isn't it?" He tasted the wine and nodded to the waiter, who poured a glass for each of them and disappeared. Rankin held up his glass, and the pale liquid sparkled in the candlelight. "To—" He paused, thinking, then smiled at her. "To the future." He lifted the glass to take a sip, but it sloshed onto his beard and dripped down his tie. "Damn!" he said, grabbing his napkin and blotting at the stain.

Delta snorted wine out her nose, and barely got her own napkin to her face in time to save herself from utter humiliation.

He finished mopping up and sat back in his chair. "I'm delighted to be such a source of amusement."

"It's not the wine," Delta said when she had regained her composure. "It's *you*."

"Oh, that makes me feel better."

She tried unsuccessfully to suppress another laugh. "I was really nervous to go out with you," she said at last. "I mean, you're a *minister*. I was afraid I'd do something stupid or say something offensive. But here you are, pouring wine down your tie and swearing."

He flushed an appealing shade of pink. "And that's a good thing?"

"It's a *very* good thing," Delta said. "You're not like any minister I've ever met."

"I'll take that as a compliment," he said. "For the sake of my poor battered self-esteem."

"It *is* a compliment. I should have known you were different when you showed up to support Bowen and Hart. But you were—well, so *impressive* that day."

"And rather unimpressive tonight," he supplied with a self-deprecating laugh.

"More human," Delta said. "More approachable."

That first dinner lasted nearly four hours. They talked about music and literature, about the uproar over Bowen and Hart (who, as it turned out, were faithful and active members of Rankin's church). When they finally did get around to talking about religion, it was Delta who raised the question, and his answer wasn't at all what she expected.

"Why did you become a minister?" she asked over key lime pie and coffee.

He thought for a moment, toyed with his pie, sipped at his coffee. "I grew up in a home that was nominally Christian but functionally atheist," he began at last. "I was baptized, taken to Sunday school when I was little, forced to endure confirmation class. But my parents never attended church, never talked about spiritual things. Never lived as if God existed, or as if that divine existence made any difference."

"Sounds pretty familiar," Delta said.

"By the time I went to college, I had rejected the whole thing as a boatload of hypocrisy. I was proud of being an atheist—it made me feel morally and intellectually superior to all those mindless sheep still claiming to believe in an invisible god."

His eyes kindled with an inner fire as he warmed to the subject. Delta leaned forward, unable to break his gaze. "So what happened?"

"I wasn't very good at it—being an atheist, I mean." He grinned and ducked his head. "I kept seeing things all around me—the beauty of nature, the goodness of the human soul, the excitement of intellectual challenge—all of which pointed me to something beyond myself."

"You're talking pantheism. God in the natural world—like Wordsworth."

"Not pantheism. Pan*en*theism. God present in all things. Separate and differentiated from created life, and yet present. The experience is difficult to explain, but once I acknowledged the possibility, I realized I had often felt God's presence.

"It wasn't a Damascus Road conversion, by any means," he went on. "More like a slow and arduous journey toward the light. By the time I finished college, I was hooked on the search."

"The search for God, you mean? But you must have found

what you were looking for, if you became a minister." Delta bit her lip, debating whether to be completely honest with him. Then she took a deep breath and said, "I'm an agnostic. I hope that doesn't offend you."

Rankin chuckled. "Agnostic. Interesting word. *Gnostic,* to know. Agnostic literally means 'not knowing.' By that definition, I too am an agnostic. A Christian agnostic."

Delta gaped at him. "But doesn't your religion tell you what you need to know? Doesn't the Bible specify what you need to believe?"

"The Bible gives me glimpses of God, hints of truth. But truth is not a treasure to be found and possessed. Perhaps the biggest heresy in the life of faith is the myth of certainty. Faith is not about knowing, about being sure. Faith is about seeking God, and continuing to seek. It's the doubts and questions and uncertainties that fuel my ongoing search for God."

He finished his pie and accepted a refill of coffee from the waiter. Slowly he stirred it, watching as the spoon created a tiny maelstrom in the center of his cup. "Tell me about this God you don't believe in," he said quietly.

Here it comes, Delta thought. *The sales pitch.*

But to her surprise it never came. He listened intently, respectfully, as she painted a picture of the God she had encountered as a child—an ancient gray-haired divinity who saw all and knew all and loomed overhead waiting to smite anyone who stepped out of line.

"Like Santa Claus without the presents," Rankin said. *"He knows if you've been bad or good—"*

"So be good, for goodness sake," Delta finished with a laugh. "I never thought about it quite like that."

"A God who lays down rules we can't possibly keep and then punishes us for violating them."

Delta nodded. "Right."

Rankin went on. "And then this demanding God further demands that we believe the incomprehensible without wavering, or we're slapped down for doubting as well."

"Yes."

He arched his eyebrows. "If that was my definition of God, I'd still be an atheist."

"But isn't that *everyone's* definition of God? And isn't your job as a preacher to get people to believe in him?"

"My job isn't to sell religion the way you sell a used car," Rankin replied. "My job—my *calling*—is to help people find their own paths. To do justice, to love mercy, to walk humbly with God. God is the ultimate mystery of life, the joyful darkness that lies beyond the edges of our sight. I hold to only one definition of God, and it can be summed up in a single word: love."

"So how did you know you had been . . . called?" Delta asked.

Rankin smiled. "I rejected the myth of certainty and embraced the mystery," he said. "It felt like driving on a country road with all the windows down. Like standing at the ocean at sunrise."

Delta gazed at him. "Like leaving home and coming home all at the same time?"

"Yes," he said. "Exactly like that."

TWENTY-SEVEN

The Minister's Wife

Despite her initial misgivings, Delta felt drawn to Rankin Ballou. Magnetized. Theoretically, she didn't believe in love at first sight, yet she had never imagined so much as a glimmer of what she experienced when she looked into this man's eyes. A feeling of rightness, a sense of destiny. It both elated and terrified her.

On so many levels, they connected. She believed she could be with him forever and never be bored, never feel like she had settled for less.

This was exactly what she had dreamed of. Still, the specter of her parents' divorce hung over her like a shroud. How could you ever know, really know, what the future might hold? How could you be certain?

Rankin would say it was a matter of faith.

But faith, when Delta tried to grasp it, slipped through her fingers like oil.

June 1973

They married on the summer solstice, outdoors in the sunshine, the year she finished her master's and turned twenty-three. Rankin was almost thirty-three, established in his life's purpose, certain about his call.

Delta didn't fully understand his sense of mission and hated the idea of moving around from church to church, but she thoroughly enjoyed the philosophical and spiritual discussions their relationship generated. He introduced her to theologians and mystics—Julian of Norwich and Teresa of Avila and the Desert Fathers and Mothers, whom he called the Abbas and Ammas. She gave him Donne and Herbert and Milton, Yeats and Auden and T. S. Eliot. He never talked down to her, never pretended to have all the answers. And yet . . .

And yet she always felt something lacking, a spiritual center he clearly possessed and she could never seem to find.

At first she tried to convince herself it didn't matter, that her identity lay in herself, not in her role as a pastor's wife. But she soon discovered a level of expectation she hadn't anticipated. Only a few members of the congregation openly criticized her for pursuing her education rather than staying home, and they kept silent once Rankin made clear his support of her. Yet the subterranean rumblings continued. Why wouldn't she organize a women's Bible study? Why hadn't she taken the lead in the Ladies' Aid? And why did she bring the same tuna casserole to every blessed potluck dinner?

The external disapproval hounded Delta, but even more the accusations of her own mind and heart.

Until she met Grandma Mitchell.

Three years into their marriage, Rankin received a call from a church in Asheville, North Carolina. Delta was halfway through her Ph.D. and had been offered an instructorship at the W. It was only an entry-level position, teaching grunt classes like freshman composition and survey of English lit, but it was her first job offer, and she loathed having to turn it down.

Intellectually, she knew that her relationship with Rankin was first priority, worth whatever rootlessness she had to endure. But emotionally, she left the college like Lot's wife abandoning Sodom, dragging her heels and looking over her shoulder, salting the way with tears of grief and resentment.

She hadn't reckoned on the grace of Gladys Elizabeth Mitchell.

They had been in Asheville less than a year when old Mrs. Mitchell first came to live with her grandson Clay and his wife, Hannah. She had just turned ninety, and her declining health prevented her from coming to church. As soon as she was settled in, Rankin made a pastoral call, and Delta went along

She had expected a frail, elderly lady whose interests ran to crocheted doilies and scrapbook photos. Instead she walked into the room to find a beady-eyed crone sitting bolt upright in her wheelchair, pointing a bony, clawlike finger into Rankin's face.

"Sit down, Sonny Boy," she commanded, taking charge of the meeting without so much as an introduction. "And you too, girl. We need to talk."

They sat.

Gladys wheeled herself over until her knees nearly touched Rankin's. "So you're the preacher my grandson has been telling me about." She looked him up and down with a critical eye. "Tell me, what exactly do you believe?"

Delta watched Rankin's face. She didn't know quite what Mrs. Mitchell expected, but she was pretty certain a ninety-year-old woman would not cater to a liberal-thinking, justice-minded minister who stood in stark opposition to the conservative perspectives most people in the South clung to. How would he cushion the truth so that she wouldn't be offended?

The old lady saved him the trouble. "You stand up for the rights of Negroes, I hear."

"Ah, yes, ma'am."

"Ever been arrested?"

Rankin quailed visibly under her unflinching scrutiny. "Well, ah, yes, ma'am, I have, but it was—"

She interrupted him before he could finish. "My granddaughter-in-law Hannah is a member of your ministry council. I take that as an indication you don't agree with the biblical injunction against women speaking in the church."

Rattled by this inquisition, he hedged again. "Well, Mrs. Mitchell, there are various interpretations—"

"For God's sake, Sonny Boy!" she screeched. "Get a backbone! Whatever you stand up for, stand up for it, and don't let anyone push you around, least of all a mule-headed intractable old broad like me."

Delta suppressed a laugh and did her best imitation of a supportive wife. Never in his life had Rankin Ballou been called spineless. More times than she could count, he had been arrested at civil rights protests and antiwar rallies. He had always put himself on the line, had risked himself for the causes he espoused. It was part of his calling.

But this old woman had nailed him. Stunned into speechlessness, he stared at her. Then, after a moment or two, he said, "Forgive me, ma'am. I was trying to be considerate of your perspectives."

For the first time she smiled, and her face softened into a lattice of wrinkles. "Never judge perspectives by appearance," she said. "In 1917 I went to jail with Margaret Sanger over the issue of birth control. In 1920 I stood on the steps of the Capitol lobbying for the ratification of the Nineteenth Amendment. In 1923 I helped draft the equal rights amendment proposed by the National Woman's Party. In the sixties I campaigned for the passing of the Civil Rights Act. I was over eighty years old, and my children and grandchildren thought I was out of my mind." She gazed placidly at him. "I can assure you I was never more sane."

Delta looked at her, then slanted a glance at Rankin. She could almost see his internal battle. Caught in the web of his preconceived notions—his assumptions, his *prejudices*—he struggled to free himself, to find the words to make amends.

Again the old woman helped him. "All those years on the front lines," she said, "all those decades of fighting for justice, and rarely did the church step forward to help. Now the time has come to pass the torch, and I'm wondering—what do you intend to do about it? What's your plan, Sonny Boy, to make the world a different place?"

He considered her question carefully before answering. "We're going to affirm the essential worth of all people," he said at last. "We're going to shout at the top of our lungs until everyone has a voice. We're going to say 'No' to images of God that are violent and cruel and judgmental."

As he spoke, Delta could see a change coming over him. She could feel his conviction swelling in his words until renewed passion swept over him like high tide. "We're going to overturn the moneychangers in the temple and make sure the widows and orphans get more than the crumbs that fall underneath the table. We're going to redefine what it means to be a Christian."

"About damn time," she murmured. "Jesus would turn over in his grave if he could see what has been done in his name."

The image, so outrageously irreverent, hit Delta full in the gut, and she let out a bark of a laugh. The old woman winked at her and laughed too—not the harsh croaking laugh of an ancient crone, but a young, vibrant sound like chapel bells ringing on the night air. Then she turned and fixed Delta with her beady eye.

"And what about you, girl?"

Delta faltered. "What about me?"

"I hear tell you're not much of a preacher's wife."

Delta fought back the temptation to make excuses for herself. Instead, she looked Mrs. Mitchell square in the eye and responded, "That's probably right."

Rankin opened his mouth to defend her, but she waved him off. "I know a lot more about literature than I do about the Bible," Delta went on. "I don't play the piano or teach Sunday school. I'm not much of a cook. I'm not much of a Christian either, if you get right down to it. I guess you'd call me a seeker."

The old woman narrowed her eyes. "What is it exactly you're seeking?"

"My own path," Delta responded after a moment's thought. "My own experience of God's presence. I suppose you'd say I have a lot more questions than answers."

Mrs. Mitchell grinned broadly, showing a gold-capped tooth. "I'd be interested in hearing those questions someday, if you'd care to spend a little time with a crusty old hag like me."

Delta nodded. "I'd like that. I'd like that a lot."

The woman leaned forward and patted her hand, then turned toward Rankin again. "You got a cigarette?"

Rankin stared at her. "No, ma'am. I don't smoke. But, Mrs. Mitchell, do you really think you should—"

"Call me Grandma," she said. "Mrs. Mitchell was my mother-in-law, and I'd rather not go to my reward with *that* picture in my mind." She arched an eyebrow. "What, you think a cigarette or two is going to kill me? For God's sake, boy, I'm ninety years old. I'm living on borrowed time as it is."

"Yes, ma'am," he said meekly.

"Camels," she ordered. "Unfiltered. Bring 'em with you next time you come, along with those wafers and wine."

TWENTY-EIGHT

Going Out and Coming In

Asheville, North Carolina
Spring 1976

In Grandma Mitchell, Delta found both a willing ear and a compassionate heart. And more. Much more. For almost two years she had been going every week to visit, and every time she came away feeling as if she had knelt at the feet of the oracle. A visionary who helped her shape her own vision.

"I love Rankin," Delta confessed one afternoon. "And I love being married to him. But I still don't think I'm cut out for this pastor's wife thing."

The old woman had transferred herself to a porch chair and now sat there rocking and smoking her Camels. "Those old biddies still giving you hell?"

Delta shrugged. "A few. I've learned to turn a deaf ear, for the most part. But that's not the real issue. This is not about running bake sales and chairing the Ladies' Aid. It's about me. My faith—or lack of it. People expect me to be some kind of expert." She sighed. "I used to say I didn't believe in God. Now the most I can say is that I don't understand God."

Grandma Mitchell leaned back in the rocker and puffed on her cigarette. "One of the great forbidden pleasures in life." She sighed. "How old are you, girl?"

"Twenty-eight. Almost twenty-nine."

"And how long have you and Rankin been married?"

"Six years in June."

Grandma Mitchell smoked some more and rocked some more. Delta waited in silence. Patience, she had learned, brought its own rewards. Despite the old woman's crusty exterior, she harbored a deep well of wisdom and a fiery spirit.

"I've lived ninety-three years on this earth," Grandma said at last. "And they've been full years too. I haven't wasted a lot of time on trivialities. And yet I can't shake the feeling that if I lived another ninety, I'd still go out with unanswered questions and an unfinished faith." She stopped rocking and fixed her watery blue eyes on Delta's. "Where do you find glimpses of this God you don't understand?"

Delta thought about this for a minute. "In nature. In poetry. In people. In Rankin's love for me." She averted her eyes. "In you."

She half expected this last declaration to draw a protest, but instead the old woman just laughed. "And where else?"

"Well, in some of the stories from the Bible, I suppose. Rankin and I always discuss the texts he's going to preach on each week. Some of them, frankly, baffle me, but I see images of the divine there too. Jacob wrestling with God, for example. That's a metaphor I can get my mind around—wrestling with an invisible foe and holding on for the light."

"That's one of my favorites too. Just remember that even after the dawn comes, the wrestling never ends." She smiled, and the web of wrinkles deepened. "You're young, my girl. Too young to realize that faith is the work of a lifetime."

"But some people seem so *sure!*" Delta protested.

"The problem with being sure," the old woman said, "is that you quit seeking. You quit growing. Life gives us two choices: change or die. My best advice is not to die until you're dead."

September 1976

Delta sat upright in the hospital bed and gazed down at the curve of the baby's cheek, the delicate lashes, the soft sucking motions as she nursed. A ripple of pleasure coursed through her as her newborn daughter's mouth worked the nipple, an unexpected arousal.

How could it be that all the mysteries of the universe were wrapped up in such a small package? Here, in this defenseless infant, lay the ultimate metaphor. Incarnation. Resurrection. Divine made human, and human become divine. The face of God, the Creator's touch and breath, a new world burst forth from the womb of the Holy.

Delta's own journey of faith might be a work in progress, a labyrinth of intellectual and emotional and spiritual questions, a seeker's way. But as she held the weight and warmth of her tiny daughter and fed her from her own body, she knew that one truth stood firm when everything else was shaken: God had a name, and that name was love.

The hospital room door opened slightly, and Rankin's grinning face poked through the crack. "Daddy's home."

Delta laughed and motioned him in. He looked handsome and formal in a black clerical shirt with black slacks and a gray tweed jacket. Just briefly, she wondered what the occasion was.

He usually wore khakis to the office and rarely donned clerical garb except on special occasions. Now she found herself wishing he would wear a collar all the time. She found it oddly stimulating.

He moved closer to the bed. "How's my little Sugar?"

Delta rolled her eyes. What was it about men and their penchant for nicknames? Rankin Ballou would be thirty-nine this year, and to all appearances an intelligent, mature, sensible man. But the moment their daughter had emerged from the womb, he had taken that round, wide-eyed baby girl in his arms, stroked her fine fuzz of white-blonde hair, and dubbed her "my little sugar pot."

The child would no doubt be called Sugar until her dying day, but her given name was Mary Elizabeth. Delta knew the exact date and time of the conception—a rainy afternoon in December, the fourth Sunday of Advent, during halftime of the football game. The lectionary text for that Sunday was Mary's visit to her elderly cousin Elizabeth after the annunciation. Rankin had backed up and told the story of the old priest Zechariah, Elizabeth's husband, visited by the angel of God in the temple and told he was going to have a son. In the face of the impending miracle, the old man had been rendered speechless.

Perhaps men were always struck dumb by the mysteries of birth, Delta thought. Or maybe just struck stupid, so that they insisted on saddling their offspring with idiotic nicknames that stuck with them forever.

But she wasn't really annoyed with Rankin. How could she be, when he was the answer to every prayer she never dared to pray?

Faith, Grandma Mitchell insisted, was the journey of a lifetime. Certainty was a myth. The wrestling would go on forever. And yet as Delta glanced back over the past seven years, she could make out the faint outline of a serpentine path, drawing her on to where she was meant to be. She might not be able to see beyond the turns ahead, but she had become convinced that, in Dame Julian's words, "All shall be well, and all shall be well, all manner of thing shall be well." And if she'd ever needed evidence of the wellness of all things, she only had to look down, for she held the proof in her arms.

THE BABY HAD FALLEN ASLEEP, and Rankin took her, cradling her against his chest. "I'm afraid I have some bad news," he said quietly. "Grandma Mitchell died."

A cold emptiness rushed into Delta, a winter blast through an unseen crevice. "No!"

"I'm afraid so."

"How? And when?"

He edged onto the bed next to her. "The night before last, while you were in labor. Her heart gave out, apparently. She died peacefully in her sleep. I'm on my way over to Clay and Hannah's now."

"When's the funeral? I want to go."

"A couple of days, maybe three. The family's coming in tonight and tomorrow."

"I'll be out of the hospital tomorrow."

Rankin stroked an errant lock of hair out of her eyes. "Sweetheart, it's too soon—"

"I feel fine. I'm going, Rankin, and I don't want to argue about it. I need to say good-bye."

He nodded. "All right. I know how much you loved her. Death was a release for her, I'm certain. But it will be a loss for the rest of us. I'll give your condolences to the family."

He kissed her—twice—and left her alone with the baby, and with her grief.

THE GATHERING at the funeral home felt more like a church coffee hour than a visitation. Delta recognized almost everyone except for five or six people gathered around Clay and Hannah Mitchell, whom she assumed to be their extended family.

Few of the church members knew the deceased, as she had been homebound. And yet half the congregation seemed to be there, not so much out of personal sorrow but out of loyalty. Clay and Hannah had been members of the church long before Rankin had come to be their pastor.

As if some invisible cue had been given, the hubbub died down and all eyes turned in their direction the moment Delta and Rankin walked through the door. Clay made his way through the milling crowd. "Delta! I didn't really expect you, but thanks for coming. Grandma would have wanted you here."

"I'm so sorry, Clay," she said. "I'll miss her so much."

Clay bent down over the blanket-wrapped bundle Delta held in her arms. Unshed tears glistened in his eyes. "So this is the new one. She's beautiful, Delta. I wish Grandma had lived to see her."

"Six pounds seven ounces," Rankin said, beaming over Clay's shoulder. "Her name's Mary Elizabeth—I call her Sugar."

Clay ran a hand through his hair. "The cycle of death and life," he mused. "I wonder if it's true, that when one person dies as another is being born, part of the dying person's soul remains with the newborn."

Delta smiled. "I devoutly hope so," she said. "If a bit of your grandmother slips into our daughter, she will grow up to be a very fortunate woman indeed."

Clay turned to Rankin, drew him into a hug, and held him there for a minute. "Grandma was ready to go, but still we're going to miss her."

"So will we." Rankin nodded. "I'll come by the house later and we can finish up details for the funeral." He gripped Clay's forearm and looked into his eyes. "You guys doing all right? You know, food and all that?"

Clay barked out a laugh. "Lord, yes. Vinca Hollowell's inundated us with so many casseroles that we'll need to buy a second freezer. I suppose you'll be getting some of Vinca's lasagna too."

Clay moved back to his family, and Delta and Rankin began to thread their way across the room, greeting people with hugs and handshakes as they went. Everyone stopped them, wanting to *ooh* and *ahh* over the baby.

At last they got to Vinca Hollowell. Vinca was the chair of the social committee, a rotund little woman with bright darting eyes, a tireless worker. She squeezed Delta's hand and congratulated her on the baby, promising that someone would come by the parsonage in the morning to bring food.

"We're fine, Vinca," Rankin assured her. "Delta and I can fend for ourselves. Don't kill yourself trying to get everything done all at once."

"Nonsense, Pastor," she said, fidgeting with his lapel and brushing an imaginary piece of lint off his shoulder. "I just—well, you know. I like for things to be done right."

"And you always do them beautifully, Vinca." Rankin smiled down at her. "Once we get the baby settled into a routine at home, I'd like to come visit you."

Vinca gave a quick glance at Delta, and she saw a shadow move behind the woman's eyes. "Well, I—that is—you know, my husband, Ham, he's not a churchgoing man, and he doesn't like to have—" She paused. "I'll come to the church instead, all right? I'll call you next week. See you at the funeral, Pastor." And she was gone, flitting with surprising speed back toward the refreshment table.

"Are you all right?" Rankin said when Vinca had disappeared into the crowd. "You look tired."

"I'm fine. You go do your pastor thing. I want to pay my respects to Grandma, and in a few minutes you can take me home."

He bent down and kissed her on the cheek. "Okay. But don't stay too long."

NEAR THE OPEN CASKET the scent of lilies nearly overwhelmed her. The smell reminded her of Easter, of resurrection, of hope and a new beginning. She gazed down at the face of Gladys Mitchell, serene in death as she had never been in life. No one—not Clay, not even Rankin—could ever comprehend what this woman had meant to Delta.

On the way in, Delta had overheard someone describe Grandma Mitchell as "that sweet old lady," but it was hardly an accurate portrayal. The woman was an institution, a matriarch—by her own admission a "mule-headed intractable old broad."

Delta stared at the emaciated body. How could such a frail shell contain that flaming spirit and not be burned to ash? She had given Delta so much—wisdom, enlightenment, a sense of direction. And now that bright soul was extinguished.

She heard the old woman's words echo in her mind:

Faith is the work of a lifetime. . . . Life gives us two choices: change or die. My best advice is not to die until you're dead.

Delta gazed down on the lifeless face in the coffin and cuddled the sleeping newborn close to her breast. "This woman," she whispered to her infant daughter, "is the wisest person I know. She gave me permission to seek, to grow, to wrestle, and to change. I'll do my best to pass those lessons on to you."

Then she reached with one hand and felt inside her purse to find half a pack of Camels still there.

No one was looking. She palmed the pack and slipped it under the satin pillow.

TWENTY-NINE

The Ghost of Christmas Yet to Come

December 1977

Delta sat cross-legged on the hardwood floor of the living room and considered the huge box in front of her—a dollhouse for Sugar, lovingly crafted by her doting grandfather. She had just enough of the Snoopy wrapping paper left, she thought, to go around three sides of the cardboard box. She could make it work.

From the hallway, she heard a commotion, a high-pitched shriek. Fifteen-month-old Sugar hurtled unsteadily into the room, fresh from her bath and stark naked. Hot on her heels was Nanny, the six-month-old golden retriever puppy.

Nanny had been Rankin's idea. Every child needed to grow up with a dog, he insisted. And the truth was, Nanny and Sugar adored each other. The dog was sweet-tempered and patient, if not the brightest star in the firmament.

"Twee!" Sugar yelled with delight. She headed straight for the Christmas tree, grabbed a light string, and began to pull.

Delta lurched to her feet in time to save the Christmas tree, but just as she scooped her daughter up in her arms and turned, she caught a glimpse of Nanny, squatting her golden haunches directly over the Snoopy paper laid out on the floor.

"Nanny, no!" she yelled. "Rankin!"

Rankin appeared in the doorway with a towel thrown over his shoulder and a diaper dangling from one hand. But too late. Nanny had already left a wide puddle square in the middle of the wrapping paper.

He shrugged and grinned. "At least she went on the paper. That's progress."

Delta glared at him. "Very funny."

"I'll take her outside. Leave the mess. I'll clean it up in a minute."

Sugar was squirming to get down, flailing her pudgy arms. Delta set her on the floor and reconsidered the large cardboard box, wondering where on earth she would find enough paper to wrap it now.

Her back was turned only a second or two, but it was enough.

"Peeee!" Sugar squealed. "Nanny peeee!"

Delta wheeled around to see Sugar squatting on the paper, peeing in exactly the same spot Nanny had chosen, and puddling her hands in the mess.

"Shit," she groaned.

Sugar looked up. "Sit," she repeated with a wide smile.

Rankin chose that moment to return. With a single glance he took in the situation, then began to laugh.

"Yeah, it's hilarious," Delta said, shooting daggers at him. "You take her back to the bath, and I'll clean up the paper."

Rankin scooped up their daughter and, holding her dripping at arm's length, dashed for the bathroom.

Delta had finally learned to cook. The parsonage kitchen emanated the smells of Christmas—turkey roasting in the oven, apple and pumpkin pies cooling on the counter, cornbread dressing awaiting its turn in the oven. Cinnamon and sage and allspice. On the stereo Bing Crosby was singing "White Christmas."

Delta opened the oven door and inhaled the fragrance as she squeezed drippings from the baster over the sizzling bird. Perfect. Another hour, and it would be done, right on time. At two, the guests would start to arrive—members of the congregation who had no family, nowhere else to go. Millicent and Stella, widows whose grown children lived in California and Florida. Ron and Edie, newly married. Walter, whose divorce had just been finalized and whose two sons would be with their mother for Christmas. Libby and Sandra, whose parents had rejected them. James, the homeless man who sat in the back row at church every Sunday. Rankin referred to him as "James the Brother of Jesus." He always went away with a huge bag of leftovers to share with his friends on the streets.

It was a grand custom, Delta thought, this gathering of the outcasts. Since their first year in Asheville, she and Rankin had hosted this traditional Christmas dinner, and although the guest list changed from year to year, it always proved to be a time of great joy and gratitude. Exactly the kind of Christmas celebration, Rankin said, that God would have planned. Plenty of room in the inn.

In the breakfast nook Sugar napped in her playpen with Nanny dozing on the floor beside her. Delta watched her daughter for a moment, her cheeks flushed pink with sleep, a delicate line of silver drool at one corner of her mouth. Her pudgy baby hands closed and opened again, grasping at some bright plaything in her dreams.

A warmth filled Delta—a radiance that had nothing to do with Christmas. But then again, perhaps it had everything to do with Christmas. Maybe every birth was an incarnation.

She leaned down to slide the turkey back into the oven, and as she did so she bumped butts with Rankin, who stood opposite her in the narrow kitchen. She gave a little laugh and turned.

Her face was flushed from the heat of the oven, the front of her blouse dusted with flour. Yet the expression on his face told her he had never seen anyone as beautiful in his life. He gazed at her, and his eyes went soft and liquid.

"Care to dance?" Rankin held out his arms and she came to him, flour and all. They waltzed around the cramped kitchen in a rhythmic embrace and he kissed her while Bing sang softly in the background.

Just as the dance might have developed into something else—something neither of them had time for, given that Millie and Stella would probably get there half an hour early—the telephone rang.

"I'll get it." Delta lunged for the kitchen phone. Sugar stirred in her sleep but did not wake, and she breathed a sigh of relief. She picked up the receiver. "Merry Christmas."

"Delta?" a tentative voice said. "I'm sorry to bother you on Christmas day. This is Vinca Hollowell."

"It's no bother, Vinca." This wasn't the complete truth, of course—the dinner was half done and time was slipping away. But Delta didn't say so.

"I—ah, as I said, I'm sorry to bother you, but—" She hesitated. Delta heard something in her voice, an edge of desperation. "I didn't know who else to call."

"What's wrong, Vinca?"

"It's Ham. He's—he's been drinking. Again."

"Is he there?"

"Yes. It was all my fault. I burned the turkey roast, you see, and—"

Delta closed her eyes and prayed for wisdom, not to mention patience. Hamlin Hollowell was a nasty drunk, a cruel man who apparently delighted in making Vinca's life miserable. Through sheer repetition he had her convinced that she was worthless, even though she was as close to a saint as anyone Delta had ever met.

In the background behind Vinca's sniffling Delta heard a crash. "What's happening?"

"He's breaking up the kitchen," she admitted. "Throwing stuff, dishes and the like."

"Has he hurt you?"

"Oh, no, he would never—" Another crash, and Vinca broke into sobs.

"Vinca, go outside. Never mind Ham, just get out of the way. We'll be there in ten minutes."

Delta hung up the telephone and gave Rankin a thirty-second summary of what was going on.

"You stay here. I'll go get her."

This was the part of a pastor's life Delta hated most. Not the interruption of schedules—she was used to that by now. But the realization that Rankin could at any moment walk into a situation that could get nasty in a heartbeat.

She couldn't have stopped him from going even if she had wanted to. This was who Rankin was, what he was called to do. Being a minister—at least according to Rankin's definition—was not just about preaching on Sunday mornings, marrying and burying and visiting people in the hospital. It was about standing up for those who couldn't fend for themselves. About justice. About showing mercy, even in the midst of risk.

Delta might not be a pastor, but she understood that sense of call. How many times had she faced down racists and hostile policemen at voter registration rallies? How many times had the Delta Belles continued to sing in the midst of booing and jeers and shouting? Still, she couldn't help worrying when Rankin went off into what might turn into a volatile situation.

"Get Sugar's blanket," she said. "The turkey will keep. I'm going with you."

RANKIN DROVE A LITTLE too fast, snaking around the mountain roads on his way to Vinca's house. Once he nearly missed a curve, sliding sideways onto the shoulder.

"You won't do anyone any good if you kill us all getting there," Delta muttered grimly.

He took his foot off the gas.

Grandma Mitchell had once warned Delta about Vinca. "Keep an eye on that girl," she had said bluntly. "Her husband's no good."

How Grandma knew this, Delta had no idea, but the old woman knew many things, and when she spoke, Delta listened.

Ham Hollowell was a big burly man, an unemployed construction worker with beefy arms and a protruding belly and red spider veins spreading across his cheeks from a lifetime love affair with liquor. Hollowell had been laid off, Delta knew, after sustaining an injury to his back, and had sued the company for worker's compensation but never collected. Vinca hadn't said why. Delta suspected the man might have been drinking on the job. For the past year Vinca had been supporting them with temp work, and Ham had been drinking up most of what she earned.

Delta had never been told how Vinca and Ham had gotten together, but her imagination had pieced together a story that seemed altogether logical. She could envision a young Ham, masculine and muscular, a man's man whose tastes ran to monster truck rallies and demolition derbies and guzzling a few brewskis with the guys after work. The kind of man who refers to his wife as "the little woman" and whistles at long legs in a short skirt. He might have been handsome in years gone by—a shadow of it still lingered in his strong jaw line and reddish blond hair.

Vinca, small and round and maternal, with bright optimistic eyes that saw the best in everyone, would have been a pushover for a man like Ham. She would have seen the need in him—the need for love, for a wife, for a home. She would have been convinced that faithfulness could change him, that if someone believed in him and loved him, he wouldn't need to drink and swagger so.

Unfortunately, Delta mused, love was not always enough. Not even the most devoted wife could compete when her husband's mistress was alcohol.

They pulled into the gravel driveway of the shambling unpainted house and Delta wondered, just briefly, if the severity of Hollowell's injuries prevented him from keeping up his own place. *"The cobbler's children have no shoes,"* she heard Grandma Mitchell whisper inside her head.

Vinca sat on the lopsided porch steps, clutching a paper grocery sack. When she saw them pull up, she rose and came toward them, casting furtive glances back toward the house.

Delta stayed in the car with the sleeping child on her lap. Rankin got out. "Come on, Vinca," he said. "You'll spend the day with us. Have dinner. We've got plenty."

She thrust the paper bag in his direction. "It's mincemeat pie and corn casserole. For your dinner." She turned as if to go back into the house.

Rankin caught her arm. "No, Vinca. Leave him. Come with us."

Vinca hesitated. The screen door swung open and Ham lurched out onto the porch, reeling drunkenly. "Bitch!" he yelled. "Stupid worthless bitch!"

He lunged toward the edge of the porch, and for just an instant Delta glimpsed a vision of a full-blown attack, with Ham Hollowell bearing down on Rankin intent on breaking bones. Then Hollowell took a step back, swayed, and collapsed into a rusted metal glider.

"He's out now," Vinca said. "He'll sleep it off. I'll be fine. He'll be sorry when he wakes up. He always is."

"Let's go, Vinca," Rankin said again.

She let out an enormous sigh, bit her lip, and followed him to the car. "Thank you, Pastor. I needn't have called, but thank you all the same." She slid into the backseat.

Delta turned and looked into her eyes. Unshed tears pooled there, and an expression of stolid resignation. "You have to leave him, Vinca. You have to keep yourself safe."

She looked up, and the tears fell, sliding down her cheeks in wide tracks. "He'd never hurt me, Delta."

"He hasn't hurt you *yet,* you mean," Delta said. "At least not physically. But what has he done to your spirit, Vinca? To your soul?"

She gulped back the tears. "He loves me—he does, in his own way," she insisted. "And I can't leave him, Delta."

"Why not? You've got plenty of reasons, plenty of justification."

Vinca smiled and patted Delta's shoulder—a gesture that said Delta could never understand, not in a million years. "I'm his wife," she said simply, as if that explained everything. "And he needs me."

Somehow they managed to get through Christmas and New Year's without another incident. But the third week in January, Vinca Hollowell called again. This time Ham *had* hit her—beaten her so badly that she ended up in the emergency room with a broken wrist and three bruised ribs. They kept her overnight for observation, to make sure she showed no signs of internal injuries. At noon the next day he appeared, hung over, disheveled and sheepish, pleading with her to forgive him and swearing it would never happen again.

Rankin and Delta had been at the hospital when Ham arrived. Delta greeted him coldly, without a shred of Christian grace. Her concern was for Vinca's soul, not Hollowell's, for Vinca's battered mind and broken heart, her crippled spirit and pummeled body. Delta gazed at the livid plum-colored bruises across her face and arms, the plaster cast running from fingers to elbow, and could not find it within herself to show mercy to the beast who had inflicted those wounds.

Ham eyed the two of them with suspicion.

"I wanta talk to my wife—alone," he said.

Rankin flicked his eyes from Hollowell's face to Vinca's. She looked at him, entreating, but said nothing. Delta could not tell if she was begging them to stay or go.

"We'll be right outside if you need us," Rankin said, and ushered Delta out of the hospital room.

He stood with his arms crossed and his back to the door. Delta leaned on the wall beside him. With the door ajar, they could hear every word. Vinca silent, sniffling a bit, uttering a little sob or two now and then; Ham by turns gruff and insisting or whiny and beseeching, vowing he'd quit drinking, get a job, straighten up and fly right, demanding that she come home where she belonged.

To her credit, Vinca made no such promise.

When Ham was gone, muttering curses to himself as he stumbled down the hallway toward the elevators, Delta and Rankin reentered the room.

Vinca lay motionless with her eyes closed, the bruising vivid against the stark white pillowcase. Without looking up she said, "I guess you heard all that."

"We weren't trying to eavesdrop," Delta said. It wasn't the whole truth, but she figured God would forgive her such a small prevarication.

"What am I going to do?"

Rankin stepped forward and took her hand. "I think you should press charges," he said. "But that's your decision, Vinca. I can't make it for you."

She sighed and reached for the tissue box on the table next to the bed. Delta saw her wince as her torso twisted. "You've been very patient with me, Pastor. Both of you. You warned me this would happen. I was just too stupid to listen."

Rankin gave a half-smile. "A good pastor never says 'I told you so.' "

"But you did tell me so." She blew her nose and wadded up the tissue. "I've always believed it was a wife's duty to stick by her husband for better or worse," she said quietly. "It's in the Bible."

"A lot of things are in the Bible, Vinca," Rankin replied.

"Slavery, violence, incest, the subjugation of women and children as property. That doesn't mean God condones them."

"So you don't think I have an obligation to stay?"

"We've talked about this before," Rankin said. "No child of God needs to subject herself to such treatment."

Vinca nodded slowly. "But where will I go? What will I do?"

"You'll go to a shelter or a safe house; I'll arrange it. When you're feeling better we can talk about options."

January 1979

Delta sat in the courtroom behind Vinca, listening as Rankin testified against Ham Hollowell. As it turned out, Vinca didn't have to press charges against her husband. While she was still healing in the safe house, Ham had gone on another roaring drunk, attacked a guy in the bar, and left him beaten to a bloody pulp in the parking lot. By the time the police got there, the fellow had gone into a coma and died two days later.

It took a year to get to trial. The prosecutor told them that, given the dozen or so eyewitnesses to the bar fight, there would be no doubt about Ham's conviction. But the case would be infinitely stronger and the sentencing more stringent if they could demonstrate a pattern of violence from a hostile, volatile, unpredictable abuser.

Rankin testified. Ham got fifteen to twenty.

After the sentence was read, Vinca Hollowell sat dry-eyed and stony-faced as her husband was led away in handcuffs. Then she broke down and bawled.

"It's not your fault, Vinca," Delta said helplessly. "Ham did this to himself. You have nothing to feel guilty about."

"It's not guilt," Vinca said between sobs. "It's *relief.*" She heaved a deep breath and got control of herself. "But I do feel a little guilty about feeling so relieved."

Delta laughed, and the tension inside her own chest released. She hadn't known, until that moment, how scared she had been. Scared for Vinca. Scared for Rankin too, and for herself and Sugar.

And now, thank God, it was over.

THIRTY

Broken Bread and Poured-out Wine

April 1994

Early Sunday morning was Delta's favorite time. The sanctuary, not yet filled with milling, chatting parishioners and their energetic children, seemed a hushed and holy place. Morning sunlight filtered through the stained glass and arched across the empty pews in vibrant shapes and colors. Two pots of lilies left from last Sunday's Easter celebration emanated the fragrance of new life throughout the room.

Delta let her eyes take in the brilliant hues, the serenity of the space. She had quarreled with Rankin this morning, over something utterly insignificant, and as a result had come to church stressed and harried. Now the peace of this place worked into her, calming the storms of her inner sea. They would make it up, as they always did. Everything would be fine.

She went into the sacristy, a small room to the left of the

altar, and turned on the light. She took down the rough crockery chalice and paten, laid out the bread, and poured the wine.

In the years they had been here, the church had grown, the faces had changed. But the spirit of the place had remained. Like bread from many grains and wine from crushed grapes, diverse individuals blended together into one. One community. One heart.

Including, much to her own amazement, Delta herself.

She still wasn't quite certain how it had happened. She had learned much from Rankin over the years, certainly. Through him, and in him, she had discovered and embraced an image of God far different from the vindictive and demanding deity of her childhood. But the real beginnings of the change, she believed, went back to Grandma Mitchell and her practical wisdom about faith and life. Somehow in Grandma's acceptance Delta had found permission to be a perpetual seeker. She didn't have to have answers, did not even have to know the right questions. All she needed to do was be open to the mystery, the miracle.

Perhaps it was just this openness that had made the difference. Shortly after Ham Hollowell's trial and conviction, Vinca had come to her and asked if the two of them could meet to talk about faith. Her own trust in God had suffered in the face of Ham's abuse, and Vinca felt that Delta was a person who could understand that struggle without condemning it.

Vinca came. Then Mary Beth, a single woman who desperately wanted to be married. Then Connie, angry with God over her miscarriage. Kathleen, who agonized over her son's problem with alcohol. And Deb, battling the enduring wounds of an emotionally absent mother.

Dozens of women cycled in and out of the group, all asking the same questions in different ways. Where is God? Who is God? How can I trust? What is faith all about?

Delta had no answers, but needed none. The important thing

was to provide a safe place for the questions to be raised and the issues discussed. And if tears fell or voices were raised in anger, nobody got upset.

Gradually, almost without her noticing, Delta's own faith began to take shape. She became aware of a gracious presence that surrounded these women and the way their labyrinthine discussions always worked them back around to God. There was an invisible nucleus here, a force that held them all together. A center that could be trusted.

She mounted the two shallow steps to the altar and set out the elements for communion. The scent of the yeasty loaf and the tang of the grape reached her nostrils, and her heart leaped.

More than any other aspect of worship—more than the music, the scriptures, even more than Rankin's preaching, the sacrament of communion brought the Presence alive. For a long time she hadn't understood the ritual, but gradually the truth dawned on her. This was a palpable experience of connection with God and the community. The center was here. The nucleus. The still point of the ever-changing world.

On occasion Delta had stood with Rankin and served communion, and it was an experience she would never forget. One by one the people came forward, looked into her eyes, heard the words of hope and dipped the bread into the cup. They often sloshed wine onto the hand that held the chalice, and for hours afterward she could feel it, smell it, could touch it to her tongue and taste the grace that had dripped down her fingers. Broken bread and poured-out wine. The loaf of life, the cup of the covenant. The unmistakable flavor of love.

Behind her, she heard the door to the sanctuary creak on its hinges.

"Pastor?"

It was Vinca Hollowell. For years now Vinca had served

as part-time secretary, and although she struggled with the computer and still didn't quite understand the intricacies of the voice mail system, Rankin liked having her around. Fleshier than she had been fifteen years ago, and grayer, she nevertheless exuded a buoyant energy, and she always made Delta smile.

"It's me, Vinca. Rankin's around somewhere."

Vinca nodded. "I just needed to make some last-minute photocopies for the adult Sunday school class. Tell him I'll be in the office if he needs me."

She turned and exited again. Delta heard the front door shut as Vinca headed over to the church offices, on the main floor of the parish house next door.

She finished the communion preparations and went back into the sacristy for the white cloths to cover the bread and chalice. The communion wine was running low; she'd need to remind Vinca to tell the chair of the Altar Guild.

The door between the narthex and sanctuary squeaked again. It was probably Rankin, coming in to get ready for service. She peered out the sacristy door and saw him behind the pulpit, going over his sermon notes.

She stood and watched him for a moment. An apology for her crabbiness this morning could come later. She wouldn't disturb him now.

Then at the edge of her peripheral vision she saw something else—a movement in the shadows, under the overhang of the balcony.

Rankin saw it too, and looked up. "Can I help you?" He glanced at his watch. "Worship isn't until ten thirty. There's Sunday school in the parish hall, starting in about half an hour—"

"Where is she?"

It was a man's voice, and something about it chilled Delta to the core. He stepped out of the shadows into the carpeted center aisle. He looked to be fifty, perhaps, but a very fit fifty, with close-cut gray hair, a broad chest, and muscular forearms. He wore blue jeans and a black T-shirt.

"Excuse me?" Rankin came down from the altar and stood at the base of the steps, where the carpet runner ended in a T with its arms stretching left and right in front of the first row of pews.

The man advanced. Something about him nagged at the back of Delta's mind, as if they had met before, but she couldn't place him.

"I said, where is she? My wife."

The voice. Delta knew that voice. Then the stench wafted toward her—the unmistakable, sickly sweet odor of whiskey—and the bottom dropped out of her stomach.

It was Ham Hollowell. And he had been drinking. In one hand he carried a half-empty bottle of Jack Daniel's. In the other, a tire iron.

"Ham," Rankin said.

"Ah, so you *do* remember," Ham slurred, his lip curling. "You cost me my life, Preacher. Fifteen years and four months of it, give or take a day or two."

"You don't want to do this, Ham," Rankin said, trying to keep his voice calm.

Delta looked about frantically. The sacristy was in the far corner of the sanctuary behind the organ console. There was no way to get out, and no telephone.

"What else have I got to lose?" Hollowell's voice rose and echoed off the vaulted ceiling. "I already lost everything. She divorced me, did you know that? Of course you did. You probably put her up to it. Soon as I got released, I went home. The place is empty and falling down. Now, answer my question. Where is she?"

"She's not here," Rankin said. "Put down the tire iron, Ham, and let's talk about this like reasonable men."

The sanctuary door swung open, and Delta caught a glimpse of Vinca's round red face. She dropped the papers she was holding, and they scattered.

Hollowell turned his head, just slightly.

"Run!" Delta screamed. "Vinca, run! Call the police!"

But Vinca stood frozen, rooted to the spot.

Rankin's head snapped around, and his eyes fixed on Delta. At last Vinca fled.

For a man of his bulk, and in his condition, Ham Hollowell moved with surprising speed. "Goddamn interfering preacher!" he shouted. "I swore if I ever got out—" He lunged and swung the tire iron.

Rankin put up his hands to defend himself. The weapon connected. Blood ran like wine down his useless fingers and dripped onto the carpet. Delta felt the jolt as if in her own body.

The second blow caught Rankin in the side, just under his arm.

"No!" Delta lunged forward, crashed into the organ bench, and went down. As she fell she caught sight of Hollowell—red-eyed, crazed, full of rage and drink, closing in on Rankin. The tire iron rose and fell again as if in slow motion; Delta thought she could hear the crack as a shinbone broke.

"God!" Rankin cried. "God!"

Then the weapon found its mark and sank into his skull.

She scrambled to her feet and dashed toward him, but it was too late.

Sirens screamed. Ham ran for it, out the front doors onto the church porch. But Delta didn't follow.

The sanctuary had gone eerily silent. Across the front pews the stained glass windows split the sun into shards of green and blue and purple. The heavy odor of Easter lilies hovered on the morning air, mixed with the scents of bread and wine.

And all the while Rankin lay motionless at the foot of the altar with his arms outstretched, a pool of red-black blood gathering under his skull.

SEPTEMBER 1994

Delta stared down at the puddle of ketchup on her plate.

How long had she been sitting here, remembering? The Park Bench Tavern had cleared out; only a handful of students still clustered here and there around the dark wooden tables. The remains of her french fries had congealed into a greasy mess.

She pushed the plate to one side.

"Anything else you need?"

Delta blinked and looked up. *Yeah,* she thought. *An angel from on high telling me what I should do with my life.*

The waiter rocked back on his heels and regarded her. The fellow who had served her had been short and dark. This was a skinny blond kid in his twenties with a name tag that read Gabe. Her mouth went dry.

"What happened to the other guy?" she asked.

"He had class at one," the waiter said. "I usually tend bar, but occasionally I pitch in and serve when they need me. I'll be sure he gets his tip." He picked up the plate. "Want some more Diet Coke?"

"That would be great. Thanks."

He disappeared, and a few minutes later set a fresh drink down in front of her. "Are you a student?"

Delta gave an involuntary chuckle. "Me? No. I'm a—" She swallowed down the rest of her answer. "Should I be?"

He shrugged and grinned. "Lots of old folks are coming back to college."

Delta cringed inwardly. *Old folks.* She was not yet fifty, but she supposed she seemed ancient to this twenty-something waiter. "I studied literature," she said. "Got my master's and did some work on my Ph.D. I was planning to be a professor, but—"

"You got married and had kids instead," Gabe supplied.

"Something like that."

"And now you've got an empty nest and don't quite know what to do with yourself."

Delta's mind flashed back to Bowen and Hart, to Rankin, to Grandma Mitchell, to Vinca Hollowell and the others who had gathered to talk about their questions and doubts. "I—I'd just like to be useful. To help people, you know?"

The young blond waiter nodded and laid her check on the table next to the Diet Coke. "You don't need a degree to help people," he said as he turned to go. "Even a bartender can listen."

THIRTY-ONE

The Invisible Hand

New Orleans
September 1994

Rae Dawn DuChamp sat on the empty stage of Maison Dauphine, fiddling with the piano keys. Delta's call—which she had never returned, even though it had been two weeks—had exhumed years of ancient memories, recollections she'd just as soon keep buried.

Why did she torture herself like this? At night, with the lights and the music and the raucous noise of the crowd, the club came alive, and she could almost make herself believe that going on was worth the effort. But in the harsh light of day she could not ignore the scars across the table tops, the stains in the rug. The place seemed vacant and sad, like an old chorus girl without her makeup. Across the silence of midafternoon, she could almost hear voices in the *whoosh* of the air conditioning, ghosts come back to haunt her. *Choices,* the eerie whispers chanted. *Choices, choices. . . .*

Fulfillment, Dr. Gottlieb had told her years ago, was in the choices. You couldn't determine what life handed you—that part of the equation was out of your control. But you could choose what you did with it.

And what, exactly, had she chosen? Two decades ago, in her twenties and full of righteous defiance, she would have said that she chose integrity above all else.

Then her career had rushed upon on her like a freight train on the downslope of a mountain, with all her dreams and aspirations on board. The confluence of work and talent finally paid off. It hadn't been so easy then to choose between success and love.

Nobody had told her that the real challenge in life was not the choice between good and evil, between right and wrong. The real challenge was the decision between good and good, between one dream and another. The real challenge was the fact that, unless you paid close attention, sometimes you made choices without even realizing you had made them until it was too late.

The telephone behind the bar rang, and Nate the bartender answered. "Maison Dauphine." A pause. "Hold on a minute and I'll see if she's here."

He covered the mouthpiece and held the receiver out in her direction. "Phone for you, Rae."

She shook her head. "Whoever it is, tell them I'm not available." She lowered her head over the piano keys and heard Nate murmuring to the caller.

Nate interrupted again. "Remember that call you got a few weeks ago, from a Delta Ballou?"

Rae Dawn sighed. She wasn't ready yet. "Take a number and tell her I'll call her back."

"I already gave you her number," he said. "Besides, it's not her. It's her sister."

A cold premonition slithered through Rae's veins. "It's Delta's *sister*? She wouldn't be calling me unless—"

She went to the bar and snatched up the receiver. Nate made himself discreetly busy washing glasses at the opposite end.

"Rae, this is Cassie," said the low female voice on the line. "I'm Delta's—"

"Her sister," Rae interrupted. "I remember. The little kid who wrote stories and drew pictures of a big rock when we were in college."

A chuckle. "I'd forgotten about that."

"What's wrong?" Rae said impatiently. "She called me several weeks ago and I haven't had a chance to return her call. Is she sick? Is she . . . ?"

"No, she's all right," Cassie assured her. "I mean, well, she is and she isn't."

Rae frowned into the telephone as if Cassie could see her. "You want to explain that?"

"Let me start at the beginning," Cassie said. "You remember Rankin, Delta's husband?"

"The minister. Sure, of course. I haven't seen either of them in years—"

"Rankin's dead, Rae. Murdered, actually. It happened back in April, the week after Easter."

The chill in Rae's veins turned to ice, and for a moment she couldn't speak.

"Are you there, Rae?"

"Yes, I'm here," she managed. "I had no idea, Cassie. She didn't call, didn't write. Nothing."

Rae listened while Cassie related a tale of unspeakable horror, about an abusive husband who took out his rage on the pastor who tried to help his wife. "Delta saw it all," she concluded, "and couldn't do anything to stop it."

"God help us," Rae murmured. "She must be devastated."

"She's putting on a good front," Cassie said, "but she's spinning her wheels. I wouldn't normally interfere—"

Rae ran a hand through her hair. "How can I help?"

"You were her best friend in college. As a pastor's wife, it's been hard for her to make close friends over the years. There are so many boundary issues—not getting too close to parishioners, conflicts of interest, that sort of thing. Rankin was her dearest friend as well as her husband."

"I understand," Rae said, willing her to get to the point. "What do you want me to do?" She paused, and then it hit her. "I get it. The reunion."

"Yes," Cassie said. "This idea of—what was her name?"

"Tabby? Tabitha Austin?"

"That's it. Tabby. She wants to get the Delta Belles together for one last concert. And although Delta's been resistant to the idea—to the entire reunion, actually—I think it could be a turning point for her. It would give her something to focus on besides her anger and grief. And it would be good for her to reconnect with old friends."

"But the reunion is less than a month away," Rae protested.

"I know," Cassie said. "The weekend of the reunion happens to be the six-month anniversary of Rankin's death."

Silence stretched between them—a deliberate silence, Rae felt sure, a silence designed to emphasize the importance of Cassie's request.

"If the three of you say yes," Cassie said at last, "I think you can convince Delta to join you."

Rae hesitated. If she agreed to do this, to go back to the reunion, to play the piano and sing, there was a good chance she would be recognized as Dawn DuChante, the Grammy-nominated torch singer. There would be questions: Why had she quit recording? What happened to her career? Why wasn't she . . . married?

And yet how could she refuse? Delta had been her best friend, had accepted her and believed in her and stood by her at one of the most crucial moments of her life.

"All right," Rae said at last. "I'll contact Lacy and Lauren and see what I can work out."

LACY PUT DOWN THE PHONE and sank onto the sofa next to Hormel, who purred and rubbed his head against her thigh. Rae Dawn had sounded stressed and worried, and after hearing what Delta had gone through with Rankin's death, she understood why. Lacy didn't want to do this, but how could she possibly say no?

Still, a heavy lump formed in her stomach at the idea of getting the Delta Belles back together again. Since she had come home to Hillsborough—almost ten years—only once had she faced Lauren alone. Always she had the buffer of family around her, and as if by mutual consent, she and Lauren had kept things cordially superficial.

Besides, Lacy could tell that Lauren was uncomfortable in her presence. The two of them danced around each other like fire-walkers, forcing themselves across the hot coals and trying desperately not to get burned.

It wasn't an issue of forgiveness. Lacy had forgiven Lauren long ago and was glad to see that somehow Lauren and Trip had stayed together. But all of them put on such well-crafted fronts that she could never see behind the mask enough to know what her twin was really thinking.

Now Lacy had really stepped in it. She had agreed to join

Rae Dawn in reuniting the Delta Belles for their twenty-fifth reunion. She would have to call Lauren and convince her to come, and then once the four of them were together, she would have to face Lauren without the rest of the family as a shield.

She blew out a breath and picked up the phone. Putting it off wouldn't make it any easier. She just had to remember they were doing this for Delta.

DELTA FUMED AND MUTTERED to herself as she packed.

How had she let herself get talked into this? She had never intended to go to this reunion, never expected that any of the other Delta Belles would even consider getting back together. And now, suddenly, they were all gung-ho about it, and Rae Dawn had talked her into committing to the insane notion as well.

Rae had been extremely persuasive, Delta had to admit. But it wasn't the persuasion that had won her over. It was the shadow behind Rae Dawn's voice.

Rae hadn't wasted any time in small talk but got straight to the point. She and Lacy and Lauren wanted to do the reunion concert, she said, and thought it would be fun to get them all together. Rae had even called Tabitha Austin to make sure she could still get them on the program for the anniversary banquet. Tabby, of course, had been thrilled.

The reunion was Friday night through Sunday noon, on campus. The anniversary banquet for the class of '69 was scheduled for Saturday night. The plan was for the Belles to meet on Friday evening at a bed and breakfast Rae Dawn had reserved. That would give them most of Saturday to catch up and practice.

Delta had hesitated, until at last Rae had said the words that convinced her. "We need you, Delta. *I* need you. I really want to see you again."

I need you.

"Is everything all right, Rae?" Delta had asked.

Rae hadn't answered right away. Then: "We'll talk when we see each other."

What was going on in Rae's life? Delta hadn't been in contact with her in a long time. Ten years or more with only a card at Christmas. She knew that Rae had been successful with her music—successful enough to own the club where she once played as a backup pianist. Her dreams had come true. And yet Delta had gotten the impression, largely unspoken, that Rae was in some kind of turmoil.

She wasn't quite sure what she could do to help. She was dead certain she didn't have Grandma Mitchell's wisdom. And yet, despite her misgivings and against her better judgment, she had finally agreed to join the Delta Belles for one last concert.

You don't need a degree to help people, the waiter Gabe had said. *Even a bartender can listen.*

A fool's errand, a voice in the back of her mind nagged.

Maybe so. But she'd rather be a fool than let down a friend who needed her.

Once the suburbs of Atlanta had receded in her rearview mirror, Delta began to feel herself relax. She adored Cassie and Russell and Mouse, and appreciated their generosity in inviting her to stay with them until she got her feet under her. But only when she got away did she realize how deeply affected she was by the harried pace of the South's largest city.

Growing up next door in Stone Mountain hadn't prepared

her for life in Atlanta. The city had mushroomed in the past twenty-five years, and the traffic—eight lanes on the perimeter loop going seventy-five miles an hour bumper to bumper—scared the life out of her. For all its talk of southern hospitality and casual elegance, Atlanta seemed to Delta to be a rushed, angry place where tempers seethed just below the surface.

The trip to Mississippi would take a little over five hours, not counting food and potty breaks. Delta had left early in an effort to beat rush hour, only to discover that rush hour started at six a.m. and lasted until ten. It had taken her more than an hour to get around the northern perimeter and out onto open road.

Now at last the traffic had begun to thin out. Exhaling tension on a sigh, Delta pointed the minivan west toward the Alabama line.

Here and there along the highway she could see hints of coming autumn. At home in Asheville, where the air was cooler and the altitude higher, the trees would be at their peak in mid-October, color creeping down the mountainsides like a spill of brilliant paints against a sky of clearest blue. A longing rose up in her, a palpable yearning for the Blue Ridge Mountains, for the beauty and serenity and protection those hills afforded.

Cassie had offered to cancel her appointments and come with her on the trip—an offer Delta quickly, and probably not graciously, refused. She had not wanted to be shut up in the car with her sister for six hours, but she hadn't counted on what it would be like to be locked in alone, with only her own thoughts for company. For the first twenty miles she had tried to listen to the radio, but no one played the kind of music she liked anymore, and by the time she got out of the city, she had become increasingly irritated with the puerile, asinine conversation on the morning shows. Even NPR couldn't hold her attention, and she hadn't yet figured out how to use the CD changer.

At last she turned the radio off and listened to the silence inside the car. Her mind drifted, predictably, to her college years with Rae Dawn and the others, to the early days with Rankin, to her life over a span of two and a half decades.

Through the years her contact—in Cassie's language, her *connection*—with her college circle had been sporadic at best. Lauren's marriage to Trip Jenkins had evidently caused an uncomfortable rift between her and Lacy. Somehow Lauren and Trip had managed to make it work; they had stayed together, anyway, and had a grown son. Lacy had gone away and come back still unmarried, and although Rae had said she seemed upbeat and enthusiastic about this reunion, Delta wondered whether the optimistic outlook was real or just a front, a posture assumed for an estranged friend. Theoretically she believed that a person could make a happy, fulfilled single life, but as she had never lived that kind of life, an experiential understanding of it was beyond her comprehension.

What would her own life have been without Rankin? The question disturbed her more than it should have. On one hand, she had been disgustingly happy with him—so happy, in fact, that Sugar as a teenager would feign retching every time she walked into a room and saw them kissing. The memory made Delta smile, and on the heels of the recollection came the palpable feeling of Rankin's arms around her, warm and inviting.

She had been so lucky. No, not lucky. *Blessed.*

It was a word Delta rarely used because of the sappy religious connotations it conjured up. People regularly talked about being blessed with a good parking space or a short line at the ATM. As if God rode around on a Mardi Gras float, throwing down trinkets from on high.

No. Being blessed was not about trivial answers to equally trivial prayers. It was about being graced with something so unexpected and undeserved that the only possible response was overwhelming gratitude.

Tears stung Delta's eyes as she recalled the years of unexpected grace with Rankin. The mountaintop experiences—their wedding day, the birth of their daughter, their recommitment ceremony after twenty years of marriage. The transfigurations, when truth pressed in upon her as they discussed theology and philosophy and poetry, those moments when she had, palpably, felt the presence of God. And the huge slices of ordinary time that make up a life together—such as that snowy night, so clear in her memory even after all these years, when they had held each other after making love and wept for the sheer joy of their oneness.

Yes, she had been blessed. And then the blessing had been snatched away.

Her mind began to veer in the direction of anger—the seething, simmering rage toward God that had burned inside her ever since her husband's death. Spiritual and theological dilemmas haunted her—questions of theodicy, of why terrible things happened to faithful people; questions of omnipotence and impotence, omniscience and ignorance; the reality of tragedy and the unquestioned assumption of divine love.

She had heard the question asked before, usually voiced by people in great pain: *If God loves me and has the power to intervene in my life, why did this happen? Why did my baby die? Why did my wife get cancer?* And now Delta herself was asking the unanswerable question: *Can God be at once omnipotent and loving?*

Rankin, in his wisdom, never let this surface question get in the way of real responses. This was the "presenting question," as he called it, this apparent dichotomy between power and love. People in crisis didn't want or need a theological treatise on natural law and the broken world. They didn't really want to know why. They wanted to know that God hadn't abandoned them.

She shook her head and forced her mind back to Rankin, back to the initial issue that had sent her down this path: What would life have been like without him?

The other side of the question nagged at her more than she wanted to admit. For all the joy and love and blessing of their years together, how much of her life had been sublimated to his? What had she missed of her own cognitive and spiritual development?

She remembered early discussions with Rankin, conversations that centered around her Ph.D. work and her sense of mission or calling as a college professor. He had agreed, quite vehemently, that she should have a life of her own, that his work in ministry should not dominate their lives or absorb her personality and gifts.

And yet it hadn't turned out quite that way, had it? Gradually—especially after Sugar's birth, when all her attentions turned to being Mommy to this needy little bundle of warm energy—Delta had become Rankin's second. The woman behind the man. The pastor's wife. And most incredibly, neither of them realized it was happening. They just went along, ushered forward by the flow of life's stream, until the rapids took Rankin and Delta was left alone in the shallows with no idea how she got here.

And so, a thousand times since Rankin's funeral almost six months ago, she had asked the question. Another question with no answer, the cry of an anguished heart:

What the hell am I supposed to do now?

THIRTY-TWO

Highgate House

Mississippi College for Women
October 1994

Delta had forgotten—or perhaps hadn't noticed when she was a student here—how many antebellum homes the town boasted. All along College Street and in a wide perimeter around the campus, enormous mansions kept watch over the old Southern way of life—lush gardens, broad porches, elegant columns rising toward the sky. Most were on the pilgrimage tour, she suspected. Several had been turned into B&Bs, with small tasteful signs out front, and a few were open to the public all year long.

Highgate House, a brick Greek Revival mansion two blocks from the college, sat back from Third Street on a shaded lot surrounded by magnolia trees. Somehow Rae Dawn had managed to get reservations there, booking its only three rooms with private baths.

Delta pulled into the driveway at Highgate and parked next

to the carriage house. Her small rolling suitcase bumped noisily as she made her way around the brick sidewalk to the front door.

The door swung open and a small, birdlike woman with silver hair stepped out onto the porch. "Welcome to Highgate!" she said, opening her arms wide. "I'm Matilda Suttleby, the owner." She squinted at Delta. "Are you Dawn? You look . . . different."

"Do you mean Rae Dawn? No. I'm Delta Ballou."

"Of course, of course!" The woman beamed and swept Delta into an effusive hug which Delta, encumbered by the suitcase and a purse, endured but did not return. "Do come in."

Matilda led the way into a wide foyer dominated by a plush oriental rug and an enormous grandfather clock. To the right was a large parlor, decorated all in pink, with several uncomfortable-looking settees surrounding a marble fireplace. In a corner next to the window sat a very old and richly inlaid piano.

Delta abandoned her suitcase in the foyer and followed as Matilda turned to the left. Two steps down, the room opened into an enormous den with a low-beamed ceiling, another fireplace—fieldstone this time—and an assortment of deeply cushioned leather armchairs.

"You'll be in the Jefferson bedroom, up the stairs and to the right," Matilda was saying as she rummaged through a pile of paperwork spread out on a huge walnut desk in the corner. "I've put Dawn in Robert E. Lee, just opposite yours, and the other two, the sisters, in the large Stonewall room down the hall."

Jefferson Davis. Stonewall Jackson. Robert E. Lee. Delta's mind flashed to the Stone Mountain carving, and she suppressed a smile.

"I'm sure you girls will have a lot of catching up to do," Matilda was saying. "So you just make yourselves at home.

Through there"—she pointed to a swinging door at the end of the den—"is the grand dining room, where breakfast is served at eight. Beyond that you'll find the kitchen. After hours feel free to forage for snacks. My room is the door to the right off the back porch. Call on me if you need anything." She got up and came toward Delta, who was still standing in the middle of the room, and pressed a large key into her hand. "This unlocks the front door, in case I'm in bed when you come home. There's a very nice enclosed garden out back—the weather is lovely in October, don't you think? Oh, and I serve tea from two thirty to three thirty," she finished breathlessly.

Delta struggled to take all this in. Finally she said, "Ah, thanks, Mrs. Suttleby."

"Matilda!" the woman corrected with a little bob of the head. "You must call me Matilda. I like to think of my guests as friends, you know."

She swooped out of the den and back into the foyer, hauling Delta behind her. "Now, up the stairs with you. Let's get you settled. I'm sure your friends will be here soon."

The Jefferson bedroom reminded Delta a little of rooms she had seen at the Biltmore House in Asheville—garish flocked wallpaper in shades of powder blue and green, dark mahogany furniture, and a bulbous blue floor lamp on a brass base. The carved rice bed was so high that she'd need a running start to get into it. From the wall above the fireplace a pen-and-ink portrait of Jefferson Davis, President of the Confederacy, scowled down upon her.

"All these bedrooms have private baths," Matilda was saying as she laid Delta's suitcase on the cedar chest at the foot of the bed and began to unzip it. "They weren't original to the house, of course. We converted the maids' sleeping chambers years ago."

Through a door to the right, Delta caught a glimpse of an expanse of white tile and a clawfoot tub large enough to swim in. When she turned back, Matilda had opened her suitcase and was beginning to transfer underwear to a dresser drawer.

"No, I can do that," she protested, returning to the woman's side and shutting the suitcase lid with a slap.

Matilda pulled back abruptly and gazed dolefully at Delta with the expression of a four-year-old who has just had her favorite doll snatched away. "As you wish," she murmured.

"I've had a long drive," Delta said apologetically, "and I'd like to freshen up before the others get here."

"Certainly." Matilda backed out of the room with a broad smile pasted on her face, a smile that did not quite meet her eyes. "I do hope you'll come down for tea."

"Of course," Delta said. "Two thirty, right?"

Matilda nodded and disappeared down the stairs.

Delta looked at the clock on the mantel under Jefferson Davis's picture. It was almost quarter to two. She'd have half an hour, at least, to rest before having to face the indomitable Matilda Suttleby again. She hung a few things in the narrow closet, climbed the wooden step stool, and collapsed on top of the enormous bed.

Only when a noise downstairs awoke her did Delta realize she had fallen asleep. As if from a great distance she heard the front door opening and shutting again, Matilda's piping voice, the sonorous chiming of the grandfather clock.

She struggled to wakefulness and peered at the mantel clock. It was two-fifteen. The half-hour nap had done nothing to refresh her; on the contrary, she felt groggy and drugged. She had drooled on the satin bedspread and tried in vain to wipe the stain off with her hand.

"Delta!" a voice called up the stairs, followed by the pounding of feet. "Delta! Are you here?"

Delta slid off the bed and willed herself awake. She was just running her fingers through her hair as a petite figure with short blond hair burst into the room.

"Lacy!" Delta grinned. "Damn woman, you look just the same."

Lacy launched herself across the room and hugged Delta hard. "So do you."

"Not really," Delta said. "But thanks for saying so."

"Is Rae here yet?"

Delta shook her head. "She called last night and said she'd be late getting in."

Matilda cleared her throat to get their attention. She was still standing in the doorway guarding a small bag, a bulky guitar case, and a large traveling crate that housed an enormous cinnamon-colored cat. "Your room is down the hall, Miss Cantrell," she said.

"Oh! Sure, all right." Lacy edged back to the doorway and retrieved her luggage She motioned to Delta with a snap of her head. "Come on. See my room."

Delta picked up the guitar and followed. Matilda ushered them into a huge square bedchamber that must have taken up one entire wing of the house. Dormer windows on three sides let in a golden afternoon light. The ceilings, painted in a pale heathery purple, slanted upward from side walls about seven or eight feet high. There were four double beds in the room, one in each corner, matching canopy beds covered with handmade quilts in shades of lavender, purple, and sage green. In the center of the room, on a floor of wide pine planks, a large floral rug flanked by two velvet love seats created a conversation area.

Lacy looked around. "Jeez. My whole house would fit in this room."

Matilda glared at the cat carrier. "I normally don't allow—"

"His name is Hormel. He's very sweet, really." Lacy opened the crate. Hormel streaked out, made one circuit around the room, and settled himself in a slant of sunlight at the foot of one of the canopied beds. "He won't be any trouble, I promise," Lacy said. "I've got a litter box down in the car, and he'll stay in the room with me."

"Well," Matilda said, "I'll make an exception this one time." She did not attempt to unpack Lacy's bag for her. Instead she placed it on a suitcase rack in the corner. "Tea in ten minutes," she said, and left the room.

"This is a great place," Lacy said when she was gone. "I feel like I'm in a time warp, gone back a hundred years." She turned a broad smile on Delta. "I'm so glad you're here."

"Me too." Delta sat on the edge of the bed and rubbed Hormel's upturned belly. He squeezed his eyes tight shut and purred loudly. "You're earlier than I expected."

"I left yesterday, spent the night along the way," Lacy said. "I'm too old for a twelve-hour road trip alone."

"Alone? Didn't Lauren drive down with you? You're sharing a room, right?"

A shadow passed behind Lacy's eyes, a brief cloud filtering the sun. "We didn't have a choice about the room," she said, "but we, ah, came separately. She'll be here by dinnertime, I think." The shadow retreated. "It looks like we get the luxury suite, anyway."

"Lace," Delta began, not knowing quite where to start, "is there something—"

Lacy held up a hand. "Later," she said. "After we have tea with Scarlett O'Hara."

It was three thirty by the time they were finally alone in Lacy's room. Hormel had discovered the window seat and was snoring loudly.

"All right," Delta said. "Tell me what's going on."

Lacy shook her head. "You first. When Rae Dawn called, she said Rankin had died. Delta, what happened? Why didn't you call us? We would have been there for you."

Delta fought for air against the heavy weight that settled on her chest. "There was this woman in our congregation—Vinca Hollowell. Her husband was a violent drunk and an abuser. Rankin was trying to help her. Anyway, Hollowell killed a man in a bar fight, and at his trial Rankin testified. Hollowell got fifteen years, and when he got out—"

She shrugged helplessly, unable to go on. "It's been awful," she said at last. "I keep trying to get a handle on this for my daughter's sake, for my own sake. But I'm so *angry,* Lace. Angry and depressed. I can't seem to get past it."

"Angry at this Hollowell guy?"

"At him. At Rankin, for leaving me. At God, for letting it happen." Delta exhaled. "Ham Hollowell beat my husband to death with a crowbar in front of the altar. I saw it all and couldn't do anything to stop it."

"Shit," Lacy said.

Delta looked up and saw tears standing in Lacy's eyes. An unexpected warmth washed over her. Someone else—someone not directly related to Rankin's death—could weep with her. Someone else could say it was shit and never should have happened. The effect was instantaneous. The tension clenching at her gut released. Just a little, but it was enough.

Lacy sat there, stunned, as she tried to absorb the specifics of Delta's husband's death. Nothing in her realm of experience enabled her to understand such grief, and yet the tears came. Now she understood, though Rae Dawn had not told her the details, why it was so important for her to come to this reunion.

Delta began to cry too. For a long time they just held hands and wept together. When the tears at last subsided, Lacy spoke.

"I have a friend in Kansas City," she said. "My best friend. Her name is Alison Rowe. She was widowed at twenty-nine, her husband killed in Vietnam. Friendly fire, they called it." She paused, remembering. "He was halfway through medical school when his number came up, and he went as a medic. One day while his unit was on patrol, they got pinned down in the jungle by snipers. Somehow he managed to get out, to radio for help. Then, while the helicopters were on their way, he went back in. Pulled three wounded men to safety and was shot in the back by one of his buddies who panicked and thought he saw the sniper."

She looked up at Delta, who nodded for her to continue.

"At the funeral, Alison told me, people kept assuring her there was justification in her husband's death. The religious folks said it was God's will, God's time, that God had reasons beyond what we could understand. The military contingent said he was a hero who had given the ultimate sacrifice for freedom."

"Sounds familiar," Delta said in a choked voice. "Everyone told me that Rankin was in God's hands, that everything happens for a purpose. That Rankin died the way he lived, standing up for those who had no power, no voice."

"Not much comfort, is it?" Lacy said. "Alison told me she

didn't want a hero. She didn't want God's will. She wanted her husband back."

Delta nodded. "She's more honest than most. Most of us can't deal with the paradox between an omniscient God and an omnipotent one. We believe—we *have* to believe—that God, or fate, or karma could have intervened, could have stopped the tragedy from happening. But when the miracle doesn't come, what kind of God does that leave us with? What kind of God stands idly by in the midst of pain and suffering? Not a loving God, but a monster, a tyrant. Or an impotent weakling."

"So what's the answer?" Lacy asked.

"That's the million-dollar question," Delta said slowly. "The question I've been asking myself for months—why a supposedly loving God would allow a man like Rankin to meet such a violent and undeserved death. So far I've only come up with one answer."

Lacy leaned forward. "And that is?"

Delta shrugged. "Shit happens."

THE MOMENT THE WORDS left Delta's mouth, some tightly wound spring inside her let go. It was so simple, really. She didn't have to blame God for Rankin's death. She didn't have to blame anyone.

Not even herself.

"So," Delta said after a while, "tell me what's going on with you."

Lacy hesitated. "I'm all right. I've been teaching in Hillsborough, and—"

"I know what you *do*, Lace," Delta interrupted. "I want to know how you *are*."

Lacy ducked her head and grinned. "All right. You want the real story, here it is."

Delta listened while Lacy told about her midnight run on the bus from Hillsborough, about the chance meeting with Alison, about her years in Kansas City. "She's a wonderful person, Delta. A great gift to my life. She helped me find purpose and direction. Alison drew me out of myself, helped me learn to live again."

"After Trip, you mean."

Lacy nodded. "When Lauren and Trip ran off to get married, I was pretty sure my life was over. It was hell. For years I had been competing with Lauren. When I met Trip and fell in love, I finally had something that was all my own. I was going to marry Trip, raise a family. When that didn't happen, I ran away. Resigned myself to being miserable."

"And Alison changed all that?"

"*I* changed," Lacy corrected. "Alison was a catalyst." She got up from the love seat and paced across the room. "On the surface, being a martyr or a victim seems very fulfilling, but it gets old after a while. Rage can be cleansing, but it only takes you so far. Sooner or later you have to let it go, get on with the business of finding purpose and meaning apart from the dreams that have died."

Lacy knew little of what Delta had been through the past few months, and yet Delta felt as if she had peered into her very soul. The effect was unnerving. "Go on," she said when Lacy sat down again. "You were talking about purpose and meaning."

"I found meaning—at least in part—in teaching. Ironic, isn't it? I took the job at the high school not because I felt called to teach, but because Trip was going to be in law school at Duke. Then I abandoned it and ran. Once I was in the classroom in Kansas City, however, I began to realize that my job wasn't to drill dates and facts into resistant young minds, but to challenge these kids to learn to *think*. To help them find the connection between their own experience and what has happened in the past." Her gaze drifted past Delta and fixed on the window that overlooked the garden. "The best days were the days when students came to me just to talk. I didn't need to have answers. I simply needed to hear them out, to be trustworthy. They got pretty honest about their lives when an adult they trusted would just shut up and listen."

"How long were you in Kansas City?"

"Almost fifteen years. When Dad had his stroke, Lauren had Ted to think about and couldn't spare enough time. I came home to help. But I had also hoped—" She shrugged and fell silent.

"Hoped things wouldn't work out with Lauren and Trip?" Delta ventured. "Hoped you might have a chance with him after all?"

Lacy's head snapped around, and she fixed Delta with an incredulous look. "Lord, no!" she burst out. "I don't want Trip. I want my *sister* back."

Delta frowned. "Wait. I'm confused. You came back to Hillsborough ten years ago. You and Lauren—"

"Lauren and I see each other," Lacy said. "We do family things together. We're very polite and courteous to one another. But it's all surface, all a sham. We're not sisters anymore. We're simply . . . acquaintances."

"I don't understand," Delta said. "That one time Rankin and I came through Durham—when was it? Four years ago?—you and Lauren seemed okay. A little distant, maybe. But you acted like it was no big deal."

"We acted. Leave it at that." Lacy fell silent for a moment, and when she spoke again her voice sounded hoarse, cracked. "This isn't about forgiveness, Delta. I forgave them years ago. I've moved on. I just want things to be normal between us. But it's not normal. She never talks about Trip or their marriage. I know she's unhappy, and I'd be there for her, except that she avoids me whenever possible and keeps things superficial when we're forced to be together. She won't open up to me. And it seems like that's the way she wants to keep it."

"Sounds like a recipe for stress," Delta said.

Lacy nodded. "It's killing me," she said. "I'm sick of walking around on eggshells with her. It's worse than not having any contact at all. I can't do it anymore."

"What are you going to do?"

"The only thing I *can* do," Lacy said. "My car is packed. I've quit my job. I'm leaving straight from this reunion to go back to Kansas City."

THIRTY-THREE

The Eleventh Hour

Lauren did, indeed, arrive in time for dinner—in a limousine from the airport.

Delta and Lacy watched from rocking chairs on the covered porch as the long black limo pulled into the driveway. "One of Trip's business partners owns a private plane, I think," Lacy said.

Delta got up and went down the steps to greet her. When she turned back, Lacy was still sitting on the porch, waiting.

Lauren lingered in the back of the limo, peering into the gilt mirror from her purse, checking her hair and makeup. She looked all right, she guessed, but her face showed every single day of her forty-seven years. She looked closer. When her reflection caught in the beveled edges of the glass, the angles magnified her crow's feet and distorted the sagging skin around her jaw line.

Jowls. For God's sake, she was getting *jowls!*

She patted a little more powder on her nose and scowled at

her reflection. Why she had agreed to this gig in the first place, she couldn't tell to save her soul. It was Rae Dawn's fault. Rae and her sense of nobility, her damned persuasiveness.

Lauren had no illusions about what Rae and Delta must think of her. The brazen hussy who seduced her twin sister's boyfriend and stole him away.

Brazen hussy? Where did that image come from? The Smithsonian, no doubt. Lauren would have laughed at herself if the language hadn't made her feel so abominably ancient. Might as well have called herself a tart or a strumpet.

At last she saw the front door of the limo open and the driver come around to her side. She plastered on a smile, wiped damp hands down the front of her skirt, and took the hand he offered her.

Delta was standing on the bottom step of the porch. The expression that flitted across her face was brief but unmistakable—the look of a visitor coming to a dying person's bedside for the first time. The oh-my-God glance that quickly rearranges itself into a false smile.

A lead weight dropped into Lauren's stomach and tears pricked at her eyes. To cover her distress, she reached out and drew Delta into a perfunctory hug. "I'm so happy to see you," she murmured into the air at Delta's ear. "It's been too long."

DELTA WAS GLAD for the hug, not because it communicated any real warmth, but because it gave her a chance to collect her wits. Coming on the heels of her time with Lacy, the sight of Lauren Jenkins shocked her to the core.

Had she expected Lauren to look as young and vibrant as her sister? They were twins, after all. A shadow of Lacy's natural attractiveness still lingered about the edges of Lauren's appearance, but anyone who saw them together would more likely take them for mother and daughter than for sisters born from a single egg.

Delta could only hope Lauren hadn't noticed her reaction. She patted Lauren's back and extricated herself from the hug.

Lauren was dressed in a gray skirt and lavender cashmere sweater set, the cardigan arranged with careful indifference across her shoulders. A string of perfectly graduated pearls at her neck caught the fading afternoon light. Real pearls, Delta thought. Real cashmere.

"You look marvelous," Delta lied.

"Thank you." Lauren took her arm and steered her toward the porch. She waved at Lacy, still seated in the porch rocker, then quickly averted her gaze. "Where's Rae Dawn?"

"She probably won't get here until midnight," Delta said. "We're supposed to go on to dinner without her."

"Then let's take the car and go." Lauren pointed toward the limo. "I can settle in later."

The driver extracted two matching leather suitcases from the trunk and handed them to Matilda Suttleby, who fluttered nearby as if in the presence of royalty. "I'll just take these up," she said at last when no one was paying any attention to her. "You girls have a nice dinner."

The limo—apparently at Lauren's disposal for the weekend—took them to an upscale restaurant called Riverbend, on the edge of town where the river made a wide horseshoe curve to the north. The back of the restaurant, a wall of glass facing the river bend, opened onto a slate patio and a lighted garden sloping down to the water.

The evening was mild, so they opted for a table on the patio. Their driver, whose name Delta had yet to hear, installed himself in the bar with a burger and an O'Doul's to watch clips from last year's Super Bowl.

Dinner, at Lauren's insistence, included a lobster appetizer, wine, and a decadent chocolate torte for dessert—all delicious and outrageously expensive. As a minister's wife, Delta wasn't accustomed to such extravagance, and she was certain Lacy couldn't afford it on a teacher's salary. But Lauren coerced them into letting her buy and encouraged them to get whatever they wanted. Delta chose a fresh trout amandine with brown rice pilaf and caesar salad. Lacy, much to her sister's displeasure, ordered the fried catfish special.

Delta had anticipated a quiet dinner and even hoped for some meaningful conversation. Shortly after the salads arrived, however, so did a gray-haired, round-faced man with a portable keyboard. He had been hired, no doubt, to provide live music for the entertainment of the diners, but his imitation of Frank Sinatra turned out to be so abominable that no one within earshot could talk of anything else.

Halfway through the meal, five ducks waddled up from the river to gorge themselves on bread hand-fed to them by indulgent patrons. When a waiter tried to shoo them back down the hill to the water, a large green-headed drake went on the attack and sent him scurrying back to the kitchens.

It proved to be an entertaining evening, certainly, but not a profitable one. The most Delta was able to accomplish was to ask Lauren about her family. She responded by passing around photographs of her son and his fiancée. Lacy barely glanced at them.

By the time they all climbed into the limo for the silent ride back to the B&B, Delta half wished she had joined the chauffeur for a burger and Super Bowl reruns.

Matilda Suttleby might be annoying, but she hadn't lied about the beauty of Highgate's small garden. Completely enclosed by a vine-covered stone wall, the place seemed miles away from the rest of the world. Stone walkways wound among the azalea bushes and dogwood trees. At the center, where Delta now sat on a carved wooden bench, a three-tiered fountain tinkled and shimmered in the moonlight.

Muffled footsteps sounded behind her, and she turned to see Lauren in navy satin pajamas, robe, and slippers.

"Have a seat," Delta offered, scooting over to make room.

Lauren edged onto the bench.

"What time is it?"

"Almost eleven. Lacy's asleep." Lauren fiddled with the sash of her robe. "It's very peaceful here."

"Yes it is," Delta agreed.

Unfortunately, the serenity hadn't seemed to rub off on Lauren. She shifted on the bench, crossed her legs, waggled one foot, agitated as a June bug battering itself against a window.

Suddenly a rush of compassion welled up in Delta, the desire to have a look into her friend's heart and find out what anxieties had aged her so. Was she still carrying around the shame and guilt of what she had done years ago? Was she afraid of what Delta might think of her? And did she know that her sister bore her no ill will?

She touched Lauren's arm. "How are you?" she asked. "We didn't get to talk much at dinner."

At the gentle touch, Lauren jerked back as if she had been stung by a scorpion. "I'm fine. Everything's fine." She stared up at the stars. "It's very peaceful here, isn't it?"

"You already said that."

Lauren got up and began picking fallen leaves out of the fountain. Delta followed.

"Stop," she said, taking hold of Lauren's hand. "I want you to talk to me."

Lauren relented, albeit reluctantly. She went back to the bench, sank down, and began to jiggle her foot again. But still she didn't speak.

"I don't mean to pressure you," Delta said, although she suspected that a little pressure wouldn't do any harm at the moment. "But clearly something's wrong."

"Am I ill, you mean?" Lauren finally said with a note of bitterness in her voice. "I caught the expression on your face when you first saw me. I look like crap, I know. Like an old woman."

"If you *are* sick, I want to know it," Delta responded. "But I'm not talking about your appearance. Hell, we're all getting older. I'm talking about your *soul*. Your heart." She looked into Lauren's shrouded eyes and opted for the direct approach. "You've been faking it since you stepped out of that limo. Like the last thing in the world you wanted was to see me again." She pressed her lips together. "Now, if you want me to shut up, say so. But at least be honest. We were friends once, Lauren, and might be again. But if all we do is make small talk—" Delta shrugged and lapsed into silence.

Lauren's countenance had taken on a fixed, stricken expression, the look of a small animal that wants to be comforted but is afraid of being hurt. She shook her head and shoved her hands into the pockets of her robe.

"No!" she said at last. "It's not you, Delta. It's me. You say I acted as if I didn't want to see you. But that's not the truth. I—I didn't want to see *myself*, reflected in your disapproval."

Delta sat back, floored by this unexpectedly profound insight. "Have I communicated disapproval?"

"No, not at all," Lauren admitted. "And that makes it even worse."

Delta shook her head. "I'm sorry, Lauren, I'm not quite following you. Talk to me, please. And start at the beginning."

LAUREN FIXED HER EYES on the fountain. *Start at the beginning.* But where was the beginning, exactly? More than twenty-five years ago, when she seduced her twin sister's boyfriend on a secluded bank in the park? Or long before that, all the years of competition between herself and Lacy, the years of vacillating between jealousy and intimacy?

"Being a twin," she finally began, "is a strange life. In many ways it's wonderful, having someone so close, someone who understands you right down to your genes. But there are also stresses unlike those faced by normal siblings. Or maybe they are the same stresses, but infinitely magnified by the similarities between the two of you."

She paused, stared at the fountain, then took a deep breath. "I was always jealous of Lacy."

"Wait a minute," Delta interrupted. "I thought I remembered that Lacy was jealous of you. You were the one who was more outgoing, had all the boyfriends, the popularity."

Lauren waved a hand impatiently. Now that she had started, she didn't want her train of thought to be derailed. "Surface stuff. Superficialities. Lace and I shared the same DNA; we should have been just alike, right? But I knew better, even when I was very small. Lacy had something different, something I only later learned to name. She had character. Substance. Not that she was smarter than I was; our intelligence level was pretty comparable, I think. But she was . . . deeper."

This time Delta didn't interrupt. "I had loads of friends as we grew up—and later, boyfriends," Lauren said. "Adolescent boys don't usually value depth. But the few friendships Lacy formed were more significant, so still I felt jealous. I compensated by competing."

Delta listened intently, both surprised and impressed by Lauren's depth of insight.

"I've never been able to talk about this except to my therapist," Lauren said, slanting a glance at her.

"Therapist?" Delta repeated. "You've been in counseling?"

"Don't look so shocked. I'm forty-seven years old. I like to think I've grown up a *little* since the sixties."

Delta suppressed a smile. "Please continue. I'm riveted."

Lauren went on with her story. "What I did to Lacy was unforgivable."

Unforgivable. The melancholy word echoed inside Delta's head, desolate, hopeless, heartbreaking. If Lauren truly believed her actions to be unforgivable, it was no wonder a reconciliation had never taken place between the twins.

She opened her mouth to protest, but Lauren was speaking again.

"Trip and I almost divorced once, when Ted was fourteen. At the time I was, frankly, amazed he had hung on that long. He stayed with me out of guilt at first, and then out of a misguided sense of loyalty. I stayed with him out of shame, because I couldn't bear to face the enormity of the mistake I had made."

"That's why you didn't want to see me," Delta murmured. "And why all these years you've avoided any real relationship with Lacy. Shame."

A flash of the old Lauren-fire returned. "What do you mean, I've avoided a relationship with Lacy?"

"Lacy told me that you kept everything superficial at your family gatherings. That you never talked about your husband or your marriage. I assumed it was because you were still nurturing shame over the, ah, the situation with Trip."

"For God's sake, Delta, give me a little credit. It's been twenty-five years. I laid down the burden of shame years ago. I avoided talking about my family not because I was ashamed, but *because I didn't want to hurt my sister.*"

Delta had no idea how to respond. Lauren saved her the trouble. "When Trip and I separated—or, I should say, when he left me—I went to visit Lacy, to tell her face to face that Trip had left. To be perfectly honest, I expected her to jump at the chance to get back together with him, if for no other reason than revenge for what I'd done. Instead, she asked me if I loved him. That question shocked me into admitting my true feelings for my husband, even if I didn't believe I deserved his love in return.

"When Trip returned, we agreed to go to counseling together, to try to sort things out. He didn't love me at the time, and I knew it. He had never really loved me. But gradually, as time went on and we got honest about ourselves, something changed. Love grew between us. Not just heat or physical passion, which I had once mistaken for love, but real love. Real intimacy. We let go of the guilt, the shame, the duty. And after more than fifteen years of marriage, we fell in love."

Delta hadn't expected this. She had anticipated a confession of blame and remorse, more than two decades of it. She had been prepared to talk to Lauren about putting the past behind her.

"My relationship with Trip," Lauren went on, "has been the saving grace of my life. Better than anything—except perhaps having Ted. Trip is an incredible father, a loving, attentive husband. We talk, we laugh, we love being together. All our friends are desperately envious of how well we communicate and how much we adore each other after twenty-five years."

Lauren turned to look into Delta's eyes. "I'm aware that the years have not been kind to me. But Trip still thinks I'm beautiful."

Delta could understand. The facade was gone, the mask set aside. Despite the crow's feet and the sagging skin, Lauren *was* attractive, lit from within with the confidence only an older, more settled love can bring.

"Then why—" she began.

"Why have I kept at arm's length the one person more important to me than anyone except my husband and son?"

Delta nodded.

"Precisely for that reason. Because she *is* so important to me. You've seen her, Delta. She lives alone except for that cat of hers. She's never married. The only close friend she has lives halfway across the country. I didn't *want* her to see how happy my relationship with Trip has become, to be confronted with our love for each other. It would just make her life seem that much more miserable by comparison. Even if it means keeping an emotional distance, the last thing I want in this world is to hurt Lacy. To make her feel left out."

Lauren bit her lip and blinked back tears. "I love my sister, Delta. I will always love her. I miss the closeness we once had. The craziness. Even the fights. But I'll go on missing her, if that's what it takes to keep from hurting her."

Delta thought about Lacy, what she had said about forgiveness, about moving on. All this time Lauren had believed her sister to be living in perpetual grief, heartbroken and tormented over the loss of Trip's love. She had withdrawn herself so as not to pour acid into the wound.

" 'The Gift of the Magi,' " Delta said.

"Excuse me?"

"It's a short story by O. Henry, about a desperately poor

couple who have only two prized possessions—Della's lustrous hair and Jim's gold watch."

Lauren frowned. "And your point is?"

"In the story, Della sells her hair to buy him a gold watch chain, and Jim sells his watch to buy her a pair of expensive hair combs. In the end, both have lost their treasures, but they've gained something even more important. The gift of the Magi, the wisest gift of all. The noble but ironic sacrifice of love."

"I don't get it," Lauren said.

Delta stood up and put a hand on her friend's shoulder. "Go talk to your sister," she said. "Really talk. Be honest with her. Tell her what you've told me tonight. Then you'll understand."

THIRTY-FOUR

The Blues Singer

Rae Dawn pulled up in front of Highgate House at ten minutes to midnight. The front porch light was on, and a sleepy, rumpled-looking Matilda Suttleby answered her quiet knock.

"Ah, Miss DuChante!" she said, coming instantly awake and pushing her hair back into place. "You finally made it."

"DuChamp," Rae corrected. "I'm sorry to arrive so late, but—"

"Not to worry," Matilda said. "I wasn't in bed yet."

Rae Dawn let the lie pass, although she couldn't have gotten a word in edgewise if she had been so inclined.

"I've reserved the best room for you," Matilda was saying. "The Robert E. Lee. Very spacious, and quite lovely. It's such an honor to have you here. I have all your albums—"

Rae arched an eyebrow. "All two of them."

"Yes, and I simply love your music," the woman went on without missing a beat. "All my friends will be absolutely green with envy when they find out I've hosted Dawn DuChante. You don't mind if I call you Dawn, do you?"

"Ah, it's Rae," she said.

"Of course, of course," Matilda gushed. Then, as if she had only now realized that she was still blocking the doorway, she gave a little jump. "Do come in. Are you hungry? I can whip up a snack, if you like. A sandwich, or some scrambled eggs—"

"No, thank you," Rae said wearily. "I'd just like to go to bed, please."

Matilda's face crumpled with disappointment. "Certainly. We can talk in the morning. I have a fine piano in the parlor if you—"

"Bed, please," Rae repeated.

"Yes, yes. Follow me." Matilda put a finger to her lips and dropped her voice to a whisper. "The other girls are already asleep, I believe. Up the stairs. This way."

Rae hefted her bag and dragged herself up the stairs, noticing as she went how flat Matilda Suttleby's feet were, her heels rough and red where they stuck out the back of her slippers.

"Here we go," the woman said when they reached the landing. She opened the door to the right and flipped on the light with a flourish. "Ta da!"

"Thank you." Rae entered the room and slung her suitcase on an overstuffed armchair in the corner. "Thank you, Mrs. Suttleby," she repeated. "Good night."

Matilda Suttleby's eager eyes were still peering at her when she shut the door.

Rae stripped off her jeans and sweater, rummaged in her bag for a nightshirt, then went into the bathroom and brushed her teeth. She was exhausted, and expected to fall asleep as soon as she climbed into the big bed, but once she had turned out the light, she found herself staring wide-eyed at the ceiling.

If it hadn't been for Delta, she would never have made this trip. Would never have driven up Interstate 59 past the exit for

Picayune, Mississippi. Would never have been inundated by memories of Noel Ridley and the love they once shared.

Illumination from a streetlamp outside the window cast a cold blue light into the room, cut into shifting shadows by the trees and the sheer lace curtains. She stared at the chandelier suspended from the center of the room. Traced the curlicues in the round plaster medallion that surrounded it. Tried to construct a pattern from the random flowers that dotted the wallpaper.

Who was she kidding, anyway? This pain—the sucking sensation in her gut when she passed by the Picayune exit, that sense of all the life being drained out of her in a single gurgling moment—was nothing new. Had there been a single day in the past ten years when she hadn't thought of Noel and cursed herself, cursed her career, cursed her own stupidity for letting the love of her life slip through her fingers? Had there been a night when she hadn't dreamed of Noel? A song she hadn't written with Noel in mind?

The music began to drift through her mind, songs of loss and longing, songs of joy and heartache and love gone wrong.

Did you ever sing the blues?
Did you ever wind up thinking
You're the only one who's sinking,
You're the only one to lose?
Does that melancholy music
Pull your heartstrings out of tune . . .

She hummed the tune in her head, fingered the piano riffs in her imagination, and finally, as the clock downstairs chimed two, fell into a restless sleep.

Soft knocking awoke her from yet another dream of Noel Ridley—this time a nightmare in which the Airstream trailer was burning and Noel was trapped inside. Rae's mind swam to the surface of consciousness, and she pried open her eyes to see golden autumn sunlight streaming into the room. On the bedside table sat the framed photo she always carried with her when she traveled.

"Rae Dawn?" the whispered voice came again. "Are you awake?"

Rae sat up and looked around. "Delta? Is that you?"

The door opened a crack and Delta's face peered around the door jamb. It was an older Delta, a bit plumper, with a few streaks of gray hair at the temples. But the eyes were the same, and the smile. "Come in."

Delta, in blue flannel pajamas with fluffy little cloud-shaped sheep on them, tiptoed barefoot into the room and shut the door. She launched herself onto the bed and her arms went around Rae in an enthusiastic embrace.

Had it been so long since Rae had been touched? She savored the hug, not wanting to let go, feeling the warmth of Delta's arms through the flannel, through her own nightshirt. Tears stung at her eyes.

"Don't go anywhere," she said over Delta's shoulder. She slid out of bed. "I have to pee, and you really don't want to talk to me with morning breath."

In the bathroom, with the water running, Rae took a moment to compose herself. She doused her face and brushed her teeth, and by the time she was ready to go back into the room, she had gained control over the unexpected tears.

Delta was sitting upright, leaning against the headboard with a pillow behind her back.

"What time is it?" Rae Dawn asked, climbing back into bed.

As if in answer, the grandfather clock downstairs gave out a full sixteen-note Westminster chime, followed by seven sonorous bongs.

"Seven o'clock. I'm sorry if I woke you. Breakfast is at eight, and I wanted to see you before everybody else did."

"Seven A.M.?" Rae repeated. "I didn't know there *was* a seven A.M." She pointed to the window. "I'm to assume this is sunrise?"

Delta laughed. "That's right. You're the night person."

"Occupational hazard of being a lounge singer."

Although Delta was still smiling, her eyes were not focused on Rae Dawn but at a point just past her shoulder. She reached out for the photo on the nightstand. "You've been holding out on me."

"No, I haven't," Rae said. "I wrote to you—"

"Generalities, not details," Delta said. "Come on, give, who is she?"

Rae took the picture and looked at it. It was a candid shot of herself and Noel, taken by a stranger during a rare and brief vacation in the Bahamas. The two of them were perched on the windblown seawall with the brilliant blue waters of the Caribbean in the background, Noel seated behind with her arms around Rae Dawn. Rae was smiling at the camera, but Noel, with her head turned slightly, was looking at Rae. The expression captured in that split second of film never failed to take Rae's breath away, the utter adoration and commitment that shone in those tawny eyes, the contentment, the rightness of their love.

They had walked along the beach that evening, basked in the purple aura of sunset, held hands, eaten mountains of fresh shrimp and crab at a thatch-roofed beachfront restaurant. "It doesn't get any better than this," Noel had said.

Rae Dawn closed her eyes and inhaled a ragged breath as the memories flooded in. Bits and pieces of an ordinary life, like millions of other lives. Waffles and scrambled eggs on the balcony overlooking the courtyard fountain. Redfish fresh from the outdoor market. Wednesday movie matinees, Sunday afternoon football, Christmas carols at the piano. Arguments about time or money or who left the shower dripping. Long conversations, cuddling in bed while a white winter sun crept its way across the ceiling. And that one unimaginably beautiful afternoon, standing at a secluded river bend surrounded by a small group of friends, when they joined their hands and pledged to love each other for a lifetime.

It was all still here, so close—the sound of Noel's laughter, the warmth of her smile, her touch, her scent, her nearness. So painfully close that in the early hours of morning Rae could feel an arm wrapping around her, a breath on the back of her neck, a body curled around her in sleep.

And then some noise would wake her—

"Rae?" Delta's voice brought her back from the brink. "Are you all right?"

Rae Dawn blinked. "Yeah."

"Who is she, Rae?"

"Her name was Noel Ridley. She was a doctor." Rae avoided Delta's eyes but could not escape her voice. The voice urging her to spill all the emotion she had been hoarding these past ten years. A voice gentle and full of compassion.

"Tell me about her."

Rae Dawn had come here to support Delta, to help her through her grief over Rankin's death. She certainly hadn't intended to talk about Noel. But it was the first time in years anyone had asked what she was feeling. Besides, pressure was building behind the floodgates, and she wasn't at all sure she could stop it now.

"Noel was my mother's doctor," she began. "I'd been in New Orleans for five years, working to build my career, when the call came that Mama had suffered a heart attack. It was so strange—there I was, in the hospital, watching my mother die and falling in love all at the same time."

"So you knew from the beginning that Noel was the one?"

"I suppose I did—subconsciously, anyway. After they took Mama's body away, she drove me out to the trailer. It was the middle of the night, and at the sight of it, all those horrible memories came flooding back and I just went crazy. Raged, screamed, cried. Noel accepted all of it in stride and didn't think I was crazy at all, even when I set a torch to the place and burned it to the ground."

Delta's eyes grew wide. "You burned it down?"

"Yes, I did." Rae smiled in spite of herself. "Did me more good than a year's worth of therapy too."

"That took a lot of courage."

Rae shook her head. "Not really. It was mostly instinct. But I did manage to get out some of what I was feeling, and I discovered that Noel could accept me at my worst. It was quite a revelation."

She went on talking, telling Delta about the development of their relationship, Noel's decision to move to New Orleans, the good years.

"She moved down, and we lived together for—" Rae paused. "Almost ten years. Our life together was wonderful."

Delta reached out a hand and squeezed Rae's arm. "I know how hard it is to lose someone you love so much."

Rae Dawn froze, and at that moment she realized her

mistake. Past tense. She had been speaking of Noel in past tense. And now she had to backtrack, to correct Delta's misconception.

"She didn't *die*, Delta," she said, trying hard to keep her voice from shaking. "She left me."

Delta looked up at Rae and then back down at the photograph Rae still held in her hands. She had known enough gay and lesbian couples through the years to realize that their relationships were subject to pressures most heterosexual couples couldn't even imagine. There was no societal structure to support gay relationships. No marriage bonds, no civic connection, no protected rights. Virtually no public support, and often little acceptance from families and friends. And although Delta knew that paperwork did not a marriage make, the lack of legal status rendered same-sex relationships all too susceptible to easy dissolution when things got difficult.

Still, in this photograph, Noel's eyes were alight with love. It couldn't have been clearer if she had been wearing a sign. The woman was in love with Rae Dawn.

"Impossible," Delta breathed, half to herself.

"I'm afraid it's very possible," Rae shot back.

Delta leaned back against the headboard. "What happened?" she blurted out, and then, realizing what an impertinent question it was, tried to take it back. "Sorry, Rae. You don't have to—"

Rae picked at a knobby place on the coverlet. "No, it's all right. I might as well just get it all out."

Get it all out and be done with it, she was thinking. But if she wasn't done with it after ten years—

She pulled in a deep breath and set the photograph back on the bedside table. Noel's golden eyes, bright with love, shone back at her from the picture. Rae jerked her gaze away and faced Delta. "When I finished college, I went to New Orleans to play as a backup pianist."

"At Maison Dauphine. I remember. The year Rankin and I moved to Asheville, we came down to visit. That was, what, four years after graduation?"

"Something like that." Rae nodded. "It was before everything happened, at any rate. My mother died in 1974; that's when I met Noel. The following spring she moved to New Orleans and worked at the clinic while I played at the club. For a few years things were great. We didn't have much money, but we got by, and we had each other. Then—" She paused. "I don't know whether to say that my career took off or my life began to fall apart. Both, really."

She summarized those difficult years leading up to the separation—the launch of her first album, the long months on the road. "It would have been hard enough just being separated like that. But to have to hide our relationship—"

"Why did you have to hide it?" Delta asked. "I thought the music industry was pretty open-minded."

"It's not the industry," Rae said. "It's the fans. My agent, Arista Records, even Chase Coulter, who owned the club when I first went to work there—they all believed my career would crash and burn if people knew I was writing and singing all those love songs to a *woman*." She shook her head. "You have to remember, Delta, this was years ago. Things have changed—" She grimaced. "Well, a little."

"Not enough," Delta said. "Please, go on."

"Anyway," Rae continued, "the last straw came with the Grammys."

Delta's eyes widened. "You have a Grammy?"

"I was *nominated* for a Grammy," Rae corrected. "Best R&B female vocal album. I didn't win."

"Yes, but you were *nominated,*" Delta said. "That means more records, fame and fortune—" She stopped suddenly. "Why didn't I know any of this?"

"You'd have to be a big R&B fan, I guess." Rae Dawn shrugged and held up her fingers in a V. "Two albums. Two. I suppose you would say I was moderately well known in very small circles for a very short time." She gave a self-deprecating grin. "But success can be both a blessing and a curse. Noel and I had both sacrificed so much for my career, and when the Grammy nomination came, I fully intended to share that moment with her no matter what. But my agent set me up with a date and absolutely refused to let me be seen in public with Noel. She didn't even go to L.A. with me. When I got home, she was packed to leave."

"Just like that?"

"It wasn't *just like that,*" Rae said. "It had been coming on a long time. We had tried to work through the problems, but I was too shortsighted to see that I was choosing my career over the person I loved." Remembered pain stabbed at her, and she sighed. "It took several more years for me to see what I had done, not just to Noel and to our relationship, but to myself, allowing myself to be locked in that closet. A soul needs light and air and honesty, Delta. Living a lie isn't living at all, even when the money's good."

DELTA WATCHED RAE DAWN'S FACE as she spoke, saw the agony and regret and raw longing that filled her eyes. She knew the pain of loss, certainly, but it was a pain tempered by the joy of more than twenty years with the man she loved. Good years, happy years. Years filled with a love unencumbered by discrimination and prejudice.

"And there was no one else," she said at last.

"I dated a little, now and then. Two or three of the women I met seemed interested in pursuing a relationship, but I didn't have the heart for it. It was hard to tell, by that time, whether they really cared about me or were simply in it for the money. Besides," she finished with a sigh. "Once you've known real love—"

"It's hard to settle for anything less," Delta supplied. "Rae, whatever happened to Noel?"

"She went back to Picayune, to her old practice. As far as I know she's still there."

"And you've never tried to reconcile with her?"

"At first, when I quit touring and came home, I thought about it. I wanted to. But I was ashamed that I had let my career get the better of my values. And then, as time went on, it just seemed like there was too much baggage between us."

"I'm sorry," Delta said. She wished she had more to offer. Silently she cursed her own helplessness. From the hallway downstairs she heard the clock chime seven thirty.

"Listen," Rae said, straightening up with a sigh, "that's enough of my sob story. I didn't come here for myself. I want to know how you're doing. I was so sorry to hear about Rankin's death."

Something clicked in the back of Delta's mind—something Lacy had said yesterday afternoon. Rae Dawn had told Lacy that Rankin had died. But how had Rae known?

She narrowed her eyes and glared at Rae. "What do you mean, you didn't come here for yourself?"

Rae blanched. "Well, I—"

"You came here for *me*? Because of Rankin?"

The color returned to Rae's face in a rush. "Yes."

"You put all this together—talked Lacy and Lauren into doing this reunion gig—and then convinced me to come? Why, Rae?"

"Because—" She hesitated. "Because you needed your friends."

Delta puzzled over this for a moment. Then the lights went on, and she understood.

Cassie.

"ALL RIGHT, I ADMIT IT," Rae Dawn said to Delta as they joined Lacy and Lauren around Matilda Suttleby's breakfast table. "Your sister did call me. She seemed to think you would agree to come if the rest of us did, and that it might be good for you."

Delta helped herself to a waffle. "Then you phoned Lacy and Lauren."

"She called *me*," Lacy interjected. "*I* called Lauren."

"And then Rae called me," Delta continued, "and convinced me that everybody else was enthusiastic about doing this reunion banquet, but couldn't do it without me."

"Yeah, something like that." Rae scooped scrambled eggs onto her plate and took a biscuit. "This breakfast is excellent, Mrs. Suttleby," she said as Matilda came in with a fresh pot of coffee.

The woman beamed and bobbed her head. "It's my pleasure, Dawn. It's such an honor—oh my, I forgot the apple butter. Homemade, you know, from apples off my own tree. I'll be right back." She skittered off into the kitchen.

"If she adds one more thing to this table, it'll collapse," Rae said. "Look at this—eggs, bacon, sausage, biscuits, waffles." She spooned a glob of blackstrap molasses over a biscuit and laughed. "I won't be able to sing a note, but it sure is good."

Lauren motioned for Lacy to pass the syrup. "Why does she keep calling you *Dawn*?"

"I was wondering the same thing," Lacy said, handing the pitcher to her twin. "She acts like you're some kind of big celebrity."

Rae Dawn rolled her eyes. "I'll explain later."

"Yes, don't get her off the subject," Delta said. "Right now she's explaining how she manipulated us all into being here." She shot a mock scowl in Rae's direction. "When you never returned my call—any of you—I assumed you didn't want to do this."

"I *didn't*," Rae said.

"Me either," Lauren and Lacy said in unison.

"That makes four of us," Delta chuckled. "So, how come we're all here, sitting at Matilda's breakfast table on Saturday morning and scheduled to do a concert tonight?"

Rae Dawn shrugged. "God, fate, destiny—"

"Coercion?" Delta supplied. "Conspiracy?"

Lacy grinned at her. "I'd say it's poetic justice, given how we started with the Belles in the first place. If you recall, Delta, *you* were the one who signed us up for that first talent show without our permission—"

"That's right," Lauren added. "You're just getting what you deserve."

DELTA WAS THANKFUL she'd had a chance to talk privately with the twins last night and Rae Dawn this morning. All during breakfast Matilda Suttleby hovered nearby fawning over Rae, her ubiquitous presence offering little opportunity for any real conversation.

After breakfast and showers, they gathered in the parlor to rehearse. Lacy brought out her guitar, and as she tuned up and went through the music with Rae, Delta watched them. She sensed a change coming over her. Ever since her arrival here, she had found herself thinking less about the horrible details of Rankin's death and more about the rich years of love they had shared. A love that now spilled over onto these friends she hadn't seen in ages.

She wondered if Lauren had had time to talk to Lacy about the misunderstanding between them. They appeared to be all right—laughing together, poking fun at one another, just as they had in college. It might be an act, but it seemed real enough. At least they were on speaking terms.

Delta was more concerned about Rae Dawn. A shadow lurked around her, a phantom that haunted her, hovering behind her eyes in unguarded moments. This reunion concert was costing her. She had agreed to it for Delta's sake, because she wanted to help a friend, but Delta suspected she was paying a high price in disturbing and painful memories.

"All right, let's get started," Rae said. "It's been a long time, and I didn't know how much you'd remember, so—" She handed out photocopies of several songs, including "Blowin' in the Wind" and "Where Have All the Flowers Gone."

"What about 'If I Had a Hammer'?" Lauren asked. "That's one of my favorites."

"We'll do it, if you like," Rae said. "I don't think we need music on that one." She sat down at the keyboard and prepared to play.

Just then the front door opened and a noisy gabble blew into the parlor from the foyer. Matilda Suttleby swept into the room, followed by a gaggle of tittering gray-haired ladies decked out in their Sunday best.

"I didn't think you'd mind," Matilda said, reaching a hand in Rae's direction. "They're such great fans of yours." She cleared her throat and turned toward the knot of old women in the doorway. "Girls, *this* is Dawn DuChante."

Delta saw the roll of the eyes as Rae plastered on a smile. She left the piano and shook hands with each of the ladies in turn.

"Oh, would you mind autographing a few things?" one of the ladies said, holding out a couple of CD cases. "We brought our DCs with us, just in case."

"It's *CD*, Mildred," another woman corrected archly. "She is so technologically challenged that her grandson has to load the CD player for her."

"That's true," Mildred confessed. "But it doesn't matter, Miss DuChante, because I keep both your DCs in there all the time. You have such a *beautiful* voice."

"Thank you," Rae said graciously. Behind her back, Delta caught a glimpse of the twins' faces, which bore identical expressions of utter astonishment.

Rae perched on the edge of a pink velvet settee and accepted a pen from one of the ladies. "I'm Sarah, with an H," the woman said. "Sarah Thomas." Rae inscribed the CD case and autographed it. Sarah took it and peered at the signature. "Oh, honey, you've made a mistake. I want you to sign your *real* name."

"That *is* my real name. Rae Dawn DuChamp."

"Your name's not Dawn DuChante?"

"No, ma'am. That's a stage name."

"But if you sign it this way, nobody will believe it's really you."

Rae took the CD back and made the correction. The rest of the ladies lined up for their autographs. One exceedingly old woman who reminded Delta a little of Grandma Mitchell had a vinyl album of Rae Dawn's first recording. She leaned on her cane and held it out.

"I haven't seen one of these in a long time," Rae said as she scrawled her signature across the cardboard cover.

"Thank you, dearie," the old woman screeched. "An autographed copy will bring twice as much at the flea market."

Matilda brought up the rear, preening herself importantly. "I told the girls you might let them sit in on your rehearsal," she said to Rae in a stage whisper. "We'll be quiet as mice."

Delta suppressed a laugh. The old women were clustered together, chattering about what an honor it was to have an autographed album and speculating loudly about the demise of Rae Dawn's recording career.

"She hasn't had a new album in years," one woman declared as she peered back over her shoulder. "Was it drugs, do you think? Or an unhappy love affair?"

Rae stood up. "Ladies, it's been a genuine pleasure meeting all of you," she said smoothly, "and I appreciate so much your taking the time to come. But if you'll excuse us now, we do need to rehearse for tonight's banquet. *Without* an audience."

Crestfallen, the old women slumped toward the foyer, casting venomous glances back at Matilda Suttleby as if she had deliberately plotted this turn of events to keep the star all to herself. When they had finally shut the door behind them, Matilda settled herself on one of the sofas and smiled. "Now that the groupies are gone," she said, "I suppose we can get on with the rehearsal."

Delta came over and sat down next to her. "Matilda," she whispered, "could I speak with you for just one moment?"

"Of course, dear." Matilda waved a hand.

"Ah, privately?"

Delta got to her feet and jerked her head toward the door. Matilda followed as she crossed the foyer and went through the den into the dining room.

"You know, Matilda," Delta said, putting an arm around the woman's narrow shoulders, "artists can be, well, a little eccentric.

Rae—I mean *Dawn*—tends to get nervous before a concert, and she prefers not to have anyone present at her rehearsals. And even if it seems silly to us, we need to honor a star's requests in a matter like this."

"Oh," Matilda said. "Well, of course, she wouldn't want all those old biddies gaping at her."

"I knew you'd understand. I'll tell you what. If you sit in the den, you'll be able to hear her just fine, and she won't even know you're there. It'll be like—like a private concert, especially for you."

"Oh, the girls will be so *jealous*."

"Yes, they will," Delta agreed. "They'll be talking about nothing else for weeks."

Matilda nodded. "And how about if I make some coffee and cinnamon rolls for later? Say in an hour?"

Delta gaped at her. After that enormous breakfast, who could eat again? "That would be lovely," she said. "You'll join us, won't you? I'll call you when we're ready to break." She turned to go. "Oh, one more favor, if I may."

"Certainly. Anything." Matilda gave her a wide smile.

"Could I use your telephone for a moment? Someplace private?"

"Use the one in the kitchen." Matilda pointed. "I'll be in the den if you need me."

THIRTY-FIVE

The Final Gig

It was a glorious October evening, cooler than Delta had anticipated, an early fall by Mississippi standards. At six, Lauren's limousine driver pulled to the curb and let them out. They walked through the iron gates, past the Kissing Rock, and around front campus, pausing for a moment to look up at the spreading ginkgo tree.

The leaves had already turned to yellow, waving like tiny fans in the autumn breeze. Through the amber curtain Delta could see dapples like gold coins from the last of the sunlight, and slivers of a deepening blue sky.

There, under the tree, was the spot where she had first met Tabitha Austin and signed up the Delta Belles for their initial gig at the Harvest Fest Talent show. Up above, the round tower on the third floor, had been Rae Dawn's old dorm room.

It had been a rainy summer throughout the southeast, and the grass underfoot was rich and lush as they walked across the lawn toward the banquet hall.

"Delta?"

The voice came from behind her, and she turned. It was a déjà vu two decades in the making—a voluptuous redhead running across the campus, waving to her.

"Delta!"

It was Tabby. Everything about her seemed to have enlarged and magnified over the years—her hair redder than it had once been, her figure rounder and pudgier.

"I saw you arrive," she said breathlessly. "Did you just get out of a *limo*?"

"Well, yes," Delta said. "We, ah—" She pointed in Lauren's direction.

But Tabby wasn't looking at Lauren. She was staring at Rae Dawn.

"I know you!" she squealed. "You're—you're—"

"Rae Dawn DuChamp," Rae said formally, extending a hand toward Tabby and giving Delta a sly wink.

"Well, yes, of course," Tabby said. "I know *that*. But you're also Dawn DuChante. I watched on television the night you were nominated for a Grammy—that was years ago, wasn't it? I have one of your albums too—one of the old ones. But on the cover you looked so—so *different*."

"Makeup artists," Rae said. "Between them and photographers, they can make anyone look good."

"I wish I'd realized," Tabby grumbled. "I would have advertised Dawn DuChante singing at our banquet."

"Oh, that would have drawn a crowd," Rae said. "Maybe two or three more people would have shown up."

Tabby ignored this, looked around, and finally realized that the twins were standing there. "Oh, hey, Lace. Lauren."

Lacy grinned. "Nice to see you too, Tabby." She turned

toward her sister. "Speaking of makeup," she said, "your mascara is smeared right here—" She licked her thumb and rubbed at a smudge on Lauren's cheek.

"Will you quit spitting on me?" Lauren pulled away and slapped at her hand. "Jeez, you're worse than Mama ever was."

Everyone laughed. *Just like old times,* Delta thought. It felt good to be back again, good to be together.

She turned and gazed across the green expanse of front campus. In her mind's eye she could see them all—young and innocent, joyous, ready to take on the world. Nostalgia overwhelmed her, the bittersweet memories of those golden days. Laughter and heartbreak, love and longing, the passionate conviction that they could, indeed, make a difference.

The youth, of course, was long gone; their lives were mostly behind them now. And had they made a difference?

Delta didn't know. She thought about Rankin, about the causes he had stood for in his life. Equality. Justice. Inclusivity. She thought about Vinca Hollowell. About Grandma Mitchell. About Rae Dawn's story of love lost and Lacy and Lauren's tale of sisters separated.

Life was such a huge, complex puzzle. Perhaps all you could do was attend to your own small pieces and try to find the pattern in them.

"Come on," she said, pulling herself out of her reverie, "let's go make some music."

THE BANQUET HALL was packed. From backstage, Rae Dawn could hear the low roar of conversation filling the room. In a corner Lacy leaned over her guitar for a last-minute tuning.

Tabitha, looking frazzled and disjointed, rushed over clutching a clipboard to her chest.

"Are you ready?" She looked around.

"We're fine, Tabby," Lacy said. "Chill out."

"All right. Now, I'm going to give out some alumni awards first, and then I'll introduce you. Five minutes. Ten, tops." She muttered something inaudible and disappeared.

"This is going to be fun," Lacy said.

"Have you been to the bathroom?" Lauren asked with a wicked grin.

Lacy curled her lip in a mocking sneer. "I'll pee on *you* if you don't shut up."

Rae felt butterflies—or maybe it was caterpillars—moving around inside her stomach. She didn't know why she was nervous. She had done this a thousand times, in front of huge concert halls filled with fans, in the more intimate setting of Maison Dauphine. Besides, it didn't matter how good they sounded. It only mattered that they had done it for Delta.

Five minutes passed. Six. Seven.

"And now," Tabitha's amplified voice boomed into the hall, "the entertainment you've all been waiting for. From the class of 1969—we know her as Rae Dawn DuChamp—but she is a Grammy-winning writer and recording star—"

"Nominee!" Rae hissed.

"Please welcome Dawn DuChante and the Delta Belles."

A wave of applause, hoots, and whistles greeted them as they came onstage from behind the curtain. Lauren and Lacy took one mike and Delta moved to the other one, beside the piano. Rae looked over the crowd but could make out only shadowy figures in the darkness.

Then, as her eyes grew accustomed to the stage lights, she saw movement. Someone threading among the tables, coming from the back of the room to the front table where Tabitha Austin sat. As the figure drew closer, Rae Dawn could see that it was a woman, small, petite. She crossed to the table, ducking down, and the spotlight caught in her auburn hair.

Then she slid into a chair, turned, and faced the stage.

It had to be an optical illusion, a trick of the light, a projection of a dream. All the air went out of Rae Dawn's lungs and tears stung at her eyes.

It couldn't be. But it was.

Noel Ridley.

And she was smiling.

The Delta Belles, like the audience, were waiting for the concert to begin. Delta followed the direction of Rae Dawn's gaze. She recognized Noel instantly, from the framed snapshot in Rae's room.

Rae turned to Delta and motioned her over to the piano. "Did you do this?" she murmured.

"I didn't drag her here bodily, if that's what you mean," Delta whispered back. "But my sister Cassie isn't the only one who knows how to use a telephone."

Her eyes drifted to Noel again, who sat at the edge of the stage with her hands clasped in her lap and her eyes fixed on Rae Dawn's face. She was wearing the same expression as in the photo—the look of love, as if she might take off flying at any moment.

Rae reached out and squeezed Delta's hand. "Thank you," she said. And then, without taking her eyes off Noel, she launched into the introduction to the first number.

They played through all the old standards—"Blowin' in the Wind," "Where Have All the Flowers Gone," "If I Had a Hammer"—much to everyone's delight. Rae sang a couple of solos too, and as she wowed the audience with a smoky, steamy version of "Come Rain or Come Shine," only Delta knew she was singing for Noel.

The crowd loved it. Yet it wasn't so much the applause and cheering that moved Delta, but the music itself. The songs that years ago had molded a generation of activists and informed her own social conscience now gave her a fresh infusion of faith. Those who had paid the ultimate price for what they believed—famous people like Dr. King and the Kennedys, ordinary people like Rankin—weren't really gone. They were here, in the music, in the hearts of those who loved them and remembered them. Still inspiring, still empowering. Still hammering out justice and freedom and love.

Before she knew it, the concert was over. The audience was on its feet, demanding more.

Lacy stepped over to the piano. "We don't have an encore," she muttered to Rae and Delta. "We've sung everything we know."

Delta exchanged a glance with Rae, who nodded.

"I'd like to play one last song for you," she said into the microphone. The crowd hushed and resumed their seats. "It's a piece I wrote years ago, when I was a student here, and it reminds me of things my heart needs to remember. Of love and friendship, of hope when all seems hopeless, of healing that appears when we least expect it."

Delta knew what was coming. She stepped back from the microphone and closed her eyes as Rae Dawn launched into the opening measures of "Woman on the Wind."

She recalled, quite vividly, the night she had first heard this music. That night so long ago when Rae Dawn had opened her heart and revealed the truth about herself. The night Rae had declared her independence from the past.

The music surged around Delta like a mighty wind, bearing

her soul aloft. First the haunting, minor-key section, the song of a caged bird. And then the release, the letting go, the setting free. The climax she herself had once described as "making love with God and the universe."

She hadn't felt it for a very long time, that sense of Presence. She had held onto her anger, nursed it, unable to reconcile the unanswerable dilemmas that surrounded Rankin's death. But now, as the music soared, she began to rise above the questions and see things from a different perspective.

Inside her head, Delta could almost hear the tumblers of the lock falling into place, the door creaking open. She had blamed God for Rankin's death, as if God sat up there pulling the strings like some cosmic puppeteer, for good or ill. But now she understood: God wasn't *up there* at all, but down here, in the trenches, experiencing life's joys and agonies with us and within us.

The liberation came like a healing flood. Within the deep recesses of her soul, a cold, dark place suddenly illuminated and warmed as if a fire had been lit.

Shit happens, Delta thought. *Chaos impinges upon order. We live in a bent and broken world.* Whatever language you used, the reality was the same: Suffering was as much a part of life as joy. And for those who believed, or *tried* to believe—for seekers of truth and of holy love—there was only one conclusion. In our suffering, God suffers too, and when we weep, God's tears drip down like rain.

Now, on the other side of her anger, she saw her husband's death in a different light. And not only his death, but his life—their life together, with all its purpose and significance. At last Delta understood the wholeness of the gift they had been given, more than twenty years of joy and grace and love.

The music soared to its glorious crescendo, and Rae began to sing words Delta had never heard before. Instinctively she surmised that they were a recent addition—written, perhaps, during Rae Dawn's dark years alone. They blended flawlessly into the piece, rising upward on the final notes:

Reach and keep reaching,
Touch and keep touching,
Fear not the future, the pain, or the loss.
Sing and keep singing,
Hope and keep hoping,
Love and keep loving whatever the cost.

The music echoed into silence, and the house lights came up. No one applauded; no one even breathed. Stunned and astonished, the audience sat motionless. Some of the faces were streaked with tears.

The silence went on for a full two minutes, and then, as if on cue, the entire audience rose as one and began clapping.

Delta looked around the stage. Lacy and Lauren gripped each other's hands and gave a little bow. She moved closer.

"Have you talked with Lacy?" she said into Lauren's ear while the noise of the crowd roared around them. "About—you know. You and Trip."

"Not yet," Lauren said. "But I will." She turned away to take another bow.

Delta wanted to grab her, shake her, tell her that this time tomorrow might be too late. But she didn't. She had done all she could. She had been there. She had listened. The rest was up to them.

Rae Dawn was standing next to the piano with her arms around Noel. Rae motioned Delta over. "This is Noel!" she yelled over the chaos. "Honey, this is Delta."

"Thank you!" Noel shouted.

"My pleasure," Delta murmured. No one heard her, but it really didn't matter.

Just as they were about to leave the stage for the last time, the door to the banquet hall burst open and a flushed, fresh-faced young girl rushed in. She reminded Delta of the four of them more than twenty years ago—ardent and enthusiastic, full of the promise of an unknown future.

"The ginkgo tree is shedding!" the girl shouted. "If you catch a leaf by moonlight, you'll find your one true love!" And she dashed out again.

Delta looked at Rae Dawn and Noel, at Lauren, at Lacy. In unison, they shook their heads in disbelief and began to laugh.

And then, still laughing, the Delta Belles joined hands and took one final bow.

Epilogue

Emory University
April 1997

Delta booted up the computer and opened her e-mail files. In addition to the usual run of interdepartmental memos, she had three personal messages.

She clicked on the first, from Lace49KC:

Delta—

Just returned from my honeymoon and back to teaching first of next week. Hank sends his best, also Alison. So glad you could come for the wedding. Rae's song was beautiful, wasn't it? We're all so blessed.

Lacy

The message evoked both a smile and a pang of regret. Lacy had, as planned, returned to Kansas City immediately after the twenty-fifth anniversary reunion. A bittersweet decision that had led to love for Lacy but no real reconciliation between her and Lauren. They had made up, Delta thought, but long-distance forgiveness was never quite the same.

The second e-mail, from Lauren, confirmed her suspicions:

Hi Delta—

Sorry I missed the wedding. Would love to have seen you. Lacy's invitation was very gracious, but Trip and I felt it might be uncomfortable for her. We've talked, sort of, although e-mail and phone isn't the same as face to face. I missed my chance, I guess. Less stress here now that she's moved, but I wish it could have been different. Call me sometime.

Love, Lauren

And the last, from CrescentCityBlues:

Delta—

Great to see you at Lacy's wedding. Wished there had been more time to talk. How about coming to visit us soon? We'll make waffles and scrambled eggs and have brunch on the patio.
Thanks for everything. Noel sends her love.

R & N

P.S. We adopted a dog, a sweet little shelter mutt. His name is Gottlieb.

Delta leaned back in her chair and grinned at the screen. Life didn't always work out the way you hoped, but sometimes, sometimes. . . .

A knock on the door arrested her thoughts. She turned and looked up.

It was Lily Quentin, a student from her English lit class. An exceptional student, for the most part, although she seemed distracted since returning from spring break.

"Dr. Ballou?"

Delta held up both hands. "This time next week you can call me *Doctor,* if all goes well. I still have to get through my dissertation defense."

Lily edged into the room and stood shifting from one foot to the other. "Did you know that T. S. Eliot never finished his doctorate? Wrote his thesis, but then wouldn't show up to defend it. Apparently he said that anything he wrote needed no defense."

Delta laughed. "If you're T. S. Eliot, maybe. I don't suppose he mentioned how many footnotes were necessary to make *The Wasteland* comprehensible."

Lily gave a weak smile and fidgeted with her backpack. "I don't mean to interrupt."

"What's up, Lily? Have a seat."

Lily sighed and sank into a chair. "I probably shouldn't be bothering you. This is not even about lit class. I just wanted to talk, if you have time."

Delta gazed at her desk. Two dozen ungraded term papers littered the surface. She had an exam to write, a composition class at two, a faculty meeting at four, and she still hadn't fully prepared for her dissertation defense.

But in the back of her mind she remembered Drs. Bowen and Hart, all those dinners and late-night coffees and conversations over brunch on the patio with the dogs at their heels. She saw the image of a skinny blond waiter named Gabe, remembered his smile, heard him say *Even a bartender can listen.* The echo of a feeling washed over her, like standing on the beach at sunrise. Like driving through the country with the top down. Like leaving home and coming home all at the same time.

And deep inside, she felt the spark as flint struck steel.

She clicked out of the e-mail program, stacked the term papers, and leaned forward to fix her gaze on her student's face.

"Talk to me, Lily," she said. "I've got all the time in the world."

SURA'S

South India

(A journey into Peninsular India)

Sura Books (Pvt) Ltd.
Chennai • Bangalore • Kolkata • Ernakulam

Price: Rs.125.00

SOUTH INDIA

This Edition : April, 2006

Size : 1/8 Demy

Pages : 308

Price: Rs.125.00

ISBN: 81-7478-175-7

SURA BOOKS (PVT) LTD.,

Head Office:
1620, 'J' Block,
16th Main Road,
Anna Nagar,
Chennai - 600040.
Phones: 26162173, 26161099.

Branch:
XXXII/2328, New Kalavath Road,
Opp. to BSNL, Near Chennoth Glass,
Palarivattom,
Ernakulam - 682025.
Phone: 0484-3205797

Printed at Novena Offset, Chennai - 600 005 and Published by V.V.K.Subburaj for Sura Books (Pvt) Ltd., 1620, 'J' Block, 16th Main Road, Anna Nagar, Chennai - 600 040. Phones: 91-44-26162173, 26161099. Fax: (91) 44-26162173. email: surabooks@eth.net; website: www.surabooks.com

04 06 2000

South India

Although India is one nation, for convenience of analysis we divide it into South India and North India. The Southern part of India is called South India which mainly comprises States of Tamil Nadu, Kerala, Karnataka, Andhra Pradesh and the Union Territory of Pondicherry. It is also known as 'Peninsular India' lying south of Vindhya Satpura mountains.

HISTORY

The prosperity of the ancient South India was due to its trade links with other civilizations. South India had trade contacts with Egypt, Rome and South-east Asia.

Indonesian islands where Buddhism and Hinduism flourished looked at South India as its mentor. One of the famous Hindu epics, Ramayana is told and retold in different forms in many South-east Asian countries. South India was affected by several outside influences. There is a Christian influence in Kerala even to this day because of St.Thomas, the Apostle's visit nearly 19 centuries ago in 52 A.D.

Cholas, Pandyas, Cheras, Chalukyas and Pallavas were the chief rulers of the South. The Chalukyas to a great extent ruled over the Deccan region of Central India, at times, they extended their power further to South. They had Badami of Karnataka as their Capital. They ruled from 550-753 A.D. and fell to the Rashtrakutas. Their reign which was 'Crucified' in 753 A.D. resurrected in 972 A.D. and continued its spell upto 1190 A.D.

The Pallavas were superseded by the Cholas in 850 A.D. The temples at Thanjavur reveals the splendour and wealth of Chola power.

The Cholas invaded Sumatra, Ceylon and Malay. They also, at times ruled over some parts of these places which they invaded.

The Vijayanagara Empire which had its sway between late 14th and 16th centuries reached its pinnacle of expansion and glory during Krishnadevaraya (1509-29 A.D.) He maintained cordial relations with the Portuguese. Religious harmony was order of the day. The Vijayanagara rulers were patrons of art and architecture. The famous Hazara Ramaswami temple built by Krishnadeva Raya is a perfect specimen of Hindu temple architecture.

Neither the Aryan nor the Muslim invasion affected the Southern part of India. Mohammed Tughlaq's invasion of 1328 rang the death knell of the Hoysala Empire which spanned over 1000 to 1300 A.D. which had its centres at Belur, Halebid and Somnathpur.

SOUTH INDIAN SPICES

South Indian food is often flavoured with the non-scalding spices such as cinnamon, cardomom, ginger, cloves, garlic, cumin, corriander and turmeric.

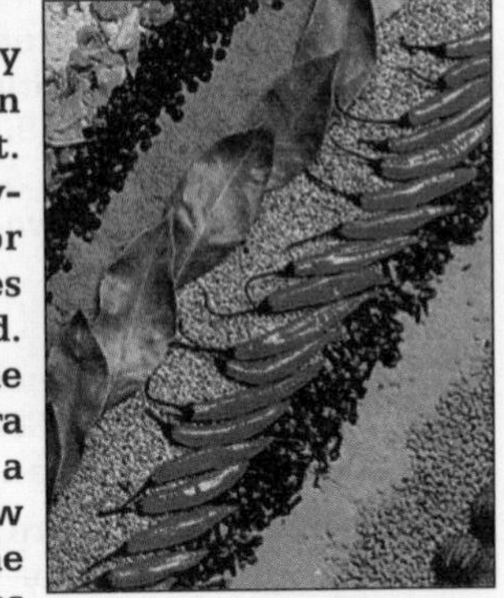

The story of the Indian spices dates back 7,000 years into the past. It is a chequered history of lands, discovered or destroyed, kingdoms built or brought down wars won or lost, treaties signed or flouted, favours sought or offered. Even today, Indian spices hold the same spell. In Tamil Nadu, Karnataka and Andhra Pradesh, the cultivation of paprika and a chilli variety with high colour value and low pungency is increased. Within the past one decade, the international trade in spices has grown by leaps and bounds.

SILK WEAVING

Today, the entire output of mulberry silk in India is produced in the three southern states of Karnataka, Andhra Pradesh and Tamil Nadu. It is considered as the queen of natural fabrics. The domestic production merely meets two-thirds of demand. The most popular varieties continue to be the native Mysore races. Kanchipuram (Tamil Nadu) silk saree is a 150-year old weaving tradition that has come to represent an art collectible more than mere clothing. Embroidery or crystal embellishments are made to the silk, or even in cotton and silk-polyster versions for the lower end of the market. The pallu of the saree carries designs of temple towers, palanquins, elephants, birds and creeping lotuses.

The export of silk goods is increasing every year by earning some crores of rupees as foreign exchange.

Tamil Nadu

Add 2 with all Phone Numbers in T.N. except Chennai for which we have already added.

General Information

Capital : Chennai • Area : 1,30,058 Sq.kms. • Population : 6,21,10,839 (2001 census) • Language : Tamil • Districts : 29 • Density (People in Sq.Kms) : 478 (2001) • Literacy : 73.47% - Male Literacy : 82.33% - Female Literacy : 64.55% • Lok Sabha Seats : 39 • State Assembly Seats : 234 • Sex Ratio (Male:Female) : 100 : 98

Tamil Nadu, a place of peace and serenity in the far south of the Indian sub-continent with its feet washed by the Indian Ocean, is a paradise for tourists. People, who come here, go back with an everlasting memory cherished forever of the land and its people. It is a land of magnificent temples that remain intact exposing the marvel and glory of the Dravidian culture, art, architecture and spiritual values. Not only temples but churches and mosques too declare the inborn secularism of the land. Numerous festivals and fairs, throughout the year add colour and mirth wherever you go. The ancient glory and modern hub of life mingle amazingly well, giving joy and soothing comforts. Long, sandy and sunny beaches abound to brace your health and enhance your happiness.

It is also a land of sanctuaries for birds and animals, forests, mountains, hill stations, natural sceneries and waterfalls - enough to forget everything and be immersed in enchanting beauty. Modern amusement theme parks have come up in various places to provide heart-throbbing and thrilling experience to young and old. The people are traditionally hospitable - the very meaning of a newcomer is 'guest' in the Tamil language - and friendly making you feel at home wherever you go. Comfortable and efficient public transport systems, air, road and rail links are available in almost all places. Good hotels, restaurants, lodges and guest-houses are available in all tourist centres affordable to your purse. From time immemorial, Tamil Nadu has been attracting travellers from abroad and the various accounts they have left are credible documents prized by the historians of this land. Tamil Nadu with such a hoary past in entertaining visitors and tourists welcomes you wholeheartedly. The moment you enter the land you enter a tourist paradise.

HISTORY

Tamil Nadu is considerably older than North India. North India and the Himalayan ranges appeared on the globe quite recently in terms of geological time scales. Even before that, Tamil Nadu existed as part of the continent that linked Africa and Australia together. It was called 'Lemuria' or 'Kumarik Kandam'. So, the origin of the first man should have taken place somewhere in this continent, and later, the race should have migrated to various parts of the world. The Tamils or the Dravidians are therefore one of the earliest races of the world. Prehistoric tools and weapons and burial sites have been discovered in various parts of Tamil Nadu.

THE SANGAM AGE

The earliest known period of organised life and history of the Tamils belong to the 'Sangam age'. Though the exact dates are disputed, it is pre-Aryan, non-Aryan and roughly goes back to 4000 B.C. The first, second and third Sangams flourished during this period and the Tamil poets of these 'Sangams' or Academies produced numerous literary works. Though most of them have been lost, a few anthologies are available in printed form. They throw considerable light on the everyday life of the people of those times and also reveal their culture, polity and social set-up. The country was ruled by three kingdoms called the Pandyas, Cheras and Cholas. The Chera Kingdom is the modern Kerala state. The Pandyas ruled the south and the Cholas the north. The Sangam Age is supposed to be the Golden Age of Tamils.

POST-SANGAM AGE

After the Sangam age, there is a dark period and the land comes under the domination of an alien race called the 'Kalabras'. There was chaos and confusion and instability with the result we get little evidence of the happenings of this period. This period was followed by the Pallavas who ruled the country for over two centuries (600 AD to 800 AD). Though the Pallavas were also alien, there was stability, peace prevailed and a lot of constructive works followed. Kanchipuram was their headquarters and the Pallavas were patrons of art, architecture and literature. The advent of rock temples by the Pallavas is a break- through in the construction of temples which were hitherto been built with wood, bricks and mud. Even today, these rock-cut temples can be seen in their pristine beauty in various places.

Rock-cut cave temples of Five Pandava Rathas of Pallava period carved in single granite boulder belonging to the 7th century AD are still a tourist attraction.

The 8th century Shore Temple built by Pallavas of Kanchipuram withstands even today the fury of sea tides and erratic weather conditions and not to say of miscreants. The temple has a Dravidian style Vimana of 60 ft. high. In the Sanctum, Vishnu - the preserver, is seen reclining on the ground.

The carvings represent Arjuna's penance praying to be blessed by Lord Siva to gain strength and vigour to win over his enemies. Some are of the opinion that it is Bagirath's penance to bring the celestial Ganges to the earth. However, the scenes in the rock are a superb poetry in sculpture which no visitor can miss.

The Pallava period was followed by the later Cholas. They ruled the country from 9th century A.D. to 13th century A.D. They gave a clean administration and people were free from

Gangaikondacholapuram Temple built by the Chola emperor Rajendra (1012-1044 AD) is a Siva temple. The rulers of many kingdoms near the Ganges (Ganga in Tamil) were won over by him. They were made to bring Ganga waters to be emptied into a huge tank near the temple. Hence the name 'Gangaikondacholapuram.'

Darasuram Temple built by Raja Raja II (1146-72 AD) was dedicated to Iravatheeswara. The reliefs sculptured in the basement walls depict the 63 Saivaite saints and the episodes in their lives.

Brahadeeswara Temple, Thanjavur represents the perfect example of Dravidian art and architecture. Begun in 1003 AD and completed in 1010 AD by Raja Raja Chola, the great King of Tanjore, the gopuram rises to a height of 208 ft. with 14 tiers. Though the temple is full of Saivaite iconography, there are Vaishnavaite and Buddhist themes also.

worries. They were great conquerors and builders of great temples. Art, architecture, literature and spiritualism flourished during the Chola reign. The art of metal casting and bronze icons were a speciality of this period. The amazing product is the icon of the cosmic dancer - 'Nataraja' - the presiding deity of Chidambaram Temple.

The Cholas were overthrown by the later Pandyas for a brief period in the early 14th century. During this period, the Khiljis invaded the south and the Pandya capital was sacked and a sultanate was formed which was destroyed by the rise of the Hindu Vijayanagar empire. The Vijayanagar empire prevented the spread of the Muslim rule south of river Thungabadra and thus was able to preserve temples and deities from being razed by the iconoclastic frenzy of the Mohammedans.

The Vijayanagar kings and their governors renovated most of the

Gingee Fort was bastion of Chola Kings during 9th century AD. Later Vijayanagara Kings fortified and made it impregnable. This fort is built on 7 hills – the most important being Krishnagiri, Chandragiri and Rajagiri.

Ekambareswara Temple, Kanchipuram, is the largest Siva Temple spread over 9 acres. Its huge gopuram (192 ft. high) and its massive walls were constructed by Krishnadeva Raya in 1509.

temples damaged by the earlier Muslim invaders. The main feature of their temple works was the erecting of 'Raja Gopuram' or the tall temple towers at the threshold of the temples. As a result of their supremacy, the Nayak dynasty adorned the thrones of Madurai, Thanjavur and Tiruchi. Their contribution to temple architecture was considerable and a valuable addition to those already done by the Pallavas, Cholas and the Pandyas. The Nayaks continued long after the fall of the Vijayanagar empire. The rise of the Marathas had its impact on Tamil Nadu and there was Maratha rule for a brief period in Thanjavur and its neighbourhood. After this, Tamil Nadu was under the muslim rule of the Nawab of Arcot. The advent of

Ten giant gopuram towers beckon the faithful to worship at the Meenakshi Temple in Madurai, one of Hinduism's busiest centres. Madurai is considered the heart of Tamil country. Goddess Meenakshi is the presiding deity with her consort Lord Sundareswarar. Lord Nataraja dances in Velliambalam, the dance hall here, in a different style, raising his right leg up instead of left.

Mariamman Teppakulam, Vandiyur, Madurai, was built by Thirumalai Naicker. The tank is a natural evolution when earth was digged out to make bricks to construct Thirumalai Naicker Mahal. The tank is almost a square with 1000 ft. long and 950 ft. wide.

Thirumalai Naicker Mahal, Madurai, constructed in Indo-Saracenic style was the palace of Thirumalai Naicker. Its gigantic granite pillars cased in mortar and imposing arches are of engineering marvel and fine example of the architectural style of Naicker dynasty.

the Europeans and their struggle for supremacy resulted in the founding of the British empire. The first presidency established by them was Madras i.e. Tamil Nadu. The British rule ended with India attaining its freedom on 15th August 1947.

During the Pallava period Buddhism, Jainism, Vaishnavism and Saivism had ardent following. Then came Islam and Christianity. Thus, a secular seed of tolerance was sown in Tamil Nadu and places of worships of all of them flourished. Today, one can find monuments and temples of all sorts throughout Tamil Nadu.

Kailashnatha Temple, Kanchipuram, *was built by Rajasimha Pallava in the late 7th century AD. The front was added by Mahendra Varma Pallavan later on. It is a fine piece of early Dravidian architecture and we can say, the only piece of the original Pallava temple architecture.*

TEMPLES AND DEITIES

There are over 30,000 temples in Tamil Nadu. "Don't live in a place where there is no temple" is the motto of the people of Tamil Nadu. Therefore, you cannot find a hamlet, a village, a town or a city here without a temple. Each place and temple has its own presiding deities. Almost all the temples have similar features - the gopuram or the Portal Tower from all four directions, the vimanam or the Tower over the sanctum sanctorum, spacious halls and corridors. Besides a place of worship, the temple also serves as a community centre. All activities like education, fine arts, functions, marriages, festivals, etc. were performed, and they served as hospital, dharmasala, storehouse and during emergencies and wars it also served as a bastion. The Marathas practically utilised the temples at Thiruvannamalai and Chidambaram as their barracks for a prolonged period.

The ***Arunachaleswarar Temple*** *of* ***Tiruvannamalai*** *is dedicated to Jothi lingam (God incarnate of fire). The temple was constructed and extended by the Cholas, Vijayanagar Kings, Hoysalas and the Nayaks. The underground lingam where sage Ramana Maharishi did penance is a great attraction.*

The main deity of the Tamils is Lord Muruga who is called 'Seyon' in Tamil literature and is the God of hills. The God of forests is called 'Mayon' or Vishnu, Siva is worshipped in the form of 'Lingam'. 'Kottravai' or 'Kali' is the Goddess of 'Palai' or arid lands. Indra is the God of fertile lands and Varuna is the God of rain. Only these deities were worshipped in the Sangam period. Vinayaga or 'Pillaiyar' who is the most worshipped God nowadays, is a later addition brought to Tamil Nadu by Mahendra Varman, the Pallava king, from Badami. There are no temples at present for Indra and Varuna. Besides, there are umpteen number of lesser deities and local 'devathas'. Arupadai Veedu of Lord Muruga-Thiruttani, Swamimalai, Palani, Thiruparamkundram, Pazhamudirsolai and Thiruchendur and the Pancha Bootha Sthalam or the five exclusive

Swamimalai is also an abode of Lord Muruga. Lying 6 kms west of Kumbakonam, the temple has 60 steps to represent the cycle of Sixty Tamil Years. Another abode of Lord Muruga at Tiruttani in Thiruvallur district has 365 steps to represent the days in a year. Swamimalai is the ideal place for craftsmen who shape the metal of bronze into idols.

The Srirangam temple situated on an island formed between Cauvery and Kollidam rivers is the abode of Lord Ranganatha (Vishnu) who is reclining on Adhisesha (Serpent) majestically. The sanctum is surrounded by 7 large enclosures and 21 majestic gopurams. Almost all the Kings who ruled Tamilnadu, spent lavishly to enrich the grandeur of the shrine.

centres of worship of Lord Siva, representing the five elements of Lord Siva, Chidambaram (sky), Thiruvanaikkaval (water), Thiruvannamalai (fire), Kanchipuram (earth) and Kalahasti (air) now in Andhra Pradesh, are famous pilgrimage centres of the Saivaites. The Vaishnavaites have 108 sacred abodes of Vishnu most of which are located in various places like Kanchipuram, Madurai, Srirangam etc. The consorts of Vishnu, Sridevi and Bhoodevi, Lakshmi and the consorts of Siva, Parvathi, Kamatchi, Abhirami, Meenakshi also have separate temples in various places. The temples of Kali are varied like Durgai Amman, Mariamman, Angalamman etc. They are found all over Tamil Nadu.

Besides these Hindu deities, churches of Virgin Mary, Shrine Velankanni, St. Antony have large following in Tamil Nadu. People of all religions and sects visit them.

Muslim durgahs at Nagore, Chennai, Madurai etc., are also worshipped and visited by people of all sects and religions. Wherever and whenever there are festivals in these places of worship, people throng without any distinction of their native religion or faith - a unique feature in Tamil Nadu manifesting the religious tolerance of the Tamils.

GEOGRAPHICAL FEATURES

Tamil Nadu is located in the Northern hemisphere in the torrid zone between 8° and 13° N. latitude and between 78° and 80° E. longitude. It is bounded by the states of Karnataka and Andhra Pradesh in the north and Kerala in the west. The southern tip is in the Indian Ocean and the long eastern coast is lapped by the Bay of Bengal. Point Calimere forms the easternmost tip and the Mudumalai wildlife sanctuary is the westernmost tip. The northern extreme touches lake Pulicat. The southernmost tip is Cape Comorin or Kanyakumari.

Tamil Nadu, the 11th largest state in India has a population over 6 crores and occupies an area of 130,058 sq. kms. The union territory of Pondicherry is a tiny pocket within the boundaries of Tamil Nadu near Cuddalore district; Karaikal, a little away from Pondicherry is near Nagapattinam district.

The ancient Tamils divided the land into 5 major physiographic parts as follows: Kurinji - mountainous region, Mullai - forest region, Marudham - the fertile plains, Neidhal - the coastal region and Palai - the arid region.

The Western ghats and the Eastern ghats meet in the Nilgris of Tamil Nadu. The hill stations of Tamil Nadu, Ooty, Kodaikanal, Kothagiri and Yercaud are situated in this region. Though the Eastern ghats is broken and appears to be a residual mountain, the Western ghats stretches along almost as an unbroken chain except for a 25 km gap at Palakkadu and a still lesser gap in Shencottah. These gaps are the entry points to the state of Kerala.

Ooty lake is an artificial one created by Sullivans. Boating is the privilege of all with a fee but fishing can be done only with the permission obtained from Assistant Director of Fisheries.

High in Tamil Nadu's Nilgiri Hills (Blue Hills), women pluck tea leaves from cultivated bushes on a tea plantation. Nilgiri-grown tea is considered to be one of the world's finest. One must visit Kodanadu viewpoint to have breathtaking view of the river Moyar.

Ooty is connected to Mettupalayam by narrow gauge rail track of 89 kms. Though the train mainly carries railway employees, the tourist must travel atleast once to have the panoramic view of Ooty hills and feel the richness of fauna and flora.

Unlike the Eastern ghats, the Western ghats receive abundant rain and are full of evergreen forests and the valleys of Cumbum and Pollachi besides having picturesque sceneries contain tea, coffee and spice plantations. The upper reaches of the Eastern ghats are called the Shervaroys famous for their fruit gardens and coffee plantations. Yercaud is situated in this region.

Tamil Nadu has a rich variety of flora and fauna. Indira Gandhi wildlife sanctuary in Anaimalai and Mudumalai wildlife sanctuary are situated in the Eastern ghats. Elephants, tigers, bisons and a variety of monkeys and deer roam about freely in them. Over 3000 plant species are also found there. The most important of them is the Kurinji plant which blooms once in 12 years. The name Kurinji to the hilly region is derived from this flower. Various medicinal herbs are also found in Palani hills and Courtallam. Palmyrah groves are abundant in Tirunelveli district which is the major source of a plethora of

***Mudumalai Sanctuary**, is the most important in South India. It borders with Bandipur National Park in Karnataka and Wyanad sanctuary in Kerala. The nights of April are lit by millions of glow-worms which look like a dream world of illuminated paradise.*

cottage industries. Rubber plantations abound in Kanyakumari district and sandal trees are grown in Javvadu hills of the eastern ghats near Vellore.

The rivers of Tamil Nadu are not perennial and one could only see a sandy dry river bed in summer. The Cauvery is the longest and most important river originating in Coorg in the state of Karnataka. Its water is utilised for cultivation in the deltaic region of Thanjavur and Nagapattinam districts. The other rivers are the Palar, Pennar, Vaigai, Tamiraparani which are flooded during the rainy season.

The only arid region or Palai is found in Tirunelveli district. It is called *Theri* by the natives. Tamil Nadu has a long coastal line, about 912 km which is named coromandal coast or *cholamandalak karai* in the northern half and the southern coast is the pearl fisheries coast. Mylapore, Poompuhar, Mamallapuram and Kayalpattinam were the ancient seaports along the coromandal coast. Maritime trade flourished between these ports and the ports of Rome, Greece and the East Indies. Mangrove forests found at Pichavaram near Chidambaram, Pulicat lake and Vedanthangal are important bird sanctuaries.

CLIMATE

As Tamil Nadu falls in the torrid zone, the climate is tropical and there is little difference between the summer and winter. April, May and June are the hottest months during which time the mercury may soar above 40° C. Near coastal regions, the climate is warm and humid and one cannot avoid perspiring. But, sea breeze sets in in the afternoon making the evenings and nights cooler. A mild winter falls between December and February, the most ideal time to visit Tamil Nadu. The weather is then pleasantly cool with no perspiration. The rainy season is marked by the onset of the north-east monsoon between mid-September and mid-December. Cyclonic storms occur during this time due to bay depression.

WHAT TO WEAR

Summer garments and cottons are ideal throughout the year if you do not visit hill stations where mild woollen clothes may be needed during summer and heavy woollen clothes during winter. Raincoats and umbrellas will come in handy during the monsoon i.e. mid-September to mid-December.

FOREIGN TOURISTS

Customs - A green channel is available for tourists without any dutiable or contraband articles. High value articles have to be entered on tourist baggage i.e. export form.

Passport, visa: Citizens of all nations barring Nepal and Bhutan and South Africans of Indian origin require valid passports and visas.

INDIAN CURRENCY

The hundred paise worth rupee is the Indian currency. The denomination of coins comes in 5, 10, 20, 25 and 50 paise and 1, 2 and 5 rupees. Currency notes are available in denominations of 1,2,5,10,20, 50,100 and 500 rupees.

Foreign currency notes and traveller's cheques brought by the tourists should be entered in the currency declaration form issued to tourists on arrival by airport officials.

FESTIVALS OF TAMIL NADU

Tamil Nadu is a land of festivals. Umpteen festivals are observed throughout the year and no fortnight ever passes without a festival. Most of them are associated with religion and temples. People celebrate them with gay and enthusiasm. A brief narration of a few festivals are given so that tourists can enjoy them realizing their significance. The tourism department too arranges festivals periodically so that the visiting guests may enjoy them and understand the cultural and spiritual values embedded in them.

January

Pongal

This is the most important of all festivals to the people of Tamil Nadu. It is often called as **"Tamilar Thirunal"** or the Prosperity Day of the Tamils. It comes in the middle of January. It celebrates the arrival of fresh harvest and everyone appears in new garments with a beaming smile greeting each other on this day. New earthen pot is put on a hearth in a central place in a open corridor and newly harvested rice and milk are cooked. As the milk boils over, people shout in chorus **"Pongalo Pongal! Pongalo Pongal!!"**. Pongal literally means boiling. The preceding day of Pongal is called **'Bhogi'**. It means Bogam or enjoyment and was originally devoted to Indra who is the Bogi or supreme enjoyer. Nowadays, old unwanted things are heaped on the middle of the road and a bonfire is made. Children beat hand drums and go round the roads beating the drums and shouting 'Bhogi Bhogi!'.

It is a three-day festival. The second day is called **Mattu Pongal**. Bullocks and cows are taken care of on this day and they are worshipped and given nourishing food called **'Sarkarai Pongal'**. **Poet-Saint Thiruvalluvar Day** is also celebrated on the 15th of January. The third day is called 'Kanru Pongal' or Calf Pongal. On that day the calves are fed. It is also called **'Kanum Pongal!'**. 'Kanum' means seeing and people visit elders or relatives and friends and seek their blessings.

Jalli Kattu - Bullfight

On the second day of the Pongal i.e. on Mattu Pongal day, Jalli Kattu or bullfight takes place in almost all villages. Youths come forward to tame the bull as they come ferociously rushing on them. It is a traditional, spine-chilling fight. The winner gets the prize money tied on the horns. Alanganallur near Madurai is famous for this sport.

Republic Day

The Republic Day falls on 26th January. It is a national festival. Spectacular march past, cultural and gay pageantry mark the celebrations in the state capital and the capitals of the districts.

Tourist Fair - Chennai

During January, Tourist Fair is conducted at Island Grounds in Chennai by the Tamil Nadu Tourism Development Corporation. All government departments and public sector enterprises take part in it. Every day folk dances and dramas are conducted. It presents a bird's eye view of Tamil Nadu. All the places of tourist interest and a wealth of information about the progress of Tamil Nadu besides cultural shows and food fairs form part of the fair. The fair lasts for nearly 3 months.

Dance Festivals - Mamallapuram

This festival conducted by the Department of Tourism is generally held at Mamallapuram where monolithic rock sculptures of the Pallava kings are built on the shore. The dances are held on an open-air stage near these sculptures. A spectacular dance festival in a beautiful surrounding that brings everlasting joy to the onlookers. Bharatha Natyam - the classical dance of Tamil Nadu, Kuchipudi - similar dance of Andhra Pradesh, Kathakali of Kerala and Odissi the dance of Orissa are performed by renowned artistes. Folk dances also form part of the festivals. Mamallapuram is just 58 km. south of Chennai, capital of Tamil Nadu.

February, March & April

Sivarathri

A festival observed in all Siva temples and Saivaite families. Special poojas and chanting of 'Siva Siva' are done throughout the night. Devotees observe fasting and remain awake throughout the night. Special abhishekam or holy anointing and ablution of Lingams are done from midnight.

Chitthirai Festival: Brahmothsavam or Chitthirai festival is the chief festival celebrated in all temples for 10 days. Every day 'urchavar' or the processional deity is carried in procession on different *vahanas* like horse, bull, swan, lion, sun, moon etc. The one at Madurai is indeed spectacular with Lord Vishnu landing on a golden horse for His sister Meenakshi's marriage. One major festival day of the 10 days is the 'Arubathumoovar Festival' day on which day all 63 Saivaite saints are taken in procession along with Lord Siva. The one at Kapaliswarar temple, Chennai, is very famous. The 63 bronze idols of the 'Nayanmars' or Saivaite saints are taken in procession - a magnificent sight. Lakhs of people throng during these festivals.

Tamil New Year's Day

It comes in the middle of April heralding the spring season. The Sun rises from the 1st constellation Aries on this day. The year's astrological prospect is read and people worship their family deity and visit temples. The neem flower is used in one way or other as a side dish and eaten alongwith sweet kheer called *payasam*. Huge queues will be found in all important temples on this day. Tamil New Year greetings will also be exchanged. This month is called *'Chitthirai'* and in olden days, on the full moon day of this month a great festival was celebrated, called *Indra Vizha* or *Vasantha Vizha* (spring festival).

Sri Rama Navami

It is celebrated in all Vishnu temples and at homes. It is the birthday of Rama, one of the Avatars of Vishnu. The Ramayanam is recited on this day.

Good Friday

The holy day of the Christians is observed throughout Tamil Nadu. Churches all over Tamil Nadu would conduct special masses on this day.

May, June & July

Summer Festival

The summer festival is celebrated in hill stations like Ooty, Kodaikanal, Yercaud etc. It is mainly a tourist festival. It is called 'Kodai Vizha'. Boat races, flower and fruit shows, are arranged. Cultural programmes are conducted. Trekking in hill stations are also done - a unique thrilling experience. There are competitions of flower arrangements, Rangoli and vegetable and fruit carving - an enticing feast to the eyes.

August, September

Adi Perukku

It is the eighteenth day of the Tamil month *Adi*, on which most of the rivers will be in spate after rains. People go to the river banks and worship the river goddess and float their offerings on river. They also carry different varieties of cooked rice and eat them on the banks and spend their time merrily.

Independence Day

15th August is the day on which India won Independence. It is a national festival. The National Flag is hoisted every year on this day. Processions and meetings are held. Flag hoisting ceremony at Fort St. George, Chennai and cultural pageantry mark the occasion. It is a public holiday and public buildings are illuminated colourfully on this day.

Krishna Jayanthi

It is the birthday of Lord Krishna. It is celebrated in all Vishnu Temples and at homes. People prepare different delicacies and offer them to Lord Krishna. Balls of butter are also offered.

Vinayaka Chathurthi

The birthday of Lord Vinayaka or the elephant-headed god. It is celebrated in all homes as well as in all Saivite temples and temples of Lord Vinayaka. The one celebrated at Pillaiyarpatti shrine of Lord Vinayaka is very famous. A gigantic *'Modhaga'* or *'Kolukkattai'* using about 80 kilos of rice, jaggery, coconut and dhall is prepared. It is baked for 3 days and offered to the deity. Lakhs of people from all over Tamil Nadu throng there on that day. Pillaiyarpatti is near Karaikudi about 500 km. from Chennai.

In all cities and district headquarters, giant Vinayaka statues ranging from 10 feet height to 32 feet are erected in public places. On the last day which varies from the 3rd day to the 10th day, big processions are held and the image is immersed in the sea, lake or nearby rivers. The procession will be colourful with various folk dances, nadhaswaram etc. performed enroute. In houses, clay image of Vinayaka is worshipped and immersed into wells, tanks or ponds the next day. The image is invariably adorned with a colourful umbrella called *'Pillaiyar Kudai'*.

September & October

Navarathri

Festival of nine nights: 'Navam' means nine and 'rathri' means night. It is the festival of Goddesses Durga, Lakshmi and Saraswathi. The first 3 days are devoted to Durga or Parvathi, the goddess of valour. The next 3 days are devoted to Lakshmi or goddess of wealth and the last 3 days are devoted to Saraswathi, the goddess of learning. On the ninth day, a pooja for Saraswathi is performed in a traditional way by piling up books in an orderly way. This day is called *'Ayudha Pooja'* - on this day all the machines, tools, instruments and vehicles are cleaned and arranged in order and worshipped. The vehicles are adorned with flowers and plantain saplings. This festival is also known as **Dussehra**. It is also called Durga Pooja. The next day is called 'Vijayadasami' or the day of victory.

During this period, most of the Hindus celebrate Kolu festival and even in temples Durga or the main female deity is specially decorated in various ways and kept in the main hall for worship. In the houses, dolls are arranged on steps numbering 3, 5, 7, 9 or 11 and the hall is decorated with festoons. Dolls of different deities and ordinary life scenes and of a secular nature are also erected. Every day visitors are invited and *Prasadam* is also given. The origin of this festival is traced to the Vijayanagar period. Doll exhibitions and sales are also arranged during this time. Especially the ones at Khadi Bhavan and Kuralagam in Chennai are feast to the eyes. People throng in large number to these places to see and enjoy them and also to purchase the dolls, the prices of which range from Re.1/- to Rs.5,000/-. The Ramakrishna Mutt at Mylapore celebrates the Durga Pooja during these ten days, as it celebrates the festivals of all religions and faiths, and on the final day a big image of Kali is taken in procession and immersed in the sea. These ten gay days are full of visitors, visitings and feasts. Children wear fancy dresses. The temples overflow with devotees.

Shrine Velankanni Festival

The renowned church of Shrine Velankanni near Nagapattinam has wondrous legends. The 16th century ship-wrecked Portuguese sailors had built this shrine in gratitude for saving and guiding them to the shore during a severe cyclone. Thousands of people visit the place during the festival, clad in orange robes to the sacred location where the ship landed. The Virgin Mary Church is the *'Courdes of the East'* and is believed to have miraculous power of healing. This festival attracts peoples of all religions: Hindus, Muslims and of course Christians - it is rather a secular gathering.

Kanthuri Festival

This too could be said to be of a secular nature since people of all faiths flock to the shrine of saint Quadirwali believed to be doing good to all. One of the descendants of the saint is chosen as the spiritual leader or 'peer' and honoured with offerings. The tenth day is most important. On that day, the tomb of the saint is anointed with sandal paste and later it is distributed to one and all. This holy paste is believed to possess healing powers as it is considered a remedy for all ills. The festival is celebrated at Nagore durgah near Nagapattinam.

Mahamagam Festival

This festival comes once in 12 years. This period is called 'Mamangam' in Tamil. This occurs once in 12 years when planet Jupiter enters the constellation of Leo. It is believed that all the holy rivers of India bathe in the sacred tank here at Kumbakonam on this holy day to wash away their sins - accrued from the devotees who bathe in them. The Mahamagam tank is situated in the temple city of Kumbakonam. The legend has it that a few drops of divine nectar from the 'Kumba' (pot of nectar) has fallen into this tank. Lakhs of people take a holy bath on this day. The unique feature is that residents of the whole city become hosts to the visitors. Lord Siva called *Adhi Kumbeswara* is worshipped here. Kumbakonam derives its name from this 'Kumba' or pot.

October - November - December

Deepavali

This is the most important festival that brings joy to both the rich and the poor. This is also called *'Naraka Chathurdasi'*, on which day the fearsome giant Narakasura was killed by Lord Krishna. According to his last wishes his death day is celebrated with festivity. People take oil bath in the early hours of the day, called

"Ganga Snanam" or holy dip in the Ganges, wear new clothes, fire crackers and eat sweets. The following new moon day is observed as "Kethara Gowri Viratham" and ladies observe this for the longevity of their husbands. In North India, it is observed as Ramlila on which day great fireworks are a feast to the eyes; they mark the defeat of Ravan by Sri Rama. It is said that it is a day of triumph of the good over the evil. In the North, lamps are also lit in a row in the houses. 'Deepam' means lamp and 'Avali' means row. On this day, sweets are prepared and distributed. People greet each other with a traditional question "Ganga Snanam Aachcha?" which means 'Have you finished your holy Ganges bath". People visit temples in large numbers on this day.

Vaikunta Ekadasi

This festival is a Vaishnavite festival and it is believed that the gates of Paradise are thrown open on that day. In all Vishnu temples, a decorative gate is erected called 'Vaikuntha Vasal' or the threshold of paradise. Thousands of people come to pass through the threshold of paradise. Bhajans are held and the day is a fasting day. During the night most people stay awake and end their fast with a feast the next morning. The Srirangam temple on the island of Srirangam near Tiruchirappalli and the Parthasarathi temple built by the Pallavas at Triplicane in the city of Chennai attract lakhs of people. It is an interesting sight to see Bhajan groups called 'Bhajanai Koshti' singing the names of Lord Vishnu in high pitch and dancing in a trance around the temple.

Arudra Darshan or Thiruvadhirai Festival

It is a festival observed by Saivaites or the devotees of Siva. The cosmic dancer Lord Siva gives darshan on this day. It is observed in all Siva temples. Very early in the morning special ablutions are done to the dancing idol of Siva and He is taken in a procession. On this day in the houses, people prepare a sweet called 'Kali' a mixed vegetable dish called 'Koottu' and offer it to the deity and eat and distribute. Arudra Darshan is very famous in the Nataraja temple at Chidambaram.

Natyanjali Festival

It is a dance festival at the Nataraja temple at Chidambaram. It is a homage paid by all the dancers to the cosmic dancer, Lord Nataraja. It is celebrated near the thousand-pillared hall of the temple where 108 dancing poses of Lord Siva are depicted. The poses are from Tamil Nadu's classical dance Bharatha Natyam. Dancers all over India come to pay their tribute by performing dances. A colourful and enchanting programme of dances like Bharatha Natyam, Kuchipudi, Kathakali, Odissi and Kathak are performed.

Karthigai Deepam

It is one of the most ancient festivals of Tamil Nadu. We have references to this festival in Sangam literature. It is the festival of lights of Tamil Nadu. Deepam means light. Rows of earthen lamps are lighted in front of houses in the evening. Traditional snacks called Appam, Pori and Adai are prepared and offered to deities. The festival is celebrated in all Siva temples. The one at Thiruvannamalai temple is most famous. It is called Annamalayar Deepam. A big lamp on the rocky top of the mountain is lit. A big wick is prepared and 100 litres of ghee is poured and the lamp is lighted. It glows throughout the night. Despite heavy downpours, the light will be burning. Lakhs of devotees gather for this festival from all over India. Thiruvannamalai is one of the Pancha Bootha Sthala or five element places and the element represented here is the fire. A big bonfire is made in front of temples. In houses, crackers are fired. This festival marks the end of the rainy season in Tamil Nadu.

Saaral Vizha

This is a unique festival of recent origin. It is celebrated in Kuttalam or Courtallam where there is a number of waterfalls. During the season, water will be abundant in them and thousands of people gather there to bathe in them. The water has healing powers as it passes through various medicinal herbs before the fall. Courtallam is near Tenkasi in Tirunelveli district. The Saaral Vizha is a unique festival which invigorates our body. The water pours on us like thousand slaps and relieves our pains and aches and makes us fresh. Proper safety arrangements are made and there are separate places for men and women.

Kavadi Festival

This is a religious festival. Kavadi is a flower-decked decoration carried on the shoulders. There are different types of Kavadies called Pal (milk) kavadi, Panneer (rose water) kavadi, Pushpa (flower) kavadi, Mayil (peacock feather) kavadi etc. Devotees of Lord Muruga dancing in a divine trance to the rhythm of beating drums carry this on their shoulders and climb the mountain. The kavadi festival is very famous in Palani, Tiruthani and Tiruchendur and the other shrines of the Arupadai Veedu or the six abodes of Lord Muruga which are mentioned earlier under the sub-heading Temples and Deities.

Music Festival

The music festival is celebrated every year in the capital city, Chennai. During December, all the 'Sabhas' or Music clubs arrange for this. The Music Academy, Annamalai Mandram, Narada Gana Sabha, Indian Fine Arts Society and other sabhas arrange for this festival in various places. At Kalakshetra, a dance festival is also conducted during this time. It is a festival for lovers of music. Research scholars and renowned musicians render vocal and instrumental recitals in various sabhas from the afternoon till late in the night. It is a festival that reflects the culture of Tamil Nadu. Music lovers from all over the world participate in it.

Besides, all the Muslim festivals like Ramzan, Bakrid, Milad-un-Nabi etc. and all the Christian festivals like the New Year Day, Ash Wednesday, Good Friday, Christmas etc. are also celebrated in Tamil Nadu. Thus, Tamil Nadu abounds with national, secular and religious festivals of all sorts - and it is apt to call it 'a land of colourful festivals and unbiased gaiety'.

LIP-SMACKING CULINARY OF TAMIL NADU

From time immemorial Tamil Nadu is noted for entertaining the guests with sumptuous feasts. It can provide a wide variety of lip-smacking, tasty, delicious food both vegetarian and non-vegetarian to visitors. With plenty of vegetables in its blend. Tamil Nadu provides a healthy fibrous food. Grams, lentils, rice, greens and vegetables with spices add aroma and taste to the food.

Breakfast

It is known as 'Kaalai Chitrundi' in Tamil. The main items of the breakfast are:

1. Rice idlies (steamed rice and orid dhal battered into fluffy cakes), 2. Dosai (A pancake of the same batter

fried crisp in a pan), 3.Vadai (deep fried doughnuts of a batter of lentils), 4. Pongal (cooked rice with lentils and flavoured with ghee, pepper, cumin seeds, cashewnuts, ginger bits and curry leaves), 5.Uppuma or Kitchedi (cooked sooji or semolina with oil, mustard, cumin seeds and lentils), 6. Idiappam (steamed rice noodles), 7. Appam (a similar preparation like Dosai but baked). Side dishes - all these items are eaten with Coconut Chutney, Sambar (seasoned lentil broth), and chilli powder (a powder mix of various dried lentils, chilly and salt with oil poured on it). Finally, coffee is served.

Lunch or Meals

This consists of cooked rice, dhall, ghee, vegetable side dishes, Sambar and Rasam (pepper water), curd, pickles and pappads or appalam. A sweet dish, payasam or kheer, is also served. In the case of non-vegetarian, various non-vegetarian side dishes of mutton, chicken, egg, prawn, crab, fish etc. are available.

Tamil Nadu dishes are mildly hot and aromatic and tasty.

Chettinadu cuisine

It is a speciality of Tamil Nadu both vegetarian and non-vegetarian and suitable to those who like hot and spicy stuff.

Besides, all varieties of other food items are available in hotels. In Star hotels, Continental, Chinese and Indian dishes are available.

Tamil Nadu is famous for its filter coffee. The coffee seeds are roasted and ground. The powder is put in a filter and boiling water poured over it. In about 15 minutes, the coffee decoction is collected in the lower container of the filter. It is taken and added to milk with sugar and served hot. The coffee aroma and its taste gives a new pep to those who drink it.

Now we shall pass on to the places of tourist importance in Tamil Nadu. This tourist guide is intended to give comprehensive details of places, their location, how to reach them, what to see there, what to buy and other useful tips to tourists with contact telephone numbers of public utility and emergency services. We shall begin with the state capital - Chennai.

Chennai

(Madras City)

Chennai hitherto known as the city of Madras is the capital of Tamil Nadu and the fourth largest city of India. It is the capital of Tamil Nadu and the gateway to the south. Francis Day and Cogan, the then East India Company officials who obtained a grant from the local chief Iyappa Nayak on August 1639 to build a factory were the founding fathers of the city. Various records showed the origin of the name and definitely the name Madras existed even before the Englishmen landed there. It was then called 'Madras Patnam'. A fort was built by the Englishmen and called Fort St. George as portions of it were completed on St. George's Day, the patron saint of England. After the fort was built, Iyappa Nayak insisted that the new settlement be named Chennappatnam after his father Chennappa Nayak. Thus the name 'Chennappatnam' came into being. In due course, Madras became the English name and Chennai the native name. Chennai lies on the 13° N. Latitude and 80° E. Longitude on a 17 km. stretch of the Coromandel coast and is virtually trisected by Adyar and Cooum rivers and the Buckingham canal. The present population is over 42 lakhs. Though its beginnings were a humble hamlet, it has now grown into a cosmopolitan metropolis by taking up the adjoining villages like Thiruvallikeni, Mylapore, Thiruvanmiyur etc. which are thousands of years older than the recent city of just 360 years. Thus a tiny hamlet hardly a sq.km. area has now become a city of 174 sq.km. It is still an expanding city and one cannot rule out its scope of further extension in north, south and west as the Bay of Bengal grudges its expansion to the east.

Chennai presents a distinctive variation to North India in music, dance, art forms, food, language, people, habits, customs and costumes. Besides modern development in industries and commerce, its traditions and conventions still continue side by side making life wonderfully charming. One can see a harmonious blend of the old and the modern in all things - conventional vegetarian fare to fast foods, traditional nine yard sarees to the latest fashion designs, ancient temples to modern multi-storeyed buildings, Indo-Saracenic and Victorian architecture to modern, classical music and dance to ultra modern pop music and disco dances. It is, in short, a kaleidoscope of harmony in contrast.

Unlike most other modern cities with a smoky sky, Chennai is a modern city with a clear sky, long sandy beaches, parks, landmarks of history, rivers, temples, churches, mosques, dance and drama theatres, cinema houses, star hotels, lodges and other tourist infrastructural facilities that make a more convenient entry point and to initiate your tour of the land of the Tamils and South India.

How to get there?

Chennai has road, rail and air links to all parts of India and the world and easily accessible from anywhere under the sun. The international airport here, is connected by several international airlines. The international terminal provides flights to several cities around the world. The domestic terminal has daily flights to all important centres in India. Domestic air traffic is handled by Indian Airlines and the international one by Air India. Besides Chennai, local airports are located in Trichy, Madurai and Coimbatore.

Two major railway terminals are there in Chennai - Central railway station and Egmore railway station. Central has broad gauge and connects Chennai to all major cities and towns of India. Egmore has both broad and metre gauges and links Chennai to all important places of Tamil Nadu and the neighbouring state of Kerala.

National highways and state highways connect the city with all important state capitals and cities of India and all district headquarters and towns of Tamil Nadu.

Air: Anna International and Kamaraj National Airports at Meenambakkam about 20 km. can be reached by suburban trains, city buses and taxis.

Rail: Central – trains to all parts of India moving north and west. Just a km. away from Central is Egmore, from where trains to all parts of Tamil Nadu and to the neighbouring state of Kerala are available. Suburban services are also available from Beach railway station to Tambaram and from Central to Tiruvellore. A new flying rail service is now available from Beach station to Mylapore.

Road: There are highways connecting Chennai to all places in India and also all parts of the state. State transport long distance coaches, private omni buses and taxis are available to any place. Prepaid taxis and airport coaches are available at airport. City buses, auto- rickshaws and taxis are available for travelling within the city and neighbouring places.

What to see in Chennai?

Fort St. George

Fort St. George is an important historical landmark in Chennai. It was built by Francis Day and Andrew Cogan, the founding fathers of Chennai and officials of the British East India Company. It was the first British settlement and was under French occupation for a brief period.

The Fort Museum formally opened in 1948 houses the fine collections of original writings of the various personalities who made Madras history for about a century. Portraits of past governors, painting of the storming of Srirangapatna and scenes of earlier Chennai adorn walls. Medieval weapons, collection of coins, silver wares, porcelain, manuscripts, engravings etc. are on display. A spectacular history of the past rolls in our minds. The marble statue of Cornwallis (1880) and Tipu handing over his children depicted on its pedestal bring before our eyes the Carnatic wars.

The flag staff on the ramparts facing the sea and atop the main gate is over 150' high and is still the tallest in India. Daily flag hoisting is done. It is said the Governor Yale was the man who first hoisted the Union Jack over Fort. St. George in 1687.

St. Mary's Church

It is the oldest Anglican church in the city built inside the fort. The foundation was laid on Lady's Day in 1678 and completed in 1680. It stands much the same as it was when built barring the spire and the tower which are later additions. It is full of mementoes of men who made the history of early Madras, and the narrow yard has tombs of various ages with inscription in several languages. These stones were presumably removed from an earlier grave. Its outer walls are four feet thick and bombproof. It is said to be the oldest Protestant church east of the Suez. A huge painting of the Last Supper in the Raphael style brought from Pondicherry when it was plundered in 1761 is a prized possession of the church. The marriage register of this church records the illustrious marriages of Elisa Yale with Catherine Hynmers and Robert Clive with Margaret Markeylyne. The Register of Baptisms, marriages and burials of the church are presented in the Fort Museum.

Other things to see in the fort are Administrative House where Robert Clive lived (at present occupied by the Pay and Accounts office), Wellesley House, King's Barracks and Cornwallis Cupola.

Now, the state legislature and secretariats are housed here besides the defence department offices.

High Court

The imposing Indo-Saracenic building of the High Court is an important landmark. Its stained glass arches and minarets are wonderful. The foundation was laid in 1889 and completed in 1892. Besides taking four years, it has consumed 13 lakhs. In its tallest minaret rising 160 feet above sea level, the Madras lighthouse was erected in 1894. It was a big gas-mantled lighthouse with huge reflecting discs. Formerly people were allowed to climb its spiralling staircase to have a bird's eye view of the city. The present new lighthouse is on the Marina. The former one called Esplanade lighthouse after being dismantled remains as an ornamental Doric column in the High Court compound itself. During the First World War in 1914, the German cruiser Emden bombarded near this place causing damages to the walls. Even today, a plaque in the eastern compound immortalises the event bearing the date 22 September 1914.

There was an imposing temple, where the High Court stands today, called Patnam Perumal Temple or Chennakesava Perumal Temple erected by Beri Thimmana in 1648. It was demolished by the Company and historical records reveal that the Company paid a compensation of 565¼ pagodas to the Hindus of Chennapatnam providing alternative site near flower bazaar where Chennakesava and Chennamalleswara temples were built side by side in 1780 and survives to this day. Another Indo-Saracenic building adjacent to the High Court on the western side is the Law College established in 1892. It was originally the first burial ground of the White Town and even today we can see the arched and spired memorial of David, son of Elihu Yale, the illustrious former governor. Just opposite the high court stands another building of sandstone built in the Jaipur-Jaina style - the Y.M.C.A. building. Another tall building which was once the tallest in the city - the 'Rare House' could also be seen in the Parry's Corner.

The Harbour

Chennai is today one of the major ports of India. In the beginning, ships used to be anchored off the Fort and landed passengers and goods in a narrow sand bank. The second Lord Clive shifted it to the present place and built a pier in 1789. Subsequently works began in 1897 to ensure safe anchorage and was completed in 1910. Thus was formed the man-made harbour of Chennai (Madras) which today stands first in India in handling container carriages–on an average about 2 lakhs container traffic a year. Opposite the harbour on the North Beach Road, stately buildings like the Collector's Office, the General Post Office, the State Bank of India building etc. entice the visitors.

Museum

The Government Museum is on the Pantheon Road in Egmore. National Art Gallery, Gallery of Contemporary Arts, Children's Museum, the Museum Theatre and the Connemara Public Library also lie in the Museum Complex. The museum was a gift to the government in 1851 by the Madras Literary Society which gave its valuable collections of geological specimens. It is the first government-sponsored museum in the country. It has the most beautiful bronze collection of international repute, numismatic and arms collection with various departments like Natural History, Comparative Anatomy, Systematic & Economic Botany, Mineralogy, Geology, Industrial Arts, Ethnology, Antiquities and Archaeology. The old building of the Connemara Public Library is a wonderful piece of architecture of Indo-Saracenic interior and stained glass roof. The museum theatre is a typical old English theatre with a pit and is a semi-circular amphitheatre.

Victoria Memorial

It houses the National Art Gallery. It is a fine building of the Mughal style of North India adapted to Madras requirements. It is faced with a pink-coloured sandstone characteristic of Mughal buildings. Its fine gateways resemble that of Akbar's dream palace at Fatehpur Sikri; and its large hall has a marble floor and a fine ceiling with relief ornaments in chunnam. The foundation stone was laid by George V who visited Madras as Prince of Wales. The exhibits include a fine collection of bronze images belonging to 10-13th centuries, 16-18th century Deccan paintings, 11-12th century splendour of handicrafts and superb Ravi Varma paintings. The whole compound of the Museum is adorned with cannons captured in various battles by the British army. These is also a sculpture park in the rear and a rare 18th century horse-coach which were common in the early colonial period.

The Marina Beach

Any tourist to Chennai should not miss this beautiful spot – a long stretch of sandy beach, the second longest in the world. A drive along the Marina is a fantastic ride. On one side you can see stately historic buildings and on the other the vast stretches of sand lashed by the Bay of Bengal. It is the real lungs of the city and people come in large number to enjoy the calm cool breeze - especially in summer there will be a sea of people. One can see long row of ships waiting to enter the harbour and catamarans returning to the shore with the bounty of their toil. Edibles and snacks are available and people enjoy them while they enjoy the cool breeze. The main attraction of the Marina are the Samadhis of two charismatic former chief ministers of Tamil Nadu, Thiru. C.N.Annadurai fondly called "Arignar Anna" (Intellectual elder brother) and Thiru. M.G. Ramachandran fondly called "Puratchi Thalaivar M.G.R." (Revolutionary Leader MGR). Even today, you can see large number of people paying homage to their beloved leaders. Opposite the Anna Samadhi, the Senate House, the Convocation Hall, the Library and the new centenary building of the first university of south India - the Madras University, are situated. The Senate House is a good specimen of Indo-Saracenic architecture with minarets, domes and stained glass windows. On the north, we have a modern swimming pool, the river Cooum and the Victory Memorial between Fort St. George and the iron bridge at a point called Cupid's Bow built by a committee of citizens of the city of Madras to commemorate the victory of allied armies in the First World War (1914-18). It is a beautiful monument with a planned garden and later victories of the Indian army are also recorded here.

On the southern side, a row of beautiful buildings which house government offices could be seen, Ezhilagam - 'the abode of beauty' is the first and foremost of them. But, the most beautiful ones are the Khalsa Mahal built between 1864 and 1868 and the tall tower adds grace to the Marina. These buildings were once the harem of Arcot Nawabs. Adjoining it, is the Presidency college where one can see the statue of Dr.U.V. Swaminatha Iyer, the Tamil scholar who brought to light Tamil classics of the Sangam age. Lines of glorious tributes paid to this Tamil savant by the national poet Bharathiar are inscribed on the pedestal. There is an old aquarium opposite this college. Upto this junction, the area is called Chepauk; beyond that is Thiruvallikeni with Marina Cricket Grounds, Warlock Park, University Examination Hall and Vivekananda House or Ice House where once the icebergs cut and brought from the lakes of Canada used to be stored. The beautiful statue of Dr. Annie Besant and the statue of Swami Vivekananda as an itinerant monk adorn this place. After Queen Mary's College, we have the state police headquarters and the Chennai station of the All India Radio. Opposite the radio station is the new lighthouse.

Along Marina's park-fringed promenade one could see stately statues of doyens of Tamil language and literature. They include Caldwell, Kambar, Ilango Adigal, Bharathiar, Bharathidasan, Thiruvalluvar, Avvaiyar, G.U.Pope and Fr. Beschi (Veeramamunivar). The Triumph of Labour, Mahatma Gandhi and Kamaraj are the other statues adorning the Marina. The Marina is maintained as litter-free zone by Chennai Corporation.

Valluvar Kottam

What was once a lake in the heart of the city and later a garbage-dump was reclaimed and refurbished by Chennai Corporation and on it was built the **Valluvar Kottam** – a fitting memorial to the greatest poet-saint of Tamil Nadu. It is shaped like the old and one of the biggest temple chariots, in fact a replica of the one at Thiruvarur. It is 33m tall with a life-size statue of Thiruvalluvar on its seat. In the front hall corridors of the chariot, all the 1330 Thirukkurals with their 133 chapters have been depicted in bass-relief. Its auditorium is the largest in Asia and about 4000 people could be accommodated. It is a befitting modern memorial erected in the Dravidian and Pallavan style of architecture. Thirukkural is a unique work translated in almost all the major languages of the world.

The Birla Planetarium

A Planetarium - one of the most modern - is located in Kotturpuram between Adyar and Guindy. With a seating capacity of 236, it is a boon to research scholars of Astronomy, Astrophysics, Space Science etc. Every day barring Mondays, two programmes depicting the position of constellations, moon panorama, galaxies, comets, occurrence of solar and lunar eclipses, space travel etc. are on show to the public. It is a modern tourist attraction and gives a new experience that dispels all superstitions about the heavenly bodies. Adjacent to it is the Periyar Science and Technology Museum, useful and interesting to students and lovers of science especially to those who wish to know scientific principles and techniques that govern our life.

Kalakshetra

Meaning 'Temple of Art', it is a cultural institution of international repute. It is renowned for Bharatanatyam, the classical dance of Tamil Nadu and 'Kuravanji', a dance drama of Tamil Nadu. It was founded by Rukmini Devi Arundale in 1936 to train, encourage and revive interest in the dances and traditions of Tamil Nadu. It is run on the ancient Gurukulam system where students stay with the gurus or teachers and learn the art treating them as their foster parents. Throughout the year, Kalakshetra performs dance and music recitals in different parts of the city. The venues and timings are published in all major newspapers and also available from the India Tourism Office at Anna Salai and from the Tamil Nadu Tourism Office, Saidapet. It is an interesting sight to see the students learning and performing arts under a sylvan setting, most of the time under the shades of trees in the open air. Dr. U.V. Swaminatha Iyer manuscript library could also be seen in the complex. It is a rare library of its kind preserving traditional literature on palm leaves. They are microfilmed and kept in the library for the use of research scholars of posterity. A number of ancient and rare books have also been published by the library and are available in the sales depot.

Theosophical Society

The Theosophical Society to help and encourage the study of comparative religion, philosophy and science was founded by Madame Blavatsky of Russia and Col. Olcott in the U.S.A. in 1875 and later moved its headquarters to Adyar in 1882. It is on the southern bank of the river Adyar at its estuary. The serene place of this retreat is amidst 270 acres of gardens and estates. The shrine of all faiths, the Garden of Remembrance and a century-old library having invaluable collection of oriental palm-leaf manuscripts and parchments and the Big Banyan Tree, one of the largest in the world are the main tourist attractions here. Every year towards the end of December, the annual convention of the Society is held.

Elliot's Beach

The Elliot's Beach is the place where former governors used to go for sea bathing and relaxation. The Schidt's Memorial on the shore washed by the waves is a favourite shooting location for Tamil movies. It was once a calm place of relaxation and a bathing spot but the old charm of it is gone due to crowded residential colonies that have come up. The major attractions nearby are a modern temple and a church – the Ashta Lakshmi Temple dedicated to the goddess of wealth is a multi- storeyed building different from the traditional temples and the church is the Shrine Velankanni. Both attract large number of crowds during festive occasions. The Elliot's Beach is in Besant Nagar.

Ripon Buildings

Fondly called the White House of Madras opened in 1913 by Lord Hardinge, the then viceroy of India, it has been built of brick and chunnam with little stone and has been surmounted by a graceful tower with a big clock resembling the Big Ben of London. The stately building has been built in the British style. The Chennai Corporation, the City Council and the Mayor's Office function here. The white building is a graceful landmark and during full moon days its charm increases and it looks like a dream palace.

Covelong (Kovalam Beach)

A small fishing village with a beautiful beach and backwaters on the way to Mamallapuram. A quiet spot for rest, relaxation and sea bathing. An excellent beach resort of the Taj Group, Fisherman Cove, is there. The ruins of a fort and a Muslim Durgah nearby are also worth visiting.

Muttukadu

It is about 36 km from Chennai on the Mamallapuram Road. It has been developed as a scenic picnic spot and a centre for water sports by the Tamil Nadu Tourism Development Corporation. The backwaters of Muttukadu provides ample scope for them. In February each year wind surfing regalia with competitions are held. Training and demonstration programmes are also held.

Gardens and Parks

Chennai was once a garden city – even though the gardens have vanished, the names of them, Kilpauk Garden, Sylvan Garden, Poes Garden etc. still cherish the memory. Though most of them have gone there are still some with the name. The Chennai Corporation maintains about 80 small and big gardens. **"My Lady's**

Garden" is the chief garden. It is a well laid-out flower garden where the Corporation holds its annual flower show – a feast to the eyes indeed, usually inaugurated by the Governor of Chennai. Prizes will be given to the best maintained traffic islands and gardens. There will also be a show of flower arrangements, Bonsai trees, musical fountain, vegetables carving etc. during the flower show.

Napier Park in the heart of the city near Anna Salai beside the river Cooum, is another big Corporation Park with May Day Memorial. The **Panagal Park** in T.Nagar and **Nageswara Rao Panthulu Park** at Mylapore are other important major parks of the Corporation, that attract crowds. The Corporation band will play Carnatic music during evenings by rotation on a weekly basis.

The Guindy National Park is a deer sanctuary and an abode of a variety of birds, the black buck, spotted deer, civet cats, jackals, mongoose and monkeys. Adjacent to it is the **Snake Park** and reptilium where about 200 species of snakes including King Cobras and black serpents are reared besides lizards, chameleons, crocodiles and spiders. Snakes in cluster on tree branches and pits thrill the visitors. Venom extraction from snakes is done on Saturdays between 4.00 and 5.00 p.m. – a really heart-chilling experience to witness.

Children's Park

An amusement park for children is adjacent to the snake park with various types of play materials really enjoyable to children. And one can see large number of tiny tots brought to the place on excursion.

Gandhi Mandapam

A stately memorial of the citizens of Chennai to the Father of the Nation has a gallery and five-pillared Mandapam with exquisite carvings. Gandhi Jayanthi and other important functions are held here and on every Sunday between 9.00 a.m. to 10.00 a.m. a large number of devotees of Sri Aurobindo and the Mother of Pondicherry gather to pray and meditate. Rajaji, Kamaraj and Bhaktavatsalam memorials are adjacent to it.

Vandalur Zoo

The zoological garden maintained by the Corporation of Chennai in the People's Park was handed over to the government and shifted to Vandalur. It is named as Anna Zoological Park and spread over an area of 1,265 acres. It is the largest in South Asia and has a rich variety of different species of mammals, reptiles and birds. The animals roam in natural surroundings. A battery-operated car is available to go round. There is a special enclosure for nocturnal creatures. Safari parks, an aquarium and a natural museum are the other attractions in the zoo. Buses ply from all places in the city to the zoo.

Theme Parks around the City

Kishkinta

It is situated about 4 km away down Rajaji Salai at Tambaram. Suburban trains and buses take you to Tambaram. From there buses are available to Kishkinta. It is spread over 110 acres of land providing exciting high-tech amusement park set in beautiful surrounding. One can experience the never-before fun sensation here. The latest attraction is a man-made waterfalls called Chennai Courtallam.

V.G.P. Golden Beach

It is about 21 km on the road to Mahabalipuram south of Chennai. Buses are available from Adyar. It is another amusement and theme park with artificial beautiful settings and sceneries and structures. Many films are shot here. A number of exciting games and high-tech entertainment equipments and super-fast giantwheel are a speciality. Sea swimming is another attraction here. Pongal festival and flower and vegetable shows are also conducted here.

MGM Dizzy World

Further south to V.G.P. Golden Beach is the Dizzy World. A high-tech amusement park with thrilling and heart throbbing entertainments which makes one really dizzy.

The Crocodile Bank

It is another place of excursion about 34 km from Chennai and located between V.G.P. Golden Beach and Dizzy World. Here several species of crocodiles are reared in natural surroundings - the crocodiles basking in the sun and their sudden movement is an exciting sight. One can see crocodile eggs and feel the rough back of the crocodile here.

Temples in and around Chennai

There are over 700 temples in and around Chennai. Some of them are old, some built during the colonial periods and some modern. We shall here take up some selective temples known for their antiquity, sculptural beauty and popularity.

Kapaleeswarar Temple

Mylapore is one of the oldest towns of Tamil Nadu. Ptolemy, the Greek and the Arabs of the 11th century have mentioned it in their writing. It was an ancient seaport and appears to have existed for over 2000 years. Earlier, it was a Jain settlement and even before that the Buddhists were here. They called it 'Mayura Sabdha Pattinam' (The town of peacock sound). In Tamil, it has been called "Mayil Arpu" (Mayil means peacock and Arpu means sound). And Mayil-Arpu-oor became Mylapore in due course. There was a shrine on the shore dedicated to Thirthankarar Neminathar. The famous Jain scholar Mayilai Nathan had lived here. He has written a commentary to "Nannool", a popular grammar of the Tamil language. Until recently a few mutilated Jain and Buddhist statues could be seen in a compound opposite to the Santhome Basilica.

The original Kapaleeswarar temple was built by Pallava but it might have been eroded by the sea or demolished by the Portuguese who settled here in 1522. Saint Thirugnana Sambandar and Appar are believed to have visited that temple. The present temple is supposed to be an exact replica of the old Pallavan temple built about 300 years ago. The temple's 120 feet gopuram (Portal tower) was built in 1906 and the stucco figures adorning it speak of puranic legends. The temple has a big tank. One of the 63 Nayanmars, "Vayilar Nayanar" was born here and a separate shrine exists for Him. Bronze images of the 63 Saivaite saints adorn the outeryard of the temple and "Arubathu Moovar" festival is the most famous attracting lakhs of people. The legend of this place is that the consort of Siva, Parvathi, worshipped Siva in the form of a Peacock (Mayil); hence the place is called Mylapore. Another legend is that one of the Saivaite saints, Thirugnana Sambandar performed a miracle by giving life to a girl named Poombavai whose ashes were kept in a pot.

There are also other temples dedicated to Lord Siva. In one of those temples, the Lord manifests as Lord Veerabadra, wielding a sword, a shield, bow and arrow in His hands.

He wears a Chain of skulls around His legs. One of the earrings is of the type worn by women, and the other by men. Ganga and Moon can be seen on the Lord's head.

Mylapore is associated with Vaishnaviate traditions too and there are two Vaishnavaite temples, Madhava Perumal and Kesava Perumal in Mylapore. One of the first three Alwars – Peyalwar was also born here in a well. Even today, the birth of this Alwar is celebrated near a well in Arundale Street which is the birthplace of the Alwar. Saint Thiruvalluvar, the author of the illustrious Thirukkural was also born here and a temple dedicated to Him also exists.

Parthasarathi Temple

This temple also was built by the Pallavas in the mid-eighth century. Its tank is beautiful with lilies, hence this place is called Thiru - beautiful, Alli-Lily, Keni-Tank. Parthasarathy means the chariot driver of Partha or Arjuna and it denotes Lord Krishna. The image in the sanctum sanctorum is scarred with arrow wounds - testimony of the sculptor to the veracity of the chariot driver of the Mahabharatha war. One of the 12 Alwars (Vaishnavaite saints) Thirumangai Alwar of the 8th century had sung hymns on this shrine. The Chola, Pandya and Vijayanagar kings have made endowments and grants to this temple. Behind the temple is Bharathiar Memorial building – the place where he lived during his last days.

Temples of George Town

Unlike these two old temples, the temples of George Town were built after the new European settlement came into being. Chenna Kesava Perumal and Chenna Malleeswarar temples in Flower Bazaar, Kalahasteeswarar temple in Coral Merchant Street, Mallikeswarar temple in Lingi Chetty Street, Chintadri Pillaiyar Koil in Muthialpet, Kachchalleeswarar temple in Armenian Street, Krishnaswami temple in Muthialpet, the Kandasami Koil in Rattan Bazaar and the Kalikamba Kameswarar Temple in Thambu Chetty Street are some of them. The last one dates back to 1678 and Emperor Shivaji once worshipped Goddess Kalikamba here. One of the temples was built by prosperous merchants of the 18th century. The Adikesava Temple in Acharappan Street too belongs to this period.

Vadapalani Andavar Temple

It is located in Kodambakkam - the Hollywood of Chennai where many of the cinema studios like Vijaya, Vahini, A.V.M., etc. are located. The temple is dedicated to Lord Muruga. It is considered a very important shrine and on par with the shrine at Palani - the original Padaiveedu of Lord Muruga in the district of Dindigul. On Krithigai and Sashti days, one can see devotees carrying various types of Kavadis to pay their offerings.

Siva-vishnu Temple

It is in the busy area of Thyagaraya Nagar. Both Siva and Vishnu have separate shrines here. The temple is crowded during evenings. The Kasi Viswanatha temple in Kuppiar Street, W.Mambalam belongs to the 17th century. When it was built it was called "Mahabilva Kshetra". "Mahabilva" was in later days corruptly pronounced as Mambalam thus giving this name to this area. The Karaneeswarar temple at Saidapet is dedicated to Lord Siva.

The Mundaka (Lotus) Kanni (Eyed) Amman temple at Mylapore is the most famous Mariamman temple where animal sacrifice was performed before it was banned. The Mariamman is supposed to be a very powerful deity capable of fulfilling the just desires of the devotees. There is another old temple of the colonial period located in Pudupet near Harris Road called Kamaleswar Temple. Pachaiappa Mudaliar, the famous "Dubash" of the Company used to take his holy dip in the Cooum river daily – the river was so clean in those days – and worship the deity in this temple.

Villivakkam

This place, about 10 km by rail from Chennai Central, has to its divine pride two ancient temples, one dedicated to Lord Siva and the other to Lord Vishnu. The presiding deity of the former is Lord Agastheeswara and that of the latter is Lord Dhamodhara. Villivakkam is also connected by buses to other important parts of Chennai.

Jain Temples in the City

In George Town area near Adhiyappa Naicken Street, a Jain Mandir was built in 1899 in typical north Indian style. There are two more Jain temples in Mint Street. Another new Jain temple built in 1979 at G.N.Chetty Road in T.Nagar is of dazzling whiteness. A magnificent flight of steps lead to the sanctum sanctorum where the 16th Tirthankar Shanthinatha is seated. This temple belongs to the Svetambara sect of the Jains. It is two tiered and 70 feet high – the first of its kind in the south. Two more Jain temples are there in Chintadripet and another at Veppery.

A Sikh Gurudhwara is also located nearby behind the Teynampet Congress Ground. A modern Gurudhwara where the Sikhs of the city throng on festive days. The only Buddhist temple is at Egmore in the lane opposite the Egmore Railway Station.

Some Important Temples around the City

These temples are easily accessible either by buses or by taxis.

Tiruvotriyur

This ancient temple is about 10 km on the Northern Trunk Road. It was once a part of Chennai city but then excluded. It is a Saivite shrine predating the Pallava period. Adi Sankara, the founder of Advaitham has visited this temple and has sung in praise of the deity. Saivaite saints Sundarar and Gnanasambandar too have visited this temple. It was rebuilt by Rajendra Chola I. It is also associated with Pattinathar of the 18 Siddhars. He attained salvation here and his Samadhi too could be seen. The presiding deity is Thyagarajaswami. It was a vedic centre during Chola period and the temple architecture is superb and belongs to the Chola period.

Thiruvanmiyur Temple

Another old temple exists in Thiruvanmiyur on the road to Mamallapuram. It is a 11th century Chola temple and the presiding deity is Lord Marundeeswarar. The author of Ramayana, Valmiki is said to have worshipped here.The name is due to his association. "Valmikiyur" in due course became "Vanmikiyur" and finally "Vanmiyur" There is also a shrine dedicated to Valmiki. Pamban Swamigal samadhi is also found near this shrine.

Thirupporur Temple

About 40 km south of Chennai is an old temple dedicated to Lord Muruga. "Soora Samharam", the defeat and salvation to the demon

Soorapadman is an important festival. The temple contains several inscriptions.

Pallavaram Cave Temple

Pallavaram is a place of historical importance. Prehistoric tools were found here. During the Pallava period, it was a flourishing town called Pallavapuram. Mahendra Varma Pallavan has built a rock-cut cave temple on the slopes of the Pallavaram hill which is now a muslim durgah. It is about 15 km from Egmore and can be reached by suburban electric trains from Beach railway station or by buses.

Thirisoolam Temple

It is a Chola Temple with 11-12th century inscriptions. It is dedicated to Lord Siva and the "Sivaratri" festival is very famous. The railway station is opposite the airport and called "Thirisoolam". The name is said to have been derived from Tirichuram, one of the family names who held sway on Chennai.

Thiruneermalai Temple

It is a nearby place of Pallavaram. A shrine is dedicated to Vishnu whose deity is called "Nirvannapperumal" from which the name "Thiruneermalai" is derived. It was once a forest shrine about which Alwars have sung hymns. The bronze images in this temple are very beautiful. This is an old temple of the Pallava period. The main temple is at the foot of the hill. There is also a shrine up the hill which can be reached by a flight of steps.

Kunrathur Temple

This place is adjacent to Thiruneermalai. It is the birthplace of saint Sekkizhar, the author of "Peria Puranam", a sacred book revealing the history of the 63 Nayanmars (Saivaite Saints). It was He who built the Nageswara temple here. It belongs to the 12th century. About a km away is the ancient hill shrine of 'Kunrathur Kumaran' sung by Arunagirinathar. There is a round rock here which produces musical notes when one strikes it with a stone.

Mangadu Bangaru Kamakshi Amman Koil: It is an ancient temple of Pallava times near Porur. Mangadu has golden idol of Kamakshi doing penance. People throng this temple on Fridays and hoildays.

Thiruverkadu Temple

It is a Mariamman temple just 5 km away from city limits, a famous temple that attracts thousands of devotees on holidays especially on the 1st of January.

Koyambedu Perumal Koil

There is an old temple at Koyambedu where the city's main vegetable market is located. It is dedicated to Vishnu. There is an underground mandapam with a secret underground passage. It is said that during the muslim invasion, the idols were kept in this mandapam and later, after the danger was over they were taken out and installed.

Singaperumal Koil

About 48 km on the Grand Southern Trunk Road is this Vishnu shrine on a hillock covered by dense shrubs. This shrine houses a huge image of Yoga Narasimhar (the Lord with a lion's head and a human body) one of the 10 avatars of Lord Vishnu carved out on the face of the rock, the sanctum sanctorum shelters the god in the act of doing penance. The stucco image was fashioned by Pallava kings who built many cave temples in this area. The Chola kings were also patrons of this temple as inscription of the Chola King Rajaraja I (1000 AD) is also found here.

Thirukkalukkundram Temple

It is an important shrine on a 500

ft. hill midway between Mamallapuram and Chengalput. Buses from city ply to that place. Two eagles come every day to have a morsel of food at noon time. The Pandaram always comes with an umbrella and a potful of food and waits for the eagles. They come appearing as two tiny dots in the horizon loom large and swoop down on a boulder and inch their way to the Pandaram who offers food pouring ghee on it. After pecking a morsel they disappear as they arrived. This is a daily ritual and people throng there to see it every day. No one knows from where they come and where they go. But hearsay offers they come from Banares after a holy dip and come here for the paltry morsel on their way to Rames-waram. Hence, this hill is called the Sacred Hill of the eagles (Thirukkalukkundram). The other name of this place is Pakshi (bird) Theertham.

Pallavas have built a shrine at the top of the hill and reliefs of Ardhanariswarar, Dakshinamurthi and Somaskandar could be seen on the rear and northern walls of the sanctum and Vedagireeswara lingam occupies the centre. Abutting the flight of steps on the way leading down, is another Pallava rock-cut cave etched with Dutch inscriptions exposing the later link with Dutch occupation. The Dutch establishment was in the nearby Sadras where even today one can see the remains of an old Dutch fort – it is about 10 kms from here.

At the foot of the hill stands big Siva temple with a majestic gopuram piercing the sky. Paintings and sculptures of Vijayanagar adorn the temple. On the east of the temple is the sacred tank "Sangu Theertham" or tank of conch. Once in 12 years, a conch appears in this tank and it is used as a vessel of oblation. One can see a large collection of conches in the temple said to have appeared in the tank.

Uttiramerur Temple

Uttiramerur could be reached by bus. It is on the road to Vandavasi from Chengalputtu. There are several ancient temples here. The Sundaravaradaperumal temple of the period of Dantivarma Pallava is of complex design. Three sanctums one above the other in storeys house Vishnu seated, standing and recumbent. The idols all are brick in stucco. In another shrine of the Chola period are the famous inscriptions that speak of the elected panchayat raj of the Cholas. The method of election, the qualification of the contestants etc. are clearly indicated. It exposes that local administration was purely a democratic set-up.

Thennangore Radhakrishna Temple

Further on the road to (Wandiwash) Vandavasi about 15 km from Uttiramerur, one can find the recently built beautiful temple of Radhakrishna in Thennangore. The temple is built like the Puri Jagannath temple and the idols are exact replicas of Panduranga of Pandaripur in North India. The temple was built by Haridoss Giri Swamiji, the disciple of Gnanananda Giri Swamiji. There are beautiful sculptures depicting scenes from the life of Lord Krishna. The sanctum has graceful idols of Panduranga and there is a Bhajan Hall, the pillars of which are nothing but statues of saints of the Bakthi cult. There is also a shrine for Gnanananda Giri and a Siva temple. Foreigners throng during Krishna Jayanthi festival and beautiful lodges are provided to them. Daily Bhajans are a speciality and so is every day free feeding of devotees. It is a most modern temple and a visit is rewarding.

Mamallapuram

It is popularly called Mahabalipuram and is 58 km south of Chennai. It can be reached by bus or taxi. A beautiful spot of wonder and amazing sculptures which no tourist to Chennai should miss.

Mamallapuram was once the flourishing port of the Pallavas – an old lighthouse built of stone exists intact till date, proclaiming the glory of Pallava trade and maritime supremacy. It is also the birthplace of one of the first three Alwars – Boothathalwar. Since Pallava kings were both Saivaites and Vaishnavaites, Mamallapuram has shrines of both beliefs. Though no formal worship is done today, large number of visitors come every day to enjoy the sculpture and splendour of Pallava art and architecture. The monolithic and scooped out cave temples are of different dates, 10 centuries old.

The Shore Temple: Lapped by the surging sea it stands gloriously on the verge of the Bay of Bengal. It has a Dravidian style vimana towering over 60 feet built in basaltic rock. A prismatic lingam is on the sanctum facing the sea and Vishnu is seen reclining on the ground (Stala sayana) in his chamber in the rear.

Pandava Raths or Monolithic Shrines are five in number out of which four are carved, out of a single rock, while the fifth is scooped from a small rock.The hut-like Draupadi Rath sports door-keepers, Durga with a worshipper cutting and offering his neck, and the outer walls of Arjuna's rath have most lovely and graceful figures of gods and mortals carved by a skilful sculptor. Nakula-Sahadeva rath stands with a huge monolithic elephant in front. Bhima's rath has two storeys and lion-based pillars. Dharmaraja's rath is the biggest and has 8 panels of exquisite sculptures.

Arjuna's Penance is the splendour of Mamallapuram. It is a huge rock in the canvas unfolding a scene of gods and demigods, birds, beasts and natural scenery. Some are of the opinion that it is in fact Bagirath's penance to bring the celestial Ganges to the earth. A natural cleft in the rock has been cleverly carved into the turbulent river Ganges with serpent gods worshipping like devotees along the banks frozen in their prayer – a superb poetry in sculpture which no visitor should miss.

The Mahishasuramardhini cave is carved into three shrines a bass relief of Somaskanda in the rear, Anantasayana - Vishnu canopied by Shesha, reclining on the serpent bed. Mahishasuramardhini is struck in bold relief in such an awe-inspiring way with the thrill of the beholder in the battlefield.

Krishna Mandapam is a rock-cut temple with pastoral scenes depicting the life of Lord Krishna.

Varaha Cave illustrates the legend of rescuing the earth Bhoodevi by Vishnu incarnated as a boar.

Besides one would be wonderstruck to see Krishna's butter ball a huge boulder with just a tip of it touching the rock giving the on- looker an impression that it may roll on him any moment. There is a huge rock tub said to be the bathing tub of Draupathi. Above, on the rocky hill is a shrine of Vishnu without the deity. One can also see the old rockbuilt lighthouse and the modern lighthouse side by side. Mahabalipuram is a real feast to the eyes that could read an epic in lively sculpture.

Thiruvidandai is a few kilometres north of Mamallapuram where stands a famous Vaishnavaite shrine built by early Cholas. A huge stucco image of Varaha holding Bhoodevi (Earth) can be seen.

The **Tiger Cave** is located a couple of miles in the south on the seashore – facing the sea. There is a beautiful monolithic stage where cultural programmes were held in olden days.

Kanchipuram Temples

75 km from Chennai, Kanchipuram is one of the great mythological cities and "Nakareshu Kanchi" is a popular saying in Sanskrit that means "Kanchipuram is the best city". It was the capital city of the Pallavas and the northern capital of the Cholas. Even during the Vijayanagar period, it was an important centre. It was also a centre of learning and a centre for Buddhists and Jains in early time. The Chinese traveller Hieun-Tsang who has visited Kanchipuram praises its glory and painfully notes the declining trend of Buddhism in his accounts. It is also a world famous centre for silk weaving. Kanchi Pattu – 'the silk of Kanchi' – is cherished by one and all and one can really see silk looms in action and find out how beautiful sarees are made. It is a temple city and innumerable ancient temples could be seen at every turning. A selective list of most important temples are given here. The whole city is divided into Siva Kanchi, Vishnu Kanchi and Jain Kanchi.

Kailasanathar Temple

This Siva temple is one of the earliest temples built by Rajasimha Pallava in the late 7th century A.D. The front was added by Mahendra Varma III later on. It is the only temple of the original Pallava architecture without additions by Cholas and Vijayanagar kings and remains a fine specimen of freshness and simplicity of early Dravidian architecture. True to its name, Kailas or Paradise, it shelters all the gods in various aspects in several niches along the circumambulatory path around the sanctum sanctorum. One has to crawl through a small opening to enter it and has to come out of a pit at the end. It is believed that by doing this exercise one will reach Kailas after one's sojourn on the earth. Puranas unroll themselves through sculptures to our view. Pallava paintings are also visible in fragments in some niches. These murals remind us the magnificence of the temple as it would have looked when it was first built. The office of the Archaeological Survey of India is nearby and one could get more details about the history and importance of Kanchipuram.

Vaikunthaperumal Temple

This Vishnu shrine was built between 674-850 AD by the Pallava king Parameswara Varman and Nandivarman II. Here the Pallava history is revealed in reliefs all along the corridors. Their dresses, costumes, jewellery and habits are captured in exquisite splendour. The shrine has two storeys and enshrines Vishnu in them. Such storeyed temple is called "Maadak Kovil" in Tamil. The walls have rich puranic sculpture. Lion pillars adorn the cloisters inside the outer wall.

Ekambaranathar Temple

This Siva temple is the largest and is spread over nine hectares. Its huge gopuram or portal tower is 192 feet high and its massive outer walls were constructed by Krishna Devaraya, the great Vijayanagar king in 1509. The original shrine dates back to the

Pallava period, additions have also been made by Cholas. Five separate enclosures and a thousand-pillared hall and a beautiful big tank are inside the temple. **'Eka Amra'** means a single mango tree and the lord is known as Ekambaranathar. It is one of the five element (Prithvi or earth) shrines of Siva and the Lingam is made of earth. A single mango tree is seen behind the sanctum – a very old tree indeed the age of which is fabulously said to be 35,000 years, with four branches representing the four Vedas. It is also said that the fruit of each branch has a different taste. Near the tank is a small cell for Valiswara, erected by Mahendra Varma Pallavan. At the back of the Lingam, Siva and Parvathi image is sculptured. The hall of Nataraja, the cosmic dancer has some interesting frescoes in the ceiling. The 'Mavadi Sevai' festival attracts huge crowds.

Kamakshi Amman Temple

This is the most important temple and the chief deity of Kanchipuram. 'Kanchi Kamakshi' is a popular saying and it has been sanctified by Adi Sankara and He has stationed before the goddess a Sri Chakra said to be containing the efficiency of power of the Devi. There is no separate sanctum for Siva here. There is a separate sanctum for Adi Sankara.

Varadaraja Perumal Temple

This Vishnu temple was built during the Vijayanagar period. This is another big temple having 5 enclosures with massive outer wall and a hundred-pillared hall. One exquisite, sculptural marvel is a huge chain carved out of single piece of stone. The sanctum on a small hillock faces west and displays murals in its ceiling. One should not miss to see the golden lizard here. The 100-pillared hall is a perfect specimen of Vijayanagar art and architecture.

Muktiswarar and Matangeswarar temples are also Pallava relics with fine specimens of art and architecture. Ashtapujam temple is in the heart of Vishnu Kanchi where the multihanded Vishnu armed to the teeth with various weapons is seen in the act of rescuing Gajendra, the elephant devotee from the clutches of the crocodile. There is another temple dedicated to Lord Vishnu called "Ulagalantha Perumal" which depicts the Viswaroopa taken by Vishnu to defeat Mahabali, the demon king. The deity raising one of its legs measuring the space (sky) is featured here – an awe-inspiring and thrilling sight. The famous commentator of Thirukkural, Parimel Azhagar was once the Poojari of this temple.

Jain Kanchi

In the south-west beyond the river Vegavadhi – one of the tributaries of Palar – stands a group of Jain temples. This place is known as 'Tiruparuthi Kundram'. This belongs to the early Chola period. There is a sangeetha mandapam (music hall) in this temple dedicated to Vardhamana Mahavira – the roof of which is adorned with paintings, illustrating the lives of Tirthankaras. Rare Jain manuscripts are also preserved in this temple.

There are a few of the most important temples in Kanchipuram and there are many of them old and new. The most important of the recent ones is the Kumarakkottam - a temple dedicated to Lord Muruga. The divine abode of the holy Sankaracharyas called Jagadgurus who reside in Kanchi at Their headquarters and give darshan to devotees is popular as 'Kanchi Kamakoti Peetam'. Tourists can reach Kanchipuram by rail or by bus and hiring a taxi or autorickshaw will do to cover the temples mentioned, in a single day.

Maduranthagam - Erikatha Perumal Koil

Maduranthagam is about 80 km south of Chennai on the trunk road to Tiruchy. The biggest lake of the district is here, with a bund of about 13,000 ft in length and a depth of about 100 ft when full. It irrigates about 3000 acres of surrounding villages. This lake was cut by the Cholas. In the close of the 18th century when Colonel Lionel Place was the collector, furious monsoon brought unprecedented rains and the lake was full and there was danger of the bund giving way at any moment. When the collector encamped here and was examining the bunds he saw the huge figure of Rama with his bow in his hand on the bund. The rain stopped and the breach was averted by divine grace. The collector, in token of his respect and gratitude built a sanctum for Sita – the consort of Rama – in the temple that stands near the bunds of the lake. Lord Rama here, is hence known as 'Eri Katha Rama' or Rama, the one who guarded the lake.

There is also a Siva temple and the Bairava statue here which are of exquisite splendour. There once flourished a vedic centre in this place.

Vedanthangal Bird Sanctuary

Vedanthangal, the paradise of ornithologists, is five km away from Maduranthagam. It is one of the largest bird sanctuaries in India. It is spread over 30 hectares and a lake full of trees half submerged is a convenient breeding site for birds of all feathers. Over 1,00,000 migratory birds visit every year. The season for bird-watching is mid-October to mid-February. The varieties include herons, spoonbills, pelicans, sandpipers, white gulls, cormorants, blue-winged teals and swans. Though this sanctuary has been existing for a very long time, only in 1798 was this fact publicised. There is a watch-tower to see the birds. The ideal time is the afternoon when diurnal birds begin to return and the nocturnal birds leave.

Sriperumpudur Temple

It is midway between Chennai and Kanchipuram and the birthplace of saint Ramanuja, the propounder of Vishistadvaita philosophy. The shrine has been improved by Vijayanagar kings. The pillars are exquisite and bear testimony to Vijayanagar architecture. The image of Ramanuja is also installed in this Vishnu shrine.

Rajiv Gandhi Memorial

It is located here in the spot where he was killed by the human bomb – one can always see a stream of visitors to this memorial paying homage to their departed charismatic leader.

Tirutthani Murugan Temple

This famous Murugan shrine is about 80 km from Chennai and can be reached either by train or by bus. It is the place where Lord Muruga, after killing Demon Surapadman, softened His fury. The shrine stands on a basaltic hill reached by a flight of steps or by vehicle through a road. On New Year Day, lakhs of pilgrims climb the steps chanting Bhajans. The temple is of Pallava origin. Saints like Arunagirinathar, Kachiyappa Munivar, Muthusami Dikshitar and Ramalinga Adigal have sung songs in praise of Tirutthani Lord Muruga. During Krithigai days, kavadis are taken up the hill by a large number of devotees. On the slope of the hills is a herbal farm.

In the eastern end of the town downhill on the river bank is a temple dedicated to Siva. Veerattaneswara is the presiding deity. This was built by the Pallava king Aparajitha. It is a black granite temple of the closing years of Pallavas with an apsidal vimana with parivara devathas in niches all round the outer wall. The sanctum here is a forerunner of present-day shrines.

Thiru Alangadu Temple

This is a unique Siva temple 37 miles west of Chennai. The Nataraja bronze idol is with the rare dancing pose called Oorthuva Thandava lifting his leg upwards. This was done to subdue Kali in a dance bout as being a female She could not do so out of modesty. An image of dancing Kali is also kept here. It is the place where Karaikkal Ammaiyar one of the 63 Saivaite saints attained Mukthi. Her image is a unique piece of art exposing the features of an old lady, bones protruding, shrivelled bosom and sunken eyes.

Tirupathi Temple

This temple town is in the state of Andhra Pradesh 180 km from Chennai. Daily 2 train services and every half an hour bus services are operated from Chennai. Besides, private vehicles and tourist coaches are also available. Down the hill there is a shrine for Alarmelmanga Thayar, the consort of Lord Vishnu and Govindaraja temple. 13 kms up the hill Tirumala, is the famous shrine of Sri Venkateswara popularly known as Balaji. In Tamil, this is called 'Vengadam'. One has to cross seven hills to reach the temple. Pucca road is available, besides many pilgrims prefer to climb the seven hills on the steps.

Lakhs of people throng from all parts of India every day and one has to wait in the queue for 3 or 4 hours and on festive occasions more than 8 to 9 hours to have darshan of the deity. Thousands of devotees tonsure their heads here and they make a vow to do so if their desires are fulfilled. Tirupathi temple has the largest revenue everyday touching several lakhs of rupees. Each day is a wedding day to Lord Venkateswara and by contributing a fixed sum one can perform this ceremony to the Lord. Tirupathi laddu and vada – the prasadams of this lord are sold to public. Laddu is a popular item and no pilgrim ever misses to buy it, standing for hours in long queues. Umpteen lodges and Devastanam (temple) guest houses and cottages are available.

The places mentioned above and located around Chennai could easily be reached by bus or taxis and after a day trip tourists could return to Chennai for their night stay.

Churches in and around Chennai

Santhome Cathedral Basilica

Santhome Church is associated with the apostle doubting Thomas. He is believed to have landed here in 52 AD to spread Christianity. At that time, this part was known as Mylapore. It is said that he used to preach on the sands of old Mylapore which has been devoured by the sea. Later on, he had some enemies and had to live in a cave near Saidapet about 6 km away from Mylapore on the banks of river Adyar, called Little Mount. From there, he had to retreat further to a hill now called St.Thomas Mount where he was killed in 72 AD. His mortal remains were buried on the beach where he preached. Later on, a church was built over it. Afterwards it was transferred to another church built further inland. In 1606, it was rebuilt as a cathedral and in 1896, it was made into a basilica. The church is a magnificent building built in Gothic style with beautiful stained glass windows portraying the stay of St. Thomas. The central hall has 14 wooden plaques depicting scenes from the last days of Christ. A three feet statue of Virgin Mary believed to have been brought from Portugal in 1541 adorns the church. In this basilica, a small hand bone of St. Thomas and the head of a lance are kept as sacred relics.

St. Mary's Church

It is the first Anglican church built inside the Fort St.George, details of which can be had under the heading Fort St. George.

Portuguese Church

This is the church of Our Lady of Assumption and is the first church built in British India (1642 AD). It was in existence before Mary's of Fort. St. George. Even now it survives on Portuguese Church Street in northern George Town .

Church of St. Mary of the Angels

This is the Catholic church built with the permission of the Company. It was built on the site of a Portuguese cemetery in 1755. The inscription on the gates of it dates back to 1642, and it is still preserved at the cathedral's entrance. In this cathedral are some beautiful oil paintings of the crucifixion and Mary Magdalane. The movement chapel attached to it is the last resting place of the Embience, Armenian family of that name. It is popularly known as St. Antony's Church.

St. Mary's Armenian Church

This was built in 1772 on the site of the old Armenian cemetery. A courtyard garden and gleaming pews of this church are wonderfully preserved. This church has the biggest bells in Chennai. This church of the Armenian orthodoxy is next door to the Church of St. Mary of the Angels.

St. George's Cathedral

This Anglican church was built in 1814-15 and consecrated in 1816. It was considered at that time the finest, outside London. Its spire is 140 feet high and used to be an imposing majestic monument in those days with its broad green lushy open space on Anna Salai near the Gemini Circle. Now the church has lost its panoramic appearance as a major portion of the open space is occupied by the American Consulate and the Anna flyover raising high nearby. The spire which was visible on all sides could now be seen only at a narrow point in the Cathedral Road.

Luz Church

This church in Mylapore on the Luz Church Road is the oldest church construction still in existence. This is popularly known even today as 'Kaattu Koil' (Forest Temple) in Tamil as there was a thick jungle around it in those days. There is a legend behind the construction of this church. Some Portuguese sailors in danger on the sea were guided by a divine light to safety. After they landed on the beach, they saw the light still glowing and followed it till it disappeared. On that spot they built the Luz Church and dedicated to 'Our Lady of Light'. There is an inscription bearing the date 1516. Luz Corner the busiest part of Mylapore got its name from the church.

St. Andrews Kirk

The Scots built this Kirk on the Poonamallee High Road (now Periyar E.V.R. Salai) and consecrated in 1821. It stands with an imposing look near the Egmore Railway Station. Its dome is unique and the marble paved aisles are magnificent.

Little Mount Church

This is half way between Santhome

and St. Thomas Mount. It is the place where St. Thomas took asylum when he was pursued by enemies. It is called Chinna Malai in Tamil. There are two churches here, the new one built half way up the hill in 1971 has been dedicated to Our Lady of Health. Another church built by the Portuguese earlier in 1551 is the blessed Sacrament Chapel still in existence, connected to the new church. The old one is a cave in which St. Thomas was hiding and doing prayers and penance. To the east of the cave is an opening with a palm print nearby. Legend says that this narrow opening was the portals of a tunnel through which St. Thomas escaped to St.Thomas Mount and the palm print is the hand print of St.Thomas. A cross cut into the rock is believed to be the cross before which St. Thomas prayed. There is also a spring nearby which St. Thomas is supposed to have struck to quench the thirst of his followers. It is said that the water has curative powers even today. Every year on the fourth Saturday and Sunday after Easter, the Little Mount festival is celebrated and thousands of devotees throng on these days.

St. Thomas Mount Church

St. Thomas Mount is a 300 feet hill called "Parangi Malai" in Tamil, on the verges of the present city limits. The Portuguese had rebuilt a church here at the behest of King Emanuel. It was originally a chapel of the Nestorian Missionary. It was on this mount that St. Thomas is said to have been speared to death. 'The Bleeding Cross' here is a miracle. Hearsay tradition says that it was chiselled by St. Thomas. During May in 1558, it first publicly bled and is said to have bled periodically ever since. There is a painting of Virgin Mary and child Christ, supposed to have been painted by St. Luke and brought to India by St. Thomas. A flight of steps lead to the top of the mountain.

Shrine Velankanni

This modern church is in Besant Nagar (vide Elliot's Beach).

Important Mosques

Wallajah Mosque

It is popularly known as the Big Mosque on the Triplicane High Road in Chepauk. It was built in 1789. It is the biggest in the city with a spacious open space. All the muslims in the city gather here on important days. It is an impressive and historic mosque associated with Nawab Wallajah's family. There is another mosque in the muslim area nearby, called Zam Bazaar historically associated with the Prince of Arcot family in a crowded part of the city.

Thousand Lights Mosque

This historic mosque stands on Thousand Lights area at the junction of Peters Road and Anna Salai. This area with numerous lanes and narrow streets is associated with members of the Nawab family as the street names reveal. The name is derived from the lighting of a triangular wedge of a building constructed by Nabab Umdat-ul-umrah around 1800 for Shias assembling during Moharram. It is one of the major mosques of the city.

Kasi Viranna Mosque

It is in Moore's Street in George Town. Kasi Viranna, a chief merchant was very close to the Golconda Sultan and he even had a muslim name Hassan Khan. He built the mosque in 1680 before he died.

Besides these temples, churches and mosques, numerous in each category have come up in various parts of the city. Only a few of them very important and having historical background have been listed here.

Chennai is still an expanding city and new residential colonies are springing up every now and then and with them the places of worship also multiply.

Shopping

Several state-run and private emporia in Chennai sell handicrafts of different kinds – rose-wood, sandal-wood, ivory, bronze, silver, leather, silk and handwoven fabrics, sarees and jewellery are also available.

Where to stay in Chennai

HOTELS

Five Star Deluxe

- **ITC Hotel Park Sheraton and Towers,** 132, T.T.K. Road, Chennai-600 018 ✆ 24994101 Fax: 044-24997101 Email:parksheraton@writeme.com
- **Le Royal Meridien** 1, G.S.T. Road, St. Thomas Mount, Chennai - 600 016. ✆ 22314343, Fax: 044-22314344 Email:reservation@royalmeridian_chennai.com
- **Taj Coromandel,** 17, Mahatma Gandhi Road, (Nungambakkam High Road), Chennai - 600 034. ✆ 28272827 Fax: 044-28278547, 28257104 Email: tajcorom@md3.vsnl.net.in

Five Star

- **Connemara,** 2, Binny Road, Chennai - 600002. ✆ 28520123 Fax:044-28523361 Email:tajcon@giasmd01.vsnl.net.in
- **The Fisherman's Cove,** Covelong Beach, Kanchipuram Dist. Tamilnadu - 603 112. ✆ 04114-72304-310
- **The Trident,** 24, GST Road, Chennai-600 027. ✆ 22344747. Fax: 044-22346689 Email: vkher@tridentch.com
- **Welcomgroup Chola Sheraton,** 10, Cathedral Road, Chennai-600 086. ✆ 28110101. Fax: 044-28278779. Email: chola@welcomgroup.com

Four Star

- **Ambassador Pallava,** 53, Montieth Road, Egmore, Chennai - 600 008. ✆ 28554476, 28554068 Email: pallava@vsnl.com
- **GRT Grand Days,** 120, Sir Thyagaraya Road, Pondy Bazaar, T.Nagar, Chennai - 600 017. ✆ 28220500, 28236789, 28267509 Fax: 044-28230778. Email: grtgranddays@vsnl.com
- **Hotel President,** 16, Dr. Radhakrishnan Salai, Mylapore, Chennai - 600 004. ✆ 28532211, 28526633 Fax: 044-28532299, 28533336. Email: reserve@president.com
- **Quality Hotel Aruna,** 144, Sterling Road, Nungambakkam, Chennai - 600 034. ✆ 28259090, 28233561-565 Fax: 044-28258282. Email: qiaruna@ satyam.net.in
- **Savera Hotel,** 146, Dr. Radhakrishnan Road, Mylapore, Chennai - 600 004. ✆ 28114700 Fax: 28113475. Email: hotsave@md2.vsnl.net.in

Three Star

- **Ambica Empire Best Western,** 79, 100 Feet Road, Jawaharlal Nehru Salai, Vadapalani, Chennai - 600 026. ✆ 23721818, 24813986 Fax: 044-24817708. Email: ambicaem@md4.vsnl.net.in
- **Breeze Hotel,** 850, Poonamallee High Road, Kilpauk, Chennai - 600 010. ✆ 26413334-37, 26428202, 26430593, 98400 60616. Fax: 044-26413301 Email: breeze@vsnl.com
- **Hotel Abu Palace,** 926, Poonamallee High Road, Chennai - 600 084. ✆ 26412222, 26431010 Fax: 91-44-26428091. Email: abuin@giasmd01.vsnl.net.in
- **Hotel Aadithya,** 155/1, Arcot Road, Chennai - 26. ✆ 24880488, 24881803, 24881089 Fax: 044-24844303 Email: aadithyamdsind@eth.net
- **Hotel Dee Cee Manor,** 90, G.N. Chetty Road, Chennai - 17. ✆ 28284411, 28282696 Fax: 044-28282775 Email: dcmanor@vsnl.com
- **Hotel Ganga International P Ltd.,** 47, Bazullah Road, T. Nagar, Chennai - 17. ✆ 28231340-44. Fax: 044-28235193
- **Hotel Kanchi,** 28, Ethiraj Salai, Egmore, Chennai - 600 105. ✆ 2827 1100 (10 lines). Fax: 044-28272928 Email: reservation@hotelkanchi.com
- **Hotel Mars** 768, Pammal Main Road, Pallavaram, Chennai - 600 043. ✆ 22402586, 22404161, 22368523 Fax: 044-22404064 Email: hotelmars@yahoo.com
- **Hotel Maurya International,** 168-169, Arcot Road, Chennai - 26. ✆ 24840049 (8 lines). Fax: 044-24840052
- **Hotel Palmgrove,** 5, Kodambakkam High Road, Nungambakkam, Chennai - 600 034. ✆ 28271881 Fax: 044-28231977
- **Hotel Radha Park Inn International,** 171, J. Nehru Salai, Inner Ring Road, Arumbakkam, Chennai - 600 106. ✆ 24757788 Fax: 044-24756644 Email: parkinn@vsnl.com
- **Hotel Royal Southern,** S.R.M. Nagar, Chennai - 603 203. Email: srmhotels@net4india.com
- **Hotel Shelter,** 19-21, Venkatesa Agraharam St., Mylapore, Chennai - 600 004. ✆ 24951919 Fax: 044-24935646. Email: shelter@vsnl.com
- **Madras Hotel Ashoka Private Limited,** 33, Pantheon Road, Chennai - 600 008. ✆ 28553377 Fax: 044-28553668
- **Mowbrays Inn** 303, TTK Road, Alwarpet, Chennai - 600 018 ✆ 24970555, 24984326,

24993915. Fax: 044-24984319, 24971764 Email: mowbrays@md3.vsnl.net.in

• **New Victoria Hotel,** 3, Kennett Lane, Egmore, Chennai - 600 008. ✆ 28253638 (10 lines). Fax: 044-28250070 Email:hotelnewvictoria@vsnl.com

• **New Woodlands Hotel (P) Limited,** 71-72, Dr. Radhakrishnan Road, Mylapore, Chennai - 600 004. ✆ 28113111 (26 lines). Fax: 044-28110460 Email: murali@newwoodlands.com

• **The Dakshin** 35, Venkatanarayana Road, Nandanam, Chennai - 600 035. ✆ 24330866/ 0871/0948/6574/6575 Fax: 044-24322639 Email: deokarg@hotmail.com

• **The Grand Orient,** 693, Anna Salai, Chennai - 600 006. ✆ 28524111 Fax: 044-28523412. Email: empeegrandorient@vsnl.com

• **The Residency,** 49, GN Chetty Road, T.Nagar, Chennai - 600 017. ✆ 28253434 Fax: 044-28250085. Email: resmds@vsnl.com

• **The Sindoori Hotel,** 24, Greams Lane, Chennai-600 006. ✆ 28271164.

• **Windsor Park,** 349, Poonamallee High Road, Aminjikarai, Chennai - 600 029. ✆ 23741999, 23741071-73 Fax: 044-23743369 Email: ampa@md3.vsnl.net.in

Two Star

• **Hotel Atlantic Private Limited,** 2, Montieth Road, Egmore, Chennai - 600 008. ✆ 28553914/ 19. Fax: 044-28553239

• **Hotel Dasaprakash,** 100, Poonamallee High Road, Chennai - 600 084. ✆ 28255111 (8 lines).

• **Hotel Maris,** 9, Cathedral Rd., Chennai - 600 086. ✆ 28110541 (10 lines). Fax: 044-28114847

• **Hotel Pandian** 15, Kennet Lane, Egmore, Chennai - 600 008. ✆ 28252901, 28226558 Fax: 044-28258459 Email: hotelpandian@vsnl.com

• **Hotel Peninsula,** 26, GN Chetty Road, T.Nagar, Chennai - 600 017. ✆ 28252770, 0853/4743/ 4826/4824/4728 Fax: 044-28254745 Email: peninsul@ md3.vsnl.net.in

• **Hotel Premier,** 22, Poonamallee High Road, Chennai - 600 003. ✆ 25383311.

• **Hotel Ranjith,** 15, Nungambakkam High Road, Chennai - 600 034. ✆ 28270521, 28277688. Fax: 044-28277688 Email: hotelranjith@yahoo.com

• **Hotel Sindoori Central,** 26/27, Poonamallee High Road, Chennai - 600 003. ✆ 25386647. Fax: 044-25387022 Email: sindhotels@vsnl.com

One Star

• **Hotel Swagath,** 243-244, Royapettah High Road, Chennai - 600 014. ✆ 28268422 (21 lines).

• **Tourist Homes Private Limited,** 45, Gandhi Irwin Road, Egmore, Chennai - 600 008. ✆ 28250079.

• **VGP Golden Beach Resort Limited,** East Coast Road, Injambakkam, Chennai - 600 041. ✆ 24491115, 24491101, 24491446 Fax: 044-24490514

Others

• **Admiralty Hotel,** 5, Norton Road, Mandaveli, Chennai - 600 028. ✆ 2494 1249.

• **Beverly Hotel** 17, Rajarathinam Road, Kilpauk, Chennai - 600 010. ✆ 26612772 Fax: 044-26612545 Email: beverly@vsnl.com

• **Buena Vista,** Beach Road, Neelangarai, Chennai - 600 041. ✆ 24492222 Fax: 044-24490301. Email: buenavista@apexmail.com

• **Buharis Blue Lagoon Hotel,** 79-A, East Coast Rd., Neelankarai, Chennai - 600 041. ✆ 24491425.

• **Guru Regency** No. 8 to 12, Balfour Road, Kilpauk, Chennai - 600 010. ✆ 26449090, 26449191 Fax: 044-26453298. Email: pmg22@hotmail.com

• **Hotel Blue Diamond,** 934, Poonamallee High Road, Chennai - 600 084. ✆ 26412244.

• **Hotel Days Inn Shan,** 85, Poonamallee High Road, Chennai - 107. ✆ 26221212.

• **Hotel Garden,** 68-A, Purasawalkam High Road, Chennai - 600 007. ✆ 26422677, 26422188, 26424484, 26424540, 26424492-93, 26424547

• **Hotel Impala Continental,** 12, Gandhi Irwin Road, Egmore, Chennai - 600 008. ✆ 28250564, 28251778.

• **Hotel L.R. Swami Narayanan,** 83, Usman Road, T.Nagar, Chennai - 600 017. ✆ 24339796

• **Hotel MGM Grand,** New No. 31, Santhome High Road, Mylapore, Chennai - 600 004. ✆ 24980320/99/11 Fax: 044-24980360 Email: hotelmgm@yahoo.com

• **Hotel Nayagara** 2, 3 & 4, II Cross, United India Colony, Kodambakkam, Chennai - 600 024. ✆ 24891209.

• **Hotel Peacock,** 1089, Poonamalle High Road, Chennai - 600 084. ✆ 25322981 (8 lines), 25321080 (10 lines).

• **Hotel Picnic Plaza,** 2, RK Mutt Road, Mylapore, Chennai - 600 004. ✆ 24941730.

• **Hotel Srilekha Inter-Continental Limited,** A564, Anna Salai, Teynampet, Chennai - 600 018. ✆ 24349125 (30 lines)

• **Kings Park** 216, E.V.R. Salai, Chennai - 600 010. ✆ 26414243. Fax: 044-22404064 Email: kingspar@md2.vsnl.net.in

• **Nilgiri's Nest,** 105, Dr. Radhakrishnan Road, Mylapore, Chennai - 600 004. ✆ 28115111, 28115222/28110716, 28111772-73 Fax: 044-28111719 Email: ndfchmyl@vsnl.net

• **Picnic Hotel,** 1132/1, Poonamallee High Road, Chennai - 600 003. ✆ 2538 8809/28 Fax: 044-25366850 Email: pnichotl@vsnl.com

• **Quality Inn MGM Beach Resort** 1/74, New Mahabalipuram Road, Muttukadu, Chennai - 603 112. Email: qimgnbr@md5.vsnl.net.in

• **Y.W.C.A. Guest House** 1086, Poonamallee High

Road, Chennai. ✆ 25323120.

- **Youth Hostels** Indira Nagar, Chennai - 600 020. ✆ 24420233.

Important Information

- Govt. of Tamil Nadu Tourist Office, Panagal Building, Saidapet, Chennai-15. ✆ 24321122.
- Tourist Information Centre, Central Railway Station ✆ 25353351.
- Tourist Information Centre, Egmore Railway Station ✆ 28252165.
- Tourist Information Centre, Domestic Terminal, Chennai Airport ✆ 22340569.
- Tourist Information Centre, International Airport ✆ 22349347.
- Tamil Nadu Tourism Development Corporation, Head Office, ✆ 28545684.
- Tamil Nadu Tourism Development Corporation, Dr. Radhakrishnan Salai, Chennai - 4. ✆ 28547346 Fax : 28546620.
- Govt. of India Tourist Office, 154, Anna Salai, Chennai-2 ✆ 22852429, 28254785 Fax : 28252193.
- Tourist Information Centre (Govt. of India), Domestic Terminal, Chennai Airport. ✆ 22340386.
- Tourist Information Centre (Govt. of India), International Terminal, Chennai Airport ✆ 22345801.
- King Institute (for Yellow fever vaccination), Guindy, Chennai-32. ✆ 22341026.
- Maharashtra Mandal, 61, E.V.K. Sampath Road, Chennai ✆ 22560328.
- Publications Division, Sales Emporium, 731, Anna Salai, Chennai ✆ 28267643.

State Information Centre (Govt. of Tamil Nadu)

- Mahakavi Bharathiyar Memorial House, T.P.Koil St, Triplicane, Chennai-5. ✆ 28591393.
- Hindu Religious & Charitable Endowments, Nungambakkam High Rd., Chennai-34 ✆ 28279402.
- Music College, Chennai-28. ✆ 24937217.
- Iyal Isai Nataka Mandram, Chennai-28 ✆ 24936848.
- Kalakshetra, Tiruvanmiyur, Chennai. ✆ 24911936
- Automobile Association of South India ✆ 28521162
- Youth Hostel Association of India ✆ 24820976
- State Guest House, Chennai. ✆ 22566920

Kanchipuram

(Temple Town)

How to get there?

It is 75 km. away from Chennai and well connected by a network of good roads. Frequent bus services are available from Kanchipuram to Chennai, Bangalore and other places. There is a Railway Station. Nearby Airport: Chennai Tirisulam Airport. Rail link from Chennai via Chengalpattu upto Arakkonam. Road link to all major cities.

Places to see:

TEMPLES

1. Ekambaranathar temple
2. Vaikunta Perumal temple
3. Kailasanathar temple
4. Varadarajaswami temple
5. Kamakshi Amman temple
6. Muktheeswarar temple
7. Mathangeswarar temple
8. Ashtabujam temple
9. Ulagalanda Perumal temple
10. Kumarakottam
11. Jain temple, Thiruparankundram
12. Kanchi Kamakoti Peetam Math.

Full details about these temples can be had under the heading 'Temples in and around Chennai' in the chapter 'Chennai'.

CHURCHES

Protestant Church - near Railway station; Roman Catholic Church - Konerikuppam.

MOSQUES

Jama Masjid, Hajaratha Burhana, Avulia Durgah and Hamid Avulia Durgah.

ANNA MEMORIAL

It is in Little Kanchipuram or Vishnu Kanchi. Dr. C.N. Annadurai, the former Chief Minister of Tamil Nadu and the founder of D.M.K. was born here. His ancestral house here has been converted into a memorial. Various exhibits like photographs, the articles used by him and important events of his life are portrayed here. As he is associated with the Dravidian movement and the nationalist movement one can see the evolution of these important movements which made a breakthrough in the lives of the Tamils who hailed him as their elder brother – 'Anna'.

HISTORICAL IMPORTANCE

From time immemorial it has been hailed as one of the holy cities of India. Buddhism, Jainism, Saivism and Vaishnavism thrived here. It was the northern capital of the Cholas, the main capital of the Pallavas and even during the Vijayanagar period, it was an important centre. The Pallava, Chola and Vijayanagar art and architecture flourished here and the temples of this city are living monuments of them. It is at present the headquarters of Kanchipuram district and the Collector's office is located here.

HANDLOOM INDUSTRIES

Kanchipuram silk sarees are known all over the world. Beautiful high grade pure mulberry silk of various hues are woven into sarees by traditionally trained weavers reputed for texture, lustre, durability and fine finish. These sarees are exported to foreign countries. About 5000 families are engaged in this industry. Sarees are available at loom prices here and through cooperative societies.

NEARBY PLACES OF EXCURSION

•Sriperumpudur - 29 km. •Tirutthani - 42 km. • Vedanthangal bird sanctuary - 60 km.

Full details of the above places are given under the heading 'Temples in and around Chennai'.

Where to stay?

• **Hotel Tamil Nadu (T.T.D.C.)**, 78, Kamakshi Amman Street, Kanchipuram. ✆ : 222533. Grams: Tamil Tour

• **Municipal Rest House.**

• Umpteen hotels and private lodges are also available.

Mamallapuram

(The splendour of Pallava art)

How to get there?

It is 60 km away from Chennai and linked by a good road running along the coast of the Bay of Bengal connected to Chengalpattu and Kanchipuram via Thirukkalukkundram. Nearest railway station: Chengalpattu. Nearest Airport: Chennai. Daily tourist coaches of T.T.D.C. and umpteen bus services are available.

Places to see

1. Shore temples, 2. Pandava raths, 3. Krishna Mandapam, 4. Rock-cut caves – nine in number, 5. Old lighthouse & new lighthouse, 6. Krishna's butter ball, 7. Tiger's cave.

Full details about them can be had under the heading 'Temples in and around Chennai'.

Historical importance: This was a flourishing port during the Pallava period and later Chola period. The birthplace of one of the first three Alwars – Boothathalwar. The Pallavas made this place a unique centre of art and architecture. At every turning, one could find amazing skills of the sculptor. It is now only a village and a centre of tourist attraction.

Festival: Pongal harvest festival is celebrated on a grand scale in January and February. The dance festival of Mamallapuram is unique during this time. They are mostly arranged during week-ends. Bharatanatyam, Kuchipudi, Kathakali and Odissi – all the types of the dances of the south are performed. The monuments are floodlit during nights and appear superb even after dusk.

Shopping: Many small shops sell decorative articles made of sea-shells, granite and small statues carved out of soft stones. Poompuhar the government-run emporium has a branch selling variety of handicrafts.

NEARBY PLACES OF EXCURSION

• Kanchipuram - 66 km. • Vedanthangal bird sanctuary - 53 km. • Covelong (Kovalam) - 20 km. • Crocodile Farm - 14 km • Muttukadu - near Covelong, ideal location for boating and water sports. • Thirukkalukkundram - 30 km. • Thiruvidandhai - 5 km.

Details of the above places can be had under the heading 'Temples in and around Chennai'.

Where to stay?

• Hotel Tamil Nadu Beach Resort, • Hotel Tamil Nadu Youth Camp, • T.T.D.C. Temple Bay Beach Resort, • Silver Sands Beach Resort, • Golden Sun Hotel & Beach Resort, • The Ideal Beach Resort, • Mamalla Bhavan, • Mamalla Lodge, • Marina Lodge.

MEDICAL FACILITIES

1. Hospitals, Government Primary Health Centre - near Township office.
2. St. Mary's Church Dispensary

IMPORTANT TELEPHONE NUMBERS

- Tourist Office: 242232
- Temple Bay Ashok Beach Resort: 242251
- Hotel Tamil Nadu Beach Resort: 242362
- Hotel Tamil Nadu Youth camp: 242287
- Ideal Beach Resort: 242240

Pondicherry

(The lingering French Culture)

Pondicherry is 162 kms. south of Chennai. It was the former French settlement. Even before that, it was known as Vedapuri and once maritime trade flourished here. Roman coins, wine jars and other articles reveal Roman connections and its antiquity is considered to be before the Christian era. It was under the rule of the Cholas, Pallavas and the Vijayanagar kings. Later it came under the Golconda Sultan and the French bought it from him in 1763 and founded their settlement. Besides Pondicherry, another place Karaikal about 150 km south of Chennai on the seashore and Yenam in Andhra Pradesh and Mahe in Kerala also form part of the Union Territory of Pondicherry. Even after Indian Independence, Pondicherry remained under French rule and only in 1954 was the de jure transfer to India made by France.

How to get there?

Pondicherry is linked by a good network of roads to almost all the important places in South India. Buses ply every half an hour to Pondicherry from Chennai. It is also linked by rail with Chennai, Trichirappalli and Villupuram. A small airport has also come up in Pondicherry.

Places to see

Sri Aurobindo Ashram: The main attraction of Pondicherry is Sri Aurobindo Ashram. Sri Aurobindo who was the stalwart freedom fighter of the pre-Gandhian era, following spiritual Adesh (voice or order) came to Pondicherry in 1910, then a French territory, and remained here for ever practising Yoga. He was later joined by a French lady, Mirra known as the Mother. After the mother's coming, the followers increased in number and the Ashram came into being. After Sri Aurobindo's retirement to recluse in 1926, Mother shouldered the entire responsibility of the Ashram. Ever since, the Ashram has grown in leaps and bounds and today there are about 2000 inmates - Sadhakas practising in action the integral or supramental yoga of Sri Aurobindo.

The main Ashram building where Sri Aurobindo and the Mother's samadhis are enshrined is open to public from 8.00 a.m to 5.00 p.m. with a recess from 12.00 noon to 3 p.m. Anyone who happens to be there by 9.00 a.m. can take special permit and visit the room where Sri Aurobindo resided and did his splendid spiritual work. The things used by Sri Aurobindo and a rare collection of beautiful artifacts are kept there. In the reception counter the books of Sri Aurobindo are on sale. One could also buy pictures, calendars and diaries there – all connected with Sri Aurobindo and the Mother. The information centre will give you all details. The educational institutions run by the Ashram, the gymnasia and the playground activities and the cultural programmes and exhibitions organised every now and then by the Ashram could also be seen after obtaining permit from the reception counter. One can also take one's breakfast, lunch and dinner in the Ashram dining hall by paying a small amount. Ashram guest-houses scattered nearby provide accommodation too at reasonable rates and most of them would be full – only early birds will find a niche in them.

There are some important days observed in the Ashram and public are allowed to have darshan of Sri Aurobindo's and the Mother's rooms. Thousands of devotees will gather on those days. The most important days are:

(i) January 1st - Prosperity Day

(ii) February 21st - Mother's Birthday

(iii) August 15th - Sri Aurobindo's Birthday

(iv) November 17th - The Mother's Samadhi Day

(v) November 24th - Supramental Day

(vi) December 5th - Sri Aurobindo's Samadhi Day

Beach: Pondicherry is on the coast of the Bay of Bengal and the 1500 metre stretch beach is an ideal place for swimming and sunbathing. 4 metre tall statue of Mahatma Gandhi, a beautiful artificial mountain park near the Ashram playground, the statue of Pondicherry's illustrious governor Dupleix and the War Memorial built by the French to commemorate the soldiers who sacrificed their lives for the victory of the First World War, the 150-year-old lighthouse are other attractions of the beach. The beach is maintained clean and of late boulders have been erected to prevent sea-erosion. Sri Aurobindo Society's beach office and the Pondicherry Government Tourist Office are on the beach road.

French Institute: The only present link with France in Pondicherry is this institute. It is an internationally acclaimed institute on Dumas Street founded in 1955 by Dr. J. Fillozet, the renowned French Indologist. It has a brilliant collection of rare books on Science, Technology, Ecology, Cartography, Pedagogy, Indian languages and culture. The Romain Rolland Library run by the government has a collection of 60,000 books some of them being rare French volumes.

JIPMER : Jawaharlal Nehru Institute of Post-graduate Medical Education and Research, started in 1979, it is one of the most prestigious institutions of its kind in India. This is one of the foremost medical institutions in the country and is located at the western entry point to Pondicherry. This place is called Gorimedu.

Botanical Garden : The botanical garden planned by C.S.Perrotet in 1826 is near the old bus stand off the West Boulevard. It has a good collection of exotic flower plants, both alien and indigenous. There is a toy rail to amuse children and the Jawahar Bal Bhavan - a unique all-India organization to train children in various arts is also located here.

Aquarium : Another attraction in the Botanical Garden is the aquarium which has some rare species of ornamental fish.

Museum : The 1984 museum near the park facing the beach houses the antiques apart from the Roman coins and other articles of Roman origin unearthed from Pondicherry. This reveals the connections of ancient times. There are also sections of archaeology, geology, and sculpture, handicrafts, artifacts, ornaments and things obtained in Arikamedu, a place in the nearby village Ariyankuppam. The bed used by Dupleix, a palanquin and a pousse-pousse that resembles a hand-pulled rickshaw are also on display.

Park : There is a well laid out park facing the beach and opposite the governor's residence. Most people take rest during the afternoon under the shady trees. The statues of Bharathiar and Bharathidasan have been erected here. One main attraction is the sculpture park interspersed in the garden with beautiful images and ornamental pillars looted by Dupleix from Gingee. In the centre is a cenotaph, raised by Napoleon, called Ayi Memorial - a woman who donated her tank to quench the thirst of people which is now the symbol of Pondicherry.

Bharathiar & Bharathidasan Memorials : The national poet Bharathi took asylum in Pondicherry when the British atrocities against freedom fighters were rampant. The house where he lived in Pondicherry on the Dharma Raja Koil Street has been converted into a fine memorial by the Pondicherry government. Rare photographs, manuscripts written in Bharathiar's own hand, volumes of his works and the papers he published are on display. Some of the things he used and some rare photographs of his associates are also on display.

Bharathidasan, the true revolutionary poet and disciple of Bharathiar is a native of Pondicherry. The house where he resided has also been converted into a fitting memorial in Bharathidasan Road.

Anandharangam Pillai's House: The famous dubash who was right hand to Dupleix and who recorded the events of his days in his diary. Anandharangam Pillai's house could be seen in Ranga Pillai Street. The beautiful ornamental carvings on tables and stately doors with carvings and the articles used by him are on display here.

Temples : There are several temples in Pondicherry town and nearby villages built by the Cholas between 10th and 12th centuries dedicated to local village gods.

In Madagadippattu village, a beautiful temple with excellent art works was found in the excavation. In Bhahur, another village, once a centre of Sanskrit-learning flourished during the Pallava period. The **Varadharaja temple** in the heart of the town is a Vishnu shrine of the Chola period built in the 12th century. There is a Chola inscription here that speaks of a Sanskrit University. There is a Siva temple known as **Ambalathu Adigal Mutt temple** nearby. The **Kimbili Swami Mutt temple** a little away has a rare sculpture which is a unique pose of Siva and Mahakali dancing together in unison. The **Siddhanta Swami Samadhi temple** near the burial ground is famed in one of the songs of poet Bharathiar. One can see the statues in stucco of all the siddhas and saints in this temple where people of all faiths visit. **Thirukkameswara temple** in the nearby Villiyanur is a Siva temple built by the Cholas in the 12th century. The annual festival of this temple held in May-June attracts thousands of devotees. The most famous and important temple of Pondicherry is the **Manakkula Vinayagar temple** near Aurobindo Ashram. It was originally an idol planted near a 'manal kulam' - sandy tank. The legend is that the early European settlers wanted to remove it from there and they had actually thrown it several times into the sea. After each throwing, the deity appeared in the same place the next day. This caused some concern among them and they abandoned the idea. Later on, the Mother of Sri Aurobindo Ashram donated lands for building the temple in a fitting manner. Poet Bharathiar has sung a beautiful prabhandam (poetic work) on this deity. Mural painting of all Ganapathis could be seen around the corridors.

In Thiruvamathur village is the famous **Vattaparai Amman**. It is a round-shaped rock and in olden times if any dispute arose instead of going to court they came here and standing before the deity will tell only the truth and nothing but the truth. The deity is supposed to be so powerful that any false witness would be severely dealt with by Amman, so none dared to utter falsehood. Many disputes were thus solved here.

Churches : There are a number of beautiful churches in Pondicherry. The most beautiful is the Church of the Sacred Heart of Jesus on south boulevard. It is a Gothic style church with three stained glass panels in a corridor behind the altar depicting the life of Christ. The Englise de Notre Dam des Anges on Dumas Street built in 1865 has an oil painting of Our Lady of Assumption donated by Napoleon III. Another famous church is the one called the Englise de Notre Dame des Lourdes in Villiyanur. It has been built exactly as the Basilica at Lourdes in France. The local Tamilians call it Villiyanur Madha church. The church festival in June attracts lakhs of devotees of all faiths. There is also a tank, the only one of its kind in a church in India.

Auroville : The city of dawn is the brainchild of the Mother designed by the well known French architect Roger Ongar. Its aim is an international community living in amity despite all creeds, politics and nationalities. The inauguration was on 28 February 1968 when the President of the Indian Union and representatives of 121 nations came to pour the soils of their lands in a lotus-shaped urn symbolic of universal oneness. About 500 people from different countries live in 40 settlements of Auroville. The best way to go round this vast area is to hire a bicycle and set on an adventurous expedition. Near Matri Information Centre is a 25 hectare farm and orchard successfully practising organic agriculture without using chemicals and factory fertilisers. The produce is utilised in the kitchens at Auroville as well as the Ashram.

Matri Mandir is the main attraction of Auroville. It is a huge globe-like structure visible everywhere in Auroville. Its construction is still going on and it is a place of meditation. In the hall, a huge crystal ball is kept which glows absorbing the natural light – a crystal to gaze and meditate. When it is completed it would be one of the wonders of the world. The Mother has conceived it as a temple of truth and inaugurated the work which still continues. Public are allowed to have a look at the progressing mandir and at particular hours to meditate before the crystal ball – a unique experience indeed!

NEARBY PLACES OF EXCURSION

• Gingee • Thiruvannamalai • Sathanur Dam • Panamalai • Melsittamur • Thiruvakkarai • Sanyasikuppam • Nandaga Pattu • Cuddalore • Thiruvahindrapuram • Vadalur • Thiruvadigai

For details 1 to 8, see Thiruvannamalai; 9 to 12, see Cuddalore.

Where to Stay?

- **Govt. Tourist Home,** Uppalam Road.
- **Pondicherry Tourism,** Development Corporation, Tourist Home, Near Thiruvalluvar Bus Stand.
- **Hotel Mass,** Near New Bus Stand.
- **Hotel Ram International,** West Boulevard.
- **Guest Houses of the Ashram**
- **Park Guest House,** Goubert Avenue on the Seaside.
- **International Guest House,** Gingee Salai.
- **Cottage Guest House,** Raja Pillai Street.
- **Youth Hostel,** Solai Thandavan Kuppam.
- **Hotel Jayaram,** Nehru Road.
- **Auroville.** (9 Guest Houses are attached to Auroville.)
- **Anandha Inn,** 154, S.V. Patel Road, Pondicherry - 605 001. ✆ 330711 Fax : 0413-331241 Email: checkin@anandhainn.com
- **Jayaram Hotel,** 90, Kamaraj Salai, Pondicherry - 605 001. ✆ 227191-98 Fax: 0413-336877
- **Hotel Annamalai International,** 479, Kamaraj Salai, Saram, Pondicherry - 605 013. ✆ 247001 Fax: 0413-247015 Email: info@hotelannamalai.com
- **International Guest House,** 47, N.S.C. Bose Salai, Pondicherry - 605 001. ✆ 336699, 221812 Fax: 0413-334447 Email: mother@sriaurobindo society.org.in
- **Hotel Pondicherry Ashok,** East Coast Road, Kalapet, Pondicherry - 605 014. ✆ 655160-167 Fax: 0413-655140 Email: itdchpa@satyam.net.in
- **Seaside Guest House,** 14, Goubert Avenue, Pondicherry - 605 001. ✆ 336494, 221825 Fax: 0413-334447 Email: sasocty@md2.vsnl.net.in
- Besides, umpteen lodges are available in Raja Pillai Street, Patel Road Mission Street, Nehru Road and near the new bus stand.

Cuddalore

(The land of Vallalar)

Cuddalore, about 180 km south of Chennai, is a minor port on the shores of the Bay of Bengal. It is about 20 km from Pondicherry. It has played a prominent role in history and religion. Cuddalore literally means city near the sea. It played a vital part in battles during the colonial period. Fort St. David, the fort built by the British near the sea was once a strategic point of vital importance. One could now see the ruins of this fort on the shore. There is a palm fringed backwater in the old town which is now a fishing village and the port is located here. It was once a dominant Jain Centre and in the new town called Thiruppathiripuliyur, there once flourished a Jain Centre. Loka Vibaga, a famous Jain treatise was written here. The famous Pataleeswara temple dedicated to Lord Siva has an imposing tower and beautiful sculptures of the Pallava and later Chola periods. It was here that the famous saint Appar was proselytized from Jainisim to Saivism. Legend has it that he was tied to a huge boulder and hurled into the sea and by singing hymns on Siva, escaped unscathed. Later, the Pallava king Mahendravarman who embraced Jainism was reconverted to Saivism by Appar. The river Gedilam passes through Cuddalore.

Thiruvahindrapuram : It is on the banks of Gedilam about 6 km from Cuddalore. There is a Vishnu shrine here and the bronze image of Rama in this temple is very beautiful – a rarity that cannot be seen anywhere else. Devanayaka Perumal is the presiding deity. There is a picturesque bathing ghat in the temple. Sri Vedanta Desikan, a famous Vaishnavaite saint is said to have lived here for 15 years.

Thiruvadigai Temple : It is a beautiful Siva temple on the banks of Gedilam about 15 km from Cuddalore in Panrutti town – a place renowned for cashewnuts and jackfruits. The Pallava Viruttaliswarar is the presiding deity. It was originally a Jain temple and Mahendravarman, the Pallava king demolished it and built this beautiful temple. It is renowned for its artistic images and stucco figures on the vimanam and gopuram. Even now a big Jain statue in sitting posture could be seen unsheltered in the temple. Some frescoes could also be seen on the ceiling of this temple, though damaged. A Vishnu temple and Gunapara Iswaran another Siva temple built with the demolished Jain temple could also be seen in the vicinity. Manavachagam Kadanthar's samadhi is also located in Panrutti town.

Vadalur is an important place associated with saint Ramalinga Adigal, southwest of Cuddalore. He is the author of Thiruvarutpa and a spiritual superman of yester years. He finally settled in this place and built an octagonal structure called 'Satya Gnana Sabha' here. This spot was chosen purposefully by him because one could see all the four towers of Chidambaram temple from here. The sanctum of this sabhai or temple is separated from the main hall by seven screens and only on 'Thai Poosam Day' in December-January all of them are lifted, otherwise only three will be removed. Jothi or eternal light is worshipped here. There is also a dharmasala which feeds all the people who come here. It is said that the hearth lighted by Ramalinga Adigal is still kept burning. Nearby is Mettukuppam where one can see the room in which the saint locked himself and instructed not to open it till a stipulated time. People in anxiety opened it before the due date and to their surprise no trace of him could be seen there.

Neyveli - the Lignite Town : The lignite town Neyveli is near Vadalur and one can see the giant bucket wheel excavator digging the earth to reach the coals. Another attraction is the Artesian wells. It is a planned township. Thermal electric power is also produced here. With permit, one could visit the open mines and see the busy activities of the digging of the brown coal and the pumping of water on which the coal deposit is virtually floating under the earth. The high pressure water underneath has to be pumped before the coal is cut.

Devanampattinam Beach : It is a fine beach with sandy stretches and an ideal location for sea bathing. Since Cuddalore is a minor harbour one could see a row of ships anchored at a distance which are reached by catamarans and boats. New housing colonies are coming up here now.

How to Reach?

Cuddalore can be reached by rail and buses. Road link to all important places are available. Umpteen buses ply every day to Cuddalore or via Cuddalore.

Where to Stay?

Though it is the district headquarters, good lodges worth the name are not available. The best is to stay at Pondicherry and visit Cuddalore and the nearby places. There are also some lodges and food is available in many hotels.

Thiruvannamalai

(The Place of Salvation)

Thiruvannamalai is a historic holy place, about 175 km from Chennai. It is the 'Mukthi Sthalam' (Place of Salvation) for several saints like Gugai Namachivayar, Seshadri Swamigal, Ramana Maharishi, Arunagirinathar etc. and the place is studded with caves and shelters of holy men. It is one of the 'Pancha Bootha Sthalams' (places of five elements) and the element here is Fire or Agni. It is called 'Sonachalam' in Sanskrit meaning red mountain – symbolic of fire.

How to get there?

It is about 175 km from Chennai and many buses ply daily. It is 66 km from Pondicherry and 68 km from Villupuram. As it is on the Katpadi-Villupuram meter gauge railway track, one can also reach it by train.

What to see?

Arunachaleswarar Temple : This is the most famous Siva temple and as mentioned earlier, one of the five element forms of Siva. It is at the foot of the hill - Thiruvannamalai. The temple is dedicated to Jothi Lingam or God incarnate as fire. It is an ancient temple. The Cholas, Vijayanagar kings, Hoysalas and the Nayakas of Thanjavur have all done various works and extended the temple to the present magnificence. It has imposing gopurams (portal towers) on all four sides and provides a majestic look. It is said that there are about 100 temples here but the chief one is this. The main gopuram is 66m high and has 13 storeys. The work was started by Krishna Devaraya and completed by Sevappa Nayaka of Thanjavur. There are many circumambulatory corridors and two large tanks inside the temple. There is a 1000-pillared mandap with floral paintings in its ceiling. Inscriptions of various rulers and chieftains abound the temple walls. Legend has it that Lord Siva stood in the form of a huge pillar of fire and the attempt of Vishnu to find his feet and the attempt of Brahma to find his head were futile. The lofty mountain is symbolic of this incident. Every year during Karthigai Deepam (November-December) a huge bonfire atop the hill is lighted in a cauldron serving as a lamp and thousands of tons of ghee poured in it with bales of cloth for wick. Lakhs of people from all over India throng to have a darshan of the sacred fire – Annamalai deepam which is visible around for many days despite heavy rains. The Kili Gopuram or parrot tower inside is very auspicious since Saint Arunagirinathar is said to have taken the form of a parrot while attaining salvation shedding his mortal coils. A sculptural representation of this could be seen on this gopuram. The Pathala Lingam or underground Lingam where the Saint Ramana Maharishi did penance is a main attraction in this temple. The samadhis of Seshadri Swamigal and Ramana Maharishi on the path round the mountain attracts streams of pilgrims - graceful places of peace and serenity. On full moon days, people throng here to walk round the mountain and reach the temple for worship. This is known as 'Girivalam' or going round the mountain. The Tamilnadu Tourism Development Corporation runs special buses from Chennai on these days.

A few kilometres east is a hamlet where the parapets of a tank is profusely covered with erotic sculptures rivalling Khajuraho. The legend has it that a Vijayanagar chieftain in order to enlighten his daughter who was averse to earthly pleasures, caused this to be carved on the parapets of the tank where she used to take her bath.

Sathanur Dam : It is a place of relaxation and rest, 22 miles away from Thiruvannamalai. The dam is constructed across the river Pennar submerging a huge forest between two mountains. A well laid out garden and well lit fountain enchant the visitors. A swimming pool, a crocodile park and motor launch also attract the tourists. Separate cottages with boarding are also available. If one wishes one may stay a day or two in the beautiful place and relax forgetting all his commitments.

Thirukoilur : 25 km down on the banks of Pennar stands a temple dedicated to Thirivikrama the Lord who measured the entire earth and sky with just two strides of His feet. It is an ancient temple with beautifully carved pillars. The temple tower on the eastern side is one of the tallest in South India. On a rock in the river bed stands another temple worth visiting. **Gnananandagiri's Tapovanam** is a main attraction in this place. Gnanananda Giri, the guru of Haridoss Giri is a well known saint of yester-years and he was supposed to possess occult powers and was a renowned telepathist. His samadhi and Brindavan are here. Every day Bhajans are held and there is free feeding for the devotees. Even today people from every nook and corner of the world visit this place to get peace and consolation.

Arakandanallur: Another place nearby where stands a Siva shrine of olden times with three caves carved by the Pallavas. The saint Ramana Maharishi got his first vision of supreme truth here and was drawn to Thiruvannamalai.

Kuvakam Koothandavar Koil: 22 km south of Thirukoilur stands this village famous for its annual festival of Aravan, the son of Arjuna. It occurs in May and the unique feature of this festival is that eunuchs from all over India assemble here to perform a vow to get married to Koothandavar at night and to be widowed by next dawn. Thousands of them visit and perform this vow.

Gingee Fort (Senchikkottai): It is about 150 km away from Chennai on the road to Thiruvannamalai. This fort was a stronghold of the Cholas during the 9th century. The Vijayanagar kings later fortified and made it an impregnable citadel. This fortified city has been built on seven hills, the most important being Krishnagiri, Chandragiri and Rajagiri.

Rajagiri is the tallest rising 600 ft. It is enclosed by massive granite walls pierced with gates and towers occupying about an area of 12 sq. km. The ascent to citadel is through a serpentine flight of rough steps. Granaries, dungeons, queen's quarters, cool pools and a temple called Kuvalakanni temple could all be seen on the way. The citadel is unapproachable being perched on a steep cliff surrounded by deep chasms. The only access is by an artificial bridge thrown across one such yawning gap of 25 ft. wide and more than 80 ft. in depth. A big cannon is quartered in a mandap there facing the plains which once might have roared emitting volleys of fire on the enemy army approaching the plains. Beehives cling to the precipitous sides and one can witness a thrilling sight of the hill tribes extracting honey dangling in the air. The Cholas,

Vijayanagar kings, Rajputs, Marathas, French, Nawabs, the Nayaks and the English evinced keen interest in keeping the strategic citadel.

The small hill is ascended by a flight of steep steps cut on the buttress of the fort. There is an audience hall atop and one could experience the cool fast winds embracing him/her. The fort is immortalised in the ballads of Raja Desingh – a hero of the Moghul period who with undaunted courage defied the Moghuls. When he was killed treacherously, the entire harem committed sathi – self immolation. Even today a pit near the tank called 'Chakkara Kulam' is shown as the place where it happened.

The tutelary deity of Raja Desingh was Lord Vishnu called Ranganatha and can be seen on the hill at **Singavaram**, 32 kms north. It is a cave temple furnished by Mahendra Varma Pallavan. The God is in the recumbent posture here. In the prakara of this temple, one could see the relief of a chilling spectacle of a devotee severing his head as an offering to Durga.

Panamalai : On the road to Villupuram from Gingee on the southern side lies this place. Here Pallava king Rajasimha has built a famous temple to Thalapuriswara–a Siva temple. There are some fine frescoes existing in good condition illustrating the Pallava style.

Mandagappattu : About 17 km on the way to Gingee from Villupuram stands this famous rock-cut cave temple of Pallava king Mahendra Varma who had the nom-de-plume of Vichitra Chittan and who boasts that he has built temples that will last for ever as they are made without mud and wood.

Mel-Sittamur : It is on the way to Tindivanam from Gingee. Temples dedicated to Jain Tirthankaras could be seen here. It is the headquarters of the chief Jain monk and possesses rare Jain manuscripts. In the beginning of Christian era when portions of Mylapore were submerged under the sea, the Jain temple that existed there was shifted to this far-off place inland. Whatever could be salvaged were removed and brought to this place. There are some fine carvings in the temple. Jain research scholars visit this temple. A good number of Jains scattered nearby come for worship.

Dhalavanur : Another rock-cut temple exists here, built by Mahendra Varman, the Pallava king. The temple is called Satru Malleswaram. The name derives from Satrumalla one of the titles of Mahendra Varman.

Thiruvakkarai : It is near Tindivanam on the banks of the river Varaha Nadhi. Here is a temple, part of which was erected by Sembian Mahadevi, the Chola queen. It is curious in many respects. The entrance way is not aligned in a line. The Nåndi of this temple is planted away from its usual place in front of the sanctum. There is an unusual mudra of the Chathura Dance pose of Nataraja. It is a place famous for trees that have become rocks and fossilised due to passage of time. They are displayed in a special park. During full moon days, hundreds of people gather here to worship the multi-handed Kali known as Vakra Kali Amman enshrined near the front gopuram.

By a strange convention, in this temple, the regular Pooja is performed in the period known as 'Ragukalam' or the period under the influence of Ragu.

Sanyasikuppam : On the way to Pondicherry from Tindivanam one can reach this place where an elaborately carved stone bull stands. **Valudavur**, a nearby place has the ruins of a fort, once the residence of Mahabath Khan, the minister of Raja Desingh.

Where to Stay?

In Thiruvannamalai, you can stay in Park Hotel or Modern Cafe. From there, you can visit the places mentioned above in excursion. At Sathanur dam, P.W.D. cottages are available.

☛ We have covered here almost all the important places of tourist interest on the way to Thiruvannamalai and the nearby places that could be covered en route to Thiruvannamalai.

Vellore

(The Fort Town)

Vellore is 145 km from Chennai. It was the last capital of Vijayanagar empire, now a busy town, a market for various agricultural commodities and the district headquarters. There are some rare places of tourist importance in and around Vellore. One could stay here comfortably and visit the places. The climate is generally hot with cool nights–a typical example of inland climate where there is considerable difference between high and low temperatures. 'A temple without idol, A river without water and A fort without forces' is a local saying about this town.

How to get there?

Vellore is very well connected with important places by good roads. There are buses every half an hour to Vellore from Chennai. There is also a rail link on Chennai-Bangalore route. Katpadi is the nearby junction and from Katpadi there is a metre gauge link to Vellore. The nearest airport is at Chennai.

Places to See

Vellore Fort : It is a moated fort of the Vijayanagar period built around the 16th century preserved in good condition even today. It was built of granite blocks with a moat watered from a subterranean drain fed by a tank. It was built by Chinna Bomminayaka, a chieftain of the Vijayanagar emperors, Sadasivaraya and Srirangaraya. It was later in the hands of Muthraza Ali, the brother-in-law of Chanda Sahib. It then passed into the hands of Marathas from whom it came under David Khan of Delhi in 1760. Then it was under Tipu Sultan. Finally, it came to the British after the fall of Srirangapatnam. At first, Tipu's children were kept in safe custody here. It is like the Windsor Castle of South India and the only one of its kind. Even before the first war of Indian Independence in 1857, a revolt against the British broke out here in 1806 which is in fact the harbinger of the 1857 Sepoy Mutiny. Various public buildings and private offices including the police training centre and a jail are inside the fort.

Jalakanteswara Temple : A Siva temple that was built at the same time the fort was built around 1566. It is a fine specimen of the later Vijayanagar architecture. The carvings are superb and even today looks fresh. One can't see Vijayanagar relics of this sort outside Hampi. The British were so enthralled by the wonderful sculpture that they contemplated to shift the temple completely to a museum in England, but fortunately a severe storm intervened and the project was dropped. Following the occupation of Muslim rulers, it was used as a garrison and desecrated. The idol was removed and worship terminated. It went under the custody of the Archaeological Survey of India and is preserved as a museum. In 1981, the idol which was removed by the threat of Muslim invasion was moved back into the temple and worship carried on.

C.M.C. Hospital : The Christian Medical College Hospital having over a thousand bed strength is renowned all over the world. Even patients from Malaysia, Sri Lanka and the Middle East come here for treatment. Founded by an American missionary in 1900, it has the support of 74 churches and organizations worldwide.

Places around Vellore

Dr. Vainu Bappu Observatory: This observatory at Kavalur has the biggest telescope in Asia. It is a powerful 2.34 metre telescope. One can observe heavenly bodies clearly from here. It is named after the great Indian astrophysicist Dr. Vainu Bappu who was responsible for the erection of various observatories in this country and the Indian Institute of Astrophysics was founded by him. He also discovered a new comet named after him as Bappu-Boll-New Kirk, the other two suffixes stand for the other two scientists who added more details to the newly found comet. There is a beautifully laid out garden in front of the observatory which was designed by Vainu Bappu himself. He also made important contributions in calculating the luminosity and distance of stars with his colleague Wilson and it is known all over the world as 'Bappu–Wilson Effect'.

Thiruvalam : An ancient Siva temple where the Nandi, instead of facing the deity faces the opposite direction. It was once the capital of Banas, who were vassals to Pallavas and the temple was built by them. The puranam of this place narrates the story of contest between Lord Muruga and Lord Ganapathi for the fruit presented by Naradha to Lord Siva. Ganapathi got the fruit by just going round His parents Siva and Parvathi while Muruga who literally went round the world was outwitted. Till recently it was the abode of Mouna Swamigal.

Vallimalai : A few miles off Thiruvalam and 25 kms from Vellore lies this hilly range which was once an abode of Jain monk and even today one could see the relief images of Tirthankaras carved on the slopes. At the bottom of the hill and in a cave on the top are temples dedicated to Lord Muruga. Vallimalai is also called as Parvatharajan Kundram. In the interior of the wooded slopes lived Vallimalai Swamigal who introduced the novel system of visiting temples on the New Year's Day.

Ratnagiri : This is about 15 kms from Vellore and there is a Murugan Temple on the top of Ratnagiri and by a flight of steps from the roadside one could reach this temple. It is an old temple but recently renovated with additions.

Sholingar : Here the low range of hills culminates in an arc and thus forms a sort of natural fortification. The Cholas and Banas keeping its strategic value formed a settlement here and four temples have come up here, two on the hills and two on the plains. This range is also called Gadikachalam in Tamil. The tall hill rising like a spire has the Lord Yoga Narasimha Swami, one of the incarnations of Lord Vishnu and the temple is reached by a stiff climb. The deity is a huge idol in

Yogasana pose. The small hill adjacent has the Hanuman temple. In a cleft, there is a pool of curative water. Mentally afflicted people stay here for 40 days and get cured of their illness. On the plains stands a Vishnu shrine improved by Vijayanagar kings and a Siva shrine of the Chola period.

Arma Malai : This hill is between Kudiyattam and Vaniyambadi and a little north of the highway. There is a cave with Pallava paintings of Jain character.

Kadambur Hill : This is near Ambur where one can see the natural cave where Anvaruddin was hiding. There is a beautiful Siva temple with a tank on the top. There is also a cool spring in a cleft. The cave about 200 sq. ft. with a small cleft through which cool breeze enters is worth a visit.

Elagiri : It is on the west of Vellore, an isolated attractive picnic spot. It is in the Eastern ghats at an elevation of 1000 metres. It is popularly known as Poor man's Ooty. A salubrious climate, beautiful sceneries and a temple to Lord Muruga attract visitors. Especially in summer, people in large numbers visit this place. Since this place is an ideal location for organising one day or two day trekking, often trekking expeditions are arranged. The Chairman, Youth Hostels Association of India, Tamil Nadu Branch, 24, 2nd Street, Balaji Nagar, Chennai - 600 014 could be contacted for further details.

Pallikonda : On the way back to Vellore one can alight at Pallikonda where Lord Ranganatha lives in an island (Ranga), in Palar. A beautiful Krishna idol dancing with a ball of butter adorns a cell in the prakara.

Thirumalai : It is 10 km north of Polur near Vellore. Two Jain temples are located in the hill. A Jain temple could be seen here. The main attraction is the paintings of Jain figures, monks, serpents, gods etc.

Padavedu : It is 10 km west of Arani near Vellore. It was the original home of the Sambhuvarayas who ruled independently this area as feudatories of the Cholas. There are two temples here, one dedicated to Renukadevi and the other to Ramaswami. In the Ramaswami temple, Hanuman is holding a book in his hand – a very unusual idol. He is supposed to be reading the Ramayana.

Thiruparkadal : It is an island in the river Palar and near Arcot on the way to Vellore. There are two shrines here, one dedicated to Lord Siva called Karapuriswara, built by early Cholas, and the other dedicated to Lord Vishnu. There are two idols in the Vishnu temple – one a recumbent Ranganatha and the other, Lingodhbhava, where out of the Lingam emerges Lord Vishnu.

Arcot : It is on the Chennai-Vellore road. It is aptly called a City of Durgahs, for at every turning one will stumble on a durgah – a tomb of a Muslim saint. The tomb of Sadatullakhan, an edifice of green polished marble, the ruined palaces of the Arcot Nawabs, the English fort on the banks of Palar could all be seen here.

Where to Stay?

- **Hotel Prince Manor,** 83, Katpadi Road, Vellore - 632 004. ✆ 227106 Fax: 0416-253016 Email: hotelprincemanor@vsnl.net
- **Hotel River View,** New Katpadi Road, Vellore. ✆ : 225047, 225251, 222349 Fax: 0416-225672
- **Palace Cafe,** 21, Katpadi Road, Vellore - 632 004. ✆ 220125

Many hotels and lodges are available in Vellore. Hotel Sangeet, the India Lodge, Palace Lodge and Venus Hotel are some of them. Staying at

Vellore one could easily visit all the places mentioned above. So far, we have covered almost all the important places of north Tamil Nadu. Now, we shall see the most important places in mid-Tamil Nadu (Nadunadu).

Chidambaram

(The abode of the Cosmic Dancer)

Chidambaram is a major tourist centre that opens the real gateway to the land of temples. It is the abode of the cosmic dancer Sri Nataraja. It is also a centre of learning, a centre of culture, a centre of pilgrimage, and a centre of Dravidian art and architecture. The original name of this place was Thillai Vanam (Forest). Thillai (Excecasia Agallcha) is a kind of thick shrub. The real meaning of Chidambaram is conciousness of the sky (space) [cit - consciousness, ambaram - sky (space)]. It is one of the five element places of Lord Siva and the element represented here is the sky (space) - ambaram. Hence, the name Chidambaram. The Pandyas, the Pallavas, the Cholas, the Vijayanagar kings have all worshipped the dancing Nataraja and enriched the temple with various works including the gold plating of the vimanam (dome)of the sanctum. Besides, the temple was also used as a garrison by the Marathas, the French, the British and by Hyder Ali for over 35 years during the Carnatic Wars. The famous Natyanjali festival is held here every year to pay homage to the Cosmic Dancer.

How to get there?

Chidambaram is 245 kms from Chennai and is well connected with several towns in the state. From here, there are bus services to Chennai, Pondicherry, Nagapattinam and Madurai. It is also connected with metre gauge rail link, main link going to Rameswaram via Kumbakonam, Thanjavur and Trichirappalli. The nearest airport is at Trichirappalli from where Indian Airlines connections are available to Chennai, Madurai and Sri Lanka. Umpteen buses ply daily to Chidambaram and via Chidambaram to various places.

Places to See

The Nataraja Temple : The temple called Ponnambalam or Kanaga Sabai is one of the oldest temples of the Chola period. It is a unique temple where Lord Siva is worshipped in an idol form instead of the usual 'Lingam'. It is spread over an area of 40 acres with 4 tall portal towers piercing the sky on each side having five sabhas or courts. The towers were built by Kulotunga Chola, Kopperumchinga, Vikrama Chola and Krishna Devaraya in the East, South, West and North respectively. The eastern gopuram (tower) is 40.8 metres high and carved on it are 108 dance poses of Bharathanatyam, the classical dance of Tamil Nadu. The western tower has also similar carvings. The other two depict the various Thiruvilaiyadalgal or puranic Holy Pranks of Lord Siva. The tallest is the northern tower soaring to a height of 42.4 m.

The presiding deity is Lord Nataraja installed in the Kanaga Sabha, the roof of which is gold-plated. The icon is the most bewitching dancing pose of Lord Siva. Adjacent is the shrine of Govindaraja (Vishnu) reclining on the serpent Adisesha and from His naval rises a lotus stem with a bloomed lotus on which is seated Brahma with His four heads. Therefore one can worship all the trinity of the Hindu faith – Brahma, Vishnu and Siva, at the same time, in this temple. In no other temple, it is possible. Two other shrines, one dedicated to Subrahmanya and the other to Ganesha could also be seen in this temple. A huge Nandi looks devotedly on His Lord and master through an aperture on the wall. As already stated Lord Siva is represented in the form of 'Akasha' - Sky (space), and it is one of the Pancha Bootha Sthalas of Lord Siva. Behind the idol, a screen conceals a mystery popularly known as Chidambara Rahasyam (mystery). While burning camphor is shown to the idol, the screen is removed momentarily to reveal a sparkling light which is symbolic of the removal of the sheath of ignorance to understand the Supreme Truth. There are two mandapams inside the complex, one 100-pillared and the other 1000-pillared. There is a big tank mirroring the north gopuram. The Nrithya Sabha is an artistic work of elegance with its minutely chiselled pillars carved to resemble a chariot drawn by horses.

The Srimulanatha complex and the shrine of goddess Sivakami contain beautiful paintings in the ceiling.

Festivals in the temple

1. Arudhra Darshan in December-January
2. Aani Thirumanjanam in June
3. 10-day Panguni Uthiram festival in March-April

Natyanjali Festival : It is jointly organised by the Department of Tourism, Govt. of Tamilnadu, The Ministry of Tourism, Government of India and Natyanjali Trust in Chidambaram. It is generally held in February and opens on the Maha Sivarathri Day. Prominent dancers of India perform their dance and offer it to the cosmic dancer Nataraja in the vicinity of his sanctum sanctorum. It is a unique tourist attraction and all the dances of India, both classical and modern, are performed.

Thillai Kali Temple : Kali was the original Goddess of Thillai Vanam i.e. Chidambaram. Lord Shiva had to perform Urdhuva Thandava by raising one of His legs up, to subdue Her in a dance competition. Hence, She has to leave the place offering it to Nataraja. So, Her temple is located in the northern outskirts about 1.6 km from the shrine of Sri Nataraja.

Annamalai University : This university is located on the eastern side of the railway station. It is a residential university founded by Raja Sir Annamalai Chettiar. It is renowned for Tamil research studies and Tamil music. It offers education in various faculties like Arts, Science, Medicine, Agriculture, Fine Arts and Engineering. There is also a marine biology department at Porto Nova.

Places around Chidambaram

Pichavaram : 16 kms east of Chidambaram lies a most beautiful scenic spot spread over 2800 acres of mangrove forest. It is formed in the backwaters which are interconnected by the Vellar and Kollidam systems offering abundant scope for water sports, para-sailing, rowing and canoeing. The Pichavaram mangroves are the healthiest mangrove occurrences in the world. A number of islands interspersing vast expanse of water covered with green trees make this place enchanting. The backwater is separated by a sand bar from the sea making it an extraordinary place of loveliness. Tamil Nadu Tourism Development Corporation offers boating, accommodation and restaurant facilities.

Sri Mushnam : It is located northwest of Chidambaram. There is a big Vishnu temple of Bhuvarahaswamy (incarnation of Vishnu as a boar) here. It is one of the eight Swayam

Vyaktakashethra (Spontaneous manifestation without being installed by anyone) in the south.

Melakadambur : It is located west of Chidambaram. The temple here is of the Pala art. Pala dynasty ruled over Bengal and produced masterpieces of art of a unique style. The Nataraja found in this temple dances on a bull and the idol belongs to Pala art.

Sirkazhi : Another Siva shrine 20 km from Chidambaram. It is the birthplace of one of the top 4 Saivaite saints named Thirugnana Sambandar and the legend proclaims that Goddess Parvathi breastfed the child Gnanasambandar as he was crying in the tank bund. The tank is inside the temple and is known as 'Mulaippal Thirtham' (Breast Milk Holy Water). During the month of April, a festival in memory of this legend is celebrated here. The temple is a Madakkoil – a structure with a storey attached.

Thiruvenkadu (Swetharanyam): It is 28 km from Chidambaram. The temple is dedicated to Agora Virabadra - a fierce aspect of Siva. An image of Bhikshadanamurthi (Mendicant Siva) unearthed here is an early Chola bronze casting of Lord Siva as a nude mendicant with the writhing cobra clinging on his thighs. The image is now in safe custody in the Thanjavur Art Gallery. This is also the abode of Budha (Mercury) one of the Navagrahas (nine planets).

Vaitheeswaran Koil : Down south of Chidambaram is located this temple of Lord Siva. The presiding deity is called Vaitheeswara - Lord of Healing. There is a tank inside the temple free from frogs called Siddha Amritha Theertha – a sacred pool reputed to contain nectar which has curative powers. Another name for this place is Pullirukku Velur. The sculptures are very wonderful here. It is the place of one of the Navagrahas - Angarahan (Mars).

Tirupunkur : It is the place where Lord Siva's mount Nandhi moved a little away from obstructing the Darshan of Lord Siva to Nandanar, the harijan devotee.

Mayiladuthurai (Mayavaram): This town can be reached by bus from Chidambaram. The river Cauvery bisects the town into Uttara Mayuram and the town proper. A fine bathing ghat is provided to bathe in the river. Dakshinamurthi shrine is famous here and the God of Wisdom sits in yoga pose on a Nandhi. At the bathing ghat, there is another Nandhi in the mid-stream where the waters swirl around him. It is said that it is a punishment to the arrogant Nandhi. Nandhi realised his fault and became repentant. He was allowed to stay in the middle to attain liberation on the full moon day of the month of Aippasi (November-December) when all the holy rivers converge here. A dip in this place on that holy day is believed to be as holy as a dip in the river Ganges.

The Mayuranathaswamy temple is in the heart of the town. It is a Siva temple with an imposing nine-storeyed tower. The goddess Durga in the northern niche is a fine piece of workmanship and differs from Durgas of other temples. A chilling sight is the offering of a devotee who is in the act of severing his head.

Vazhuvur : This place on the southern side of Mayavaram is about 12 km away. It is renowned for its bronze images of exquisite splendour. The Lord of this temple is called Krithivasa, one who wears the elephant skin. This is one of the eight places where Siva danced to destroy demons. The dance hall is called

Gnana Sabai - Hall of Wisdom. Behind Gajasamharamurthi is kept a Yantra which is known as Vazhuvur Rahasyam (mystery). The Gajasamharamurthi idol is a bronze image of the 11th century and is also the only one of its kind – a fusion of grace and vigour. The Bikshadana or Siva as mendicant is another marvel in bronze. He holds the Damaru (Hand-drum) in one hand, the Kapala in the other and is seen feeding a deer with His fingers with flowing locks of hair on which are perched the Crescent and the Ganges and the coy Uma with Skanda cuddled in Her arms makes the onlooker spellbound.

Perambur : 14 km away from Mayiladuthurai is a Subramania temple. Though small, the image is of granite and beautifully carved with 6 faces in the pose of Samharamurthi. Snakes abound this place, but no one has so far been bitten. The snakes just hiss at those who enter the Iluppai garden stealthily to pilfer.

Therazhundhur: The birth place of Kambar who rendered the epic Ramayana in Tamil, is 10 km away from Mayiladuthurai on the way to Poompuhar. There is a temple of sculptural value here and people point out a place called Kamba Medu as the birthplace of Kambar.

Vriddhachalam: The Vriddhagiriswarar temple with high enclosing walls and four tall gopurams is a big shrine. The mandapam here is carved like a chariot with wheels and horses. 24 delicately carved pillars with Yalis support the roof. The chains of the temple car were donated by Charles Hyde, the Collector during 1813.

Nannilam: 25 km from Mayiladuthurai is the place called Nannilam. It is here in Narimanam we get petrol. The crude petroleum pumped from the oil wells here is taken to the refinery at Ennore, Chennai. The installations of ONGC for drilling oil wells could be seen here.

Thiruppanaiyur : 3.5 kms from Nannilam, the temple has palmyra tree as the sacred tree. It is said the great Chola king Karikala, standing under a palmyra tree, was picked up by the royal elephant and taken to the palace to be crowned as king. Hence, it has become the sacred tree and the place also got the name Thiruppanaiyur (panai-palmyra).

Engan : The most beautiful and captivating idol of Lord Muruga is located in this temple, 6 miles from Koradacheri on the Nagore-Thanjavur railway line. The idol of Shanmuganathar has been carved with minute details – even holes are pierced in His ears to insert ear-rings. The same sculptor who made the idol at Sikkil cut off his right thumb to avoid carving another image superior to the Singaravelar. But Lord Muruga appeared in his dream and bade him to make another image at Ettukkudi. He then blinded his eyes as it excelled Singaravelar of Sikkil. Again he had a command to commission another image at Engan. He sought the help of a woman to assist him as he was blind. While working, his chisel cut the finger of the lady and the spurting blood fell on his eyes. His eyesight was immediately restored and he exclaimed 'Engan' (my eyes) and completed this superb idol. Hence, the place got its name 'Engan'.

Thiruchenkattankudi : It is about 13 km from Nannilam famous for Asthamurthi Mandapam. The image of Seeralan, the son of Siruthonda Nayanar, who was cooked for meals to Siva and resuscitated by Siva, is in the prakara. Its idol of Ganapathi is said to have been brought from Vatapi of the Chalukyan kingdom after an expedition by Chola and installed here. Siruthonda Nayanar was the General Paranjothi who led Chola's forces. Thiruchenkattankudi is the place where Siruthondar lived and the episode of Seeralan's resurrection happened. Tiripurantaka and Nataraja in this temple are fine specimens of Chola art.

Thiruvanjiam : It is 10 kms west of Nannilam. The sandalwood tree is the Sthala Viruksha here. Images of Durga, Bhairavar, Rahu and Kethu are of fine workmanship in this temple. Vanjinatha the deity is mounted on the Yama Vahana during Masi Dhasami festival (February-March).

Vidyapuram : 4½ kms from Koradacheri is this place where Rajaraja I has built a beautiful Siva temple. The presiding deity is called Meenakshisundareswarar. The idol of Meenakshi, the consort of Siva is noted for its artistic perfection and grace.

Gangai Konda Cholapuram : It lies 50 kms away from Chidambaram. The Chola emperor Rajendra I (1012-1044) built this temple dedicated to Siva with an imposing gopuram that can be seen miles around. It is a replica of the Brihadeeswarar temple at Thanjavur built by his father. There are many beautiful sculptures on the walls of the temple and its enclosures. It was built in commemoration of his victory over the kingdom abutting the Ganges. The waters of Ganges were brought in huge vessels by vassal kings and emptied into a huge tank more or less a lake named Cholagangam which literally means the Ganges of the Cholas. A big Nandhi in front of the temple made of brick and mortar, a lion-faced well with yawning mouth through which a flight of steps lead to the water beneath and gigantic dwarapalakas (gate-keepers) are the other thrilling features of this temple.

Kalvarayan Hills : They lie 150 km northwest of Chidambaram on the western side of Kallakurichi taluk. Spread over an area of 600 sq. kms and heights ranging from 315 to 1190 metres, they offer a temperate climate and quite solitude. It is an ideal place of retreat and peace. A well laid botanical garden pleases the eye. There are two waterfalls for taking a refreshing bath. It is an ideal location for trekking too. Every year in May, a summer festival is held.

All the above places around Chidambaram could easily be visited as there is a good road link to these places and buses too ply to all these places from Chidambaram.

Shopping : A number of shops are located in the Car Street around the temple. Many curious things can be purchased from Khadi Craft Emporium. Shops are available in all tourist centres around Chidambaram.

Where to Stay?

- **Hotel Tamil Nadu,** Railway Feeder Road, Chidambaram. ✆ 20056 to 20061
- **Hotel Saradha Ram,** 19, VGP Street. ✆ 04144-21338 (5 lines), Fax : 04144-22656, Email: hsrcdm@vsnl.com
- **Hotel Akshaya,** East Car Street. ✆ 22181
- **Star Lodge,** 101, South Car Street. ✆ 22743
- **Ramya Lodge,** South Car Street. ✆ 23011
- **Kalyanam Boarding & Lodging,** VGP Street. ✆ 22707
- **Shameer Lodge,** 6, VGP Street. ✆ 22983
- **M.A.T. Lodge,** S.P.Koil Street. ✆ 22457
- **Everest Lodge,** 55, S.P.Koil Street, ✆ 22545
- **Railway Retiring Room,** Rly. Feeder Road, ✆ 22298
- **O.S.Deen Lodge,** West Car Street, ✆ : 222602

<u>For Tourist Information</u>

- Govt of Tamilnadu Tourists' Office, Chidambaram. ✆ : 04144 - 22739

Poompuhar

(The Glorious Port of the Sangam Age)

Poompuhar or Kaviripoompattinam as it was known manifests the ancient glory of the Tamils. It was the chief port of the Chola kingdom during the Sangam Age. Sangam literature and the two great epics Silappadhikaram and Manimekalai give us glimpses of its glory. It was an international seaport and one could hear there many languages spoken by the merchants of various countries. The city contained separate quarters for foreigners and both day and night bazaars called Nalangadi and Allangadi were busy selling a plethora of articles like spices, gold, fancy wear, garments, liquor, pearls and precious stones and various edibles. Vast emporia were dealing on these goods. There were organised syndicates of merchants who also participated in the polity of the Cholas. Though it is reduced to a small village today, one could see evidences of its past glory in and around Poompuhar.

How to get there?

Poompuhar is in the Sirkazhi taluk of Nagappattinam district. Tourists have to alight at Mayiladuthurai Junction and proceed to Poompuhar by road. Those who come from Chennai have to alight at Sirkazhi and proceed by road. Poompuhar is linked to Mayiladuthurai as well as Sirkazhi by road, the distance being 24 kms and 21 kms respectively.

Tourists from Chennai to Poompuhar by private carriers can take the route via Tindivanam, Pondicherry, Cuddalore and Sirkazhi. Those coming from Madurai, Ramanathapuram and Tirunelveli may proceed via Melur, Tiruppattur, Karaikudi, Tharangampadi and Akkur. They can also come by Pudukkottai, Thanjavur and Mayiladuthurai .

Distance by rail route is as follows:

Chennai-Sirkazhi 260 kms; Chennai-Mayiladuthurai 281 kms; Thanjavur-Mayiladuthurai 70 kms; Trichy-Mayiladuthurai 120 kms.

One can also travel by bus to Mayiladuthurai or Sirkazhi from anywhere in Tamil Nadu and reach Poompuhar from there.

Antiquity of Poompuhar : Foreign notices of this ancient port could be seen in the travelogues of Periplus and Merris Erithroly, Ptolemy and Pliny. Pali literature like Milindapanha, Buddha Jataka tales, Abithama Avathar and Buddha Vamsakatha too mention this place. Buddhism flourished here 2000 years ago and evidences have been found out of the donation of a pillar by a Buddhist Somaya Bikkuni of Poompuhar during the second century B.C. Brahmi inscriptions dating back to 2nd century B.C. too speak of the city. The inscription at Sayavanam temple in Poompuhar also records its history. The Chola kings of the Sangam Age ruled the city with pride and embellished it in various ways. Most of them speak of a great festival called 'Indra Vizha' devoted to Lord Indra. Evidences have been found of its continuance till the later Chola period.

The plan of the city : From literary evidences, the plan of the city has been elicited as follows: (1) The city was divided into two well marked divisions as Pattinappakkam and Maruvurpakkam. (2) The market-place of Poompuhar was sandwiched in between Nalangadi, the day market and Allangadi, the night bazaar. (3) The seashore was occupied by ferocious undaunting fisher folks.

(4) The warehouses were also located there. Artisans, merchants, sweet-vendors, butchers, potters and diamond-cutters lived in Maruvurpakkam. (5) Kings, nobles, elite citizens, rich traders and farmers, physicians, astrologers, the king's barracks and court dancers lived in Pattinappakkam. (6) Vellidai Murugan, Elanchi Mandram, Nedunkal Mandram, Bootha Chatukkam and Pavai Mandram were located in Pattinappakkam. (7) The city also had well laid-out gardens like Elavanthigai Cholai, Uyya Vanam, Champapathi Vanam and Kaveri Vanam. (8) Temples for Lord Siva, Chathukka Bootham, Indra, Balarama, Soory (Sun), Machathan, Chandra (Moon), Arugan (Jain), Thirumal (Vishnu) were there besides Buddha stupas and seven Buddha vihars, Champapathi Amman temple, brick idols and Ulagu Arivai Mandram. (9) There were avenues and separate sacred passages for temple idols to take bath in the river. (10) There were ring wells on the fringes of the city. (11) There was a separate quarter for foreigners besides separate market-places. (12) All along the river banks, cool and shady trees were planted. This in short is the plan of Kaviripoompattinam or Poompuhar. 'Puhar' means estuary and the city was at the estuary of the only perennial river of Tamil Nadu - Cauvery.

Excavation at Poompuhar : Archaeologists have unearthed interesting evidences supporting the literary evidences. The excavations were initiated in 1910. The Archaeological Survey of India found out several ring wells near the seashore. The excavations near Champapathi Amman and Pallavaneswaram temples brought to light the existence of various buildings. Remains of a brick building and a boat jetty were discovered in Keezhaiyur. A water reservoir and the remains of several buildings were also found. Relics of a sixty feet Buddha vihar was found in Pallavaneswaram. A Buddha marble paadha (feet of Buddha) of the size 3½′ × 2½′ with holy symbols akin to those at Amaravati and Nagarjunakonda. The coins that were in use during the early Chola Karikalan period were also found out. An ancient Roman copper coin too was unearthed at Vellaiyan Iruppu. Copper coins of Rajaraja Chola were also unearthed. An eighth century gold-plated copper statue of Buddha in meditation was also unearthed in Melaiyur in 1927. The Tamil Nadu Archaeological Department has discovered the remains of several buildings recently. This department in collaboration with The National Institute of Oceanography, Goa, has launched an offshore exploration of Poompuhar. This venture, it is hoped will bring out the magnificence of this erstwhile international seaport of South India.

Revival of Poompuhar's Ancient Glory : Dr. Kalaignar Karunanidhi, the illustrious statesman cum literateur and Chief Minister of Tamil Nadu who evinced keen interest in reviving the past glory of Poompuhar gave a crystal form to the lost city on the basis of literary evidences and through his initiation and efforts rose Silappathikaram Art Gallery, Ilanji Mandram, Pavai Mandram, Nedungal Mandram and Kotrappandal, in this place, with artistic splendour. Streams of visitors pour in every day.

What to see in Poompuhar

Silappathikaram Art Gallery: It has a beautiful seven-tier building of exquisite sculptural value. The first storey is 12′ high and the following storey each has a height of 5′ atop of which is erected a kalasam with a height of 8′ - the total height being 50 feet. The art gallery depicting scenes from one of the five major epics of Tamil 'Silappathikaram' was opened in 1973. These lovely scenes are lovingly immortalised in stone on the walls of the gallery. It is in short a treasure-house of Tamil Nadu.

The Makara Thorana Vayil at the entrance of the Art Gallery gives an imposing look to the whole structure. It has been designed on the model of Magara Thorana Vayil found in Surulimalai Mangala Devi temple and rises to a height of 22½′. There is an anklet-shaped tank in the art gallery with statues of Kannagi (9½′) and Madhavi (8′) on both sides of it.

Ilanji Mandram, Pavai Mandram, Nedungal Mandram and Kotrappandal have been reerected here and they remain here attracting the public with their artistic splendour. All these public places have been mentioned in Silappathikaram, the epic poetry of the Tamils. They served various purposes besides being ornamental. For instance, Ilanji Mandram is a place of beauty with a miracle tank which cured all illnesses. Nedungal Mandram is a pillar of splendour and those afflicted with mental disorder or those who have been poisoned or bitten by snake, if they go round and worship they will be cured. Pavai Mandram is a place of justice and if injustice is done the Pavai (idol) there would shed tears. Kotrappandal was the ornamental shamiana presented by the king of the Vajjra country.

One can also stroll along the Bay of Bengal which appears to be washing the shores in repentance of its cruelty devouring this glorious land. The estuary where the river Cauvery enters the sea could also be seen.

Other Places of Interest around Poompuhar

Thirusaikkadu (Sayavanam): Situated 2 kms away from Poompuhar estuary is this Siva temple of Thiru Sayavaneswarar and Kuyilinum Inia Nanmozhi Ammai. The Saivaite Saints or Nayanmars have sung hymns in praise of this temple. Chola inscriptions are also found here.

Thiruppallavaneswaram : This is an ancient and beautiful temple in Poompuhar. Iyarpagai Nayanar and Pattinathar and the hero and heroine of Silappathikaram, Kovalan and Kannagi were also born here. This temple was built by the Pallavas. The inscription of Vikrama Chola calls this place 'Puharnagaram' - Puhar city.

Melapperumpallam and Keezhapperumpallam : These two places are situated very near to Poompuhar and Thiruvengadu. The Valampurinathar temple at Melapperumpallam has Chola inscriptions. Nayanmars have sanctified this temple in their hymns. Keezhapperumpallam is at a distance of 2 km from Poompuhar and one of the Navagrahas, Kethu (serpent's tail), has a separate sanctum here.

Thiruvakkur : A famous Siva temple is here. It is constructed on Madakkoil (Storeyed Temple) pattern. Nayanmars have sung hymns on this temple. Sirappuli Nayanar, one of the 63 Saivaite saints, was born here.

Semponnarkoil : A temple of historic significance, it is called Thirusemponpathi in Thevaram. It is near Poompuhar on the bus route to Tranquebar (Tharangambadi).

Punjai : It is near Semponnarkoil. A beautiful Siva temple sung by Nayanmars. It is hailed for the architectural wonders of the Cholas.

Thirukkadaiyur : It is on the road to Tranquebar from Mayiladuthurai. It is one of the eight temples (Atta Veerattanam) glorifying the heroic victories of Lord Siva. Siva released Markandeya from the clutches of Yama, the God of Death and made him a perpetual youth. A beautiful bronze representation of this event could be seen here. The lingam here bears the rope marks of Yama. This place is also known for its fame in patronizing Bharathanatyam as evidenced by the inscription of Kulottunga Chola III. It is also a famous Sakthi Sthalam. The holy hymns of Abirami Anthathi was sung here by Abirami Bhattar, whose devotion made the Goddess bring the full moon on a new moon day. The Lord of this place is known as 'Amirthagateswara' (Lord of the nectar pot and people select this place to celebrate their 60th birthday so that they be rewarded with longevity by the grace of this God.

Anantha Mangalam : This place near Thirukkadaiyur is famous for its 'Dasa Bhuja Veera Anjaneya' (Ten-headed Hanuman).

Nangoor : Eleven of the 108 holy places of Vaishnavaites are near Nangoor. The Nangoor Vishnu temples were sanctified by Thirumangai Alwar, one of the 12 Vaishnavaite Saints. The stucco figure of Nara Narayana in one of these temples is an architectural marvel. Some of them are Madakkoils (storeyed temples) and date back to the early Chola Paranthaga, 907 A.D. Evidences are available in Siam for its flourishing as a centre of trade in those days.

Thalaignayiru : This temple nearby contains an interesting inscription prescribing rules for the election of the village assembly. Those who were not members for the previous ten years and above 40 years alone are eligible to contest an election.

Tharangampadi (Tranquebar): It is on the coast of the Bay of Bengal, south of Poompuhar. It is the place where the first Tamil printing press was erected and casting of Tamil alphabets were done. The Christian missionary brought out The Bible here as the first printed book in Tamil.

It was a site of Danish settlement and has the remains of the Dansborg Fort built by Ore Godde, the Commander of the Royal Dutch Navy in the 17th century. This fort was constructed in 1620 with two storeys and the top echelons of the Dutch officials resided here. Though the ramparts are ruined, the rest of the buildings are in good condition.

The Church of Zion : It was built in 1701 in the corner of King Street and Queen Street. After several modifications in 1782, 1784, 1800 and 1839, the church as it stands today has an impressive vaulted roof.

The Town Gateway : It is 200 years old and has historical and architectural values.

Danish Fort : Even today it exhibits Danish architecture and is under the control of Tamil Nadu Archaeological Department and has an archaeological museum open to public on all days except Fridays.

Masilamaninathar Temple : It was built in 1305 AD by the Pandya king Maravarman Kulasekara. Its outstanding architectural beauty spellbind the onlookers, despite the front portion damaged due to sea erosion.

Rehling's Gaid : It is named after Johannes Rehling who was the Danish governor and owned this house between 1830 and 1841. It is the biggest building in Tranquebar. Presently St. Theresa's Teachers Training College is functioning here and it is well preserved.

British Collector's House : It is on the eastern end of King's Street opposite the Dansborg Fort. It is another important landmark 150 years old with beautiful round columns, a central courtyard and a garden.

Transport: Buses ply frequently from Poompuhar, Sirkazhi, Mayiladuturai and Nagappattinam to Tranquebar.

Where to stay

Lodges and cottages maintained by Tamil Nadu Government Tourism Department.

- Shell Type Cottage I (Sangu), Rs. 150/- (Two Beds-A/c).
- Shell Type Cottage II (Sippy), Rs. 50/- (Two Beds)
- Tourist Lodge, Rs. 25/- (Two beds with common toilet)
- Shell Type Cottage, Rs. 120/- (Two beds A/c)

Visiting Time:

Silappathikaram Art Gallery

8.30 a.m. to 1.00 p.m. - 2.30 p.m. to 8.30 p.m.

Entrance Fee : Adult Rs. 2/-

Child (5 to 10 years) Re. 1/-

Nagappattinam
(Maritime Supremacy)

Historical Antiquity: This town was known from very early times as a trading centre and even today it is a minor port. It was the headquarters of a region during the Chola period and was a pride of the Cholamandalam coast. The other name of this place is Cholakula Vallippattinam. The Burmese historical text of 3rd century B.C. mentions this place and gives evidence of a Buddha vihar built here by the emperor Ashoka the Great. The Chinese traveller Hiuen Tsang also mentions it in his travel accounts.The ancient Buddhist literature names it as 'padarithitha'. Avurithidal, the name of a part of Nagappattinam might have been derived from padarithitha, the name of a fruit tree common in this region.

Buddhist monks of Sri Lanka had close connection with this place. Anaimangalam copper plates of Kulothunga Chola mentions that 'Kasiba-thera', a Buddhist monk renovated this Buddhist temple in 6th century A.D. Pallava king Rajasimha (695-722 A.D.) permitted a Chinese king to be buried in a Buddha vihar in Nagappattinam. The Anaimangalam copper plate also reveals that Vijayathunga Varman of Sri Vijaya kingdom built two Buddha vihars in the names of Rajaraja and Rajendra named respectively Rajarajapperumpalli and Rajendrapperumpalli. The latter was also called Soodamani Vihar. Excavations by the Archaeological Department at Velippalayam in Nagappattinam unearthed more than 300 Buddha statues. They are kept in the Govt. Museum at Chennai. Kayaroganam Shiva temple here existed in the 6th century and was sanctified by the hymns of three Nayanmars.The Vishnu temple here has been sung by Thirumangai Alwar of 9th century. This town was a famous trading centre during the Vijayanagar period. The Portuguese settled here in 1554 during the Thanjavur Nayaka rule. Then Christianity began to take root and the famous Velankanni church came into existence.

In 1658, the Dutch supremacy prevailed and ten Christian churches and a hospital were built by them. They also released coins with the name 'Nagappattinam' engraved on them. The British were the last owners of this place after a prolonged struggle in 1781. Gold coins bearing the name of East India Company were issued from here. They were called 'Nagappattinam Varagan' and 'Nagappattinam Sornam' and were in circulation during the Thanjavur Maratha rule. Nagappattinam has thus a vast history of over 2000 years. Today, it is the headquarters of Nagappattinam district.

How to get there?

Nagappattinam is very well connected to all important places in Tamil Nadu by rail and road. Buses ply every hour from Chennai to Nagappattinam. Train facilities are also available from Nagappattinam to Thanjavur, Trichy, Nagore and Chennai. Bus services are also available for these places. Tamilnadu State Transport Corporation operates tourist buses to nearby places. Hired vehicles are also available. Cars and autorickshaws could be hired to visit places around Nagappattinam.

The nearest airport is at Trichy, a distance of 141 kms. Air Lanka and Indian Airlines operate services to Sri Lanka. The Indian Airlines operates services to Chennai and Madurai from Trichy.

Places to see in Nagappattinam

Harbour, Lighthouse and Beach : Nagappattinam is a minor port of India today. Hence, the harbour which was once a maritime pride is busy even today. The lighthouse is nearby and could be climbed. The beach, a fine stretch of sand is worth visiting. Sea bathing could also be done.

Temples

Kaayaroganam Siva Temple: The three Nayanmars, Appar, Sambandar and Sundarar have sung the hymns in praise of this temple. It is an old temple existing from 6th century A.D. This is a Karonam and one of the Vidanga Sthalams. A cult called Lakulisa - the mendicant aspect of Siva - spread from Karonam in Gujarat to all parts of India. In South India, two temples of this cult came into being, one at Kanchipuram and the other here. The Thyagaraja here is known as Sundaravidangar. It is made up of a precious stone Komedhagam (lapis lazuli). The Nagabarana Vinayagar and the bronze Panchamuga (five-headed) Vinayagar on a lion mount are of exquisite workmanship in this temple.

The image of Thyagaraja in a niche of Thyagaraja Sabha is of excellent craftsmanship.

Neelayadakshi Amman temple is more familiar to devotees than Kaayaroganam.

Soundararaja Perumal temple is the Vishnu temple glorified by Thirumangai Alwar of the 9th century. This temple has a unique bronze of Narasimha slaying Hiranya, the demon and blessing his son Prahalada the devotee, of Narayana.

Mosques

1) Durgah at Nagai Pudhur Road

2) Durgah near new bus stand

3) Durgah at Moolakkadai Street

Churches

1) Lourdhu Madha Church

2) Maharasi Madha Church

3) T.E.L.C. Church

4) Protestant Church

Library

The District Library

OTHER FACILITIES

Telephone, telex and courier services are available. Hospitals and private clinics and pharmacies too are available.

Places around Nagappattinam

Nagore : It is 5 km north of Nagappattinam. The Durgah of Saint Hazareth Syed Shahul Hamid Quadir Wali is here. He is believed to shower His grace without distinction of caste, creed, colour or class. People of all faiths flock here to get solace. Hindus call him Nagoor Andavar. The Kanduri festival during October and November is very famous. Four minarets serve landmark to this durgah and the biggest one of them was built by Pratap Singh, the Thanjavur ruler and his son Tulajaji endowed it richly. The tomb of the saint in the centre is approached by seven silver-plated doors.

Velankanni : It is on the coast of the Bay of Bengal 14 kms south of Nagappattinam. The shrine basilica of Our Lady of Velankanni here on the shore is popularly called 'Sacred Arokkia Madha Church'. The church is dedicated to Virgin Mary and has an imposing façade with tall spires and the wings present the shape of a cross. In a niche in the altar is enshrined the statue of Our Lady of Health. Numerous legends prevail of the miraculous power of this lady, and lakhs of people converge here during the 'Feast' festival occurring in August. The greatest of miracles is the offerings thrown into the sea by devotees in Myanmar, Malaya and South Africa reaching this churches safely being picked and conveyed by fishermen. Such articles are exhibited in a hall here.

Sikkil : This place is on the bus route from Nagappattinam to Thiruvarur. Here is an age-old Siva temple in which the Sikkil Singaravelar bronze idol is so beautiful that it spellbinds the onlooker with rare craftsmanship and grace. This deity, Lord Muruga attracts crowds from far and near. The presiding deity of this temple is Navaneethes-warar. The festival in Chitthirai (April-May) is most famous. In the car festival, the bejewelled idol of Singaravelar receives the Vel (spear) from Parvathi - Vel Nedum Kanni (Long spear-like eyed) Amman to destroy the demon Surapadman. It is said that the idol profusely perspires at that time.

Thiruvarur : The most ancient temple patronised by almost all the kings reigning the south is the Thyagarajaswami shrine of Thiruvarur. This temple is associated with the legend of Sundarar to whom the God served as a messenger of love and arranged his marriage with Paravai and Sangili Nachiars. Thyagaraja like Nataraja dances — He performs the Ajapa dance here. Hence, He is known as 'Ajaba Natesar'. However, the presiding deity is Lord Vanmikanatha.

The temple complex is spread over 20 acres with the eastern gopuram dominating. In front of the western gopuram is the Kamalalaya Tank covering an area of 25 acres with an island temple in the centre. Vanmikanatha shrine is the earliest edifice, Akileswari a coming next and Thyagaraja the last. Many mandapams crowd the temple. The biggest one is the Devasiriya Mandapam. The Akileswara shrine contains beautiful sculptures of Ardhanareeswara, Durga, Karkalamurthi and Agastya in its niches. Paintings of Vijayanagar period adorn the ceiling of Devasiriya mandapam.

Outside the temple is a beautiful sculptural representation of Manuneedhi Chola who ran his chariot on his own son to mete out justice to the cow whose calf was killed by his son, caught under the chariot.

The temple car here is a beautiful structure and the biggest on which model is the Valluvar Kottam in Chennai built. The car festival is famous and attracts large crowd. The original car was burnt in 1922 in an accident and is now replaced in all its original grandeur. As in Srirangam, here the goddess Piriyavidai Amman is called 'Padi Thandal' (one who never goes out of the portals) and is never taken out in procession.

The Nandhi in this temple, unlike the other Nandhis in sitting pose, is seen standing before Thyagaraja. The deity is on Ratna Simhasana (throne made of precious stones). In the southwest corner of the inner prakara Nilotpalambigai is seen blessing her child Muruga sitting on a maid's shoulder. Goddess Kamalambigai is in yogasana pose during penance in another sanctum. Navagrahas are not as usual in a circle around the sun but standing in a row.

Thiruvarur is the birthplace of musical trinity Thyagaiah, Shyama Sastri and Muthusamy Dikshithar. Rare musical instruments — Panchamuga vadyam with five heads representing the five heads of Siva and a nadaswaram called Barinayanam — could also be seen in this temple.

Keevalur : A mile from Keevalur station on the Tiruvarur-Nagore line is a temple of Agastyalinga. The Nataraja image here is unique having ten heads, all armed with trident, round, shield, mazhu, noose, club etc. - a craftsmanship of inimitable intricacy. There is a separate sanctum here for Kubera the God of fortune, rare indeed in the south.

Ettukkudi : 28 kms away from Nagappattinam this temple is famous for Lord Muruga. Saint Arunagirinathar has sung hymns on the Lord here.

Vedaranyam (Thirumaraikkadu – Forest of Vedas): This place is 58 kms from Nagappattinam. The author of Thiruvilaiyadal Puranam Paranjothi Munivar (13th century A.D.) was born here. It is an ancient temple and the earliest inscription dates back to Parantaka Chola (905-945 A.D.). The presiding deity is Vedaranyeswara and it is one of the 'Saptha Vidanga Sthalams'.The miracle of this place is that the Vedas after worshipping the Lord had locked the main gates of this temple and worship had to be conducted through another passage. When Appar and Sambandar came here, the former sang hymns at the request of the latter to open the gates and thus the gates were automatically opened.

During the independence struggle this place attained fame because of Gandhiji's Salt Satyagraha. Sardar Vedaratnam Pillai and Rajaji took part in the Satyagraha (1930-32) and courted arrest. A memorial has been erected to commemorate the event.

Kodikkarai (Point Calimere): Just 10 kms from Vedaranyam and 68 kms from Nagappattinam is this sanctuary famous for birds. Black bucks, spotted deer, wild pigs and vast flocks of migratory birds like flamingoes could all be seen here. In winter, the tidal mud-flats and marshes of the backwaters are covered with fowls like teals, curlews, gulls, terns, plovers, sandpipers, shanks and herons. Most of them are sea birds. At a time, upto 30,000 flamingoes could also be seen here. In the spring, quite different set of birds like koels, mynas and barbets are attracted by the profusion of wild berries. The best time to visit is November to January. April to June is the lean season with very little activity.

The main rainy season is from October to December.

A forest rest-house is available. You can get to Kodikkarai by bus from Nagappattinam, Thanjavur, Mayiladuthurai and by train through Mayiladuthurai-Thiruthuraipoondi section.

Koothanur: 45 kms from Nagappattinam is the renowned place associated with the Tamil poet Ottakkoothar. There is a unique temple here to Goddess of learning - Saraswathi. The idol in sitting posture is elegant and artistic.

Thirunallaru : The famous Siva temple lies 5 kms from Karaikkal, a Pondicherry Union Territory off Tharangampadi. The Siva temple is a Dharbaranyam and the presiding deity is Dharbaranyeswara. His consort is Bhogamanantha Poornambikai Amman. In the prakaram niche at the entrance is Lord Saneeswarar (Saturn) and lakhs of people worship here to propitiate Him when He enters a particular constellation of the zodiac once in 2½ years. Nala Theertham is a famous tank where the devotees take a dip smearing oil on their body. The original Nataraja idol of this temple is at Thiruchendur with the engravement Thirunallaru on it. It is said that the Dutch removed this idol from here and reaching Thiruchendur, they also removed the idol of Muruga of that temple and when they set sail, a fierce storm appeared and they dropped them into the sea and escaped. Later, the idols were rescued from the sea by a miracle and both of them have been installed at Thiruchendur.

Thillai Vilagam : This place is about 25 kms south of Thiruthuraipoondi. It is a famous Vaishnavaite sthalam visited by all. The image of the presiding deity Kothandarama is of intricate workmanship even the veins are beautifully exposed. There is a sanctum for Nataraja too in this Vishnu temple. There is another shrine of Kothandaramar at Vaduvur on the Mannargudi route. This village is also known as Dakshina Ayodhya.

Mannargudi : The most important Vaishnavaite shrine is here. It has the name Raja-mannargudi as the presiding deity here is Rajagopalaswamy. The shrine is spread over 15 acres. The image of the presiding deity Rajagopalaswamy is 12 feet tall. There are 16 gopurams, 7 prakarams with 24 shrines, 7 beautiful mandapams adorning the inside and 9 sacred theerthams. There is a Garuda Sthamba, a monolithic pillar 50 ft. tall in the forefront with a miniature Garuda shrine on the top. The sacred waters Haridra Nadhi is only a tank but bigger than Kamalalayam at Thiruvarur. The place is also called Dakshina Dwaraka – Dwaraka of the South.

Once Jainism seems to have flourished in this part as there are evidences of Jain statues in the vicinity. Mallinathaswami Jinalayam is in the middle of a Jain locality. Meru Parvatham, Padmavathi Amman, Nandiswaradeepam and Trikala Tirthankarar are worth seeing in this Jinalayam.

Where to Stay?

• **Quality Inn MGM Vailankanni,** No. 64, F/2, Nagapattinam Main Road, ✆ 63900, 63336, Fax: 04365-63336 Email: qimgmv@vsnl.net

Thanjavur

(Legacy of the later Cholas)

Thanjavur properly situated in the Cauvery delta is the rice - bowl of Tamil Nadu. A fertile land that was also fertile for art, architecture and culture. Though it was a famous city from early times, its importance was fully understood only by the later Cholas (AD 846-1276) who built an empire making it their capital. It was Vijayalaya who founded the later Chola kingdom here and Rajaraja the Great (AD 984-1014) and his son Rajendra I (AD 1012 - 1044) were the real architects of the Chola empire that held sway over India upto the Ganges in the north and held colonies in Myanmar, Malaya and the East Indies. It became the centre of Tamil learning and culture. It became the original home of the Dravidian art and architecture besides being the centre of Tamil classical dance which is now known as Bharatha Natyam all over the world. Even today, the teachers of Bharatha Natyam hail from Thanjavur. Its further glory is the Carnatic music which in essence is nothing but classical Tamil music. The only remains of its glorious past are the beautiful temples that were built by the Cholas known for their amazing architectural wonder, and not less than 74 of them are around Thanjavur itself. The Pandyas, the Nayaks and the Marathas ruled the city after the later Cholas and finally the British made it a district.

How to get there?

Thanjavur is directly connected by rail with Chennai, Nagore, Trichy and Madurai. It is connected to all major cities with road. The local transport system runs buses to all places in and around Thanjavur. Autorickshaws and taxis are also available. Frequent bus services are available to Chennai, Trichy, Madurai, Dindigul. The nearest airport is at Trichy, 58 kms away. The Indian Airlines and Air Lanka operate flights to Sri Lanka. Indian Airlines operates flights to Chennai and Madurai. It is about 350 kms on the meter gauge main line from Chennai.

What to see in Thanjavur?

The Big Temple (or) the Brahadeeswara Temple : This temple, the marvel of Dravidian art and architecture needs several days to go round and enjoy inch by inch, even then one would not go with complete satisfaction. It was built by the Great Rajaraja I the nonpareil of the later Chola dynasty. Begun in A.D. 1003 it was completed in 1010. He was a king of magnificence and his temple also stood magnificent, true to its name Dakshina Meru. Unlike other temples the vimanam (the tower over the sanctum) soars higher than the usual gopuram or portal tower. It soars to a height of 64.8 m (208 ft.). It rises from a square base and shaped like a pyramid with 14 tiers, on the top of which is a higher monolithic cupola carved out from a 81.3 tonne block of granite. It was perched there from the village, 'Saarappallam' by rolling it along a ramp of earth six km long like the way in which the Egyptian pyramids were built. It is set on a spacious prakara of 240m by 125m. The Lingam in the sanctum is 3.70m high. The huge bull (Nandhi) in the outer courtyard is monolithic 3.70m high, 6m long, and 2.50m wide which is the handiwork not of Chola but added by the Vijayanagar rulers. It is the second largest in India, the first being the one at the Lepakshi temple in Andhra Pradesh.

The dwarapalakas flanking the doorways are 5.50m in height. The complex is flanked with various mandapams. There are three gateways with gopurams to enter the temple. The basement is crowded with inscriptions telling the various grants and gifts offered to Brahadeeswara by innumerable kings, chieftains and nobles. The establishment of the temple had 1000 persons, 400 of them were female dancers. The outer side of the exterior wall is divided into 2 storeys with niches filled with images of Saivaite iconography. There are also Vaishnavaite and Buddhist themes in sculptures. One difference here is that even the sculptor's name is engraved.

While the outer walls is ornamented with stone images, the inner wall of the sanctum is covered with Chola murals. They were concealed by the superimposition of Vijayanagar Nayak paintings. It was only in 1930, the originals were brought to light by a special chemical process. Sundaramurthy Nayanar, Cheraman Perumal, Tiripuranthaga, Rajaraja, Karuvur Thevar and Dakshinamurthi were thus discovered to the world manifesting the marvel of Chola painting. With permission from the archaeological department one could see them dazzle in floodlight inside the inner corridor. The outer wall of the upper storey is carved with 81 dance poses of Bharatha Natyam, the classical dance of the Tamils. A look at the inside of the spiralling 14 tiers is quite amazing and the precision of the engineers of the Chola period makes one spellbound. Another wonder is that the shadow of the cupola never falls in the ground – a testimony to the engineering skills of the Chola architecture.

The shrine for the Goddess was added by Pandian rulers in the 13th century A.D. The Subramania shrine was added by Vijayanagar rulers. Sambaji, the Maratha ruler of Thanjavur renovated the Vinayaka shrine.

Nidamba Sudini : This is the earliest image of Kali in Potters Street 1.6 km to the east of the Big Temple.The image of the Goddess is five feet tall wearing a garland of skulls, a snake covering Her breasts, teeth protruding and in unbearable wrath trampling the two demons Chandan and Mundan. This image was installed by Vijayalaya Chola in commemoration of his victory over the Mutharayas which enabled him to found the later Chola kingdom.

The Palace : Not far from the temple and in the heart of the old tower lies the palace with vast labyrinthian buildings, enormous corridors, big halls, watch-towers, moat, fort and courtyards. The palace was built by the Nayak rulers around 1550 A.D. and subsequently renovated and enlarged by the Maratha rulers of Thanjavur. Though a portion is in ruins, much of it is still in its original beauty. Some government offices are located inside besides an art gallery, a library, the hall of music, the audience hall and even today in a portion lives the present legal heirs of the Thanjavur Marathas.

The Rajaraja Chola Art Gallery: It is inside the palace. It has a beautiful collection of granite and bronze idols from the 9th to the 12th centuries. They are fine pieces of workmanship of Chola art. Most of them were brought from the temples in and around Thanjavur and preserved here. The collection holds the onlooker spellbound with their minute details and grace.

The Saraswathi Mahal Library: This is also inside the palace. It was founded in 1700 A.D. by the Maratha kings who ruled Thanjavur. There are over 30,000 palm leaf and paper manuscripts in this library. Books both in Indian languages and European languages are preserved here. In one section on the walls are displayed pictures of Chinese torture of prisoners.

Sangeetha Mahal : It is inside the palace and a specimen of soundproof and acoustically perfect music hall. It is tastefully decorated with fine etchings.

Church : Inside the palace could also be seen a church on the eastern side. It is called Schewartz Church and was built in A.D. 1779 by Raja Serfoji in honour of revered Schewartz of Denmark.

Royal Museum : This is another museum in the palace complex, very interesting to see. It contains a good collection of manuscripts, weapons, dresses, utensils and musical instruments used by the members of the royal family of Thanjavur.

Rajagopala Beerangi : On the eastern rampart of the fort is this big Beerangi (cannon). It is called Beerangi Medu or Dasmedu.

Sharja Madi : It is also located in the palace complex. It is a storeyed building opened for tourists to have a panoramic view of Thanjavur city. There are beautiful wooden carvings and sculptures inside the Sharja Madi.

Rajarajan Manimandapam : This was built during the 8th World Tamil Conference. There is a small garden with children's play materials in it.

Rajarajan Museum : It is in the ground floor of the Manimandapam and under the control of the State Archaeological Department containing interesting exhibits, charts, maps etc. on the history of the Chola empire.

Tolkappiyar Sadukkam : During the 8th World Tamil Conference the Sadukkam (square) was built to commemorate the memory of the ancient grammarian Tolkappiyar who was the author of Tolkappiyam, the oldest Tamil grammar available now in full form in print. From this tower, one can have a panoramic view of Thanjavur.

Sivaganga Park : It is a beautifully laid-out park with a tank known for its sweet water and children's play materials are also kept there.

Timings

Art Gallery : 9 a.m. to 1 p.m.
2 p.m. to 6 p.m.
Entrance Fee: Adult Rs.3/- & Child Re.1/-.
Holidays : National Holidays only.
Phone : 22823

Saraswathi Mahal Library : 10 a.m. to 1 p.m.
1.30 p.m. to 5.30 p.m.
Holidays : Wednesdays & National Holidays
Phone : 20107

Royal Museum 9 a.m. to 6 p.m.
Entrance Fee : Adult Re.1, Child–Re.0.50.
Holidays : No Holidays
Phone : 31486

Sharja Madi : 10 a.m. to 1 p.m.
2 p.m. to 5 p.m.
Entrance Fee: Re.1.

Rajarajan Manimandapam : 10.00 a.m. to 8.00 p.m.
Entrance Free

Rajarajan Museum : 10 a.m. to 5 p.m.
Entrance Fee : Adult Re.1/- and Child Re.0.50.

Tolkappiyar Sadukkam : 9 a.m. to 7 p.m.
Entrance Free

Tamil University : Founded in 1981, this University specialises in research and advanced study of the Tamil language. It is 7 km away and located in a vast area with beautiful buildings. A very good library with a good collection of English and Tamil books is functioning in the University complex.

Places around Thanjavur

All the places mentioned hereunder can be reached mostly by town buses or by hired vehicles without any difficulty.

Mariamman Temple : It is at Punnainallur 6 kms away from Thanjavur. It is one of the local temples of Thanjavur and attracts enormous crowd.

Thiruvaiyaru Temple : 13 kms from Thanjavur on the banks of the river Cauvery lies this ancient temple dedicated to Panchanadiswara (Lord of 5 rivers). Cauvery, Vennaru, Vettaru, Kudamurutti and Vadavaru form a network like garland to this Lord. Thiruchattruruthurai, Thiruvedikkudi, Kandiyur, Thiruppoonthuruthi and Thiruneithanam are Saptha Stalas to which the Deity of Ayyaru proceed during Chitthirai (April-May) festival which attracts great crowd. On the way to Thiruvaiyaru at Kandiyur one can see the beautiful image of Brahma and at Thiruppoonthuruthi the superb panel of Ravana lifting Kailas, Siva mounted on the bull with Uma, Ardhanari and Dakshinamurthi with veena in His hands are fine pieces of art that should not be missed. In Panchanadiswara temple that contains spacious halls and corridors, the idol of Lord Brahma is very exquisitely executed. Some sculptures here are of Chalukyan style having been brought as war trophy.

One of the musical trinity, Thyagaraja's samadhi is on the banks of the river. Near the Siva temple is a one-roomed house where Thyagaraja composed some of his greatest works. The samadhi itself is a fitting tribute to the saint and one can see almost all the scenes of Ramayana as they appear in his songs beautifully sculptured in black marble by Bangalore Nagarathinammal, a devotee of Thyagaraja. There is also the samadhi temple with the saint's statue. The Thyagaraja Aradhana festival is held in January when most of the leading exponents of Carnatic music come to perform and are listened to by lakhs of ardent fans of classical music. A huge complex is under construction here to accommodate the ever increasing number of devotees.

Grand Anicut (Kallanai) : This barrage was built at the delta head of Thanjavur by Karikal Chola of the Sangam Age and serves even today. This was built by slave labour, the slaves being the prisoners of war from Ceylon. Stones were piled up across the river for 1080 ft. It was 60 ft. wide and about 20 ft. high. That it stood the ravages of time and floods for over 1500 years is a testimony for the skills of ancient engineering. It is fully made of stones and earth. In 1805, the dam was repaired by Captain Caldwell. It is the overhead regulator of the water of Cauvery for irrigation. Excessive flood waters were left in Kollidam. There is a park and it is a nice picnic spot. Buses are operated from Thanjavur and Kumbakonam. It is about 48 km from Thanjavur.

Thingalur : This Siva temple is about 18 kms from Thanjavur. There is a separate shrine for Chandra (Moon God) in this temple and it is one of the nine places of Navagrahas. It attracts pilgrims on all days.

Ganapathi Agraharam : It is about 5 kms east of Thingalur. A famous Vinayaka temple is here. Next to it is a Vishnu temple. The Vinayaka Chathurthi festival (August-September) is very famous and thousands of people gather here at that time.

Alangudi : This famous Siva temple is 43 kms from Thanjavur and near Kumbakonam on the Mannargudi Road. It is one of the temples of Navagraha (Nine Planets) and this place has the shrine of Guru (Jupiter). On all days, pilgrims throng this temple from all over India. The temple is of the Chola period and exposes Chola architecture.

Papanasam : It is 30 kms from Thanjavur. It is a historic town. There are two temples here, one Pallavanatha Swamy temple constructed by Chola king and the other is called 108 Sivalingam. There is a granary here of 80 ft. breadth and 36 ft. height for storing 3,000 'kalams' of paddy. It was constructed by the Nayak kings in A.D. 1600-1634. It has been declared as a monument by the state archaeological department. The 108 Sivalingams in one temple is in the Papanasam town. There is also a famous temple at Thirukkarukavur nearby dedicated to Mullaivananathaswamy.

Thiruvalanchuzhi : This place near Swamimalai has a shrine for Vinayaga. The temple is an architectural marvel. As the river Cauvery changed the course to the right (valam) the place came to be known as Thiruvalanchuzhi. The image of Vinayaga is in the form of a sea foam. It is named Swetha (white) Vinayaga. Beautifully chiselled stone pillars and stone lattice work of intricate design could be seen here.

Poondi Madha Shrine : This village is about 3.5 kms from Thanjavur. The nearest railway station is Budalur. It is a Roman Catholic pilgrim centre like Velankanni and people from all over India visit this place. The church authorities provide accommodation to pilgrims.

Manora : It is 65 kms on the way to Kodikkarai in Saluvanayakkappattinam. A 11 storeyed tower stands here built by Raja Serfoji in 1814 to commemorate the victory of the British over Napoleon in the battle of Waterloo. It served as an observatory and a lighthouse for some time. The tall tower could be seen from a distance of 5 kms. It was utilised to keep books on shipbuilding, by the king.

Kumbakonam : It is 36 kms from Thanjavur linked by road and rail. It is the biggest town in Thanjavur district and a commercial centre for silk, utensils and trade. It is the treasure-house of art and architecture, because almost all the important temples are in and around Kumbakonam. It is a focal point from where all the Chola temples could easily be visited.

Mahamagam, the Kumba Mela of the south which occurs once in 12 years when the planet Jupiter enters the constellation Leo and the Sun in Aquarius is famous here, and lakhs of people from all over India throng here to have a holy dip in the Mahamagam tank which is located in the middle of the town. It is believed that the holy Ganges flows into this tank on that day. Bordered by exquisite mandapams, the tank bears an imposing look with stone-cut steps leading to water level. There are umpteen spring wells in the bed of the tank, called 'Theerthams' or holy waters.

Temples in Kumbakonam

Adikumbeswara Temple : It is an

ancient temple, very huge spreading over 4 acres with a gopuram 125 ft. high. The Mahamagam tank itself is its Theertham (holy water). The Navarathri Mandapam with 27 'Stars' and '12 Rasis' (constellations) carved in a single block, the idol of Shanmuga with only six hands instead of usual 12, two stone Nadaswarams and Kiratamurti are the main attractions in this temple. They speak volumes of the artistic attainment of Chola sculptures.

Sarangapani Temple : It is the Vaishnavaite shrine equally famous as the Adikumbeswara temple. The temple has Hema Pushkarani as its holy tank. The inner shrine has a unique feature is being fashioned like a chariot with galloping horses; besides, it has two entrances – Uttara Vasal in the north and Dakshina Vasal in the south. The northern gate is opened for entering the sanctum when Sun reaches the Tropic of Capricorn and the other one closed, until the Sun reaches the Tropic of Cancer. Afterwards, it is repeated vice versa. The gopuram with 12 tiers (150 ft. high) has the dancing poses of Siva — a strange feature in a Vaishnavaite shrine.

The deity Aravamudhan in the sanctum inside the temple is in the act of rising from His Snake-couch to give darshan to His ardent devotee Thirumazhisai Alwar. The Komalavalli Thayar image is very charming, true to the name of 'Komalam'. The Vaishnavaite literary work Divya Prabhandham 4000 in number was brought to light in this temple just like the Thevaram of Saivism brought to light at Chidambaram temple.

Ramaswami Temple : It is near the Adikumbeswara temple. The Mahamandapam has exquisite sculptures, each a class in itself, the noted ones being Vibhishana Coronation, Trivikrama, a dancer with Veena and Manmatha. The idol in the sanctum installed by Ragunatha Naik of Thanjavur had been found from a tank. Lord Hanuman image in this temple can be seen playing a Veena. The corridor walls are painted with sequences of Ramayana.

Chakrapani Temple : The temple is noted for its exquisite pillars. The presiding deity Chakrapani has eight arms. There is a bronze image of Raja Serfoji worshipping the Lord as he is said to have been cured of an illness by the grace of this God. A panchamukha (five-faced) Hanuman is erected in the prakaram.

Brahma Shrine : The Brahma temple is very rare in India and the Brahma temple here is in the place where He performed a penance.

Nageswaraswami Temple: The temple is so aligned that the rays of the Sun falls for 3 days on the Lingam in the sanctum in the first Tamil month (April-May). The Nrithya Sabha (dance hall) is a typical example of the Chola art.

Temples around Kumbakonam

Oppiliyappan Koil : Hardly a km from Thirunageswaram is the Vishnu shrine, Oppiliappan temple. It ranks equal to Thirumalai in Thirupathi and many perform their vows here which they made to perform at Thirumalai. The idol is just like the one at Thirumalai. Salt is not added in the daily food offered to this deity in deference to His consort's ignorance of cooking. An image of Vedanta Desika is found in this temple. There is also a tank inside. Tasting the Prasadam (food offered to the deity) inside the temple one never gets the feeling that it has been prepared without salt but on coming out one finds out the difference.

Thirunageswaram Temple : This temple is another masterpiece of Chola art. It was built by Aditya Chola in 10th century A.D. Later rulers have also improved the temple with additions. It is called Bhaskara (Sun) Kshetram. The niches contain Vinayaka, Ardhanariswara and a maiden – all a splendour in stone. This is also one of the Navagraha sthalams for Raghu (dragon's head) and a beautiful sanctum for Him with His consorts attracts thousands of pilgrims each day during the Raghu Kalam (inauspicious time) when holy Abishekam (ablutions) is performed to the deity.

Thiruvidaimarudur : It is 10 kms north of Kumbakonam with an imposing gopuram. A huge Mahalingam is the presiding deity here. He is supposed to be the main deity (Moolavar) of Tamil Nadu as the other temples around it houses only the Parivara Devathas as main deity. Marudur is derived from the holy tree of the place called Marudha maram. From time immemorial, those afflicted with evil spirits circumambulate the Aswamedha Prakaram and get cured. On the eastern tower is the sculpture of Brahmahatthi, a brahmin murdered by a king waiting to take revenge. The king who entered the temple to escape from the sin of killing a brahmin was asked to go out through another gate as he was a devout Siva Baktha. The shrine of Mookambika here is in the northern style of architecture. A library is attached to this temple possessing Saiva Siddhanta and Agama palm-leaf manuscripts. There is a Theertham called Singha Thirtham inside the temple. Pattinathar stone image and Bhadragiriyar stone image are in the eastern and western gateways of the temple. Thai Poosam festival (January-February) is very famous attracting huge crowds.

Thirubhuvanam : It is 8 km from Kumbakonam. It has the 13th century A.D. Chola temple of Kambahareswara built by Kulottunga III. It is a colossal stone edifice raised as a memorial of the victory of his North Indian campaign. The whole temple including the gopuram has stone relief, of the legends of Siva. The Sarabha Murthi bronze idol is the unique feature here. It is a fusion of human, bird and beast supposed to have been incarnated by Lord Siva to release the Devas from the unabated fury of Narasimha - the avatar of a human lion of Vishnu - after he slayed the demon Hiranya. Near the Sarabha sanctum can be seen two exquisite sculptures of Sridevi and Bhudevi — the consorts of Vishnu. The place is famous for silk weaving.

Suriyanar Koil (Sun Temple) : This temple is 22 kms from Kumbakonam and even before the great temple for Sun god at Konarak was dreamed of, a temple for Sun and the planets that move around Him was built here. It was built by Kulottungan I. A fifty feet gopuram stands here and passing through it the image of a horse and the chariot of Surya appears into view. The planets have different shrines around the Sun's sanctum which is in the centre. This is one of the Navagraha sthalams and people pour here daily to propitiate Sun God, the chief of the planets according to Indian Astrology. Ratha Sapthami (January - February) is the day of the change of Sun's course (Starting His northern course from Capricorn) and that day is celebrated as a festival day.

Ammangudi : This is farther off to Surianar Koil on the north-east. The famous Ashta Bhuja Durga temple is in this place. It is the birthplace of Krishnan Raman, Chief Minister to the Chola Emperor Rajaraja I. The idol is a splendid specimen of Chola art and Goddess Durga is seen slaying the demon from Her lion mount.

Thiruppurambiam : About 13 kms to the north of Kumbakonam is the place which was a fierce battlefield in the 9th century deciding the bright future of the Cholas. Chola king Aditya built a temple in sweet remembrance of the turn of tide in his favour and named it Aditeswaram. The present name of the presiding deity is Sakshinatheswarar and the consort bears the beautiful name Kuraivila Azhagi (Beauty Unsurpassed). The sanctum for the Devi was built by Rajaraja I. The sanctum wall contains beautiful sculptures of Parivara Devatas. Lord Ganesa here is performed honey ablutions on the Vinayaka Chathurthi day and all the honey passed on Him is absorbed by Him.

Swamimalai : It stands 6 kms west of Kumbakonam on the banks of the river Cauvery. It is one of the six abodes (Arupadaiveedu) of Lord Muruga. 'Malai' means hill but there is no hill here but an artificial hill is built and the deity enshrined on the top. There are 60 steps, each step for a year of the Tamil Year-series which has a cycle of 60 years. Here, before the idol stands an elephant instead of the usual peacock, the mount of Lord Muruga. The deity is called Swaminatha as He explained the meaning of Pranava Mantra to His father Lord Siva and also got the nickname 'Thagappanswami' – God to Father. This is the only shrine where Lord Muruga is seen with his consort Devayani.

Darasuram : 4 kms on the south-west of Kumbakonam is this famous temple dedicated to Iravatheeswara noted for its sculptural wonder. It was built by Rajaraja II (1146-72 A.D.). The original name was Rajarajeswaram which was later corrupted as Darasuram. The shrine is a square panchadhala vimanam, and the mandapam is raised with its basement walls carved with exquisite sculptures. The reliefs depict the 63 Saivaite saints and the episodes in their lives. The Badra Koshtas have Dakshinamurthi, Lingodhbhavar, Brahma and Vishnu carved beautifully. Different forms of Siva adorn the Karna Devakoshtas. In the north wall, Mahishasura - the buffalo demon is shown in full human form, not to be seen anywhere else. Even narrow spaces are filled with Kiritarjuna and Ravana lifting Kailas. The cell in the second floor contains Umamaheswara with king Rajendra II. The king wanted to make this temple unique in every respect, so he has lavished it with intricate artwork, even paid attention in the choice of stones for carving the images.

The balustrades of steps reaching the mandapam too are wrought with elaborate sculptures. The middle Ghoshta in the south wall has an awe-inspiring image of Sarabha pacifying Narasimha. In the north-east mandapam, the pillars contain Natya poses and the ceiling with dancers. Even the Balipeetam facing the temple is an ornate structure with a flight of steps (9 nos.) each producing a musical note when struck. The Dwarapalakas that adorn the temple were brought from the western

Chalukya capital Kalyanapuri as trophy of victory.

Pazhayarai : About 7 kms from Kumbakonam is this old Chola capital. Rajarajan II has built a temple here for Somanadiswarar. Formerly it had a palace where the Chola kings resided. It was called Cholan Maligai but now no trace of it is left. Life-size image of Durga, chariot-like mandapam drawn by galloping horses, Ardhanariswara (half Parvathi, half Siva form), and Narasimha (human-lion avatar of Vishnu) are most exquisitely carved here.

Kizha-Pazhayarai: On the eastern side of Pazhayarai was a Kailasanathar sculpture. Ravana is seen lifting Mount Kailas, the abode of Siva only to be trapped under its weight when Lord Siva presses it down with the thumb of His right foot - a remarkable sculpture. Saint Appar one of the 63 Nayanmars of the Siva cult is said to have observed a hunger strike here to establish it as a Siva temple.

Pattiswaram : This temple is 8 kms from Kumbakonam. The presiding deity is Dhenupuriswarar. The right of this temple is imposing with five gopurams piercing the sky. A life-like statue of the great scholar and minister Govinda Dikshithar of the Thanjavur Naick kings is in this temple. The important idol here is the Kattaivasal Durga at the entrance of the northern gopuram. It was the guardian deity of the palace of the Cholas and after the disintegration was brought with Bhairavar and installed here. Vishnu Durgai is very famous here and pilgrims throng here every day. A little to the west is Ramanathar temple dedicated to Vishnu, which contains niches on the walls housing images of fine artistic skill.

Where to stay at Thanjavur?

- **Hotel Parisutham,** 55, G.A. Canal Road. ✆ 31801, 31844 (10 lines) Email: hotel.parisudham@vsnl.com
- **Hotel Oriental Towers,** 2889, Srinivasa Pillai Road. ✆30724, 31467, Fax: 04362-30770, Email: hotowers@tr.dot.net.in
- **Pandiyan Residency,** Cutcheri Road. ✆ 30514
- **Ashok Lodge,** Abraham Pandithar Rd. ✆ 30022
- **Kasi Lodge,** Ezhadi (seven feet) Rd. ✆ 31721
- **Hotel Valli,** N.K.M.Road. ✆ 31584
- **Hotel Karthik,** South Rampart St. ✆ 30116
- **Hotel Sangam,** Trichy Road, ✆ 39451, Fax: 04362-36695, Email:hotelsangam@vsnl.com
- **Hotel Ganesh,** 2905/3 & 4, Srinivasanpillai Road, Railway Station,) 31113, 32861, 72518, Fax: 04362-72517, Email: hotelganesh-97@hotmail.com
- **Yagappa Lodge,** Trichy Road. ✆ 30421
- **Hotel Tamil Nadu I,** Gandhi Road. ✆ 31412
- **Hotel Tamil Nadu II,** ✆ 30365
- **Rajasekar Lodge,** South Rampart St. ✆ 30496
- **Tamil Nadu Lodge,** Trichy Road. ✆ 31088
- **Rajarajan Lodge,** Gandhi Road. ✆ 31730
- **Raja's Rest House,** Gandhi Road. ✆ 30515
- **Ajanta Lodge,** South Rampart St. ✆ 30736
- **Eswari Lodge,** South Rampart St. ✆ 30488
- **Safire Lodge,** South Rampart St. ✆ 30970
- **Youth Hostel,** Medical College Road. ✆ 23591
- **Ganesh Lodge,** Gandhi Road. ✆ 30789

What to buy?

Thanjavur is famous for repousse (metal work with raised relief) and copper work inlaid with brass and silver. The Thanjavur plates are noteworthy. Bronze images are made by traditional craftsmen at Swamimalai.

The Poompuhar Emporium on the Gandhi Road is ideal for buying them. Besides repousse, wood carvings like temple cars and pith models of Thanjavur temple etc. are stocked here. Ancient brass betal boxes, cutters and Chola bronze pots are also available.

RECREATION

Cultural Programme : South Zone Cultural Centre (Phone : 40072) organises cultural programmes in Big Temple premises on every second and fourth Saturday. Admission free.

Clubs : Cosmopolitan club. Rotary and Union club (On Trichy Road).

Library : District Central Library near State Bank, Opp. to Government Hospital. Phone : 30397.

Municipal Library is situated inside the Sivaganga Park.

Bookshop: Appar Book Stall – situated in South Main street. New Century Book House - Rajarajan Vaniga Maiyam, South Rampart Street, Thanjavur. Higginbothams Book House, inside Railway Junction, Thanjavur.

Swimming Pool: (1) Government Stadium, Thanjavur, (2) Hotel Parisutham, (3) Hotel Oriental Towers.

FESTIVALS:

Saint Thyagaraja Aradhana Music Festival - Thiruvaiyaru - January.

Pongal (Tourist) Festival - Thanjavur - 14th to 16th January.

Mahamagam Festival at Kumbakonam - February & March once in 12 years. Last held in 1992.

Annai Velankanni Festival - August-September.

Arulmigu Thyagarajaswamy Car Festival at Thiruvarur - March and April.

Muthu Pallakku Thiruvizha, Thanjavur - May.

Rajaraja Chola's Birthday - Sathaya Thiruvizha - October every year at Thanjavur.

Places of Worship

Temple - Sri Brahadeeswarar Temple, Mariamman Koil, Bangaru Kamakshi Koil, etc.

Church - Sacred Hearts Church, St. Mary's Church etc.

Mosque - Durgah near bus stand and Irwin Bridge.

Tourist Information

● Government of Tamilnadu, Tourist Office, Jawan's Bhavan, Opp. Head Post Office, Thanjavur - 1. ✆ : 39084

● Tourist Information Centre, Hotel Tamil Nadu Complex, Gandhiji Road, Thanjavur - 1. ✆ : 31421.

Other Information

Post/Telegraph/STD/ISD/Telex/FAX etc. : Available

Courier Service : Available

P.M.G.H. Raja Mirasdar Govt. Hospital, Thanjavur - 1.

Medical College Hospital, Thanjavur-7.

Chemists and Druggists : Available

Important Telephone Numbers

Tamil University ✆ : 22221
Art Gallery ✆ : 22823
Public Relations Office ✆ : 22645
State Bank of India ✆ : 20082
Town Police Station ✆ : 22200
Rural Police Station ✆ : 2377
Railway Station ✆ : 22416
Cholan Roadways Corp. ✆ : 21999
Thiruvalluvar Transport Corporation ✆ : 20666

Thiruchirappalli

(The Rockfort City)

Thiruchirappalli derived its name due to Jain association with this place. Buddhism and Jainism thrived in Tamil Nadu before the renaissance of Hinduism in the form of the Bhakti cult which popularised Saivism and Vaishnavism and exterminated these anti-Hindu religions. So, we find numerous Jain and Buddhist traces scattered in remote and unapproachable spots throughout Tamil Nadu. 'Chira' is actually the name of a Jain monk and once in this rock was his 'palli' (abode). Therefore, it came to be known as Chirappalli and Thiru was added to it as it is an adjective of reverence in the Tamil language. Now nobody takes pain to pronounce its full name and reduced the beautiful name to 'Trichy' properly pronounced as 'Trichy'–these popular shortening of place names is a peculiar character of the Tamils, e.g. Kovai for Coimbatore, Mayilai for Mylapore, Tharai for Dharapuram, Thanjai for Thanjavur etc. There is a special rule in the Tamil grammar for shortening names like this – it is called "Maruvu".

Even before its association with Jains, it was a famous place in the Sangam Age and the capital city of Cholas, called 'Uraiyur'. It has a prime place in the history of Tamil Nadu. The Cheras, the Cholas and the Pandyas have all held sway and after them, the Pallavas, the later Pandyas, the later Cholas, the Vijayanagar rulers, the Marathas, the Nawabs, the French and finally the British–all of them coveted to possess this strategic place which is more or less centrally located place in Tamil Nadu. This was the scene of the decisive Carnatic War which enabled the British to emerge as the future undisputed masters of the Indian sub-continent. It is at present the fourth major city of Tamil Nadu and the headquarters of Trichy district.

How to get there?

Trichy is very well connected by a good network of roads to all the important places in Tamilnadu. Umpteen bus services with high frequencies ply buses to all major places in Tamilnadu. Town buses ply to the nearby places of tourist importance. It is also a major junction for both metre gauge and broad gauge lines of the Southern Railway and is linked to Chennai, Madurai, Thanjavur, Bangalore, Mysore, Tirupathi, Rameswaram, Thiruvananthapuram and Kochi. The Trichi airport has flights to Chennai, Sharjah, Kuwait and Colombo.

Places to See

Rock Fort : This is the important landmark of Trichy. It is an 83 metre (237 ft.) high rock that is the only outcrop in the otherwise flat land of the city. This is perhaps the oldest rock in the world as old as the rocks of Greenland. The Himalayas are infant rocks compared to its age. There are fascinating temples with brilliant architecture in it: Thayumanavar temple, a Siva shrine in the middle and a Ganesa temple at the top called 'Uchipillaiar Koil'. Two Pallava cave temples, one on the way to the Pillaiar Koil and the other in the northwest end of the street around the hill. A flight of steps leads to the Thayumanava Swami temple the presiding deity of which is a projection of the rock itself. There are on the whole 437 steps cut into a tunnel through the rock. There is a 100-pillared wall and a vimanam covered with gold in the Thayumanavaswami temple. The cave temple belongs to the Pallava period and Pallava king Mahendra Varman (6th century A.D.) built this cave temple inside which is a beautiful carving of Gangadhara. The image must have been the first one fashioned by the Pallavas. From the Uchipillaiar Koil one can have a panoramic view of the city on all the four sides.

The winding river Cauvery and the temples of Srirangam and Thiruvanaikaval can be seen from the northern side. The view is spectacular and a fitting reward for the painstaking ascend. The Teppakulam built by Viswanatha Nayak is another landmark. This tank with the background of the fort is vey imposing. Teppakulam is the float festival tank.

Nadirshah Mosque : To the west of the city is this mosque containing the remains of Nawabs Mohammed Ali and the headless body of Chanda

Sahib who were the principal cause for the Carnatic Wars. The tomb of saint Babbayya Nadir Shah attracts devotees of all faiths in large number.

Srirangam : 'Rangam' means island and Srirangam is the island between Cauvery and Kollidam (Coleroon) where Sri Ranganatha is lying on His Adi Sesha (snake) couch. The main sanctum of Sri Ranganatha is surrounded by 7 large enclosures and 21 majestic gopurams. On the south is Ranga Vilasam and Seshagiri Royal Mandapam with marvellous sculptural splendour. The main deity is enshrined within the first Corridor. The vimanam shaped like Omkara is plated with gold. The temple was constructed by the Chola King Dharmavarman and even before that, it is said that the temple existed buried under the sand. Almost all the kings who held sway in Tamil Nadu have spent lavishly to embellish the temple and even the British King Edward VII has presented a gold plate. Saint Ramanuja, the author of Vishistad-vaitham tenet functioned from here to spread Vaishnavism and His mortal remains are entombed in a sanctum here.

The unfinished tower started by Krishna Devaraya has now been completed (1987). It is the tallest in India rising 73 m high with 13 tiers. The other gopurams were built between the 14th and 17th centuries by various kings.

The artistical splendour of this temple excels beyond description. The east-facing Krishna shrine is a display of feminine grace in stone. The Seshagiri Rayar Mandapam opposite the 1000-pillared mandapam is unique with its equestrian statues. The tiger hunt sculpture is a marvel in stone. The hall is a living testimony to the dexterity of the Vijayanagar craftsmen. The Amirta Kalasa Garuda is a superb carving in the vehicle mandapam. The eight-armed Venugopala and Lakshminarayana on Garuda are inimitable.

Vaikunda Ekadasi festival is very famous in this temple. At that time, the Paramapada Vasal (Paradise Gate) is opened and lakhs of pilgrims rush to enter it as it is believed that one who enters here will reach Vaikunta after death.

Thiruvanaikkaval : This Siva temple too is in the same island on the other side of the railway line. This is one of the Pancha Bootha Sthalam (five elements) and it is called Appu (water) Lingam. The element represented here is water. The deity is in water. A perennial subterranean spring gushes around the lingam. A peculiar practice observed in this temple is that while performing the midday puja the priest wears a woman's dress. Another peculiarity is the presence of Eka-Pada-Tirumurthi in which the trinity Siva, Vishnu and Brahma are combined in one. It is not found in any other temple in Tamil Nadu except in Thiruvottriyur near Chennai.

The temple has five enclosures and the walls reach a height of 35 ft. Numerous sculptures of rare beauty could be found everywhere in the temple. The figure of a nomadic gypsy with her palm-leaves woven basket holds the onlooker spellbound. It is near the sanctum of Sri Sankara.

Samayapuram Mari Amman Koil : This is a very famous temple near Thiruvanaikkaval. The grace of Mari Amman here, has turned an illiterate fool into a poet. This temple attracts thousands of devotees every day.

Vayalur : It is 8 kms from Trichy

and a famous Murugan temple is seen here amidst bushy green fields. The gopuram of this temple was built by the famous devotee of Lord Muruga, Sri Kripananda Variar.

Mukkombu : It is a very beautiful picnic spot about 18 kms from Trichy. Green carpeted fields fill the route. Here the river Cauvery branches off into Kollidam (Coleroon). There is a well laid-out park. There is a barrage called Upper Anaicut. A beautiful spot of picturesque scenery.

Thiru Erumbur : 10 kms from Trichy is the famous place where an ant (erumbu) worshipped Lord Siva and got bliss. The temple has 3 prakaras or enclosures, one down the hill and the other two up the hill. The temple belongs to the Chola period. There is a beautiful sculpture of Gangalamurthi here not to be missed by any lover of art.

Thiruvellarai : About 15 kms from Trichy is Thiruvellarai, famous for its Pallava cave temple and a strange swastika well belonging to the period of Dantivarman.

Pullamangai : This place near Trichy is famous for an early Chola temple built by Parantaka I known for its sculptural splendour. The presiding deity of Pullamangai is Brahmapuriswara. One can see how the Chola sculpture gave life to stone as even the ganas or demons that worship Siva are carved with minute details – expressive faces, pot-bellied in fantastic poses. They embellish the roof of the Ardha Mandapam. Brahma, Lingodhbhava, Dancing Siva, Eight-Armed Durga are the other entrancing sculptures here.

Elakurichi : At Elakurichi nearby is the famous church built by the well known Catholic missionary, Constantine Joseph Beschi, popularly known as Veeramamunivar. He has done yeoman service to Tamil and even the first modern Tamil dictionary called 'Chathur Agarathi' was compiled by him.

Besides, there are several other churches, colleges and missions dating back to 1760's. As excellent infrastructural facilities are available in Trichy, it can be a convenient place to see east-central Tamilnadu.

Some Important Festivals

Mohini Alangaram, Vaikunda Ekadasi, Garuda Sevai, Flower Festival and Car Festival at Srirangam - (December-January).

The float festival at Teppakulam - (March-April).

Samayapuram Mari Amman flower festival - (April).

Where to Stay at Trichy?

- **Hotel Tamil Nadu,** MC Donald Road. ✆ 460383
- **Hotel Sangam, (4 Star),** Collector's Office Road, ✆ 414700, 414480, Fax: 0431-415779 Email: hotelsangam@vsnl.com
- **Vignesh,** Dindigul Road. ✆ 461991
- **Hotel Aristo,** Dindigul Road. ✆ 461818
- **Hotel Madura,** Rochin Road. ✆ 463737
- **Hotel Ajanta,** Junction Road. ✆ 460501
- **Gajapriya,** Royal Road. ✆ 461144
- **Hotel Anand,** Racquet Court Lane.
- **Vijaya Lodge,** Royal Road. ✆ 460512
- **Hotel Arun,** State Bank Road. ✆ 461421
- **Hotel Rajasugam,** Royal Road. ✆ 460636
- **Hotel Raja,** Junction Road. ✆ 461023
- **Jenneys Residency,** 3/14, Macdonalds Road, Tiruchirapalli - 620 001. ✆ 414414, Fax: 0431-461451, Email: jenneys@satyam.net.in
- **Royal Southern Hotels,** Race Course Road, Khajamalai, Tiruchirapalli - 620 023. ✆ 421303 Fax: 0431-421307, Email: royalsouthern@eth.net
- **Abbirami Hotel,** No. 10, McDonalds Road, Contonment, Trichy - 620 001. ✆ 415001, Fax: 0431-412819
- **Femina Hotels,** 14-C, Williams Road, Contonment, Tiruchirapalli - 620 001. ✆ 414501, Fax: 0431 - 410615, Email: femina@tr.dot.net.in

• **Hotel Aanand,** No.1, V.O.C. Street, Tiruchirapalli - 620 001. ✆ 415545 Fax: 0431-415219, Email: hotelaanand@hotmail.com

• **Ramyas Hotel,** 13/D-2, Williams Road, Trichy - 620 001. ✆ 415128 Fax: 0431-414852 Email: ramyas@ramyashotel.com

• **Ashby Hotel,** 17-A, Rockins Road, Tiruchirapalli - 620 001. ✆460652, 460653 Email: chinoor@yahoo.com

• **Sri Raajaali Hotel,** 8/6, 3A, Tanjore Road, Near Chennai Byepass Road, Tiruchirapalli - 620 008. ✆ 200470, 200439 Fax: 200470

Pudukkottai

(Archaeological Treasure-house of Tamil Civilization)

Pudukkottai, the former princely state that was the first to join the Indian Union after breaking away from foreign yoke, is indeed the archaeological treasure-house of Tamil civilization. Pre-historic and proto-historic finds like megalithic burials, dolmens stone circles etc. in the district blaze forth the civilization of the Tamils of the past. Sangam classics mention this tract as a notable place of highly cultured elites. The rich cultural heritage of this district is also evidenced by the archaeological and cultural remains of Kodumbalur, Narthamalai, Kudumiyanmalai, Kunnandar Koil, Sittanna Vasal, Thirumayam and Avudayar Koil. Its emergence as a princely state occurred in the 17th century and even before that, from time immemorial, it has been a centre of culture, civilization, art, architecture, fine arts and polity. It is therefore no wonder that historians, anthropologists, archeologists and lovers of art have an absorbing interest in Pudukkottai.

This town lies on Chennai-Rameswaram line, 390 kms away from Chennai, 53 kms from Thiruchirappalli and 57 kms from Thanjavur. The rulers of Pudukkottai have left historical landmarks like buildings, temples, tanks, canals, forts and palaces.

How to get there?

Air : Nearest airport–Trichy 53 kms, from where flights are available to Chennai, Sri Lanka, Sharjah and Kuwait.

Rail : Chennai-Rameswaram railway line will take you to Chennai, Trichy, Thanjavur, Madurai and Rameswaram.

Road : It is well connected to Chennai, Thanjavur, Trichy, Madurai and Rameswaram by road. Town buses are available to all tourist centres in and around Pudukkottai. Besides, taxis, private vehicles and contract carriages are also available.

Shopping

• **Poompuhar Handicrafts,** 851, North Road.

Working Hours : 9 a.m. to 1 p.m. & 2 p.m. to 8 p.m.

Handicrafts, handlooms, silk, paper-mache, cane articles, mats made from korai grass etc. are available.

• Karpagam Palm-leaf Products near Anna Statue, Pudukkottai.

Working Hours: 9.30 a.m. to 1.30 p.m. & 4 p.m. to 8 p.m.

Places to See

Sri Kokarneswar Temple : This temple of Pallava period is a rock-cut cave temple of Mahendravarma Pallava. The presiding deity is Kokarneswarar and His consort Brahadambal. Some later additions have also been made. The idols of Ganesa, Gangadhara, Saptha Kannikas are artistic creations of perennial value. An image of the saint Sadasiva Brahmendra is seen at the foot of a Bikula tree. The deity is the family deity of the Raja and in reverence of Brahadambal, coins called 'Amman Kasu' were released by the king. The place is called

Thirukkokarnam and is about 5 kms from the railway station.

Government Museum : It is also located in Thirukkokarnam. It contains a wide range of collections in the sections of Geology, Zoology, Paintings, Anthropology, Epigraphy, Historical Records etc. which are very interesting. Fine sculptures and bronzes of various periods exhibited here are the main attraction.

Timings : 9 a.m. to 5 p.m.
Admission : Free
Holiday : Friday
Phone : 22247

Places of tourist interest around Pudukkottai

Sittannavasal : 16 kms from Pudukkottai is this ancient abode of Jains dating back to the 2nd century B.C. The main attractions are the rock-cut cave temple with its beautiful paintings in natural colours akin to the ones at Ajanta and stone beds called Eladipattam and a cave where the Jain monks sought refuge in those days. An Ardha Mandapam and inner shrines of the cave temple contain images of Jain Tirtankaras in the niches. But the ceilings and walls contain frescoes that resemble Ajanta paintings. Though partially damaged they are quite absorbing. Flowers, calves, elephants, geese — all executed in inimitable poses and all relate to the Jains. They were believed to be a Pallava creation, but later discovery of inscriptions proved it to be the work of Pandyas.

As this place has been developed under the District Excursion Project, it is easily approachable by road and frequent bus services are available. In places around Sittannavasal, there can be sighted many pre-historic burial sites consisting of Kurangup-pattarai, cairns, burial urns, cists etc.

Kudumiyanmalai : 20 kms from Pudukkottai. There are exquisite sculptures and a 1000-pillared hall in the temple of Sikharagireeswarar. Inscriptions abound in this temple and the quite interesting one is that of Mahendra Varma Pallavan who has actually made a treatise on music here - especially on the seven notes called Saptha Swara. He is a versatile man and calls himself 'Vichitra Chittan', 'Chitthirakkarappuli' (Man of Wonderful Mind and Adept Painter). He has also done research in music especially on the saptha swaras in a veena called 'Parivadhini' with 8 strings. There is also a rock-cut temple above called 'Melakkoil' which too was scooped by Mahendra Varma Pallavan. The Anna Agricultural Farm and Agricultural Research Institute located here indicates that even today the place is not bereft of research - the former was a cultural research though the present one is on agriculture.

Kodumbalur: 36 kms from Pudukkottai, this place is also known as Moovar Koil. Irukku Velirs, an illustrious warrior clan related to the Cholas once ruled over this place. Of the Moovar Koil (Three temples) only two exist now. They were built by Boodhi Vikrama Kesari, a general of the Chola army in the 10th century A.D. One of the Irukku Velirs who ruled this place, named Idangazhi Nayanar is included in the canons of the 63 Nayanmars. This place was also a stage of fierce battles between the Pandyas and the Pallavas. The architecture of this temple is unique among the temples of south India. The sculptures of Kalarimurthi, Gaja (Elephant) Samharamurthi, Gangadaramurthi etc. are unique masterpieces. Nearby is the temple dedicated to Muchukundeswarar of the early Chola period.

Viralimalai : The temple of Lord

Muruga is built here on a hillock. It has been existing from the 15th century. The presiding deity is seated on a peacock mount with His two consorts Valli and Deivayanai. There is also a peacock sanctuary. It is 30 kms from Trichy and 40 kms from Pudukkottai.

Narthamalai : It is 17 kms from Pudukkottai. It contains several Jain monasteries on the hill sides. Rare medicinal plants and herbs such as black gooseberry (Karunelli), Jathi tree etc. could be seen in the forest. This is also a place of historical importance and the capital of Mutharaiyar chieftains who had an upper hand in the polity of Tamil Nadu before the rise of the later Cholas. The earliest structural stone temple, circular in shape built by Mutharaiyars, the Vijayalaya Choleswaram cave temple built by Vijayalaya the first king of the later Cholas and Kadambar Malai temple are worth a visit in this place.

Thirumayam : It is 19 kms from Pudukkottai. The fort, the Siva and the Vishnu temples are the tourist attractions here. The fort played an important role in the history of Tondaiman rulers of Pudukkottai and the British. This 40 acre wide fort was built by Vijaya Ragunatha Sethupathi of Ramanathapuram in 1687 A.D. On the hill, there is a rock-cut Siva temple with inscriptions on music. There are the relics of another fort. At the foot of the hill are the Siva and Vishnu temples. The Vishnu temple houses the largest Anantasayi in India. It is a natural cavern which has been changed into a shrine. It was in this fort that the brother of Kattabomman, Oomaithurai was ensnared and imprisoned. An old chain armour used by him is exhibited here.

Avudayar Koil : It is 40 kms from Pudukkottai. It is also called Thiruperunthurai. The presiding deity is Atmanatha. This temple is unique in many ways. There is no Lingam in the sanctum, only the Avudayar or its bottom pedestal is worshipped. Even the Goddess is not displayed by any form. No Neivedyam of food is offered to the deity. Even Nandhi the mount of Siva usually in front of the deity is absent. There is deep spiritual significance in the queerness. Hinduism allows idol worship only for the beginners in the initial stage. As the devotee and his devotion mature he has to realise the absolute truth as formless. Simply to illustrate this, this temple has been modelled like this on monistic principles. This is the only Saivaite shrine in the whole of India to portray the supreme truth symbolically. Since the soul (Atma) has no form, the deity is called Atmanathar. This temple is supposed to have been built by Manicka Vasagar, one of the 63 Saivaite saints who spent all the money he got for purchasing horses for the Pandya king in building this temple. As he was bereft of money, God played one of His Thiruvilaiyadal by transforming foxes into horses and once they were entrusted to the king, they were reconverted into foxes again. Many legends vividly describe this.

Besides the legendary and spiritual fascination, the temple is also unique and unrivalled from the sculptural point of view. The temple is noted for its zephyr (granite roof) work. The ceiling of the Kanaka Sabhai is a grandeur creation in stone – the rope, rafters and nails are all in granite. The bow wielding Muruga, Kali and Siva's Rudra Thandavam are the finest specimens in sculptural art.

Avur : 28 kms from Pudukkottai lies this place famous for churches. The old chapel was constructed in 1547 A.D. by Fr. John Venatius Bachet and the new Roman Catholic Church was built in 1747 A.D. The renowned Tamil scholar Rev. Father Joseph Beschi (Veeramamunivar) also served in this church. The Easter passion play followed by car festival in summer attracts people of all faiths.

Kumaramalai : About 10 kms from Pudukkottai is located a temple for Lord Muruga at a small hill. Kumaran is another name for Lord Muruga, hence the name Kumaramalai. The tank water of this hill is considered to be holy.

Kattubava Pallivasal : 30 kms from Pudukkottai is this important Islamic pilgrim centre. Located on the Thirumayam-Madurai highway, it is visited by devotees of all faiths. The annual 'Urs' occurs in the month of Rabiyul Ahir.

Vendanpatti : It is 40 kms from Pudukkottai on the way to Ponnamaravathi. The Nandhi known as Nei Nandhi (Ghee Bull) in the Meenakshi Chokkeswarar temple is very famous. Though made of black granite, it shines like marble due to frequent ablutions with pure ghee. One more astonishing feature is the absence of flies and ants despite the Nandhi being showered with pure ghee daily. Every day large number of devotees visit this temple.

Aranthangi : It is the second largest city in Pudukkottai. There is a ruined fort here that attracts people, the walls of which are not constructed with bricks or stones. Large interstices are filled with mud. Inside the fort, there are no ruins of palaces or any striking building. The date of the fort is not known. But a line of Tondaimans who had no connections with those of Pudukkottai were in power during the 16 and 17th centuries. They are believed to have constructed it. There is also a eleventh century A.D. temple built by Rajendra Chola Varman.

With this we have covered all the important places for tourists in mid-east Tamil Nadu and we now move to the mid-west part of Tamil Nadu which contains Salem, Dharmapuri, Erode, Coimbatore and Nilgiri districts.

Salem

(The Steel City of Tamil Nadu)

Salem got its name from the Sanskrit word 'Sailam' which means mountain. As this area is surrounded by hills, it is apt to be called Salem. It is a land of minerals. The hills around Salem has iron ore, bauxite, limestone, precious stones etc. Salem is the fifth largest city of Tamilnadu. It was originally got by the British from Tipu Sultan as Bara Mahal which contained 12 localities. This district was later divided into three: Dharmapuri, Namakkal and Salem. Another speciality of the name is that it is made up of the initial letters of its dominant specialities: S - for steel, A - for aluminium, L - for limestone, E - for electricity (There is hydro-electric power generation in Mettur) and M - for mango (Salem mangoes are famous). Yercaud, a beautiful hill station, is located here. Since Salem is a city with infrastructures well developed, tourists can stay in this place and visit the places in the neighbouring districts of Namakkal and Dharmapuri.

How to get there?

Salem is on the Chennai broad gauge line, 335 kms from Chennai. The train services are available from here to Chennai, Kochi, Coimbatore, Ooty, Thiruvananthapuram and Bangalore. It is well connected by road with all the major towns in Tamil Nadu. Local buses are available to all the places of tourist interest from here.

Nearest airport is at Coimbatore, 162 kms from Salem. Flights are available from here to Madurai, Chennai, Bangalore, Kochi and Mumbai.

Places to see in and around Salem

Yercaud : This charming hill station is about 8 kms from Salem at an altitude of 5000 ft. The temperature never rises beyond 29° C and never falls below 13° C. There is neither a biting winter nor a scorching summer. An ideal place to visit throughout the year. It is on the Shevaroy range of the Eastern ghats. It was brought to light by Sir Thomas Munroe, the erstwhile Governor of Madras in 1824. A fine motorable ghat road with several hair-pin bends links the top after a 23 kms ride through coffee plantations. Fruit plantations like apple, cherry, orange also abound. 'Yer' means beauty in Tamil, 'Kadu' means forest. Hence, Yercaud in Tamil means 'beautiful forest'. Some say that the word was a corruption for Erikadu which means forest full of lakes and true to it there are a number of lakes big and small and waterfalls on this hill. A beautiful lake with boating facilities adorns the centre. Yercaud is also ideal for trekking.

How to get there?

Frequent bus services are available from Salem to Yercaud. Private carriages like taxis, vans and buses are also available from Salem.

What to see in Yercaud?

Yercaud Lake : The lake is centrally located and is the centre of attraction. It is a cool clean sheet of water surrounded by well laid-out gardens and woods. Boats are available and boating in the chill water is an enchanting and refreshing experience.

Anna Park : It is a beautiful, well laid-out garden near the lake and a dream land of fragrance and colour with buzzing bees busily seeking honey in the flowers.

Lady's Seat : It overhangs on the winding ghat road and is a spectacular viewpoint. The panoramic view of the plains down the mountain is breath-taking and dizzy if you look down the steep gorge. At night with the twinkling lights, Salem city looks like a far-off dream land — an unforgettable spectacle. The telescope mounted at Lady's Seat gives a picturesque view of the valley below.

The Pagoda Point, Prospect Point and Arthur's Seat are the other vantageous viewpoints to look and enjoy the magnificent thrilling sights.

The Kulliar Falls : This 3000 ft high waterfalls among sylvan surroundings is a beautiful sight for spending hours together without boredom.

Bear Cave : It is formed of two huge boulders and is situated near Nation Bungalow — an oldest bungalow here. Special arrangement has to be made to reach this place.

Servaroyan Temple : It is at the top of the Shevaroys. It is said that this is the third highest peak in the range. Special arrangement with local guides have to be made as no regular transport services are available to reach this place. The annual festival is observed in May and all the hill tribes around assemble to celebrate it.

Montfort School : It is a famous public school and the Sacred Heart Convent is another school imparting education to boys and girls respectively.

The Retreat : This institution started by brothers of Don Bosco in

1945 serves as a Novitiate house where students of the religious order stay and study.

Places of Worship

Temples : Servaroyan temple and Sri Rajarajeswari temple.

Churches : Sacred Heart Church, The Retreat Church, St.Joseph's Church, Holy Trinity Church, C.S.G. Church and Lutheran Church.

Mosque : Yercaud Mosque.

Other Places of Interest in Yercaud: Ornamental Plants & Tree House, Orchard cum nursery of rose plants, Silk farm, Horticultural Research Station, Orchidorium, Mettur View, Cauvery Peak and Salem View.

Festivals : Summer festival during middle of May.

Transport

Rail : Nearest rail-heads are Salem Junction (36 kms) and Salem Town (33 kms).

Bus : Bus services operate from Salem Junction and Salem bus stand to Yercaud frequently. There is no town bus service in Yercaud, but certain buses coming from Salem ply through Yercaud and connect the important villages like Cauvery Peak, Valavanthi, Nagalur, Velakkadi, Swinton Bridge with Yercaud.

Where to Stay

- **Hotel Salem Castle,** A/4, Bharathi Street, Swarnapuri, Salem - 636 004. ✆ 446102-03, 448702, 444774, Fax: 0427-446996, Email: salemcastle@eth.com
- **Hotel LRN Excellency,** No. 7, Sarada College Road, Salem-636 007. ✆ 414411/66, 412383-86
- **Hotel Shevaroys,** Hospital Rd., Yercaud Hills. ✆ 22288, 22383, 22386, Fax: 04281-22387
- **National Hotel,** 132/18E, Bangalore Road, Salem - 636 009. ✆ 353800, 353900
- **Hotel Sri Chandra,** 231, Cherry Road, Salem - 636 001. ✆ 415775, Email: cafechandra@yahoo.com
- **Hotel Tamil Nadu,** ✆ 22273 Fax : 04281 22745
- **Sterling Holiday Resorts,** (Near Lady's Seat). ✆ 22700-22707. Fax : 04281 22537
- **Hotel Shevaroys,** Hospital Road, Yercaud. ✆ 22001
- **Hotel Select,** Near Bus-Stand, Yercaud. ✆ 22525
- **Hotel Shoba,** Near Bus-Stand, Yercaud. ✆ 22409
- **Township Rest House,** ✆ 22223

Mettur Dam : Mettur about 30 kms from Salem is connected by rail. Buses also ply from Salem to Mettur. Mettur dam is one of the largest of its kind in the world. It is constructed in a gorge where the river Cauvery enters the plains. Its height is 65 metre, length 1616 metre, area 15,540 hectare and capacity 2648 cubic metre. This is a hydro-electric power station producing 240 mega watt power. Water is stored here during floods and rains and let out for irrigating to the deltaic regions of the Cauvery. There is a beautifully laid-out garden. The Cauvery crossing is the place where a canal crosses over Cauvery–the water of the canal is carried by overhead pipelines to the other side. There are a number of factories here like soaps and detergent manufacturing factories, galvanizing plants, Vanaspathi units etc. and with permit, visitors could see them. With permit, visitors could also enter the tunnel of the dam and also witness the hydro-electric power station.

Belur : It is 25 kms away from Salem on the banks of river Vashistanadhi. There is a white rock north of Belur which is said to represent the ashes of the Yagam (Sacrificial fire) performed by Vashista.

Kolli Hills : Another hill station at an altitude of 1190 mts. The terrace type 70 hair pin-bend road leads you to this place. Fruit orchards abound in this place. Still the tribes here are unchanged and follow meticulously their traditional customs and practices–an astonishment to the modern men.

Namakkal : Formerly a part of Salem District, it is now the headquarters of the newly formed district Namakkal. It lies at the foot of a rock 200 ft high and half a mile in circumference. The Hanuman statue that stands 20 ft high is the centre of attraction. It is carved out of single piece of rock.There are two unique cave temples here. These temples were the works of 'Adhia' rulers containing relief sculptures of unrivalled beauty. The caves dedicated to Narasimha and Anantasayi (Vishnu on his snake-hooded couch) are cut on the sides of the hill. Inscriptions reveal that it was built by Gunaseelan of the Adhiakula (Adhia clan) (784 A.D.). The Narasimha cave has an enormous rock with the image of Lord Narasimha tearing the entrails of Hiranya the demon - a splendid sculpture that chills the heart of the beholder. The mandapa of the side of the cave reveals three forms: Narasimha Avatar, Vamana Avatar, Varaha Avatar. The images of Vaikunta Narayanan, Bala Narasimha, Brahma, Chandra, all reveal the dexterity of master hands. The two Vamana Avatar idols in Narasimha cave and Anantasayee cave differ from each other in that the former has a parasol and a sacrificial horse which is absent with the latter. The hollows in the rock have become sacred pools, one of them is named Kamalalayam.

Tharamangalam : It is a paradise to lovers of sculpture. The Kailasanathar temple here vividly portrays the dance competition between Siva and Kali. The two sculptures depicting the episode make us spellbound and we even forget that we are spectators of mere sculptures and think we are actual participants of that event — so lively are they done. The Bikshadana is another marvel, the Rishipatni who offers food for the mendicant Siva has forgotten herself in His beauty without even knowing the pilfering parrot that pecks at the alms. The God of Love, Manmatha releasing His shafts of flower from his sugarcane bow and Rati (the Goddess of Love) beside him, Dakshinamurthi, Valivadham, stone chains and various other sculptures are a feast to the eyes with their minute details and lively expression.

Thiruchengodu : In the southwest of the district is an important shrine dedicated to Ardhanariswarar (Siva and Uma in one form) situated at a height of 2000 feet. Flights of winding steps lead to the temple. Along the steps by the side is a huge hooded serpent-sculptured so real that it creates awe in our face. A huge Nandhi faces the hill presuming it to be Lord Siva. Mr. Davis, a former collector has renovated the partially damaged Ganesa Mandapam of this temple and his relief portrait adorns a pillar. Climbing still further one can reach Maladi (a barren woman) hills, where a huge boulder is precariously perched on the tip of an edge of an abyss of 800 ft threatening each moment. Barren women crawl around it three times to be blessed with pregnancy. The famous Gandhi Ashram founded by Rajaji is still functioning actively at Thiruchengodu.

Sankari Durg : The Someswar temple attracts large crowds. Here too we can see a boulder akin to one at Maladi hills. It is about 40ft. high and almost equally broad. There is a well known cement factory since limestone is enormously found here.

Dharmapuri : This was once part of Salem district but now its headquarters. During the Sangam Age it was called Thagadur. It was the capital of Adiaman Neduman Anji. The 7 ft. high Hanuman in the temple of Anna Sagaram is the main attraction here. The curious feature about Him is that He has no tail at all.

Hogenakkal : The main picnic spot in Dharmapuri is Hogenakkal, the place where the Cauvery enters Tamil Nadu. It is one of the most beautiful places in the state with picturesque scenes. The broad stream of the river Cauvery gets forked at this point, forming an island from where one stream continues and plunges into a deep chasm to create a lovely waterfalls. As the spray of this waterfall raises clouds of droplets resembling smoke this place is known as Hogenakkal (Hoge means smoke, Kal - rock) – smoking rock. Earlier above, the river Cauvery flows in a particular narrow gorge so narrow that it could be easily leapt by a goat and hence the name of that place is Meka Dhattu (Goat's leap). Since the water of Cauvery flows through a herbal forest before it reaches Hogenakkal, bathing in the falls here is considered good for health. A large number of people gather here daily to have bath in river. A bath after a malish with oil (smearing of oil) is very refreshing. One can find malish experts are busy here minting money. If one wants to taste the thrill of adventure one can hire a 'parisal' (round basket-like boats) to ply in the river. Hogenakkal offers a quiet holiday in comfort. The magnificent, rugged mountain scenery around the falls can be better enjoyed by long walks and treks.

Hosur : Though this place is very well known as a centre of industries, it does not lack the charms of being a tourist centre. Thali located nearby is known as 'Little England' to the British because of its beautiful green downs and salubrious climate.

The Tamil Nadu Tourist Development Corporation arranges for student package tours–

For details, contact: Ph : 60-91-44-582916, 584356, 560294. Fax : 561385.

Erode

(Paradise of Handloom Textiles)

Erode occupies the 5th place for handloom textiles in India. It is a business centre and the birthplace of Thanthai Periyar, the greatest social reformer and father of the self-respect movement in Tamil Nadu. It was formerly part of the Coimbatore district and became a separate district in 1979. The river Cauvery flows through Erode. Erode got its name from the famous Arthra Kapaleeswarar. Arthra means wet. The Tamil word is 'Iram' (ஈரம்) and 'odu' means kapala or the skull. So, the word Ira-Ottu-Isar in due course was corrupted to be pronounced as Erode. This district contains some important temples and places of tourist importance.

How to get there?

Erode is on the broad gauge railway line and can easily be reached by numerous trains that pass through this important junction. It is 398 kms from Chennai. Almost all the trains to the west coast pass through this junction. It is connected to Chennai, Arakkonam, Salem, Coimbatore and Nilgris by rail. The town is connected to all important towns in Tamil Nadu by good roads. Umpteen town buses also ply to places of tourist importance. Private vehicles and taxis are also available to any place in the district.

Bannari Mariamman Koil : It is on the western side of Erode about 10 kms from Bhavani Sagar. Goddess

Mariamman is famous here and attracts thousands of pilgrims. During the month of Adi (August-September) the festival at this temple is attended by large number of people. The fire walk by the devotees is very thrilling.

Bhavani Sagar : Bhavani town is situated at the confluence of the river Cauvery and Bhavani one of its major tributaries. The Sangameswarar temple is at this confluence. This place is also known as the 'Thriveni of South India'. It is an important pilgrim centre and also an important picnic centre. Lord Sangameswara with His consort Vedanayaki is the presiding deity. Legend goes that once the collector of the Coimbatore and Salem districts of the colonial period, William Garraw was directed by the Goddess Vedanayaki to immediately vacate the building in which he was staying. The collecter obeyed and immediately after vacating, the building collapsed. In reverence of this miracle, the collector presented an ivory cradle to the temple which even today can be seen there with the collector's signature on it. People also visit the Bhavani Sagar Dam which presents a beautiful feast to the eyes. There is a swimming pool and a park. Bhavani is known the world over for its blankets with floral designs.

Kodumudi : It is situated 40 kms from Erode. A special feature of this place is that the Trinity of the Hindu faith Siva, Vishnu and Brahma all have their shrines in a single temple complex. Muchukundeswarar is the name of Siva and Veera Narayana Perumal is that of Vishnu here. This is an important temple in Erode district.

Chennimalai : It is located 30 kms from Erode. There is a famous temple dedicated to Lord Muruga on the top of Chennimalai (Mountain). Rare forms of Muruga – Agni Jather - with two faces and eight arms; Gourapeyar - with four faces and eight arms, as hunter with a single face and six arms – can be seen here. Originally the presiding deity had the idol of Subramanya with six faces. As it was damaged, a Dandayuthapani idol like the one at Palani has been installed as the presiding deity. Chennimalai is an important handloom weaving centre.

Kangeyam : It is 40 kms from Erode. A famous Muruga temple is located here. It was once famous for bullocks called Kangeyam Kalai. From here, on the Muthur Road about 10 kms is situated Kuttappalayam where a modern Dhyana Mandapam (Meditation hall) is built dedicated to Sri Aurobindo and the Mother of Pondicherry. The mandapam is located amidst a spacious 5 acre land which is being developed as a beautiful garden. Inside the mandapam is an exact replica of the Sri Aurobindo and Mother samadhi found in Pondicherry. The relics of Sri Aurobindo and the Mother have been enshrined in the samadhi here. Every month on the 2nd Sunday, group meditation is conducted from 9.00 a.m. to 12.00 noon which attracts large gathering from far and near.

Dharapuram Siva Temple : Dharapuram is about 70 kms from Erode. An old Siva temple is located here on the northern banks of river Amaravathi. The temple has Lingam and Devi shrines. There is a separate shrine for Bhairava. A flight of steps lead to the river. On the southern side also there is a Siva temple quite older than this one containing several inscriptions. The Dhakshinamurthi in the niche here is different from the usual one. The idols are beautifully carved in this temple.

Thindal Malai Murugan temple, Pariyur Amman temple, Sivanmalai Arthra Kapaleeswarar temple, Kooduthurai, Kodiveri, Varattuppallam, Kunderippallam and upper dams are the other places of tourist attraction in this district. Bus services are available to all the places. The Thalavadi hills and Andhiyur forests border this district.

Where to Stay

- **Hotel Oxford,** 120, Park Approach Road, Erode - 638 003. ✆ 226611, Fax: 0424 - 226618, Email: oxford-mohan@yahoo.com
- **Hotel Sivaranjani,** 177, Brovgh Road, Erode - 638 001. ✆ 257880, Fax: 0424-255278

Coimbatore

(The Manchester of Tamil Nadu)

Coimbatore is the 3rd largest city of Tamil Nadu. It is the district headquarters and the most industrialised and commercialised city in Tamil Nadu. It is the textile capital of the south and called the Manchester of Tamil Nadu. It is on the banks of Noyyal, a tributary of the river Cauvery. The hinterland with black cotton soil and the ideal climate are suitable for the development of textile industry. It was in existence even before 2nd century as the capital of Kongu kings. It came under the reign of Karikal Chola of the 2nd century A.D., the Rastrakutas, Chalukyas, Pandyas, Hoysalas and Vijayanagar rulers, and Mysore Wodeyars too held sway in this region. When it finally fell into the hands of the British, its name was perpetuated as Coimbatore. As it is located in the shadows of the western ghats, it enjoys a very pleasant climate throughout the year with the fresh breeze that blows through the 25 kms wide Palakkad gap which is the main link to the neighbouring state Kerala. The first textile mills came up here as far back as 1888 but now there are over hundred mills in Coimbatore. Mettuppalayam (35 kms from Coimbatore) that borders the Nilgiris district, is the disembarking point to board the mountain train that goes to the 'Queen of Hill Stations' - Ooty.

How to get there?

Coimbatore is 497 kms from Chennai. It is connected by road to all major places in South India. There are regular bus services from Chennai, Madurai, Trichy, Salem, Erode, Udagamandalam etc. Inter-state buses also run from Palakkad, Ernakulam, Thrissur, Bangalore and Mysore. It is a major railway junction on the Southern Railways and has trains to Chennai, Rameswaram, Madurai, Bangalore, Mumbai, Kanyakumari, Kozhikode, Mettupalayam, Kochi and Delhi.

There is an airport here at Sulurpet and flights go to Chennai, Mumbai, Madurai, Kochi and Bangalore.

Local bus transport and private vehicles and taxis are also available to go to all the places of tourist importance in the district.

Places to see

Perur : This place 7 kms from Coimbatore junction is the most important place to be visited for its sculptural splendour. It is often called the Mecca of Art Lovers. The other name of this place is Mel-Chidambaram. The Perur temple was built by Karikal Cholan of 2nd century A.D. There are shrines to the presiding deity Patteeswarar and his consort Pachainayaki. The Kanaga Sabha pillars are chiselled with images of unsurpassing beauty. The images of

Gajasamhara, Veerabadra, Bikshadana, Oorthuva Thandava, Veena Pani Saraswathi, all rival with one another in artistic perfection. Imposing corridors with numerous carvings is a feast to the eyes. The Panguni Uthiram festival in March-April attracts thousands of people every year. Nearby flows the Noyyal river with green lushy banks. One can also visit the Santhalinga Adigalar Mutt and Tamil College here.

Agricultural University : The most famous Agricultural University, the best in South East Asia, is located here. It was originally established as an agricultural farm in Saidapet, Chennai and later moved to Coimbatore in 1907. The name got changed first as Agricultural College and it developed into the Agricultural University. It is 5 kms from railway station.

G.D.Naidu Industrial Exhibition : G.D. Naidu the famous technocrat of yester-years was a legend in his own time. His contribution to automobile, electronics, mechanical and agricultural sectors are invaluable. He founded a technical institute and the Industrial Exhibition is located here. It is a splendid exposure to science, technology and modern industry.

V.O.C. Park : Named after the eminent freedom fighter and patriot V.O.Chidambaram Pillai, this huge park is maintained by the Municipal Corporation. There is a mini zoo, and a joy train in this park amuses children as well as the grown-ups.

Forest College : It is just 3.5 kms from the railway station. It is one of the oldest institutes of its kind in India. It trains forest rangers. The college museum has wonderful collections and demands a visit.

Places of Worship

Koniamman Temple, Big Bazaar Street, Town Hall.

Thandu Mariamman Temple, Avinashi Road, Uppilippalayam.

Rathina Vinayagar Temple, R.S.Puram, D.B.Road.

Sri Ayyappan Temple, Sithapudur, Satyamangalam Road.

Kamatchi Amman Temple, Ukkadam, near B-2 Police Station.

Mundhi Vinayagar Temple is in the heart of the city. This gigantic statue of Vinayagar is a modern attraction and landmark.

Ichanari Vinayagar Temple : This modern Vinayagar temple on the outskirts is becoming famous nowadays. The temple is kept spotlessly spick and span with modern facilities.

Churches

St. Michael's Cathedral, Big Bazaar.

St. Antony's Church, Puliakulam.

Christ King Church, Dr. Nanjappa Road.

Fathima Church, Gandhipuram.

Mosques

Big Mosque, Oppanakkara Street.

Big Mosque, Kottaimedu.

Mosque, 1st Street, Gandhipuram.

Shopping

Big Bazaar, Oppanakkara Street,

Raja Street, Ranga Gounder Street,

Sukravarpettai (for handloom goods)

Chintamani Super Market (Main), North Coimbatore

Poompuhar Handicrafts Emporium

Co-optex
Khadi Crafts
TANSI Sales Centre

Places around Coimbatore

Marudhamalai : 12 kms away from Coimbatore is this hill- top temple dedicated to Lord Subramanya. Devotees throng this temple as the Lord Dhandayuthapani of this temple has performed several miracles to devotees. The temple is reached by a flight of steps. There is also a motorable road and temple buses are available to reach the top. Marudhamalai is a mountain full of rare herbs. One of the 18 siddhars, Pampatti Siddhar has resided in this place. The cave where he resided is now a shrine of worship. Thai Poosam (January-February) and Thirukarthigai (November-December) festivals are very famous here. They are celebrated with pomp and gaiety. The greenery of this mountain is pleasing to the eyes and the chill breeze atop is quite refreshing.

Vaideki Waterfalls : It is 30 kms from Coimbatore via Narsipuram village. A beautiful picnic spot and a heaven for trekkers. A perennial waterfalls is the chief attraction of this place.

Sengupathi Waterfalls : The Sengupathi waterfalls are located 35 kms from Coimbatore on the Coimbatore-Siruvani main road. It is a nice picnic spot and people come in large number to bathe in the falls.

The Siruvani Waterfalls and Dam: The dam and waterfalls are at a distance of 37 kms from Coimbatore on the western side. The water of Siruvani river is known for its taste and mineral properties. The panoramic view from the dam and the falls enchant the visitors.

Parambikulam-Aliyar Dam : This dam is a multi-purpose project. It consists of a series of dams interconnected by tunnels and canals for harnessing waters of Parambikulam, Aliyar, Nirar, Sholaiar, Thunnakadavu, Thekkadi and Palar rivers, lying at various elevations, for irrigation and power generation. The scheme is an outstanding example of engineering skill and inter-state relationship. It is in the Anaimalai range at the foot of the entrance to Valparai. It is about 64 kms from Coimbatore. There is a park and boating can also be done. The early morning mist that hangs over the Aliyar Dam is an enchanting dreamy sight.

Monkey Falls : This falls is ideal even for children to bathe. It is located on the Pollachi-Valparai High Road just on entering the ghat section after passing the Aliyar-Parambikulam multi-purpose project. An entrance fee of Rs.2/- is collected.

Valparai : It is 102 kms from Coimbatore in the Western ghats of the Anaimalai range. A ride in ghat road that passes through the Indra Gandhi Wildlife Sanctuary is fantastic. The flora of this place is quite interesting and a paradise for botanists. All along the road one can see innumerable tea plantations. The Kadambarai power project is on the way and could be visited with permit. On the top is a Balaji temple built by the Birlas. A beautiful and neatly kept temple with an enchanting idol. One can also see plantation workers busily picking tea leaves and smoking the area to ward off insects and flies. It is a nice place and a developing hill station. The scenery and the murky sky with intermittent drizzle is quite enjoyable. Valparai is really the Princess of Hills as it is called.

Mazani Amman Temple : This is near the highway to Anaimalai Topslip from Pollachi. It stands on the banks of river Amaravathi. It is a renowned local temple. The main feature in this temple is the grinding of red chillies by devotees. It is said that the deity here is Goddess of revenge and would punish severely the enemies of Her devotees if they grind the chilly on a stone grinder kept here for that purpose. The devotee chants the name of the deity and prays for the ruin of his enemy while grinding the chillies. The chillies to be ground are available in the temple.

Topslip : It is a picturesque spot in the Anaimalai Hills about 37 kms from Pollachi. There is a waterfalls on the top, an ideal picnic location. Arrangements are made at Topslip to take tourists around the sanctuary on elephant's back or in a van.

Thirumoorthy Temple & Waterfalls: It is about 96 kms from Coimbatore and 20 kms from Udumalaipet at the foot of the Thirumoorthy hills. The presiding deity is called Ammanalingeswarar. True to the name, the main deity is left nude (Ammanam) without any clothes on. It is an old temple with beautiful setting and some rare sculptures with a spacious front hall. There are some inscriptions too. A perennial stream flows by the side of the temple. Just a km from the temple on the hill is a beautiful waterfalls. There are bathing arrangements and one can hold the iron chain fastened to the walk beneath the waterfalls and enjoy the thrill of a chill water massage. Above, after a strenuous climb lies another waterfalls which is more vigorous and refreshing. It is an ideal place for trekking too. At the foot of the hills lie the Thirumoorthy dam with boating facilities. There is also a swimming pool and a well laid-out garden. Local buses ply from Udumalaipet to this place. There is rail link to Udumalaipet from Coimbatore on the metre gauge line.

Amaravathi Dam : The steep Amaravathi dam across the river Amaravathi is just 25 kms from Thirumoorthy Dam. Buses from here and Udumalaipet ply to this place. There is a well laid-out park and on climbing the steep dam on steps, one can have a picturesque view. There is a crocodile farm nearby and umpteen crocodiles of all sizes basking in the sun and suddenly making a stride or piled up on one another could be seen.

The Anaimalai Wildlife Sanctuary: The Indira Gandhi Natural Park and Anaimalai Wildlife Sanctuary is at an altitude of 1400 metres in the western ghats near Pollachi about 90 kms from Coimbatore. The area of this vast sanctuary is 958 sq. kms. The flora and fauna of this place is very unique and rare varieties which are fast disappearing could also be seen here. The fauna consists of elephant, gaur, tiger, panther, sloth-bear, deer, wild boar, wild dog, porcupine, flying squirrel, jackal, pangolin, civet cat, snakes and birds like rocket-tailed drango, red-whiskered bulbul, black-headed oriole, tree pie, spotted dove and green pigeon. A large number of crocodiles are seen in the Amaravathi reservoir in Anaimalai. Places of scenic beauty are Karainshola, Anaikunthishola, grass hills, waterfalls, groves, teak forests, estates, dams and reservoirs. Rest houses and safari sightseeing are available at Topslip, Vanagaliar and Mount Stuart. The sanctuary can be visited any time of the year but the best time is to go in the very early morning or late evening. Transport through the sanctuary is arranged by the forest department. The reception centre is at Parambikulam dam.

Black Thunder : A water theme park named Black Thunder is located at 8 kms from Mettupalayam (35 kms from Coimbatore) - Ooty ghat road at the foot of the Nilgiris. It is a fine amusement park and said to be Asia's number one theme park. Numerous tourists visit daily. The entrance fee is Rs.150/-.

Tiruppur : It is 50 kms from Coimbatore and is associated with the illustrious freedom fighter Kumar called 'Kodi Katha Kumaran' (Kumaran who saved the honour of the flag). A statue is erected for him in this place. It is an important textile centre and famous the world over for hosiery products.

Where to stay at Coimbatore?

- **Cag Pride,** 312, Bharathiar Road, Coimbatore - 641 044. ✆ 497777 Fax: 0422-491763 Email: sales@cagpride.com
- **Heritage Inn,** 38, Sivasamy Road, Ram Nagar, Coimbatore - 641 009. ✆ 230011, 231451 Fax: 0422-233223 Email: heritageinn@vsnl.com
- **Hotel Surya International** 105, Race Course Road, Coimbatore - 638 452 ✆ 217751-55 Fax:0422-216110 Email: suryaint@md2.vsnl.net.in
- **Resort Black Thunder,** Ooty Main Road, Mettupalayam, Coimbatore - 641 305. ✆ 26632-40, 25739 Fax: 04254-25740
- **Sree Annapoorna Lodging** 75, East Arockiasamy Road, R.S.Puram, Coimbatore - 641 002. ✆ 547621/547722 Fax: 0422-547322 Email: apoorna@md2.vsnl.net.in
- **The Residency** Avinashi Road, Coimbatore - 641 018. ✆ 201234 Fax: 0422-201414 Email: rescbe@vsnl.com
- **Nilgiri's Nest** 739A, Avinashi Road, Coimbatore - 641 018. ✆ 217247, 214309, 217130 Fax: 0422-217131 Email: nilgiris@md3.vsnl.net.in
- **Hotel Seetharam** 67, Malaviya Street, Ram Nagar, Coimbatore - 641 009. ✆ 230724-25, 231086 Fax: 0422-233328
- **Hotel Indrapuri** K.V.K. Complex, 91, S.S. Kovil St., Pollachi, Coimbatore Dist., ✆ 04259-25550, 26550
- **Howard Johnson The Monarch Resort,** 286, Off Ponnuthu Road, Pannimadai, Coimbatore - 17. ✆ 858413, 858416 Fax: 0422-858411 Email: themonarch@vsnl.com
- **Annalakshmi Foods,** 106, Race Course Road, Coimbatore - 641 018. ✆ 212142, 217770-72 Fax: 0422-217810
- **Bombay Anand Bhavan,** 293, Big Bazaar Street, Coimbatore - 641 001. ✆ 0422-397949
- **Dakshin The South** Sree Annapoorna Annexe, 75, East Arokiasamy Road, R.S. Puram, Coimbatore - 641 002. ✆ 437722, 431722 Fax: 0422-437322
- **Sree Annapoorna Park Restautant** 75, East Arokiasamy Road, II Floor, R.S. Puram, Coimbatore - 641 002. ✆ 547722, 541722 Fax: 0422-547322
- **Sri Krishna Sweets** 137, D.B. Road, R.S. Puram, Coimbatore - 641 002. ✆ 472458 Fax: 0422-473416
- **Hotel Tamil Nadu** ✆ : 236311
- **Hotel City Tower** ✆ : 230641
- **Hotel Alankar** ✆ : 235461
- **Hotel Thaai** ✆ : 302736
- **Hotel Diana** ✆ 230982
- **Hotel Meena** ✆ : 235420
- **Jyothi Hotel** ✆ : 300077
- **Ambika Lodge** ✆ : 231660
- **Sahri Hotels** ✆ : 232866
- **Park Inn** ✆ : 301284
- **Mangala International** ✆ : 232012
- **Hotel Devi** ✆ : 301667
- **Hotel Vishnupriya** ✆ : 233652
- **Hotel Pushpam** ✆ : 234366
- **Hotel Maruthi** ✆ : 471270
- **Elite Tourist Home** ✆ : 303607
- **Cheran Palace** ✆ : 300211

The Nilgiris (Ooty)

(The Queen of Hill Stations)

Udhagamandalam or Ooty is rightly called the 'Queen of Hill Stations' on account of its unrivalled beauty and everlasting charm. It is in the Nilgiris where the western and eastern ghats meet. The mystic beauty of Ooty lied unknown to the rest of India until it was discovered by the British in the early 1800s. Though the whole area was inhabited by hill tribes like the Todas, the Kotas, the Kurumbas, the Badagas, the Panias and the Irulas, it was only after the first railway line was constructed that much of its enchantment was revealed. Its popularity grew because of the gold hunt pursued by early colonialists in the Nilgiris. Though the gold hunt was given up in the early 20th century, its rich endowments of nature came to the limelight and Europeans and the well-to-do natives settled there. It became the summer capital of the then Madras Presidency. It is known as 'Nilagiri' meaning 'blue mountain' because of the blue haze that prevailed to look at from a distance. It is at a height of 2240m, and is the headquarters of the Nilgiris district. Besides coffee and tea plantations, eucalyptus, pine and wattle dot the hill sides of Udhagamandalam. The summer temperature is rarely higher than 25°C with a minimum of 10° C and winter with a high of 21°C and a low of 5° C, rarely it touches O° C.

Settlement in Ooty began in 1822 with the construction of the Stone House by John Sullivan the erstwhile collector of Coimbatore. It was locally called 'Kal Bangala' and is now the chamber of the Principal of Govt. Arts College. Following this, several English cottages with pretty gardens sprang up. Even today, the atmosphere of the British Raj lingers in places like the club where snooker was invented by a subaltern Neville Chamberlain, the Nilgiris library with rare and invaluable collection of books on Ooty and St. Stephen's Church which was Ooty's first church.

How to get there?

Rail : Ooty is on the narrow gauge railway connected to Mettupalayam which is directly connected to Coimbatore and Chennai. Mettupalayam 89 kms from Coimbatore is the downhill railway station.

Road : It is also connected by good motorable road. It is 535 kms from Chennai via Salem and Mettupalayam. From Coimbatore (89 kms) road link is available to Mettupalayam and umpteen buses ply from there to Ooty and the surrounding places in Ooty. Private vehicles and taxis are also available. There is also a road link from Mysore.

Air : The nearest airport is at Coimbatore (100 kms) and flights connect you from there to Chennai, Mumbai and Bangalore.

Places of Worship

Temples : Murugan temple, Elk Hill, Venkateswara Perumal temple, Sri Mariamman temple, Subramaniaswamy temple, Vittobha temple, Muniswara temple.

Churches : St. Stephen's Church, Union Church, Holy Trinity Church, Sacred Heart Church, St. Mary's Church, St. Thomas Church and Kandal shrine.

Mosques : A few mosques are also available.

Places to see in and around Ooty

The Botanical Garden : The Botanical Garden maintained by the Horticulture Department is a unique place containing a wide range of plants that include different kinds of roses, important shrubs, rare flowering plants, eucalyptus trees, several old trees and even a fossilised tree trunk that has become a hard stone in about 20 million years. A beautiful Italian garden, green carpets of well maintained lawns attract the visitors inclined to relax. The summer festival is held here annually in the month of May, surely an added attraction to tourists. The annual flower show is the pride of this festival, besides, cultural programmes are also organised to bring to light traditional classical arts. Adventurous sports like trekking also form part of the festival.

Mini Garden : It is about 1 km from the railway station. This mini garden also called 'Children's Lake Garden' is on the way to Boat House. There is a children's amusement park here. A snack bar is also available. Maintained neatly by the Tamil Nadu Tourism Development Corporation, the garden is open from 8 a.m. to 6 p.m.

Entrance fee Rs.2/-, Camera fee Rs.5/-, Video Camera fee Rs. 100/-.

Ooty Lake : It is an artificial lake created by Sullivans. It has boating facilities. Even fishing can be done in the lake with a permission by the office of the Asst. Director of Fisheries.

Rose Garden : Just 3/4 kms from the Railway Station is the Rose Garden. It is about 10 acres full of roses of 1419 varieties–a real feast for the eyes.

Entrance fee Rs.5/- per adult and Rs.2/- per child.

Timings : 8 a.m. to 6 p.m.

Art Gallery : Lalitha Kala Academy is about 2 kms from Ooty in the Mysore Road. The Art Gallery is located here. It has various collections of contemporary paintings and sculptures from all over India.

Timings : 9.30 a.m. to 5 p.m.

Government Museum : The government museum is on the Mysore road. Items of tribal objects, district's ecological details and representative sculptural arts and crafts of Tamil Nadu are on display.

Admission : Free

Timings : 10 a.m. to 1 p.m. & 2 p.m. to 5 p.m. It is closed on Fridays, 2nd Saturdays & national holidays.

Wenlock Downs : It is a heaven for nature lovers, sprawling over 20,000 acres. It was the famous erstwhile Udhaga-mandalam Hunt. The Gymkhana Club, the Hindustan Photo Films Factory, The Government Sheep Farms and the Golf Course are all in the Wenlock Downs.

The Viewpoints around Udhagamandalam : Elk Hills, Green Valley View, Snowden Peak and Doddabetta Peak are the most important viewpoints and the chief among them is the Doddabetta peak which is the highest and is at a height of 2623m. If the day is clear, one can see as far as the plains of Coimbatore and the plateau of Mysore.

Coonoor : 17 kms from Udhagamandalam, Coonoor is at an altitude of 2000 ft and is the first of these hill stations. It is a small town with an equable climate that has made it popular. The Sim's Park is the major attraction, though small it is well maintained and contains varieties of plants not to be found in other hill stations. Lamb's Rock, Lady Canning's Seat, Dolphin's Nose, St Catherine Falls, Law's Falls, Rallia Dam, The Droog, Pomological Station, Kallan Agricultural Farm, and Burliar Agricultural Farm are the other important view points, picnic spots and places of tourist interest in Coonoor.

Mudhumalai Wildlife Sanctuary: Mudhumalai Wildlife Sanctuary is the most prominent in the state and the most important in the southern region. The thickly forested Mudhumalai borders the Bandipur National Park in Karnataka and the Wynad Sanctuary in Kerala. Tiger, spotted deer, elephant, gaur, sambar, barking deer, wild boar, civet cat, flying squirrel, four-horned antelope, bison, mouse deer, common langur, bonnet macaque, pangolin, the scaled ant-eater, panther, leopard, hyena, sloth-bear and jackal roam about the forest. The birds of the forest include peacock, woodpeckers, several species of owls, vultures, buzzards and the grey jungle fowl. During the April nights, the whole sanctuary is lit up by millions of glow-worms which look like a dream world of illumined quiet.

Theppakadu is an elephant camp within the sanctuary.There is a rest-house here — besides, accommodation is also available in TTDC youth hostel and rest-houses in Masinagudi, Abhayaranyam, Kargudi and Bamboo Banks Farm. The best season is between January-March and September-October. The Wildlife Warden at Coonoor Road, Udhagamandalam can be contacted for further information.

Ketti Valley Viewpoint : Located on the road to Coonoor, this idyllic spot is a cluster of tiny villages that extend to the plains of Coimbatore and Mysore plateau.

Glenmorgan : It is about 17kms from Ooty. Ecologically it is a rich forestry spot. From here, the Electricity Board winch carries staff from Glenmorgan Viewpoint to power house at Singara. All the 4 km of the winch track passes through undisturbed sholas and wildlife habitats. Prior permission of the E.B. is necessary to enter the viewpoint zone.

Upper Bhavani : It is about 10 kms from Korakundha and 20 kms from Avalanche. This spot is a naturalists' paradise. This is also a rich and undisturbed wildlife habitat. From Bangithapal via Sirpura one can trek to Silent Valley. The permission of the forest department is necessary to go there.

Kalhatty Falls : It is on the Kalhatty slopes, 13 kms from Udhagamandalam on the Mysore-Kalhatty ghat road. The height of the waterfalls is 100 ft. Kalhatty- Masinagudi slope is rich in wildlife such as panthers, bisons, wild buffaloes, wild dogs, spotted deer, sambars and different varieties of hill birds.

Cairn Hill : It is about 3 kms on the road to Avalanche and is one of the few surviving original walks. The entrance road to the hill is flanked by dense cypress trees. The clearing underneath them make good picnic spots. The quietitude and silence of the cypress woods is broken by the chirping of birds in the shrubs –an experience unforgettable.

Kandal Cross Shrine : This Roman Catholic church is to the Nilgiris Catholics 'The Calvary of Tamilnadu'. It is about 3 kms from Ooty railway station on the western side. A relic of the true cross is here and it cures the sick, bestows peace and joy to the visitors. Special prayers and holy masses are offered every Friday. The annual feast falls on 3rd May each year.

Kamaraj Sagar (Sandynallah Reservoir): The Kamaraj Sagar dam is a nice picnic spot. It can be reached via Kandal amidst old trees and green shrubs of various terrains via the Hindustan Photo Films in Gudalur road. Apart from studying nature and the environment, fishing provides excellent game in the dam. Upper Bhavani and Avalanche are also good places for fishing. The trout fish abounds in them.

The Mukurthi Peak and Mukurthi National Park : It is about 40kms from Ooty. It is located on the south-eastern corner of the Nilgiris. The area contains a large number of Nilgiri trees (Hamitragus hilverius). The Silent Valley is located on the western side of these ranges. The main feature of Mukurthi Sanctuary is its variety and similarities to Himalayan flora and fauna.

Pykara : It is 21 kms on the Ooty-Mysore road. Pykara has a well protected fenced sholas, Toda settlements, undisturbed grassy meadows and wildlife habitat. The Pykara dam, Pykara falls and Pykara reservoir attract many tourists. T.T.D.C. maintains a boat house and restaurant here. The Pykara power station to which water is carried through pipelines along the slope is a fascinating sight.

Avalanche : It is 28 kms from Ooty. A beautiful lake teeming with a thick shoal where even sunlight cannot penetrate and abundant with a wide variety of avifauna – really a paradise for nature lovers.

Western Catchment : It is 28 kms from Ooty. It contains rolling grassy downs interspersed with temperate shoals occupying depressions and valleys.

Kotagiri : It is 31 kms from Ooty. It is 6503 feet above sea level. The climate here is very salubrious. It is shielded by the Doddabetta ranges which receives much of its rain from the north-west monsoon. One can enjoy a pleasure ride on roads flanked by green tea beds on either side.

Kodanadu Viewpoint : It is about 16 kms on the eastern edges of the Nilgiris. On either side is a panoramic view of tea estates and the river Moyar is breathtaking. A watch-tower is there to view the panoramic view of Rangasamy peak and pillar. Bus services are available for Kotagiri.

St. Catherine Waterfalls : From Dolphin's Nose, Coonoor, one can have a magnificent view of St. Catherine waterfalls which is about 250 feet high. But it can't be reached from Kotagiri which is 8 kms from here. To reach the top of the hills, tourists should take a diversion at Araveni on the Kotagiri-Mettupalayam road.

Gudalur : It is 51 kms from Ooty. It is the gateway to Nilgiris from Kerala and Karnataka. Ooty, Coonoor and Kotagiri lie in the upper plateau of Nilgiris while Gudalur lies in the lower plateau. The Ooty-Calicut road and the Ooty-Mysore road meet at Gudalur town. Most of this area is a green carpet.

Frog Hill Viewpoint : It is 14 kms from Gudalur on the way to Ooty. From here, one can see the gigantic frog shape of a hill view.

Needle Point Rock View : It is 12 kms on the way to Ooty from Gudalur. From here, one can enjoy panoramic views of Mudhumalai wildlife sanctuary and Gudalur town.

Numbal Kattah : 8 kms from Gudalur. A shrine of Battarayaswamy (Lord of the hunts) with sub-shrine built in Kerala style is situated here. Wynad scenes are visible from here.

Nellakotta : 15 kms from Gudalur. A dilapidated old fort is seen here.

Nellialayam : 20 kms from Gudalur. Ruins of the historical Ummathur dynasty can be seen here.

Cherambadi : 35 kms from Gudalur. It is the extreme western corner having plantations and mica mines. Sultan Bathery is very near this place.

Hanging Bridges : It is 14 kms from Gudalur on the way to Mudhumalai wildlife sanctuary. A Siva temple at Baro Wood Valley, Marava Kandy Dam at Masinagudi and Moyar waterfalls are the other places of tourist attraction here.

Summer Festival : The Summer Festival in Ooty is the best event during the season in May. Regular cultural programmes, fashion shows, flower and fruit shows, boat races, boat pageantry, dog shows etc. are held during the festival. It is a gay occasion of fun and frolic and enjoyment of never - forgettable experiences.

Where to stay

Coonoor

• **Taj Garden Retreat,** Church Road, Upper Coonoor, Coonoor - 643 101. ✆ 230021, 230042 Fax: 0423-232775
• **Velan Hotel Ritz,** Ritz Road, Bedford, Upper Coonoor, The Nilgiris - 643 101. ✆ 230484, 230084, 230632 Fax: 91(95) 423-230606
• **Hotel Tamil Nadu Youth Hostel** Mount Pleasant ✆ 232813
• **Sri Lakshmi Tourist Home,** Kamaraj Ngr. ✆ 231022
• **Hotel Blue Hills,** ✆ 231348
• **Vivek Tourist Home,** ✆ 231292
• **Venkateswara Lodge,** ✆ 234309

Ooty

• **Savoy Hotel** 77, Sylks Road, The Nilgiris, Udagamandalam - 643 001. ✆ 444142, 444147 Fax:0423-443318 Email:savoy.ooty@tajhotels.com
• **Holiday Inn Gem Park Ooty,** Sheddon Road, Udagamandalam - 643 001. ✆ 442955, 443066, 441761, 441762 Fax: 0423-444302 Email: higp@vsnl.com
• **Hotel Sinclairs Ooty,** 153, Gorishola Road, Udagamandalam - 643 001. ✆ 441376-80, 444309 Fax: 0423-444229 Email: sinooty@sancharnet.in
• **Howard Johnson The Monarch,** Church Hill, Off Havelock Rd., Udagamandalam - 643 001. ✆ 444306, 443655 Fax: 0423-442455 Email: themonarch@vsnl.com
• **Nahar Hotels (Nilgiris),** 52 A, Charing Cross, Ooty, The Nilgiris - 643 001. ✆ 443685, 442173 Fax: 0423-44751, 445173
• **Welcomgroup Sullivan Court,** 123, Selbourne Road, Udagamandalam - 643 001. (441415-16 Fax:0423-441417 Email: wgsull@md5.vsnl.net.in
• **The Willow Hill,** 58/1, Havelock Road, Udagamandalam - 643 001. ✆ 442686, 444037, 444758 Fax: 0423-442686
• **Merit Inn Southern Star,** 22, Havelock Road, Udagamandalam - 643 001. ✆ 443601-06, 440240 Fax: 0423-440202, 441098 Email: dean@md3.vsnl.net.in
• **Fernhill Palace Hotel,** Fernhill Post, Udagamandalam - 643 004. ✆ 0423-443910-15
• **Hotel KHEMS,** Ettines Road, Udagamandalam - 643 001. ✆ 444188, 441265/66, 441635/36 Fax: 0423-442461 Email: khems999@yahoo.co.in
• **Hotel Lakeview,** West Lake Road, Udagamandalam - 643 004. ✆ 443580-82, 443904, 440978-83 Fax: 0423-443579 Email: lakeview@md3.vsnl.net.in
• **Howard Johnson The Monarch,** Safari Park, Bokkapuram, Masinagudi - 643 223. ✆ 526250, 526343 Fax: 0423-526326 Email: themonarch@vsnl.com
• **Regency Villa,** Fernhill Palace, Fernhill Post, Udagamandalam - 643 004. ✆ 442555, 443098 Fax: 0423-43097
• **Sterling Holiday Resorts (India) Ltd.,** P.B. No. 73, Kundah House Rd., Fernhill, Ooty - 643 004. ✆ 441073, 450948, 450949 Fax: 0423-445890 Email: sterling@md4.vsnl.net.in
• **Sterling Holiday Resorts,** ELK Hill P.B. No. 25, Ramakrishna Mutt Road, Ramakrishna Puram, Udagamandalam - 643 001. ✆ 441395 Fax: 0423-444265 Emal: sanjeevfernhill@rediffmail.com
• **The Nilgiri Woodlands,** Ettiness Road, Udagamandalam - 643 001. ✆ 442551, 442451 Fax: 0423-442530
• **Charring Cross Dasaprakash,** 343/1, Garden Road, Charing Cross, Udagamandalam - 643 001. ✆ 44803, 40184
• **Hotel Dasaprakash,** ✆ 442434
• **Hotel Tamil Nadu,** ✆ 444370
• **Hotel Sowbagya,** ✆ 443353
• **Railway Retiring Rooms,** ✆ 442246
• **Central Park Guest House,** ✆ 444046
• **Seetalakshmi Lodge,** ✆ 442846

With this, we complete the places of tourist interest in Mid-Tamil Nadu and move to the south Tamil Nadu consisting of Dindigul, Madurai, Theni, Tirunelveli, Tuticorin, Ramanathapuram, Virudhunagar and Kanyakumari districts.

Dindigul
(The City of Locks)

Dindigul is the district headquarters now. Formerly it was part of Madurai district. Dindigul played a strategic role during the colonial period. Tipu Sultan wielded this fort under Wodeyar period, he strengthened the Dindigul fort and trained an excellent army which stood him in good stead during the Carnatic War. The fort on the Dindigul hills was built by Muthu Krishnappa Nayaka who hailed from the Madurai Nayaka clan. This district is number one in the production of flowers and grapes in Tamil Nadu. The Dindigul locks are world famous. It is also famous for tobacco and silk sarees especially the Chinnalappatti (artificial) silk saree. Kodaikanal, the 2nd important hill station and Palani temple which is next to Tirupathi in generating revenue are other highlights of this district. It was originally a Jain settlement and the Jains who stayed on the mountain had beds made of rock for their use. Hence, the place came to be known as (dindu - bed, kal - rock) Dindigul .

How to get there?

Dindigul is very well connected by national highways to all the important towns of India. It is 430 kms from Chennai. Buses are available from Chennai, Madurai, and Trichirappalli to Dindigul. It is also having a rail link in the Chennai-Madurai chord line and can be easily reached. Besides, many omnibuses and private transport go to Dindigul from Chennai and other places. Local transport is available to all the places in and around Dindigul. The nearest airport is at Madurai (62 kms), from where Indian Airlines operate flights to Trichy, Chennai and Coimbatore. Recently, it has been linked to the broad gauge line from Chennai to Kanyakumari via Erode and Karur.

Places to see in and around Dindigul

Dindigul : There is a fort on the hills visible from the town. It was built by the Nayaks of Madurai and strengthened by Tipu Sultan. It is now in heavy ruins and practically there is nothing left in the fort except a magazine built with mud and bricks which remains unplastered. Even the stone beds of the Jains could not be found now. Only heaps of rubble could be seen exposing the fury and revenge of the colonial rulers who vowed to destroy all the forts in the southern part of Tamil Nadu which did not bow down to them posing a stiff resistance. The ruins of a temple also could be seen. The Mariamman temple that was on the hill has been shifted down. Even today, people throng there to worship the Goddess. The Abirami Amman Temple is also famous.

Tadikombu : It is about 8 kms north of Dindigul. There is a temple here dedicated to Sundararaja Perumal possessing exquisite sculptures, monolithic pillars 12 ft high – all of excellent workmanship. Though carved in one stone, they present several designs. Garuda, Rudhrathandava, Kali, Chakkarathalwar, Vaikuntanatha, Rama mounted on Hanuman – all make the onlooker spellbound. The hill of 250 ft height 'called Anaimalai' looks like a recumbent elephant (Elephant Hill). At the bottom is the temple of Narasimha Perumal built by Paranthaka Chola I. South-west of this shrine is a cave temple. The deities and other figures are cut out of solid rock. Farther off are relics of a Jain monastery with Tirthankaras on a boulder. The boulder is quite astonishing–precariously over-heading and forming a cave. Besides several Tirthankara figures vatteluthu inscriptions are also found here. A pool filled with water is pointed out as the eye of the reclining elephant.

Gandhigram University : It is a rural university 15 kms from Dindigul near Ambathurai railway station. Named after the father of the nation Mahatma Gandhi, it was inaugurated by Pandit Jawaharlal Nehru. The university is located in a spacious area covering 300 acres. Rural demography, rural development, foreign and Indian languages and rural upliftment are the main subjects taught. It is a central university and the Vice President of India is the ex-officio Chancellor of this university.

Rajakaliamman Temple : This famous temple is located 22 kms from

Dindigul on the Palani-Dindigul-Madurai road near Kannivadi.The place is called Thethuppatti. The story goes that the guardian-deity of Madurai named Madurapathi shifted here from Madurai after it was partially burnt by Kannagi's curse who lost her husband as the king gave him capital punishment without proper enquiry, deciding him to be a thief. It is also said that one of the 18 siddhars Bogar did penance here before making the idol of Palani Andavar in 'Navapashanam'. The presiding deity Rajakaliamman is seen with a sceptre in Her hand. Besides the principal deity, there are sanctums for Bogar, Anjaneya, Navagrahas, Ayyanar and eight-headed serpent called Ashta Nagu. The peculiarity of this temple is, there are two sanctums of Navagrahas, one in the usual way and the other in the Kochara style i.e. the Navagrahas are placed in the constellations they are at present staying on date. With the result we can see two or three planets of the zodiac in one 'House' or 'Graha' (constellation) according to their wandering positions. Navagraha Santhi Yagam is performed here. Sri Chakra which wards off the evil eye is also available here. On Tamil New Year Day (April), there is a flower festival. The Siddhar festival is celebrated on 18th of Adi (August). Besides, Navarathri is also celebrated here. People throng this temple in large numbers. Town buses ply from Dindigul to this place.

Gopinathaswamy Temple : Popularly known as Kopanaswamy Koil, this temple is also at Kannivadi about a km from Rajakali Amman temple. It is on the top of a hill called Varahagiri. It is also called Harikesa Parvatham or Kannivadi hills. A flight of steps leads to the temple. There is a beautiful idol of Lord Krishna called Gopinatha in the sanctum. Though the idol is about 2½ ft., its grace and beauty can't be described by words. This temple is considerably older than the other one.

Palani : Palani the most important temple of Tamil Nadu which is second only to Balaji temple of Tirupathi is about 68 kms from Dindigul. It is dedicated to Lord Muruga here called Dhandayuthapani as He just has a staff in His hand. The idol installed by Bogar one of the 18 siddhars is made of Navapashana - 9 medicinal herbs that have curative powers and together a panacea. Hence the abluted water of this idol is supposed to be a cure for all diseases. The temple is on a steep rocky hill 450 ft high at the mouth of the Vaiyapuri valley. It is a major pilgrim centre and each day is a festive day here. A winding flight of steps leads to the Palani Andavar shrine. There is also the elephant path through which elephants go up, which is easier to climb than the steps. An electrically operated winch is also available to go up. Palani Andavar is known as Palani Babha to the Muslims since the deity here is an Andi (Fakir). There is a shrine for Bogar who installed the idol here. 'Panchamirtham' a mixture of Sirumalai plantains, honey, sugar, dates etc. is offered to Lord Muruga and after ablution, the 'Panchamirtham' is distributed. Another important Abhisekam is the pouring of sacred ash. The deity looks beautiful with the ash covering His body. Tonsure and carrying of Kavadi (a balance held on the shoulder with hanging basket filled with offerings like milk, rose water, flowers and sandal etc.) are performed as vows by devotees. One can find the place full of tonsured heads smeared on with sandal paste.

Nearby are its constituent temples Avinankudi where Lord Muruga as a child is seated on His mount Peacock. The place is also known as Thiru Avinankudi. It is one of the six abodes of Lord Muruga called Arupadai Veedu. Perianayaki temple is also nearby where one can witness rare pieces of sculpture especially that of Uchchimakali. Since Palani is a pilgrim centre one can always find enormous crowd of devotees from all over India.

Where to Stay at Palani?

STD Code : 04545

- **Hotel Ganapathi,** Adivaram. ✆ : 42294
- **Rajalakshmi Hotel,** ✆ : 43313
- **S.K.N.Lodge,** Dindigul Road. ✆ : 43237
- **New Thiruppur Lodge,** Adivaram. ✆ : 42303
- **Hotel Subham,** Adivaram Road. ✆ : 42672
- **Sitaram Lodge,** ✆ : 42856
- **Hotel Karpagam,** Adivaram Road, ✆ : 42544
- **Modern Home,** Railway Junction Road. ✆ : 42376
- **Hotel Tamil Nadu (Near the Winch),** ✆ : 41156

Kodaikanal : It is Dindigul's pride to have this beautiful hill station – the princess of hill stations – included in the district. It is about 60 kms from Dindigul and 120 kms from Madurai. Of all the three major hill stations of Tamil Nadu — Ooty, Kodaikanal and Yercaud–it is definitely the most beautiful and unlike Ooty does not warrant heavy woollen clothes during winter. It is located on the western crest of the Palani hills amidst thickly wooded slopes, precipitous rocky outcrops, waterfalls, fragrant and colourful flowers with astonishing viewpoints that is incomparable to any place in India. Unlike Ooty where you have to travel long distances to see the places of tourist interest, here you can visit all the places within walking distance. This is a nice place not only to escape the heat of the tropical summer and a perennial place of relaxation.

Kodaikanal means a cool resting place in summer (Kodai). The hill is of 7000 ft height (2133m) and was discovered by the Madurai American missionary around 1820. The erstwhile collector of Madurai Vere Leving constructed several roads and dug the lake. The climate is quite ideal for blossoms to bloom and the Pambar stream provides excellent water. One of the world's oldest solar observatories (1899) is also located here.

How to get there?

There is no rail link to this hill station. Those who come by rail have to get down at Kodaikanal Road railway station on the Chennai-Madurai line and take buses from there. Umpteen buses ply to Kodaikanal from Madurai which is 120 kms away. From Trichy also buses are available via Dindigul. It is well connected by roads to Palani, Pollachi, Valparai, Dindigul and other places. Private vehicles and taxis are also available.

Places to See

Kodai Lake : The lake skirted by a 6.4 kms road is the chief attraction. This artificial lake was dug in 1820 by the erstwhile collector of Madurai, Mr. Vele Leving. It is a star-shaped lake spread over 24 hectares. Boating and fishing are allowed. The lake glitters like sapphire embedded in emerald green. It is nice experience to stroll along the road or to row a pleasure boat.

Bryant Park : It is on the eastern side of the lake. A well laid-out park with exotic and native flowers, hybrid varieties etc. The flowers are even cut and exported. The annual horticultural show is held here in May.

The Solar Observatory : This is one of the oldest observatories in the world that came into being in 1899. The solar observatory is being used to observe sunspots and their behaviour. Solar Physics, Astronomy and Meteorology are the main concerns. It is about 850 ft higher than the lake.

Coaker's Walk : It is about a km from the lake. It runs along a steep slope on the southern side of the hill. It is a semi-circular beautiful path overlooking the plains. The view from here is simply captivating. The distant plains appear to be a dream land.

Kurinji Andavar Temple : Kurinji is the name of a flower of the hills. That is why in Tamil, the mountainous region is called Kurinji. It is a small bush and blooms once in 12 years. The flowers are a delicate mauve and during the flowering season the hill sides look completely mauve and look like a mauve-tinted fairy land. Near the Prospect Point is the Kurinji Andavar temple. The presiding deity is Lord Muruga just like Lord Dandayuthapani of Palani. The site for the temple was picked by a Ceylonese named Sri Ponnambalam Ramanathan simply because of the visibility of Palani 60 kms away and 6000ft below. One can also get a glimpse of the Vaigai dam which is 3.2 kms from here.

Telescope House : Two telescopes are erected in two different viewpoints in Kodaikanal to have a clear view of the plains and valleys. One is near the Kurinji Andavar temple and the other is at Coaker's Walk. Entrance fee has to be paid to look through them.

Green Valley Viewpoint : It is about 5.5 kms from the lake and near the Golf Club. It commands a beautiful view of the entire Vaigai dam.

The Pillar Rocks : 3 massive granite rocks about 400 ft high standing abreast on an edge by the Coaker's Walk are called the Pillar Rocks. The sight is quite enchanting. It is about 7.5 kms from the lake and a nice road passing through a charming greenery takes you there.

Waterfalls : Fairy Falls, Silver Cascade, Glen Falls and Bear Shola Falls are the main falls that serve as good picnic spots. Bear Shola Falls is about 1.5 km from the lake and can be reached by a picturesque ragged path. Silver Cascade is on the ghat road to Madurai 8 kms from Kodaikanal. The other falls are also within walking distance from the lake. They are beautiful and charming as their names indicate.

Dolphin's Nose : It is 8 kms from the lake and is a plateau with steep chasms on either side. The yawning chasms below is quite breathtaking and dizzy. A thrill passes through the veins that makes one tremble for a while.

The Perumal Peak : It is a trekkers' paradise, situated 11 kms from Kodaikanal. Its height is 2400 metres. It is a day's trip on foot and one feels little strenuous as the path is quite bewitching and absorbing with beautiful sceneries all through. The actual climb begins at a point called Neutral Saddle.

Berijam Lake : This lake is beyond Pillar Rocks at a distance of 21 kms. It supplies drinking water to Periakulam town. It is a fine picnic spot offering picturesque scenery.

Kukkai Cave : About 40 kms from Kodaikanal is this natural cave where cavemen dwelt..It is a nice camping centre with ample scope for trekking.

Shenbaganur Museum : Located

about 5.5 kms from Kodaikanal is this museum devoted to the flora and fauna of the hills. The museum is being run by the Sacred Heart College, a seminary founded in 1895. Some of the archaeological remains are also exhibited here. It is a must for every visitor as it enlightens on subjects very interesting to hilly habitat.

Orchidorium : This is also maintained by the Sacred Heart College. It is one of the best of its kind and contains about 300 species of orchids.

Important Telephone Numbers

- Astrophysical Observatory ✆ : 41336
- Office of the Sub-collector ✆ : 40588
- Govt. Hospital ✆ : 41292
- T.V. Relay Monitor ✆ : 41026
- Inspector of Police ✆ : 40262

Where to Stay?

- **The Carlton,** Lake Road, Kodaikanal-624 101. ✆ 40056, 40071, Fax: 04542-41170, Email: carlton@krahejahospitality.com
- **Paradise Inn,** Paradise Compound, Laws Ghat Road, Kodaikanal - 624 101. ✆ 41075, 41175, Fax: 04542-41024
- **Hotel J's Heritage,** P.T. Road, Near Seven Roads, Kodaikanal - 624 101. ✆ 41323, Fax: 04542-40693, Email: jaherit@md5.vsnl.net.in
- **Hill Country Holiday Resorts,** Attuvampatti P.O., Kodaikanal - 624 101. ✆ 40949/45/63, Fax: 04542-40947, Email: hillctry@md3.vsnl.net.in
- **Hilltop Towers,** Club Road, Kodaikanal - 624 101. ✆ 40413, 42253-54, Fax: 04542-40415, Email: httowers@md3.vsnl.net.in
- **Hotel Jewel,** 7, Road Junction, Kodaikanal - 624 101. ✆ 41029, 41185, Fax: 04542 - 40518, Email: glentravels@vsnl.com
- **Hotel Kodai International,** 17/328, Lawsghat Road, Kodaikanal - 624 101. ✆ 45190-92, Fax: 04542-40753, Email: hki@vsnl.net
- **Somam Apartments,** Fernhill Road, Kodaikanal - 624 101. ✆ 40562, 40731, 40421
- **Hotel Tamil Nadu,** Fern Hills Road. ✆ 41336
- **Valley View,** Post Office Road. ✆ 40181
- **Hotel Astoria,** Near bus stand. ✆ 40624
- **Hotel Sivapriya,** Convent Road. ✆ 41144
- **Hotel Jayaraj Annexe,** Bazaar Road. ✆ 40178
- **Garden Manor,** Lake Road. ✆ 40461
- **Sterling Holiday Resorts,** ✆ 40313

Sivagangai

(The Land of Marudhu Pandyas)

Sivagangai is the land of Marudhu Pandyas who opposed the colonial power with patriotic fervour. They were a nightmare to the British who in the guise of traders grabbed the whole of India and founded an empire here. Had there been many Marudhus, the history of India would have been different from what it turned out to be. Sivagangai is now the headquarters of the district. It was formed out of Ramanathapuram as a separate district in 1985.

How to get there?

It is 531 kms from Chennai on Chennai-Rameswaram metre gauge main line and can be reached by train via Chidambaram, Mayiladuthurai, Thanjavur, Trichy, Pudukkottai and Karaikudi. It is connected by road to all the important towns in Tamil Nadu. Bus services are available from Chennai, Thanjavur, Trichy, Madurai and Rameswaram. Private carriages, omnibuses and taxis could also take you there from anywhere in Tamil Nadu. The nearest airport is at Madurai which can be reached by bus. From Madurai, flights are available to Chennai, Coimbatore and Trichy.

Places to see

The Sivaganga Palace : The old royal palace, besides being magnificent, is full of historical association.

Tondi : Tondi was a maritime trade port several centuries before the first century A.D. It is also an ideal location for sea-bathing and boating.

Karaikudi : This town is 41kms from Sivagangai. Magnificent mansions have been built here by Chettiars — a merchant class known for their wealth and magnificence. Though the owners have left, still these palatial wonders with beautifully carved woodwork, stone and mortar works are amazing and attract visitors. The Alagappa University founded by Dr. Alagappa Chettiar is functioning here.

Pillayarpatti : It is 12 kms from Karaikudi on the national highway proceeding to Thiruppathur. There is an old Ganesa or Pillayar temple. It is a beautiful cave temple of the Pandya period exhibiting fine architecture. The presiding deity, Pillayar is a bas-relief sculpture on the wall of the cave and named as Karpaga Vinayagar. It is different from other pillayar idols in having only two hands instead of the usual four, besides there are no weapons in His hands, quite different from the others. It is said to have been the earliest image that would have been made when Pillayar worship was introduced in Tamil Nadu. This is also attested by the inscriptions of this temple. During the 12th century, this temple came under the administration of the Nagarathar community and the temple is still in their hands. Siva is always represented with four arms but queerly in this temple He is found with two arms. There are vatteluthu inscriptions in this temple dating back to 7th century A.D. The mandapam has the sculpture of Ashta Lakshmi. The Vinayaga Chathurthi day (August-September) and January 1st are very famous in this temple. Lakhs of people visit and worship Lord Pillayar here on these days. A giant size Kozhukkattai (Modhaga) is made weighing several kilos and offered to the deity on the Vinayaka Chathurthi day. It takes 3 or 4 days for steaming the Kozhukkattai.

Kundrakkudi : It is hardly 2 km from Pillayarpatti. This temple dedicated to Lord Muruga is also a rock-cut temple of the Pandya period. It is on a hill called Mayuragiri and the hill is shaped like a peacock. Lord Muruga the presiding deity with six faces and twelve hands is mounted on a peacock atop the hill which could be climbed over a flight of steps. The vibudhi (sacred ash) of this temple is believed to have curative powers. Marudhu Brothers of Siva gangai were patrons of this temple and have done improvements to it. In another cave, the eight-armed dancing Nataraja is sheltered. Another attraction is the very rare image of Gaundaku Vishnu.

Thenithangal : This ancient rock-cut shrine is also near Pillayarpatti. The presiding deity is Veera Narayana Perumal. Inside the sanctum, images of Garuda, Pradyumna, Nila-devi, Usha-devi and Jambagavathi are beautifully sculptured.

Madurai

(The Athens of the East)

Madurai which is usually called 'Nanmadakkoodal' in Tamil literature is an ancient city more than 4000 years old. Koodal means assembly and as all the 3 Tamil Academies (Sangams) were established in Madurai, it got the name Koodal. Literary evidences prove that the first Madurai was devoured by the sea and what we now see is the second Madurai founded by the Pandya king Kulasekara in 6th century B.C. The culture of Tamil Nadu is woven with the history of Madurai in all aspects–history, religion, art, legend, polity, learning and so on. It was the city of elites and learned men, so it is aptly called the 'Athens of the East.'

The name Madurai is associated with 'Maduram' meaning nectar. The legend is that when Lord Siva came here to marry Devi Meenakshi, few drops of nectar fell from His locks and therefore named as Madurapuri, the land of nectar which was shortened later as Madurai.

From the Sangam Age, it was the capital of the Pandyas and except for a brief spell under the Cholas till the Muslim invasion by Malik Kafur (1290-1320 A.D.), it was ruled by the Pandyas. Afterwards, it came under Vijayanagar rule and their governors, the Nayaks from 1371. The Nayaks ruled for over 200 years and their reign is the golden age when Madurai was at its height in art, architecture and learning. They embellished Madurai with temples and buildings, including the Meenakshi temple, which are landmarks of the city. Madurai now is the 2nd largest city of Tamil Nadu very much modern and progressive.

How to get there?

Madurai has an airport and flights from Chennai, Mumbai, Trichy and Coimbatore arrive here. It is very well connected by roads to all major cities in India. Buses ply from Chennai, Thanjavur, Dindigul, Palani, Rameswaram, Tirunelveli and Kanyakumari to Madurai. It is linked to all the places in Tamil Nadu by both the metre gauge and broad gauge of the Southern Railway. Bus services are available to all the places in and around Madurai. Taxis and private carriages are also available in plenty to take you to all the places of tourist importance.

Places to see in Madurai City

Meenakshi Temple : It is in the midst of the city. The entire city is planned keeping the temple as its core like a lotus. The city is planned according to the silpa canons and the other city that has the same basis is Kanchipuram famously known as 'Nagareshu Kanchi' in Sanskrit. The temple is an important landmark and nucleus of the life of the city. The temple has 11 gopurams and the tallest of them is at the southern portal rising to a height of 200 ft. This portion is exclusively dedicated to Goddess Meenakshi. The shrine is usually entered from Vittavasal Street the entrance of which is adorned by the Ashtalakshmi (eight forms of Goddess Lakshmi) Mandapam. Scenes of Kumara Sambhava and the marriage of Goddess Meenakshi with Sundareswara are painted on the ceiling. At the entrance are the statues of Subramanya and Vinayaka and on the passage is the beautiful sculpture of Siva and Meenakshi as a huntress. An exquisite brass-faced doorway gifted by the rulers of Sivaganga is the inlet to the mandapam lined with sculptures of Siva in various poses. It leads to the Pottramarai tank with arcades all around. The corridors of the tank display the 64 Leelas called Thiruvilaiyadalgal of Siva. The doors in the shrine display poses of Bharatha Natyam. The temple having been built in several epochs reveal different styles of architecture. There is a musical pillar near the north tower corridor which emits the seven musical notes when struck.

The thousand-pillared mandapam is a veritable museum of Dravidian art and architecture. Goddess Saraswathi arrests our attention in Her demeanour, folds of dress and the grace with which Her fingers play the instrument Veena. Thirumalai Nayak has carved the Ardhanari idol (both male and female in left and right halves) that spellbinds the onlooker. In Kambathadi Mandapam, Agni Veerabadra and Agora Veerabadra speak volumes of their valour and fiercesome look. The wedding of

Meenakshi with all the important participants in the marriage is a lively sculpture each one expressing apt feelings in one's face – Siva with His magnanimity, Meenakshi with Her coyness, Vishnu with His grace, Malayatwaja Pandya with His joy, Brahma with rapt attention in observing the rites and the others looking on without winking their eyes in gaiety. All these make one feel that he/she is a participant in the event.

Lord Nataraja dances here in a different style instead of raising His left leg up, He plays it vice versa. The dancing hall is called Velliambalam and the idol is plated with silver.

The Temple Museum is housed in the 1000-pillared mandapam. There are 985 richly carved pillars each one surpassing the other in elegance. The Vasantha Mandapam or Pudumandapam has more scenes of the wedding ceremony. The spring festival is held here in April-May.

Oonjal Mandapam : It is on the western end of the tank called Pottramarai Kulam. There is a swing on which Goddess Meenakshi and Her consort Lord Siva are seated and worshipped every Friday. Adjacent is the Kilikoottu Mandapam or hall of parrots having beautiful sculptures with caged parrots that chant the name of Meenakshi.

The Madurai temple is a twin temple complex and Meenakshi Sundareswar temple is across the courtyard. The corridor outside the shrine has the stump of a tree under which Indira (the head of Devas) is said to have worshipped a Lingam.

Out of the 12 gopurams, the tallest four stand at the outer walls. The southern gopuram, the tallest of them is the most spectacular and has over 1500 sculptures. From its top one can have a panoramic view of the city. The Rayagopuram on the eastern side is still unfinished having a base of 174 sq.ft. and had it been completed it would have been the tallest (The unfinished tower with only the base and initial super- structure is called Rayagopuram and the finished one is called Rajagopuram). The eight smaller gopurams are within the compounds of the twin temples. There are few temples in India which share the grandeur of this twin temple complex. It is so huge that newcomers will be upset to find their way proper, hence, it is better to go with a guide or with a person who had already been there several times.

The Mariamman Teppakulam: This tank is also known as Vandiyur Teppakulam and is about 5 kms east of Meenakshi temple. It occupies an area equal to the twin-temple complex. This tank was also built by Thirumalai Nayakar. In the middle is an island with a temple for Ganesa. The tank was created due to digging of earth to make bricks for the Thirumalai Nayak palace. It is 1000 ft long and 950 ft wide and four white turrets border the garden of the island. The float festival of the Meenakshi Amman temple is held here in January-February.

The Thirumalai Nayak Mahal: This is the palace of Thirumalai Nayak, just a km away from the temple. This Indo-Saracenic marvel was constructed in 1523A.D. It has pillars of granite cased with mortar and supporting arches which present a majestic view. The corner of the east face has towers. On three sides of a quadrangle 250 ft. by 180 ft. are corridors with arches supporting roof. The most remarkable part of the structure is the Swarga Vilasam or the audience hall.

Its dome is 60 ft in diameter and 70 ft in height. Such a lofty dome stands firm without any support revealing the engineering skill of its builders. Circling this is the zenana from where the royal ladies witnessed the durbar. It is a fine example of the architectural style of the Nayaks.

It is open to public from 9 a.m. to 1 p.m. and from 2 p.m. to 5 p.m.

Entrance fee is Re.1/- per head.

Sound and light shows on the life of Thirumalai Nayak and the story of Silappathikaram (one of the 5 major epics of Tamil) are held every day.

Timings: English – 18.45 hrs
Tamil – 20.15 hrs

Fee : Rs.5, Rs.3 & Rs.2

Koodal Azhagar Temple : Lord Vishnu in Madurai is called Koodal Azhagar and His temple is as ancient as the Meenakshi temple. Though tall Gopurams are absent, the Vimana called Ashtanga stands in the centre with diminishing tiers under which is the sanctum. Ferguson, the connoisseur of arts, estimates that it surpasses anything of its kind to be found in South India. The base has excellent carvings. There are three sanctums where the deities are seen in sitting, standing and recumbent postures one above the other.

The Tamakam : It is a beautiful relic of Thirumalai Nayak resembling his palace, the Mahal. The Lotus Hall here has a dome with ceiling, shaped like an inverted lotus. It was the Nayak's summer palace.

Goripalayam Mosque : There is a large mosque in Goripalayam containing two tombs of two Delhi Sultans of the Madurai sultanate. The amazing thing about it is that the dome which is 70 ft. in diameter and 20 ft. in height is made of a single block of stone. It is said that it was built by Thirumalai Nayak for his muslim subjects.

The Gandhi Museum : It contains a picture gallery, a gallery of relics, a Khadi and Village Industries section and a South Indian handicrafts section. It is located in an old palace.

Timings : 10 a.m to 1 p.m &
2 p.m to 5.30 p.m.

Phone : 531060

Places around Madurai

Thiruparankundram : One of the abodes of Lord Subramanya is located 8 kms south of Madurai. The six abodes are known as Arupadai Veedu. Out of the six, two are near Madurai, the other Padaiveedu is **Pazhamudirsolai**. It is a cave temple. It is known from the Sangam times and one of the Sangam poets Nakkiran has sung a long poem about this temple called Thirumurugatrupadai. As in the case of other temples, new structures have been added later on. There are a series of mandapams one above the other in elevation in this temple. There is a shrine dedicated to Nakkirar. The front mandapam contains the marriage of Deivayanai and the sculptures of Thirumalai Nayak and Mangammal. In the descent from the mandapam are caves with images of Annapoorna, Varaha Avataram, Narasimha Avataram, Mahalakshmi etc. The Sivathandavam is a masterpiece sculpture of the group and Uma is witnessing it reclining on the bull. The Kudarmugha drum is also seen being beaten by a celestial attendant. The important feature is that Siva is holding the flag of Rishaba in His hand while dancing — a rarity, not to be found elsewhere. Separated by a wall is another group of sculptures with Nandhi standing in bull-head and human-body form beside some sages. About 7 km away is another cave with images of Nataraja, Sivakami, Heramba Ganapathi, dancing Sambandar etc.

Kallazhagar Koil : 21 kms from Madurai is this important Vishnu temple at the foot of a wooded hill. 'Azhagu' in Tamil means beauty and true to its meaning, everything here is a thing of beauty and a joy forever. The main deity is Paramaswami and the itinerant idol is Kallazhagar. It is a beautiful idol made of pure gold. The other temple having a gold idol is at Thiruvananthapuram. Barring these two, no other temple has an idol made of pure gold. The ablution water for this idol is brought from Noobura Gangai - a perennial waterfall 3 kms up on the hill the water of which contains copper and iron minerals. The Vimanam of this temple is called Somaskanda Vimanam (tower over the sanctum) and a unique one of its kind. The Kalyana Mandapam contains sculptures that rival the one at Madurai—the images of Krishna, Rathi, Manmatha, Garuda Vahana, Trivikrama, Lakshmi and Varaha Avatar are really masterpieces in stone. The British contemplated to shift the temple in toto like the one they wanted to shift at Vellore to one of the museums in England, but anyhow the attempt was failed.

Pazhamudir Solai : It is about 4 kms above on the hill. Beautifully situated amidst sylvan surroundings, the temple has to be climbed through thickly shaded woods through which the rays of sun rarely peep in. On the way, there are several perennial springs and beyond the Muruga temple is the Noobura Gangai. It is one of the 6 abodes of Muruga. Lord Muruga stands with His 'Vel' (spear) in His hand. The ruins of a fort built by Thirumalai Nayak can also be seen here.

Thiruvedagam : About 15 kms north-west of Madurai on the left bank of the river Vaigai is the place where Saivite supremacy over the Jains was established by performing Punal Vadam i.e. each contestant will put into the stream sacred palm leaves on which are written hymns and if the palm leaves do not sink or get carried by the running stream but sail upstream the one who set it sail is the winner. The palm leaves of the Jains were carried away by the stream and the palm leaves of Gnanasambandar sailed upstream thus proving Saivite supremacy over the Jains.

Thiruvadhavur : This place is about 9 kms from Melur near Madurai. One of the Saivaite saint Manickavasagar was born here. He was the minister to a Pandya king. He built a temple for Siva with the money he was entrusted to buy horses for the king. A miracle was performed by Siva in which foxes were transformed into horses and after they were taken by the king and sent to the stables they again turned into foxes. The site of the house of His birth is pointed out to visitors.

Madappuram Badrakali Amman Temple : This famous temple visited often by V.I.Ps, cine stars and I.A.S. officers is at Madappuram about 20 kms from Madurai near Thiruppuvanam. It stands on the banks of the river Vaigai on the northern side of Esanar Koil. It is amidst a cool coconut grove. The first idols that greet the visitor here are that of Lord Ayyanar and His horse. The horse with its protruding teeth and bulging eyes and Lord Ayyanar with fierce looks really make one tremble. The horse is of a height of 30 ft which wears a garland of lemons. The devotees pray to the Goddess, the presiding deity of this temple, for creative comforts, promotions in job and for the ruin of their enemies. One curious practice in this temple is to cut a coin and offer it to the deity to get relief from being bullied by the mighty. A gunny bag full of cut coins can be seen here. The presiding deity Badrakali Amman is armed to the teeth and seen standing at the breast of a horse with fierce looks amidst a group of demons-really awe-inspiring.

Vaigai Dam : The dam across the river Vaigai is 69 kms from Madurai. In order to augment water supply, a dam has been constructed across Periar of Kerala state and the water from there is diverted through tunnels to flow into the river Vaigai. The height of the dam is 106 ft and its breadth is 11,657 ft. Its capacity is 58,000 cubic ft. It irrigates about 2½ lakh hectares of land. There is a beautiful garden laid out here. It is a popular picnic spot.

Cumbum Valley : The Cumbum Valley located in the newly formed Theni district could easily be reached from Madurai. The Cumbum valley offers beautiful scenic spots like Kandamanur, Kadamalai Kundu, Mayiladumparai and various streams like Varaha Nadhi, Mullaiyar etc. and various hills and estates. It is really the catchment area of river Vaigai and a beautiful place with frequent drizzles. There are various barrages across the streams and picturesque sceneries greet us everywhere. The chief attractions are the Suruli Falls and Thekkady on the verge of Kerala.

Suruli Falls : It is 128 kms from Madurai on the way to Thekkadi. It is a sacred spot visited by pilgrims on specific days. Of late, it is becoming a picnic spot. Though of lesser height than the Courtallam Falls, the water gushes with great force out of caves. It is a fine place for bathing and arrangements are made for the safety of the bathers. There is a rope rail from Suruli dam to Moonaru for about 50 kms distance for the quick transport of tea leaves from the estates.

Periar Wildlife Sanctuary (Thekkady) : It is on the verge of Kerala about 155 kms from Madurai. The sanctuary is between Tamil Nadu and Kerala. It is formed around Periar reservoir and dam spread over 729.29 sq.km. The animal watchers have to go by a motor boat along the Periar lake and watch them on the hills surrounding the lake. Many animals come for drinking water at various places. Boats can be hired from which the animals could be watched in their natural habitat basking in the sun, adult elephant helping elephant calves to climb the slopes, bathing in the water, preying, frolicking etc. Tigers, elephants, bisons, deers and boars could all be seen by lucky tourists. The most common sight is the elephant herd with elephants of all sizes. The route from Madurai to Kumizhi is itself a picturesque ride through the slopes of western ghats. On entering Kumizhi one can breathe the fragrance of cardamom and other spices that emanates from the estates around. Kumizhi is the border line and from there Thekkady can be reached by a short walk amidst sylvan surroundings.

Buses are available to visit all the places mentioned here from Madurai. Staying at Madurai all these places could be visited.

FESTIVALS

Avani Moolam Festival – August-September.

Float Festival – January-February.

Chitthirai Festival – April-May.

Government Chitthirai Exhibition – April-May.

The dates in each year will vary as the festivals are observed based on the lunar months and not as per the Gregorian calender which is universally followed.

Where to Stay?

- **Taj Garden Retreat,** No. 40. T.P.K. Road, Pasumalai, Madurai - 625 004. ✆ 771601, Fax: 0452-771636, Email: retreat.madurai@tajhotels.com
- **Hotel Madurai Ashok,** Alagarkoil Road, Madurai - 625 002. ✆ 537531, 537675, Fax: 0452-537530 Email: ashokmadu@vsnl.com
- **Hotel International,** 46, West Permaul Maistry St., Madurai - 625 001. ✆ 741552-55, Fax: 0452-740372
- **Hotel Supreme,** 110, West Perumal Maistry St., Madurai - 625 001. ✆ 0452-743151, Fax: 0452-742637, Email: supreme@md3.vsnl.net.in
- **New Arya Bhavan,** 241-A, West Masi Street, Madurai - 625 001. ✆ 740577, 740345, Fax: 0452-744481, Email: 9843010430@bplmobile.com
- **Hotel Tamil Nadu,** Azhagar Koil Road. ✆ 537461.
- **Hotel Tamil Nadu,** West Veli Street, Madurai.
- **Hotel Blue King,** Near airport. ✆ 620511
- **Railway Retiring Rooms,** Railway Station, Rani Mangammal Choultry, (Opp. Railway Station).
- **T.M.Lodge,** 50, West Perumal Maistry St., ✆ 741651
- **Jupiter Rest-house.** ✆ 543786
- **New College House,** Town Hall Road. ✆ 742971
- **Hotel Prem Nivas,** 102, West Perumal Maistry St.. ✆ 742532
- **Hotel Grands Central,** 47-48, West Perumal Maistry Street. ✆ 743940
- **Pandyan Hotel,** Race Course, ✆ 537097
- **Hotel Empee,** 253, Nethaji Road. ✆ 741252
- **Hotel Aarathy,** 9, Perumal Koil West Mada Street, ✆ 731571
- **Hotel Sulochna Palace,** 96, West Perumal Maistry Street, ✆ 741071-3
- **Hotel Dhanamani,** Sunnambukara Street. ✆ 742703
- **Hotel Chentoor,** 106, West Perumal Maistry Street. ✆ 747022
- **Hotel Park Plaza,** 114-115, West Perumal Maistry Street. ✆ 742112
- **Hotel Vijay,** 122, Tirupparankundram Road. ✆ 736321
- **Hotel K.P.S.,** 8-9, West Marret Street. ✆ 741541
- **New Modern Lodge,** 10, Perumal Tank East. ✆ 742797
- **Laxmi Towers,** 40A, Koodalazhagar Perumal Koil South Mada Street. ✆ 732069
- **Hotel Boopathi International,** 16-17, Perumal Tank (E). ✆ 743627
- **Hotel Thilaga,** 111, West Perumal Maistry Street. ✆ 743383
- **Classic Residency,** 14-15, West Marret Street. ✆ 743140
- **Hotel Ramson,** 9, Perumal Tank East. ✆ 743406
- **Ashoka Lodge,** 12, Perumal Theppakulam East, Town Hall Road. ✆ 740282
- **Hotel Gangai,** 41, West Perumal Maistry Street. ✆ 742180
- **Prabhat & Co Lodging,** 15, Perumal Theppakulam. ✆ 740810
- **Kavery Mahal Annexe,** 35-37, Pachai Nachiyamman Koil Street. ✆ 742368
- **Hotel Keerthi (P) Ltd.,** 40, West Perumal Maistry Street. ✆ 741501
- **Hotel Blue King,** Near Airport, ✆ 620511

Besides, there are umpteen lodges and boarding houses in Madurai. Madurai is also famous for open-air catering stalls on pavements after 6 p.m.

Virudhunagar

(The Grocery Town)

Virudhunagar was formerly part of Ramanathapuram district and now a new district and its headquarters. It was under the Pandyas and passed into the Paligars known as 'Palayakararkal' in Tamil. They showed stiff opposition to the colonial supremacy and finally were subdued by the British. Now Virudhunagar is a very big grocery centre in Tamil Nadu and plays a vital role in edible oil business too and a number of cement factories are also located here. It is the birthplace of Kamarajar, popularly known as Kala Gandhi (kala–black), who played a vital role in freedom struggle and at one time became the king-maker of India. The house where he lived is preserved as a monument and memorial. It is 44 kms from Madurai and 536 kms from Chennai.

It can be reached by rail or by bus from Chennai and other important towns. The nearest airport is at Madurai which connects to Coimbatore, Trichy and Chennai.

Aruppukkottai : It is 20 kms from Virudhunagar. It is an important weaving centre and grocery trade centre.

Thiruchuzhi : This place is so-called because it was saved from being sucked into the earth during the deluge. It is 33 kms from Virudhunagar. Several sacred pools are scattered here. This is the birthplace of the great saint Ramana Maharishi.

Sivakasi : It is a town of cottage industries engaged in the manufacture of safety matches and fireworks. It is also famous for litho-printing and calendar manufacture. Out of 3932 match factories more than 80% are located here. There are about 120 litho printing presses located here. It is 25 kms from Virudhunagar.

Srivilliputhur : This is the most important tourist attraction because of the ancient Andal temple. It is the birthplace of Andal, one of the twelve Vaishnavaite saints called Alwars. Alwar means one who is immersed and since they are immersed in Vishnu Bhakti they are called Alwars. It is the 60 metre tower of this temple that has been portrayed in the insignia of the Government of Tamil Nadu. The residence of Perialwar, the foster father of Andal, has now become the Nachiar Koil and the other part of the temple is known as Vadabhadra Sayi temple.

The temple has beautiful sculptures and the delicacy of carving is more dominant in the coiffure of feminine images - Andal's hair style and head ornamentation are a speciality of South India and it is this style on which the sculptors have lavished their skill. The images of Rathi, Swan, Parasakthi, a lady playing the Veena, a warrior brandishing his sword are superb examples of embellishments in stones. The scene of the mutilation of Soorpanaga's nose and breast in the Ramayana has so well been captured by the dextrous hands of the sculptor that it should be seen to be believed of its excellence. The temple is one of the biggest and has beautiful wood carvings. It is 71 kms from Madurai and about 48 kms from Virudhunagar.

Rajapalayam : It is close to the temple town of Srivilliputhur and the coolest place in the district located almost on the western ghats. Rajapalayam dogs are known for their ferocity. It is an industrial centre and famous for teak industry. The Gandhi Kalai Mandram and Library are very popular here. They are the gift of the late Chief Minister of Madras and the Governor of Orissa, Mr. P.K.Kumaraswamy Raja.

Rameswaram

(The Lifeblood of National Integration)

India is a land of variations and multiplicity, the one chain of integration that binds India together is Hinduism. Though the people speak different languages, eat different kinds of food, clothe differently and differ in habits and customs, still they are united by religion and spiritualism. From Varanasi to Rameswaram, a chain of holy shrines unite the Indians into a single entity. The lifeblood of national integration runs thus. For every Hindu, Varanasi or Kasi in the north and Rameswaram, in the south are indispensable. Those who go to Kasi have to consummate their pilgrimage at Rameswaram. The north Indians and south Indians thus emerge as true Indians by this integration.

Rameswaram the holy island is in the district of Ramanathapuram, the land of Sethupathi who sent Swami Vivekananda to the Parliament of Religions held at Chicago. It is 167 kms from Madurai and 666 kms from Chennai. It is sacred for both Vaishnavites and Saivaites. Never ending pilgrims from all quarters of India is the greatness of this place. It is also the seaport from where the ferry to Sri Lanka port Thalaimannar is operated throughout the year barring November and December when the sea turns rough.

How to get there?

Rameswaram is connected by train from Madurai and Chennai. It is also connected by road to all towns and bus services from Chennai, Madurai, Coimbatore and Trichy etc. are available. Train services are operated from Rameswaram terminal to Chennai, Madurai, Coimbatore, Trichy and Thanjavur. The main island is connected by the Pamban bridge. The nearest airport is at Madurai (167 kms) from where flights are available to Chennai, Coimbatore and Trichy.

Places to see in and around Rameswaram

Ramanathaswamy Temple : This temple is the centre of attraction and thousands of pilgrims pour in daily. It is a gem of Dravidian architecture. It is known worldwide for its magnificent corridors running 4000 ft (1220 metres) in length and 30' in breadth lined by massive sculptured pillars. Figures representing elephants lifting their trunks caught between the paws and fangs of rampant lions, hunters and warriors riding on horses or elephants are favourite themes. The temple was built by Sethupathis, the rulers of Ramanathapuram district between 1414 A.D. and 1649 A.D.and it has grown in leaps and bounds to the present stage. The statues of Sethupathis line the corridor at the eastern gate before the Nataraja shrine. Some are found in the Kalyana Mandapam too. They are all lifelike in appearance. The gopuram on the east facing the sea front rises to a height of 126 ft. and is 100 metres away from the sea. Devotees bathe in the sea water here which is considered to be sacred and called Agni Theertham. Sacred pools or Theerthams like this are innumerable in Rameswaram and the pilgrims plunge into them with untiring zeal and devotion. The temple is built at the spot where Rama worshipped Lord Siva after slaying the demon Ravana, king of Lanka, who was a great devotee of Siva. In order to worship Siva, Hanuman was sent to Kailas to bring the Lingam. It so happened that Hanuman could not return before the arrival of the auspicious hour; so Sita Herself moulded a Lingam for Rama. When Hanuman arrived later, He was consoled and the Lingam brought by Him was given precedence over Ramanatha and made to worship first before the worship of Ramanatha by the devotees.

Kothandaramaswamy Temple: This Vishnu shrine is located 18 kms away on the southern tip of the island called Dhanushkodi. This temple is the only structure that survived the 1964 cyclone which washed away the rest of Dhanushkodi. It can be reached by road from Rameswaram and buses ply to this place. It was the place where Vibishana the brother of Ravana is said to have surrendered to Rama. The temple has beautiful idols of Rama,

Sita, Lakshmana, Hanuman and Vishnu. On the very tip of Dhanushkodi is a sacred pool - a lovely bathing ghat.

The Gandhamathana Parvatham (Hillock) : It is in the north-west of the island and the most elevated point of the island. It is a two-storeyed structure with a ruined fort. Hanuman is said to have leapt from this point across the sea to reach Lanka. The feet of Rama is in the centre of the lower storey. It is also known as Ekantha Rameswaram and contains handsome idols of Rama, Sita and Lakshmana. Here, Rama is seen raising one of His arms. From this elevated place, one can have an excellent view of the whole island.

Coral Reefs : The coral reefs of Rameswaram is another attraction mainly for marine biologists, who throng these islands for research and observation. There are sandy beaches fringed by coconut palms and swaying tamarind trees. A wide variety of sea creatures live in these reefs. The Kurusadai Islands on the west and the Pamban bridge are ideal places of exploration. The Gulf of Mannar has been declared as a bio-sphere reserve and is being developed as an ecologically sensitive area. It is about 20 kms from Rameswaram via Mandapam. The permit of the Fisheries Department is necessary to go there.

Adam's Bridge : It is 26 kms at the eastern edge of Rameswaram. It is also called Thiruvanai, Adhisethu, Nalasethu and Rama's bridge. This is formed like a bridge between Dhanushkodi and Thalaimannar. It is said that Rama crossed this way with his Vanara sena (army of monkeys) to Lanka. Till 1480 A.D. this was a land route to Lanka. Series of cyclones have washed away the continuous stretch and broken them into islands. Most of them are submerged under 3 to 4 ft water. The sandy banks of these islands quickly change and some may even vanish. There are at present about 19 islands on the route interspersed with gaps the longest of them being 19 kms in length. They are called 'Theedai' by the local fishermen. In some of them shrubs can be seen. The depth of the sea here is between 7 ft and 11 ft only. Hence, big boats cannot reach there. Swift sea currents flow in the canals between the islands. This place is full of different varieties of fish and they are being caught only by using small country boats. A lot of birds also can be found here and some varieties of migratory birds too throng here.

Mandapam : It is the end of the mainland from where people have to proceed for the island of Rameswaram either by road, rail or by boat. A boat-ride to Kurusadai Island can be arranged from here. The Indo–Norwegian Fisheries Project is located here. During the colonial period, this was the quarantine camp for passengers proceeding to Ceylon.

Thiruppullani : It is 14 kms from Rameswaram. It is a Vishnu shrine. It is also called Dharbasayanam as here Rama took rest on a couch of grass. Lord Rama here is seen lying on a couch of grass. Thiruvadanai, Pularanyam, Adhisethu and Ratnaharam are the other names of this place. The presiding deity is Adhi Jagannatha Perumal who was worshipped by Rama before launching His Lanka expedition. The temple has a gopuram and after crossing it one reaches the sanctum of Goddess Padmasini Thayar. A pipal tree is the tree of this place and we can see it behind the sanctum. There are over hundred Nagas (serpents) in stones around the tree. After this, one has to go to the sanctum of Adhi Jagannatha. Following this is the sanctum of Rama lying on the grass couch, three stems of lotus branch from His naval and on each of them are seated Brahma, Siva and Moon. At the feet of Rama, Sugabrahmar, Charapar and Brigu Maharishis are seated. In the mandapam is a sculpture in which Vibishana, the king of Lanka and his Devi worship Vishnu. It is a masterpiece which no tourist should miss. The temple was built by the Pandyas, Vanadhirayas and Sethupathis. Life-size statues of Sethupathis could also been seen here. Those who do the pilgrimage to Rameswaram visit the temple too.

Devipattinam : This place is also known as Navapashanam. This coastal village is 15 kms from Rameswaram and there is a temple here dedicated to Devi. It is the place where Mahishasura was slayed by Goddess Durga Devi. Rama is said to have set up stones here for the planets. Besides, there are two temples here, one dedicated to Thilakesava and the other to Jagannatha. The beach is full of multicoloured shells and corals of varied forms thrown by the waves of the sea. Hence, it came to be called also as Ratnakara Kshetram.

Ervadi : It is 21 kms from Rameswaram. The tomb of Ibrahim Syed Aulia is located here. It is visited by Muslim pilgrims from other states and countries like Sri Lanka, Malaysia and Singapore. The annual festival is celebrated in December. It is 8 kms from Keezhakarai.

Ramanathapuram : This is the district headquarters and 55 kms from Rameswaram. The Sethupathis ruled their territory from here. This place is also known as Sethupeetam. A fort is at the centre of this town and inside the fort is Ramalinga Vilasam, the palace of the Sethupathis. It is built in Moorish style with Byzantine arches. Murals of historic scenes adorn the walls. Inside is a crude platform surrounded by a square block of stone on which the first Sethupathi is said to have been crowned by Sri Rama Himself. The successors sat there as the viceroys of Rama. The tomb of the philosopher-saint Thayumanava Swamigal is also in the town. Both the palace and the tomb are worth visiting.

Kanchirankulam : This is about 35 kms from Rameswaram. A water-bird sanctuary is located here. Migratory water fowls from far-off places visit this place from November to February.

Valinokkam : It is a seaside village, 90 kms from Rameswaram. The beach is verdant with natural scenery. The sea here is very calm. It is an ideal location for sea bathing.

Nainar Koil : It is 14 kms from Ramanathapuram on the western side. A dumb Muslim girl recovered her speech by the grace of Lord Siva here. The Muslims call Him Nainar–'Father', hence the name Nainar Koil. This temple is hailed and visited by Muslims.

Tourist Information

- Tourist Office, 14 East Car St, Rameswaram. ✆: 21371
- Tourism Information Centre, Railway Station Compound. ✆ : 21373
- Temple Information Centre, inside the temple, east side, Ramanathaswamy temple. ✆ : 21246

SHOPPING

Local handicrafts include sea-shell articles, palm leaf articles, corals and conches.

Where to stay in Rameswaram

- **Hotel Tamil Nadu (TTDC)** ✆ : 21277 Rameswaram ✆ : 21064 to 69 Fax : 04575-21070
- **Hotel Maharaja,** ✆ : 21271
- **Hotel Venkatesh,** ✆ : 21296
- **Lodge Sandhya,** ✆ : 21329
- **Hotel Chola** ✆ : 21307
- **Hotel Tamil Nadu (Mandapam)** ✆ : 41512

Festivals in Rameswaram

Thai Amavasai - January
Maha Shivarathri - February-March
Thirukalyanam - (July-August)
Mahalaya Amavasai - (September)

Thoothukudi

(The Gateway of Tamil Nadu)

Tuticorin is properly called Thoothukudi in Tamil. As Mumbai is the Gateway of India, Thoothukudi is the Gateway of Tamil Nadu. It is a major seaport in India. It is also called Pearl City as pearl fishing is a major occupation and the oysters yield a fine quality of pearl. It is a major industrial centre too. SPIC fertilizer plant, a heavy water plant, a thermal power station, chemical factories etc. are all located here. It is also a major salt producing centre in Tamil Nadu. It was made into a new district from Tirunelveli and is the district headquarters. It is 48 kms from Tirunelveli.

How to get there?

It is linked to Tirunelveli by road and rail. From Chennai you can reach by train directly to Thoothukudi. Thoothukudi is also linked to other places by road. It will be convenient to visit all the places in this district by making Tirunelveli as the headquarters and staying there one can visit all the places around Tirunelveli and Thoothukudi.

Tiruchendur : It is 56 kms from Tirunelveli and can be reached by train and by buses. It is the most important tourist attraction in Thoothukudi district. It is one of the six abodes of Lord Muruga called Arupadai Veedu. Of them, this is the only one standing on level ground, the others are on hills or elevated places. It is the place where Lord Muruga offered His thanksgiving prayers to His father Lord Siva for gaining victory over the demon Surapadman by slaying him. The temple is on the edge of the sea and the main deity has been cut on a rock lying on the shores. The idol of the Urchavar or festival-deity is kept in a separate shrine facing the opposite direction. This idol was recovered from the sea by a local chief called Vadamalai and installed there. The silver vessels presented to the shrine by the erstwhile collector of this district, Lushington expose the devotion of foreigners too. Kumarakuruparar (17th century A.D.) the famous saint and poet who was originally dumb got his power of speech in this temple and sung hymns on the deity.

Srivaikuntam and Alwarthirunagari : These two Vaishnavaite shrines are on the way to Tiruchendur from Tirunelveli. Srivaikuntam is also known as Kailasapuram and has in the Nataraja shrine, 8 artistically carved pillars. The most famous is the Kallapiran, the festival- deity and the presiding deity is called Vaikuntanatha. On the 6th day of the Tamil month Chitthirai (April), the sun rays fall on the main deity as token of worship. The idol is most exquisitely carved with club in hand. Lions, Yalis and Elephants are carved in the pillars of the mandapam. The temple served as a fort during the patriotic war of Kattabomman with the British.

In the north of the town is a mud enclosure of 10 ft high running round with a gate in the middle. The women of this fort never stir beyond the wall. The outside world is sealed for them. Kattai pillaimars as they are called never marry outside their clan.

Nava Thiruppathis : The nine holy shrines of Vishnu called Navathiruppathis are in this district. Thiruvaikundam, Thiruvaraguna-mangai, Thiruppulingudi, Thirukkulandai, Thirutholaivilli Mangalam, South Thirupperai, Thirukkolur, Alwar Thirunagari are their names. The Sri Aravinda Lochana sanctum in Thiruvaikuntam is also counted as one Thiruppathi. Thus, the Nava Thiruppathis are near one another in this district.

Panchalamkurichi : It is 54 kms from Tirunelveli and 3 kms from Ottappidaram. It is the home of the patriot Kattabomman, a 17th century freedom fighter. The original fort of Kattabomman is now in ruins and under the custody of Archaeological Survey of India. The Kattabomman memorial fort was constructed in Panchalamkurichi by the Government of Tamil Nadu in 1974. Near the fort is the temple of Jakkamma, the family deity of Kattabomman. A cemetery of British soldiers too is found near the fort. Ottappidaram is the birthplace of V.O.Chidambaram Pillai, the freedom fighter of the pre-Gandhian era. Kayatharu is the place where Kattabomman was hanged to death by the British. There is a Vishnu temple in this place.

Ettaiyapuram : The birthplace of the national poet Bharathiar. Ettaiyapuram is 71 kms from Tirunelveli. Here, Manimandapam is constructed for Bharathiyar. There is also a memorial for Bharathiyar. His patriotic songs aroused the Tamilians from slumber and made them conscious of the evils of foreign dominators and inspired them to fight relentlessly for freedom.

Manappadu : This place is 71 kms from Tirunelveli on the shores of the Bay of Bengal. There is a 400-year-old Holy Cross Church here. Some fragments of the True Cross from Jerusalem are enshrined here. It is one of the churches connected with St. Francis Xavier.

Tirunelveli

(The Cradle of the Dravidian Civilization)

Tirunelveli district in the south is really the cradle of the Dravidian civilization, supported by the excavations of Adichanallur. The burial urns discovered here proclaim the antiquity of this region made fertile by the Thamirabarani river. The Tamil hill called Podiyamalai is on the western border with evergreen vegetation. It is the abode of Agastya who is said to be the father of Tamil Grammar. Even Buddhists make a claim to this hill calling it Bodhi Malai which was later corrupted as Podhiamalai. They argue it was the seat of Avalokideswara and go to the extreme that Potala of Tibet took its name only from Podhikai. It was the land of the Pandyas, so Pandya art and architecture and cave temples abound in this district. The district headquarters is Tirunelveli.

Tirunelveli stands on the banks of Thamirabarani river. Its history goes back to the Sangam Age and beyond it to pre-historic times. It is now the headquarters of the district and the 6th major city of Tamil Nadu.

How to get there?

Tirunelveli is well connected by road with all the towns of Tamil Nadu, Chennai, Madurai, Trichy, Coimbatore and Kanyakumari. It is a major junction on the Southern Railway and has rail connections to all important places in the country. The nearest airport is at Madurai in Tamil Nadu, 157 kms from Tirunelveli. Flights are available to Coimbatore, Trichy and Chennai. Umpteen bus services are available to all the places of tourist importance in the district and the neighbouring district of Thoothukudi which formed part of this district before it was formed as a new district.

Places to see in and around Tirunelveli

Tirunelveli City : The city is situated on the banks of the river Thamirabarani. There is a legend to the name of the place. Vedasarma an ardent devotee of Lord Siva went to bathe in the river after spreading paddy in the open space to dry. As he was bathing, a heavy downpour came and Vedasarma simply prayed Lord Venuvana Nathar and after his bath went back. To his surprise not a drop of rain had fallen on the paddy. All the rain poured avoiding the paddy that was put to dry. As the Lord guarded the paddy like a fence (veli) the place got the name Tirunelveli (nel-paddy) and the God came to be known as Nellaiyappar. The twin temple of Kanthimathi (Goddess) and Nellaiyappar is the main attraction in the city. The gopuram was built in 1606 A.D. The Nandhi idol in stucco is huge as at Rameswaram. There are 46 musical pillars in the mandapam. The sculptures here are delicately carved — Yalis (lion-headed elephant), Purushamirugas (half human and half animal forms), the Pandavas and Anjaneya (Monkey God) are some shining examples. The Thamira (copper) Sabha (hall) is nicely adorned with wood carvings. The beautiful bridge across the river was modelled after the Waterloo bridge on the river Thames and stands on two arches. Dalavai (General) Arianatha Mudaliar designed the town and built a fort at Palayamkottai.

Krishnapuram: The Krishnapuram temple dedicated to Vishnu lies about 13 kms from Tirunelveli and should not be missed by lovers of art. As there are Belur and Halebid in Karnataka and Tadpatri and Lepakshi in Andhra to boast of the art and architecture, Tamil Nadu has Krishnapuram to brag. This temple dedicated to Lord Venkatachalapathi is filled with sculptural beauties of excellent workmanship. Krishnappa Nayak (1563-73) a connoisseur of art has built this edifice of beauty. The Ranga Mandapam is a theatre of arts. Mythological scenes are beautifully portrayed with expressions suiting the moods in which they are captured. Even contemporary social life is not left out. A gypsy woman with a child on her back while a toy is held before it by a man to keep it from crying, a Korava kidnapping a princess, being rescued by the prince wounding the Korava in the encounter and the wound profusely bleeding are examples. One wonders how the red tint of the gushing blood was introduced within the sculpture! Unlike Belur with its dwarf-like figures, here the figures are of life-size carved with intricate delicacy.

Sankarankoil : It is 56 kms north of Tirunelveli. The Sankara Narayanan temple is famous here. A fusion of two faiths Saivism and Vaishnavism is aimed at in this temple by presenting an image combining both aspects. The right half has all the symbols of Siva, deer, cobra, moon etc. while the left half has all the symbols of Vishnu like Chakra, conch etc. There are fine paintings in the

'Prakarams' (corridors). Goddess Gomathi's penance called 'Adi Thapasu Vizha' and the car festival celebrated in June-July attract nearly 3 lakhs people to this place. Sankarankoil is connected by road and rail to important places in the state. The nearest places are Tirunelveli, Thoothukudi, Tenkasi, Kovilpatti, Srivilliputhur and Madurai.

Courtallam Waterfalls : Courtallam 59 kms from Tirunelveli is the "spa of the south," situated at an elevation of 170 metres, on the western ghats. Besides being a tourist spot, this is also a health resort. The waters of Courtallam has therapeutic value to cure physical ailments as the water flows through a herbal forest. During the season (June to September) thousands of tourists from far and near visit this place. There are nine waterfalls here: 1) Main falls, 2) Chitraruvi, 3) Shenbagadevi falls, 4) Thenaruvi (thèn–honey, aruvi–waterfalls), 5) Aindharuvi (five falls), 6) orchard falls, 7) New falls, 8) Tiger falls and 9) Old Courtallam falls.

The place itself is picturesque with a mountainous backdrop (6000 ft). The main fall is formed by Chithra Nadhi dropping 300 ft down a precipice, a trough called Pangimangodal, then falls out into beautiful cascades for the visitors to bathe. Cloud capped peaks, inspiring temples, evergreen and lush verdure, salubrious climate, snow-white waterfalls and their gurgling noise with the chirping of birds, rare fruits mangosteen and durian make this place a paradise on earth. The rain too is not torrential here but a soothing drizzle called 'saral'. Drenching in saral combined with the cool breeze braces the body.

The deity of the temple is called 'Kutralanathar' and the stunted jack-fruit tree is the tree of the temple. Therefore, he is also called "Kurumpala Easar". The Lingam of this temple is carved on the face of a rock. The temple is called Chitra Sabha - 'Chitram' means paintings – and the Chitra Sabha (hall) contains a number of mural paintings of rural deities and episodes from epics. The sabha is one of the five sabhas where Nataraja performed His cosmic dance. Chitra Sabha is made of medicinal herbs. The wooden carved door itself is a wonder. The painting of Lord Nataraja is another marvel.

Tenkasi : Tenkasi means Dakshina Kasi – Varanasi of the south. Pandya king Paranthaga Pandiyan after his return from the Benaras created this temple dedicated to Viswanatha and called it Tenkasi. The inscriptions of this king reveal his spiritual ardour and his concern for future maintenance. The temple for a very long time had its gopuram damaged by lightning but now it has been completely renovated. There are beautiful sculptures in the temple besides a flag staff 400 years old. It is 53 kms from Tirunelveli and 7 kms from Courtallam.

Thirumalaiappan Pozhil : 15 kms from Courtallam is this beautiful temple dedicated to Lord Muruga atop of a hill rock.

Kazhugumalai : It is 76 kms from Tirunelveli and 24 kms from Sankaran Koil. A huge rock has been shaped into a shrine here. The unique feature is, the temple instead of rising from the foundations has been chiselled from the top. This temple is called Vettuvar Koil by the local people.Two friezes of ganas (demons) line the front porch. Even the tiniest of them has received full attention from the sculptor. A musical soiree of these ganas is portrayed, one playing a musical instrument, another dancing etc.

The top of the vimana (tower over the sanctum) of any temple could be appreciated from a distance but here it is topsy-turvy. It is octagonal and embellished with lion heads. Four vimana deities, Siva and Parvathi in the east, Dakshinamurthi in the south, Narasimha in the west and Brahma on lotus in the north, are the peaks of art. Lord Dakshinamurthi here is unique playing a mirudangam (drum), which cannot be seen anywhere. The image of Lord Siva holding a Naga displays His 'Vishabarana' aspect. The cobra seems to wriggle out of His hold - so lifelike! Nearby is a big rock containing Jain figures like Tirthankaras, Yakshas and Yakshinis. These Jain temples are among the oldest in the country and the bas-relief sculptures mentioned above are excellent pieces of art.

Thirumalaipuram : It is 6.4 kms from Kadayanallur (16 kms from Tenkasi). There is a rock-cut temple here with Ganesa, Vishnu and dancing Siva. The dance of Siva here is different from the usual types - in chatura pose, with His right hand thrown in a 'Mirgasirsha' attitude. A dwarf near His feet plays the instrument called Chandala Vallaki (something like veena). Murals in the ceiling are badly damaged.

Kalakadu Wildlife Sanctuary: It is 47 kms from Tirunelveli. This is renowned for its flora and fauna. Botanists and ornithologists throng this area. Tiger, panther, jackal, wild dogs, cobra, python and several snakes and other reptiles, the lion-tailed monkey—all could be sighted in the thick forest. The best season is between March and September. The temple near Kalakadu has 16 musical pillars.

Shengaltheri : It is located in the Kalakadu mountain area. It is 20 kms from Kalakadu village and 68 kms from Tirunelveli. It is in the area of wildlife sanctuary. It is an important picnic spot and also popular for its natural scenery and salubrious climate. There is also a perennial waterfalls. There is a rest house and a watch-tower. Manimutharu originates from this place. There is also a P.W.D. inspection bungalow near the bus stop. This place is connected to all important pilgrim and tourist centres by road. The nearest railway station is Valliyur. For going there, prior permission of the Deputy Director of Wildlife, Ambasamudram, Mundanthurai and Kalakadu Wildlife Sanctuary is necessary.

Pathamadai : This hamlet 13 kms from Tirunelveli is renowned for weaving mats of korai grass. One can see the beautiful korai mat manufacturing unit here. Some of the mats can be folded like cloth. This is also the birthplace of Swami Sivanandha.

Thirukkurungudi : It is located in the western ghats about 52 kms south of Tirunelveli. It is one of the 108 divine Vishnu shrines. It is also known as Vamana Kshetram. The temple is spread over 18 acres. It is dedicated to Azhagiya Nambi and shelters splendid sculptures. The images of Varuna, Dakshinamurthi, Vamana, and Gajendra Moksha are best specimens. A lady's horror at seeing a scorpion makes the heart flutter. Generally, Lord Vishnu in any shrine can be seen only in one of the forms, standing, sitting or lying. But here, He is seen in five forms as Standing Nambi, Sitting Nambi, Lying Nambi, Parkadal Nambi and Thirumalai Nambi. There is a sanctum for Siva also in the temple exposing the Saivaite-Vaishnavaite unity. There are more than 90 vatteluthu inscriptions in this temple. The temple is surrounded by tall granite walls. It has been sanctified by four Alwars in Nalayira Divya Prapandham.

Kunthakulam Bird Sanctuary: It is situated 33 kms south of Tirunelveli in Nanguneri taluk. It is a small and beautiful village of natural scenery. It is covered with natural forests and ponds. During the season from January to April, more than 10,000 birds from various countries like Pakistan, Myanmar, Sri Lanka, U.S.A. and Australia migrate to this place. Daily over 5000 people come here to watch them. Ariyankulam is another bird sanctuary 13 kms east of Tirunelveli.

Shenbagarama Nallur : It is near Nanguneri and the temple here has a stone pillar with a conical bore in the centre about a foot long. When blown from one end which is bigger the sound of a conch and from the smaller end the sound of an ekkalam (a long pipe-like musical instrument) is produced. The sculpture in the Vishnu temple is marvellous, each image producing a musical note when struck. The sculptor's dexterity is revealed in the nerves and nails of the sculpture. It is astonishing that even these things could be produced in stone.

Thiruvalliswaram : It is on the Tirunelveli-Ambasamudram (35 kms) road and contains many exquisite images. On the upper tier, the figure of Nataraja is a feast for the eyes. The sway of His dress in the whirl of His dance, the locks crowning His head, His slender waist of a dancer are all brought out skilfully by the sculptor. Gangadhara, Dakshinamurthi and Ardhanari images too enchant us.

Cheranmadevi : It is 18 kms from Tirunelveli on the Tiruchendur M.G. railway line. There are eight beautiful shrines here. Of them, the Milagupillayar shrine is the most famous and unique too. When the water level in the village channel drops, pepper paste is plastered over the idol and lo! miraculously enough, the water overflows.

Papanasam : It is located 60 kms from Tirunelveli. The famous Siva temple is located at the bottom of the western ghats and also very near to the origin of river Thamirabarani. Every year, the Chitthirai Vishu festival is celebrated in the month of April and another festival Adi Amavasai is celebrated in July. About 2 lakhs people congregate at these festivals. It is also a picnic spot.

Kalyana Theertham : It is reached after a strenuous trek of 24 kms through the wilds. The river cascades into a drop of 125 feet vertically. This falls is the Papanasam waterfalls. There is a pool of the falls. This is called Kalyana Theertham. Near the pool is a temple dedicated to Lord Siva.

Pana Theertham : The river Thamirabarani originates and commences its course from Pana Theertham. It is located just opposite to the upper dam. One has to reach this place crossing the dam by boat. During festival days, local tourists around Papanasam will visit this place.

Agasthiyar Temple and Falls : This temple adjoining the falls named Agasthiyar Falls is located half way to the Pana Theertham which is 4 kms from Papanasam Siva temple. One can reach the falls and the temple by trekking 3 kms. Regular buses are available to these temples.

Upper Kodaiyar and Manjolai: This is a quiet hill station in the western ghats about 6000 ft. above sea level. Manjolai is the nearby town and an ideal summer resort. It is 50 kms from Ambasamudram (35 kms from Tirunelveli). The hill station may also be reached from Nagercoil. One can reach lower Kodaiyar by winch. There is also a road from Balmore to upper Kodaiyar. The hill resort with panoramic views is a tourist's heaven. Oothu and Kuthiraivetti are excellent viewpoints. The guest-house of the Travancore royal family located here is called "Muthukuzhi Vayal". The approach road begins from Manimutharu and Ambasamudram to Kodaiyar Manjolai. Regular bus services are available from Manimutharu and Ambasamudram.

Mundanthurai Wildlife Sanctuary : This sanctuary is situated 42 kms from Tirunelveli. It is mainly a tiger reserve forest. Anyhow one is likely to see other animals like leopard, sambar, sloth bear, cheetah and a wide variety of Indian primates including bonnet macaque, common langur, Nilgiri langur and lion-tailed macaque. The best time to visit is between October and January. The sanctuary lies on the mountains verging Kerala. The nearest railway station is Ambasamudram from where regular bus services are operated. Since, tigers are likely to be seen only in the very early morning or late evening, a stay for the night is essential. The forest department will arrange to take tourists round the sanctuary. There is a forest rest house for accommodation that could be reserved earlier.

Uvari : It is a village on the shores of the Bay of Bengal on the way to Tiruchendur from Kanyakumari in Tirunelveli district, 40 kms from Kanyakumari, 50 kms from Tiruchendur and 72 kms from Tirunelveli. Nadar Uvari is famous for Swayambulingaswamy Siva temple. 3 important festivals are held here every year. Bharatha Uvari is a Roman Catholic Centre where one can see an ancient church as well as a modern church. The structure of the modern church is like that of an aeroplane. The annual festival falls in mid-January attracting over 2 lakh pilgrims.

Aathankarai Pallivasal : This pallivasal is between Tiruchendur and Kanyakumari coastal road in Tirunelveli district. It is 30 kms from Valliyur. There are two tombs belonging to 2 sufi saints Syed Ali Fathima and Hazarath Sheik Mohammed. It is a pilgrim centre for all faiths. More than 50,000 visit during the festival held in September.

Places of worship

Temples: Kanthimathi Nellaiyappar temple, Tirunelveli; Salaikumaraswamy temple, Tirunelveli Junction; Subramanyaswamy temple, Kurukkuthurai.

Churches : C.S.I. Church and Roman Catholic Church.

Mosque : One in the town and the other near Tirunelveli Junction.

Shopping Centres in Tirunelveli and Thoothukudi Districts

Poompuhar Handicrafts Emporium, S.N.High Road, Tirunelveli Junction.

Khadi and Village Bamboo Industries, Sengottai.

Bell Metal Industries, Vagaikulam, Ambasamudram taluk.

Mat Knitting Industries, Pathamadai and Kayathar.

Terracotta Industries, Thenpothai in Tenkasi taluk.

Nellai Super Market, S.N.High Road, Tirunelveli Junction.

Important Private Travel Agencies

- Standard Cabs, S.N. High Road, Tirunelveli. ✆: 337666

• Ambika Cabs, Trivandrum Road, Vannarapettai, Palayamkottai. ✆ : 576664
• Regaul Travels, Madurai Road, Tirunelveli Junction. ✆ : 339172
• Air King Travels, S.N.High Road, Tirunelveli Jn. ✆ : 334846
• Premier Cabs, Trivandrum Road, Vannarapettai, Palayamkottai. ✆ : 581666
• India Cabs, East Great Cotton Road, Thoothukudi.
• Professional cabs, Madurai Road, Tirunelveli Jn. ✆ : 331627

Important Hotels (with Bar)

• **Hotel Tamilnadu** T.T.D.C. unit, Beach Road, Tiruchendur.
• **Hotel Aryaas,** Madurai Road, Tirunelveli Jn.
• **Hotel Venkateswara,** Main Road, Opp. to Bus Stand, Valliyur.
• **Hotel Sugam,** Charles Theatre Road, Thoothukudi.
• **Hotel Alwin,** Thoothukudi.
• **Hotel Tilak,** Near New Bus Stand, Thoothukudi.
• **Hotel Geetha International,** Near New Bus Stand, Thoothukudi.
• **Visaka Lodge,** Near Old Bus Stand, Thoothukudi.

Important Silk Emporiums

R.M.K.V. Cloth Merchants, North Car Street, Tirunelveli Town. ✆ : 333105

Pothy's Cloth Merchants, North Car Street, Tirunelveli Town.

Nalli Silk House, S.N.High Rd., Tirunelveli Town.

Ganthimathi Co-optex, Raja Building, Near bus stand, Tirunelveli Junction.

D.Arumugampillai Cloth Merchants, East Great Cotton Road, Thoothukudi.

Abirami Textiles, East Great Cotton Road, Near Sivan Koil, Thoothukudi.

Seematti Textiles, East Great Cotton Road, Thoothukudi.

Jewellers Park

M.K.M. Jewellers, S.N.High Road, Tirunelveli Junction.

M.H.Jewellers, West Car Street, Kuzhakadai Bazaar, Tirunelveli Town.

Ameer Jewellers, West Car Street, Kuzhakadai Bazaar, Tirunelveli Town.

V.R.C.Jewellers, Hotel Aryaas Complex, Madurai Road, Tirunelveli Junction.

A.V.R.M. Jewellers, Thoothukudi.

Alagiri Chettiar Jewellers, Thoothukudi.

Somasundaram Chettiar Jewellers, Thoothukudi.

Important Festivals in Thoothukudi and Tirunelveli Districts

JANUARY: Pongal Tourist Festival.

FEBRUARY: R.C. Church Car Festival at Uvari.

APRIL: Papanasam Chitthirai Vishu Festival.

MAY: Veerapandia Kattabomman Vizha - Panchalamkurichi.

JUNE: Lord Murugan Temple Car Festival at Tiruchendur, Kazhugumalai and Thirumalaiappan pozhil.

JULY: Saaral Thiruvizha, Courtallam.

Nellaiyappar Ganthimathi Car Festival - Tirunelveli.

Adi Thapasu Festival - Sankarankoil.

Govt. Exhibition at Tirunelveli.

AUGUST: Adi Amavasai Festival at Papanasam.

SEPTEMBER: World Tourism Day at Tirunelveli.

Pottal Pudur - Mask Sandanakoodu Festival.

OCTOBER: Tiruchendur Lord Muruga Temple Kandasashti Festival.

Aathankarai Pallivasal Mask Sandhanakoodu Festival.

NOVEMBER: Kulasekarappattinam Dhasara Vizha.

DECEMBER: Kurukkuthurai - Tirunelveli Junction Karthigai Deepa Thiru Vizha.

IMPORTANT HOSPITALS

Tirunelveli Medical College Hospital, High Ground Road, Palayamkottai.

Get-Well Hospital, Raja Buildings Compound, Bus Stand Road, Tirunelveli Junction.

Annai Velankanni Hospital, Tiruchendur Road, Murugankurichi, Palayamkottai.

Indirani Chelladurai Hospital, Thoothukudi Road, Samadhanapuram, Palayamkottai.

Dr. Agnes Hospital, Murugankurichi, Palayamkottai.

Lakshmi Nursing Home, Madurai Road, Tirunelveli.

Ganthimathi Hospital, East Car Street, Tirunelveli Town.

Krishna Hospital, High Ground Road, Palayamkottai.

CLUBS

Rotary Club, High Ground Road, Palayamkottai.

Lions Club, S.N. High Road, Tirunelveli Jn.

Innerwheel (Ladies Club), Ganapathi Mills Compound, Vannarapettai, Palayamkottai.

District Club, High Ground Road, Palayamkottai.

IMPORTANT MONEY CHANGERS

State Bank of India and other nationalised and scheduled banks are transacting foreign exchange.

Note : Foreigners are advised to get their currency forms endorsed by the money changers at the time of exchanging their currency.

IMPORTANT BANKS

- State Bank of India, S.N. High Road, Tirunelveli Junction.
- Canara Bank, Raja Buildings, New Bus Stand, Tirunelveli Junction.
- Indian Bank, Near Bus Stand, Madurai Road, Tirunelveli Junction.
- State Bank of Travancore, S.N.High Road, Tirunelveli Junction.
- Union Bank of India, S.N. High Road, Tirunelveli Junction.
- Indian Overseas Bank, Near Super Market Building, Madurai Road, Tirunelveli Junction.
- Central Co-operative Bank, Vannarapettai, Palayamkottai.

POSTS & TELEGRAPHS

- Head Post Office and Telegraph Office, S.N. High Road, Tirunelveli Jn.
- R.M.S. Post Office, Railway Station, Tirunelveli.

IMPORTANT AUDITORIUMS AND MARRIAGE HALLS

- Sangeetha Sabha, Kailasapuram, Tirunelveli Junction.
- Municipal Kalyana Mandapam, Near Palayamkottai Bus Stand.
- Rose Mahal Marriage Hall, Near Science Centre, Kokkirakulam.
- Raj Mahal Marriage Hall.

Kanyakumari

(The Confluence of A Sea, An Ocean and A Bay)

Kanyakumari is the land's end and at the confluence of the Bay of Bengal, Indian Ocean and the Arabian Sea. On full moon days, one could see the moonrise and sunset at the same hour. The full moon day in the month of Chitthirai (April-May) is the best time, since on that day the sunset and moon-rise take place when the sun and moon are face to face in a straight line along the horizon. It is the tip of the Indian peninsula and its antiquity goes to pre-Himalayan days. Actually, it is the residual part of the lost Lemuria which extended up to Africa and Australia. So, the rocks are geologically the oldest of their kind. It was ruled by the Pandyas and later, parts of it were in Kerala and after the reorganisation of the states, all the Tamil speaking areas were seceded and the district was formed in 1956. Natural vegetation abounds on the western side and the eastern side is a fertile plain. It has 68 kms length of sandy seashore rich in atomic minerals. The sands of the beach are of different hues due to the mineral content. It is the meeting place of Tamil and Malayalam and even Tamil is spoken differently, like Malayalam with nasalized accent. As it is surrounded on three sides by sea, it enjoys a temperate climate. Besides, it is a major pilgrim centre with a heavy floating population.

How to get there?

Kanyakumari is connected with Tirunelveli, Chennai, Thiruvananthapuram and Coimbatore by broad gauge railway. Tirunelveli (83 kms) is connected to Chennai, Madurai etc.

It is well connected to almost all the towns in India by road. The nearest airport is Thiruvananthapuram (87 kms) from where flights are available to Coimbatore, Madurai, Bangalore, Chennai and Mumbai. Local buses are available to all the places of tourist attraction in the district.

In Kanyakumari

Kanyakumari Amman Temple: This temple is associated with the Goddess Parvathi doing a penance for the arrival of Her consort Siva to claim Her hand in marriage. She is doing the penance daily and at the same time guarding the country. There is another legend on the diamond nose stud of the Goddess which misguided many a ship with its lustre resulting in a tragedy with the ships hitting the submerged rocks. Hence, the door on the side facing the sea has been closed for ever. This Devi in Her fiercest aspect killed Banasura and in the Tamil month of Purattasi (September-October) during the festival, a drama of this event is enacted. The virgin Goddess Kanyakumari is standing with a rosary in Her hand bestowing benediction.

Gandhi Memorial : There is a memorial mandapam to the Father of the Nation, Mahatma Gandhi, erected on the place where his ashes were kept for public homage before being immersed at the confluence of the 3 seas. There is an architectural brilliance in the construction that it has been so designed that the rays of the sun fall on the same spot where the urn was kept exactly, on the 2nd of October every year i.e. on the birthday of Mahatma.

Vivekananda Memorial : The Vivekananda Memorial has been built on the Vivekananda Rock, so called because Vivekananda used to swim to the rock and meditate there hours together during his sojourn at Kanyakumari. It is one of the two rocks jutting out of the ocean and providing the visitors a view of the land's end of India.

The memorial is a blend of all the styles of the Indian architecture and was completed in 1970. A statue of Swami Vivekananda is installed. Ferry services are available to go to the memorial from 7 a.m. to 11 a.m. and from 2 p.m. to 5 p.m.

Close to it is another rock called Sripadaparai with the footprint of the Goddess who guards India from the southern tip. Both these rocks offer a good view of the land's end.

On this rock, a memorial to Thiruvalluvar, the unmatched poet-saint who gave to the world his immortal work, Thirukkural, which shows a right path for leading a good life, has been erected. The statue is made of a titanesque size rising 133 ft. which is a world wonder of this millennium. The statue was unveiled on January 1, 2000 A.D.

Guganathaswami Temple : This temple built by Rajaraja Chola I is about 1000 years old. The Siva Lingam at the sanctum sanctorum of this temple is 1.4 metre high. It is near the railway station.

Vivekananda Kendra : It sprang up after the Vivekananda Memorial in a spacious area of over 100 acres. Its aim is to give a practical shape to Swami Vivekananda's message of service. The headquarters is named Vivekanandapuram. It is a spiritual retreat and a centre of service to humanity.

Government Museum : The Government Museum is near the Transit Office, Beach Road. It contains bronzes, tribal articles, wood carvings and zoological and botanical specimens. The Samythoppu temple car is also exhibited. A whale's bone obtained from Manavalakurichi is another attraction.

Timings : 9.30 a.m. to 5.00 p.m.

Holiday : Fridays & Second Saturdays.

Entrance fee : Re.1 for Adults, 0.50 N.P. for Children and 0.25 N.P. for School Children.

Around Kanyakumari

Suchindram : It is 13 kms from Kanyakumari. The famous Thanu-Mal - Ayan (Siva, Vishnu, Brahma) temple is located here. The temple has a 7 tier gopuram, from the top of it the cape is clearly visible. There is a musical pillar inside the temple. The temple corridors are second only to

Rameswaram in magnificence. Inscriptions belonging to 9th century A.D. could be seen in the temple. Two chief attractions are the giant size Statue of Hanuman (Monkey God) rising 25 ft. and the statue of Vinayaki (female form of Vinayaka) as bas-relief.

Nagercoil : The name is originated from the temple here dedicated to Nagaraja (Serpent God). The temple is full of images of snakes. Even the gate keepers of the sanctums are two snakes. Besides Nagaraja, there are sanctums for Lord Siva and Anantakrishna too. Images of Jain Tirthankaras, Mahavira and Parswanatha are seen engraved on the pillars of the temple. The entrance to the temple is reminiscent of the Chinese architecture of Buddha Vihara. Nagercoil is the headquarters of the district. There are frequent buses from Nagercoil to all other parts of the state and to Thiruvananthapuram in the neighbouring state of Kerala.

Thirupathisaram : It is north-east of Nagercoil and the temple is 5000 years old. King Kulasekara has renovated this temple and even Thirumalai Nayak has done repairs here. There is no separate sanctum for the Goddess in this temple. Thiruvazhimarpan (Vishnu) is the chief deity. The idol is 9 ft. tall and made of a special element called Kadusamagayogam and no ablutions are performed to it. Dasavathara (Ten incarnations of Vishnu) paintings adorn the Indra Kalyana Mandapam of this temple.

Olakkay Aruvi (Waterfalls): The Olakkay Aruvi Waterfalls is about 8 kms north of Azhagiya Pandyapuram, 14 kms from Nagercoil and 35 kms from Kanyakumari. The waterfalls is surrounded by beautiful sceneries. It is a picnic and trekking spot attracting good crowd. A small Agasthiyar temple is near the falls and on the full moon day in the Tamil month of Chitthirai (April-May) devotees throng here to worship the deity after a bath in the falls.

Kumarak Koil : It is 34 kms from Kanyakumari, 15 kms north–west of Nagercoil and 3 kms east of Thukkalay. It is on the Vellimalai hills in Kalkulam taluk. The temple is on a hillock 200 ft. high amidst paddy fields, plantain and coconut groves. It is noted for its fine sculptures. There is a separate sanctum for Goddess Valli besides the presiding deity Lord Subramanya (Muruga). There is a big lake nearby suitable for bathing.

Mandaikadu Bagavathi Amman Temple : Mandaikadu is 41 kms from Kanyakumari situated on the sea coast north–east of Colachel port. A motorable road connects this place with Nagercoil and Thiruvananthapuram. There is a famous temple here dedicated to Bagavathi Amman dating back to 7th century A.D. The deity is in the form of an ant hill which is about 12 ft. high with 5 heads and is believed to be growing gradually. The annual festival called Mandaikadu Kodai, falls in March and is celebrated for ten days. At that time, over two lakhs of people assemble here for worshipping the deity. The Tourism Department of Tamil Nadu conducts an exhibition at that time. Though the temple is not big, it attracts huge crowds from all over the district and from Kottayam in Kerala about 160 kms from Mandaikadu.

Thengaipattinam Beach : It is 54 kms from Kanyakumari and 35 kms from Nagercoil. As coconut trees abound, this place is called Thengai (coconut) Pattinam. In ancient times, this was a busy maritime trade centre doing business with foreign countries especially with the Arabs. The mosque here was erected by Arab merchants 1200 years ago. Bus services are available to this place from Nagercoil and

Thiruvananthapuram. There is a fine backwater and an excellent beach and large number of people go there for relaxation and fun. Seabathing and boating are specialities of this place. It is a fine picnic spot.

St. Xavier Church, Kottar (Nagercoil) : It is 15 kms from Kanyakumari. An old church dating back to 15th century A.D. is built here. A ten day festival from 24th November to 3rd December attracts hugh crowd.

Curusadi St. Antony's Church: This church near Nagercoil is said to be 400 years old. Once a Hindu Nadar, found a stone with a cross embossed on it. He had dreams and received orders from a form of light to build a church. Worship began in a humble manner and the place came to be called Curusadi (Curusu–'cross'in Tamil). Later on after 21 years of construction, a new church came into being in 1911. It has two beautiful towers rising high. People from far and near visit this church with faith. St. Antony being a miracle saint has worked wonders among the devotees fulfilling their desires.

Pechipparai Dam : The dam is 75 kms from Kanyakumari. It is a popular picnic site. There is a park and boating facilities are also made here. Buses ply from Kanyakumari to the dam. Dormitory accommodations are available.

Udayagiri Fort : This fort built by king Marthanda Varma (1729-1788 A.D) is about 34 kms from Kanyakumari. The fort was popularly known as a foundry for casting guns. The grave of De Lennoy, the Dutch General, one of the most trusted generals, of the king lies within the fort.

Padmanabhapuram : This was the capital of Travancore till 1333. It is 45 kms from Kanyakumari. There is a palace inside a fort covering over 6 acres. There is also a temple inside. The palace is an art museum with mural paintings and exquisite wood carvings. Many objects including an armour of the royal family are exhibited. A clock made 400 years ago and a cot made of herbal wood used by the Maharaja to sleep on, can also be seen. The Ramasamy Temple inside has beautiful wood carvings depicting scenes from Ramayana, like Sita's wedding, Ravana's end etc. In the Neelakantaswamy temple, the image of a fierce Nataraja – the only one of its kind – is seen.

Thirupparappu Waterfalls : It is 60 kms from Kanyakumari. An ancient temple dedicated to Mahadeva is located here. It is a picnic spot. People throng in large numbers to bathe in the waterfalls.

Thiruvattar : The place is 60 kms from Kanyakumari. The Thiruvattar temple is one of the 13 Divyadesams (holy country) of Vishnu in Malai Nadu. Chaitanya of the Bhakti Cult movement has visited this place. The temple is in picturesque setting surrounded on three sides by 3 rivers (Kottaiyar, Paraliyar and Thamirabarani). The Lord is lying on His snake couch and has to be viewed through three doors. Deepalakshmis are many but none resembles the other. The Otraikkal Mandapam (Single Stone Hall) made of single stone 3 ft. thick is a marvel. Oorthuva Thandavam, Venugopala, Rathi, Manmatha, Lakshmana and Indrajit are excellently carved. The temple is also renowned for its murals.

Thirunandikarai : This place is near Thiruvattar. There is a rock-cut temple here. Once in 12 years, the Lingam is anointed with ghee on the Mahasivarathri day (March-April). The sanctum is circular with a conical dome in the typical Kerala style with the roof copper plated.

Thirucharanathumalai (Chitharal) : Thirucharanathumalai is located in Chitharal village 6 kms from

Kuzhithurai and 55 kms from Kanyakumari. It is a hillock. On the top of the hill under a path that seems naturally hanging there is a temple with mandapam, corridor and Balipeetam with a Madappalli (Kitchen). There are 3 sanctums housing Mahavira, Parswanatha and Padmavathi Devi. The idol of Bagavathi was installed instead of Padmavathi Devi by Sri Moolam Thirunal, King of Travancore in 1913 A.D. Above the hanging path, there is a dilapidated tower on a rock on the northern side. Bas-relief sculptures of all the 29 Tirthankaras are found. Some inscriptions belonging to the 9th century A.D. are also found here. It was a Jain training centre for both men and women in those days.

Government Fruit Farm : This farm is located 2 kms from Kanyakumari on the road to Suchindram. All kinds of plants and rare species can be seen here. Tourists are allowed to go around the farm.

Muttam : Muttam is 32 kms from Kanyakumari. A beautiful beach with fine rocky backdrop near the shore and a lighthouse make it a fine picnic spot. The place is a favourite haunt for cine technicians to shoot films.

TOURIST INFORMATION

Govt. of Tamil Nadu Tourist Office, Beach Road. ✆ : 71276

Information Centre, Vivekananda Rock Memorial, Beach Road. ✆ : 71250

Tour Operators

Triveni Tours & Travels ✆ : 71383, (Agent for TTDC Ltd) 71483, 71152

SHOPPING

Souvenirs and handicraft articles made from sea shells, and palm leaf articles are the main items to buy at Kanyakumari. Trinklets and packets of coloured sea sand for children can also be bought here. There are several shops selling these articles. Prices vary depending upon your bargaining power.

OTHER INFORMATION

Communications : Post/Telegraph/STD/ISD/Telex/Fax etc. –Available

Banks/Money Changers : State Bank of India, Canara Bank, State Bank of Travancore.

Medical Facilities : Hospitals, Chemists - Available.

Yoga : Classes are organised at Vivekanandapuram.

For details, please contact : The Secretary, Vivekananda Kendra at Vivekanandapuram, Kanyakumari.

Where to Stay at Kanyakumari?

- **Hotel Singaar International,** 5/22, Main Road, Kanyakumari - 629 702. ✆ 347992, Fax: 04652 - 347991, Email: singaar@sancharnet.in
- **Hotel Tamilnadu,** ✆ 346257
- **Manickam Tourist Home,** ✆ 346387
- **Youth Hostel,** Govt. of Kerala
- **Guest House,** ✆ 346229
- **Hotel Sangam,** ✆ 346352
- **Lakshmi Tourist Home,** ✆346333
- **Viveka Tourist Home,** ✆346192
- **Sankar's Guest House,** ✆ 346260

At Nagercoil : STD - 0465

- **Hotel Ganga,** ✆ 232999
- **Parvathi International,** ✆ 233020

Important Telephone Numbers

- Police Station ✆ : 71224
- Railway Station ✆ : 71247
- Bus Stand ✆ : 71285
- Tourist Office ✆ : 71276
- Kumari Amman Temple ✆ 71223
- Vivekanandapuram & Information Centre ✆ : 71250

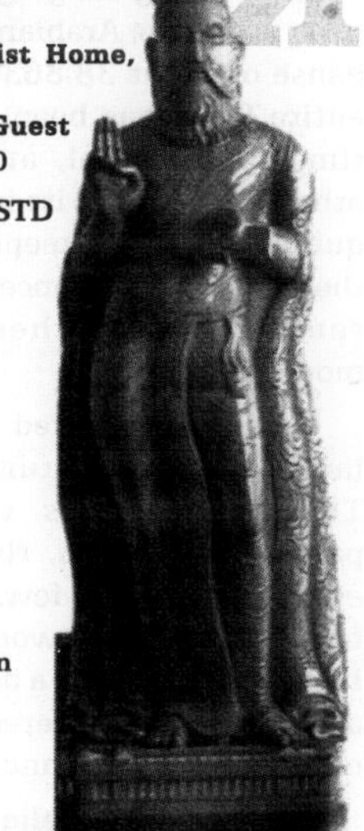

Kerala

General Information

Facts and Figures

Capital	:	Thiruvananthapuram
Area	:	38,863 Sq.kms.
Population	:	3,18,38,619 (2001 census)
Length	:	575 Km
Language	:	Malayalam, English
Literacy	:	90.92
Sex Ratio	:	(Females per 1000 males) 1058
Temperature	:	21°C to 35° C
Monsoon	:	June to October
Tourist Season	:	October to March
Major Port	:	Kochi
Other Seaports	:	Vizhinjam, Neendakara and Beypore
Airports	:	Thiruvananthapuram, Kochi and Kozhikode.

Kerala, one of the southern States of India is situated along the gregarious shores of the Arabian Sea at an expanse of about 38,863 Sq. Km. The entire State has been known since time immemorial, among myriad other features, for its inherent tranquillity. Although keeping pace with the present day advancements, Kerala remains unscathed by the modernisation.

Kerala is endowed with various landscapes and natural resources. The western ghats, thick forests, palm-fringed lakes, rivers, lagoons etc. are to name a few. The coconut farms of Kerala are world renowned. It is no surprise that a domain of such a rich heritage fostered the growth of religion, culture and art.

All the major religions co-exist harmoniously in Kerala inasmuch as it is no exception to following the ideal of secularism of the nation - India, of which it is a part. Here temples greet mosques, mosques wish churches and churches welcome temples. Ancient temples, mosques and churches are dissipated all over the State. The synagogues stand tall as reminiscences of the ancient Jewish settlers. It was here that the famous dance drama 'Kathakali' evolved from an ancient form of Sanskrit drama called "Kudiyattam". It has been a centre of Sanskrit, the language of Indian culture. "Silapathikaram", an ancient marvellous Tamil literary work of perpetual glory cites evidences of the "Kudiyattam" having been in vogue here for more than 20 centuries.

The State, much longer than it is wide, is about 580 km. in length and is flanked by Karnataka in the north and the north-east and Tamil Nadu on the east and the south. The western ghats, with an average height of 900 mts and peaking from 1800 mts to 2400 mts at places, run all along

Mohiniyattam *- a fusion of Bharathanatyam and Kathakali exudes enchantment, grace and passion. It literally means 'Dance of the Temptress'. In Mohiniyattam, the 'lasya' element of dancing is predominant and the mood created is 'Sringaram'. The dance admixes the elegance and grace of Bharathanatyam and dynamic vigour of Kathakali.*

the eastern border of the State, thus forming a natural cordon. The highest South Indian Mountain peak known as the **Anamalai Peak** which is about 2689 mts in altitude is situated here in Idukki district. Kerala, the smallest of the South Indian States, makes up to 1.3 per cent of the total area of the nation.

History has it that Kerala has been an irresistible temptation to visitors right from the ancient times. Here, phoenicians had traded in ivory spices and peacocks as long back as 3000 years ago. Many historic visitors to Kerala have adored its indisputable greatness in ways which came to them naturally.

Behold! a few of such historic utterances.

"When you leave the islands of Seilan and sail westwards about 60 miles, you come to the great province of Malabar which is styled India the greater. It is the best of all the Indus and is on the main land... There is in the kingdom a great quantity of pepper and ginger and cinnamon and nuts of India".

- *Marco Polo in his books of Travels (1292 AD)*

"We next come to Kalikat, one of the great ports of the district of Malabar and in which merchants from all parts are found. They put a thief to death for stealing a single nut or even a seed of any fruit; hence thieves are unknown among them. The greatest part of Mohammedan merchants of this place are so wealthy that one of them can purchase the whole freightage of such vessels as put in here.

- *Sheik Ibu Batuta (1342-47 AD)*

"Such security and justice reign in Malabar that rich merchants bring to it from maritime countries large cargoes of merchandise which they disembark and deposit in the streets and market places and for a length of time leave it without consigning it to any one's charge or placing in under guard".

- *Abdur-r-Razzak (1442 AD)*

"There was one point in regard to the inhabitants of Malabar, on which all authorities, however diametrically opposed to each other on other points agreed and that was with regard to the independence of mind of the inhabitants. This independence of mind was generally diffused through the minds of the people."

- *Lord William Bentinck (1804 AD)*

"Some of the more remarkable of the vegetable and the animal productions of the Malabar Coast have been known to the Western Nations from times antecedent to Christian era, and have been the objects of maritime enterprise and commerce through all the succeeding centuries".

- *William Logan (1887 AD)*

While high mountains form the border on one side of the State, the deep blue Arabian Sea does on the other. And obviously there is no scarcity for beaches. The beaches here are quite different from most of those at other places since what gives them the border lining for a length, longer than one's imagination, is lavish palmgroves. This enthralling uniqueness add to the beauty and attract a lot of visitors. Some of the famous beaches in the State are at Kovalam, Papanasam (Varkala) Shanghumugam, Vizhinjam, Alleppey Kappad, Bekal and Payambalam.

The mountains have gentle contours and rounded tops and sharp peaks are hardly seen. This is a characteristic of the Himalayas. The mountain range is a treasure from tip to toe as the tops are covered with evergreen forests while all along the incline are valuable teak, rich plantations of cardamom, tea, rubber, coffee and pepper. The southwest monsoon, between May and August, fetch more shower than its ironical rival, north-east, in October. The heavy downpour and the broken terrains give rise to a number of rivers and brooks whose beauty has besotted many a visitor.

Naturally enriched with minerals Kerala has an abundance of 'Monazite' on its beaches which is converted into a radioactive material called 'thorium' used as an atomic fuel.

In the retrospect, Kerala has been ruled over by a number of dynasties. It had been under the empire of Ashoka in the 3rd century BC. Then the historic battles had continually placed it under the control of several heroes. The rulers of the three great Tamil dynasties viz., the Cheras, the Cholas and the Pandyas had succeeded in turns, to bring the coveted region under their belts. Then the Islamic emperors conquered it and then it went to the hands of Vijayanagar Kingdom which offered resistance to the iconoclastic approach of the Muslim rulers.

PEOPLE

Exotic, about the people of the State is their classification and the factors upon which it is based.

The sect of people who have devoted themselves to religion and vedic practices, popularly known as the Brahmins is called Nambudris. They excel in Sanskrit studies and are patrons of a number of fine arts.

Wielding their swords and shielding their sods in the hierarchical era were the sect known as the Nairs who have thereafter taken to various other occupations. They adhere to the joint family traditions with an unrelenting family bondage. The oldest male member of the family, the 'Karnavar', is looked upon with reverence by the rest of the family.

Reference to Mahatma Gandhi's words "India lives in Her villages" seems imminent looking at the 'Thiyas or Ezhavas'. They are traditionally the cultivating class engaged in coconut farms.

Among others are a large number of Hindu class distributed all over the State. These include several hill tribes, Uralis, Ullatans and Mudrans.

The Christians again in several classes and groups, have their indispensible contributions to the greatness of the State in the field of 'Education', 'Industry' and 'Economic development'.

'Moplas' as are called, the Muslims of Kerala are an industrious lot, their main occupation being trade. However, Kerala also hosts a small colony of Jews.

CULTURE

Kerala has established its name in the fields of music, dance, architecture, painting and other forms of artistic expression.

Malayalam, the vernacular of the region, rich in its literature, has imbibed vocabulary to a substantial extent from the ancient and yet not obsolete language, Sanskrit. The translations of the Ramayana, the Mahabharatha and the Bhagavata (from Sanskrit to Malayalam) by Ezhuthachan in the 16th century are still adored by the pious people. Thus it has been a land of a number of genii in almost all the fields.

AYURVEDA

The traditional form of medicine and treatment is yet another feather to the hat. 'Ayurveda', the English for which is 'Knowledge of life' has flourished here since very ancient times. 'Ayurveda', the system of treatment

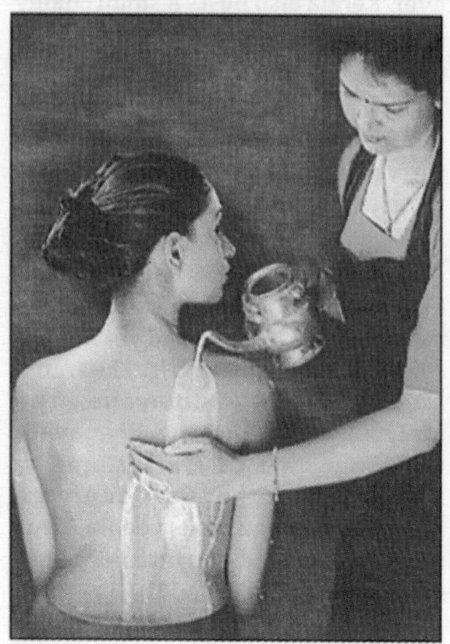

believed to be older than 5000 years is based on the philosophy, "Prevention is better than cure". However, it offers a lasting cure to patients suffering from various diseases.

It is not only a system to cure diseases but the system teaching us how to achieve 'Perfect Health' for diseased or abnormal conditions and how to lead our life, both physical and mental, to attain the bliss of real life.

It is almost as old as mankind and at the same time so new as modern man that no disease is there which is incurable or uncontrollable unless missed too much.

According to ayurveda, human body is composed of three fundamental elements called *'Doshas'* - which represent the physico - chemical and physiological activities of the body, *'Dhatu'* which denotes the materials entering into the formation of a basic structure of the body cell, thereby performing some basic actions and *'Malas'* the substances which are partly used in the body and partly excerted in yet another form after serving their physiological activities.

'Doshas' are three - *vata, pitta,* and *kapha* and they may not be equal and same in all. According to the dominance of each dosha every man is categorised to different types.

Physical and mental co-operation of the patient to make necessary changes in his life style and food habits also are essential to attain the natural dynamic balance of the doshas and once that balance is maintained the illness is gone.

It describes how to live to avoid disease in each climate and how can perfect health be maintained throughout the life. Ayurveda has a separate branch called 'Rasayana' to maintain youth and vitality to recover lost health in diseased conditions.

In Ayurveda, all treatment is aimed at building up the strength of the person which would help him to lead a health and happy life.

Methods of Ayurvedic treatment are primarily classified into three.

1. *Antharparimarjanam*
2. *Bahirparimarjanam*
3. *Sastrapranidhanam*

It lays more emphasis on the promotion of positive health and prevention of diseases.

Yoga and Tantra which are primarily meant for spiritual attainments have also certain prescriptions for the prevention and cure of psychic, somatic and psychosomatic ailments.

The unique features of Ayurveda treatment of medicine are:

1. Treatment of individual as a whole, ie. not only the condition of other parts of his body but also the condition of his mind and soul.
2. Medicines are available on reasonable prices.
3. No import involved ie. medicines are vegetables, metals, minerals and animal products which are available in nature.

BOAT RACES

In the months of August and September, over hundred thousand men and women gather on the banks to

Bursting with energy, team members paddle a high-sterned snake-boat at an exciting race on a palm-fringed canal at ***Alleppey*** *to win Nehru Trophy on Onam Day.*

witness a spectacular water regatta **the Snake Boat Races**. The most famous one is the **Nehru Trophy Boat Race** which began in 1952 on the occasion of the visit of India's first Prime Minister, Jawaharlal Nehru to Alappuzha. It is now a major event held on the second Saturday of every August and features the gigantic snake boats of Kerala, the Chundans - once the battleships of the Malayalee King of Yore. Now, the boat race has grown as most important tourist even with boats being sponsored by

different villages. Another traditional boat race, Champakulam Moolam Vallam Kali is connected with a temple festival. There are other snake boat races too.

The chief competitors of the trophies are *Champakulam, Kavalam, Karichal, Jawahar Thayangari, Kallooparamban, Pulinkunnu, Nadubhagam, Cheruthana, Kandangari and Paippad.*

AMUSEMENT PARKS

The first theme park in India is **Essel World** in Mumbai established in 1981. But now, South India itself has more than twelve such parks.

Fantasy Park: It is the first amusement park in Kerala located at Malampuzha in Palakkad district. Entry fee is separate for each items. (Address: Fantasy Park, Malampuzha, Palakkad. Ph: 0491-2815122, 2815123).

Veega Land: It is located 12 km from the Ernakulam bypass (Kakkanad route). Time: 10.30 am - 6.30 pm on weekdays. 10.30 am - 9.30 pm on weekends and holidays. Address: Veega Land, Pallikkara, Kakkanad, Kochi-683 565. Ph: 0484-2684001, 2684002. www.veegaland.com

Veega Land

Silver Storm: This park is situated 19 km from Chalakudy in Trissur district. Address: Silvern Storm, Athirappally Road, Vettilappara, Chalakudy, Trissur - 680 721. Ph: 0488-2769116.

Dream World: It is located near Chalakudy on way to Atirappally and Vazhachal falls. It is 8 km from the town. Address: Dream World, Athirappally Road, Kanjirappalli, Chalakudy, Trissur-680 721. Ph: 0488-2766935, 2766955, 2767665. www.dreamworldkerala.com

RIVERS AND BACKWATERS

There are forty four rivers in Kerala. Out of 44 rivers, forty one rivers are west flowing and 3 are east flowing rivers which cut across Kerala with their innumerable tributaries and branches. It turn into rivulets in summer.

The backwaters from a specially attractive and economically valuable

The high-range forests of Kerala are rich in teakwood, rosewood, ebony, sandalwood etc. Tucked in between are the small hill stations, plantations, wild-life sanctuaries etc. Adding to these natural riches, is a water fall in ***Munnar*** *- a cascade from Heaven.*

feature of Kerala. The biggest backwater is the Vembanad Lake which opens out into the Arabian Sea at Cochin port. The other important backwaters are Veli, Kadinamkulam, Anjengo, Edava, Madayara, Paravoor, Ashtamudi, Kayamkulam, Kodungallur and Chetuva. The deltas of the rivers interlink the backwaters and provide excellent water transportation.

FESTIVALS

When one thinks of the festivals of Kerala, the one that spontaneously springs to the mind is **'Onam'**, though there is a long list of others too! It marks the beginning of the new year in the Kerala's aboriginal calendar. It falls in the month of August-September which is called the month of Chingom. It is obviously celebrated with enthralling pomp and show.

'Ammankudam', Arattu', Chandankudam, 'Chuttuvilakku,' Ezhunallathu', 'Pallivetta', 'Paraveppu, 'Pongala', 'Seeveli', Thalappoli', 'Velichappadu' (Komaram) are some of the unique Hindu rituals, performed regularly with fabulous fan-

The Pooram temple festival at Thrissur.

fare apart from the festivals like Diwali, Dasara etc.

The Christian festivals, the **Christmas**, the Good Friday and the Easter are cherished with equal zeal and zest all over the State and the Ramadan and the Bakrid bring about no less joy to the people of Kerala.

Thiruvananthapuram

FACTS AND FIGURES

Area : 2,192 Sq.kms. • Population : 2,105,349 (2001 census) • Headquarters : Thiruvananthapuram • Tourist Season: September to May.

Thiruvananthapuram is the State capital. Trivandrum Central Railway Station and Central Bus Station is at Thampanoor. It has rail links with Bangalore and Chennai. Fine roads branch out of the city connecting it to all southern parts of India. Trivandrum Airport (International) linked by flights to Cochin, Chennai, Delhi, Goa and Mumbai. International flights also operate to Colombo, Male, Dubai, Abudhabi, Kuwait and Singapore.

Bounded on the east and north east by the mountain ranges of Western Ghats, in the South by the fertile rice bowl district of Kanyakumari presently in the State of Tamil Nadu and on the west by the Arabian Sea. The hillocks stand majestically right on the shore (Arabian Sea) as though beckoning to the sea and hence the rains run down the hills caressing every inch of the incline, to the sea. The city has a lot to offer to the voracious eyes of the tourists. The modern style of architecture seems to compliment the antique monuments.

TOURISTS' INTEREST

Sri Padmanabha Swamy Temple: It is situated in the heart of the city. It would rather be more pertinent to say the city had been built around the temple as it is believed to have come into existence on the first day of 'Kaliyuga' era, (28-12-3101 BC). The presiding deity is, as the name implies, Lord Padmanabha, one of the variations of Lord Vishnu. The deity can be seen reclining on serpent 'Anantha'. The 'Dharshan' (reverential sight) can be had through three doors, the face through south door, the navel through the middle and the feet through the North. This venue is one of the exquisite group of 108 Temples dedicated to 'Maha Vishnu'. Two festivals are held annually. Only Hindus are allowed inside the temple. Wearing of shirt or any attire to cover the upper part of the body by MEN inside the temple premises is strictly prohibited. Thus men are restricted to 'Dothi' (Pants not allowed) and women to sarees and blouse. (Chudidhar, pants, shirts etc. not allowed).

Dharshan
Hours : 04:15 - 05:15 hrs,
06:45 - 07:30 hrs,
08:30 - 10:30 hrs,
11:30 - 11:45 hrs,
17:15 - 19:30 hrs.

Sri Subramaniyaswamy Temple - Ullur: This temple dedicated to Lord Subramaniya (Murugan) is situated 7 kms from Thiruvananthapuram.

Bhagawathy Temple - Attukal: Located 2 km from the State capital is this temple dedicated to Goddess Bhagawathy. The famous 'Pongala Utsavam' popularly known as 'Attukkal Pongala' lasts for 10 days.

Sarkaradevi Temple - Chirayinkeezhu: This temple is, again, dedicated to Goddess Bhagawathy. It is situated 18 km from Thiruvanantha- puram. Bharani Utsavam - a 10 day festival Kaliyoothu Mahotsavam - a folk ritual are celebrated annually.

Siva Temple, Aruvippuram: The idols in this temple were installed by Sri Narayana Guru. 'Sivarathri' festival, during which devotees observe fast and forgo the night's sleep and perform puja (offer prayers and worship) and adore Lord Siva, is famous here.

Thiruvambadi Sri Krishna Temple, Varkala: Sri Krishna, one of the 10 'Avathars' (Divine incarnations) of Lord Vishnu is the presiding deity. It is located at Manthra near Varkala. A festival to mark the birthday of Lord Krishna is celebrated here, in a grand manner.

Kuthiramalika (Puthenmalika) Palace Museum: At a stone's throw from Sri Padmanabha Swamy temple this marvellous specimen was built by Maharaja Swathi Thirunal Balarama Varma. The workmanship, traditional style typical of Travancore Architecture, captivating wood carvings and the importance given to every minute detail of the construction, all reflect the grandeur of the construction techniques of the olden times. The 'Maharaja' (King) was himself a great poet, musician, social reformer, and statesman. In the palace to be seen are breathtaking paintings and invaluable collections of the royal family.

Visiting
Hours : 08:30 - 12:30 hrs,
15:30 - 17:30 hrs,
Closed on Mondays.

Entrance Fee :
Adults : Rs. 5/-
Children : Rs. 3/-
Foreigners : Rs. 20/
Camera permit : Rs.25/-

IN AND AROUND THIRUVANANTHAPURAM

Thirunavaya: Overseeing the gushing river Bharatapuzha is the historical city of Thirunavaya. This city was the ancient venue for an exotic festival called 'Mamankam'.

It is apposite to call it the 'Sport of Kings' for this festival was indeed a stiff contest between the rulers of various parts of Kerala to declare the emperor among them. The last 'Mamankam' was celebrated in the year 1755. The place can also be reached from Tirur in Malapuram district which is about 8 km away.

The Government Art Museum (The Napier Museum): Built in the year 1880 by an English architect in honour of Lord Napier, Governor of Madras, this museum is situated on the crest of the public gardens near the observatory hills. The structure has a built-in natural air-conditioning system and a good collection of archaeological and historic artefacts, bronze idols, ancient ornaments, a temple chariot, ivory carvings, sculptures, models and zoological specimens. A clock about 4 centuries old and a cot made out of herbal wood for the king are among those exclusive ones. The zoological gardens with beautiful meadows and attractive landscapes surround the structure. The use of plastic in the museum premises is prohibited.

Napier Museum has built-in natural air-conditioning system and of course good collection of rarefacts such as bronze idols, ancient ornaments, ivory carvings etc. It houses a four centuries old clock and a cot made of herbals.

Visiting Hours : 10:00 - 17:00 hrs, closed on Mondays and forenoons of Wednesdays.

Sree Chithra Art Gallery: With- in the periphery of the compound of Napier Museum is yet another piece of beauty to behold - Sree Chithra Art Gallery. It contains a large collection of paintings of various Indian and South Asian Schools. There is a good number of paintings of the veteran, Raja Ravivarma - a name worshipped by many artists. Copies of Kerala's exquisite murals, paintings of the Rajput, Mughal and the Tanjore Schools, reproductions of murals of Ajantha, Bagh, and Sittannavasal, paintings from China, Japan, Tibet and Bali - all add to the decorum. The canvases of Roerichs, vividly capturing the colours of the Himalayas, can also be seen.

In a nutshell, it is a visual banquet to any pair of connoisseur's eyes.

Visiting Hours :10:00 - 17:00 hrs, closed on Mondays and forenoons of Wednesdays.

Veli lagoon: The seemingly placid sheet of water that backed away from the visibly reverberant sea offers a general idea of the famous backwaters of Kerala. Boating facilities are also available. Pedal boats, row boats and motored boats are available on hire. Children, in particular have a lot of fun and frolic climbing over the huge sculptures which dot the landscapes, and riding a ferry.

Visiting Hours : 08:00 - 18:00 hrs
Boat Rentals : 10:00 - 17:30 hrs

Rate Tariff :

Safari boat	-	Rs.10/-(per head)
Speed boat	-	Rs. 120/-
Pedal boat (4 seater)	-	Rs.50/- (for half an hour)
Pedal boat (2 seater)	-	Rs.40 (for half an hour)

The Public Park: The public park encompasses some vital attractions like the zoo, the botanical gardens and the observatory atop a hill, popular as 'observatory hill'.

The Zoological Park: This is one of the pioneer zoos in India, located amidst a wonderful botanical garden. The tall, huge and massive trees, wild bushes, shrubs and lawns, the lake strewn with wild fowls and mild ducks give the visitors a glimpse of the jungle in the city. Different varieties of snakes, poisonous and non-poisonous, inherently active and sluggish can also be seen.

Visiting Hours :10:00 - 17:00 hrs, closed on Mondays.

The Connemara Market: This is the city's colourful market forum. Its grandness is overt from the archway entrance near the Secretariat and is often a tourists' hang out. Hence everything from 'A' to 'Z' is available in this market.

The Observatory: On the top of the observatory hills at the vantage point, 60 mts above the sea level which is also the highest point in the city, the observatory, carrying out extra-terrestrial observations, offers to the visitors, a panoramic view of the city.

The Kanakakunnu Palace: The palace and its vast grounds provide the stage for many cultural meets and programmes.

The Science and Technology Museum Complex: The museum contains articles of science and technology, modern and old, including all branches of science. Educative, informative and interesting as it is to the young and old alike, it inculcates a quest for science and a passion for technology in the young minds.

Visiting Hours : 10:00 - 17:00 hrs closed on Mondays
Entrance Fee : Adults - Rs.2/-, Children Re. 1/-.

Shankumugham Beach: 8 km off the city, abutting Thiruvananthapuram airport and Veli tourist village, this beach is the ideal spot for watching Sunset. The glorious sight of the mighty Sun submerging into the conspicuously endless expanse of the blue waters in the far-away horizon sending out His golden yellow and orange rays is relished, time and again, by visitors of all sorts. Those who are looking for a diversion or a relaxation can just step into the recreation club at the beach. A gigantic sculpture of a mermaid, 35m long can also be seen apparently in the posture of taking a well deserved rest after a tiring swim. A huge starfish, several times bigger than the ones found in the sea made not of flesh and skin but of bricks and concrete but there is a restaurant for the visitors to satisfy their hunger. The 'Chacha Nehru Traffic Training Park', here, helps children learn the traffic rules.

Priyadarshini Planetarium: The planetarium helps the viewers get a glimpse of the magnificent extraterrestrial happenings beyond the average human perception.

The show takes the viewers light-years into the incomprehensible space. They are sure to loose themselves in the narration and the movements of the replica of the heavenly bodies on the dome shaped screen overhead.

Show Schedule : 10:30, 12:00, 15:00 and 17:00 hrs

Entrance fee : Adults - Rs.10/- Children - Rs.5/- (from 3-10 yrs)

Chacha Nehru Children's Museum: The museum is named after the first Prime Minister of India, late, Sri. Jawaharlal Nehru. It is well known that he doted on children and even a quick glance through his biography would reveal many an incidence that alludes to this fact. And quite rightly the museum is intended for kids. It has a large collection of dolls (nearly 2000), stamps and masks.

Visiting Hours: 10:00 - 17:00 hrs, Closed on Mondays

The Secretariat: This is an edifice of the Roman architectural style. The government administration is carried out here. The offices of ministers and bureaucracy are also present.

The Kerala Legislature Complex: Complex, as is the construction of auditoriums with minimal noise levels, optimum feed back etc., meticulous care has been exercised in maintaining the acoustic properties of the hall with advanced acoustic treatments and latest sound system technologies. Though equipped with modern facilities, the structure bears a resemblance to the classical form of grand architecture with its dome-tower, carved galleries and the ornamental work on the teakwood panel and the ceiling.

Akkulam Tourist Village: This is a picnic-makers' paradise. Boating is popular here. Children love the spot and it is always seen swarming with children revelling in joy. There is also a swimming pool to add to the fun.

Visiting Hours : 10:00 - 17:00 hrs

Boat Rentals :

Safari boat - Rs.15/-(per head)

Speed boat - Rs. 150/ (for four passengers)

Children's Park -

Visiting Hours : 09:30 - 19:30 hrs

Entrance fees : Adults - Rs.2/- Children - Re.1/-

Swimming pool -

Visiting Hours : 07:30 - 18:30 hrs

Entrance fees : Adults - Rs.15/- Children - Rs.10-

Thiruvallam: It is situated 10 km off the city. Canoeing is popular in the calm stretch of backwaters between Thiruvallam and Kovalam.

Lord Parasuraman's Temple is here by the river at Thiruvallam, Chithranjali, the State Film Development Corporation's studio is at Thiruvallam.

Aruvikkara Dam: This beautiful dam is just a half an hour's drive from the city, 16 km away. It is situated on the banks of the river Karamana. A temple dedicated to Goddess Durga can also be seen. A stream near the Temple is abundant in fish that dauntlessly near the shore to be fed by the visitors. The visitors seem to enjoy feeding them too.

The Kovalam Beach: A half-an-hour drive from the city covering 16 km leads to this Nature's marvel of international acclaim. It has been a tourists' favourite since long past. Visitors from all over the globe throng to the resort and spend days together trying to grab every bit of the joy it proffers. There are also three crescent beaches; the most popular being the southernmost known as the 'light house beach'. Accommodation is available. Boarding and lodging is available at different rates to cater to the needs of all the visitors.

Vizhinjam Rock Cut Cave: 17 km from the city, it takes about half an hour to reach the spot. The awe-inspiring cave temple here comprises of splendid sculptures cut out of rocks in the 18th century A.D. The cave encloses a one-celled Shrine with a loose sculpture of Vinandara Dakshinamurthi. The outer wall of the cave depicts half complete reliefs of Lord Siva with His consort Goddess Parvathi. In short, it is a place to admire and worship.

The Koyikkal Palace - Nedumangad: Situated at the place called Nedumangad 18 kms from the city which is again around half an hour's drive it is also enroute to the Ponmudi hill station and the Courtallam Waterfalls. This ancient palace dates back to the 15th century. The traditional 'Nalukettu' building here is two storeyed with inclined gabled roofs, an inner courtyard and museums of folklore and numismatics set up by the department. 'The Folklore Museum' established in 1992 is a treasure house of quaint musical instruments, occupational implements, household utensils, models of folk arts, etc.

The Numismatics Museum houses rare and historically valuable coins evidencing the trade relations of the State.

Sri Mahadeva Temple: It is believed that this temple dedicated to Lord Siva, located at Kazhakuttom, had been built in the 14th century. Mitramandapuram Temple is another old temple and is situated on the outskirts of the city.

Neyyar Dam: It is a picnic spot about 29 km from the city. There is a watch tower. Just as crocodiles are attracted to the water, the visitors are attracted to the crocodile farm, here. The majestic 'King of the forest' - Lions can be sighted on a safari in the 'Lion Safari Park'. There is also a deer park. And there are also boating facilities at the reservoir.

Varkala: Situated 40 km from the city, this seaside resort is a spa and an important Hindu pilgrim spot. Near here, stands the hill Sivagiri on the top of which Sri Narayana Guru, a great social reformer had spent his last days. The coastline is famous for its high cliffs and mineral springs. The 2000 years old Sri Janardhana Swamy Temple and the Nature Care Centre are the two main attractions here.

Peppara Wild Life Sanctuary: This sanctuary occupies over a 53 sq. km of the western ghats and is about 50 km from Thiruvananthapuram, on the way to Ponmudi. It is rich in flora and fauna. It also has wide-spread hillocks, forests and eucalyptus plantations. It is a never-to-miss spot for every wildlife enthusiast.

Ponmudi : About 54 km from Thiruvananthapuram, this hill resort is about 915 mts above sea level. The pathways are narrow. The atmosphere is cool, the ground is lush green and the place is woody. The air is filled with the fragrance of mountain flowers. Exotic butterflies can be spotted. Springs and small rivulets are enchanting and enlivening.

There is a deer park close by and there are also excellent trekking trails. There is also a KTDC restaurant and a government guest house.

Accommodation : Guesthouse : Cottages & Rooms Rs.250/-, Rs.600/ - Dormitory Rs.800/-.

For reservations contact: The Secretary, General Administration Department (Political), Govt. Secretariat, Thiruvananthapuram.

The Padmanabhapuram Palace: On the way to Kanyakumari, 63 km from Thiruvananthapuram is the place called Tuckalai in which stands the magnificent palace which had been the abode of the hierarchical rulers of Travancore. This is a well preserved wooden palace and a standing testimony to the traditional Kerala school of architecture. The extraordinary murals, exquisite floral carvings and the black glossy granite floor have withstood the test of time. The palace remains closed on Mondays.

Agasthyakoodam: It is a part of the Sahyadri range of mountains and is the second highest peak in Kerala at a height of about 1890 mts above sea level, the highest one being Anamalai (2689 ft). These mountains are covered with thick forests which provide home to a large number of wildlife species. Agasthyakoodam is abundant in rare medicinal herbs with amazing curative properties. Brilliantly hued orchids and a variety of plants are also found in large numbers. Home to certain birds and a seasonal dwelling to a huge set of certain migratory ones; this mountain attracts professional as well as occasional birdwatchers. This legendary mountain can also be accessed on foot from Kotoor, near Neyyar dam and also from Bonacaud. The ideal season for trekking is from December to April. Trekkers need to obtain a forest pass from the wildlife warden, Forest Department, PTP Nagar, Thiruvananthapuram.

Somatheeram: Somatheeram is also known as 'The Tropical Garden of Eden'. It is an Ayurvedic Beach resort which preserves the age old heritage of Kerala. It is 21 kms. from Thiruvananthapuram and 9 kms. south of the Kovalam Beach. Somatheeram, 15 acres of green garden terraced heights sloping down to the sandy beach stretching to the tranquil, turquoise sea changing colour and mood momentarily as the white clouds sail past over it.

Somatheeram has an Ayurvedic Centre, where several rejuvenative therapies based on the Vedic science Ayurveda are undertaken.

Ayurvedic treatment with herbal preparations directed towards strengthening the immune system, preventing curing diseases without any side effects. Somatheeram Ayurvedic Hospital and Yoga Center has been selected for the Award of Excellence in the category of Best Ayurvedic Centre.

Manaltheeram Ayurvedic Beach Village: Manaltheeram is a picturesque beach resort and near to Somatheeram Beach Resort.

FESTIVALS

India is known for Her festivals. Thiruvananthapuram as all other parts of India celebrates a number of festivals almost all through the year though they occur in a quicker succession in one part of the year than the other.

Christmas, Easter, Good Friday are celebrated with much fanfare by the Christian community here and the exchange of greetings and wishes among the Christians and their Hindu and Muslim brethren, is a commonsight.

Muslims, have their heyday during Bakrid and Ramadan. The air is filled with serenity as they observe fasting during Ramadan month. The celebrations are coupled with piety and stoicity. Warm greetings exchange kind hearts regardless of religion or caste.

Hindus make merry of a number of festivals. Apart from the functions like Diwali, Dasara. etc. which are celebrated with equal pomp and show throughout the Nation and with hearty greetings, gifts and wishes being conveyed among kith and kins and to the friends belonging to other religions, with equal zest, there are a few unique to the State.

Onam: This is celebrated in the months of August-September. It commemorates the reign of the legendary king Mahabali in the Hindu Mythology.

One week is earmarked for tourism during the peak of the festive season to enable the tourists as well as the inhabitants to move about and have their slice of the hilarity.

Arattu: Vetta and Arattu occur twice a year. Holy processions are held from Sri Padmanabha Swamy Temple to Shangumugam Beach led by the members of the royal family of erstwhile Travancore.

The idols from the Temple are taken to the sea for a holy dip. Cultural performances including the Kathakali are part of the celebrations.

Attukal Pongala: Thousands of female devotees throng the 'Bhagawathy Amman' Temple at Attukal, just a couple of kilometers from Thiruvananthapuram, for the 10 day Pongala festival. As it is a 'Ladies' Special' festival, men are not supposed be in the proximity. 'Pongala', considered to be the Goddesse's favourite, is in fact a kind of sweet porridge. The long line of women absorbed in devotion, preparing this ritual offering can be seen all the way till the East Fort and farther.

Chandanakudam Mahotsavam: This is a colourful Islamic festival. Devotees bring offerings in the form of money in pots decorated with flowers and incense sticks and sandalwood paste sending out their sweet aroma, to the tomb of an austere lady, Bee Umma, at Beemápally, near Thiruvananthapuram.

Nishagandhi Dance and Music Festival: The 'Nishagandhi Open Air Theatre', Kanakakunnu Palace, Thiruvananthapuram hosts this festival of Indian classic dance and music from the 22nd to the 27th of February every year. The evenings are filled with, Bharathanatyam, Kathak, Kathakali, Kuchipudi, Manipuri, Mohiniattam, Odissi and traditional dance forms of classical music and Jugalbandi, etc.

Gramam: This is a 10 day (Jan. 14-23) village fair along the beach at Kovalam. The venue is provided by the quadrangular penthouse courtyard with an open centre, called the Nalukettu. Arts and Crafts fair, Kathakali, Thiruvathirakali, Mohiniyattam, Oppana Kalaripayattu, Theyyam Kumettikali, Kakkarisi Natakam, Panchavadyam, Chakyarkoothu, Ottanthullal, etc. deserve special mention.

Flavour Food Festival: Celebrated from 5th to 11th April by renowned hotels across Kerala at the Kanakakunnu Palace Grounds, Thiruvananthapuram, this festival is the time for various cuisines of the world, titillating dishes and inviting delicacies.

Accommodation

Thiruvananthapuram (STD: 0471)

- **The Muthoot Plaza,** Punnen Road, Thiruvananthapuram-695 039 ✆: 2337733; Fax: 0471-2337734; Email: muthoot@eth.net
- **Hotel Saj Lucia,** East Fort, Thiruvananthapuram-695 023. ✆: 2463443; Fax: 0471-2463347; Email: sajlucia@md2.vsnl.net.in
- **Surya Samudra Beach Garden,** Heritage, Pulinkudi, Mullur P.O., Thiruvananthapuram-695 521; ✆: 2480413, 2267333, 2481825; Fax: 0471-

2267124; Email: suryasamudra@vsnl.com

- **Best Western Swagath Holiday Resort,** Kovalam, Thiruvananthapuram-695 527 ✆: 2481148/49; Fax: 0471-2481150; Email: swagat. esort@satyam.net.in
- **Hotel Chola International, Aristo Junction,** Thampanoor, Thiruvananthapuram ✆: 2334334, 2334601-04; Fax: 0471-2473172
- **Hotel Kadaloram Beach Resort,** G.V. Raja Road, Kovalam, Thiruvanathapuram-695 527 ✆: 2481116-20; Fax: 0471-2481115; Email: kadaloram@vsnl.com
- **Samrat Hotel,** Thakaraparambu Road, Thiruvananthapuram-695 023 ✆: 2463314, 2463214, 2460167; Fax: 0471-2570432
- **Hotel South Park (4 Star)** ✆: 2333333 Fax: 2331861 Email:southpark@vsnl.com
- **Hotel Luciya (4 Star)** ✆: 2463443 Fax: 2463347 Email:sajluciya@md2.vsnl.net.in
- **Horizon (3 Star)** ✆: 2326888 Fax: 2324444 **Email**: hotelhorizon@vsnl.com
- **Hotel Pankaj (3 Star)** ✆: 2464645 Fax: 2465020
- **Mascot Hotel (3 Star)** ✆: 2318990 Fax: 2317745 **Email**:ktdc@vsnl.com
- **Jass** ✆: 2324881 Fax: 2324443 Email:jas@md2. vsnl.net.in
- **Ariya Nivas** ✆: 2330789 Fax: 2330423 Email:www.ariyanivas.com/index.html
- **Residency Tower** ✆: 2331661 Fax: 2331311 Email:rtower@md2.vsnl.net.in
- **Chaithram** ✆: 2330977 Fax: 2331446 Email:chaithra@md3.vsnl.net.in
- **Geeth** ✆: 2471987 Fax: 2460278
- **Oasis** ✆: 2333223 Fax: 2328054
- **Paramount Park** ✆: 2323474 Fax: 2331311
- **Prasanth** ✆: 2316189 Fax: 2316407
- **Thampuru** ✆: 2321974 Fax: 2321987
- **Hotel Pallava** ✆: 2452839
- **Amritha** ✆: 2323091 Fax: 2324977
- **Navarathna** ✆: 2330473
- **Regency** ✆: 2330377 Fax: 2331690 **Email**:hotelregency@satyam.net.in
- **Jacobs Hotel** ✆: 2330052
- **Aulakam Hotel** ✆: 2330488
- **Hotel Silver Sand** ✆: 2460318 Fax: 2478230
- **Moon Light** ✆: 2551186
- **Hotel Highland** ✆: 2333200 Fax: 2332645
- **Keerthi** ✆: 2325650 Fax: 2325792
- **President Hotel** ✆: 2313228 Fax: 2330305
- **Safari** ✆: 2477202
- **Yathri Niwas** ✆: 2324462
- **Hotel Kyvalya** ✆: 2330724 Fax: 2334176
- **Sukhwas** ✆: 2331967

Kovalam (Beach Destination) (STD: 0471)

- **Hotel Ashok (5 Star)** ✆: 2480101 Fax: 2481522 **Email**:htlashok@giasmd01.vsnl.net.in
- **Lagoona Beach** ✆: 2480049 Fax: 2462935 **Email**:davindia@hotmail.com
- **Surya Samudra** ✆: 2480413 Fax: 2481124 **Email**:suryasamudra@vsnl.net.in
- **Bethsaida** ✆: 2481554 Fax: 2481554 **Email**:saturn@md3.vsnl.net.in
- **Uday Samudra** ✆: 2481654 Fax: 2481578 **Email**:udaykov@md4.vsnl.net.in
- **Manaltheeram Beach Resort** ✆: 2268610 Fax: 2267611 **Email**:somatheertham@vsnl.com
- **Nikkis Nest** ✆: 2481822 Fax: 2481182 **Email**:nest@giosmd01.vsnl.net
- **Somatheeram Ayurvedic Beach Resort** ✆ 2268101 Fax: 2267600 **Email**:soma@md2.vsnl.net.in
- **Hotel Sea Face** ✆: 2481591 Fax: 2481320 **Email**:seaface@md4.vsnl.net.in
- **Hotel Samudra** ✆: 2480089 Fax: 2480242 **Email**:samudra@md3.vsnl.net.in
- **Bright Resorts** ✆: 2481192 Fax: 2481210 **Email**:bright@md3.vsnl.net.in
- **Coconut Bay** ✆: 2480566 Fax: 2343349 **Email**:cocobay@md3.vsnl.net
- **Ideal Ayurvedic Resort** ✆: 2481632 Fax: 2481632
- **Hotel Neelakanta** ✆: 2480321 Fax: 2480421 **Email**:info@hotelneelakant
- **Santhatheeram** ✆: 2481972 Fax: 2481972 **Email**:sntheeram@md4.vsnl.net
- **Sea Rock** ✆: 2481721 Fax: 2480422
- **Hotel Rockholm** ✆: 2480606 Fax: 2480607 **Email**:rockholm@techpark.
- **Hotel Aquarious** ✆: 2481072 Fax: 2481072 **Email**:vunus@md3.vsnl.net.in
- **Beach and Lake Resort** ✆: 2481055 Fax: 2481559 **Email**:beachandlake@yahoo
- **Hotel Aparana** ✆: 2480950
- **Hotel Blue Sea** ✆: 2480401
- **Raja Hotel** ✆: 2480355 Fax: 2480455
- **Moon Light** ✆: 2480375 Fax: 2481078
- **Neptune Hotel** ✆: 2480222 Fax: 2460187 **Email**:replica@vsnl.com
- **Wilson Beach Resort** ✆: 2480051 **Email**:wilson@md3.vsnl.net.in
- **Hotel Seaweed** ✆: 2480391 Fax: 2722698 **Email**:seaweed@md3.vsnl.net.in
- **Merriland Tourist Home** ✆: 2480440 Fax: 2481456 **Email**:kovalam@md3.vsnl.net.in
- **Hilton Beach Resort** ✆: 2481995 Fax: 2481476
- **Golden Sand** ✆: 2481476 Fax: 2481476
- **Hotel Orion** ✆: 2480999
- **Jeevan House** ✆: 2480662 Fax: 2480662 **Email**:kovalam@md3.vsnl.net.in
- **Royal Retreat Cottage** ✆: 2481080
- **Hotel Thushara** ✆: 2480692 Fax: 2481693 **Email**:hushara@md3.vsnl.net.in
- **Hotel Thiruvathira** ✆: 2450588
- **Golden Sands** ✆: 2481076
- **Sandy Beach Resorts** ✆: 2480012 **Email**:sandybeach@vsnl.net.in

• **Hotel Palmshore** ✆: 2481481 Fax: 2480495
• **Varmas Beach Resorts** ✆: 2480478 Fax: 2480578 **Email**:ushas@md4.vsnl.net.in
• **Hawah Beach Hotel** ✆: 2480431 **Email**:topic@md3.vsnl.net.in
• **Pappukutty** ✆: 2480235 Fax: 2480234
• **Lobster House** ✆: 2480456
• **Sea Flower Home** ✆: 2480554 Fax: 2481069
• **Holiday Home** ✆: 2480497
• **Hotel Deepak** ✆: 2480667
• **Swagath Resorts** ✆: 2481148 Fax: 2481150 **Email**:yajkal@md2.vsnl.net.in

Travel agents, Kovalam: Western Travel Service Ph:2481334. Elite Tours & Travels Ph:2481905, 2481405. Universal Travel Enterprises, Ph.2481729. Visit India, Lighthouse Road, Ph.2481069. Banyan Tours & Travels, Ph.:2481922. Great Indian Travel Service, Lighthouse Road, Ph.:2481110.

Convention Centre: ITDC, Kovalam Ph.: 2480101.

Cultural Centre, Kovalam: Ayyipilla Asan Memorial Kathakali School.

Two Wheeler Hire, Kovalam: Voyager Travels, Near Police Station, Ph.:2481993, Fax:2451858.

Varkala (Beach Destination) (STD: 0472)

• **Taj Garden Retreat (4 Star)** ✆: 2603000 Fax: 2602296 **Email**:retreat.varkala@tajhotel.com
• **Hill Top** ✆: 2601237 Fax: 2601237 **Email**:kutty@techpark.net
• **Sea Pearl** ✆: 2660105 Fax: 2605049 **Email**:seapearl@md3.vsnl.net.in
• **Preeth** ✆: 2600942 Fax: 2600942 **Email**:preethonline@sathyam.net.in
• **Thiruvambadi** ✆: 2601028 Fax: 2604345
• **Skylark Cliff Beach Resort** ✆: 2602107 Fax: (0473) 2601311

Kottayam

FACTS AND FIGURES

Area : 2,203 Sq.kms. • Population : 1,952,901 (2001 census) • Headquarters : Kottayam • Tourist Season: September to March.

About 154 kms in the Northwest of Thiruvananthapuram and about 64 kms in the Southeast of Kochi spanning the foothills of the unrelenting range of gigantic mountains, the Western Ghats, stands the city of Kottayam with its captivating mangrove forests, lush green paddy fields and a generous expanse of coconut groves rightly punctuated by enthralling brooks amidst teeming white lilies. Among the agricultural produce of the place are cashcrops like rubber, tea, pepper and cardamom. No wonder that a place of such picturesque beauty with tall trees, wide area and so on forms the natural habitat for scores of birds. There are many places which would interest tourists of varied tastes.

The religious harmony of the district can be sensed from the presence of over 50 Temples, 70 Churches and several Mosques including the one 1000 years old. It is also the gateway to a number of pilgrim centres like Sabarimala, Mannanam, Vaikom, Ettumanoor, Bharananganam, Erumeli, Mannarkad, Aruvithura, Athirempura, Perunna Vazhapalli and Thrikkodithanam near Changanachery.

Air: The nearest international airport is at Nedumbassery, Ernakulam, 90 km North.

Ferry Station: Boats are available here to Alleppey, Nedumudi, Kumarakom and Kavalam.

TOURIST INTEREST

Mahadeva Temple: This Temple, situated in the busy area of Kottayam is dedicated to Lord Siva. The legend has it that the idol here is 'Swayambu' (Self-manifested) and not installed. A 12 day festival is celebrated annually.

Sri Krishnaswamy Temple: Just 8 km from Kottayam, this temple is famous for the festival, Ezhunallathu procession in which Elephants have their own part to play along with humans. The festival goes on for 10 days and so does the ritual procession. Kathakali, Ottamthullal and other classical art forms of Kerala come alive during the festival.

Bagawathy Temple: About 6 km from Kottayam is the place called Kumaranallur where this temple stands with the architecture of the 'Gopurams' (Temple-Tower, Portal Tower) of Tamil Nadu. The idol is made of 'Anjanakkal' (antimony sulphate) and a 9 day festival is held every year.

Dakshina Mookambika Saraswathy Temple: This temple dedicated to Goddess Saraswathy- the Goddess of Arts and Learning and the consort of Lord Brahma - the God of Creations, is situated 10 kms from Kottayam at Panachikkadu in Chingavanam. The nine day festival 'Navarathri' (nine nights) is famous here.

Mahadeva Temple: Ettumanoor, 12 km north of Kottayam, is where this temple is dedicated to Lord Siva is situated. Here, the deity is in two forms, Vallya (Love) and Rudhra (Fury). The mural paintings of the temple especially that of Nataraja on the 'Gopuram' (Tower) and the ezharaponnana (7½ Elephants finished in gold) are famous. The festival 'Ezhara- ponnana Ezhunallathu' lasts for 10 days in February/March.

St. Mary's Church: Situated at Mannarkad, 8 kms from Kottayam, this church is dedicated to St.Mary. This is one of the most important churches of the Malankara Jawbite Syrian Christians. The 'Ettunompu', a festival of fasting for 8 days is held annually during which devotees from far and wide pour in to take part in rituals and prayers.

St. Mary's Forane Church: About 20 km from Ettumanoor, this church at Bharananganam, is one of the oldest churches in Kerala. The feast of carmel and that of St. Sabastian are held, annually.

Panchalimedu: Situated 7 km from the Mundakkayam - Kuttikanam stretch on the Kottayam-Kumili road lies Panchalimedu, at an attitude of about 2500 feet above the sea level. A three hour trek from Valliankavy, which is connected by bus service from Kottayam takes you to the spot. According to legends, the Pandavas stayed here and the pond beside a small temple is where Panchali is said to have bathed.

Kesari Falls: The Kesari Falls otherwise known as Valanjamakanam Falls lies in between Kuttikanam and Murinjapuzha on the Kottayam-Kumili route. Valanjamakanam is a three-hour journey from Kottayam by any bus to Kumili.

In and Around Kottayam

Kumarakom: The breath-taking beauty of the mangrove forests, the green sea of paddy fields and the vast, fantastic coconut groves benevolently accommodating eye-pleasing and thirst-quenching rivulets, canals, channelled between wild flora and mild lilies extend a warm welcome to every nature-loving tourist. The resorts nearby offer comfortable accommodation and exclusive leisure options like an ayurvedic massage, yoga, meditation, boating, fishing, angling and swimming. This place is 10 km from Kottayam on the Eastern bank of Vembanad lake.

The Vembanad Lake: This lake at about 16 km from Kottayam is the repository to myriad rivers, rivulets and canals of Kottayam. This enchanting tourist spot is fast turning out to be known also as a backwater tourism destination. The fish-rich lake offers excitement not only to fishing hobbyists but also to boating maniacs. The sights here are to be seen and enjoyed. House boat cruises and holiday packages are offered by the Kumarakom Tourist Village. The placid lake turns vibrant with the arrival of Onam as it is the place for spectacular regatta (the snake boat races)

Kumarakom Bird Sanctuary: About 16 km from Kottayam, on the banks of the splendid lake of Vembanad is this ornithologists' lure - the bird sanctuary where a number of species of birds flock in and flock out during migration. Popular among the migratory birds are Siberian stork, egret, darter, heron and teal. Some of the other common varieties are woodpecker, skylark, crane, waterhen and parrots. Taking a cruise on the Vembanad lake, the curious visitor, could catch a glimpse of a few of the endless species of living flying machines whose mysteries have been puzzling expert ornithologists across the globe ever since the study began. Pathiramanal, an enchanting island can be reached by boat.

Tariff for Houseboat cruises

One day cruise on full board basis: Single apartment houseboat for 2 persons - Rs.5,000/-

Twin apartment for 4 persons including food - Rs.6,000/-

One night, 2 days cruise on full board basis: Single apartment houseboat for 2 persons - Rs.12,500/ - Twin apart houseboat for 4 persons including food Rs.14,500/-

Stationary houseboat on room only basis: Single apartment houseboat for 2 persons - Rs.1195, twin apartment houseboat - Rs.995/= (per apartment)

For reservations please contact: KTDC Kumarakom Tourist Village, Kavanattinkara Ph. : 2525861, Central Reservation, KTDC, Mascot Square, Thiruvananthapuram. Phone: 2318976.

Pathiramanal: Pathiramanal, which means sands of midnight, is a wonderful island on the backwaters. According to mythology a young Brahmin once, dived into the Vembanad lake to perform his evening ablutions and the water made way for the land to rise from below to form this beautiful island which is now the abode of a variety of migratory birds from different parts of the world. The area of the island is about 10 acres.

Nattakom and Panachikad Reservoirs: In the lush green environ, the marvellous reservoirs add lusture to the calm village. The landscape here again is an invitation to scores of migratory birds. The boat ride from Kodoorar in Panachikad to Kumarakom is very popular. Other interesting features are Ayurvedic massages, boating, fishing and swimming.

Vaikom Tourist Land: This piquant picnic spot is ideal for langorous break. Various recreations including boat cruises on the Vaikom lake are on offer.

Mannanam Tourist Home: It is 8 km from Kottayam. It sites the St. Joseph's Monastery associated with the name of Fr. Kuriakose Elias of Chavara (1805-71). One of the saintly figures of the Syrian Catholic Church of Kerala. An intricate network of shimmering waterways embroider the richly green landscape, making the place ever so charming. There are boat cruise packages, ingenuously devised to make the tourists' experience most exciting. Through the Pennar canal, the cruise does not forsake the scenic backwaters of Alappuzha and Ernakulam.

Anchuvilakku: Anchuvilakku, meaning five lamps where five is the English for 'Anchu' and lamp for 'Vilakku' was built near the boat landing pier at Changanacheri by the great freedom fighter 'Veluthampi Dalawa'. He was also the one who established the Changanacheri market, one of the largest in Kerala. Five lamps are lit on this stone lamp post using kerosene. It is 22 km from Kottayam.

Nadukani: A fabulous hill-top-spot with abundant stretches of beautiful meadows and gigantic tenacious rocks is this place Nadukani which offers a overall view of the immensely beautiful land lying below.

Aruvikkuzhi Waterfalls: 18 km. from Kottayam and 2 km along a narrow muddy terrain this spot of boundless charms receives visitors looking for sheer enjoyment. The awe-inspiring streams jink their way through the benign landscape and the gushing waters cascade down the mountains with relentless fury and fall with a majestic roar from a height of 100 ft. The enormous rubber plantations here provide shade for Sun-beaten tourists.

Kariambukayam: The glorious Manimala river embellishes the elegant spot, Kariambukayam, Meloram in between the panchayat jurisdictions of the town known for its plantations Kanjirapalli and the pilgrim spot Erumeli. Enriched with rich natural features, the place has quite a few reservoirs on which, at occasions, aqua banquets are organised. The natural reservoirs and waterfalls at Melaruvithodu on the Ernakulam-Thekkady road play a substantial part in glorifying Kottayam.

Erumeli: 'Unity in Diversity', one of India's hallmarks, is well evident here as thousand upon thousands of Hindu pilgrims, fasting and observing strict austerity for a specific number of days, traditionally worship and offer prayers at a Mosque in Vavarambalam, on their way to Sabarimala which is another pilgrim spot. The mosque is dedicated to 'Vavar' a thick crony of Lord Sree Ayyappa, the presiding deity of Sabarimala.

Erumeli, the village with a natural bliss is situated 60 km South-east of Kottayam.

Maniamkunnu: The tenacious mountains characterised by wild plants and trees, shrubs and bushes, exotic flowers prudently part at places giving rise to astounding valleys of natural splendour. The higher the mountains soar the deeper the valleys dive.

Kayyoor: The ghat region with its own aspects of natural charms, and blanketed by lush green hilly vegetation is the pride of the Bharanganam panchayat in Kayyoor. A temple dedicated to the Pandava brothers (5 sons of the couple King Pandu and Kunthi in the legendary epic 'The Mahabharatha') is also found here. The temple lamps are lit only with ghee as in the temple at Sabarimala. Women are not allowed inside the temple.

St. Mary's Church: At Bharananganam, the church dedicated to St. Mary entombs the mortal remains of the benedicted Alphonsa and is now a popular pilgrim centre where multitude of devotees throng during the festival called the 'Feast of the Blessed Alphonsa' which is held in the month of July every year.

Illaveezhapoonchira: 'The valley where leaves do not fall' is what the very name of the domain means as it is devoid of trees. The startlingly beautiful valleys of here spanning over thousands of acres contribute in great deal to the natural attractions of Kottayam. The four distinct mountains soaring to heights of around 3200 ft, completely green deserve special mention. The valleys look entirely different when the gracious rains fill them up to form awesome lakes. This is one of the ideal spots to watch both Sunrise and Sunset. Thus the place offers dawn to dusk enchantment. Accommodation is provided by a DTPC rest house nearby.

Kannadipara: This place derives its name from the exotic rocks it possesses. 'Kannadi' which means mirror and 'para', 'rock' have merged together to christen the unique place whose rocks shine and reflect the Sun like mirrors. It is also the highest point in Ilaveezhapoonchira. Pazhakakanam plateau through which the resplendent river Kadapura flows is about 3 km from here. The place is rich in bamboo grooves, captivating meadows and eye-catching wild flora. The Kazhukankulimali waterfalls, here, as though tired of its long trek down the unyielding mountains thuds into the river below. To the east of the place, steep rocks enclose a natural fort.

Mankallu Mudikal: There are three magnificent hills in the region which are not too faraway from one another. Verdant and flat landscape marks the hilltops. An areal view of the place reveals a cauldron like formation. The place has no trees on the hilltops.

Illickal Mala: This mountain peak, soars to about 6000 ft above sea level. A lot of typical mountain streams, apparently emerging from the oblivion, merge merrily with one another to give rise to the all but calm Meenachil river. Here, the tranquil atmosphere, sought-after solitude, gentle breeze, picturesque environs and an endless list of natural features make the region all the more salubrious. Reaching the hilltop calls for a trek of about 3 km up the hill which will get amateurs a feel of mountaineering.

Illickal Kallu: This mammoth hill is made of three distinct hills averaging about 4000 ft and above, above the sea level. These hills or rocks are named after their own strange countenance. The umbrella shaped rock, locally called 'Kuda Kallu' resembles an umbrella. Among other common and rare herbs, a medicinal herb called the 'Neela Koduveli' which is, according to a common belief, blessed with paranormal powers to yield a rich harvest, is seen in large numbers here. 'Kunnukallu' which means hunch-back rock has a hunch on its sides. The supposedly ominous bridge of just about ½ a metre is called 'Narakapalam' which means 'bridge to hell'. The sight of Sunset and Moonrise, partially simultaneous happenings on fullmoon days is simply astonishing on the hilltops. The thin thread like lining of blue beauty, seen from the hilltops, at a faraway horizon is indeed the vast Arabian Sea.

Ayyapara: This spot extends to about 20 acres in area and is about 2000 ft in altitude. The legend says that 'The Pancha Pandavas' the five Pandava brothers, sons of King Pandu and his spouse Kunthidevi spent certain number of days here during their tenure of exile. It is also believed that the name of the place was originally, 'Anchupara', meaning five rocks and has later become to be known by the present name as time rolled by. However, some attribute the name to the temple dedicated to Lord 'Ayyappa' here. Four sturdy pillars support the rock-roof of the Temple. The mountain and every part of the nature here condition the wind into a pleasantly cool breeze. There is also a cave which can hold upto 15 persons. This is also a spot to admire Sunset.

Kolani Mudi: This is also one of the extravagant peaks, with an inviting cave, in the seemingly limitless range of Ilaveezhapoonchira mountains.

Marmala Stream: This is a place of streaming enjoyment. The startlingly beautiful stream leads to a roaring waterfalls, squired by the jungle around. The water falling from a height of about 200 ft. after taking an arduous course along the hillocks has with meticulous care and an architectural expertise, sculpted on the rocks down below a deep pond whose beauty speaks for itself. The natural bridge right under the waterfalls is yet another example of natural splendour.

Vazhikkadavu: The all but calm Meenachil river flows on one side of a medley of hills and rocks on the suburbs of the main district. This hill station comprises huge rocks, magnificent and elegant. The extremely tall rocks on one side of the main rock form spine-chilling abyss. Come December and January, the entire region is invaded by flora and fauna, the eyecatching colours and orchids, and so are the onlookers.

Kurisumala: This is a popular pilgrim centre of the Christians, about 3 km from Vazhikadavu. During and after the Holy week the place is filled with thousands of devotees, their souls soaked in faith, carrying small wooden 'Holy Crosses' up the hill in awesome reverence to the Almighty and offer prayers while the air is filled with divinity. There is also a Holy Monastery of the Jews atop the hill. The eastern side of the hill known as the 'Murugamala' has to its pride a temple dedicated to 'Lord Muruga' the son of 'Lord Shiva' in Hindu Mythology. The enchantment seems to begin the moment one sets off on the road to Kurisumala as the houses of European style alongside the path and an artificial lake, both designed by the famous architect, Larie Baker are sights never-to-miss.

Thangalappara: Situated near the resplendent hill resort of Karuthikallu and the alluring Kottathavalam, this is a Holy place of Islamic pilgrimage as it is here that the mausoleum of Sheikh Fakruddin is located.

Kottathavalam: This is another place of archaeological interest as the legends allude that the royal family from the town of Madurai in Tamil Nadu, rested here on their way to Poonjar. A magnificent cave which can be reached by the rock cut steps near the Murugamala, is an addition to the natural attractions. The cave contains rock cut chairs and couches and carvings of the figures of Goddess Madurai Meenakshi, Lord Ayyappa, Lord Muruga and the legendary personality known for her chastity, Kannaki and also the weapons and armoury.

Poonjar Palace: This palace stands tall as a genuine repository to a rare and a large collection of regal antiques, pristine artifacts, extraordinary furniture etc. A fabulous palanquin, a 'Thoni', made out of a single piece of quality wood ad hoc for 'Ayurvedic' massages, a hanging light with arms for holding lamps, traditional palm leaf scriptures, decorated jewel boxes, sculptures of Lord Nataraja, the dancing form of Lord Siva, grain measures of the olden days, statues and armoury are to name a few.

As part of an annual ritual, a conch is taken on a procession. At a stone's throw from the palace, there stands a temple identical to that of Madurai Sri Meenakshi. The wall sculptures tell stories from the Puranas. Another temple in the proximity is the 'Sastha Temple' dedicated to Lord Ayyappa in which a rare row of stone wall lamps known as the 'Chuttuvilakku' is famous.

Vagamon: Situated on the border of Kottayam and Idukki, this place is the breeding centre of 'Kerala Livestock Board'. This is again a typical hill station with bountiful tea-gardens and stimulating meadows.

The greatest attraction of the place in Kurishumala, a sky scraping mountain with a small church on its peak and the Kurishumala Ashramam, a monastery atop another hill.

Pala, Kanjirapally, Vayaskara and Chirattamon: The two former towns are known for their rubber plantations watered by the generous rivers Meenachil and Manimala. The later two, house 'Ayurvedic Rejuvenation Centres'.

St. Mary's Church: Located at Cheriapalli, 2 km from Kottayam town, this church of splendid architectural value, dedicated to St.Mary, is the result of coalition of the Kerala and Portuguese styles. Built by Thekkumkoor Maharajah it dates back to the year 1579. The wall paintings reveal general themes and the ones relating to the Holy Bible.

Thazhathangadi Valiapalli: About 2 km on the west of Kottayam town, this ancient church of the 1550's stands as a living monument of the Knanaya Orthodox Syrian Community. The Persian Holy Cross here is believed to be one of the seven brought by St. Thomas Pahlavi inscriptions can also be found.

There is yet another structure of ancient glory. A Holy Mosque, believed to be of the last millennium is also seen here.

Dharmasastha Temple: Dedicated to Lord Ayyappa at Pakkil, about 3 km from Kottayam. This temple is one of the eight established by Parasurama the legendary founder of Kerala. 'Sankranthi Vaibhavam' - an annual festival in which a fair of household articles comes up is celebrated in the month of June and July.

St. George's Church: This church situated at Puthupalli, believed to have been built by the rulers of Thekkamkoor has a famous golden cross. An annual festival known as the feast of St. Geroge (Gee Varghese), is famous.

Siva Temple: This temple at Thalikkotta, 2 km from Kottayam, is dedicated to Lord Siva. The royal families of Thekkamkoor have worshipped here. Sivarathri festival in January-February and another 10 day festival in April-May are held here.

The CSI Cathedral Church: This church was built over 175 years ago during the British rule of India.

Syrian Churches: The Old Seminary, Marthoma Seminary and Vadavathoor Seminary and the Malankara Orthodox Syrian Church headquartered at Devalokam, Kottayam are places of historical, architectural and devotional interests.

St. Thomas Mount: 1200 ft. above sea level, where exclusive view of the Vaikom lake and its extraordinary surroundings are in the offing, is a

Holy place of worship and prayer for the Christians.

Siva Temple: Located at Vaikom 40 km from Kottayam, this temple dedicated to Lord Siva has a rich architecture typical of Kerala style. It is also famous as Kasi (Varanasi) of the South. Traditional art renditions and Elephant processions are famous here. November-December is the period of the annual festival known as Vaikathashtami. Legends cite Parasurama's associations with the temple.

St. Mary's Church: This church in the high ranges of Karuvilangad town was built in 355 AD. The inscription on the ancient bell of the church is yet to be deciphered.

The one at Athirampuzha renovated in 1874 was built in 1080 AD. The annual feast in honour of St.Sabastian accompanied by fireworks and decorative illuminations and privileged devotees making votive offerings of gold and silver are all part of an exclusive festival here.

The 800 year old church at Kudamaloor was built by Champakasseri Maharajah. A rope and water log used to draw water from wells is the traditional offering here. The place also has a famous temple.

St. Joseph's Monastery: Situated near the Medical College at Mannanam, this church was built by the blessed Father Chavara Kuriakose Elias whose mortal remains are preserved and revered by the multitude of devotees every day.

Kaduthuruthi Valiapalli: Situated on the MC road between Ettumanoor and Vaikom, this age-old church, built in 500 AD is famous for its huge portal cross made out of a single stone.

Vimalagiri Church: This Holy place of worship stands tall as a reminder of the grandeur of Gothic architecture with its 172 ft. tower, clearly one of the tallest church towers of the State. Every December hosts a feast.

St. Thomas Church: This is again an ancient monument, built in 1002 AD and renovated in the 18th century. This is situated at Pala.

Another church, at Cherpungal, which according to a belief was built by St. Thomas and then relocated to the southern banks of the beautiful Meenachil river with the aid of poet Kunchan Nambiar and family is another age-old worship centre. The votive oblation here is oil lamps in front of the image of Infant Jesus, much similar to Hindu faith.

Aruvithira Church: 11 km off Kottayam, this church, according to a belief established by St.Thomas, is among the churches of Kerala which have a hefty inflow of pecuniary oblations during the festive occasions. A feast is celebrated in April every year.

Pazhayapalli Mosque: In Chenganacherry, 21 km off Kottayam, this famous Mosque of central Travancore was built 950 years ago. During 'Thangal Adiyanthiram', which is the famous annual festival, two tonnes of rice and hundreds of kilos of meat pour in from devotees, with which 'Biriyani' a famous cuisine of lingering taste is cooked for a grand community feast. The Mosque also celebrates another festival, the 'Chandanakudam' festival for which devotees flock in large numbers.

Thirunakkara Mahadeva Temple: Right in the heart of the city of Kottayam, this Siva temple built in the grand architectural style unique to Kerala, by the Maharajah of Tekkumkoor is half a millennium old.

The walls are adorned with exquisite paintings. The 'Koothambalam', the grand edifice ad hoc to cultural congregation is one of the highlights.

Pathenpalli: In Erattupetta, this place is famous for the festival 'Chandanakudam', 'Chandan' meaning sandal and 'Kudam' meaning pot, in the months of February and December.

Saraswathi Temple: This temple, situated at Panachikkad is also known as the Southern Mookambika Temple. This temple is dedicated to Goddess Saraswathi, the Goddess for arts and learning and the consort of Lord Brahma, the creator of the Universe and everything it holds. Saraswathi Pooja is celebrated every year here in October or November. 'Vidhyarambam' is also a famous festival during which the juveniles are introduced for the first time ever in their lives to letters and other arts.

The Surya Temple: The very name of the place 'Adityapuram' which means 'Abode of Sun God' signifies the presence of the Temple dedicated to the Sun God. The first and last Sundays of the Zodiacs Scorpio which falls in the months November and December and Aries in the months of April and May are reckoned to be auspicious.

Bhagavathyamman Temple: This temple, at Ambalakadavu, dedicated to Goddess Bhagavathy is where the 'Arattu' festival of the Thirunakkara Mahadevar Temple is celebrated. The Vishu festival is also celebrated here in the months April and May.

Pallipurathukavu: This place is famous for the 'Padam Udaya Mahotsavam' and the ritual offering 'Nadel Thiyattu' performance.

Bhagavathi Temple: This temple, situated at Manarkad, dedicated to Goddess Bhadrakali was built 200 years ago. 'Kalamezhuthupattu', 'Kumbha Bharani', 'Meena Bharani', 'Patham Udayam' and 'Mandalam Chirappu' are the main festivals here.

Kavil Bhagavathy Temple: Located at Changanacherry 18 km from Kottayam, this temple dedicated to Goddess Bhagavathy, was built by the Maharajas of Thekkumkoor. 'Kavilchirappu' in December-January is the annual festival here.

Kidangoor Sri Subrahmanya Swamy Temple: The annual festival takes place between middle of March.

Sree Subramanya Swamy Temple: Sree Subramanya also known as Lord Muruga, son of the Divine couple Lord Siva and Goddess Parvathi, is the presiding deity of the Temple which is situated at Perunna, 20 km from Kottayam. The annual festival 'Pallimetta Utsavam' is celebrated here in the months of November and December.

Siva Temple and Kalkulathukavu Temple: At Vazhappalli, Changanacherry, 17 km off Kottayam, this temple dedicated to Lord Siva abounds in ancient sculptures and ornate carvings.

The Kalkulathukavu Temple at Vazhappalli hosts a rare festival called the 'Mudiyeduppu Utsavam' which is celebrated at 12 year long intervals. Apart from other rituals the Holy procession carrying honey, known as 'Madhu' and plantain saplings and trees bearing fruits and flowers known as 'Kulavazha', 'Bhairavi Purapadu' and Darika Vadha Purappadu also form part of the grand celebrations.

FESTIVALS

Floral Display and Victual Banquet: With the arrival of the penultimate week of the first month of the year, rapturous memories of the exuberant celebrations of the 'New Year' still lingering in the minds, various parts of the district and inundated with flowers, wild and mild with their piquant fragrance wafting through the air.

Feasts are organised as part of the annual celebrations at a number of Churches, Mosques and Temples during their respective periods.

Erumeli Petta Thullal: Erumeli, the venue of innate congenuity between Hinduism and Islamism hosts this traditional festival. The pilgrims on their way to Sabharimala halt here, offer prayers in Vavar Mosque and indulge in the legendary 'Petta Thullal', at Sastha Temple which is, unconstrained dancing in Divine Ecstasy. This occurs in the month of January.

Vaikomashtami: This is a 12 day festival which usually falls in between November and December. Elephant processions fireworks and cultural performances like the Kathakali, Ottamthullal and musical recitals etc., are some of the highlights.

Ettumanoor Ezharapponnana: Arattu ritual, Elephant processions, procession of devotees, etc., are part of the celebrations.

Chandanakudam: The 'Chandanakudam' or 'Sandal Pot' is a 2 day festival. Cultural performances like music, dance, drama and fireworks add to the celebrations.

Ponadu Chootu Padayani: The Bhagavathy Temple at Meenachil taluk celebrates this festival annually. Devotees perform clockwise reverential circumambulation carrying lighted palm fronds and hit one another with the burning fronds as part of the ritual.

Better Home Exhibition: An exclusive fair of household articles and domestic utensils help better homes. This is held between the 2nd and the 6th October every year.

Boat Timings: The town jetty is about 1.5 km away from the KSRTC Bus Stand and during summer season the boats operates from Kodimatha Jetty is about 1 km from KSRTC Bus Terminal and 2.5 km from Railway Station.

Kottayam-Alleppey - 3 hours journey.

Kottayam-Mannar - 3 hours journey.

Kottayam-Champakulam - 4 hours journey.

Accommodation

Kottayam (STD: 0481)

- **Anjali Hotel (3 Star)** ✆: 2563661 Fax: 2563669
- **Vembanadu Resort** ✆: 2361633 Fax: 2360866 Email:vembanad@md5.vsnl.net.in
- **Hotel Green Park** ✆: 2563311 Fax: 2563312
- **Hotel Prince** ✆: 2578809 Fax: 2573138
- **Hotel Floral Park,** ✆: 2597108 Fax: 2595020
- **Hotel Aiswarya** ✆: 2581254 Fax: 2581253
- **Hotel Sakthi** ✆: 2563151
- **Hotel Nisha Continental** ✆: 2563984
- **Hotel Aida** ✆: 2568391 Fax: 2568399 Email:aida@md3.vsnl.net.in
- **Nellimuttil Tourist Home** ✆: 2560714 Fax: 2595020
- **Hotel Nithya** ✆: 2597849
- **Exon Guest House** ✆: 2564916
- **The Ambassador** ✆: 2563755 Fax: 2563755
- **Tipsy Hotel** ✆: 2535541 Fax: 2536708

Kumarakom (STD: 0481)

- **Kumarakom Lake Resorts** ✆ 2524900 Fax: 2524987
- **Golden Waters** ✆: 2525826
- **Taj Garden Retreat** ✆: 2524377
- **Coconut Lagoon** ✆: 2525834

Changanacherry (STD: 0481)

- **Hotel Vani** ✆: 2422403 Fax: 2421803
- **Hotel Breeze International** ✆: 2422909 Fax: 2421015
- **Hotel Maharanj** ✆: 2422983

Malappuram

FACTS AND FIGURES

Area : 3,548 Sq.kms. • Population : 3,629,640 (2001 census) • Headquarters : Mallappuram • Tourist Season: September to March.

This is yet another district of Kerala with places of historic and archaeological importance. The ancient temples and mosques, the traditional system of medicine and treatment practiced here, the bird sanctuary buoyed by picturesque hillocks, the festivals and the costumes of the people, all speak volumes of the rich heritage of the district which has adopted the name of one of its major cities–Malappuram. This was incidentally the military headquarters of the popular Zamorians of Kozhikode which is about 50 kms afar.

Mallappuram district is bounded by Kozhikode district on the North, The Nilgiris on the East, Arabian Sea on the West and Thrissur and Palakkad districts on the South.

Air: The nearest airport is at Karippur, Kozhikode, 36 km away.

Rail: The main railway station is at Kozhikode.

In and Around Malappuram

The Thali Temple: About 20 kms from Malappuram city is Perinthalmanna wherein this famous temple whose presiding deity is Goddess 'Durga' is situated. Angadipuram is just 3 km on the East of the place. Pooram festival is celebrated here.

Thirumandhamkunnu Temple: This temple at Angadipuram, 3 km on the west of Perinthalmanna is an important pilgrim centre, whose presiding deity is Goddess 'Durga'. In the months March and April the annual festival, Pooram is celebrated.

The Jama-at Mosque: This mosque at Malappuram attracts a large number of Muslim pilgrims from every nook and cranny of Kerala and more during the annual festival in April. The 'Mausoleum' abutting the Mosque reminisces the heroic acts of bravery of the martyrs of Malappuram - 'The Malappuram Shaheeds'.

The Pazhayangadi Mosque: This mosque is situated at Kondotti, 18 km East of Manjeri. This important pilgrim centre of the Muslims has been built 500 years ago. The annual festival unique to the place, known as the 'Valia Nercha', held in February and March is indeed a grand feast for three long days.

Tirur: (25 km West of Malappuram) The presence of the birth place of 'Thunchath Ezhuthachan', the father of the regional language of Kerala - Malayalam, is the pride of the place. The practice of acquainting toddlers with the alphabets of the fathomless Malayalam, on a small plane of sand taken from the revered spot which was once the abode of Ezhuthachan who later came to be known as Thunchan Parambu, has been going on for years together with unscathed enthusiasm.

Tanur: History suggests this coastal fishing town as one of the settlements of the Portuguese of the very early times. It is also believed that, in 1546, St. Francis Xavier visited the place.

One of the oldest temples of Kerala, 'The Keraladeshapuram Temple', dedicated to Lord Vishnu is situated about 3 km from here.

Kottakkal: The mention of the name 'Kottakkal' leads invariably to the thought of 'Arya Vaidyasala', founded by Vaidyarathnam in 1902. This pioneer institution of Ayurveda, the traditional system of health and medicine which believes in 'Prevention is better than cure' though it offers lasting cure to various diseases, has branches throughout the State and in Delhi and Chennai. Relentless in research and development the Vaidyasala runs an Ayurvedic Research Centre which also serves as a nursing home and hospital. An appointment in advance of at least 10 days is mandatory to see the chief doctor. Accommodations are available. The Ayurvedic centre is famous as P.S. Warrier, 'Kottakkal Arya Vaidyasala'.

Kottapadi: The base of the Cantonment Hill, near the health- giving Ayurvedic Centre at Kottakkal, contains cognizant evidences of an old and once magnificent fort of the Zamorins of Kozhikode. Vettakkorumakan Temple and a popular Siva Temple whose walls are adorned by the ornate paintings of Malabar are not too far away.

Kadaladi Bird Sanctuary: The sanctuary ideally studded with beautiful hillocks on a group of exhilarating islands is where the enchanting river 'Kadundipuzha' meets her destination - the Arabian Sea. It is the asylum to more than a 100 species of fascinating bird-inhabitants and 60 species of migratory birds. The awesome view of the magnificent river blending effortlessly into the mammoth sea can be had from the vantage points atop a hillock 200 m above the sea level. The place is also the fisherman's favourite as it hosts a variety of fish, mussels and crabs.

Padinharekara Beach: This place is where the fabulous rivers Bharathapuzha and Tirurpuzha combine and flow into the Arabian Sea. It is situated on the Tipu Sultan road near Ponnani.

The Vallikunnu Beach: A beach resort is a beauty by itself. And this beach is further beautified by the immense coconut grove that graces the place. One more spot of gleeful-awe to bird-admirers -the 'Kadaladi' Bird Sanctuary' is at a stone's throw from here.

Kadampuzha: (30 km from Malappuram) On the highway which passes by Kozhikode and Trissur, about 3 km on the North of Vettichira, the place, Kadampuzha is where the famous temple dedicated to Goddess Bagavathy, believed to have been established by Sri Adi Sankara, a great religious reformer of Hinduism, is situated.

Trikandiyur Siva Temple: According to the legends the idol of this temple dedicated to Lord Siva, has been installed by Parasurama, the legendary creator of Kerala. It is located near Tirur.

Mamburam: It is a frequented pilgrim centre of the Muslims in A.R. Nagar Village as it is where the Mosque and Mausoleum of the religious leaders of the Malabar Muslims known locally as the 'Thangals' is situated.

Biyyan Kayal: This place near Ponnani is famous for water-sports. The aquaduct amidst lush green surroundings is anyone's attraction.

Kodikuthimala: The verdant mountains with a variety of herbs and shrubs, the mighty rocks and the natural perennial springs whose cool waters calm minds are simply nature's marvel.

Tirunavai: On the banks of the river Bharathapuzha, 8 km South of Tirur, is Tirunavai, a place of historical and religious significance. In older days, the Mamamkam festival here was a grand assembly of rulers of Kerala, held once in 12 years. Believed to have been founded by Cheraman Perumal, it was last performed in 1755. Today, the Sarvodayamela is held in the *Navamukunda Temple* every January. This temple is said to be founded by the nine great saints and is so called the *Banares of the South*.

Nilambur: The sylvan landscape with teeming plantations of teak and bamboo on the famous canolis plot is the original abode of one of Kerala's oldest tribes called the 'Cholanaickans'.

Adyanpara: The fabulous waterfalls and the extensive woods are the natural pride of Adyanpara, located in Kurumbalangode Village of Nilambur taluk.

FESTIVALS

Nilambur Pattu: This annual festival is celebrated with great enthusiasm in the month of February.

Neercha: This festival is held by the Mosques at Malappuram and Kondotti in the month of February and March every year. Community feast is the highlight of the celebrations.

Pooram: This is an annual Hindu festival in the months March and April. A number of faithful devotees from all over Kerala take part in the celebrations.

Accommodation

Malappuram (STD: 0493)

- **Hotel Palace** ©: 2734698
- **Hotel Mahendrapuri** ©: 2734101 Fax: 2734105
- **Geemi Tourist Home** ©: 2734761
- **Maliyakkal Tourist Home** ©: 2734513

Kottakkal (STD: 0493)

- **Hotel Viraj** ©: 2744830
- **Reem International** ©: 2742302
- **Thayambagom Tourist Home** ©: 2743078
- **Sajidha Tourist Home** ©: 2742017 Fax: 2742717

Kondotty (STD: 0493)

- **Hotel Airport Plaza** ©: 2711206

Kollam

FACTS AND FIGURES

Area : 2,491 Sq.kms. • Population : 2,584,118 (2001 census) • Headquarters : Kollam • Tourist Season: August to March.

This is another prodigious part of Kerala rich in ancient monuments, historic magnificent temples, rock cut caves, picnic spots and so on. The place has historical and legendary references. There are quite a few pilgrim centres where thousands of devotees congregate and perform a variety of religious rituals. It also has a unique temple at Ochira where festivals marked by not-so-usual rites take place. The remains of an ancient fort of the 18th century can also be found here.

There is a place called Thenmala which is rapidly developing into an 'Eco Tourism Spot'. This place abounds in rubber and tea plantations. The aroma of the rejuvenating tea of Kerala fills the heart of the tea-maniacs all over the world.

Kollam is connected by rail and road with several important cities and tourist centres in India. The nearest airport Thiruvananthapuram, is 71 km away.

In and Around Kollam

Sri Maha Ganapathy Temple: Situated in Kottarakara. This temple is dedicated to both, Lord Ganapathy and His father Lord Siva. Praying to Lord Ganapathy on the commencement of every act or event is a common practice among Hindus. A festival lasting eleven days starting from the Kodiyattam is celebrated annually.

Thangasseri: This placid hamlet along the shore is one of the ancient Portuguese settlements in India. The time-worn Portuguese fort here, which stands in ruins, dates back to the 18th century. There is also a 144 ft. tall lighthouse which can be visited between 15.30 and 17.30 hrs. The town busses ply between Kollam and here every 15 mts.

Mayyanad: About 10 km South of Kollam, Mayyanad is a Holy land of Temples as there are as many as 9 of them. The Subramanya Swamy Temple at Umayanallur dedicated to the Lord Subramanya or Muruga has, according to the legends, been consecrated by the great religious and social reformer Sri Adi Sankara. There are busses in quick succession from Kollam to Mayyanad.

Sasthankotta: This is an important pilgrim spot, 29 km from Kollam, where the ancient Sastha Temple dedicated to the Lord 'Ayyappa' is situated. It is evident that the name of the town owes its origin to the temple. The place also has a wide fresh water lake, a captivating one with elegant hills aptly located on all the three sides to make every on- looker get carried away. Busses frequent between here and Kollam. P.W.D. offers accommodation at the rest house.

Ochira: It is here, 34 km North of Kollam Town that the unique 'Parabrahma Temple' is situated. The temple has no idol, no deity and is dedicated to the 'Universal Consciousness' instead. This Pilgrim Center is no less famous than any other. The Ochira Kali and the 'Panthrandu Vilakku' are the two main festivals celebrated here, the former in the middle of June and the latter in the months November and December. As part of the Ochira Kali celebrations, men form groups donning warriors attires of the historic era and enact a mock fight between themselves on the spot 'Padanilam' which means battle-field. Another strange performance is the martial dance by devotees in knee-deep water wielding their swords and flashing their shields, splashing the water all over in the process. The 'Panthrandu Vilakku' which means twelve lamps is a festival which lasts for 12 days. The place has busses frequently to Kollam and Alapuzha.

Kulathupuzha: Situated on the Senkottai-Thiruvananthapuram Road, 64 km off Kollam, this place has a temple dedicated to Lord Ayyappa or Sastha, known as the 'Sastha Temple'. The important festival here is the 'Vishu Mahotsavam' which is celebrated in April and May every year. Frequent busses are available to Kollam and Alapuzha. The nearest railway station, 'Thenmala' is about 10 km away.

Thenmala: This region has a plenty of rubber and tea plantations. The tea of the region is much sought after while the rubber has an equal appeal. Efforts are on to develop the place into a spot of 'Eco Tourism'. There is also a dam here.

Ariankavu: This is again a famous pilgrim spot of the Hindus with a Temple dedicated to the Lord 'Ayyappa' also known as Sri Sastha. Mandala Pooja and Trikalyanam are the two major festivals here. Busses from Kollam to Ariankavu, on way to Senkottai, covering a distance of 70 km are frequent.

Palaruvi Waterfalls: Located at about 75 km from Kollam, 'Palaruvi' which as a matter of fact means 'Milkfalls' is an excellent picnic spot.

Scores of picnic makers are lured by the charms of the waters making an abrupt fall from a height of 300 ft. as if relieved from the tedious roll down the robust rocks. The surrounding jungle adds to the grandeur of the area. Accommodations are available at the P.W.D. inspection bungalow and the KTDC Motel.

Matha Amrithanandamayi Ashram: The Ashram of Matha Amrithanandamayi situated at Amrithapuri near Vallikavu is also the headquarters of the Matha's Ashrams. The ashram can be reached by boat; however, there is also a road link.

Thirumullavaram Beach: This beach in recluse as if in search of solitude, is a placid picnic spot. The palm trees around add to the calm that surrounds. Frequent busses help visitors get to the spot from the town.

Picnic Village: Recreation is at a high in the Picnic Village located at Ashramam in Kollam. The back water here is typical of the Kerala backwaters. A Government guest house built two centuries ago, a tourist boat club, an adventure park, a traffic park for children imparting the important knowledge of traffic rules and their importance in the young all-grasping minds and a 'Yathri Nivas' are among the salient features.

Kottukkal Rock Cut Cave Temple: Separated from Chadayamangalam, by a mere 11 km on the M.C. Road between Thiruvananthapuram and Kottayam, this temple is an excellent specimen of rock cut architecture. Hundreds of visitors, come, stand and admire.

Jatayu Para: This is a huge rock at Chadayamangalam on which, as the legend says, the Mythical Eagle 'Jatayu' breathed His last after His bid to avert the demon King Ravana abducting Sita, Rama's spouse, went in vain. 'Jatayu' as was called the mythical Eagle and 'Para', meaning rock constitute the name of the gigantic rock of mythical importance.

Backwater tours: ATDC and DTPC operate Kollam-Alapuzha boat cruises (Departure: 10:30 hrs from the boat jetty) **Fare**: Rs.150 per person.

Half way journey from Kollam to Alumkadavu: Rs. 100 per person. Concession offered to International Student Card holders.

DTPC backwater village cruise on country boat (09:00 - 13:30 hrs, 14:00 - 18:30 hrs). **Fare:** Rs.250 per person.

DTPC pleasure boating on Thenmala Lake.

Houseboat Operators: Tour India, Thiruvananthapuram. Ph. : 0471-2331507 DTPC, Kollam Ph. : 2742558 Fax: 2742558. Email: dtpcqIn@md3.vsnl.net.in

Soma Houseboats, Thiruvananthapuram Ph. : 0471-2481600 ATDC Ph. : 0477-2243462

Exclusive Houseboat Holiday Packages from DTPC - Kollam.

Exotic blue water houseboat cruises:

Round trip cruise: Departure: 11:00 hrs from Kollam. Arrival: 17:00 hrs at Kollam. **Tariff:** Single bedroom: Rs.3000. Double bedroom: Rs.4000.

See & Sleep cruise (Day cruise with overnight stay in the houseboat): Departure: 14:00 hrs. from Kollam. Overnight stay: 18:00-06:00 hrs. Arrival at Kollam (2nd day):08:00 hrs. **Tariff:** Single bedroom: Rs.3000, Double bedroom: Rs.4000

Star night cruise (Sunset cruise & night stay on the backwater): Departure: 17:00 hrs. from Kollam. Overnight stay: 18:30-06:30 hrs. Arrival at Kollam (2nd day): 07:30 hrs. **Tariff**: Single bedroom: Rs.2000 Double bedroom: Rs.3500.

Houseboat Cruise & Resort Stay Package

Full day cruise in Kollam DTPC's Houseboat and stay in a reputed backwater resort.

Majestic cruise: Departure: 10:00 hrs. from Kollam. Arrival: 17:00 hrs. at Ashtamudi Backwater Resort with A/c suite room. Departure from Ashtamudi Resort: 08:00 hrs. Arrival at Kollam (2nd day):09.30 hrs. **Tariff (all inclusive)**: Single family: Rs.5500. Double family: Rs.9000.

Elegant cruise & resort stay: 10:00 hrs. from Kollam Arrival: 17:00 hrs. at Palm Lagoon Backwater Resort, with natural cottage accommodation and special seafood cuisine. Departure:08:00 hrs. from Palm Lagoon Resort. Arrival at Kollam (2nd day): 09:30 hrs. **Tariff (all inclusive)**: Single family: Rs.3000, Double family: Rs.6000.

Houseboat cruise with Kathakali performance package

Full day houseboat cruise, Kathakali performance in the Sunset hours and night stay on board the houseboat. Departure: 13:00 hrs. from Kollam. Performance of Kathakali at Thouryathrika performing art centre: 16:00-18:30 hrs. Overnight stay: 18:30 - 06:30 hrs. Arrival at Kollam (2nd day): 10:00 hrs.

Tariff (all inclusive): Single bedroom: Rs.5500, Double bedroom: Rs.7000.

Royal gateway city packages

Covers all backwater towns in Kerala - Kollam, Alappuzha, Kumarakom, Kottayam and Kochi. Tariff inclusive of hire, food and bata.

Kollam - Alumkadavu - Kollam & Kollam - Amrithapuri - Kollam: Full day cruise (If trip starts at 10:00 hrs from Kollam, the boat will be back at Kollam by 18:00 hrs.). **Tariff**: Single - Rs.3750, Double - Rs.4350, Conference Hall - Rs.3500.

Kollam-Kayamkulam- Kollam: Full day cruise and night stay (If trip starts at 10:00 hrs. from Kollam it will be back at Kollam by 10:00 hrs. the next morning). **Tariff**: Single - Rs.6500, Double - Rs. 8200.

Kollam-Alappuzha (one way): Full day cruise and night stay (If trip starts at 10:00 hrs. from Kollam, it will reach at Alappuzha by 10:00 hrs. next morning). **Tariff**: Single - Rs.8175, Double - Rs.10,125.

Kollam-Alappuzha- Kumarakom/ Kottayam: Two days and one night stay (If trip starts at 10:00 hrs. from Kollam, it will reach Kumarakom/ Kottayam on the 2nd afternoon). **Tariff**: Single - Rs.12,300, Double - Rs.14,420.

Kollam-Alappuzha-Kochi: Two days and two nights (If the trip starts at 10:00 hrs. from Kollam, it will reach Kochi on the third morning at 10:00 hrs.). **Tariff**: Single - Rs.16,350, Double - Rs.17,750.

Additional day Single - Rs.500 per hour. Additional night stay (12 hours) Single - Rs.1500.

Note: Tourists can decide the departure and arrival points (Alumkadavu to Alappuzha, Alappuzha to Amrithapuri Ashram, Kollam to Alappuzha, Kochi to Kollam, Kumarakom to Kollam, etc.). Tariff subject to changes according to destination opted.

Kollam-Alappuzha/Alappuzha-Kollam cruises

The internationally popular regular one way - 8 hour - backwater cruise between Kollam and Alappuzha/Alappuzha - Kollam is specially designed on a doubledeck cruiser. Departure: 10:00 hrs. from Kollam. Arrival: 18:00 hrs. at Alappuzha. **Tariff:** Adult (per person): Full way Rs.150, Half way - Rs.100.

Children (below 12 years): Full way Rs.100, Half way Rs.100. International Student Card Holders: Full way Rs.100, Half way Rs.100.

Canal Cruises

Kayalpradakshin Backwater Village Tour: Kollam DTPC's prestigious canal cruises to the Munroe island village is the best of its kind in India. Departure: 09:00 hrs. from Kollam. Arrival: 13:00 hrs. at Kollam. **Fare:** Adult: Rs.300 per person Children (below 12 years) : Free.

Tourist boat cruises: The mechanised and motorised tour section of DTPC has a wide range of luxury boats for backwater cruises on the Ashtamudi Backwaters.

Type of boat, capacity & fare

Ashtamudi (luxury cruiser): 150 pax capacity: Rs.1000/hr. Rs.7000 for 8 hours.

Ms. Vatsala (luxury boat):
60 pax capacity: Rs.500/hr. Rs.3500 for 8 hours.

Yatrika (open safari boat):
10 pax capacity: Rs.200/hr. Rs.1400 for 8 hours.

Aranya (closed safari boat):
8 pax capacity: Rs.300/hr. Rs.2100 for 8 hours.

Pedal/Row boats: 4 persons/ 2 persons capacity: Rs.20/person/hr.

Ethnic tours

Kairali darshan: DTPC's ethnic tour of the art, culture and traditions of interior Kerala by luxury coach.(Departure: 08:00 hrs. Arrival: 19:00 hrs.). **Fare:** Rs.750 per person.

For more details, please contact:

The Administrative Office, District Tourism Promotion Council, Govt.Guest House Complex, Ashramam, Kollam Telefax: 742558 Email:dtpcqln@ md3.vsnl.net.in.

Tourist Reception Centre (DTPC), KSRTC Bus Stand, Kollam. Ph. : 745625

Tourist Information Centre (DTPC), Railway Station, Platform No.4, Kollam.

FESTIVALS

Ochira Kali: This is a festival unique to the place, celebrated in the middle of June every year.

Panthrandu Vilaku: This is a 12 day festival celebrated in November/ December.

Vishu Mahotsavam: It occurs in the months of April/May and a number of devotees eagerly take part.

Crafts Festival: It is high time craftsmen made merry. This festival is widely celebrated featuring the conscientious work of the craftsmen. It falls in between December/January.

Accommodation

Kollam (STD: 0474)

- **Aquaserene** ✆: 2512410 Fax: 2512104 Email:aquaserene.emds@vsnl.net
- **Palm Lagoon** ✆: 2523974 Fax: 2533974 Email:palmlagoon@mailro
- **Prasanthi Hotels (Quilon) Pvt. Ltd.** ✆: 2742292 Fax: 2742792
- **Sha International** ✆: 2724362 Fax: 2719435
- **Lake View** ✆: 2794669 Fax: 2795041
- **Sea Bee** ✆: 2744696 Fax: 2744158
- **Hotel Sudarshan** ✆: 2744322 Fax: 2740480 Email:comfort@md4.vsnl.net.in

Paying Guest Accommodation

- Prof. K.R.C Nair, Ambadi Lake Resorts, Asramam, Kollam. (Approved by Dept. of Tourism) ✆: 2744688

Idukki

FACTS AND FIGURES

Area : 5,019 Sq.kms. • Population : 1,128,605 (2001 census) • Headquarters : Painavu • Tourist Season: August to March.

Idukki is bounded by Kottayam, Pathanamthitta districts on the South, Trichur and Coimbatore district on the north, Madurai, Ramnad and Tirunelveli district on the east and Ernakulam and Kottayam districts on the west.

The district's name 'Idukki' is supposed to be derived from the Malayalam word 'Idukku' which means a narrow gauge.

This district is a medley of marvels. The wavy ghat regions, inhabited by a variety of flora and fauna are of bewitching beauty. The wildlife sanctuary spanning over a vast area near a huge dam forming a weir between hills, benevolently accommodates a number of wildlife species including the 'National Animal', the mighty tigers, different types of reptiles and a large number of fascinating birds. The 'National Bird' of India, the peacock is among the peaks of attraction. Earavi-kulam is known for its pedigree breed of mountain goats.

There are summer resorts of subtle beauty and cascades and waterfalls adding glitz to the glamour. The highest South Indian peak Anamalai is situated here.

Air: The nearest international airport is at Nedumbassery, Ernakulam, 107 km North west.

Rail: The nearest railway station is at Kottayam, 133 km away.

In the Vastness of Idukki

Idukki Wildlife Sanctuary: A game reserve comparable, though smaller to Periyar is the idukki Wildlife Sanctuary, just above the Idukki Arch dam. This comprises 70 sq.km. of forest land between the Periyar and Cheruthoni, situated 40 km. from Thodupuzha. There is a scenic lake around the sanctuary. The wildlife here is similar to that at Thekkady.

Idukki Arch Dam: Built across the Kuravan and Kurathi hills the huge dam, 550 ft. tall and 650 ft. wide, facilitating a regular supply of water has the credit of being the first arch dam of Asia and the second of the world.

Gracing a generous area of about 77 sq. km, from about 450 to 748 m above the sea level the wildlife sanctuary which is situated near the dam is home to a number of common and rare land creatures and fascinating birds. Three dams, Cheruthoni, Idukki and Kulamavu contribute to form a 33 sq. km. expanse of water.

In and Around Thekkady

The Periyar Wildlife Sanctuary: Redolent of spice plantation, the resplendent Thekkady is where the far-reaching sanctuary of 777 sq. km. is situated. The sanctuary having lent a sizable slice of about 360 sq. km. of its coveted landscape to a verdant, thick evergreen forest has to its credit a great number of wild lives. It was also declared a 'Tiger Reserve' in the year 1978. The grounds here flash with pride more than 1965 species of flowering plants, 143 species of orchids and 171 species of grass. Among the roaming wild-life are Wild Elephants, Gaur, Sambar Deer, Wild boar, etc., which make up to over 35 species.

The beautiful artificial lake formed by the Mullai Periyar Dam built across the Periyar river provides a spellbinding view of the nonchalantly captivating creatures of the wild, from a boat, close and yet safe. This 'Never-before' experience enthralls tourists from various parts of the Nation as much as those from overseas.

Visiting Hours: 06:00 - 18:00 hrs.

Kumily: About 4 km from Thekkady, on the outskirts of the Periyar Sanctuary, this place is known much as a plantation town, thanks to the fertility of its vast landscape. It is also a sought-after shopping centre and obviously spice trade is rampant. This is also the bus terminal for the Periyar region and accommodations are available here.

Murikkady: Situated 5 km from Thekkady, this place abounds in spice and coffee plantations. The spices have a good appeal and the flavour of the coffee of the place reaches far and wide.

Pandikuzhi: About 5 km from Kumily, this place has an assortment of eye pleasing flowers and a good lot of animals. The splashing streams of smashing beauty add to the splendour. It is near the Tamil Nadu border.

Mangala Devi Temple: Encapsuled in thick forests this ancient temple atop a peak, 1337m above the sea level is a revelation of the traditional style of the grand architecture of Kerala. It is situated about 15 km from Thekkady. The access to the temple remains cut off on all other days than the day of Chithra Pournami Festival, when there is a heavy rush of devotees.

The peak also offers a scintillating view of the inclines of the eastern ghats and hamlets of the contiguous State 'Tamil Nadu'. A visit to the temple requires permission from wildlife warden, Thekkady who can be contacted over phone : 2322027.

Chellarkovil: This placid village, 15 km from Kumily, has the riches of beautiful plains and water cascades. The slopes of this village hills lead to the famous coconut groves of cumbum in Tamil Nadu, the neighbouring State.

Vandiperiyar: This is a popular place of plantations, 18 km from Thekkady. The periyar river courses along beautifully through the centre of the town facilitating a high yield from the tea, coffee and pepper plantations of the region. The place, in which a number of tea factories thrive, is obviously an important trade centre. Rows of sparklingly beautiful beautiful rose, exciting orchids and anthuria are displayed in the government agricultural farm here.

Vandanmedu: The name Vandanmedu is familiar among the cardamom traders as it is one of the world's largest auction centres. The place is surfeited with cardamom plantations whose enchanting fragrance greets every bypasser. It is 25 km from Kumily.

Pallumedu: This stupendous hill town with the nourishment of the Periyar river is about 43 km from Thekkady. Typical of a ghat section, the region blanketed by rich greenery, punctuated with scenic hills welcomes the visitors with its exotic range of flora and fauna and natural meadows and lawns. The famous pilgrim spot, Sree Ayyappa Temple at Sabharimala where thousands of devotees throng and the Makara Jothi illuminations are sights to revere from here. Visitors to the place are required to obtain permission from the Wildlife Preservation Officer, Thekkady whose phone number is 2322027 or the Range Officer at Vallakadhavu on the number 2352515.

Peermade: Peermade is a small hill station on the way to Thekkady. It is a fertile land at an altitude of 914 metres. This tiny and cool hill station is full of *rubber, tea, coffee, pepper and cardamom* plantations, intersquessed with waterfalls and open grass lands.

In and Around Peermede

Kuttikanam: This is the place for adventurers and trekkers, and also those who love to be lost in the serene solitude of natural splendour. It is green everywhere on the picturesque hills and the cardamom plantations fill the air with their sweet scent.

Thrissanku Hills: About 4 km from Peermede and just half a kilometer from Kuttikanam is yet another astounding part of the Earth, 'The Thrissanku Hills'. The gregarious hills with a generous green coating and strong wind intercepted by the intriguing hills to form a mild breeze is an ideal spot to watch the Sunrise and the Sunset. A stroll through the place is rejuvenating.

Peeru Hills: Just 1 km from Kuttikanam and about 4 km from Peermede this place is named in memory of an Islamic Saint, Peer Mohammed. The Saint is believed to have spent his last days on this wonderful place where His Mausoleum can also be found. Near the place are the summer palace of the royal family and the residence of Diwan. Picnic-makers and trekkers frequent the place.

Grampi: Grampi, otherwise known as 'Parunthupara', meaning 'Eagle Rock' is about 5 km from Peermede and 10 km from Vandiperiyar. The high peaks here renders a panoramic view of the remarkable landscape lying below and hence the name 'Eagle Rock'. The road to Grampi passes by extensive plantations of coffee, tea and cardamom.

Pattumala: About 17 km on the east of Peermede and 28 km on the west of Thekkady, Pattumala, meaning 'Silk Mountain' with its soft and gentle landscape is an entertaining region of soaring peaks and beautiful little streams. This is a place of proliferating tea plantations. The Velankanni Matha Church, built out of granite stone, makes it a popular pilgrim centre. The flower garden nearby with its flashy colours and placid flowers, ornate orchids and anthurium is an irresistable invitation to the tourist.

Vegamon: 25 km from Peermede, the grassy hills, wide open lawns and a beautiful landscape, all constitute the splendid picnic spot vegamon. There is also a chain of three distinct hills (viz) 'The Thangal Hill', 'The Murugan Hill', and 'The Karisumala', which is considered to be a natural symbol of religious harmony. There is also a dairy farm managed by monks. This place is a confluence of religious mysticism and European legacies.

Sahyadri Ayurvedic Centre: A place that holds promise for the dismayed, the Ayurvedic Centre offers treatment packages for cure and rehabilitation. It is equipped with excellent facilities including a unit for manufacturing and processing Ayurvedic medicines. A herb museum houses over 200 varieties of rare herbs of high medicinal value as part of an attempt to perpetuate the precious herbs pushed to the verge of extinction. Over 400 herb varieties are grown here in a garden of about 35 acres in area. The garden, which belongs to the hospital, can be visited with the permission of the Director, Peermede Development Society, Peermede, Idukki, Ph. : 2332097 & 2332247, Fax : 2332096.

Munnar - Hill Station: It is 129 kms from Cochin, with an altitude ranging from 1600 to 1800 metres above sea level. Munnar boasts of the highest peak in South India. Anamudi 2695 metres high.

In and Around Munnar

Pothanmedu: Pothanmedu, possesses enormous plantations of tea, coffee and the spice cardamom. Pervaded by picturesque hills and verdant mountains, the place attracts a lot of trekkers. It can be reached from Munnar which is just 6 km away.

Devikulam: About 7 km from Munnar, this place has a natural mineral water lake known as the 'Sita Devi Lake' which lends its name to the place. Devikulam which literally means that 'the Pond of Goddess'. This is a serene hill station with all the richness of a typical ghat region.

Pallivasal: This place is situated 8 km from Munnar and is the site of the first Hydro Electric Project of the State. The place abounds in natural beauty.

Attukkal: This place, just 9 km off Munnar, is famous for its waterfalls and serene hills. This place is situated in between Munnar and Pallivasal.

Nyayamakad: About 10 km from Munnar, between Rajamala and Munnar, this naturally gifted place has all the beauties of an awesome waterfalls. The waters roll down the hills from a height of 1600 m in a splendid cascade gaining momentum with every inch of their long track.

Chithirapuram: Separated from Munnar by 10 km, this spot has beautiful little cottages, grand bungalows, old playgrounds and courts. Pallivasal Hydel Power Project is located here. There are also tea plantations.

Mattupetty: This is a wonderful place with a lake and a dam. The sheet of water squired by mighty mountains make it a fine picnic spot. There are also tea plantations, DTPC Idukki offers boating facilities. The altitude of the region is about 1700 m above sea level. There is a highly specialised dairy farm - the Indo-Swiss Livestock Project. Visitors are permitted to enter only 3 of the 11 cattlesheds here.

Visiting Hours : 9:00-11:00 hrs.
Entrance Fee : Rs.5/- per head

Echo Point: About 15 km from Munnar, this is the place where, as the name suggests, the natural echo phenomenon takes place. It is on the way to the top station from Munnar.

Eravikulam National Park: This park spans over an area of 97 sq. km in the Devikulam Taluk about 15 km from Munnar. This place again, abounds in flora and fauna. Among the exotic fauna of here are the Nilgiri Tahr and a pedigree breed of cattle. The Anamudi Peak, 2695m above the sea level is situated here.

Rajamalai: Among the original inhabitant variety of animal species of the region is the 'Nilgiri Tahr' whose population is dwindling. The total number of them according to an estimate, is a mere 1317 (subject to variations in number with time). The Rajamalai region is the only region out of the three in the park, in which tourists are allowed, the other two being the buffer and the core area.

Visiting Hours : 7:00-18:00 hrs. (Entry prohibited during monsoon)
Entrance Fee : Rs.10/- for Adults, Rs.5/- for children below 12 years and Rs.50/- for foreigners

Power House Waterfalls: 18 km from Munnar, this place is worth a halt on the way to the Periyar wildlife sanctuary. The inspiring cascade of the enormous waters down the steep rock 2000 m above the sea level is there to stand and admire. The scenery of the gregarious western mountains leave in the minds a lasting impression.

Kundala: 20 km from Munnar the beautiful town of Kundala is situated on the way to the top station. The vast Golf course located here belongs to Tata Tea Ltd. The presence of Kundala dam adds to the charm. The wonderful waterfall of 'Aruvikkad' is located near 'Kundala'.

Anayirankal: This wonderful place is about 22 km from Munnar. The delightful dam and the beautiful reservoir amidst a vast expanse of aromatic tea plantations of the Tata Tea Ltd. and the evergreen forests all combine to make it an ideal picnic spot.

Top Station: As it is rightly called, the 'Top Station', it is the highest point in Munnar, about 1700 m above sea level, on the Munnar-Kodaikanal Road, about 32 km from Munnar. The exotic flower 'Neelakurinji' is said to hail from this region. These flowers appear in brilliant blue but only once in 12 long years and when they do, the entire region gets smeared by the rare but sure beauty. An areal view of parts of the adjoining State Tamil Nadu can also be had from here.

Marayoor: The mention of the name Marayoor which is 40 km off Munnar sends the scent of sandal in the air. This is the only place in Kerala where there is a natural growth of Sandalwood Trees. The place cherishes the subtle fragrance. The Forest Department runs a sandalwood factory. There are also wonderful caves whose walls are adorned with painting and sculptures relating to the 'New Stoneage Civilization'. The children's park and a huge banyan tree are among the salient features. Thoovanam waterfalls and the Rajiv Gandhi National park are close by.

Cheeyapara: The marvellous waterfalls of Cheeyapara is simply a visual feast as the waters roll down in a seven step cascade. Cheeyapara and Valara waterfalls are located between Neriamangalam and Adimali on the Kochi-Madurai highway. This place also attracts trekkers.

Meenuli: A mammoth rock of about 500 acres in area upon which spreads two lavish acres of beautiful evergreen forest is behind the fame of the place which challenges mountaineers.

Malankara Reservoir: 6 km from Thodapuzha, this is a wonderful artificial lake. Boating and fishing are very popular here.

Thommankuthu: About 28 km from Thodapuzha, the waterfalls here again like the 'Cheeyapara falls' flow down a flight of seven steps in a captivating cascade forming a pool beneath each step. Adventurers are attracted to the place in large numbers.

Kalvari Mount: This is a famous pilgrim centre on the way to Kattappana.

Chinnar Wildlife Sanctuary: About 60 km from Munnar, on the Kerala-Tamil Nadu border, this sanctuary spreading over 90.44 sq. km. is an asylum to a number of animal and bird species.

Visiting Hours : 7:00-18:00 hrs

A visit to the sanctuary requires the permission of the Wildlife Warden, Idukki Wild Division, Painau/Wildlife DFO, Munnar, Ph.: 2530487.

TEMPLES AND FESTIVALS

Sree Krishna Temple: This temple is dedicated to Lord Krishna. It is located at Peermedu, 42 km from Kumili.

The ten day annual festival ceremoniously commences with the hoisting of the temple flag (Kodiyettam). The last two evenings are marked by lively performances of *'Ottanthullal', Kavadiyattam.*

On the last night, the *'Thidampu'* is taken out for the *'Arattu'* (holy bath). This colourful procession, with the Thidampu ceremoniously carried on a caparisoned elephant to the accompaniment of the temple music, *Panchavadyam',* marks the conclusion of the festival.

Sree Dharmasastha Temple, Vazhathoppu, Idukki: This temple is dedicated to Lord Dharmasastha (Ayyappa, son of Shiva and Vishnu in the female form of Mohini - the temptress). The annual one day colourful festival is celebrated in pomp and splendour. *'Ammankudam'* and *'Thalappoli', 'Garudanvaravu'* (a folk ritual) representing the celestial bird, Garuda (the vehicle of Vishnu) is also performed during the festival.

Sree Murugan Kovil, Munnar: This temple is dedicated to *Lord Subrahmanya,* also known as Sree Muruga - son of Lord Siva. The one day festival is known as *'Thrikkarthika Utsavam'.*

Sree Ayyappa Temple, Anachal, Munnar: This temple is dedicated to Lord Ayyappa. It is situated at Anachal, 15 km from Munnar. The six day annual festival commences with the ceremonial hoisting of the temple flag (Kodiyettam).

Santhigiri Sree Maheswari Temple, Adimali: This temple dedicated to Lord Siva is situated at Santhigiri at the heart of Adimali town. It celebrates a five day festival every year. The last day *'Sivarathri'* is considered most auspicious for worship.

Sree Parthasarathy Temple, Mundakkayam: This temple at Mundakkayam, 65 km from Thekkady, is dedicated to Lord Parthasarathy. The six day festival commences with the ceremonial hoisting of the temple flag (Kodiyettam).

Sree Krishnaswamy Temple: Thodupuzha: The temple, dedicated to Lord Krishna, is located at the heart of Thodupuzha town. It celebrates a ten day festival every year. *'Kathakali'* performances are also held on 5th and 6th days.

FOR TOURISTS' INFORMATION

A number of facilities as the local transport, communication, banks & currency exchanges, Ayurveda hospitals and Allopathic hospitals are available both in Thekkady and Munnar.

The Kerala Tourism Development Corporation (K.T.D.C.) along with other departments like the Forest Department offer a well organised network of package tours to cater to the needs of various tourists. Information about the accommodation, mountaineering, boating etc., can be obtained from the respective departments. In an attempt to facilitate the tourist, we have provided the telephone numbers then and there. And given below are two important numbers which would serve as a ready-reckoner.

The Forest Department : 2322 028

KTDC : 2322 023

BOAT CRUISES

The forest department and the KTDC conduct boating trips from Periyar Lake, Thekkady.

Entrance fee at check-post: Foreigners: Rs.50/- (valid for 3 days) and Domestic Tourists: Rs.2/-.

For advance booking contact: KTDC, Ph: 2322023 and Forest Department, Ph: 2322028.

Accommodation

Thekkady (STD: 0486)

- **Taj Garden Retreat (4 Star)** ✆: 2322401-08 Fax: 2322106 **Email**:retreat.thekkady@tajhotels.com
- **Aranya Nivas (KTDC) (3 Star)** ✆: 2322023 Fax: 2322282 **Email**:aranyanivas@vsnl.com
- **Lake Palace (KTDC)** ✆: 2322024 Fax: 2322282 **Email**:ktdc@vsnl.com
- **Spice Village** ✆: 2322314-16 Fax: 2322317
- **Cardamom County** ✆: 2322806 Fax: 2322807 **Email**:cardamomcounty@vsnl.com
- **Periyar House (KTDC)** ✆: 2322026 Fax: 2322526
- **Leela Pankaj** ✆: 2322392 Fax: 2322392

Peermede (STD: 04869)

- **Thrissanku Haven, Kuttikanam** ✆: 2322491 Fax: 2332692 **Email**:trisangu@md4.vsnl.net.in
- **Misty Mountain, Kuttikanam** ✆: 2332065

Munnar (STD: 04865)

- **Abad Copper Castle Resort** ✆: 2531201 Fax: 2530438
- **Status Resorts (Cottages)** ✆: 2530688 Fax: 2530538
- **Mahindra Resorts** ✆: 2849224 Fax: 2849227 **Email**:generalmanager.munnar@clubmahindra.com
- **Sterling Resorts** ✆: 2849207 Fax: 2849206
- **Periyar Mist Valley** ✆: 2530708 Fax: (0484) 2318664
- **Mist Valley Resort (Cottages)** ✆: 2530708
- **High Range Club** ✆: 2530724 Fax: 2530333
- **Copper Castle** ✆: 2530633 Fax: 2530438
- **Tea County** ✆: 2530460 Fax: 2530970 **Email**:teacounty@vsnl.com
- **Star Homes Igloo** ✆: 2563207 Fax: (0484) 2394681
- **B-Six Holiday Resort (P) Ltd.** ✆: 2530527 Fax: 2530193 **Email**:bsixresorts@md3.vsnl.net.in
- **Royal Retreat** ✆: 2530240 Fax: 2530440
- **Edassery East End Hotel** ✆: 2530451 Fax: 2530227
- **Elseem Garden** ✆: 2530510
- **The Residency** ✆: 2530501 Fax: 2530265
- **Surya Ayurvedic Resort** ✆: 2563204 Fax: (0487) 2331347 **Email**:surya@ayurvedaresorts.com
- **Poopada Tourist Home** ✆: 2530223
- **Spring Dale Resorts** ✆: 2564268
- **Misha Tourist Home** ✆: 2530376
- **Holiday Inn** ✆: 2563204
- **Tourist Home Accommodation** ✆: 2522506, 2522229, 2522179, 2522196, 2522177, 2522661

Kumily (STD: 04869)

- **Shalimar Spice Garden Resort** ✆: 2322132 Fax: 2323022 **Email**:shalimarresort@vsnl.com
- **Michael's Inn** ✆: 2322355 Fax: 2322356 **Email**:bvlpala@md3.vsnl.net.in
- **Tabernacle** ✆: 2322240 Fax: 2322240
- **Revathy International** ✆: 2322434 Fax: 2322436 **Email**:rissas@vsnl.com
- **Lissiya International** ✆: 2322288 Fax: 2322288 **Email**:hotellissiya@usa.net.in
- **Mukkumckal Regent Tower** ✆: 2322570 Fax: 2323270 **Email**:regenttower@hotmail.com
- **Homestays** ✆: 2322229, 2322547, 2322179, 2322196

Others

- **Carmelia Haven, Vandanmedu** ✆: 2870272 Fax: 2870268
- **Edassery Resorts, Kattapana** ✆: 2872001 Fax: 2872712
- **Idukki Tower, Thodupuzha** ✆: 2224193 Fax: 2224196
- **Gemini Tourist Home, Thodupuzha** ✆: 2222734 Fax: 2224364

Kozhikode

FACTS AND FIGURES

Area : 2,345 Sq.kms. • Population : 2,878,498 (2001 census) • Headquarters : Kozhikode • Tourist Season: September to May.

Kozhikode, formerly known as Calicut, a typical English nomenclature, gains historic importance for, among a number of diverse reasons, it is the very spot where the great explorer Vasco-da-Gama landed in 1498 AD. It was once the capital of Zamorins.

Kozhikode district is bounded on the north by Kannur district, on the east by Wynad district, on the west by Arabian Sea.

Rivers: The important rivers of the district are the Mahe river, the Kuttiady river, the Korapuzha river, the Kallai river, the Chaliyar river and the Kadalundi river. The Chaliyar river is one the major rivers of the State.

The district is gifted with natural wonders and artificial splendours. The Museum and Art Gallery here is a treasure of antique furniture and objects d'art. There are excellent boating resorts. The importance given to science, engineering and technology is apparent from the 'Regional Science Centre'. The famous 'Kozhikode Planetarium' is a source of copious arrangement. The beach resorts and the ghat sections of the district are the favourite hangouts of both the locals and the visitors. The temples of the region adorn history.

Thus places of diverse interests are dissipated all over the district which as a whole helps enhance tourism.

Air: Kozhikode Airport is at Karipur, 23 km from city centre.

Rail: Kozhikode railway station is linked with major cities in the country.

In and Around Kozhikode

Srikandeswara Swamy Temple: This temple in the heart of the city is dedicated to Lord Siva. The famous Sivarathri festival is celebrated for seven days here.

Thacholi Manikkoth Temple: Situated 2 km from Vadakara, which is about 48 km from Kozhikode, this temple is dedicated to Thacholi Othenan, the paragon of martial arts. The 'Kalaripayattu' the deftful form of the art advocated by Him has set off a tradition which is much in vogue even today. This is also the birth place of the legend.

Thali Siva Temple: About 2 km from Vadakara, this temple dedicated to Lord Siva built by the Zamorian Swamy Thirumulpad is a structure of the 14th century architectural excellence. 'Revathi Pattathanam', the annual cultural event with its cognate intellectual features is indeed a discourse in Sanskrit, the India's ancient and one of the world's first languages. The temple celebrates an eight day festival every year.

Lokarnarkavu Bhagawathy Temple: At about 6 km on the east of Vadakara, in the place called Memunda, this temple is dedicated to Goddess Badrakali, the Goddess of bravery. Another example of a splendid architecture, the temple's walls, portray ancient paintings and carvings. The 41 day Mandala Vilakku festival is famous here.

Pazhassiraja Museum and Art Gallery: About 5 km off Kozhikode, this remarkable repository of ancient murals, antique bronzes, ancient coins excavated earthenware, temple models, stone umbrellas, condescends to the present an awesome picture of a glorious past. The Art Gallery abutting the Museum brandishes with pride the much admired paintings of Raja Ravi Varma and Raja Raja Varma.

Krishna Menon Museum: A wing of this museum which is embellished by the evergreen paintings of Raja Ravi Varma and Raja Raja Varma, is set apart for the paraphernalia of V.K. Krishna Menon, the renowned statesman.

Kalipoika: 2 km from Kozhikode, this place offers an exciting boating experience.

Boating Hours : 08:00 - 19:00 hrs.

Kallai: The beautiful bridge of steel built by the British here, has stood the weather. This was once an important trading centre of Timber.

Kirtads: About 7 km from Kozhikode, the Museum contains ancient tools and devices of the tribal ancestors of Kerala. Anthropology and Sociology books are predominant in the library here.

Beypore: This place about 10 km South of Kozhikode, at Chaliyar river-mouth was an important port and fishing harbour of the olden times. The 'Uru' or the 'Arabian Trading Vessel' here is one of the by-products of a 1500 years old tradition.

Kappad: This place, 16 km from Kozhikode, commands a place in the pages of history as it is here that the great explorer Vasco-da-Gama set foot on Indian soil along with 170 assistants in three vessels on the 27th of May, 1498. The local name of the rocky beach is Kappakadavu. The temple on a rock here which protrudes into the sea, is believed to have been built about 800 years ago.

Kozhikode Beach: It is a pleasure to watch the Sunset from here. The old lighthouse and the two piers leaping into the sea each of which is over a hundred years old, the lions park for kids and the marine aquarium for the kids and the grown-ups alike, all add to the pleasure.

Velliyamkallu: The massive rock here forbade the Portuguese invaders as it offered the ideal footage to the Marrakas to counter attack the intruders. Once, the entire crew of a Portuguese warship was annihilated here. The rock with natural engravings is a real excitement.

Thikkolti Lighthouse: This lighthouse was necessiated as a ship, once, led off course had hit the shore. The tragic remains of the ship wreck can still be found. This region around the Velliyamkallu rock also serves as temporary halt for flight-weary, migratory birds.

Payyoli: This is again a beautiful beach, a favourite haunt of solitude-seekers, near Velliyamkallu.

Kadalaudi Bird Sanctuary: Exotic species of birds make their homes, between November and April at this river-mouth region. Terns, gulls, whimbrels, etc., are among those fascinating birds.

Planetarium: Located at Jaffarkhan Colony the planetarium seems to comprehend the prolific universe under one roof. The viewers are elevated to an utopian State of being lost in the mysteries of the Universe.

Show Hours: 12:00, 14:00, 16:00 and 18:00 hrs.

Regional Science Centre: Rubbing shoulders,with the 'Planetarium', the Science Centre provides an insight into the thrilling traits of 'Science'.

Kakkayam: About 45 km from Kozhikode, the beautiful dam amidst an enthralling landscape inundated with rare flora and fauna appeals not only to common tourists, but also to trekkers and rock climbers. The ideal season for an exciting visit is from November to April.

Tusharagiri: About 50 km from Kozhikode, the place is rich in rubber, arecanut, pepper and spice productions. The entire region, a trekker's attraction, is marked by excellent flora and fauna.

Two streams originating from the Western Ghats meet here to form the Challipuzha river. The river diverges into three waterfalls creating a snowy spray which gives the name Thusharagiri or the 'Snowy Peak'. Of the three, the highest waterfall is the Thenpara that drops 75 metres.

Thiruvangoor Sree Mahaganapathy Temple, Kozhikode: This temple dedicated to Lord Ganapathy - the elephant-headed son of Lord Siva, is located at Thiruvangoor, 18 km from Kozhikode. The annual festival 'Sivarathri Utsavam' of the temple lasts for two days. Theyyam, the ritual spectacle is performed on the second day watched by a large crowd of devotees, who at the end receive blessings in persons from the `Theyyam'.

Dolphin's Point: Here one can see in the early hours of the morning dolphins playing in the sea. The beach is 2 km from Kozhikode town .

Badagara: A commercial centre of martial arts, Kalaripayattu. Badagara, 48 km from Kozhikode is also the birthplace of Tacholi Othenan, whose heroic deeds have been immortalised in the ballads of North Malabar.

Peruvannamuzhi: 60 km from Kozhikode, the place has more than one reason to be proud of. The beautiful dam surrounded by picturesque hills, the serene reservoir with boating facilities, the tranquil islands free of inhabitants, the bird sanctuary wherein a large species of inhabitant and migratory birds greet each other and a crocodile farm of the occasionally sprinting and otherwise sluggish creatures, all make the experience thrilling and unforgettable. 'Samarakathottam', a garden commemo rating the freedom-fighters of the region can also be seen.

Vellari Mala: The verdant landscape, with a beauty of its own, holds aloft a sparkling waterfalls. Trekkers are naturally attracted here.

Kuttiyadi: This beautiful village is situated 78 km from Kozhikode. This is the site of Kuttiyadi Hydro-electric Power Project.

Iringal: This place is of archaeological importance. Kunjali Marikkar, the commander of Zamorians Naval fleet, who defied the Portuguese vessels for a long time, was born here on the banks of the river 'Moorad' and the site is now under preservation by the Dept. of Archaeology.

Mananchira Maidan: The king Mana Vikrama is ever remembered for the marvellous architecture on the palace tank. Traditional Kerala style is reflected on the buildings around the captivating musical fountain and the conscientiously cut lawns here.

Kuttichira: The Maccunthi Mosque here and other old Mosques in Kozhikode strike a stunning similarity in construction and architecture with that of the Hindu temples. The stone inscriptions of the Muccunthi Mosques unravel interesting vignettes of the Zamorins and their patronage of Islam.

Mishkal Masjid: This is again one of the oldest Mosques of Kuttichira. It has four storeys and sturdy wooden pillars. Rich in architecture, some parts of the Mosque had been burnt down by the Portuguese in 1510 and the charred remains can still be seen. The mosque owes the origin of its name to the rich trader who built it.

Pishakarikavu: Goddess Bhagavathy is the presiding deity of this temple. Elephant pageants are part of the celebrations of the annual festival in March/April.

Mannur Temple: 12 km from Kozhikode, the temple resembles the one dedicated to Lord Siva at Thiruvannur. The 'Gajaprathishta' of laterite structure here is over 200 years old. The legend has it that, Sri Parasuraman starts his 'Siva Linga Prathishta' at Thirvannur and finishes it here. Hence, the poojas at noon are of particular importance. The annual festival, 'Sivarathri' is famous here.

Ponneri: The ritzy paintings of the

Sri Krishna temple and the Siva temple at Karatt and Ponneri respectively portray incidences from the 'Puranas'.

Varakkal Devi Temple: Parasurama, according to the legends, the creator of Kerala, ploughed this area out of divine intuition when Goddess Devi with all Her Mercy appeared before him. This is considered to be the last of the 108 temples built by Sri Parasurama. 'Vavu Bali' during which thousands perform ancestral obsequies is the main festival here. The benevolent sea remains amazingly calm as the people carry out the rites.

Jain Temple: The two temples at the Trikkovil lane are known for their beautiful paintings and wonderful porticos.

Parsi Anju Amman Bang: This is a 'Fire Temple' on the S.M. Street. The temple is two centuries old and was built during the early Parsi settlements.

Buddha Vihar: This temple of both historic and religious interest has a number of books on the birth, life and teachings of 'The Buddha'.

Muchunthi Palli: This is a beautiful mosque of the grand traditional style of Kerala architecture. The donations to the mosque by a Zamorian is learnt from the 13th century inscription on a stone slab, 'Vattezhuthu'.

Mother of God Church: This church built in 1513 AD is an architectural splendour of the grand Roman style, the like of which can hardly be found elsewhere in Kerala. The church also has a 2 century old portait of St.Mary. It is a famous pilgrim centre.

The lagoons of Kozhikode: The backwaters of Kozhikode are thrilling holiday resorts. The estuaries, as fascinating as ever with boating facilities attract a large number of tourists. There are exciting boat house cruises to be relished.

Malabar Boat House Cruise: Ph.:2452045/2452046.

For package tours contact: DTPC, District Collectorate, Kozhikode, Ph.: 2371062

FESTIVALS

Malabar Mahotsavam: This is a grand festival of the Malabar region celebrated with much rejoice characterised by the confluence of traditional and cultural art performances. It falls between January and February every year.

Sivarathri: It is a grand affair at Sreekanteswara Temple. Ardent devotees with profound belief fast all day and perform Poojas to Lord Siva all through the night of the Sivarathri day. It occurs in the month of February.

Jalotsavam: Water fiestas are the highlight of the festival. It is held between February and March by the sports clubs at Korapuzha, Pongilodippara. This is a part of the grand Onam festival.

Accommodation

Kozhikode (STD: 0495)

- **Fortune Hotel** ✆: 2768888 Fax: 2768111
- **Taj Residency (5 Star)** ✆: 2765354 Fax: 2766448 Email:rajclt@md3.vsnl.net.in
- **Kappad Beach Resort** ✆: 2683760 Fax: 2683706 Email:moosa@kappadbeachresort.com
- **Hotel Malabar Palace** ✆: 2721511 Fax: 2721794
- **Hotel Sea Queen** ✆: 2366604 Fax: 2365854
- **Hotel Hyson** ✆: 2766423 Fax: 2766518
- **Calicut Towers** ✆: 2723202 Fax: 2720702
- **Hotel Regency** ✆: 2723121 Fax: 2722694
- **Aradhana Tourist Home** ✆: 2302021 Fax: 2302220
- **Metro Towers** ✆: 2700571 Fax: 2301647
- **Malabar Mansion** ✆: 2722391 Fax: 2721593
- **Hotel Maharani** ✆: 2723111
- **Sasthapuri Tourist Home** ✆: 2723281 Fax: 2721543 Email:sasthapuri@md4.vsnl.net.in
- **Kalpaka Tourist Home** ✆: 2720222 Fax: 2720222
- **DTPC, District Collectorate, Kozhikode** ✆: 2371062

Pathanamthitta

FACTS AND FIGURES

Area : 2,642 Sq.kms. • Population : 1,231,577 (2001 census) • Headquarters : Pathanamthitta • Tourist Season: August to March.

This forms the neighbour to the three districts Kollam, Kottayam and Idukki. There is a number of temples including the Lord Ayyappa at Sabarimala where thousands of pilgrims throng during the Makara Jothi festival. The birth place of historic personalities like Muloor and Sri Shakli Badra render honour to the region.

Rivers: Achan Kovil, Manimala and Pamba are the three important rivers that flow through this district. The second Pamba river merges beautifully with two other rivers giving the place, the name 'Thriveni Sangamam' which means 'The Confluence of Three Rivers'.

Air: The nearest airport is at Nedumbassery, Ernakulam 146 km away.

Rail: Rail link at Tiruvalla, 30 km away.

It is in this district, a huge convention of Christians takes place, which is reckoned to be the largest in Asia.

In and Around Pathanamthitta

Rakthakanta Swamy Temple: Situated in Omallur, 5 km from Pathanamthitta, this temple and the annual cattle fair attract a large number of visitors from far and wide.

Malayalapuzha: This temple, about 8 km from Pathanamthitta is dedicated to Goddess Bhagavathy. The Goddess here according to the prevalent belief, helps all the genuine dreams of faithful devotees come true.The mural paintings and excellent carvings of the temple are a visual feast.

Kadammanitta: About 8 km from Pathanamthitta, this Devi Temple celebrates a grand annual festival for 10 days in April/May.

Konni: This place is situated about 11 km from Pathanamthitta. This agricultural region has a bounty of rubber, pepper, coffee, ginger, etc. It is also the centre for training elephants where the magnificent beings of the wild are tamed and trained for useful work. Elephant is the much sought after entertainment here.

Mulour Smarakam: 12 km from Pathanamthitta, stands a memorial built after the renowned social reformer and poet Muloor at Elavamthitta.

Kodumon Chilanthiambalam: 15 km from Pathanamthitta, Kodumon is the birth place of Sree Shakthi Bhadra who authored the famous 'Aascharya Chudamani'. There is also a temple famous for its well, 'Chilanthi kinar' (spider well), whose water, it is said, has amazing curative properties against skin diseases.

Perunthenaruvi: About 36 km from Pathanamthitta via Vachoo-chira the splendid waterfalls situated on the banks of the sacred river Pamba is as much an attraction to tourists from abroad as to those from within.

Sabarimala: It is located at about 72 km from Pathanamthitta town, 191 km from Thiruvananthapuram and 210 km from Kochi. It is here the famous temple dedicated to Lord Ayyappa where thousand upon thousands of ardent devotees throng between the months November and January. The devotees undertake a vow for about 48 days during which period they stick to strict austerity before taking on the pilgrimage. The tranquil temple situated in the picturesque mountain ranges of Sabarimala, at about 914 m above sea level, which can be reached only on foot traversing about 4 km remains closed on all other days of the year except during the festive season between November and January and the first five days of every 'Malayalam' month and also during Vishu. The nearest railway station Thiruvalla is about 102 km away. The temple welcomes people of all castes and creeds; however, women between 10 and 50 years are not allowed inside.

Pamba: It is the major halt of pilgrims on the way to Sabarimala. A holy dip in the sacred waters of the river is customary among the pilgrims. The place is also known as 'Thriveni Sangamam' which means 'The Confluence of Three Rivers'.

Aranmula: About 10 km from the nearest railway station, Chengannur, 'The Parthasarathy Temple' here is dedicated to Lord Krishna. The sacred Pamba river flows by the temple. As a conclusive part of the popular Onam Festival, a boat race is conducted. The 'Vijnana Kalavedi' here is the centre for learning traditional arts like the Kathakali, classical music and dance as well as Kalaripayattu. The Parthasarathy Temple also has 18th century murals. A number of foreigners can be seen making a long stay to get an unadulterated idea of the fathomless depths of the rich traditions of Kerala.

Aranmula is famed for its hand made mirrors of polished metal called 'Aranmula Kannadi'.

Thiruvalla: The place is famed by the presence of Malankara Marthoma Syrian Church headquarters. The wall paintings of the Paliakara Church here are extraordinary. Kathakali performances are part of the daily routines in or probably only in the 'Sree Vallaba Temple' here.

Mannadi: The stone sculptures in the ancient Bagavathy temple are remarkable. This place, about 13 km from Adoor is where the renowned freedom fighter Veluthampi Dalawa who hailed from Travancore, spent his last days. This is also the venue of Folklore and Folk Arts Institute of Kerala. An annual festival is held between February and March.

Niranam: This place, 7 km from Thiruvalla, boasts of its famous poets and ancient church. The church, oldest in India, believed to have been built by apostle St.Thomas in 52 AD is situated here which is also the birth place of the poets and social reformers, popular as 'Kannassa Kavigal'.

Nilackal: Situated about 5 km from Plappally, this place is of reverence to both Hindus and Christians. The old Siva Temple is an important centre of worship for the Hindus. The Ecumenical centre of the Christians is also found here.The place is also the venue of the estate of 'Farming Corporation'.

Pandalam: This Holy town is about 14 km away from Chengannur railway station. The Valiakoikal temple on the banks of the river Achenkoil bears resemblance to the Lord Ayyappa Temple at Sabarimala. The pilgrims on their way to Sabarimala customarily worship here since this is the place, according to the legends, where Lord Ayyappa, on his human incarnation, was born as the son of the King of Pandalam. As part of the festival formalities, the sacred ornaments of the Lord Sri Ayyappa are taken in a grand procession, teemed with ardent devotees, from here to Sabarimala, three days in advance of the famous 'Holy Makaravilakku festival'.

Parumala: About 10 km from'Thiruvalla', the place is known for the grand festival 'Ormaperunal' which means 'Commemoration day'. It is the commemoration of 'Mar Gregorios Metropolitan', the declared saint of Malankara Orthodox Church, celebrated on the 1st and 2nd of November every year.

Charalkunnu: This piquant picnic spot is a picturesque hill station from where the breath-taking areal view of the beautiful valleys and other low lying lands can easily knock any one out of one's senses. The camp house here offers a feel-at-home lodging.

Cherukolpuzha: This is the place where thousands of Hindus congregate, usually in February every year and perform an important religious ritual on the river bed of the Holy Pamba.

Kakki Reservoir: The vast sheet of the serene waters is ideally encapsuled by a verdant expanse of thick forests which are homes to a number of dangerously beautiful tigers, magnificently attractive elephants and ostensibly human monkeys which can at times be sighted.

Kaviyoor: About 5 km east of Thiruvalla, overseeing the delightful Manimala river, Kaviyoor has a small hillock on which stands the gravel Hanuman Temple, dedicated to 'Lord Anjeneya', in which the marvellous triangular structures and also the rest of the wonderful architecture are much different from the usual Kerala style of splendid architecture. Just about half a kilometre from here there is yet another architectural marvel, the rock cut Siva Temple. The tranquil temple belongs to the 8th century and reflects the great Pallava architecture.

Manjanikara: Mar Ignatius Elias III, the clergy and patriot of Anthoid, on his errand to India, breathed his last here in the year 1932. His mortal remains are preserved in the church here. This place, in course of time has turned into a famous pilgrim centre. 'Ormaperunal' the annual festival is celebrated in February.

Maramon: This place is the Holy site of the christians where thousands of them from all over the world congregate for a huge religious convention. The clergy and evangelists of different parts of the world address the convention which is held in February. This is perhaps the christian convention of maximum turnout in the whole of Asia.

Vijnana Kala Vedi Cultural Centre: Vijnana Kala Vedi Cultural Centre founded by Louba Schild, a French scholar under the Indo French Cultural Exchange Programme, was started with UNESCO support. Those interested in culture and the arts would not want to miss it. The centre offers residential training courses in Kerala's traditional arts and crafts like Kathakali, Mohiniattam, Bharata Natyam, Kalaripayattu, Music, Wood carving, etc.

FESTIVALS

The cattle fair and the annual 10 day festival at Rakthakanta Swamy Temple and Devi Temple are celebrated with much fanfare.

The Makara Jothi festival at Sabarimala, between November and January is a grand one teeming with devotees from far and wide, drenched in devotion.

The boat races mark the conclusion of the grand Onam festival with a competitive and yet a congenial note.

The mammoth christian religious

convention considered to be the largest in the whole of Asia welcomes devotees from all over the world.

Accommodation

Pathanamthitta (STD: 0468)

- **Hotel May Fair** ✆: 2322894
- **Ashoka International** ✆: 2323152
- **Hotel Dolphin** ✆: 2323220 Fax: 2325661

Adoor (STD: 04734)

- **Apsara Tourist Home,** M.C. Road.
- **Fathima Tourist Home,** Pathanamthitta Road.
- **Adoor Tourist Home,** Central Jn.
- **Amritha Tourist Home,** Central Jn.

Pandalam (STD: 04734)

- **Hotel Shimi's,** M.C. Road.
- **S.N. Tourist Home,** M.C. Road.
- **Suni Tourist Home,** Medical Mission Jn.

Ranni (STD: 04735)

- **Sree Ayyappa Tourist Home,** Main Road.
- **Karakath Tourist Home,** Pazhavangadi Jn.
- **Mammukku Kalpana Tourist Home,** Pazhavangadi

Kozhencherry (STD: 0468)

- **Mothi Tourist Home,** Central Jn.

Mallapally (STD: 04738)

- **Hotel Sea Blue,** Near Private Bus Stand.

Thiruvalla (STD: 04736)

- **Hotel Panchamai,** Railway Station Road.
- **Hotel Elite,** M.C. Road.
- **Hotel Asoka,** T.K. Road.

Ernakulam

FACTS AND FIGURES

Area : 2,408 Sq.kms. • Population : 3,098,378 (2001 census) • Headquarters : Kochi • Tourist Season: September to May.

This is again a land of lavish leg ends and legacies. The towns of Ernakulam and Kochi, the almost inseparable twins, brandish ancient movements, places of historical significance and a number of ancient temples. The ancient Portugal and Dutch monuments and the early British structures are reminiscent of a glorious sequence of historical events. The colossal places of the Maharajas (Kings) of the region speak volumes of the rich architecture of the part. 'Kaladi', the birth place of the great Hindu philosopher Adi Sankarar, who promulgated the doctrine of 'Advaitha' which means 'Not Two But One', is situated in this district. Unique legends and conventions are associated with the temples and churches of the region.

The entire region is gifted with natural landscapes of enormous beauty. The sumptuous sanctuaries swarmed with capricious birds are a delight to the sight. The bird sanctuary at Thottakadu is also home to certain wildlife creatures.

Thus, this part of Kerala is always full of joyous visitors everywhere.

Rivers: Periyar and Murattupuzha are the main rivers of the district. The Chalakudi river which flows through north of Alwaye also joins Periyar at Alanthikara. The rivers of Thodupuzha, Kallai and Kothamangalam join together to form Muvattupuzha rivers.

Air: Cochin International Airport is at Nedumbassery, 33 km North east of Ernakulam city.

Rail: Kochi is connected by rail with many important cities.

Ferry; The main Ferry Station (Boat jetty) is located 1 k.m. away from Ernakulam South Railway Station. From here, boats are available to all islands.

In and Around Ernakulam

Pierce Leslie Bungalow: This grand edifice was the office of Pierce Leslie & Co., the centuries old coffee merchants, in 1862. The style of the construction seems to be the rare outcome of the fusion of three great architectural excellences - the Dutch, the Portuguese and the last but not the least, the Keralite. The verandahs are furnished with waterfronts.

Koder House: This is again an 18th century edifice of elegance built by Samuel S. Koder of the Kochin Electric Company. The architecture here emphasises the advent of Indo-European style over the colonial style.

Delta study: The High School here is part of the magnificent bungalow built in 1808 which was once a warehouse.

St. Francis Church: This ancient church, reckoned to be the oldest European church in India, has a long history of construction and re-construction. Originally built of wood and timber by the Portuguese in 1503, the church was rebuilt by the Dutch protestants with stone masonry in 1779 and then converted into an Anglican church by the British in 1795. It is now under the Church of South India Council. The tombstone of the great historic voyager Vasco-da-Gama can be seen here since it was here he was laid to rest in 1524 before his remains were removed to Portugal.

Santa Cruz Basilica: This ancient church built by the Portuguese was consecrated as a Cathedral by Pope Paul IV in1558. Eventually, when the British annexed Kochi in 1795, it was demolished. Then Bishop Dom Gomez Ferreira established a new building at the very site in 1887. Pope John Paul II declared the church, Basilica in1894.

Vasco House: This 16th century building with typical European glass paned windows, balcony and verandahs is believed to have been the residence of Vasco-da-Gama.

VOC Gate: This huge wooden gate in front of the parade grounds was built in 1740. The monogram VOC by which the gate is called, can be seen carved on it. The parade ground spreads over 4 acres and was once the venue of the military parades of the Portuguese, the Dutch and then the British. Now, it serves as a sports ground.

The Bishop's House: This beautiful building on a small hillock near the parade grounds, built in 1506 as the residence of the Portuguese Governor has its facelift embellished by Gothic arches and a tread-worthy path along a circular garden leading to the inviting portal. The building then went into the possession of Dom Jos Gomes Ferreira, the 27th Bishop of the Diocese of Kochi.

Fort Immanuel: What looks today as a reticent remnant of a mighty structure along the beach was once a magnificent fort. The bastion here signified the alliance between the then rulers of Kochi and Portugal. It was built in 1503 and fortified in 1538. The beautiful fort walls and bastions were destroyed by the Dutch and the British in the 1800's and after.

David Hall: It was built in the later part of the 17th century by the Dutch East India Company. David Koder, a Jewish businessman, by whose name the building is known today was one of the later occupants. The famous Dutch Commander Hendrick Ardiaan Van Reed Tot Drakestein who was originally linked with the hall was the pioneer who compiled the flora of Malabar coast. The compilation is known as Hortus Malabaricus.

The Cochin Club: It started functioning in the 1900's. The club houses an impressive collection of sporting trophies. It is situated in a meticulously beautified park.

Mattancherry Palace: Also known as the Dutch Palace, this beautiful structure renovated by the Dutch in 1663 was originally built by the Portuguese in 1557 and presented to Raja Veera Kerala Varma of Kochi. Today, it is a 'Portrait Gallery' of Kochi Rajas. There are beautiful wall paintings here. Old Dutch maps of Kochi, royal palanquins and other ancient materials add to the attraction.

Visiting Hours : 10:00 to 17:00 hrs. Closed on Fridays.

Synagogue: Built in 1568, this is the oldest synagogue in the Commonwealth. It was destroyed in 1662 during the Portuguese raid and rebuilt after 2 years by the Dutch. Among the exquisite elements are a clock tower, stone slabs with Hebrew inscriptions, great scrolls of Old Testament, copper plates bearing ancient scripts, etc.

The floor tiles here are willow patterned and hand painted of the 18th century China style, brought from Canton.

Visiting Hours: 10:00 - 12:00 hrs. and 15:00 - 17:00 hrs. Closed on Saturdays and Jewish Holidays.

Jew Town: The area around the synagogue is known as Jew Town. It is the centre of spice trade and curio shops.

Cherai Beach: This beautiful beach along the border of the placid island Vypeen is ideal for swimming. The maritime friend of humans, the Dolphins can occasionally be sighted. Paddy fields and coconut groves are abundant.

Bolghatty Island: This wonderful holiday resort is where the Bolghatty Palace was built in 1744 by the Dutch which was then taken over by the British. Now, it serves as a hotel managed by the K.T.D.C. A small golf course and honeymoon cottages are special features.

Gundu Island: With an area of 5 acres, Gundu Island is the smallest island around Cochin.

Wellingdon Island: This artificial island in the middle of the artful backwaters is named after Lord Willingdon, a former British Viceroy of India. There are in this beautiful place, excellent hotels, trading centres, Port Trust and the Southern Naval Command Headquarters.

The Hill Palace Museum: Located at Thripunithura about 10 km from Kochi, this beautiful palace was built in 1865. This huge palace is constituted by as many as 49 extravagant buildings of traditional architectural style of Kerala. The palace has benevolently made room for an outstanding Museum in which one can relish the glory of 19th century paintings, murals, stone sculptures, manuscripts, inscriptions and a lot more. The vast area of 52 acres of terraced land around the palace has to its credit deer parks and horse riding facilities. Tripunithura is also known for the nearby Chottanikara temple and Poornathraessa temple.

Parikshith Thampuran Museum: A good number of ancient coins, bronzes, copies of murals and megalithic relics of Kerala are on display here. It is adjacent to the Shiva temple on Darbar Hall Road, Ernakulam.

Madhavan Nayar Foundation: Found in this exclusive foundation, which is about 8 km from Ernakulam town, at Edapally are life size figures revealing the historic episodes and events from the neolithic to the neoteric era. The gallery exclusive to paintings and sculptures displays more than 200 original works of the contemporary Indian artists. Among the visual arts collection are authentic reproduction of certain world masters and mural reproductions of Indian art which are larger than life size. The light and sound shows with English and Malayalam commentaries attract a number of visitors.

Vamanamoorthy Temple: This temple dedicated to Lord Vamana, one of the divine incarnations of Lord Vishnu has inscriptions spanning over three centuries from the 10th to the 13th. The deity is popularly known as 'Thrikkakariappan'. A 10 day festival is celebrated here.

Kaladi: About 32 km from Ernakulam, this place is elated to divine honours by the birth of the great philosopher and reformer of Hinduism, Adi Sankara. The place is also sanctified by the temples dedicated to Sri Sankara, Sarada Devi, Sri Krishna and Sri Ramakrishna. According to the legends, Sankara's mother Aryamba was turning down his repeated pleas to take up austerity when one fine day a crocodile caught his feet and held on until he convinced his mother and obtained her permission. The legendary spot called 'Crocodile Ghat' can also be seen.

Kodanad: It is one of the largest elephant training centres of South India. On the north of the place flows the beautiful river Periyar. The elephants are mainly trained for Safari. There is also a small zoo.

Chennamangalam: About 42 km from Ernakulam, this is a place of versatile landscape. Three beautiful rivers, one more than a half a dozen inlets, picturesque hillocks and gleeming plains of green vastness all form a rare and a rapturous combination. The Paliam Palace here representing the splendid architecture of Kerala was the official residence of the Paliath Achaus, the hereditary prime ministers to the Kings of Kochi. Many historic documents and important relics are preserved here. The noble ideal of peaceful coexistence of religions is well exemplified by the unusual presence of a temple, a church, a mosque and also a synagogue, congenially close to one another all of which can be viewed with reverence from the enthralling hillocks at Kottayil Kovilakom. The remains of the Vypeenkotta Seminary built by the Portuguese in the 16th century keeps the onlookers guessing about its wholesome grandeur.

Malayatoor: Situated about 47 km from Kochi, the place is sanctified by the presence of a Catholic church on a beautiful hill, at an altitude of about 609 m. The church, dedicated to St. Thomas receives thousands of dedicated devotees during the annual festival–Malayatoor Perunal between March and April. The Holy Saint Thomas is believed to have prayed here.

Bhothathankettu: An excellent picnic spot about 50 km northeast of Ernakulam town embedded in a vast expanse of virgin forest which is just a short distance away from another spot of endless enjoyment, the 'Salim Ali Bird Sanctuary' at Thattakkadu at Bhothathankettu is situated near the two main irrigation projects, the Periyar Valley and the Idamalayar Irrigation projects. It is also a trekkers' paradise.

Thattakkadu Bird Sanctuary: On the Kochi-Munnar road, about 20 km from Kothamangalam this scintillating sanctuary is rightly named after its discoverer Dr.Salim Ali, the renowned ornithologist. The Salim Ali Sanctuary holds a variety of native birds like the Malabar grey-horn bill, the woodpecker, the parakeet and so on. The Ceylon frog-moth and rose-billed roller are among the rare birds. A large variety of migrant birds makes itself comfortable during the season here. With luck, one can also sight wildlife.

Chinese Fishing Nets: The entrance to the Cochin harbour is dotted by the Chinese Fishing Nets called Cheena Vala in Malayalam. There are large nets which hang from bamboo or teak posts and are still used by local fishermen in Fort Cochin to catch fish attracted by the lights suspended above the net.

Munikkal Guhalayam: Located atop a hill at Chengamanad (30 kms north of Kochi), this is a place shrouded in mythology. It is believed that Sage Jangaman had lived here around 2000 years ago, and the place was initially known as Jangaman. A famous Lord Murugan temple is located on the spot where the sage is said to have meditated which was later consecrated by Chattambi Swamikal in 1898. The word 'Munikkal Guhalayam' literally means 'sages rock cave'. Another story goes that Lord Murugan also called as 'Guhalayam' had made this place as his abode and hence the word 'Guhalayam'.

In and Around Kochi

Siva Temple: This temple is dedicated to Lord Siva. The presiding deity here, one of the various forms of the Lord, is known as Ernakulathappan. An eight day annual festival is famous here.

Valanjambalam Devi Temple: This Devi temple celebrates a 2 day annual festival known as Thalapoli Utsavam marked by caprisoned elephant.

Sri Poornathraessa Temple: Lord Krishna is the presiding deity here. Three festivals are celebrated here in a grand manner. 'Athachamayam' the splendid procession on Atham which marks the beginning of the famous, long Onam festival is a beauty to watch.

Chakkamkulangara Siva Temple: Situated at Thirupunithura, this temple dedicated to Lord Siva celebrates the famous 'Sivarathri' festival for 7 days.

Mahadeva Temple: This temple situated at Nettur is dedicated to the Lord 'Sankara Narayana' who is indeed an interesting combination of Lord Siva and Lord Vishnu. It is 10 km from Ernakulam.

Baghavathy Temple: This Baghavathy Temple is situated at Thirupunithura. A seven day festival is famous here.

Sri Rajeswari Temple: This temple at Chottanikara follows a unique convention by which Goddess Saraswathi is worshipped in the morning, Goddess Badrakali at noon and Goddess Durga in the evening. The famous temple tank here is believed to act as an exorcist, as a dip in the holy tank drives away the evil spirits tormenting the possessed individuals.

Perumthrikoil Temple: Situated on the banks of the beautiful river Muvattupuzha near Piravom. The idol in this temple is made of river sand and the one winged Garuda, the mythical Eagle, carved in wood.

Bhagavathy Temple: This temple at Cheranallur is situated 12 km from Ernakulam. The temple hosts two annual festival of which one lasts for 9 days and the other for a day.

Mahadeva Temple: This temple, dedicated to Lord Siva is located 25 km from Ernakulam and hosts an eight day annual festival which comes to an end with Arattu celebrations.

Siva Temple: This temple at Alwaye has a unique feature. The Holy Siva Linga is installed on sand banks and is not enshrined in any Pagoda.

Mahadeva Temple: Situated between Thrikkariyoor and Kothamangalam, this temple dedicated to Lord Siva is one of the ancient temples. Kurathiyattam, Chakyarkoothu, Pathakam, etc., are parts of a grand 10 day annual festival.

Azhakiyakavu Bhagavathy Temple: This temple at Palluruthy celebrates a grand festival marked by sparkling fireworks for 22 days.

Thonnyakavu Bhagavathy Temple: This temple is situated at North Parur. An eight day festival marked by the 'Ezhunallathu', 'Elephant Processions' is celebrated.

Sri Venkatachalapathy Temple: In this temple at North Parur, dedicated to Lord Venkatachalapathy, one of the various forms of Lord Vishnu, a 6 day festival is celebrated in a grand way.

Mahadeva Temple: This temple at Vaikom is one of the most famous Siva temples. 'Annadhana' (feeding) is conducted here. Vaikom Ashtami festival is celebrated for 13 days.

St. Mary's Church: A small beautiful island off Kochi is the venue of this church believed to have been built by the Portuguese in 1676. A week long feast known as 'Vallarpadath Amma' is held annually.

Kadamattam Church: 35 km from Ernakulam, this church is famous for its priest 'Kadamattath Kathanar'. Two feasts are held annually.

St. Thomas Shrine: This Shrine of Malayattur is situated at an altitude of 20,000 ft. It is believed to be one of the seven churches established by St. Thomas.

Kanjiramattam Mosque: It is situated 25 km from Ernakulam. It is believed to have been constructed over the mortal remains of Sheik Fariduddin. On the 14th of January every year, the festival Kodikuthu is celebrated.

FESTIVALS

Among the Hindu festivals are the famous 'Sivarathri' celebrated at Siva shrines marked by 'Poojas and Prayers' and a number of customs and conventions, and another festival, 'The Arattu' which usually marks the conclusion of most of the festivals. There are also other festivals exclusive to the individual temples at various places. Vaikom Ashtami Festival is a grand celebration at the Mahadeva Temple.

At the St. Mary's Church, 'Vallarpadath Amma' is a week long ceremonial occasion to feast. It is an annual celebration.

Cochin Carnival Feast is observed during the last week of every year.

The Kanjiramattam Mosque celebrates the grand festival known as 'Kodikuthu' on the 14th of January every year.

Accommodation

Willingdon Island (STD: 0484)

- **Taj Malabar (5 Star)** ✆: 2666811 Fax: 2668297
- **Casino Hotel** ✆: 2668221 Fax: 2668001 Email:casino@giasmd01.vsnl.net.in
- **A T S Willingdon** ✆: 2667282 Fax: 2667043
- **Maruthi Tourist Home** ✆: 2666365

Ernakulam (STD: 0484)

- **Taj Residency (5 Star)** ✆: 2371471 Fax: 2371481
- **Hotel Mercy (4 Star)** ✆: 2367372 Fax: 2351504
- **Avenue Regent (4 Star)** ✆: 2372660 Fax: 2370129 **Email**:avenue@md2.vsnl.net.in
- **Quality Inn Presidency (4 Star)** ✆: 2394300 Fax: 2393222 **Email**:presid@md2.vsnl.net.in
- **Sea Lord Hotel (3 Star)** ✆: 2368040 Fax: 2370135 **Email**:sealord@vsnl.com
- **Abad Plaza (3 Star)** ✆: 2381122 Fax: 2370729 **Email**:abad@vsnl.com

- **International Hotel (3 Star)** ✆: 2382091 Fax: 2373929 **Email**:international@vsnl.com
- **The Metropolitan (3 Star)** ✆: 2352412 Fax: 2382227 **Email**:metropol@md3.vsnl.net.in
- **Bolgatty Palace** ✆: 2355003 Fax: 2354879 **Email**:bolgatty@md3.vsnl.net.in
- **Hotel Rajmahal** ✆: 2371054 Fax: 2355377
- **Bharath Hotel** ✆: 2353501 Fax: 2370502 **Email**:bthekm@md2.vsnl.net.in
- **Woodlands** ✆: 2368900 Fax: 2382080
- **Hotel Excellency** ✆: 2374009 Fax: 2374001 **Email**:excellency@Sathyam.net.in
- **Sun International** ✆: 2364162
- **Hotel Sangeetha** ✆: 2368487 Fax: 2354261
- **Biju's Tourist Home** ✆: 2381881
- **Hotel Mayura Park** ✆: 2390560
- **Paulson Park Hotel** ✆: 2382179 Fax: 2370072 **Email**:paulsonpark@satyam.net.in
- **Hotel Orchid** ✆: 2319135
- **Good Shepherd Tourist Home** ✆: 2381143 Fax: 2352045
- **Hotel Blue Diamond** ✆: 2382115
- **Hotel K K International** ✆: 2366010
- **Udipi Ananda Bhavan** ✆: 2382071
- **Queen's Residency** ✆: 2365775 Fax: 2352845
- **Hotel Luciya** ✆: 2381177 Fax: 2361524
- **The Avenue Regent** ✆: 2372660
- **The Best Western Viceroy** ✆: 2366477
- **Bolghatty Palace Hotel** ✆: 2355003
- **The Metropolitan** ✆: 2352412
- **Hotel Abad** ✆: 2228211 Fax: 2227163
- **Hotel Joyland** ✆: 23677664
- **Gaanam Hotel Ltd.** ✆: 2367202, 2365313, 2366848 Fax: 2354261
- **Dwaraka Hotel** ✆: 2352706
- **Maple Tourist Home** ✆: 2355156
- **Hotel Crystal Palace** ✆: 2352444
- **Hotel Blue Diamond** ✆: 2353221
- **Queens Hotels** ✆: 2365775
- **Matha Tourist Home** ✆: 2355221
- **Pamba Tourist Home** ✆: 2367111
- **Maruthi Tourist Home** ✆: 2666365
- **Pizza Lodge** ✆: 2364923
- **Elite Hotel** ✆: 2225733
- **Hotel Grace** ✆: 2354914
- **Hotel Shaziya** ✆: 2369508
- **Hotel Hakoba** ✆: 2353933
- **Grand Tourist Home** ✆: 2355206
- **Grace Hotel** ✆: 2223584
- **Delight Tourist Resort** ✆: 2228658

Fort Kochi (STD: 0484)

- **Malabar House Residency** ✆: 2221199 Fax: 2221199
- **Fort Heritage** ✆: 2225333 Fax: 2225333
- **Hotel Fort House** ✆: 2226103
- **Hotel Seagull** ✆: 2228128

Wayanad

FACTS AND FIGURES

Area : 2,132 Sq.kms. • Population : 786,627 (2001 census) • Headquarters : Kalpetta • Tourist Season: August to May.

It is bounded on the east by the Nilgiris and Mysore district of Tamilnadu and Karnataka respectively. On the north by Coorg district of Karnataka. On the south by Malappuram district and on the west by Kozhikode and Cannanore districts.

The name Wayanad is derived from the expression 'Wayalnadu' which means land of paddy fields. The Kabini river system of Wayanad is the perennial source of water to Cauvery.

This district seems to be second to none in its natural diversity of delightful landscape. The undulating region covered with thick verdant thick forests varies between 700 and 2100 m above sea level. With all the appropriate landscape and ideal environment, it is no wonder that the region accommodates some fascinating sanctuaries. The Banasura Project in this district hold an exclusive earth dam which will be the largest in India and the second largest in the world.

This is also the land of the tribals with the highest concentration of tribal population in Kerala. Tribal feasts, dances and conventions are still much in vogue here. There are a number of ancient temples, rock caves relating to the stoneage era, churches, mosques and antique monuments.

Air: The nearest Airport is at Karippur, Kozhikode, 95 kms from Kalpetta.

In and Around Mananthavady

Kalpetta: It is the headquarters of Wayanad district. The famous Ananthanathaswami Jain Temple is situated at Puliyarmala near Kalpetta.

Bhagavathy Temple: Situated at Valliyurkavu, about 3 km from Mananthavady the place is known for two temples. An annual festival for 14 days is celebrated here. Tribal dances and tribal feasts add nostalgic charm to the celebrations.

Erulam Sita Devi Temple: Situated at Pullapally about 8 km from Sulthan Bathery, the temple is dedicated to Goddess Sita the divine consort of Lord Rama in the sacred epic, 'The Ramayana' and their two Holy Sons Lava and Kusa. In the 2 day festival, Thira Utsavam, 'Theyyams' present ritual dances to invoke the deity.

Sri Maha Ganapathy Temple: Situated at Sulthan Bathery, this temple dedicated to Lord Maha Ganapathy, the God for successful initiation and thorough conduct of all events, celebrates an 8 day festival in which a variety of temple art forms takes place.

Sri Thirunelli Temple: About 30 km from Mananthavady, this temple also known as 'Sahayamalakshetra' is surrounded by beautiful thick forests. A two day festival is celebrated annually.

Kuruvadweep: About 17 km East of Mananthavady and 45 km Northwest of Sulthan Bathery is this 950 acre of gracious islands uninhabited and hence untarnished in its natural richness complimented by the serene river 'Kabini'. It is no wonder that the picnic makers are overwhelmed by the pleasant experience. This sylvan stretch is marked by orchids, herbs and birds. It is also known as Kurava islands.

Pazhassi Tomb: 32 km North- east of Kalpetta, this tomb stands majestically as the memorial of 'Veera Pazhassi Raja' who is rightly remembered as 'The Lion of Kerala' who was instrumental in the famous 'Guerilla' warfare against the East India Company. The Pullapally cave gains historic importance since it was here the British captured 'Pazhassi Raja' at last.

The Glass Temple of Kottamunda: This temple about 20 km from Kalpetta, dedicated to Parswanatha Swamy, third Thirthankara of the Jain Faith has an interesting feature. The interior walls are fixed with mirrors in such an array that they reflect the icons of the Sanctum Sanctorum.

Pakshipathalam: About 10 km from Thirunelly, this is, as the name suggests, a centre for bird watching. The watch tower offers a better view of some rare species. Reaching the place on foot is the only means to get there.

Boys Town: This beautiful town is the outcome of the conscientious efforts of the Wayanad Social Service Society. It is 15 km north of Mananthavady. Nature Care Centre, Herbal Garden, Sericulture Unit, Permaculture Centres, etc., are the treasures of the town along with Jean Park, the Indo-Danish project for promoting herbal garden.

Chembra Peak: This is the highest peak in the district at 2100 m above sea level. It is an ideal place for trekking.

Banasura Project: About 25 km North-east of Kalpetta, this place 'Padinjarathara' is where the construction of the largest earth dam in India and the second largest in Asia. The magnificent site is also the venue of a fascinating sanctuary where perpetually blooming trees with their fabulous flowers add charm to the colour.

Begur Wildlife Sanctuary: About 20 km from Mananthavady this sanctuary is home to a variety of wildlife.

Edakkal Caves: 12 km from Sulthan Bathery, the two beautiful caves with their walls adorned with pictograph of the 'New Stonage' era, at an altitude of 1000m on Ambukutty near Ambalavayal bears testimony to the ancient civilisation that thrived here. Reaching the marvellous caves calls for a trek of about 1 km from Edakkal. Morning hours are ideal for a visit and the entry closes by 17:00 hrs.

Wayanad Wildlife Sanctuary: Abundant in flora and fauna the sanctuary with a variety of wildlife forms an integral part of the Nilgiri Biosphere Reserve and in making inroads in the conservation of the regional biological heritage, the purpose it is intended for. It is adjacent to the protected area network of Nagarhole and Bandipur on the northeast and the Mudumalai of Tamil Nadu on the southwest. The life style of the tribals and others of the region have appropriately been taken into account by the management. Visitors to this sanctuary are required to obtain permisison from the Wildlife Warden, Muthanga Wildlife Sanctuary, Sulthan Bathery.

Nagarhole Wildlife Sanctuary: It is 40 km from Mananthavady. There are no bus services to Nagarhole from Mananthavady, only jeeps and trucks are available.

There is a PWD Rest House, Forest Rest House and Forest Inspection Bungalow at Mananthavady. The reservation authorities are the District Collector, Wayanad and the DFO, Mananthavady.

Brahmagiri: Brahmagiri, a trekker's paradise is a vast area of scenic wildland forming part of the Western Ghats. It is 11 km trek from Tirunelli. Brahmagiri lies 1600m above sea level. Pakshipathalam and Munimala are the other attractions. The Thirunelli Mahavishu temple, popularly called 'Thenkasi' or 'Dakshin Gaya' nestles in the lap of Brahmagiri.

Kuruva Island: 17 km east of Mananthavady and 45 km north west of Sultan Battery. But there are no good roads from Payyampalli. The best way is to trek 4 kms through the thick forest. There are six more such islands near the tributaries of the kabini river.

Lakkidi: About 5 km South of Vythiri, this calm and cool hill station, the gateway to Wayanad, at an altitude of about 700 m, forming a border to the Thamarasseri Ghat Pass is an enchanting place with looming peaks, splashing streams and thick forests.

Pooket Lake: This fresh water lake with natural intrinsic springs which never let it turn dry, in the backdrop of the sumptuous sylvan hills stands apart with boating facilities which offer thrill, a children's park where the little ones can be seen wallowing in their whims and a fresh water aquarium where the sub-marine creatures welcome the tourists.

Ambalavayal Heritage Museum: Just a little away from Ambukuty hill area, the museum tells tales of the tribe varieties of Kerala from their large collection of artefacts.

Chethalayam Waterfalls: This sensational waterfalls is located on the Pullapally Main Road, 12 km from Sulthan Bathery.

Panamaram: 29 km from Sulthan Bathery, this place holds the ruins of the once magnificent fort of Pazhassi Raja.

FESTIVALS

A grand festival which runs for 14 days marked by tribal feasts and tribal dances is celebrated annually at the Bhagavathy Temple between February and March. The Thira Utsavam is a grand festival at the Sita Devi Temple. The Thomas Church and the Pallikkunnu Church come alive with grand celebrations in the months of January and February respectively. The Verambatta Mosque and the Mardoni Mosque have their festive occasions in the months of March and April every year.

Accommodation

Sulthan Bathery (STD: 04937)

- **Dwaraka** ✆: 2620358
- **The Resort** ✆: 2620510-12 Fax: 2620583

Kalpetta (STD: 04936)

- **Green Gate** ✆: 2602001 Fax: 2603975 **Email**:greengate@md3.vsnl.net.in
- **Haritha Giri** ✆: 2602673

Mananthavady (STD: 04935)

- **Green Magic** ✆: 2330437 Fax: 0471-2331407 **Email**:tourindia@vsnl.com
- **Elite** ✆: 2540236
- **Hakson** ✆: 2540118 Fax: 2540499
- **Reviera** ✆: 2540322

Vythiri (STD: 0493)

- **Vythiri** ✆: 2655366 Fax: 2655368 Email: primeland@eth.net

Alappuzha

FACTS AND FIGURES

Area : 1,256 Sq.kms. • Population : 2,105,349 (2001 census) • Headquarters : Alappuzha • Tourist Season: August to March.

This part as any other part of Kerala has a number of ancient temples with unique legends associated with them. There is also a temple dedicated to the 'Serpent King'. One of the churches here is believed to be one of the seven established by St. Thomas.

There are enough waterways to make the region fair and fertile. Paddy, Banana, Cassava, Yam etc., are among the sumptuous produce of the region. The exciting lagoons, the delightful dikes and the cultivation below the sea level all add to the astonishing elements of the region. The coir products of the region command a huge acclaim in the international markets. There are beautiful beach resorts, alluring amusement parks and exciting canoes. The ancient palaces bearing the evidence of a grand architecture and the museum with a variety of artefacts add to the greatness of the region.

The famous regatta is a special event here. The coveted Prime Minister's Trophy donated by the first Prime Minister of India, late Jawaharlal Nehru, attracts a large number of contestants.

Air: The nearest international airport is at Nedumbassery, Ernakulam, 86 km to the North. Trivandrum International Airport is 159 kms to the South.

Boat Services: Alappuzha is linked by boat service through the backwater to Quilon, Changanassery, Kottayam, Cochin, Kumarakom and Kavalam.

In and Around Alappuzha

Mullakkal Rajeswari Temple: This temple is located in the heart of the city. The Navarathri and the Thaipoosa festivals are famous here.

Sri Bhagavathy Temple: It is situated about 3 km from Alappuzha. A three day festival marked by traditional ritual folk forms like Kudiyattam, Padayani and

Garudanthookkam is celebrated in a grand way.

Sri Mahadeva Temple: Situated, just 3 km from Alappuzha, this temple is dedicated to Lord Siva. The traditional art forms of Kerala, Ottamthullal, Kathakali, etc., are part and parcel of an eight day festival here.

Sri Karthyayani Temple: This temple is situated on the way to Alappuzha from Ernakulam at Shertallai. The roof of the sanctum-sanctorum is completely gold plated.

Sri Nagaraja Temple: Nestled in an vast expanse of verdant forests this temple is dedicated to Nagaraja, the serpent king. It is believed, by performing 'Uruhi Kamizhthal' which is placing a bell shaped vessel upside down as an oblation to the deity, childless couples are blessed with children. The sacred turmeric paste of the temple is believed to cure leprosy.

Gosalakrishna Temple: Situated on the Thiruvan Vandoor-Chengannur road, this temple is dedicated to 'Nakulan', the fourth of the five Pandava brothers of the legendary epic 'The Mahabaratha'. A 10 day festival is held every year. An exciting snake boat race is also conducted by the temple committee.

Bhagavathy Temple: At Chettikulangara, about 5 km from Kayamkulam, this temple has a huge oil lamp made of granite with more than 1000 wicks.

Sri Krishna Temple: Situated at Ambalappuzha, this temple is dedicated to Lord Krishna. A grand 10 day festival is celebrated annually. Sankaranarayana Utsavam, another 12 day festival is a musical time full of musical concerts and soirees. 'Palpayasam', a sweet milk porridge is brewed during the festival. It was in this temple, the first Ottamthullal performance of the famous poet Kunjan Nambiar was staged in the 16th century.

St. George's Church: This church is located at Edathua, about 23 km from Alappuzha. An annual feast is held in April/May.

Kuttanadu: Regarded as the 'Rice Bowl of Kerala' this place with its abundant paddy crops amazingly in the heart of the backwaters has to its credit the distinction of being the only region in the world where farming is carried out about 1.5 to 2 m below the sea level. This region with its intrinsic waterways strangely flowing above the land level with its sumptuous plantations of banana, Cassava and Yam leaves the visitors in sheer astonishment.

Alappuzha Beach: This beautiful beach is yet another crowdpuller in Alappuzha. The 137 year old pier can be seen here running right into the sea. The old lighthouse is also one of the attractions. The 'Vijaya Beach Park' here offers copious amusement which includes boating facilities. The time and tariff of the park are as follows.

Visiting Hours	: 15:00-20:00hrs.
Entrance Fees	: Rs.2/- per head and free for children below 5 years.
Boating fees	: Rs.10/- for 10 minutes.
Video Permit	: Rs. 25/-
Camera Permit	: Rs.5/-

For further details contact : 242960

Sea View Park: This is an ideal place for picnic makers. The beautiful park has a swimming pool and offers boating facilities too.

Boating fees : Rs.10/- per head, for 10 minutes on a 4 seater.
: Rs. 15/- per head on a 2 seater pedal boat.
: Rs. 25/- per head on a 4 seater pedal boat.

Champakulam Church: This church dedicated to St.Mary and also one of the oldest churches in Kerala is believed to be one of the seven established by St.Thomas. On the 3rd Sunday of October every year, a grand feast is held. The feast of St. Joseph is celebrated on the 19th of March every year.

St. Sebastian's Church: Situated at Arthunkal about 22 km north of Alappuzha the church is an important pilgrim centre. 'Arthunkal Perunnal', the feast of St. Sebastian is held in January every year.

QST and R Block Kayal: If one wants to witness something similar to the famous dikes of Holland one should go to this place. The backwaters have been pushed back to reveal vast areas of land lined around by the beautiful dikes. Here farming and habitation about 4 to 10 ft. below sea level is a surprising reality.

Chavara Bhavan: Chavara Bhavan which is now a famous pilgrim spot which receives thousands of devotees from far and wide was the ancestral home of the blessed Kuriakose Elias Chavara. The two and a half centuries old beacon here still retaining its original form can always be seen flanked by tourists. It is 6 km from Alappuzha. Boating is the only means to get there.

Krishnapuram Palace: About 47 km from Alappuzha at Karthikapalli this palace built by Marthanda Varma has murals dating back to 18th century depicting an episode from the Hindu Mythology, The 'Gajendra Moksham'. Apart from the exquisite murals which are the largest in Kerala, there are antique sculptures, ancient paintings and bronzes.

Karumadikuttan: The stately statue of Lord Buddha (made in black granite) dating back to the 11th century with a number of interesting legends attached to it makes the place a historically important one.

Nehru Trophy Boat Race: The not-to-be missed spectacle in Allappey is the Nehru Trophy Boat Race. It is a major event held on the second Saturday of every August and features the gigantic snake-boats of Kerala. Competition is severe as the boats with over 100 rowers in each.

FESTIVALS

A grand annual festival is celebrated at the unique 'Nagaraja Temple' here in October/November. 'Chirappu' Mahotsavam is a big occasion at Mullackal Temple in December. Another festival celebrated by the temple is a one day Thaipooyakavadi. The famous Chandanakudam is celebrated at the Kidangam- parampu Temple in December every year.

The churches here celebrate grand annual feasts, an occasion to regale and rejoice.

The 'Arthunkal Perunnal' is celebrated at the Jamma Masjid in Kakkazhom.

The famous regatta forms part of many festivals here at many places. A number of contestants are in the run for the famous Prime Minister's trophy, a trophy donated by the first Prime Minister of India late Jawaharlal Nehru.

Champakkulam 'Moolam Vallamkali': The traditional annual boat race of Kerala begin in July at Champakulam. This festival is known as 'Moolam Vallamkali'. 'Moolam' signifies Malayalam Nakshathram Moolam of the month 'Mithunam'.

Accommodation

Alappuzha (STD: 0477)

- **Marari Beach Resort (3 Star)** ✆: 2863801 Fax: 2863810 **Email**:casino@giasmd01.vsnl.net.in
- **Mankotta Island** ✆: 2212245
- **Kayaloram** ✆: 2232040 Fax: 2252918 **Email**:kayaloram@satyam.net.in
- **Coir Village Lake Resort** ✆: 2243462 Fax: 2241693 **Email**:coir@atdcalleppey.com
- **Alleppey Prince** ✆: 2243752 Fax: 2243758 Email: princehotel@satyam.net.in
- **Palmgrove** ✆: 2245004 Fax: 2251138
- **Keraleeyam Ayurvedic Lake Resort** ✆: 2241468 Fax: 2251068 **Email**:mail@keraleeyam.com
- **Cherukara Nest** ✆: 2251509 Fax: 2243782 **Email**:zachs@md4.vsnl.net.in
- **The Green Palace Holiday Resort** ✆: 2736262 Fax: 2245351 **Email**:greenpalace@rediff.com
- **Padippura Residence** ✆: 2244978 Fax: 2243150 **Email**:babuncm@md3.vsnl.net.in
- **Tharayil Tourist Home** ✆: 2243543
- **Sona Tourist Home** ✆: 2245211
- **Mutteal Holiday Home** ✆: 2242365 Fax: 2251961
- **Aditya Resort** ✆: 2244610 Email: sajipc@md3.vsnl.net.in
- **Hotel Komala** ✆: 2243631 Fax: 2243634
- **Arcadia Hotel** ✆: 2251354
- **Enkays Tourist Home** ✆: 2258462 Fax: 2802267
- **Santhatheeram Lake Resort** ✆: 2582333
- **Kalpakavadi Inn** ✆: 2492239

Thrissur

FACTS AND FIGURES

Area : 3,032 Sq.kms. • Population : 2,975,440 (2001 census) • Headquarters : Thrissur • Tourist Season: September to March.

Thirusiva Perur which is regarded as the cultural capital of Kerala is situated in this region. The presiding deity of the temple of this place is Lord Siva. The region is blessed with a number of temples whose architecture and sculpture would take us back by hundreds of years and a number of natural picturesque locations. The famous Guruvayur Temple is also located in this district. There are also ageold churches whose constructions and existence are landmarks in history. An ancient mosque much in conformity to Hindu temples in appearance can also be found in this region. The centre for learning traditional fine arts corroborates the rich heritage of the region. There are also museums of artefacts, art galleries and a zoo.

Besides the ancient monuments, the fascinating picnic spots like the dam, the waterfalls etc., add glitz to the glamour.

The Periyar, The Chalakudy, the Karuvannur and the Ponnani are the main river system in this district.

Air: The nearest international airport is at Nedumbassery, Ernakulam, 60 km South away.

In and Around Thrissur

Vadakkunnathan Temple: This temple is a classic example of the Kerala style of architecture. The temple contains the sacred shrines of Paramashiva, Parvathy, Sankara-narayana, Ganapathy, Sri Rama and Sri Krishna. Legend goes that this temple was founded by Parasurama. 'Thrissur Pooram' the grandest temple pageantry in Kerala, is celebrated here in April-May every year.

Sri Maheswara Temple: The Siva idol in this temple was installed by Sri Narayana Guru, a social reformer and a rationalist.

Sri Koodal Manikyam Temple: About 10 km from the nearest railway station Irinjalakuda, this temple is dedicated to Lord Bharatha, Lord Rama's brother in the great Epic 'The Ramayana'. The eleven day grand annual festival marked by the enchanting pageant of 13 caparisoned elephants celebrated in April/May forms the conclusion of the festive season in the Temples of Kerala.

Guruvayur Temple: About 29 km west of Thrissur, Guruvayur also known as the 'Dwaraka of the South' is where this famous temple dedicated to Lord Krishna is situated. A belief says that this temple was created by 'Guru' the preceptor of the vedas and 'Vayu' the lord of the winds. This is a popular pilgrim spot.

It is at this temple that Melpathur Narayana Battathiri composed his well-known Sanskrit devotional poem 'Narayaneeyam'.

Punnathoorkotta: There are over 40 temple elephants sheltered here. A number of tourists are overwhelmed at the sight of the magnificent beings.

Sri Kurumba Bhagavathy Temple: This temple at Kodungallur has access both from Thrissur and Kochi. The temple is dedicated to Goddess Bhagavathy who can be seen brandishing weapons and arms with all Her eight mighty hands keeping evil at bay.

Sri Ramaswamy Temple: Ideally situated on the banks of the enchanting river Triprayar, the temple dedicated to Lord Rama has episodes of the great epic, 'The Ramayanam' sculpted marvellously around the sanctum-sanctorum.

Mahadeva Temple: About 12 km away from Thrissur, this temple dedicated to Lord Siva is an architectural splendour of the traditional Kerala style. The temple complex spans a large area.

Puzhayannur Bhagavathy Temple: This Bhagavathy Temple which hosts a number of festivals is situated about 20 km from Ottapalam, a town near Thrissur.

Arattupuzha Temple: About 14 km from Thrissur, this temple is dedicated to Lord Ayyappa. The annual festival Pooram is a grand celebration in April and May during which the revered processions of the deities of 41 temples in the neighbourhood, to this village, take place.

Avittathur Siva Temple: About 4 km from Irinjalakuda this ancient Siva temple of architectural workmanship hosts an annual festival for 10 days.

Sri Rudhra Mahakali Temple: This temple is situated on the beautiful hills at Parthipara (Kavu-Vadakkanchery). The annual Pooram festival is a marvellous pomp and show here in April and May. Sparkling fireworks add to the colour.

Ariyannoor Temple: This temple at Kandanissery has a curved gabled entrance. The Siva Temple at Thiruvanchikulam and the Sri Krishna Temple at Thirukulashekharapuram have resemblances to the 9th century architecture.

Archaeological Museum: Situated on the town-hall road this museum houses a variety of archaeological artefacts.

Visiting Hours : 10:00 - 17:00 hrs. Closed on Mondays and National Holidays.

Zoo: About 2 km from Thrissur, the zoo has a fascinating variety of wildlife and rare species.

Visiting Hours : 9:00 - 17:00 hrs. Closed on Mondays.

Art Museum: Within the periphery of the zoo, the Art Museum has an excellent collection of rare metal sculptures, wood carvings, ancient jewellery and so on.

Visiting Hours : 10:00 - 17:00 hrs. Closed on Mondays.

Town Hall: The picture gallery here is a treasure of mural paintings of all parts of Kerala. It offers an exciting experience.

Aquarium: The beautiful aquarium near Nehru Park housing a good variety of rare species is worth a visit.

Visiting Hours : 15:00-20:00 hrs.

Vilangankunnu: About 7 km from Thrissur, this piquant picnic spot is a picturesque hill which offers the visitors a nice, pleasant time.

Peechi Dam: About 20 km from Thrissur this beautiful dam site attracts several tourists. There are boating thrills to be experienced.

Cheruthuruthy: The world famous Kathakali Training Centre, the Kerala Kalamandalam is situated here about 32 km north of Thrissur. A number of art-fascinated young aspirants are taught and trained in the classical arts like, Kathakali, Mohiniyattam, Thullal, etc. The music and dance academy was founded by the famous poet Vallathol Narayana Menon.

Athirapally: About 63 km from Thrissur, this is a famous picnic spot at the entrance of the Sholayar ranges. The rolling and gurgling waters after an arduous climb down the mountains falling from a height of 80 ft. is a glorious sight to watch.

Vazhachal: 68 km from Thrissur, this sparkling waterfalls very close to thick verdant forests forms an indispensable part of the enchanting Chalakudy river.

Shakthan Thampuran Palace: Three tombs are visible from this palace which is also known by the name Thoppu Palace which spreads over a vast area of 6 acres.

St. Thomas Memorial: This old church at Kodungalloor which, according to a belief, is where St. Thomas landed, encompasses holy relics of the olden days. The church was obviously established by the Apostle. History cites the name of the place in 52 AD as Muziris.

Cheraman Juma Masjid: About 2 km from Kodungalloor town, this mosque, perhaps to bear testimony to religious harmony, has the appearance of a Hindu Temple. This temple-like mosque was built in 629 AD. This mosque stands apart as the first in India and only the second in the world where the Juma prayers were started.

FESTIVALS

The 'Elephant Processions' are a great attraction in the festivals of the temples of the region. The Kodiyattam festival finds a grand way here. As in most parts of Kerala, 'Pooram' is celebrated with great enthusiasm. Exquisite boat races are also conducted which attract a large number of contestants and viewers.

Accommodation

Thrissur (STD: 0487)

- **Sidharth Regency** ✆: 2424773 Fax: 2425116
- **Casino Hotel** ✆: 2424699 Fax: 2442037 Email: casino@md5.vsnl.net.in
- **Luciya Palace** ✆: 2424731 Fax: 2427290
- **Manappuram** ✆: 2440933 Fax: 2427692 **Email**: director@mannapuramhotels.com
- **Elite International** ✆: 2421033 Fax: 2442057
- **Alukkas Tourist Home** ✆: 2424067 Fax: 2442003
- **Yathri Niwas** ✆: 2332333 Fax: 2371481
- **National Tourist Home** ✆: 2424543
- **Central Hotel** ✆: 2333314
- **Hotel Peninsula** ✆: 2335537
- **Hotel Shalimar** ✆: 2227744
- **Hotel Merlin International** ✆: 2385520 Fax: 2384962 Email: merlin@md3.vsnl.net.in

Athirapally

- **Hotel Richmond Resorts** ✆: 2834076
- **Hotel Spring Valley** ✆: 2834076
- **Riverock Villas** ✆: 0488-2834140 Fax: 0484-2374880 **Email**:riverokvillas@yahoo.com

Guruvayoor (STD: 0487)

- **Hotel Sopanam Heritage** ✆: 2555244 Fax: 2556753 Email: mail@sopanamguruvayoor.com
- **Krishna Inn** ✆: 2550777 Fax: 0487-2554169 Email: krishinn@md5.vsnl.net.in
- **Vyshak International** ✆: 2556188
- **Vanamala Kusumam** ✆: 2556702 Fax: 2555504
- **Elite** ✆: 2556215 Fax: 2555218 **Email**: elitechm @md4.vsnl.net.in
- **Ayodhya** ✆: 2556226
- **RVK Tourist Home** ✆: 2556204 Fax: 2554655
- **Poornima** ✆: 2556691
- **Mangalya Tourist** ✆: 2554061
- **Sreekripa Tourist Home** ✆: 2552415
- **Nandanam** ✆: 2556266 Fax: 2555513
- **Hi-power Regency** ✆: 2552296 Fax: 2556576
- **Anjanam** ✆: 2552408

Kannur

FACTS AND FIGURES

Area : 2,997 Sq.kms. • Population : 2,412,365 (2001 census) • Headquarters : Kannur • Tourist Season: August to March.

The district is bounded in the east by the Western Ghats, in the west by the Arabian sea, in the north by the Kasaragod district and in the south by the Mahe region of the Union Territory of Pondicherry.

Going about the district, one finds no paucity of entertainment and enchantment, Kannur, formerly known as Cannanore is rich in ancient temples and monuments. The 16th century Portuguese fort, the Gundert Bungalow and a number of other monuments speak volumes of important historic events which had taken place in the region. The Mosque at Madayi Para was built of gleaming white marbles brought from Arabia, the birth place of Islam. An ancient Siva temple of the district, as alludes a belief, has references of having been in existence since two milleniums.

The region also has a plenty of picnic spots, beach resorts and hill stations. The wildlife sanctuary and the snake park of the district are much favoured by the enthusiastic tourists. The region also has a centre to teach and promote the cultural and traditional fine arts.

Air: The nearest airport is at Karipur, Kozhikode about 115 km south.

In and Around Kannur

Sri Sundareswara Swamy Temple: This temple is dedicated to Lord Siva. An annual festival is celebrated here attended by several devotees.

Sri Krishna Temple: This temple dedicated to Lord Krishna is located at Kadalayi about 6 km from Kannur. An eight day annual festival is celebrated here. Traditional art performances like the Kathakali, the Ottamthullal, etc., come alive during the festival.

Sri Jagannatha Temple: This temple located about 3 km from Thalassery is dedicated to Lord Siva. The deity was installed by the famous reformer Sri Narayana Guru. An eight day festival is celebrated every year.

Malliyottu Kurumba Bhagavathy Temple: This temple at Kunjimangalam, 4 km from Payyanur is dedicated to Goddess Kurumba. A five day annual festival is famous here.

Muchilottu Bhagavathy Temple: About 36 km from Kannur, this temple dedicated to Goddess Bhagavathy is situated at Kadanapally, Payyanur. The annual festival here lasts for 4 days.

Paralessery Temple: This temple is situated at Mundalur. The presiding deity is Lord Muruga, the son of divine couple Lord Siva and Goddess Parvathy. An eight day annual festival is held here.

Sri Krishnaswamy Temple: This ancient temple which interests archaeologists and the layman alike is situated at Thrichambaram, 2 km from Thaliparamba. It is believed that the deity has been installed by Lord Parasurama.

Sri Annapoorneswari Temple: About 14 km from Kannur this is one of the temples where the grand Kerala architecture is at its best. The idols of Lord Krishna and Goddess Annapoorneswari are installed here. The annual festival here extends upto 14 days.

Kalarivathukkal Sri Bhagavathy Temple: Located at Chirakkal about 6 km from Kannur this temple is dedicated to Goddess Bhadrakali, the Goddess of 'Bravery'.

Payyambalam Beach: This beautiful beach is the favourite haunt of a number of visitors. It is situated about 2 km from Kannur.

St. Angelo Fort: This wonderful fort on the seaside is a 16th century monument of the Portuguese. Francisco De Almeda, the first Portuguese Viceroy to India raised the fort in 1505 AD with the consent of Kolathiri Raja, the then ruler of the region. The fort had then been in the possession of the Portuguese, the Dutch and the British before it came under the canopy of the 'Archaeological Survey of India' lately. Mappila bay fishing harbour is an entertaining sight from the fort.

Arakkal Kettu: Arakkal Ali Rajas, the only Muslim rulers of Kerala had their residences here. It is about 3 km from Kannur.

Kizhunna Ezhara and Meenkunnu Beaches: About 11 and 12 kms from the town respectively, these beaches are most sought-after by tourists as well as locals for their beauty and solitude.

Parassinikadavu: About 16 km from Kannur this enchanting place is nourished by the serene 'Valapattanam River' on whose beautiful banks stands the famous Sri Muthappan Temple which makes the place a popular pilgrim centre. Boating facility and accommodations are available.

There is also an entertaining snake park nearby, with 3 snake pits, 15 glass cases and 2 glass houses exclusively for King Cobras. A fascinating variety of the reptile species can be seen here. Hourly snake shows are the 'Crown' to the endless entertainment.

Visiting Hours : 9:00 - 17:30 hrs.

Muzhapilangad Beach: About 8 km from Thalasseri and 15 km from Kannur, this elegant stretch of about 4 km along the shallow waters, is probably the only drive-in beach in Kerala. Black rocks which forebode the deep currents, and clean waters are characteristic of this beautiful beach which is well suited for swimming.

Gundert Bungalow: 20 km from Kannur, near Thalassery, this mansion plays a significant role in the recent bibliography of 'Malayalam', the language of the State, since the first ever dictionary and a newspaper in the language were brought out from here. The great German missionary, scholar and lexicographer Dr. Herman Gundert had lived here for 20 years from 1839.

Thalassery Fort: The construction of this grand fort, which served as the centre of military proceedings for the British, dates back to 1708 AD. The tourists to this place also have other attractions around; the Mosque, Jagannatha Temple; Sri Rama Temple and the Gym.

Sri Ramaswamy Temple: This temple dedicated to Lord Rama, the divine Hero of the great Hindu epic 'The Ramayana', is adorned with marvellous carvings which are said to be 400 years old. This is one of the important ancient temples in Malabar situated in Thiruvangad, 23 km from Kannur.

Madayi Para: The wonderful mosque here built in the 12th century by Malik Ibn Dinar shines with white marbles imported from Arabia, the birth place of Islam. The Madayi Kavu Temple and Vadakunnu Temple add importance to the place. The ramshackle fort which had been a marvellous structure at Madayi is said to have been built by Tipu Sultan.

Malayala Kalagramam: The Kalagramam is at New Mahe, 29 km from Kannur. Painting, mucic, dance, sculpture, etc., are taught here. This renowned centre craddles arts.

Thodeekulam Siva Temple: A prevalent belief relates the existence of this ancient Siva temple to over 2000 years ago. The Pazhassi Raja family is said to have had close associations with this temple. It is situated about 34 km southeast off Kannur and 2 km from Kannavam on the Thallassery-Mananthavady road.

Pazhassi Dam: About 37 km on the East of Kannur, this picturesque region with the beautiful 'Pazhassi Dam' draws flocks of tourists. The serene reservoir paves the way for added enjoyment, the pleasure boating. The project inspection bungalow and its dormitories provide accommodation to the tourists.

Ezhimala: This is an exciting spot, about 55 km from Kannur which couples the conjuring beauty of the elegant beach and the extravagant hill of about 286 m above the sea level. The hills here are treasures of rare medicinal herbs with amazing curative property. Carved stone pillars of ancient times sprout majestically from the ground at the hillfoot and an ancient burial chamber can also be seen. This is now a restricted area which can be entered only with permission since a 'Naval Academy' is underway.

Pythal Mala: This hill resort where tourists frequent and get delighted is about 4,500 ft. above the sea level. This region, near Kerala-Karnataka border abounds in flora and fauna. An interesting aspect is that it takes a trek of about 6 km on the challenging terrain to get to the top of the hills.

Aralam Wildlife Sanctuary: This fascinating sanctuary spreads over beautiful landscape of 55 sq. km. Elephants, bears, sambars, mouse deer and a number of other animals wander in their vast territories.

Kottiyoor: The beautiful river Bavali here flows by the ancient, famous temple dedicated to Lord Siva. During May/June a long festival which lasts for 27 days is celebrated every year.

Dharmadom: About 3 km from Thalassery lies the small island of Dharmadom. A bus ride from Thalassery will take one to the place of destination. The place was earlier known as Dharmapattanam, getting its name from the popular belief that it was a Buddhist monastery as Buddha's images are said to have been excavated from this place.

FESTIVALS

A number of festivals unique to the respective shrines according to the legends and conventions associated with them takes place. These festivals vary in nature, periodicity and the time-length over which they are celebrated. Some last for just a day or two while some others go on for 2 weeks or nearly a month. For instance, the annual festival at the Siva Temple Kottiyur extends for 27 days. Most of the festivals are aptly complimented by the traditional art performances.

Accommodation

Kannur (STD: 0497)

- **Malabar Residency** ✆: 2701654 Fax: 2765456 Email: malabar@sancharnet.in
- **Mascot Beach Resort** ✆: 2708445 Fax: 2701102
- **Kamala International Tourist Hotel** ✆: 2766910 Fax: 2701819
- **Costa Malabari** ✆: 2371761
- **Hotel Palmgrove** ✆: 2703182
- **Meredian Palace** ✆: 2701676 Fax: 2701519
- **Safire Tourist Home** ✆: 2760043
- **Hotel High Place** ✆: 2700558 Fax: 2705116 Email: aquariusff@vsnl.com

Palakkad

FACTS AND FIGURES

Area : 4,480 Sq.kms. • Population : 2,617,072 (2001 census) • Headquarters : Palakkad • Tourist Season: September to February.

The district headquarters, Palakkad town is situated on the Kerala-Tamil Nadu border where the combined influence of the cultures of both the States is largely felt. A number of ancient temples and grand festivals can be seen all over the district. The district has a long and rich cultural heritage. Traditional fine arts have flourished since time immemorial. The great names in classical music like Chembai Sri Vaidyanatha Bhagavathar and Palakkad Sri T.S. Mani Iyer hail from this district.

The entire region has a remarkable landscape with magnificent mountains in a lush green cover and enchanting rivers lending fertility to the land. There are a few beautiful dams of which 'The Malampuzha' and 'The Siruvani' are always in the limelight of any tour itinerary.

There are also numerous ancient monuments some still intact and some others though in ruins throw light upon the ancient people, their life style, the architecture, and so on and so forth. There are regions of reasonably thick tribal population. The wildlife sanctuary at Parambikulam, apart from hosting a number of the exciting species, also offers boating thrills. The ghat sections of the region are indeed too compelling for trekkers to resist.

Air: The nearest airport is Coimbatore, 55 km away. To the South is Nedumbassery Airport, 128 km away.

In and Around Palakkad

Loknayak J.P. Smrithivanam and Deer Park: (22 kms from Palghat) The Smrithivanam and Deer Park extended over an area of 100 acres of reserve forest at Walayar along the Kerala-Tamilnadu border. Deer and other animals move freely in this area. Facilities for elephant rides are also provided.

Thiruvalathoor: A 10 km drive from Palakkad, Thiruvalathoor is an ancient temple with some wood carvings and stone sculptures.

Meenvallam: The little known waterfalls at Meenvallam, 8 km from Thuppanad junction on the Palakkad-Manarkad route is a combination of enchanting beauty and scenic splendour. The water falls from nearly 20 to 25 feet and the depth is around 15 to 20 feet. There are 10 steps of waterfalls, of which, eight are located in the upper hills inside the dense forest thereby remaining inaccessible. One has to hire a jeep from Koomankund junction and then trek a distance of 1.5 km by crossing the Thuppanad river.

Punarjani Guha: Situated 2 km

from the Tiruvilawamala Temple, the Punarjani Guha is a natural tunnel in the rocky cliff. Sri Raman is the temple's chief deity and the idol is believed to be 'swayambhoo' i.e. born on its own, and its abode is on the Western side.

Sri Vilwadrinatha Temple: About 15 km from Ottapalam, at 'Thiruvilvamala', this temple is dedicated to Lord Rama and Lord Lakshmana, the divine brothers in the great epic 'The Ramayana'.

Sri Thirumandam Kunnu Bhagavathy Temple: This temple dedicated to Goddess Bhagavathy is situated at Kongad about 20 km from Palakkad.

Alathur Temple Complex: This important temple complex at Alathur near Palakkad encompasses four temples dedicated to Lord Siva, Lord Krishna, Lord Varadaraja and Goddess Mahalakshmi.

Kottapuram Bhagavathy Temple: There is a temple dedicated to Goddess Bhagavathy at Kottapuram which is accessible from Palakkad.

Jain Temple: The place on the western outskirts of Palakkad town receives its name from the historic Jain Temple. 'Jainamedu', as the region around the beautiful 32 ft. long and 20 ft. wide temple is called, is where traces of Jainism having flourished in the region are explicit. The images of Jain Tirthhankaras and Yakshinis can be seen in the temple.

Palakkad Fort: The beautiful old fort in the heart of the city was built by Hyder Ali of Mysore in 1766. The British made some renovations and modifications in 1790. It is now under the protective canopy of the Archaeological Survey of India.

Fantasy Park: The amusement the park offers seems to make the fantasies come true.

Visiting Hours: 14:00 - 21:00 hrs. on weekdays 11:00 - 2100 hrs. on Saturdays, Sundays and National Holidays

Entrance Fees: Rs.20/- for adults and Rs.10/- for children. Pleasure rides and computer games carry extra charges.

Block Tickets: Rs.80/- for adults and Rs.60/- for children.

Pothundy: About 45 km from Palakkad, on the way to Nelliyampathy, the beautiful reservoir complex at Pothundy is the ideal place for short and sweet picnics.

Dhoni: This is a sumptuous sylvan region with a refreshing waterfalls. A three hour long trek has to be carried out to get to the foot of the beautiful Dhoni hills.

Malampuzha Dam: This exquisite dam and the conscientiously laid garden with a variety of brilliant and colourful flowers, the meticulously manicured grass lawn, the marvellous meadows, the fabulous fountains displaying an orchestrated water show, all that and a lot more leave the visitors spellbound.

The site lies in the cauldron formed by the western ghats. The gracious expanse of the serene lake formed by the dam provides boating facilities. The scenery of the numerous lights in a beautiful array breaking into the cool darkness of the night, like bright pearls arranged on a black sheet of cloth, is a breathtaking beauty. It is usually illuminated only in the week ends; however, it can be arranged on other days through the executive engineer on payment of a fixed fee. Adding to the fun and frolic are a swimming pool with high diving stages, an aquarium and pleasure rides like the boating and the ropeway winch and also a snake park and a children's park.

The garden opens by 10:00 hrs and closes by 18:00 hrs.

Boating	: 10:00 - 18:00 hrs.
Swimming Pool	: 12:00 - 20:00 hrs.
Aquariam	: 13:00 - 21:00 hrs.
Snake Park	: 08:00 - 18:00 hrs.
Winch	: 10:00 - 13:00 hrs. &14:30 - 20:00 hrs.
Pleasure Train	: 08:00 - 20:00 hrs.
Telescope Tower	: 10:00 - 17:00 hrs.

Kollengode: About 19 km south of Palakkad, Kollengode which literally means 'Abode of Blacksmiths' cherishes the rural beauty of Palakkad. The place also has ancient monuments like the Kollengode palace, the temple dedicated to Lord Vishnu and the memorial of the renowned poet P. Kunhiraman Nair.

Lakkidi: About 30 km from Palakkad, Killikkurissimangalam at Lakkidi has a historic monument which is preserved by the State Government today - the house of the 18th century poet 'Kunchan Nambiar' who is survived by his famous Satires and Thullal.

Meenkara: This beautiful dam across the enchanting river Gayathri which merges with Bharathapuzha is an exciting picnic spot.

Ottappalam: This town gains importance by the presence of several places of worship and a number of grand festivals during which the entire town swells in population.

Mangalam Dam: About 50 km from Palakkad the beautiful Cherukunnath river, a tributary of the glorious river Mangalam, is intercepted by the wonderful dam which makes it a popular picnic spot.

Thrithala: Ancient monuments and the dilapidated remains of the once-glorious structures signify the place. There is also a temple dedicated to Lord Siva and a ramshackle mud fort near the place. The Kattilmadam Temple, a small but subtle Buddhist monument (supposed to be of the 9th or the 10th century) made of granite on the Pattambi-Guruvayoor road, provides stuff for archaeological study. The Paakkanar memorial stands in honour of Pariah Saint near Thrithala-Koottanad Road. This place is also the old sod of VT. Bhattathiripad, the famous writer and social reformer. This place is situated about 75 km from Palakkad.

Parambikulam Wildlife Sanctuary: Numerous wildlife creatures, the rare and the common, make themselves comfortable in the enchanting expanse of about 285 sq. km. The splendid reservoir amidst a picturesque environment makes boating and cruising possible. Accommodations are available at the rest houses of State Forest Department at Thoonakkadavu, Thellikkal and Anappady. For a tree house in the forest reserve of Thoonakkadavu, advance reservation has to be made. 'Kannimari', the famous, oldest teak tree is found here. The permission to visit the 'Sanctuary' can be obtained from, 'The Divisional Forest Officer, Parambikulam, Thoonakkadavu, Ph. (0425) 2367233/2367228.

Siruvani Dam: About 48 km from Palakkad, the beautiful dam built across the serene river Siruvani is a popular picnic spot. One of the two gateways on either side of the length of the dam, is built in traditional Kerala style of architecture while the other in the traditional Tamil Nadu style. The region is also known for tribal population.

Nelliyampathy: About 467 to 1572 m above the sea level, 40 km south of Nenmara, this hill resort with its piquant evergreen forests spread lavishly along the incline and with vantage points which present to the viewer the diminished but spellbinding sight of almost a third of the distant, Pallakkad promises the tourists a memorable experience. Trekkers flock here to test their mites. For accommodation, contact the DTPC, Palakkad, Ph.: 2346212.

Chittur Gurumadam: Overseeing the benevolent river 'Sokanasini' which literally means 'Annihilator of Woes' is the memorial of Thunchath Ezhuthachan who authored the famous 'Adhyatma Ramayana'. The memorial houses a 'Srichakra' and some idols worshipped by the poet who spent his last days here. His wooden slippers and a stylus can also be seen.

Thenari: This place is famous for the temple dedicated to Lord Rama, the Hero in the great epic 'The Ramayana' and a natural spring in front of the temple. The waters of this spring is considered to be as sacred as that of the magnificent, perennial, Holy river Ganges in which a dip cleanses souls.

Mayiladumpara: Mayiladumpara which means, 'The rock on which peacock dances' abounds in the ever so beautiful bird, peacocks.

Attappady: About 38 km on the northeast of Mannarkad, Attappady is an awesome rendezvous of the magnificent natural elements like the picturesque mountains, elegant rivers and thick verdant forests. This is also the land of tribals which seems to keep the anthropologists busy. The Malleeswaram Peak which naturally resembles the Holy Sivalinga is revered and worshipped by the inhabitants. The 'Sivarathri' festival is celebrated with much enthusiasm. Accommodations are available at the PWD Rest House and a few private hotels at Agali.

Thiruvegappura Sankaranarayana Temple: The presiding deity of this temple is 'Sankaranarayana', a unique combination constituted on one half by Lord Siva and by Lord Vishnu on the other. This temple belongs to the 14th century whereas the auditorium here known as the 'Koothambalam' is believed to be a later addition in the 15th or the 16th century.

Ongallur Taliyil Siva Temple: This temple, near Pattambi, dedicated to Lord Siva displays the architectural skills of the period. Some of the most intricate laterite sculptures can be seen here. The 'Sivarathiri' festival is celebrated annually.

Silent Valley National Park: About 40 km on the northwest of Mannarkad, the once, seemingly boundless expanse of thick evergeen forests of the Sahya Ranges, now reduced to about 89.52 sq.km. has a salient feature which makes it known as the silent valley. The incessant chirping of the cicadas which is very common in sylvan regions is absent here. The beautiful river Kunthipuzha which forms a silver ornament to the valley before meeting the serene river Bharathapuzha, has its fount in the region which can be accessed. The visitors to the park must necessarily do a trekking of about 24 km since the ghat terrain makes vehicle movement possible only beyond that distance. The visitors have to obtain the permission of the Wildlife Warden, Silent Valley National Park, Mukkali, Ph. : 2453225.

FESTIVALS

Kalpathi Rathotsavam: This annual festival attended by a large number of devotees is celebrated at the 'Viswanatha Temple' in November every year. The temple Chariot Procession is the highlight of the festival.

Vela at Manappulli Kavu: This annual festival at the Bhagavathy temple is celebrated in March.

Kanniyarkali: This is an art form, patronised by the Nair Sect, which comes alive in the temples during March or April.

Nenmara Vallengy Vela: This is a grand annual festival celebrated at the Bhagavathy temple near Nenmara during February or March. Brilliant fireworks add to the holy mirth.

Pavakkoothu: This is a shadow play in the months of March/April at some Bhagavathy Temples.

Kaalapoottu: This is a thrilling race among the oxen used in agriculture. This usually falls in the month of January.

Konganpada: This is a ritual drama at the Bhagavathy temple in Chittur in the month of February/March.

Pattambi Nercha: This annual Muslim festival commemorates the Saint Aloor Valia Pookunjikoya Thangal.

Accommodation

Malampuzha (STD: 0491)

- **Govardhana Holiday Village Resort** ✆: 2815264 Fax: 2815264
- **Garden House, KTDC** ✆: 2815191
- **Hotel Dam Palace** ✆: 2815237

Palakkad (STD: 0491)

- **Walayar Motels** ✆: 2566312 Fax: 0491-2567162
- **Hotel Indraprastha (3 Star)** ✆: 2534641 Fax: 2539531 Email:eyepee@md3.vsnl.net.in
- **Kairali Ayurvedic Beach Resort** ✆: 2322553 Fax: 2322732 Email:kairlpgt@md3.vsnl.net.in
- **Fort Palace Hotel** ✆: 2534621 Fax: 2534625
- **Hotel Rajadhani** ✆: 2521314 Fax: 2537317
- **Gazala Inn** ✆: 2522044
- **Merhaba Residency** ✆: 2525262 Fax: 2537833 Email:merhaba@eth.net
- **ATS Residency** ✆: 2537477 Fax: 2537037
- **East Fort Resort** ✆: 2532507 Fax: 2526977
- **Hotel Chanakya** ✆: 2537064
- **Hotel Ambady** ✆: 2531244
- **Surya Tourist Home** ✆: 2538338
- **KPM International Hotel** ✆: 2534601
- **Hotel Hilux** ✆: 2539433
- **Royal Tourist Home** ✆: 2535012
- **Hotel Devaprabha** ✆: 2823383
- **Ashok Tourist Home** ✆: 2536661

Kasaragod

FACTS AND FIGURES

Area : 4,992 Sq.kms. • Population : 1,203,342 (2001 census) • Headquarters : Kasargod • Tourist Season: August to March.

This extraordinary part of Kerala, with its scintillating natural features is aptly marked by a number of ancient temples and festivals. Measures are on to develop the city of Bekal into a fascinating centre of tourist attraction as it already has all the prerequisites to be one. The only 'Lake Temple' of Kerala belongs to Kasaragod. This region also has centres of arts and learning. There are picturesque hill resorts in the region on par with the famous Kodaikanal and Ooty of the neighbouring State, Tamil Nadu. The departments of 'Archaeology' and 'Agriculture' find interests in the region. The picnic spots here offer an assortment of amusement.

The region also has a long history of Islamic culture and influence. The Malik Deenar Mosque is of historic importance.

'Naturopathy', the natural way to the pink of health, has Nileswaram as one of its centres of renaissance.

Air: The nearest airport is at Mangalore, 50 km away. International airport at Nedumbassery, Ernakulam is 376 km South.

In and Around Kasaragod

The Bekal Fort: About 16 km on the south of Kasaragod stands the magnificent fort with its circular laterite structure about 130 ft. above sea level. This fort overlooking the Arabian Sea was built 300 years ago. Just one kilometre from the fort is the beautiful 'Pallikere Beach' from where the fort is an overwhelming sight. The Aqua Park nearby has a variety of thrills to offer like the pedal boats, water cycles etc.

The Bekal Tourism Project is on its toes to make the naturally gifted place Bekal, one of the finest tourist centres.

Ananthapura Lake Temple: About 30 km from Bekal, this ancient temple amidst a serene lake belongs to the 9th century. The legend has it that this temple is the original abode, known as the 'Moolasthanam' of Sri Padmanabha Swamy, the presiding deity of the temple at Thiruvananthapuram.

Kappil Beach: About 6 km from Beka Fort this beautiful beach, apparently isolated, offers calm and charm. The Kodi cliff at a stone's throw, is the vantage point to get an areal glimpse of the great expanse of the Arabian Sea.

Anandasram: This tranquil place is about 15 km from Bekal. Founded by Swamy Ramdas whose spiritual aura attracted disciples and followers from India and abroad this is an ideal place for meditation and spiritual endeavours.

Valiyaparamba: This beautiful backwater resort studded with picturesque little islands, greeted by four resplendent rivers attracts a number of visitors. The resort which also offers pleasure boating is only about 30 km from Bekal.

Manjeswaram: Sanctified by several centres of worship, the place also has a high yield of the cash crop 'cashew'. The two beautiful Jain temples here are situated on the banks of the enchanting river Manjeswar. The century old Gothic styled Roman Catholic Church, known as the Mother Dolorus Church is about 11 km from Kumbla. The oldest church in the district, here, 'Our Lady of Sorrows Church' was built in 1890. Manjeswaram also has the memorial of Govinda Pai, the forerunner in Kannada literature.

Kanwatheertha Beach: This is the favourite hangout of many. The natural extension of the waters in a calm pool like formation is ideally suited for swimming.

Kanhangad Fort: Also known as Hosdurg fort, this enthralling chain of forts suggests Somashekara Nayak of the Ikkery royal dynasty should have been on a fort building spree. The 'Nithyanandasram' here is a tranquil spiritual centre of international recognition.

Sri Mahalingeswara Temple: At Adoor, about 45 km from Kasaragod, this ancient temple dedicated to Lord Siva has a transliterated inscription of Sanskrit in Kannada which is related to the Western Chalukya King Kirthivarman II of 745-755 AD. The environs of the temple are enchanting sylvan region which also has a rejuvenating river, 'The Payaswini'.

Cheruvathur: This popular picnic spot holds the ruins of the 18th century Dutch Fort in its beautiful Veeramala hills. The place has produced famous poets and scholars.

Kottancherry: About 30 km north-east of Kanhangad, this place with its picturesque undulating landscape, mountains and hills is a trekkers' paradise.

Chandragiri Fort: This beautiful fort of the 17th century forms an integral part of the chain of magnificent forts built by Sivappa Naik of Bedanore. The fort is the ideal place to admire the glorious Sunset, the enchanting river and the endless Arabian Sea. There is a temple nearby in which the festival 'Pattu Utsavam' is famous. There is also a mosque. The picturesque islands and inviting palmgroves nearby are piquant spots for the boat cruise. The Chandragiri bridge forms the boat jetty.

Ranipuram: About 85 km from Kasaragod and about 750 m above sea level, Ranipuram comprises an assortment of exclusive landscapes, the evergreen forests, monsoon forests, tall grass lands, pasture lands etc. The vast forests of Madathumala, the earlier name of the place, are contiguous to the forests of Karnataka. Mighty elephants grace the region. DTPC offers accommodation.

Madhur Temple: About 8 km north of Kasaragod, the wonderful temple known as 'Srimad Anantheswara Vinayaka Temple' is rich in its splendid architecture. The roof of the temple is elegantly copper plated. The temple is ideally situated in the pleasant environs of the beautiful river 'Madhuvahini'.

Edneer Mutt: About 10 km north-east of Kasaragod, the Mutt follows the 'Sankaracharya' tradition, an ancient tradition which has been in vogue since the period of 'Adi Sankara' the great religious reformer. This is also the renowned centre of arts and learning.

Possadigumpe: About 18 km on the east of Mangalpady, this picturesque hillock rising to a height of about 1060 ft. above sea level is a much sought-after spot for picnic.

Thulur Vanam: The temple here, about 4 km on the east of Panathur, is dedicated to 'Kshetrapalan and Bhagavathy'. This place also called 'Kekulom' is the venue of a grand 8 day festival led by the famous 'Sivarathri' which is attended by a large number of devotees.

Central Plantation Crops and Research Institute: This institute, abbreviated as CPCRI, established in 1970 has its headquarters in Kudlu, 5 km north of Kasaragod. Among its major activities are improving the genetic potential of plantation crops, production of superior planting materials, conducting research in various agrarian aspects.

Pandiyan Kallu: This rock sprouting from the sea, about 2 km from Trikkanad Temple, derives its name from the popular legend which says this rock was once a ship which was converted into a rock when one of the Pandiya Kings to whom the ship belonged, launched an attack from it, on the Trikkanad Temple. Now, this rock serves as the target of many an adventurous swimmer.

Malik Deenar Mosque: This historic mosque, the Jumma Masjid is believed to have been built by Malik Ibn Dinar. It is rich in Kerala style of architecture and is located in Thalankara, Kasaragod is revered as the west coast centre of Islam.

Madiyankulam Durga Temple: This temple dedicated to Bhadrakali, the Goddess for Bravery, hosts two grand annual festivals, one in May and June and the other in December and January. 'Bootham' a famous form of dance is the highlight of the festival.

Nileswaram: This town, regarded as the cultural centre of the district, has plenty of temples and festivals. The Kavil Bhavan Yoga and Cultural Centre here is famous for its 'Naturopathy' treatments and rejuvenation therapies. Nileswaram is also the folklore centre of the Archaeological Department. In the past, it was the home town of the great Nileswar Rajas.

FESTIVALS

Pattutsavam: This 9 day annual festival marked by cultural performances, conventions and elephant processions falls in January every year.

Chaliyaporattu: This grand festival celebrated annually at Bhagavathy Temple occurs in March.

Palakunnu Bharani: This celebration is highlighted by grand processions and sparkling fireworks usually in the first week of March.

Nileswar Poorakali: This exciting event, usually from the last week of March to the first week of April at Bhagavathy Temples is a grand folk dance of men.

Palakunnu: This festival is marked by long processions of women carrying earthen pots which are then deposited at the local temple.

There are also other festivals celebrated with much fervour at homes and at temples. Traditional art performances form an indispensable part of most of the celebrations.

Accommodation

Kasaragod (STD: 04994)

- **Apsara Regency** ✆: 2430124 Fax: 2421629
- **Hotel City Tower** ✆: 2430562 Fax: 2430235

Email: citytower@satyam.net.in

- **Enay Tourist Home** ✆: 2421164/2464

Bekal

- **Fort Land Tourist Home** ✆: 2736600 Fax: 2737471

Kanhangad (STD: 04997)

- **Elite Tourist Home** ✆: 2702276
- **Green Land** ✆: 2707203

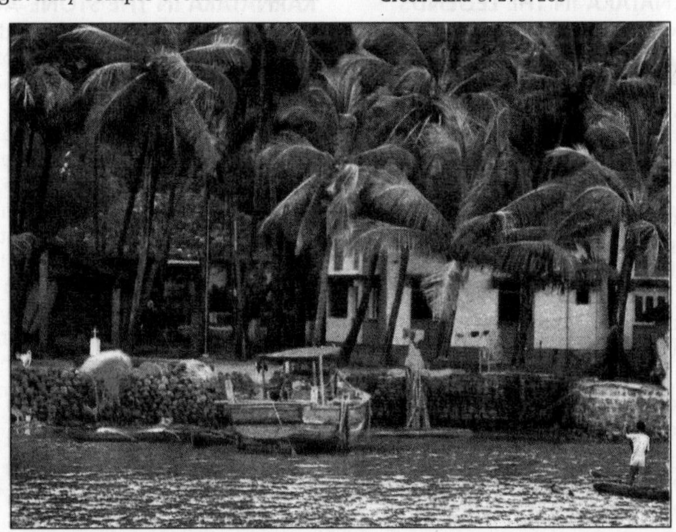

Karnataka

General Information

Facts and Figures

Capital	: Bangalore
Districts	: 27
Language	: Kannada
Area	: 1,91,791 Sq.km.
Population	: 5,27,33,958 (2001 census)
Males	: 2,68,56,343 (2001 census)
Females	: 2,58,77,615 (2001 census)
Increase in Population	: 77,56,757 (1991-2001)
Growth Rate	: 17.3%
Density (people in sq. km)	: 275
Urban Population	: 38.3%
Sex Ratio (Male : Female)	: 100 : 96
Literacy	: 67%
Male Literacy	: 76.3%
Female Literacy	: 57.5%
Lok Sabha Seats	: 28
Rajya Sabha Seats	: 12
State Assembly Seats	: 224

KARNATAKA IN THE LEGENDS

Karnataka, the state which has provided the stage to many a historic event is also in the limelight of puranic happenings. Humpi in Bellary district has a legendary reference since it is supposed to have been the capital city Kishkinda of the mythical anthropoid King Vali who was succeeded by his brother Sughriva, with the aid of Lord Sri Rama, mediated by Lord Sri Anjaneya in the great epic 'The Ramayana'. Batapi, the place associated with the mythical sage Agasthya is believed to have been the place which later came to be known as Badami in Bijapur district. Besides, several other places too have legendary reference.

KARNATAKA IN THE STONE-AGE

Even in the palaeolithic and the neolithic ages, the inhabitants of the state have shown a keen sense of understanding and innovation. The pre-historic culture here known as the hand-axe culture can be compared with the one that existed in Africa. The culture is explicitly different from that of North India. The pre-historic settlements have, as always, been along the extensive banks of the beautiful rivers in the valleys in between massive mountains. In as much as there is no scarcity of nature's bounty, there were no paucity to the places of ideal settlements. The palaeontology suggests that the antique denizens of the region had known the use of iron far earlier than their North Indian counterparts.

KARNATAKA UNDER VARIOUS RULERS

Karnataka has been in the realm of myriad heroes of various dynasties. Archives also reveal sovereign parts of the state had been under different rulers, ubiquitously. Many great royal dynasties have flourished here, the rulers of which have bequeathed treasured monuments of perpetual values. Noteworthy among those are Maurya, Kadamba, Chalukya, Ganga, Rashtrakuta, Hoysala and Vijayanagara.

Shravanabelagola, where the emperor Chandra Gupta Maurya embraced Jainism in the 3rd century B.C. was the retreat of the emperor in his twilight years while he sought solitude. Swamigiri, known as Kanakagiri situated in Raichur district was the southern capital of the Maurya rulers who ruled the kingdom of Magadha in the north. Ashoka, the grandson of Chandra Gupta Maurya had under his belt parts of Karnataka while his entire kingdom sprawled over the whole of North India. Ashoka who embraced and patronised Buddhism after the famous battle of Kalinga in which he emerged triumphant, has left behind as many as 11 edicts in Karnataka, of which one can be seen at Sannathi, Gulbarga district, three in Chitradurga district, three more in Raichur district and four in Bellary district. These edicts bear testimony to the expanse of the Mauryan empire.

'Satavahana', a new dynasty rose to power around 30 B.C. pulling the plug on the reign of the Mauryas. Extensive areas of north Karnataka belonged to these rulers. The Darwad and Bellary districts of today's Karnataka was known as 'Santhavahanihara' which means the Satavahana region and this leads to the belief that several scholars of this dynasty should have hailed from Karnataka. The rulers of this dynasty kept invasions at bay for 300 years before they conceded to two dynasties, viz. the Kadambas and the Gangas who divided the territory, the former holding the north and the latter the south. The Satavahana rulers have also made wonderful contributions to the ancient greatness of Karnataka and so have their successors in the Kadamba and the Ganga dynasties. Almost all of the rulers of all the dynasties seem to have had a passion for literature, art, architecture, sculpture and suchlike things while each of them had a unique stamping (i.e.,) their style.

At the outset of the 6th century the Chalukyas set up a new empire. The Chalukyan contribution to the grandeur of the state is also inexplicable. They remained invincible for quite some time until the Yadavas of Devagiri and the Hoysalas of Dwarasamudra took over and divided the region between them. The 14th century saw the rise of one empire and the fall of another. The one that fell was the Hindu Kingdom of Halebid conquered by Mohammed-bin-Tuglaq in 1327, who ravaged all priceless monuments leaving no trace to evince

*A temple chariot, complete with realistically turning wheels, was carved from a single stone at **Vijayanagar**, the great Hindu city of Karnataka. The city's heyday lasted from 1336 to 1565. It was then invaded by Muslim armies and fell to ruin.*

The domed elephant stables reflect Islamic architectural style. Royal mounts to carry the king and his splendid retinue were held here. Today the site of the fabled city is known as Hampi.

such a grand kingdom ever existed, and the one that rose was the great Vijayanagar empire. The Vijayanagar empire was replete with prosperity but in the 16th century, the placidity was ruptured by the foray of a confederation of Muslim Sultans and at last in 1565 the Vijayanagar empire with all its glory was annihilated in the battle of Talikota and so were a panoply of historic monuments and fabulous masterpieces of arts and architecture. The enormous ruins of Hampi today are the reticent reminders of the glories of the Vijayanagar empire.

In 1399 AD. a new dynasty came into existence founded by Yaduraya, who was the then ruler of the relatively small province of Mysore. The territories of this dynasty were furthered by 'Rajawodeyar' between 1578 and 1612 AD and the kingdom was eventually transfigured as a mighty empire with 'Srirangapatnam' as the capital. However, this rule gave way for Hyder Ali the Muslim ruler who is remembered for, among other things, his religious tolerance and appreciation of others' faiths along with son Tipu Sultan who offered a stiff resistance to the invading British. Tipu Sultan, well trained in warfare had always been a nightmare to the British until though at last the British proved too strong to resist. Then, the Wodeyar dynasty was revived but now as a feudatory of the British and Sri Krishna Raja Wodeyar III, who was a boy was made the king in 1799. Sri Krishnaraja III, himself being a scholar

*Royal elephants adorned for the ten-day **Dassehra Festival** pass through a palace gateway. Mysore's Dassehra festival pageantry, celebrating a goddess's victory over an evil demon, is spectacular.*

Gol Gumbaz, *the mausoleum of Mohamed Adil Shah II at Bijapur, built in 16th century has the second largest unsupported dome in the world.*

fond of literature founded 'The Rajah School for Teaching English' in 1833, which later became Maharaja's High School and finally in 1879, the Maharaja's college.

Durbar Hall of Mysore Palace *can accommodate thousands of onlookers. It was used much in 1930s and 40s. The palace has been the erstwhile residence of Mysore Maharajas. The exquisite art and paintings in the hall are pleasant to see.*

In 1947, when India finally broke her shackles, Mysore was conflated with Indian union as wished by the then ruler Maharaja Jayachamaraja Wodeyar sequel to a popular consensus. The Maharaja was aptly made the Governor and K.C.Reddy the Chief Minister of Mysore.

Since a number of ruling dynasties have prospered in Karnataka over the centuries, the state abounds in historic monuments. Some of them still intact in wholesome form and some others in ruins as a result of ravaging invasions.

"What a connoisseur of art and architecture this lot of lieges of yore should have been" is the spontaneous thought that overwhelms the observer of these extraordinary monuments. The Gomatheshwar statue, a magnificent monolithic stone sculpture soaring to a height of 17.5 m, perceivably the tallest of its kind conceives the patronage of the art under the Ganga dynasty, while the sculpture at Badami speaks volumes of the Chalukyas between the 6th and the 8th centuries. The grand temple architecture of the Hoysalas at places

A colonnade of pillars, ***Seshasayee Vishnu Temple*** *7th century AD at* ***Badami*** *which was once the capital of Chalukyas. 500 km. away from Bangalore. Badami has a number of cave temples dedicated to Lord Nataraja.*

like Somnathpur, Belur and Halebid are the captivating outcome of a conscientious workmanship between the 11th and the 14th centuries.

ARCHITECTURE AND SCULPTURE

The Gomatheshwar statue, a mammoth monolith built in 983 AD during the Ganga dynasty's rule, at Shravanabelagola is a standing example of the ingenious sculpture of the olden days and the admiration of the people for such huge images particularly when they are carved out of a single stone. The temple at Belur, another masterpiece of the Hoysala architecture, built by Vishnuvardhana to commemorate his victory over the Cholas, presents a different look from those of the other South Indian Temples in that the soaring Temple Towers are not seen, instead the walls of the temple and those of the Sanctorum are replete with beautiful workmanship. Besides, there are several images of deities, sculpted to a splendour. The twin temples dedicated to Lord Shiva at Halebid are also suffused with intricate and ethereal sculpture and carvings. The friezes portray scenes from 'The Great Epics' and things like the social setup, the Heavenly court, etc. The reliefs display various forms of the deities. The Parashunath Jain Temple at Halebid also falls in the spot light of temple architecture with its exquisite pillars polished to a sheen. Fascinating Jain monuments are also found in many other places. There are holy and huge statues of Sri Gomatheshwara which seem to express enormous plaudits to the devout sculptors. And there are also other evidences which corroborate the architectural and sculptural excellence of the state.

THE GEOGRAPHY OF KARNATAKA

The entire state Karnataka, which became one of the linguistic states of India in 1955 is graced by very interesting and enchanting landscape. The name Karnataka literally means 'High Land' in the language Kannada which is the vernacular. Geographically the state spreads between 11.5° and 18.5° north latitude and 74° and 78.5° east latitude. This 'Table Land'

*The **Pattadakal temple**, constructed during the Hoysala Dynasty some eight hundred years ago is a cynosure for the present day tourists. A high platform at the base of the temple provides a walkway for pilgrims making prayerful circumambulations of the star-shaped holy site while gazing at instructive sculptures.*

is surfeited with picturesque mountains, magnificent rivers, ravishing rivulets, beautiful becks, vivacious valleys, thick verdant forests and a host of other natural resources. The mighty ranges of the western ghats and the eastern ghats converge on the scenic Nilgiri Hills, along the border of the state. Beautiful ranges of rugged mountains form the border to the state on the east, west and south. The lavishly wonderful landscape of the state undulates between 600 and 900 mts above sea level. The exciting range of verdant mountains whose slopes are inundated with flora and fauna is aptly punctuated by amazing aqueducts, waterfalls and gorgeous gorges. Karnataka has Andhra Pradesh on the east, Arabian Sea on the west, Maharashtra and Goa on the north and north-west, and on the south, the states of Kerala and Tamil Nadu. The state is lined to a length of 320 km by sea coast. This coastline gives rise to some beautiful beaches. Quite a few port-cities have been centres of maritime trade since long past. The benevolent landscape of Karnataka also has a generous expanse of arable land. The fertility is primarily attributed to the wonderful rivers Cauvery, Thungabadra, etc., and a number of their tributaries. A sizeable portion of the state is blanketed by dense forests which, the environmentalists say, serve more purpose than one. 20% (i.e.) 38,724 sq. km. of the total area (i.e.) 1,91,791 sq. km. falls under the canopy of forest department. This vast area quite expectedly proffers land for a number of sanctuaries which prudently preserve a host of endangered species among other common creatures of the wild. There are also 'National Parks' in the sylvan region, meant to be more congenial.

*A waterfall refreshes the forest in the **Coorg (Kodagu)** region of southern Karnataka. The Abbey Falls situated about 3 km. from Madikere is a picnic spot. The cool sizzling waterfalls attract many tourists.*

*A herd of wild elephants forages in the forests and grasslands of **Nagarhole National Park**, Karnataka. Over a thousand of these huge beasts roam the area, one of the best remaining habitats for the Asian elephants.*

A number of steps has been taken to preserve the natural habitat of these nonchalant beings. These forests fall under an interesting classification to help the development programmes. There are reserved forests, protected ones unclassed, village and private forests. Teak, ebony, black wood and cedar find these forests their homes and so does bamboo which is equally sought-after. The sumptuous plantations of sandalwood fill the forest air with their pleasant fragrance. These forest produce play a vital role in determining the economic echelon of the state. Majestic elephants with an ambience of unquestioned awe around them, the big cats like the leopard, the panther, and cheetah with their unparalleled running speeds, the frightening and yet fabulous tigers, the wild boar, the spotted deers which have time and again held the fascination of renowned poets and a host of other remarkable creatures of the wild grace these woods galore, bearing testimony to the primordial beauty.

MODERN KARNATAKA

The Karnataka state of today which is in fact the collation of 4 districts of Mumbai, 2 of Chennai and 3 of the Nizam's territory. Coorg forms part of the Western Deccan region of Peninsular India. The state holds the 8th place in the Nation in area and people. The capital city Bangalore with more than 6 million people, is the 6th largest urban agglomeration out of the 23 in India.

The transportation in the state is aided by a cumulative length of 1.34 lakh km of road. Four important National Highways leading to the state were sanctioned by the central government in 1998. The rail route in Karnataka stretches to 3089 km. And there are airports at Bangalore, Mysore, Belgaum, Mangalore and Hubli. And the much awaited "Konkan Railway" connecting Mumbai and Mangalore, an important port city was also commissioned on the first of May in the year 1998.

INDUSTRIES

Karnataka also fosters many important industries. There are Government undertakings and also private sector establishments which play an important role in the field of employment and revenue. Bharath Earth Movers Ltd., Bharath Electronics, Hindustan Machine Tools, Bharath Heavy Electricals, Hindustan Aeronautics and Indian Telephone Industries deserve a special mention in the public sector. Besides, the proliferating medium scale industries make up to over 650 in number, at an estimate. The iron and steel industry is also thriving one here. The Viswesvaraya Iron and Steel Ltd., has a production capacity of 77,000 tonnes of special and alloy steel per year. The electronic industry is wayward putting Karnataka ahead of all other states in the production of electronic equipments. Karnataka stands first also in the production of raw silk. The sandalwood industry of the state is noteworthy. The ivory factory here produces exquisite decorative articles. The state is rich also in natural mineral resources. High grade iron ore, copper, manganese, chromite, china clay, limestone and magnetite are the important minerals found here. The state shoots the spotlight in gold production.

RELIGION AND PEOPLE

Karnataka has been the centre of religious activities which is quite evident from the ancient temples and hermitages. Sri Madhvacharya, who promulgated 'Dvaita' was born in the state. Sri Ramanuja, who spread the philosophy of 'Visishtadvaita' among the multitude of population, had a sojourn of over 12 years in Karnataka in the 11th century during which period the saint attracted scores of devotees who eventually became ardent followers. Sri Adi Sankara who upheld the philosophy of 'Advaita' has also visited Karnataka in the 8th century and established a diocese at Sringeri which imparts the essential spiritual knowledge in millions of people. Thus Karnataka has been consecrated by the religious 'Trinity' and also been one of the platforms of the three great philosophies. And in the 12th century, Basava shook off the constraints of caste and took to preaching 'The oneness of God and the Brotherhood of Man'.

The religious heads, Sri Adi Sankara, Sri Ramanuja and Sri Madhvacharya have traversed on foot the length and breadth of the Nation propagating their philosophies all along. A number of people took recourse to the saints to get over their woes. The saints have visited several temples and led their followers to eternal bliss through their spiritual aura.

Even today the influence of the saints is largely felt, predominantly the Madhva culture. The Brindavan of Sri Raghavendra, a prominent saint in the hierarchical order of Sri Madhvacharya, can be seen at many places. And devotees of Sri Raghavendra are found in every nook and corner of Karnataka.

Though Hinduism has more number of people than other religions in Karnataka, there are also considerable numbers belonging to the major religions like Buddhism, Christianity, Sikhism, Islamism and

*Tall ornate towers (gopurams) of Hindu temples testify to the faith of most South Indians. This four-hundred-year-old temple dedicated to Sri Virupaksha draws devotees at **Hampi**, Karnataka.*

Jainism. Karnataka is an anthropologically diverse region. The populace of the region is composed of various races and the conflation of various races. The distinct races in retrospect, were the Dravidians and the Indo-Aryans. However, the strains of other notable races are the Turks, Afghans, the Negro slaves known as Siddhis and Tibetans.

Bangalore

This beautiful city lends its name to the district of Bangalore to which the city is perceivably the head-quarters. The district spreads over an area of 8005 sq. km. and has a population of 65,12,356 according to the census 2001. Though the city has little to display from the antiquities, the later developments and the conscientious planning have earned a distinction to it. With the variety of its populace, the city wears a cosmopolitan countenance. If the artificial feats adorn the city, the natural traits without exception to the climate seem to have propped the artificial endeavours which had brought about the charm. About 921 m above sea level, the splendid city had been the summer asylum of the British from, the proximity. And today, it continues to be the summer resort to many.

The district has a number of industries and business establishments and consequently has people from various parts winning their bread and butter. Apart from Kannada which is the Mother tongue of the people, Urdu, Hindi and English are also widely spoken. Tamil, the language of the neighbouring State is obviously in place in many parts of the city.

The way the city was christened is quite interesting. While the King Veera Ballara of Vijayanagar was hunting in the forest, he lost his way. After exasperating attempts to make it out rendered him ravenous he was guided by the boiled beans known as Benda- kalo of a hermit and he made it out of the forest, sure and safe. An earthen fort was raised by Sardar Kempegowda to reminisce this event in 1537 AD. Then, Kempegowda founded the city which was originally called 'Benda Kalu Uru'. This name synonymous to the present name was later transformed into Bangalore. This fort was transfigured into a sturdy stone structure by Hyder Ali and later improved by his son 'Tipu Sultan'. This fort is an excellent example of the 18th century military architecture.

The tourists have umpteen places of interest. Cubbon Park, Lalbagh, Tipu's Fort, Government Museum, Venkatappa Art Gallery, Bull Temple, Viswesvaraya Industrial and Technological Museum, Ganesh Temple, Gandhi Bhavan, Ulsoor Tank, Gavipuram Cave Temple, St.Mary's Basilica Church, Aquarium, Boat Clubs, Libraries, Auditoriums, Swimming pools and a number of other places around the city as well.

The city is connected by rail, road and air with several major cities. There are also convenient and fre-

*The **Basavanagudi Bull Temple** was built by Kempegowda I (1513-1569), the founder of Bangalore. The locality derives its name from the temple.*

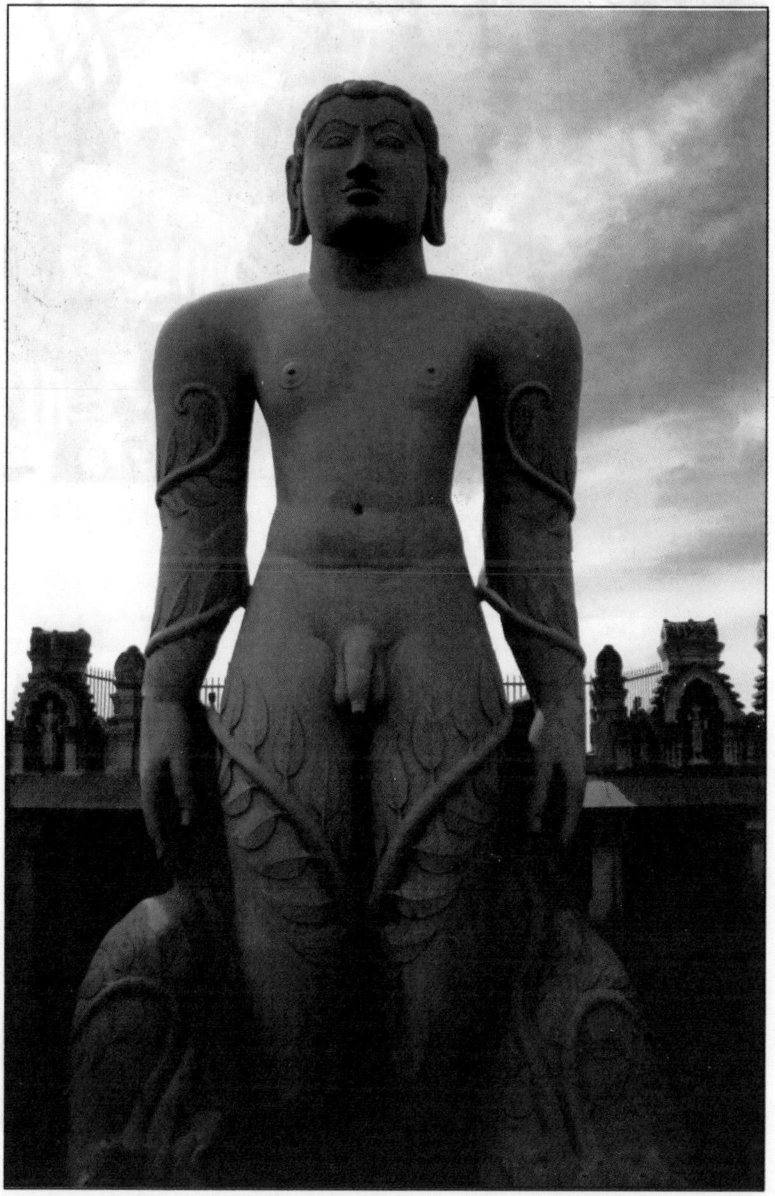

Statue of Lord Gomateswara (Lord Bahubali), Shravanabelagola.

'Lord Nandi', the holy bull of Lord Shiva atop Chamundi Hills.

Vidhan Soudha, houses both the Secretariat and the Legislative Assembly, Bangalore.

quent buses plying within the city. Other modes of transportation like autorickshaw and taxi can also be hired. Excellent accommodation to suit various budgets are available.

Cubbon Park: This wonderful park which has recently been rechristened as Jayachamarajendra Park is situated in the heart of the city about 5 km from the railway station. This 300 acres of sheer beauty was the outcome of the conscientious efforts of the British in 1864.

Beautiful roads, blooming trees and placid plains are spread in between, a memorial hall dedicated to Seshadri Aiyar, Jawahar Bal Bhavan, Children's Park and a Museum. The beautiful podium of band orchestra has around it a large soiree on Sundays. There is also a general library in the memorial hall.

The museum here set up in 1866 houses exquisite specimens of Vijayanagar and Halebid, Mohenjadaro architecture, ancient coins and stone inscriptions which takes us 5000 years back in time. The children can have a lot of fun in the Children's Park and also in the pleasure train. This beautiful museum, which comprises 18 enclosures, and which is one of the oldest ones in India can be visited on all days except Mondays between 08:00 and 17:00 hrs.

The Venkatappa Art Gallery, a recent enclosure to the park is a roomy structure which displays the exciting paintings of Venkatappa, the court painter to the Maharajah of Mysore in the early 20th century. The beautiful works of contemporary artists are also displayed. The gallery can be visited between 9:00 hrs and 17:00 hrs on all days except Wednesdays.

Viswesvaraya Industrial and Technological Museum: Attractive models are displayed here, depicting the industrial and technological developments of India. These models are illustrative of various stages of the development and the achievements thereof. It comes under the management of the 'Council of Scientific and Industrial Research', New Delhi. It is open on all working days other than Mondays. It remains closed on notified holidays. Visiting Hours : 10:00 - 17:00 hrs.

Lalbagh: About 2 km southeast of the city market, this beautiful botanical garden spreading over an area of 240 acres is a marvel laid by Hyder Ali in 1760 and beautified subsequently by his son Tipu Sultan. Later in the 19th century, the British added several beautiful features giving it a modern look. The name 'Lalbagh' reasons with the teeming red roses in the garden. And the magnificent trees seen here had been brought from Persia, France and Kabul. A beautiful glass hall built in 1890 sequel to the crystal palace in London, to serve as a wedding hall is one of the prime attractions. Captivating fountains, a placid artificial lake and an enclosure of cool waters flaunting a sumptuous lot of the lavish lotus and a deer park where the fascinating mild creatures of the wild greet the visitors all enhance the enchantment. Another piece of attraction is the gigantic clock dial installed by the HMT, embellished with eye catching artificial flowers flashing a wide spectrum of attractive colours, and measuring in diameter to a good 7 metres. This battery operated clock incorporates the precision quartz technology. The Republic Day and the Independence Day are two special occasions here marketed by the horticultural shows. Lalbagh is a frequent hangout of many locals while it is also the favourite picnic spot of several tourists.

Visiting Hours: 08:00 - 20:00 hrs.

Vidhan Soudha: This grand edifice of the Dravidian style, built of granite in 1954 occupies a gracious 5,05,000 sq.ft. The door of the cabinet room is made of pure sandalwood. The structure has four storeys and houses both the Secretariat and the Legislative Assembly. With the nightfall on Sundays and other holidays, the huge structure presents a beautiful scenery with tremendous illumination. The wonderful dome can be seen on all working days between 15:00 and 17:30 hours with the permission of the Under Secretary. On the opposite is the high court building. Visitors may get in touch with the authorities over the number 2200112.

Tipu's Fort: This fort was first raised with mud by Kempegowda in 1537. In 1761, Hyder Ali renovated it, making it a sturdy stone structure. Portions of the fort were destroyed during the battle between the British and Tipu Sultan, the son of Hyder Ali. And it was repaired by Tipu Sultan later. A temple dedicated to 'Lord Ganapathy' can also be seen inside the fort.

A beautiful wooden palace which served as the summer retreat of Tipu Sultan is situated a little south of the fort near the 'City Market' at the Krishna Rajendra and Albert Victor roads junction. The construction of this palace started by Hyder Ali in 1778 was completed by his son Tipu Sultan in 1791. This palace was one of the victims of careless neglect which has caused its destruction.

There is also a museum which houses a number of artifacts which proclaim Tipu's bravery and his deftness in warfare. These collections bring to the fore the zeal with which Tipu guarded his territory against the mighty British.

An ancient temple dedicated to Lord Venkataramana, built 300 years ago in the Dravidian style is also situated in the vicinity. The impact of the third battle of Mysore during the period between 1790 and 1792 is explicit on the stone pillars opposite the temple. These pillars bear the scar left by the cannon shots.

Visiting Hours (Fort): 08:00 - 18:00 Hrs.

Bull Temple: This marvellous temple, dedicated to 'Lord Nandi', the Holy Bull of Lord Siva, built in the grand Dravidian style by Kempegowda is situated on the beautiful "Bugle Hill" on the road which derives its name from this famous temple, 'The Bull Temple Road'. The gigantic statue of 'Lord Nandi' here is an exquisite monolithic stone sculpture which measures to a height of 6.2 m. It is believed that the statue keeps growing further and further.

The temple adjacent to this is that of 'Lord Ganesa' which has a unique feature. The image of the deity here is made once in 4 years out of 110 kg of 'Butter' and amazingly enough it never melts. At the end of the 4 years time, a ritual is performed and the butter from the old idol is distributed to the devotees. About 400 mts to the west are 4 watch towers also built by Kempegowda.

Gandhi Bhavan: The beautiful portraits here display scenes from the life of 'Mahatma'. There are also photostat copies of letters written by Gandhiji to some distinguished personalities. The picture gallery is open on all days except Sundays and Government holidays. Visiting Hours 12:00 - 18:00 hrs.

Ulsoor Lake: Situated at the centre of the cantonment area, this 1.5 sq. km. expanse of placid waters offers thrill while the beautiful scenery of the tank attracts scores of visitors from far and near. Boating facilities are available. There is also a modern public swimming pool. It can be visited on all days except Wednesdays between 09:00 and 18:00 hrs.

Overlooking this splendid expanse of water is the serene Ashram dedicated to Sri Aurobindo. This is also the centre for learning enthralling and essential things like Yoga, Naturopathy, Ikebana, Bonsai and a variety of arts and crafts in a peaceful ambience.

Gavipuram Cave Temple: This beautiful cave temple, filled with tranquility, dedicated to Lord Siva has a unique feature in that, on the 14th day of January every year, a ray of sunlight passes in between the horns of 'Lord Nandi', the sacred bull mount of Lord Siva, and falls on the 'Linga' between 17:00 and 18:00 hrs. It goes to show what an excellent astronomical knowledge and architectural skill the architects of the olden days possessed.

This temple was built by Kempegowda. The four marvellous monolithic pillars are carved with Trishula, Damaru, Suryapana and Chandrapana. The icon of 'Agni Deva', the God of Fire, here is a rarity.

St. Mary's Basilica Church: This church, situated in Shivajinagar, is the oldest church in Bangalore. It is believed that it was built in the 16th century but it was transfigured into the present shape in 1832. It is also known as the church of 'Our Lady of Health'. An annual festival is celebrated in September, marked by the grand procession of Virgin Mary followed by thousands of devotees.

Hanuman Temple: This exquisite temple dedicated to Lord Anjaneya is a relatively modern structure with a touch of the olden form of grand sculpture and environs. Gigantic figures of Lord Sri Rama hugging Lord Anjaneya can be seen on the temple roof. These statues are about 31 feet tall. Shri K. Hanumanthaiya, who is known for the excellence of the magnificent structure of 'Vidhan Soudha', was the architect behind this wonderful monument too. The temple also offers a panoramic view of Bangalore. Within the vicinity, there is another beautiful temple and this is dedicated to Lord Siva who manifests in the form of Lord 'Hariheswara'. Hanuman Temple is situated near the Cave Temple.

Nandi Hills: The beautiful town situated on the picturesque Nandi Hills at an altitude of 1478 m above sea level, is about 60 km north of Bangalore on the Bangalore-Mysore road. This sylvan region had been the summer resort of Tipu Sultan. This historic place also has Tipu's prayer hall known as Chhabotra, Kumpage Orchard, Yogananda Temple and Tipu's harem. The famous 'Tipu's Drop' here is a steep hill 600 m high from where the capital punishment was executed in Tipu's days by throwing the convicts to death. Even the British were no exceptions to be lured by the charms of Nandi Hills. This place has offered a pleasant stay to historic personalities like Mahatma Gandhi, Queen Elizabeth II, Jawaharlal Nehru, etc.

There are two ancient temples dedicated to Lord Siva, with exquisite architecture and sculpture, one at the foot and the other on the top of the hill 'Amrita Sarovar' which means 'The lake of divine nectar'. Its perennial springs with their salubrious waters never let it turn dry. It is situated near the temples. These springs also form the fount of the ravishing rivers, Pennar, Chitravathi and Palar. Grand Chola architecture is reflected in the Siva Temple atop the hill. There are also many other ancient temples, built by the kings of Chola and Vijayanagar dynasty in the wonderful region. Cottages are available here and excursions are also arranged. The interested may contact, 'Director of Horticulture', Lalbagh, Bangalore, Ph. 602 231or the 'Special Officer, Horticulture, Nandi Hills'.

Kolar Goldmines: Kolar is famed by the world's deepest and India's only goldmines. The mines go deep down to over 3 km beneath the surface of the earth. Kolar had been the capital of the Ganiya Kings for 7 centuries. There are elevators to take the visitors in and out of the mines. Visitors are required to obtain permission from 'The Secretary, Kolar Goldmining Undertaking, Kolar-563101. Entry is prohibited to children below 10 years. It is situated on the highway between Chennai and Bangalore which is about 68 km away.

Sivaganga: This is yet another beautiful hill town, 1380 m above sea level, about 60 km from Bangalore. This vivacious wooded region has a number of ancient temples of which Gangadeeswara and Honna Devi temples are very popular. There are ancient monuments like Kempegowda's Hazara, the image of Khumbi Basava and the Lingayat Mutt called 'Mahanta Mutt'. It is believed that there were 64 Lingayat Mutts here. The temples here, quite ancient, are replete with ornate carvings, rich sculpture. The image of Kempegowda can also be seen as a devotee at the Siva temple here. Another ancient temple dedicated to Lord Siva is situated below the hill. Here Lord Siva is worshipped in the form of Shanteswara. The temple has a huge tank with sculptures depicting epic events.

This picturesque hill is by itself a natural marvel since it offers a pleasant surprise to the onlooker from each of the 4 directions. It presents the look of Nandi, the sacred bull of Lord Siva, from the east. From the west, it looks like the image of Lord Ganesa. It resembles a Siva Linga to look at from the south and a gigantic cobra with its hood spread, from the north.

Chamarajasagar: The beautiful dam across the mighty river Arkavali and the artificial lake with its serene waters cater to the drinking water needs of the town. This scenic place in Tippagondanahalli is obviously a popular picnic spot. The permission of the Chief Engineer BWSSB, Cauvery Bhavan, Bangalore-560 009, is necessary to visit this enchanting place which is about 35 km from Bangalore.

Devanahalli: About 35 km from Bangalore, this historic place has the pride of being the birth place of 'The Tiger of Mysore', Tipu Sultan, son of Hyder Ali. A commemorative monument and a massive fort are among the tourist attractions here. An ancient temple dedicated to Lord 'Venugopal', one of the various forms of Lord Vishnu can also be seen. This temple reflects the grand style of Dravidian architecture. An old Mosque can also be seen here.

Hesarghatta: It is 29 km from Bangalore on way to Tumkur. A beautiful artificial lake sprawling over 1000 acres can be seen here. This place is also the venue of the Indo-Danish dairy project and the Govt. Horticultural and dairy farms. An Indo-Australian fodder seeds farms was set up here in 1979.

Mekadatu: On the Kanakapura road, 98 km from Bangalore, Mekadatu which means a "goat's leap" is where the ancient Siva temple known as the 'Sangameswara Temple' at the confluence of two beautiful rivers, is situated. This sumptuous sylvan region has a beautiful canyon through which the Arkavati river flows. Here, this river tributes the river Cauvery which courses along a ravine, so narrow that a goat can leap across. Hence, it has been named so.

Bannerghatta National Park: This picturesque sylvan region which spreads over 104 sq. km. about 20 km on the south of Bangalore is home to a fascinating variety of wildlife creatures which include the bewitching spotted deers and sambars, magnificent elephants and mighty bisons and the 'Jungle-Kings' - lions. Besides, there are varieties of venomous and non-venomous snakes. Among the unique attractions are model park of pre-historic animals, the crocodile project and the spell-binding 'Lion-Safari' which gets a 'close-up' of the majestic beasts.

The region is also graced by more than a 100 species of exciting birds. The pinnacle of two scenic hillocks, the Mirya and the Hajamanakallu provide vantage points to get a panoramic view of the national park. This park which remains closed on Mondays can be visited on all other days.

Visiting Hours: 09:00 - 17:00 hrs.

Ghati Subramanya: About 52 km from Bangalore via Doddaballapur, this famous temple is dedicated to 'Lord Subramanya' or 'Lord Muruga' and 'Makali Durga' situated on the Bangalore-Guntakkal line, is the nearest railway station.

Devarayanadurga: This beautiful place is situated about 79 km from Bangalore via Tumkur. There are two wonderful temples nestled in enchanting wooded surroundings which is home to some wildlife. There is also a scenic hill in the region at the top of which there are temples dedicated to Lord 'Ugra Narasimha', an incarnation of Lord Vishnu and at the hill-foot a natural water spring known as 'Namada Chilume'. This region with undulating landscape is a beautiful hill resort. The 'Department of Tourism' provides accommodation at the 'Tourist Rest House', Devarayanadurga.

Muthyala Maduvu: This is a piquant picnic spot situated about 44 km from Bangalore. The beautiful valley amidst picturesque mountains fills the air with tranquillity. This deep valley, rightly known as the 'Pearl Valley' is an ideal spot for solitude seekers. To compliment the captivating scenery, there is a ravishing waterfalls whose roistering waters falling from a height of 30 ft form a 'Pool of Pearls' which lends the place the name'Muthyala Maduvu'. There is a travellers bungalow, 6 km from Anekal town on the Hosur road. To reserve an accommodation, contact: The Block Development Officer, Anekal.

Savanadurga: About 58 km on the Magadi road from Bangalore, this magnificent hill fortress, formerly known as 'Nelepatna' which means 'Underground City', was the hide-out of Kempegowda. During the reign of Sawantharaya, it was called 'Savantdurg' and later modified as 'Savanadurga' during the days of Kempegowda. There is an ancient temple dedicated to Lord Ugra Narasimha', an incarnation of Lord

Vishnu with a human body and a lion's head. Another temple in the vicinity built by Kempegowda, is dedicated to Lord Veerabadra, a variation of Lord Vishnu. There are also two scenic hills adding attraction to the environs. The tomb of a Muslim saint by name 'Sayyed Ghulam Hussain Shah Qadri' is situated in between the temples.

Kanva Reservoir: This beautiful reservoir is situated 69 km from Bangalore on the road to Mysore. Accommodation is available at the Travellers Bungalow. For reservations, contact: Assistant Executive Engineer, No.2, Sub Division, Channapatna.

Ramohalli: The huge banyan tree by which the place is known spreads lavishly over a generous area of 3 acres. 'Ramohalli' which means 'An Enormous Banyan Tree' is an excellent picnic spot. A number of prop roots support the massive 400 year old tree which offers a cool shelter under the scorching Sun to the awe-struck visitors. This beautiful place is situated 28 km from Bangalore.

Magadi: This historic city, the headquarters of Bangalore Rural District, situated about 41 km from Bangalore was founded in 1139 by the Cholas, one of the three eminent Tamil dynasties. Kempegowda, the ruler of the region who was instrumental in the evolution of Bangalore as a city, was born here. He has raised in this place a number of magnificent temples with wonderful architecture and stupendous sculpture besides building a massive fort. The Indo-Saracenic architecture is reflected in the 'Someswar Temple'. The other temples include the ones dedicated to Lord Veerabadra, Lord Gangadeeswara and Lord Rameswara. All the temples are rich in architecture, sculpture and carvings; however, the wall paintings of the Rameswara temple are fading. There is also a temple dedicated to 'Lord Ranganatha' one of the various forms of 'Lord Vishnu'. This beautiful temple is situated on a scenic hill known by the name of the famous Tirumala Hills situated in Andhra Pradesh.

Vasanthapur: Located about 13 km from Bangalore, this place is famous for the ancient temple known as the 'Sri Vasantha Vallabharaya Swamy Temple'. This temple with grand architecture is believed to have been built by the Cholas. The image of the Lord here is 5 ft. in height.

There is a legend which associates the mythical sage Mandavya with this place. The sage once vanished from his 'Asram' or 'Hermitage'. Baffled by this, his 'Sishyas' or disciples set out in search of their 'Guru', (Teacher) in all directions from his 'Ashram' which was situated on the salubrious banks of the holy river Ganges. Obsessed with anxiety they screened every possible corner until at last they arrived in Vasanthapur, where the sage was found absorbed in deep meditation inside a serene cave.

The legend also adds that the Holy marriage of Lord Srinivasa with Goddess Padmavathi took place here, which the sage penchantly wanted to attend but was unable to make it here on time. Therefore, he prayed to the just-wed divine couple to perform certain rites and rituals at his Ashram which was immediately heeded to.

Now this sacred place is a popular pilgrim spot.

Bhavani-Shankar Temple: About a stone's throw from Sri Vasantha Vallabharaya Swamy Temple, this, yet another wonderful temple is dedicated to Lord Siva. Goddess Parvathi, the divine consort of the Lord manifests here as Goddess Bhavani and Lord Siva as Lord Shankar and hence the name Bhavani-Shankar Temple. An interesting feature in this temple is that there are icons of Saint Purandaradasa, one of the pioneers of 'Sangeetha' or classical music and Saint Thyagaraja, one of the three Saints regarded as the prodigious trinity of Sangeetha, the other two being Saint Muthuswamy Dikshithar and Saint Shyama Sastrigal. It is said that 'Chathrapathi Shivaji', the 'Lion of Maharashtra' who had been a nightmare to Aurangzeb, has performed worship at this temple during his southern sojourn.

Ramanagaram: This place on the beautiful banks of the river Arkavathi has 'Puranic references'. It is believed that Lord Rama with His consort Goddess Sita and His brother Lord Lakshmana had a halt here at Ramaveda Betta while they were on their way to the forests as ordained by King Dasaratha, Lord Rama's father. There is a gorgeous hill topped by an ancient temple with excellent architecture, wonderful carvings and sculpture which depict among other figures, the Hoysala Lions. The temple also has icons of Lord Rama, Goddess Sita and Lord Lakshmana. The sacred temple tank here is known as 'Laksha Theertha'.

In the proximity, there is another temple with splendid architecture. Goddess Parvathi, the consort of Lord Siva is the presiding deity here. Lord Siva is worshipped in His usual Linga form in front of the sacred bull mount, Nandhi.

Overlooking the beautiful river Arkavathi are a temple dedicated to Lord Arkeswara and the Peeran Shahwali Mosque. Ramanagaram has traditionally been a place of dextrous potters. The pottery products of this place have a wide and far-fetched appeal. A showroom and the Rural Marketing and Servicing Centre of the Karnataka State Handicrafts Development Corporation is situated here. The place excels in the production of silk, with the distinction of being the largest silk production centre in India.

Suharawardi Mosque: The fraternity between the Hindus and the Muslims is well exemplified here at this Mosque of the Muslim Saint Hazarat Tawakkal Mastan Shah Suharawardi, whose 'Urs' is celebrated every year on the 19th of the Islamic month 'Safar'. By a traditional convention which bears testimony to the religious harmony, the grand Hindu annual procession customarily visits and pays respects to the Saint at the Mosque, which stands tall as the centre of pilgrim attraction to both Muslims and Non-muslims.

This centre of worship, one of those where the ever existent congenial feelings of two major religions are brought to the fore is situated in the heart of Cottonpet.

Karnataka Folk Museum: This museum houses a number of folklore costumes, beautiful artifacts, animated masks etc., of the exciting folk dance forms. These costumes are brightly coloured and quite attractive. These masks configured to present various looks and the attires and other beautiful accessories are the outcome of the hereditary folklore. The fascinating folk-arts are still relished at various places. This museum comes under the management of 'Karnataka Janapada Trust'. The folk music has also soothed millions of pairs of ears traditionally. Audio and video tapes of the ever entertaining folk music and folk dance are available here.

Visiting Hours: 10:30 - 17:00 hrs.

Mahalakshmipuram Hanuman: This image of Lord Hanuman, 22 ft. and 6 ft. in height and width respectively was beautifully carved out of a huge granite stone slab after the Dewan of Mysore, Mizra Ismail witnessed the amazing divine phenomenon of light being emitted from the stone which had been the shooting target during the King rule in Mysore.

The gigantic statue represents Lord Anjaneya at the instant of landing with a huge mountain seated effortlessly in His mighty benevolent hand. The traditional 'Poojas' at all places to Lord Anjaneya include among other rites and rituals, anointing the image of the deity with butter fully or on the mouth and 300 kg of butter is used for the holy purpose. A number of devotees come and offer prayers and worship the Lord here.

Ramanashram: This tranquil Ashram of Bhagavan Sri Ramana Maharishi who attracts thousands of devotees of Indian and foreign origin even after His attaining the 'Divine Abode', is situated near Mekhri Circle. There are Ashrams dedicated to the Maharishi at many places and the one at Thiruvannamalai of Tamil Nadu was the first and it was where Bhagwan Sri Ramana dwelled.

This ashram has a huge polished granite hall which can hold upto 300 devotees at a time. Though relatively modern, the structure offers the serenity of an antique cave. The 'Ramana Maharishi Centre for Learning' which opens the eye of wisdom in millions of people through various means such as publishing of the Maharishi's Teachings, libraries with a good collection of priceless books and also through fine arts like music, dance and dramas, manages this ashram.

Sri Dharmaraja Temple: Situated in Nagarethpet, this temple is dedicated to 'Sri Dharmaraja' of the great epic 'The Mahabharatha'. 'Draupathi' is worshipped here as Goddess Shakthi. The famous Bangalore Karaga festival and procession starts here. A noteworthy aspect of this procession is that it visits Mosque of the Muslim Saint Hazarat Tawakkal and pays respects to Him. The mutual brotherhood of Hindus and Muslims finds a fine example here.

White Field: This place about 20 km from Bangalore city is famous as the sacred sojourn of Bhagwan Sri Sathya Sai Baba while on tour to Bangalore. The original ashram of the Bhagwan is situated at Puttaparthi in Andhra Pradesh. The devotees of Sri Sai Baba numbered to thousands upon thousands are spread all over the globe. The Bhagwan visits Bangalore quite frequently and offers darshan to the swarming devotees at Whitefield. Those who wish to know the schedule of the Bhagwan's Bangalore visits may contact Bangalore Ashram, Information Centre, Brindavan, Kadugodi, Bangalore - 560 067. Ph.: 842233.

Jumma Masjid: Situated in Taramandalpet, Pettah Area, this beautiful mosque formerly known as Sangin Jumma Masjid, with tall pillars made out of granite and adorned with ornate carvings and a spacious prayer hall, is the oldest in the city.

The Third Mysore War has left the elegant roof of the impressive mosque partly damaged due to the impact of the 'balls' from the cannon of the British. Mohiyuddin Ali Khan who was the 'Bakshi' at the court of Bangalore during the King rule, is said to have renovated the structure in 1836 AD.

Ravindra Kalakshethra: Cultural activities find patronage here in the centenary memorial of great poet and the architect of the 'Indian National Anthem' Sri Rabindranath Tagore. The massive auditorium here which can accommodate 900 people, stages a number of dance and drama events.

Contiguous to this is, Sir Puttannachetty Town Hall, an excellent Gothic Style construction with a roomy auditorium to hold as many as 1500 people, opened in 1935. It is now the venue of important public functions, lectures, meetings, seminars, conferences, exhibitions and concerts.

Chowdaiah Memorial Hall: Chowdaiah, a very popular name in 'Carnatic Music' was a renowned violinist. This memorial built in his honour, with air-conditioning and a spacious hall of 1010 people capacity designed to meet various purposes, is appropriately shaped like the ever so melodious musical instrument 'violin'.

Accommodation

5 Star Hotels

• **Curzon Court,** 10, Brigade Road, Bangalore-1. ✆ 25582997, 25581698, 25583161 Fax : 080-25582278

• **Golden Waters,** B-1266, 14th Floor, Mittal Towers, M.G. Road, Bangalore - 1. ✆ 25595031, 25591416 Fax : 080 - 25586473 Email: alexeblr.vsnl. net.in

• **Hotel Ashok,** P.B. No. 5095, Kumarakrupa High Grounds, Bangalore - 1. ✆ 22269462, 22250202 Fax : 080-22250033 E mail:htlashok@blr.vsnl.net.in

• **Le Meridien,** 28, Sankey Road, Bangalore - 52. ✆ 22262233, 22282828 Fax : 080-22267676/ 22262050 Email: leme@vsnl.net.in

• **Taj Residency (Member of the Taj Group),** 41/3, M.G. Road, Bangalore-1. ✆ 25584444 Fax: 080-25584748 Email: residency.bangalore@ tajhotels.com

• **The Leela Palace,** Bangalore, A Kempenski Hotel (Govt. Approved) 23, Airport Road, Bangalore - 8. ✆ 25564525 Fax: 080-25212323 Email: reservations @theleelablr.com

• **The Oberoi (Member - Leading Hotels of World),** 37-39, MG Road, Bangalore-1. ✆ 25585858 Fax : 080-25585960 Email:som@oberoiblr.com

• **West End Hotel (Taj Group of Hotels),** Race Course Road, Bangalore - 1. ✆ 22255055 Fax : 080-22200010 Email: v.mohan@tajhotels.com

• **Windsor Manor Sheraton (5 Star Deluxe Hotel),** 25, Sankey Road, Bangalore - 52. ✆ 22269898 Fax : 080-22264941 Email: itcwindsor@welcom group.com

4 Star Hotels

• **Bush Betta Wildlife Adventure Resorts,** 3, President Chambers, 8, Richmond Road, Bangalore - 25. ✆ 22243274, 22244795 Email:bushbetta@ vsnl.net.in

• **Gateway Hotel (Hotel & Restaurant),** 66, Residency Road, Bangalore - 25. ✆ 25584545 Fax : 080-25584030 Email:gateway.bangalore@ tajhotels.com

• **Hotel Luciya International (Boarding & Lodging),** 60, O.T.C. Road, Bangalore - 2. ✆ 22224148, 22224470 Fax: 080-22239898

• **St. Mark's Hotel (Quality Food & Service),** 4/1, St. Marks Road, Bangalore - 1. ✆ 22279090 Fax : 080-22275700 Email: stmarks@vsnl.com

• **The Park Kensington Terrace,** 14/7, Mahatma Gandhi Road, Bangalore - 42. ✆ 25594666 Fax:080-25594029 Email:admin.ban@park.sprintrpg.ems. vsnl.net.in

3 Star Hotels

• **Angsana Oasis SPA and Resort,** Main Doddaballapur Road, Addevishwanathapura Village, Rajankunte, Bangalore - 64. ✆ 28468898/ 25591080 Fax: 080-28468897 Email:prestinge1@ vsnl.com

• **Hotel Samrat Residency,** 173/1, S.C. Road, Seshadripuram, Bangalore - 20. ✆23360822, 23443199, 23364776 Fax : 080-23465657 Email: samrat@bgl.yahoo.com

• **Mercure Inn Guestline,** Plot No. 1 & 2, KIADB Industrial Area, Attibele Bangalore - 7. ✆ 08116-220430-34 Fax : 08116-220435 Email:hgalbr@bgl. vsnl.net.in

• **Museum Inn Hotel,** 1, Museum Road, Bangalore-1. ✆ 25594001, 25595272-273 Fax : 080-25581313 Email: hotelmuseuminn@rediffmail.com

• **Nahar's Heritage (Hotel & Restaurant),** 14, St. Marks Road, Bangalore - 1. ✆ 22278731-36 Fax :-2080-22278737 Email: naharblr@vsnl.net.in

• **Ramanashree California Resort,** Hotel Ananthapura Gate, Doddaballapur Road, Bangalore - 64. ✆ 28461250-53, 28461256-9 Fax : 080-28461254

• **The Central Park Manipal Centre,** 47, Dickenson Road, Bangalore - 42. ✆ 25584242 Fax:080-25588594 Email: centpark@blr.vsnl. net.in

2 Star Hotels

• **Harsha Park Inn International,** 11, Park Road, Bangalore - 51. ✆ 22865555/566 Fax : 080-22865943 E-mail:harshahotel@yahoo.com

• **Hotel Abhishek,** 19/2, Kumara Krupa Road, Bangalore - 1. ✆22262713/4707 Fax : 080-22268953 Email: hotelabhishek@vsnl.net

• **Hotel Broadway Annexe,** 19, KG Road, Bangalore - 9. ✆ 22266374-76, 22872321/3013 Fax : 080-22203661

• **Hotel GEO,** 11, Devanga Hostel Road, Bangalore - 27. ✆ 22221583/4, 22221991/2 Fax : 080-22221993 Email: hotelgeoblr@rediffmail.com

• **Hotel Indraprasta Achar Arcade,** 17/1, III Main Road, Gandhi Nagar, Bangalore - 9 ✆ 22202622-24 Fax:080-22265063

• **Hotel Ramanashree,** 16, Raja Ram Mohan Roy Road, Bangalore - 25. ✆ 22225152, 22235250 Fax: 080-22221214 Email: comforts@ramana shree.wiporbt.ems.vsnl.net.in

• **Kamat Yatri Nivas (Restaurant & Lodging),** 4, First Cross, Gandhi Nagar, Bangalore - 9. ✆ 22260088, 22263727, 22281070 Fax: 080-22281070 E-mail: kamat@blr.vsnl.net.in

• **Nalapad's Hotel Broadway Annex,** 19, K.G. Road, Bangalore - 9. ✆ 22266374/2377 Fax: 080-22872321 Email:hotelbroadway@yahoo.com

• **Nilgiris Nest (Star Hoteliers),** 171, Brigade Road, Bangalore - 1. ✆ 25588401-702-103-704 Fax: 080-25582853 Email: nilgirisnest@vsnl.net

• **Sakthi Hill Resorts,** Arunagiri, BEML Layout, Raja Rajeshwari Nagar, Bangalore - 39. ✆ 28601800, 28601801 Fax: 080-28601802, 28600027 Email:shresort@giasbg01.vsnl.net.in

• **The Club,** 7th Mile, Mysore Road, Bangalore-39. ✆ 28600665/768/769 Fax: 080-28600770 Email: theclub@bg1.vsnl.net.in

• **Woodlands Hotel Pvt. Ltd.,** 5, Raja Ram Mohan Roy Road, Bangalore - 25. ✆ 22225111 Fax : 22236963

OTHERS

• **Abhishek Hotel,** Old Madras Road, Dooravani Nagar, Bangalore - 16. ✆ 28511046.

• **Adora Hotel,** 47, SC Road, Bangalore - 9. ✆ 22872280

• **Airlines Hotel,** 4, Madras Bank Road, Bangalore-1. ✆22273783/85/86 Fax: 080-22218776

• **Amblee Hotels Ltd.,** G-6, Raheja Plaza, 17, Commissariat Road - 25 ✆ 25363722

• **Anand Bhavan Lodging,** Chickpet, Bangalore - 53. ✆ 22874313/1584, 22264037 Fax: 080-22256101

• **Anand Sagar Lodge,** Dinesh Complex, 52, Subbarama Chetty Road, Nettakala ✆ 26616626

• **Anupama Coffee Works,** 375/1, H. Siddaiah Road, Wilson Garden, Bangalore - 27. ✆ 22233295

• **Arun Lodge,** GN Tower 60, Huriopet, BVK Iyengar Road Cross, Bangalore - 53. ✆ 22876516

• **Ashraya International Hotel,** 149, Infantry Road - 1. ✆ 22261921 Fax : 080-22263982 Email: ashintel@bgl.vsnl.net.in

• **Atithya (Restaurant & Lodging),** 93, Gandhi Bazaar Main Road, Basavangudi, Bangalore - 4.

• **Atria Hotel,** 1, Palace Road, Bangalore - 1. ✆ 22205205 Fax: 080-22256850 Email:atria.blr @gnblr.global.net.in

• **Balal Residency,** 74/4, III Cross, Residency Road, Bangalore - 25. ✆ 25597277 (8 lines) Fax : 080-25597276 Email : ballalry@vsnl.com

• **Baljee's Hotel,** Harsha Park Road, Bangalore - 51. ✆ 22865566 Fax : 080 - 22865943

• **Bangalore Gate Hotel,** 9 & 12, K.G. Road, Bangalore - 9. ✆ 22204848

• **Berrys Hotel,** 46/1, Church St, Bangalore - 1. ✆ 25587211, 25587383 Fax : 080-25586931

• **Berrys Hotel (Bar & Restaurant),** Off MG Road, 46/1, Church St., Bangalore - 1. ✆ 25587211

• **Black Pearl Hotels P Ltd.,** (Restaurant/Disco) 9, Curzon Complex, Brigade Road, Bangalore - 1. ✆ 25583678

• **Bombay Ananda Bhavan (Lodge),** 68, Vittal Mallya Road, Bangalore - 1. ✆ 22214581/82/83 Fax: 080-22277705 Email:gupta.babh@axcess. net.in

• **Capitol (Hotels),** 3, Raj Bhavan Road, Bangalore - 1. ✆ 22281234/800 Fax : 080-22259911/22259933 Email : thecapitol@vsnl.com

• **Cassia Boarding and Lodging,** Near Check Post, 150/1, Hosur Main Road, Bangalore - 95. ✆ 25532252

• **Chalukya Hotel,** 44, RC Road, Bangalore - 1. ✆ 22265055/6866, 22253377 Fax : 080-22256576

• **Chancery Hotel,** 10/6, Kasturba Road, Bangalore-1. ✆ 22219067

• **Chandra Bhavan Lodge,** 380, Avenue Road, Bangalore - 2. ✆ 22237972

• **Chik Point Fast Food,** 9045th Main, Vijayanagar, Bangalore - 40. ✆ 23380992

• **Chop Sticks (Restaurant),** 68/69, 8F Main, 3rd Block, Jayanagar, Bangalore - 11. ✆ 26630225

• **Chung Wah (Hotels),** 45/1, Residency Road Cross, Bangalore - 25. ✆ 25582662

• **Citizen Lodge,** 3/4, Lady Curzon Road, Bangalore - 1. ✆ 25591793

• **Cliffton's (Excellent Non- Vegetarian Food)** 3, CMH Rd., Indra Nagar, Bangalore - 38. ✆ 25252189

• **Club India Resorts Metro Hotels P. Ltd.,** Tf-9 City Point, 13, Infantry Road, Bangalore - 1. ✆ 22862341

• **Comfort Dormitory Lodging,** (P. Krishnamurthy) 7, Sirur Park Road, Seshadripuram, Bangalore - 20.

• **Comfort Inn Infantry Court (Hotel),** 66, Infantry Rd, Bangalore-1. ✆ 22292281

• **Dasaprakash Kuteera (Hotel Services),** Manipal Centre, N - Block, Dickenson Rd, Bangalore - 42. ✆ 25588494

• **Delhi Bhavan Lodge,** Avenue Road, Bangalore - 2. ✆ 22875045

• **Delhi Restaurant,** 38, GK Temple St., Chickpet Cross, Bangalore - 53. ✆ 22870730

• **Dhwani Darshan (Hotel),** 11/A, 26th Main, SBM Colony, Bangalore - 50.

• **Direct Resort,** 9, Park Road, Tasker Town, Bangalore - 51. ✆ 22863807

• **Dosa Camp (Fast Food),** Near Complex, 4th Block, Jayanagar, Bangalore - 11. ✆ 26630742

• **Eagleton - The Golf Resort,** Bangalore-Mysore Highway, Shyawamangala Cross, Bidadi Industrial Area, Bangalore Rural. ✆ 08113-287222/33/44/55/66 Fax : 08113-287222/33/44/55/66

• **Executive Home (Hotels),** 1404, 3rd Main Road, Kacherakkanahalli, Bangalore - 84. ✆ 25462271

• **Gainwell Enterprises (Hotels),** 1113, Raheja Towers, MG Road, Bangalore - 1. ✆ 25264646

• **Ganesh Bhavan (Hotel & Restaurant),** 104, D.V.G Road, Basavangudi, Bangalore - 4.

• **Ganesha Refreshment (Hotels),** 624, Rajaji Nagar, 6th Block, Bangalore - 10. ✆ 23355612

• **Ginza Bar & Restaurant (Hotels),** 43, Church Street, Bangalore - 1. ✆ 25598598

• **Guestline Days Hotels (Hotels and Resorts Club),** 140, Hosur Road, Bangalore - 95. ✆ 25531696, 25534407

• **Gupta's Board & Lodge (Lalit Gupta),** Gupta Market, KG Road, Bangalore - 9. ✆ 22265131/32/33

• **Highgates Hotel P. Ltd.,** 33, Church Street, Bangalore - 1. ✆ 25589989, 25597172 Fax : 080-25597799 Email:highgates@bg1.com

• **Highlands Hotel,** 154-156, RC Road, Bangalore - 1. ✆ 22269235

• **Himalaya Restaurant,** (Hotel : Veg and Non-Veg) 32, 6th Main Road, Gandhi Nagar - 9. ✆ 22269535

• **Holiday Inn (Ajay Sharma),** 28, Sankey Road, Bangalore - 52. ✆ 22262233

• **Hotel Adarsha Palace,** 15, Dharmambudhi Road, Main Circle, Bangalore - 53. ✆ 22875106

• **Hotel Ajantha,** 22 A, M.G. Road, Bangalore - 1. ✆ 25584321 Fax : 080 - 25584321 Email : bagilthay@vsnl.com

• **Hotel Algate** , 93, Residency Road, Bangalore - 25. ✆ 25594786

• **Hotel Amar,** 5 & 6 T.B. Road, Bangalore - 9. ✆ 22872008

• **Hotel Amrapali,** 36, 8th F Main Road, 3rd Block, Jayanagar, Bangalore - 11.

• **Hotel Archana (Boarding & Lodging),** 23, JC Road, Archana Complex, Bangalore - 2. ✆ 22225123

• **Hotel Aruna (Non-veg Hotel),** 81, Kalasipalayam Main Road, Bangalore - 2. ✆ 26703481

• **Hotel Ashoka,** 1096, 7th Main Road, Vijayanagar, Bangalore - 40. ✆ 23301048

• **Hotel Badami Court (Quality Restaurant),** 325, CMH Road, Indira Nagar, Bangalore - 38. ✆ 25258615

• **Hotel Blue Diamond,** 8/1, Platform Road, Seshadripuram - 20. ✆ 23314515

• **Hotel Brindavan,** 1031/A 40th Cross, 26th Main, 4th Block, Jaya Nagar, Bangalore - 41.

• **Hotel Cauvery Continental,** 37/11, Cunningham Road, Bangalore - 52. ✆ 22257458, 22256966/67/68/69 Fax : 0091-80-22257460

• **Hotel Comfort Inn Vijay Residency,** 18, 3rd Main Road, Gandhi Nagar, Bangalore - 9. ✆ 22203024

• **Hotel Dwaraka,** 29, SC Rd, Anandrao Circle, Bangalore - 9. ✆ 22265011

• **Hotel Elite,** 25, Tank Bund Road, Bangalore - 9. ✆ 22877563

• **Hotel Essar,** Near Tin Factory OM Road, KR Puram, Bangalore - 16. ✆ 28512693

• **Hotel Gandhinagar,** 27, 6th Cross, Gandhinagar, Bangalore - 9. ✆ 22253624

• **Hotel Gangothri (K. G. Suresh Bhat),** 173 & 174, SC Road, Seshadripuram, Bangalore - 20.

• **Hotel Ghousia,** 115, OTC Road, Cottonpet, Bangalore - 53. ✆ 22200149

• **Hotel Hari Prasad,** 815, Church Cross Bus Stop, Chamarajpet, Bangalore - 18.

• **Hotel Hoysala,** 212, SC Road, Seshadripuram, Bangalore - 20. ✆ 23445311

• **Hotel Imperial (Lodge),** 94/95, Residency Road, Bangalore - 25. ✆ 25588391

• **Hotel India International (Lodging/Food),** 43, 44, Poorna Venkata Rao Rd, Jolly Mohalla, Bangalore - 53. ✆ 22873441

• **Hotel Janata & Janata Lodge (Boarding / Lodging),** 190, Albert Victoria Road, Bangalore - 18.

• **Hotel Janatha,** (Boarding & Lodging) KG Circle, Bangalore - 9. ✆ 22874164

• **Hotel Janpath (Boarding),** 3/1, T.S.P. Road, B/h, B.M.C. Kalasipalayam, Bangalore - 2.

• **Hotel Kanva Lodge (Anil Kumar),** BVK Iyengar Road, Near Abhinay Cinema, Bangalore - 53. ✆ 22879604

• **Hotel Kapila,** (Mr. Giridhar) 229, S.C. Road, Anand Rao Circle, Bangalore - 9. ✆ 22269434

• **Hotel Kanishka,** 2, Second Main Road, Gandhi Nagar, Bangalore - 9. ✆ 22265544, 22266843 Fax : 080-22204186

• **Hotel Kirthi,** (Quality Restaurant) Main Road, Mahadevapuram, Bangalore - 16. ✆ 28512489

• **Hotel Lakshmi,** (Lodging) 11, B B Naidu Road, Gandhi Nagar, Bangalore - 9. ✆ 22268618

• **Hotel Madhu,** (Bar & Restaurant/Lodging) 1142/A, EOC Road, Rajaji Nagar - 10. ✆ 23359278

• **Hotel Madhuvan,** N. T'Pet, Opp. Central Police Station, Bangalore - 2. ✆ 26700086

• **Hotel Mahalakshmi International (Lodge),** 208-214, Majestic Circle, Bangalore - 53. ✆ 22876069

• **Hotel Mahaveer,** Near City Railway Station, 8/1 & 9, Tank Bund Raod, Subhash Nagar, Bangalore - 53. ✆ 22870741/74, 22873670 Fax: 080 - 22870735 E-mail: bachhawat@vsnl.com

• **Hotel Majestic (Hotel/Boarding),** 3rd Cross, Bazaar St., Chamarajpet, Bangalore - 18. ✆ 26706565

• **Hotel Mangala,** 910/34, 4th Cross, Hanumanth Nagar, Bangalore - 19.

• **Hotel Manu,** Basappa Circle, V V Puram, Bangalore - 4.

• **Hotel Maruthi,** 8, SM Road, Majestic Circle, Bangalore - 53. ✆ 22876841

• **Hotel Maurya (Lodging),** 22/4, RC Road, Gandhinagar, Bangalore - 9. ✆ 22254111-119 Fax: 080-22256685 Email: hotelmaurya@hotmail.com

• **Hotel Motimahal,** 8/17, 5th Main Road, Hanumanthappa Rd., Gandhi Nagar, Bangalore - 9. ✆ 22267940

• **Hotel New Brindavan (Hotel & Catering),** 43, 2nd Main Road, Srirampuram, Bangalore - 21. ✆ 23385183

• **Hotel Pampa,** 23, 2nd Cross, Journalist Colony, JC Road, Bangalore-2. ✆ 22243753

• **Hotel Pawan Sree (Deluxe Lodge),** Opp. Kapali Theatre, SC Road, Bangalore - 9. ✆ 22870506

• **Hotel Plaza & Plaza Durbar (Lodge/Food),** 7, 6th Main Road, Gandhi Nagar, Bangalore - 9. ✆ 22263101

• **Hotel Pranam,** No. 1, YMS Building, Opp. Railway Station, Yeshwantpur, Bangalore - 22. ✆ 23372665

• **Hotel Prashantha** (Contact : Mr. K.T. Nanjappa) Gandhi Bazaar, Bangalore - 4.

• **Hotel Prince** 50, New Bamboo Bazaar, Bangalore - 2.

• **Hotel Pulikeshi (Boarding and Lodging),** 168/29, 5th Cross, Gandhi Ngr., Bangalore - 9. ✆ 22226925

• **Hotel Pushpamala,** (Puttaswamy H.M) 9, 2nd Cross, SC Road, Gandhi Nagar, Bangalore - 9. ✆ 22874010

• **Hotel Rainbow,** 14, NR Road, Bangalore - 2. ✆ 26702335

• **Hotel Rajatha (Lodging & Boarding),** 812/1, 4th Floor, Rajatha Complex, Chickpet, OTC Road, Bangalore - 53. ✆ 22281056/57/58

• **Hotel Rajatha Mahal,** (Mr. K.G. Aswathanarayana) 872, Nagarethpet, Bangalore - 2. ✆ 22275000

• **Hotel Rajkamal,** 3, 1st Main Rd., Kumara Park East, Bangalore - 1. ✆ 22263951

• **Hotel Rajputana Ltd.,** 80, Hospital Road, Balepet, Bangalore - 53. ✆ 22876897, 22873543/44 Fax: 080-22877121 Email: rajputin@vsnl.com or rajputana@hotmail.com

• **Hotel Rama P. Ltd.,** 40/2, Lavelle Road, Bangalore-1. ✆ 22273311-14, 81-84 Fax : 080-22214857 Email: ramabglt@bgl.vsnl.net.in

• **Hotel Sanman,** 19, RV Road, Basavangudi, Bangalore - 4.

• **Hotel Sapna,** 235, SC Road, Bangalore - 9. ✆ 22267338

• **Hotel Sarathi (Boarding & Lodging),** 96/1, Appu Rao Road, Bangalore - 18. ✆ 26703966

• **Hotel Select (Boarding & Lodging),** 31, Central Street, Bangalore - 1. ✆ 22864316

• **Hotel Shalimar,** 126/128, BVK Iyengar Road, Bangalore - 53. ✆ 22258063-66 Fax : 080-22282059

• **Hotel Shilpa (Lodge),** Balepet, Bangalore - 53. ✆ 22873631

• **Hotel Shiva (Lodging & Boarding),** 14, Tank Bund Road, Subhash Nagar, Bangalore - 9. ✆ 22281778

• **Hotel Shiva International,** 132, SC Road, Seshadripuram, Bangalore - 20. ✆ 23315746-50 Fax : 080-23368198)

• **Hotel Siddharth (Deluxe),** 29, 2nd Main Road, CKC Garden, Mission Road, Bangalore. ✆ 22276143

• **Hotel Sri Ramprakash Lodge,** (Mr. Neelappa Reddy) 36, 1st Main, Kalidasa Road, Gandhi Nagar, Bangalore - 9. ✆ 22262565

• **Hotel Sumanth Lodge (Boarding/Lodging),** 11/1, SC Road, Bangalore - 9. ✆ 22877041

• **Hotel Suprabatha (Refreshment Place),** Marathalli Main Road, Marathalli, Bangalore - 37. ✆ 25265499

• **Hotel Suraj,** 203, Near Cottonpet, Bangalore-53. ✆ 22874365

• **Hotel Swagath,** 75, Hospital Road, Near Majestic Circle, Bangalore - 53. ✆ 22877200 Fax: 080-22259837 E-mail: swinn@blr.vsnl.net.in

• **Hotel Telehouse International (Restaurant),** 19, K.H. Road, Bangalore - 27. ✆ 22226754

• **Hotel Tourist (Lodging),** Race Course Road, Ananda Rao Circle, Bangalore - 9. ✆ 22262381

• **Hotel Tribhuvan,** 4/1, W.H. Hanumanthappa Road, 5th Main, Gandhi Nagar , Bangalore - 9. ✆ 22263151, 22263152

• **Hotel Umesh (Hotel),** 213, Magadi Road, Bangalore - 23. ✆ 23355572

• **Hotel Vasanth,** 5, Magadi Road, Vijayanagar, Bangalore - 79. ✆ 23355757

• **Hotel Vellara,** 283, Brigade Road, (Opp. Brigade Towers) Bangalore - 25. ✆ 25369116/25369205/25369775/25365684

• **Hotel Vijaya Dakshini (Boarding and Restaurant),** 38/2, Hareram Complex, KG Road,

Bangalore - 9. ✆ 22263747

• **Hotel Vishnu Lodging,** 14, Beli Srinivasa Rao St., Bangalore - 2. ✆ 22876372

• **IFB Industries Ltd (Hotels),** 16/17, Visveswaraiah Indl. Est., WF Road, Bangalore - 48. ✆ 28511202

• **Indian Hotels Company,** 23, Race Course Road, Bangalore - 1. ✆ 22255580

• **Indra Bhavan Lodge,** 36, KV Temple St, Balepet Circle, Bangalore - 53. ✆ 22873293

• **Ivory Towers,** 84, M.G. Road, Barton Centre, Bangalore - 1. ✆ 25589333 Fax : 080-25588697 Email: ivorytower@bplnet.com

• **Jaela Restaurant,** (Hotels) 180/C, Magadi Road, Vidhyaranya Nagar, Bangalore - 23. ✆ 23355655

• **Janatha Lodge,** (Lodging and Party Hall) 6, 2nd Cross, SC Road, RK Puram, Bangalore - 9. ✆ 26708731

• **Kailas Bhavan,** Lodging 89, Hospital Road, Bangalore - 53. ✆ 22876491

• **Kamal Lodge (Hotel/Lodge),** 98, Kilari Road, Bangalore - 53. ✆ 22874591

• **Kamat Cafe (Hotels),** 815, Chickpet, DK Lane, Bangalore - 2. ✆ 22264980

• **Kamat Hotel Mayura (Boarding and Lodging),** 495/496, O.P.H. Road, Bangalore - 1. ✆ 25591811

• **Kamat Restaurant Unity Buildings,** JC Road, Bangalore - 2. ✆ 22224802

• **Kamath Restaurant (Hotel),** JC Road, Near Archana Complex, Bangalore - 2. ✆ 22222798

• **Keerti Lodge,** 1st Cross, Ist Main Road, Chamrajpet, Bangalore - 18.

• **Konark Vegetarian (Hotels),** 50, Residency Road, Bangalore - 25.

• **KTC Hotel Reservations,** 23/A, 2nd Cross, Sampige Road, Malleswaram, Bangalore - 3.

• **Lakshmi Bhavan,** (Refreshment Centre) Chandra Reddy Building, CT St., Marathalli - 37. ✆ 25263775

• **MS Resorts (Hotel Industry),** 19 & 29, HMS Complex, Cubbonpet, Bangalore - 2. ✆ 22210554

• **Madhu Lodge,** 35, BVK Iyengar Road, Bangalore - 53. ✆ 22870175

• **Maruthi Bhavan (Hotel),** 257, 8th Main, Ragavendra Block, 50 Feet Road, Bangalore - 50. ✆ 26617214

• **Mayura Refreshments (Contact: Nagraj),** 47, SC Road, Bangalore - 9. ✆ 22870072

• **Megh Darshan (Hotel),** Balepet Main Road, Bangalore - 53. ✆ 22871709

• **Mini Complex (Hotels & Lodges),** 11/21 RP Road, Yeshwanthpur, Bangalore - 22. ✆ 23371299

• **Modern Hotel (Hotel) & Modern Lodge (Parameshwar),** 207, SC Road, Seshadripuram, Bangalore - 20. ✆ : 23364269

• **Mohan Vihar Lodge,** D.K. Lane, Chickpet Cross, Bangalore - 53. ✆ 22205149

• **Nagarjuna Chimney (Hotel),** 21/22, 22nd Cross, Jayanagar 3rd Block, Bangalore - 11. ✆ 26656566

• **Nagarjuna Residency,** (Andhra Foods) 44/1, Residency Road, Bangalore - 25. ✆ 23488222

• **Nagarjuna Savoy (Hotels),** 45/3, Residency Cross Road, Bangalore - 25. ✆ 25587775

• **Nalapad's Hotel Bangalore International,** 2A-2B, Crescent Road, Highgrounds, Bangalore - 1. ✆ 22268011 (7 lines) Fax : 080-22203661 Email: nahbi@blr.vsnl.net.in

• **Navrang Lodge,** 6, Venkatachaliah Lane, Near City Market, Bangalore - 2. ✆ 22874394

• **Neeladri Lodge,** 943, Nagarathpet Main Road, Bangalore - 2. ✆ 22216201

• **New Central Lodge,** 56, Infantry Road, Bangalore - 1. ✆ 25592396

• **New Chandra Bhawan Restaurant (Hotel / Restaurant),** 380, Avenue Road, Bangalore - 2. ✆ 22236539

• **New Krishna Bhavan,** (Hotel) 417, Sampige Road, Malleswaram, Bangalore - 3.

• **New Kumar Lodge,** (Hotel/Lodge) Hospital Road, Balepet, Bangalore - 53. ✆ 22871052

• **New Light Hotel,** Old Madras Road, Dooravaninagar, Bangalore - 16. ✆ 28510696

• **New Metro Hotel (Non-Veg. Restaurant),** 31 B, Journalist Colony, AM Road, Bangalore - 2. ✆ 22221022

• **New Modern Hotel (Lodging),** AN Krishna Rao Road, V V Puram, Bangalore - 4.

• **New Nandini Restaurant,** 3, Eswar Nagar, DS Colony Main Road, Banashankari 2nd Stage, Bangalore - 70. ✆ 26632398

• **New Prakash Bhawan (Hotel/Restaurant),** Avenue Road, Bangalore - 2. ✆ 22876100

• **New Shere Punjab Hotel,** 79, 2nd Main Road, KPM Extension, Bangalore - 2. ✆ 22220354

• **New Victoria Hotel,** 47-48, Residency Road, Bangalore - 25. ✆ 25584076/77, 25585028 Fax : 080-25584945

• **Oasis Hotels Ltd.,** 1, Church Street, Bangalore - 1. ✆ 25586081

• **Orange County Resort Coorg (Hotels),** 82, The Presidency, St. Marks Road, Bangalore - 1. ✆ 22224043

• **Pai Refreshments,** 18, RV Road, Basavangudi, Bangalore - 4.

• **Parivar Restaurant (Hotels),** 50/1, Gupta Towers, Residency Road, Bangalore-25. ✆ 25588393

• **Park Residency Hotel Printo Towers,** 31, Residency Road, Bangalore - 25. ✆ 5582151/ 25596720

• **Poornima Coffee Bar (Hotel),** Mysore Bank Colony, B.S.K, 2nd Stage, Bangalore - 50.

• **Poornima Hotel (Vegetarian Foods),** 5th Cross Malleswaram Circle, Bangalore - 3.

• **Priyadarshini Restaurant (South Indian Foods),**

263, SC Road, Bangalore - 1. © 22263793

• **Quality Inn Kensington Terrace (Star Hotel),** Off M.G. Road, Bangalore - 42. © 25594666

• **R & M Manpower (India) Pvt. Ltd. (Hotels),** 104, 1st Main, 7th Cross, LPO, Bangalore - 3. © 23442334

• **Raghavendra Bhavan (Hotels)** Kumar Bldg., I Main Road, Yeshwanthpur, Bangalore - 22. © 23376249

• **Raj Residency Lodge (Lodge Homely) 260,** Bhashyam Road, Cottonpet, Bangalore - 53.

• **Raja Lakshmi Vilas (Hotel)** 15/3, Lakshminarayanapuram, Bangalore - 21. © 23421396

• **Regency (Choices & Cuisine)** 37, Lady Curzon Road, Bangalore - 1. © 25550838, 25593041

• **Renuka Lodge DR House,** 117, Kilari Road, Near Abhinaya Theatre, Bangalore - 53. © 22204590

• **Royal Lodge,** 251, SC Road, Near Kapali Theatre, Bangalore - 9. © 22266951

• **Royal Orchid Park Plaza** 1, Golf Avenue, Airport Road, Bangalore - 8. © 25205566 Fax : 080-25216247 Email: roppblr@vsnl.net

• **Safina Hotel,** 84/85, Infantry Road, Bangalore - 1. © 25581988/89/90 Fax: 080-25581984 Email: safina@giasbg01.vsnl.net.in

• **Sajjan Lodge,** 28-29, 6th Main Road, Gandhi Nagar, Bangalore - 9. © 22269613

• **Sambhrama Vegetarian,** 16, Millers Road, Vasanth Nagar, Bangalore - 52. © 22281731

• **Sandhya Lodge,** 70, SC Road, Bangalore - 9. © 22874064

• **Saptha Sagar (Hotel),** 1/3, New Guddadahalli, Mysore Road, Bangalore - 26. © 26600724

• **Sarathi Darshan (Hotel),** 22/3b, 23rd Cross, 8th Main, B.S.K. 2nd Stage, Bangalore - 70.

• **Sarathy Upahara Mandira (Hotel),** 48, 3rd Main, HM Nagar, Bangalore - 19.

• **Sarovar Park Plaza Hotels (Hotels & Resorts),** 3, Mittal Towers , MG Road, Bangalore - 1. © 25597322

• **Satyam Lodge,** KV Temple St., Balepet Circle, Opp. Cottonpet Police Station, Bangalore - 53. © 22872666

• **Shahinsa Lodge,** 10, Beli Srinivasa Rao Road, Bangalore - 2. © 22870811

• **Shakti Vegetarian (Hotel),** 2/1, Nagappa Street, Swastik Circle, Seshadripuram, Bangalore - 20. © 23342914

• **Shalimar Deluxe Lodge (Lodging & Restaurant),** 17, Court 2nd Road, Jolly Mahal, Bangalore - 53.

• **Shanbhag Restaurant,** 69, Gandhi Bazaar, Basavangudi, Bangalore - 4.

• **Shangri-la Resorts (P) Ltd (Health Resort),** 325/1, RMV Extension, 14th Main, Bangalore - 80. © 23375007

• **Sharada Darshin (Hotels),** Lingapuram, Bangalore - 84. © 25477558

• **Sharada Hotel,** 25 RK Market, KG Circle, Bangalore - 9. © 22872240

• **Sheetal Lodging,** 32/12, Seshadri Road, Ananda Rao Circle, Bangalore - 9. © 22874136

• **Shobha Lodge (Hotel),** 29/4, AM Lane, Bangalore. © 22267509

• **Shree Lodge,** 29/1, KG Circle, Bangalore - 9. © 22873529

• **Shree Sagar (Hotel),** 73, 30th Cross, 4th Block, Jayanagar, Bangalore - 11. © 26630575

• **Shri Kamal Hotel (Hotels & Lodges),** Cubbonpet Main Road, Near Ave Road Post Office, Bangalore - 2. © : 22215903

• **Silver Work (Hotel),** 85, Richmond Road, Bangalore - 25. © 22211081

• **SPR Boarding & Lodging,** 292, 12th Cross, Wilson Garden, Bangalore - 27. © 22223020

• **Sree Hotel Ganesh Bhavan (Boarding & Lodging),** 104, DVG Road, Basavangudi, Bangalore - 4. © 26615281

• **Sree Krishna Lodge,** 38, GK Temple St., Chickpet Cross, Bangalore-53. © 22870216

• **Sree Lodge,** 195/196, Cubbonpet Main Rd., Bangalore - 2. © 22212969

• **Sree Raghavendra Lodge,** 77, PC Road, Bangalore - 53. © 22872840

• **Sree Sumukha (Hotel),** 9/1, K.H. Road, Double Road, Shantinagar, Bangalore - 27. © 22222183

• **Sri Devi Cafe (Hotel),** 964, 3rd Block, Rajaji Nagar, Bangalore - 10. © 23353958

• **Sri Kenchamba Lodge,** (24 hrs room service) Ananthashrama Line, SC Road, Gandhi Nagar, Bangalore - 9. © 22254131

• **Sri Kumara Hotel & Lodge,** Hospital Road, Balepet, Bangalore - 53. © 22870365

• **Sri Manju Lodge Deluxe Hotel,** 96,97 Hospital Road, Bangalore - 53. © 22200679, 22287585

• **Sri Prasad Refreshments (Foods & Refreshments),** Garudacharpally, Madhavpura PO, Bangalore - 48. © 28511073

• **Sri Ragavendra Prasad (Hotel),** 166/B, Magadi Road, Vidhyaranya Nagar, Bangalore - 23. © 23358107

• **Sri Ragavendra Prasanna (Refreshment),** 80 Feet Road, Prakashnagar, Bangalore - 21. © 23324795

• **Sri Raghavendra Bhavan (Veg. Restaurant),** 260, 1st N Block, Rajaji Nagar, Bangalore - 10. © 23326068

• **Sri Swamy Lodge,** 135 (upstairs), AM Road, Kalasipalayam, Bangalore - 2. © 22220712

• **Srinath Deluxe Lodge (Hotels),** 142 R.T. Street, Balepet Cross, Bangalore - 53. © 22872350, 22872351

• **Srinidhi Lodge,** 4/1A, T.Extn, RK Puram, Bangalore - 9. © 22870269

• **Sterling Holiday Resorts P. Ltd.,** (Holiday Resorts) HJS Chambers 26, Richmond Road, Bangalore - 25. © 22279955

• **Sudha Lodge (Lodging & Boarding),** 6, Cottonpet Main Road, Bangalore - 53.

• **Surya Lodge,** 3rd Cross, SC Road, RK Puram, Bangalore - 9. © 22871125

• **Suvarna Sagar (Refreshments),** 60, Magadi Road, Agrahara Dasarahalli, Bangalore - 79. © 23354178

• **Swathi Hotels P. Ltd.,** 1-A, Platform Road, Bangalore. © 23360122

• **Taj Hotel,** (Contact : Anees UR Rehman) 383, OPH Road, Bangalore - 51. © 25592006

• **Thangam Lodge (Boarding),** 13, Narasimharaja Road, Bangalore - 2. © 22237952

• **The Basil,** 8, Sampige Road, Malleshwaram, Bangalore - 3. © 23315123 Fax : 080-23343904

• **The Hans Hotel,** (A unit of Hans Inn Pvt. Ltd.) Vidyanagara NH - 4, Hubli - 31. © 2374770

• **The Minerva Hotel,** (5* Luxury At less than) 34, JC Road, Bangalore - 2 © 22222992

• **The Rice Bowl (Hotels),** 215, Brigade Road, Bangalore - 1. © 25587417

• **The Richmond Hotel,** 88/2, Richmond Road, Richmond Town, Bangalore-25. © 22233666 Fax : 080-22233777 Email: restrh@vsnl.net

• **Udupi Sree Krishna Bhavan (Resi Hotels),** 124, Balepet, Bangalore - 53. © 22284777

• **Venus Hotel (Lodging),** 306, Subedarchatram Road, (Near Circle), Bangalore - 9. © 22260181

• **Victoria Hotel (New),** 47-48, Residency Road, Bangalore - 25. © 25584076-77/25585028 Fax : 080-25584945

• **Vijay Residency (S. Sharvani),** 18, 3rd Main Road, Gandhi Nagar, Bangalore - 9. © 22203025

• **Vinayaka Refreshment (Coffee, Snacks),** 747, Triveni Road, Yeshwanthpur, Bangalore - 22. © 23374958

• **Vybhav Lodge,** 60, SC Road, Opp. Movies Land Theatre, Bangalore - 9. © 22873997

• **Welcome Group (Chain of Luxury Hotels),** No. 8, Presidency, 82, St. Marks Road, Bangalore - 1. © 22217448

Mysore

The headquarters of the district known by the same name Mysore is situated about 139 km west of Bangalore. It was also the capital of the ancient rulers of Mysore. The archives allude that in their days the city was known as 'Mysooru'. The district spreads over 6,269 sq. km. Mysore has a population of 22,81,653 according to the 2001 census. Mysore has a number of places of historic importance. The Hoysalas and Chalukyas have made wonderful contributions, besides other great dynasties, to its richness through their extraordinary architecture and sculpture They have constructed a number of wonderful temples with unique designs and ornate carvings all over the walls, pillars and towers. The circumambulatory paths are flanked by walls replete with friezes.

The Mysore Palace which can always be seen brimming with overwhelmed visitors is a grand structure with some extraordinary elements. There are magnificent temples inside the palace. There is also a good collection of exquisite paintings. The scenic Chamundi Hills owes its name to the 'Chamundeswari Temple'. The deity of this temple had been adored and worshipped by the royal family for over 2000 years. The Mahabala Temple and the huge Nandi offer a unique experience. Besides there are number of places in and around Mysore which attract tourists of varied interests.

Mysore Zoo: This zoo at Mysore known as Chamarajendra Zoological Gardens attracts a number of visitors. The zoo has a good collection of animals and birds of the world. This gardens spread over 37 hectares of verdant land. There is a separate enclosure for reptiles too. Friday is the weekly holiday.

Visiting Hours : 08:00 - 11:30 and 14:00 - 18:00 hrs

Entrance Fees : Re. 1/- (for adults & Rs. 0.50 (for children)

Chamaraja Technical Institute: Some exquisite specimens of local art work are housed in an exhibition hall. The chief attractions are the ivory and sandalwood carvings and metallic images. This institute also imparts training in various crafts and manufactures excellent articles of rose wood and sandalwood.

The Mysore Palace: The magnificent palace built in 1897 incorporates a number of overwhelming features. The courtyard contains a gorgeous garden and exclusively architectural temples dedicated to Goddess Gayatri, Goddess Buvaneswari, Lord Gopalakrishna, Navagraha, the controllers of all the happenings on earth, Lord Sri Varaha and Lord Trinayaneswara. The Hoysala school of architecture has had a beautiful influence in the structure. The exquisite art and paintings, ancient swords which the kings and soldiers of the olden days wielded against their enemies, crystal furniture and such-like items in the palace takes the imagination of the visitors to hitherto unexplored dimensions. The portals with astounding workmanship are in an ideal location to view the crest of the temple coated with 18 carat gold.

There is also a 'Kalyana Mandapa' or 'Marriage Hall' adorned with fabulous murals depicting scenes of the famous Dasara procession and the Durbar of the 1930's and the 1940's. This palace has been the residence of the erstwhile rulers of Mysore.

The present structure called Amber Vilas with parts of it repaired and parts reconstructed since a devastating fire broke out causing damage to the ancient structure, was the brainchild of Henry Irwin who combined the Hindu and the Arabian style of architecture. This beautiful palace is further beautified by the lightings during holidays and festival evenings. Shoes are to be left outside the palace. Boxes and bags or any other personal belongings are also not allowed inside. Photography is prohibited.

Visiting Hours : 10:00 - 17:00 hrs.

Entrance Fees : Rs.2/-

Mysore Arts and Crafts Emporium: Alluring articles of handicrafts are displayed and sold here. The curious purchasers have a large variety to choose from, which include intricately carved products of ivory and sandalwood, lacquer toys, handloom silk, porcelain and clay articles and a host of other captivating artware. It is situated on the Mahatma Gandhi Road.

Rail Museum: Situated near the Mysore railway station, this small but yet exciting railway museum comprises a good collection of old coaches which have been put out of track by their modern rivals. The queen's royal saloon is a special attraction.

Visiting Hours: 10:00 - 13:00 hrs and 15:00 to 17:00 hrs.

The Brindavan Gardens and Krishnaraja Sagar Dam: This picturesque gardens have been conscientiously laid out in beautiful cascade. The gardens have a profusion of brightly coloured blossoms, enchanting fountains, musical fountains and slides and swings for children who can always be seen roistering in the place. These gorgeous fountains are equipped with special lights which make them a sumptuous feast to the hungry eyes. When lit at night, the entire garden is a sheer beauty to behold. An enthralling glimpse of the illuminated gardens can be had between 19:00 and 19.55 hours on week days and between 19:00 and 20:55 hrs on Sundays.

The magnificent Krishnaraja Sagar Dam built across the beautiful river Cauvery extends to 3000 m in length and 40 m in width. The serene sheet of waters in the reservoir created by the dam spreads over an expanse of 130 sq. km. and is ideally suited for pleasure boating. The construction of this huge dam, one of the biggest in South India, took 20 long years from 1911 to 1931. This dam takes care of the water supply to the Simsa Hydroelectric Power Project at Sivasamudram.

It is situated 22 km from the Mysore city, 16 km from Srirangapatnam and 153 km from Bangalore. The entrance fees is Rs. 5/-

Chamundi Hill: Atop this beautiful hill 1095 m in altitude stands a marvellous temple built by Krishnaraja Wodeyar III. The presiding deity here is Goddess Chamundeswary who killed the demon Mahishasur to save the humanity. The idol of the Goddess had been the personal property of the royal family for 2000 years before it was installed here. The Gopuram or the portal tower is 7 storeyed and 40 m in height. An old and a new image, side by side, of the demon Mahishasur can also be seen on the Gopuram along with numerous other images. A panoramic view of the beauties below can be had from the vantage points in the temple.

Mahabala Temple: Close to the beautiful Chamundi Hills, this ancient temple was built during the 10th century. It is learnt that it was formerly known as 'Marbala Betta'. A huge monolithic Nandi, the sacred Bull of Lord Siva, which measures 16 ft×25 ft with an ornamental chain around the neck with a bell attached to it can be seen on the way to the temple.

Varahaswamy Temple: This temple is dedicated to 'Lord Varaha', an incarnation of Lord Vishnu. The temple reflects the grand Hoysala type architecture. There are excellent sculptural words and inscriptions.

Sri Lakshmi Narayana Swamy Temple: This temple dedicated to Lord Lakshmi Narayana, a variation of Lord Vishnu, is believed to be the oldest in the city.

Trineswara Temple: This ancient temple of Dravidian style of architecture is dedicated to Lord Siva. It is situated facing the palace.

Prasanna Krishna Swamy Temple: Situated on the south of the main palace, this temple dedicated to Lord Krishna, an incarnation of Lord Vishnu was built in the year 1825 by Krishnaraja Wodeyar III.

The Lake of Thousand Lights: It is so named because thousand lights are lit during the 'Teppotsava' or the ceremonial sailing of the 'Holy Raft'. The grand festival with a thousand light illumination leaves the onlooker awestruck. This occurs on the full moon day during the Dasara season in the beautiful evening with the Sun filling the sky with crimson.

This lake is situated on the east of Chamundi hills.

Somnathpur: 26 km from Srirangapatnam and 40 km from Mysore, this place is sanctified by three ancient wonderful temples in a complex called Prasanna Chenna Keshab. These three temples known as 'Trikuta' built by Somnath Dhandanayaka, the commander in the army of Hoysala Narasimha III the ruler of Dwara Samudra in 1268, on an elevated star-shaped base. Reliefs of scenes from the great epics and life of Hoysala Kings can be seen on the exterior walls of this triple-shrine. The environ of the temples is beautified by the confluence of the rivers Cauvery and Kabini.

Talkad: About 30 km southeast of Somnathpur on the way to Sivasamudram, this historic place, which is now the headquarters of the Taluk was the ancient capital of the Ganga and the Chola Kings. The 'Pancha Linga' or five Lingas comprising the ones at different Siva Temples here are very famous and a grand festival 'Jatra' is held once in a dozen years in honour of these five Lingas. During this festival, the devotees have the 'Darshan' of all the 5 Lingas.

These temples are built in 'Dravidian style'. There are as many as 6 prominent temples. Talkad is one of the regions nourished by the resplendent river Cauvery. The ancient temple dedicated to 'Lord Vaideeswara', the Healer of all diseases who is a variation of Lord Siva, is a grand granite structure of the 14th century. Reliefs of Lord Siva in various postures can be seen here.

Kesava Temple: 'Lord Kesava', one of the forms of Lord Vishnu is the presiding deity of this ancient temple whose courtyard measures 215 ft in length and 177 ft in breadth. The rows of elegantly carved reliefs of various deities, Natya Ganapathi, Lord Ganesa in a dancing posture, Natya Saraswathy, the Goddess for arts and learning, Ishwara or Lord Siva, Varaha, one of the incarnations of Lord Vishnu, Indra, the head of Devas and so on depict mythical events. The outer walls are ornately sculptured and the panels bear the sign-manuals of great sculptors like Baleya, Chaudeya, Mattitamma Chamaya, Bharmaya, Yalasamayya and Nanjayya.

Jaganmohan Art Gallery: Beautiful portraits displaying eminent historic personalities and recounting the events in the history of Mysore are housed in the older of the two edifices. To the south, in an enclosure, in the ground floor, the nostalgic paraphernalia of the kings of the olden times can be seen. The marvellous carvings of 'Dasavathara' or the 'Ten incarnations of Lord Vishnu' on single grains of rice, leave the observers awe-struck.

Also known as Chamarajendra Art Gallery, it houses some exquisite articles made in 1861 for the special occasion of Maharaja Krishnaraja Wodeyar's wedding. This collection was set up in 1875. The ageless paintings of the legend Raja Ravi Varma graciously fill up a huge hall. 'Woman with the Lamp' a remarkable piece of S.L. Haldekar's paintings is a living marvel. There is also a good collection of musical instruments on display. An imposing clock can be seen at the entrance.

Visiting Hours: 08:30 - 17:00 hrs.

Entrance Fees: Rs. 5/-

Mahadeswara Betta: This is a picturesque hill resort near the mighty Eastern Ghats, about 142 km and 220 km from Mysore and Bangalore respectively. This is the favourite spot of thousands of tourists who come here to get carried away in the natural beauty. Accommodation facilities are available.

Lalitha Mahal Palace: This beautiful palace which was the residence of the royal family, situated on the highest point in the city and home offering a panoramic view of the magnificent city has been converted into a posh hotel now.

Accommodation

- **Air Lines Hotel** 1064, Jayalakshmi Villasa Road, Chamarajapuram, Mysore - 5. ✆: 2330475, 2520394
- **Best Western Ramanashree,** B.N. Road, Hardinge Circle, Mysore - 1. ✆: 2522202/65 Fax: 0821-2565781 Email: ramanmys@sancharnet.in

• **Bombay Indra Bhavan** Sayyaji Rao Road, Mysore - 1. ✆: 24205221

• **Ganesh Palace Inn** Chandragupta Road, Mysore - 1. ✆: 2428985

• **Hotel Calinga,** 23, K.R. Circle, Mysore - 24. ✆: 2431310, 2431019, 2431070 Fax: 0821-2428424

• **Hotel Chakravarthy** Ashoka Road, Mysore - 1.

• **Hotel Chalukya** Rajkamal Talkies Road, Mysore - 1. ✆: 2427374

• **Hotel Darshan Palace** Lokaranjan Mahal Road, Nazarbad, Mysore - 10. ✆: 2520794

• **Hotel Dasaprakash** Gandhi Square, Mysore - 1. ✆: 2442444, 2444455 Fax: 2443456

• **Hotel Gokul** D.Banumiah Square, Mysore - 24. ✆: 2427555

• **Hotel Highway,** New Bannimantap AP Extn. Mysore - 15. ✆: 2491117, 2491534, 2497384, 2492978, 2491984

• **Hotel Hoysala** (KSTDC) Jansi Laxmibai Road, Mysore - 5. ✆: 2425349

• **Hotel Indra Bhavan** Dhanvantri Road, Mysore - 1. ✆: 2423933

• **Hotel Kalinga** K.R. Circle, Mysore - 1. ✆: 2431310

• **Hotel Kamadenu** Sayyaji Rao Road, Mysore - 1. ✆: 2521171

• **Hotel Kanishka** 1387/1, Irwin Road, Mysore-1.

• **Hotel Krishnarajasagar** P.O. Krishnasagar-2571607

• **Hotel New Gayatri Bhavan** B/L, Danvantri Road, Mysore - 1. ✆: 2425916

• **Hotel Prakash Lodge** Sayyaji Rao Road, Mysore - 21. ✆: 2510494

• **Hotel Quality Inn Southern Star** 13, 14, Vinoba Road, Mysore - 5. ✆: 2426426/7427 Email: sstar@sancharnet.in

• **Hotel Ritz** Bangalore-Nilgiri Road, Mysore - 1. ✆: 2422668

• **Hotel Roopa** 2724/C, Bangalore-Nilgiri Road, Mysore - 1. ✆: 2443770, 2440044 Email: hotelroopamyso@eth.net

• **Hotel S.C.V.D.S.** Sri Harsh Road, Mysore - 1. ✆: 2421379

• **Hotel Siddharta** 73/1, Guest House Road, Nazarbad, Mysore - 10. ✆: 2522999, 2522888 Email: giri@giadbg01.vsnl.net.in

• **Hotel Sriram** Srirampet, Mysore - 24. ✆: 2423348

• **Hotel Sureka Lodging** 33/A, Sreenivasa Plaza, D.Devaraj Urs Road, Mysore - 1. ✆: 2422094

• **Indus Valley Ayurvedic Centre** Lalithadri Pura, P.O. Box No.3, Ittigequd, Mysore - 10. ✆: 2473437/263/220 Email: ivac@canada.com

• **Kabini River Lodge** Karapur, Nissana Belthur Post, H.D. Kote Taluk, Mysore - 571 114. Email: junglelodges@vsnl.com

• **Kadur Inn** Mysore-Mercera Highway, Hinkal, Mysore - 17. ✆: 2402210, 2402840, 2402841

• **Kaynes Hotel** 85-87, Hootagalli, EML Road, Mysore - 571 186. ✆: 2402931-33/2403104-107 E-mail:kaynes@blr.vsnl.net.in

• **Kings Kourt Hotel** Jhansi Lakshmibai Road, Mysore - 5. ✆: 2421142

• **Lalitha Mahal Palace Hotel** Siddhartha Nagar (P.O.) Mysore - 11. ✆: 2571265 (12 lines) Email: lmph@bgl.vsnl.net.in

• **Prashanth Lodge** Santhepet, Mysore - 24. ✆: 2421748

• **Maurya Palace,** 2716, Sri Harsha Road, Mysore - 1. ✆: 2435912/13 Fax: 0821-2429304

• **Rajendra Vilas Palace,** Gayathri Enterprises, The Palace, Mysore - 1. ✆: 2420664 Fax: 0821-2420664

• **Sri Balaji Lodge** 372/2, Halladakeri, Mysore - 1. ✆: 2521953

• **The Paradise** 104, Vivekananda Road, Yadavagiri, Mysore - 20. ✆: 2410366, 2515655 Email: hotelparadise@sanchar.net.in

• **The Viceroy** Sri Harsha Road, Mysore - 1. ✆: 2424001, 2428001, 2437744, 2434687 Fax: 2433391 Email: viceroymys@eth.net.

Coorg

This vivacious district is character ised by thick forests and mountains on the western ghats. Its undulating landscape varies in altitude between 823 and 2700 m above sea level. The main agricultural produce of the region is coffee and rice while orange groves are also found in plenty. This district became part of Karnataka in 1956. The headquarters Mercara which has been re-christened as Madikeri lies at an altitude of 3781 ft above sea level. Spanning over an area of 4102 sq. km. the district has a population of 4,89,000 as per 2001 census.

Coorg offers an interesting variety of landscape. The inhabitants of the district called the Kodabas are a race of soldiers. The dialect of these people is slightly different from that of others in other parts of Karnataka though the language is one and the same.

Merkara or Madikeri, the district headquarters had been the capital of the Helari Kings. This place gains historic importance from the monuments it holds. The meeting point of Cauvery and Kanike. Bagamandala has a famous Siva Temple. The Abbey Falls makes a fine picnic spot. Talacauvery, the legendary place from where the sacred river Cauvery originates, has a rare temple dedicated to Goddess Cauvery. The Bandipur Wildlife Sanctuary and the Nagarhole Wildlife Sanctuary unfold the hidden beauties of nature with the former one having been declared a 'Tiger Project' in 1973.

Madikeri: Sri Ohmkareswara Temple dedicated to Lord Siva here blends the architecture of Gothic and Islamic styles. It was built in the year 1820 by Lingaraja II.

Situated at an altitude of 3781 ft above sea level and about 250 km from Bangalore, Mercara has some interesting historic monuments. Atop a scenic hill stands the fort which was built by the kings of Kodagu and then repaired by Tipu in 1781 and from then on known as Jafarabad. The fort encompasses a church which houses the state archaeological museum, and a beautiful palace built by Lingaraja II in 1812. When the British took over the territory the fort, the palace and its apartments were all transformed into district offices. Two magnificent mortar elephant figures can also be seen inside the fort.

Another piece of attraction is the famous Raja's Seat located at the vantage point atop the hill, from where the members of the royal family used to relish the natural beauties of the valley during the Sunrise and the Sunset. This spot also offers a thrilling view of the lush green coffee and paddy plantations.

The tombs of the Kodagu kings Lingaraja and Doddaveera Rajendra which reflect the Indo-Sarcenic style are also found here.

Abbey Falls: This beautiful picnic spot is situated about 3 km from Madikeri. Here a ravishing rivulet gives rise to a sizzling waterfalls which attracts a number of tourists.

Bhagamandala Siva Temple: About 35 km from Madikeri and 288 km from Bangalore, situated at the confluence of the rivers Cauvery and Kanike. Bhagamandala hosts the architecturally beautiful temple dedicated to Lord Siva, with copper plated gabled roofs. The extraordinary carpentry and the exquisite paintings take the visitors by surprise. There are also idols of Lord Ganapathy, Lord Vishnu and Lord Subramanya.

Bhagamandala also has an important apiary for breeding bees which make sizable contributions to the repute of the famous Coorg honey.

Talacauvery: About 48 km from Madikeri, in the ranges of Kodanda, this spot is where the holy river Cauvery has Her founts. The legend has it that Lopamudra, the daughter of Lord Brahma, the creator, was given in marriage to the mythical sage Agasthya, by her foster father, another mythical sage, Kabhir Muni. Sorrowed by the marriage, Lopamudra turned herself into water and sought asylum in the 'Kunda' or the mountain cauldron. It is believed by the faithful that she still dwells in the 'Kunda' in which an amazing phenomenon occurs on the 17th of October every year without fail. The placid waters of the pond turn vibrant in the form of a bubbling spring on the day, bearing testimony to the belief. There is also a larger pool nearby in which a dip is considered sacred.

A flight of rock cut steps meanders up the sacred Brahmagiri Hill, on the top of which a beautiful temple is dedicated to Goddess Cauvery where the Goddess is worshipped with alacrity. This region also has puranic references. The 'Pandava Brothers' of the great epic 'The Mahabharatha' are said to have sojourned here. The hill offers a wonderful view of sylvan beauty.

Bandipur Wildlife Sanctuary: About 80 km from Mysore, at an altitude of about 1022 to 1454.5 m above sea level, this verdant sylvan region on the beautiful Nilgiri hills became the venue of a 'Tiger Project' in 1973 under the WWF scheme and was named 'Venugopal Tiger Project'. This picturesque region abounds in flora and fauna. Elephants, bisons, sambars, deers, tigers, panthers, cheetahs and bears grace the sanctuary. Besides, fascinating birds can also be seen here. This sanctuary also offers elephant and jeep safari.

In the 400 sq. km. lush expanse of the beautiful landscape adjacent to Mudhumalai forests of Tamil Nadu and Wynad of Kerala, there are sumptuous plantations of sandalwood, mahogany, ebony teak, bamboo, teak and deodar trees. The beautiful Mayar river acts as a boundary between the two. The maharajas of Mysore had this region as their venue for the big game, hunting. Though it can be visited throughout the year the tourist season falls between November and May while the period between January and May is all the more enchanting. For accommodation, visit and safari, contact Forest Officer, Forest Department, Woodyard, Ashokpuram, Mysore (or) Asst. Director, Bandipur NP, Bandipur - 571318.

Nagarhole Wildlife Sanctuary: The beautiful river Kabini which jinks joyfully through the picturesque region lends it the name Nagarhole, through its serpent-like zigzag. 'Nagar' means serpent and 'hole' means river. In the olden days, it was the hunting grounds of the Maharajas of Mysore. This sanctuary which spreads over 572 sq. km falling partly in the Mysore district and located at an altitude of 780 m above sea level offers shelter to a number of wildlife beings such as the elephants, bisons, panthers, foxes, deers and tigers. A large number of reptiles and fascinating birds can also be seen here. This region also has a plenty of coffee plantations. There are jeeps and minibuses which offer a thrilling browse, 'Safari', through the sanctuary. This sanctuary is situated 67 km from Mercara and 91 km from Mysore.

Accommodations are available. There are 4 forest lodges at the entrance. 'Karapur Tented Camp' is situated about 6 km inside the park and offers both boarding and lodging. For reservations, contact: Forest Officer, Forest Dept. Woodyard, Ashokpuram, Mysore (or) Range Forest Officer, Nagarhole NP Kutta.

Accommodation

Coorg

• **Kannika International,** 4-12(3), I.B. Road, Kushalnagar, Coorg-571 234. Email: kannika@rediffmail.com

• **Orange Country Resort** Karadigodu Post, Sidapur Coorg - 571 253. Email: rhrlcoorg@vsnl.com

Madikeri

• **Capital Village Resort** Sidapur Road, Madikeri. ✆: 225929

• **Hotel Cavery** Near Bus Stand, Madikeri. ✆: 225492

• **Hotel Coorg International** Convent Road, Madikeri. ✆: 228071

• **Hotel East End** Mysore Road, Madikeri. ✆: 229996

• **Hotel New Chitra** Near Bus Stand, Madikeri. ✆: 227063

• **Hotel Rajdarshan** Rajaseat Road, Madikeri. ✆: 229142

Hassan

Hassan the headquarters of the district known by the same name, is situated about 186 km from Bangalore. This city which has rail access from Mysore and Arsikere acts as the gateway to the historic cities Belur and Halebid.

The ancient Siva Temple at Arsikere with a unique frontal polygonal Mandapa reflects the architecture and sculpture of the Hoysalas. Belur at an elevation of about 775 m above sea level is yet another venue of sacred monuments. The Chennakesava Temple here, is again a masterpiece of the Hoysala rulers. Belur is historically noted as the capital of Hoysala kings. Doddagaddavalli has a temple dedicated to Goddess Lakshmi,built in the 12th century by a merchant. Halebid which has also been the ancient capital of the Hoysala rulers is where the famous Siva Temple built by Vishnuvardhana in the 12th century, stands. This temple has some unique features. The Karadeswara Temple has all but not the image of the presiding deity. Parasunath Jain Temple, noted for its beautiful sculpture has some gleaming pillars.

Hassan district which has a population of 15,70,000 according to the 2001 Census, spreads over 6814 sq. km. As it has a number of places of historic, religious and archaeological importance, good facilities for boarding and lodging have come up in almost all the places.

Arsikere: About 41 km from Hassan and 176 km from Bangalore, this commercial town abounds in coconut groves.

The ancient temple dedicated to Lord Siva, known as Kattameswara and also Chandramouliswara Temple, reflects the grand architectural style of the Hoysalas with a specially designed polygonal 'Mandapa' or 'Hall' in the front. The archives of 1220 AD refer to this temple as 'Sri Kalameswara Temple'.

Near Arsikere, is Malekal Thirupathi where the beautiful temple is dedicated to 'Lord Venkatramana', the presiding deity of the temple at Thirumala, Andhra Pradesh.

Belur: Situated at an altitude of 975 m above sea level, about 22 km from Bangalore and 40 km from Hassan, on the banks of the river Yagachi, Belur is sanctified by the ancient temple dedicated to 'Lord Chennakesava' one of the various forms of Lord Vishnu, built by the Hoysala King Bittiga or Vishnuvardhan in the year 1116 AD. It was built to celebrate his victory over the Cholas in the battle of Talikad. The architecture, typical of the Hoysalas, and the sculpture are spellbinding. Intricate carvings adorn the walls of the sanctorum. There are three entrances to the temple, on the east, north and south. There are reliefs of various deities, human forms, demons, etc. at the entrances. The figures also depict events from the great epic 'The Mahabharatha'. There are also images of Dasavathara or the 10 incarnations of Lord Vishnu, in the Temple.

The excellence of architecture is evident from the grand statues of 'Mandanikas' and the 38 sturdy pillars which support them. This exquisite piece of architecture has fascinated many a keen observer over the years. Each Mandanika can be seen in a unique elegant posture such as dancing, playing, dressing etc. It leaves one cueless when one attempts to fathom out the quantum of meticulous work that should have gone into their making. There are about 46 exquisitely carved pillars. There is a host of other features which make the structure awe-inspiring.

The other ancient monuments here are the wonderful temples dedicated to Lord Ganesa, the principal deity of all Hindu endeavours, Goddess Durga, the Goddess of valour, Goddess Saraswathi, the Goddess of Arts and Learning, Lord Lakshmi Narayana, Lord Vishnu, the protector of the universe with His consort Goddess Lakshmi, the Goddess of wealth. Besides, there are a number of other temples as well.

Belur was the flourishing capital of the Hoysala Kings about 800 years ago. It can be reached from Bangalore, Mysore or Hassan. Accommodations are available. Contact : Manager (or) Tourist Officer, Karnataka Tourism, Hassan.

Doddagaddavalli: Situated about 14 km from Hassan, this sacred place is known for the famous temple dedicated to Goddess Lakshmi, the Goddess of wealth. The unique feature of this temple is that there are five Garbhagrihas or 'Sanctum Sanctorums'. It is an important monument built in 1114 by a merchant named Kallahana Rahuta. The image of the Goddess here represents 'Saktha Lakshmi' and the temple is also known as Dakshina Kolapura.

Halebid: About 16 km from Belur towards the east and 30 km from Hassan, Halebid, the ancient capital of the Hoysala rulers is sanctified by the Siva Temple built by the Hoysala king Bittiga. This king is said to have been reconverted to Hinduism and consecrated by 'Sri Ramanuja' one of the three eminent social reformers and religious heads of Hinduism. King Bittiga was then rechristened as Vishnuvardhana. The ancient capital was called Dwarasamudra which is the present Halebid. This capital city was ravaged by Mohammad Bin Tuglaq when he conquered the region in 1327 AD. And today, the city stands as a backwater village.

The wonderful Siva temple which speaks volumes of the Hoysala architectural excellence was built by the rechristened king Vishnuvardhana in 1121 AD. The temple has two Garbhagrihas or 'Sanctum Sanctorums' and the 'Siva Lingas', the usual icon representation of Lord Siva, in these Garbhagrihas are known as Hoysaleswara and Shanthaleswara named after the king and the queen.

Though it had taken 80 long years of meticulous hard work, the temple remains incomplete in construction. Behind the sanctorum of Lord Hoysaleswara, there is a shrine dedicated to Lord Surya, the Sun God with a two metre tall image and in front, which is the enormous statue of Lord Nandi, the sacred Bull mount of Lord Siva. The walls are embellished with exquisite friezes of various deities and the marvellous sculptures of human figures are teeming. The walls with their extraordinary carvings portray scenes from 'The Ramayana', 'The Mahabharatha' and 'The Bhagavath Geetha'. While these breathtaking features adorn the outer walls, some stupendous art work decorate the lower part of the cornice. These give the observer an insight into various aspects of a glorious past which include among other facets, the social life, the dance forms, the music renditions, victories, etc. The onlooker is won over by the living evidences of the skills of the architect Yabanacharya. There are also remarkable reliefs of Lord Ganesha with an ornate Crown, Lord

Nandi and Lord Nataraja the dancing form of Lord Siva. The extraordinary portal seems to attest the marvels inside. There is a museum in front of the temple, displaying artefacts of temple architecture. For accommodation, contact: Manager (or) Tourist Officer, Karnataka Tourism, Hassan.

Karadeswara Temple: On the way to Hassan, from Hoysaleswara Temple, this is yet another Hoysala style temple dedicated to Lord Siva. It was built by King Veeravallara and his queen Abhinaba Ketaladevi in the early 13th century. The structure is again replete with sculptures recounting puranic events. The 'Dwarapalaka' or the statues of the mighty gate keepers on the southern entrance are extraordinary. All these remain but not the image of the deity.

Parasunath Jain Temple: This beautiful temple is situated, half a kilometre from the Hoysaleswara Temple. The sculpture is exquisite and the south gate is adorned with captivating art work. Here the beautifully sculpted pillars are polished to a mirror-like finish.

Shravanabelagola: This picturesque region ideally wedged in between the two scenic hills Chandragiri and Indragiri, situated about 52 km from Hassan, 84 km and 86 km from Halebid and Belur, 115 km and 155 km from Mysore and Bangalore respectively. Shravanabelagola is famed for its Jain Temple. A literal translation of 'Shravana' gives Jain Thirthankar or the stoic ascetic who has relinquished everything pertaining to the material world including the need to be dressed, and that of 'Belagola' gives a white lake.

Atop the hill Indragiri 3347 ft high, majestically stands the mammoth unclad statue of Gomatheswara or Bahubali. This monolithic statue the tallest of its kind, measures to 57 ft in height. This sacred, stately statue marks the quintessence of total renunciation. The legend has it that the king Rishaba Nath abdicated his throne in his insatiable quest for spiritual knowledge and took to doing stern penance in the uninterrupted wilderness of the forests. Consequently a stiff tussle for power ensued between his two sons, the then princes of the state, Bahubali and Bharat and though the former emerged victorious he resolved to adhere to austerity, entrusting the rule to his brother. Then, Bahubali went on 'Vanaprastha' for 1000 years.

King Rishaba Nath then became the first 'Thirthankar' of the Jains and Bahubali came to be known as 'Gomatheswara'. This collosal statue of Gomatheswara came up in the year 983. Chamundaraya, a minister of the kings of the Ganga dynasty was instrumental in its construction. And Aristonemi, was the sculptor behind this marvellous monolith.

It was here in Shravanabelagola that the emperor Chandra Gupta Maurya is said to have spent his twilight years after embracing Jainism under the auspices of his Guru Badrabahu-swami. Jainism flourished here under the patronage of the Ganga rulers between the 4th and 10th centuries.

There is a flight of uncovered steps greeted quite often by 'Belagola', leading to the statue. Dulis and chairs with bearers are available for the aged and disabled to get to the statue. 'Mahamasthakabhisheka' is a grand festival here which occurs only once in 12 long years. During this 'Abhisheka' or 'Reverential Bath' the deity is bathed in a variety of sacred stuff such as ghee, milk, curd, vermolin, honey, sandalwood paste besides 1008 pots of holy water. Money and precious stones are also showered on the statue. This festival came into practise in 1398.

During the last occasion which marked the 87th Mahamasthakabhisheka, an estimated 10 lakh devotees congregated and celebrated the festival with profound alacrity. This festival attracts a large number of devotees from far and near everytime.

A five foot tall Tyagada Brahmadev Pillar can also be seen on the rocky incline of the hill. Footwears have to be left at the hillfoot. Other belongings can also be left at the foot of the hill before climbing the hill. No charge is levied for keeping watch over the articles.

Chandragiri which rises to about 3052 feet above sea level also has many a treasured monument. There are as many as 26 Jain Bastis and Mutts and not too far away are Kalyanipukur and other Jain shrines. There are also some important monuments such as Chandragupta Basti, Bandan and Akkana in the interior village of Shravanabelagola. Accommodations are available at Karnataka Tourism Tourist Home, SPGH and Jain Dharmasala.

Accommodation

Hassan

- **Ambili Group Hotels** R.C. Road, Hassan ✆: 08172-266310
- **Abhiruchi Hotel** Hassan ✆: 08172-268885
- **Hotel Apoorva** Park Road, Hassan ✆: 08172-267153
- **Hotel Harshmahal** Hassan ✆: 08172-268533
- **Hotel Hassan Ashok** P.O. Box.121, Bangalore-Mangalore Road, Hassan - 573 201. ✆: 08172-268731-36 Email: hsnashok@sanchar.in
- **Hotel Suvarna Regency** Suvarna Arcade, B.M. Road, Hassan - 573 201. ✆:08172-266774, 264279, 264006
- **Vaishnavi Lodgings** Harshamahal Road, Hassan ✆: 08172-267413

Belur

• **Hotel Mayura Velapuri (KSTDC),** Temple Road, Belur • **Sri Gayatri Bhavan,** Main Road, Belur ✆: 08177-222255 • **Sri Raghavendra Tourist Home** Near Chennakeshava Temple, Belur. ✆: 08177-222372 • **Travellers Bungalow** P.W.D., Belur ✆: 08177-222348

Mandya

Situated about 100 km from Bangalore, Mandya is the headquarters of the 'Mandya district' which spans over 4961 sq. km. has a population of 16,44,374 as per 2001 census. There is a large sugar factory here.

This district also has a number of ancient monuments in the form of temples and palaces. While the Hoysala and Chola style of temple architecture can be found all over Karnataka along with that of other dynasties, this district is no exception. Adichunchangiri hosts the temple of 'Lord Bhairava'. The wonderful sanctuary *ad hoc* to peacocks, the beautiful birds, is also found here. Besari is where the temple of Mallikarjuna is situated. The grand Hoysala architecture adorns the temple structure. 'Arjunapuri Agrahara' as it was referred to in the days of yore as suggested by the records, Muddur has puranic references attributed to the epic hero Arjuna. The Narasimhaswamy Temple and Varadarajaswamy Temple, with exquisite sculptures and intricate carvings have larger than life size figures of the deities. 'Melukote' a famous pilgrim centre, with the temple dedicated to Lord Cheluva-narayana is where a Sanskrit Academy has been founded recently.

Srirangapatnam, a sacred island formed by the elegant division of the beautiful Cauvery river is noted for a number of aspects. The place owes its name to 'Lord Sri Ranganatha' who is the presiding deity of the ancient architectural temple here. This place holds historic monuments of Tipu which reminicise the valour and commitment of 'The Tiger of Mysore'.

Spreading over 1600 acres on the captivating island in the middle of the river Cauvery is the Ranganathittu Bird Sanctuary. Hence there are fascinating places of ancient, historic and biological importance.

Srirangapatnam: This holy place is a placid island formed by the division of the beautiful river Cauvery which surrounds the place. This is a popular pilgrim spot with the ancient temple dedicated to Lord Sri Ranganatha, a variation of Lord Vishnu. It is believed to have been built in 894 AD by Thirumalaiah. It can be seen that the entire island is known by the name of the presiding deity of this temple whose 'Gopuram' or portal tower bears the Vijayanagar architecture. This tower has 5 storeys. Here the Lord can be seen in the reclining posture. The chariot in front of the temple was gifted by Hyder Ali. Tipu Sultan, the son of Hyder Ali, was himself an ardent devotee of Lord Sri Ranganatha. The entire area around this temple is replete with temples. This temple was renovated by Hoysala and Vijayanagar Kings. A beautiful church can be seen here.

In the past, the rulers of Mysore had Srirangapatna as their capital. It was here, Tipu - "The Tiger of Mysore" fought his last battle against the British in 1799. The ruins of an ancient fort can be seen here. It was built by Hebbar Timmana in 1510. This fort had been protecting the city for a long time until the British defeated Tipu and destroyed the fort in the process. Now, the ramshackle remains of the fort are vociferous of the valour and patriotism of Tipu who fought the British with girth. Srirangapatnam is situated 15 km east of Mysore.

Dariya Daulat Baghicha: This is a picturesque garden of the Persian style laid in 1784 surrounded by the river Cauvery and one of the summer resorts of Tipu. There is a palace with beautiful carvings of the Indo-Saracenic style on teak wood. This historical structure was used by Hyder Ali and later by the British colonel Arthur Wellesley for short stays.

The spot where the 'Tiger of Mysore' Tipu was laid to rest is where an obelisk capped by a Creamdome stands now. The walls schematize events of war. These paintings were made by the East India Company. It was in this same yard Tipu's parents and ancestors were buried too. The museum in the first floor displays a number of Tipu's belongings. A Jamma Masjid built in the same year with inscriptions from the sacred Quran gracing the walls of its vestibule can also be seen. The tall minaret of this Mosque provides a good view of the ramshackle fort and the entire Srirangapatnam.

Ranganathittu Bird Sanctuary: About 3 km from Srirangapatnam, this beautiful sanctuary is at an altitude of 750 m above sea level. Since it is an island in the middle of river Cauvery, boat rides are possible around the sanctuary. A number of migratory and inhabitant birds can be seen perching here. The ideal season to witness a throng of birds is from June to September.

Adichunchanagiri: About 66 km from Mandya Town, this sacred place has a shrine dedicated to 'Lord Bhairava', the Lord created by Lord

Shiva, on a scenic hill. It is also the seat of the 'Swamiji' of the vokkaliga community. About 21 km from Nagamangala, there is a beautiful sanctuary earmarked for the fascinating birds 'Peacock'. The Mutt here offers accommodation.

Basarai: About 25 km from Mandya, here at Basarai stands the famous temple dedicated to 'Lord Mallikarjuna'. This temple is replete with the intricate carvings and stupendous sculptures of the rich Hoysala style of architecture. It was built by Harihara Dhandanayaka in 1234.

Maddur: The records reveal that the name of Maddur which is now the 'Taluk Headquarters' was 'Arjunapuri Agraha'. This name takes us back to the Puranic days. 'Arjuna' is the legendary archer in the great epic 'The Mahabharatha'. And 'Arjunapuri Agraha' means the 'Agraha' or institution dedicated to Arjuna, the epic hero. The presiding deity of the entire village is 'Goddess Maduramma' and hence the name Maddur has been given to the village.

Narasimhaswamy Temple: This temple dedicated to 'Lord Narasimha' the Lord with a Lion's head and a human body, one of the 'Avthars' or 'incarnations' of Lord Vishnu who assumed this strange, holy and fierce form to kill the demon Hiranya and save his pious son 'Prahlada', is yet another masterpiece of the Hoysala rulers. The image of the deity, a huge monolith, is 7 ft tall.

Varadaraja Temple: 'Lord Varadaraja' the presiding deity of the temple is one of the forms of Lord Vishnu, the protector of the universe. The temple structure reflects the grand Chola style of architecture. The intricate carvings, splendid sculpture, the ornamental workmanship on the walls and pillars are typical of the ancient Chola grandeur. The image of the deity here, 'Lord Varadaraja' is a huge 12 feet tall one.

Melukote: The ancient temple here dedicated to Lord Vishnu in the form of 'Lord Cheluvanarayana' makes the place a famous pilgrim centre. There is also a 'Sanskrit Academy' here, which is relatively a new establishment with modern amenities and a good collection of palm leaf manuscripts. It is believed that the rulers of Mysore have gifted many costly jewels to the temple and also the 'Vairamudi' or the diamond studded crown to the Lord.

Sivasamudram: This beautiful hilly isle formed by the wonderful branches of the magnificent river Cauvery, known as Gangachukki and Barachukki is situated about 37 km from Somnathpur and 77 km from Mysore. There are two ancient temples; one dedicated to Lord Shiva and the other to Lord Ranganatha, a variation of Lord Vishnu. Amidst the forested hills, there are two gurgling waterfalls created by the vivacious waters of Gangachukki and Barachukki which are formed by the division of the river Cauvery. The region is also inhabited by wild animals.

The Shimsa Hydel Project commissioned here at Shimsapur in the year 1902, the first of its kind in India can be visited on the permission of the Executive Engineer, Electrical Division, Shimsapur.

Accommodation

- **Hotel Mayura River View** (KSTDC), Mandya Dist. ✆: 2252114

Dakshina Kannada

Bordered on the west by the vast blue expanse of the Arabian Sea, this district, as its name 'Dakshina' which means South, suggests lies in the southern part of the state. The area of this district with Mangalore as its headquarters, covers 4,843 sq. km. The census taken in 2001 shows a population of 16,33,392. The neighbouring districts to this are Kodagu (or) Coorg, Hassan and Chikmagalur.

The language spoken here is 'Tulu' and the district is also known as the 'Land of Tuluvas', Tuluvas meaning 'Tulu speakers'. Mangalore, which derives its name from that of the Goddess Mangaladevi, is a beautiful port city with a number of interesting features. The untiring tourist has a lot to relish, in and around the city. This district abounds in holy Jain monuments. It is learnt that parts of the region had been under the realm of Jain rulers who have raised towering statues of 'Sri Gomateswara'. These huge and holy statues which mark the region with centres of pilgrimage have come into existence over a long span of time. Thus there are ancient and modern ones while all have an equal acclaim.

Udupi, the city popular for more than one reason is sanctified by the presence of the wonderful temple dedicated to Lord Krishna, founded by Sri Madhvacharya. There is also a tranquil mutt dedicated to 'Sri Raghavendra'. All the places have convenient road links with one another and good accommodations are available at all major centres.

Mangalore: The present headquarters of the district Dakshina Kannada, Mangalore known as Mangalapura had in the past been the long-time capital of the kings known as Alupas. This port city situated at the confluence of the beautiful rivers Netravati and Gurupur was also the headquarters of Canara under the British in the 18th century. The first ever newspaper in Kannada, the language of the state was brought out here in the year 1843.

This beautiful palm fringed west coast city is accessible from Mercara, the headquarters of Coorg district by a road squired by bewitching sceneries. With its lagoon, enchanting palmgrooves and interesting landscape, Mangalore bears a close resemblance to the coastal towns of Kerala and experiences a typical coastal climate.

Mangalore is one of the several places in India where religious harmony is overt with a number of ancient temples, churches and mosques. It has been an important centre of the Indian catholics since long. The university and college founded here in 1868-69 was the first one to come up in the whole of Karnataka. The city consists of a number of places of tourists' interests. There are good accommodation facilities.

Mangaladevi Temple: This beautiful temple is situated about 3 km from Mangalore. The presiding deity of this temple is Goddess Mangaladevi to whom, the city owes the origin of its name. This temple was built in the 10th century.

Ullal: This place is beautified by the enchanting beach marked by abundant fir trees and sanctified by the Sayed Mohammed Shenphul Madani Mosque. Hence this place gains importance both as a picnic spot and a pilgrim spot. It is situated 12 km from Mangalore.

Karkala: It is situated about 50 km from Mangalore. This place, which is a sacred worship centre of the Jains was the seat of the Bhairasas or Shantarsas, the royal Jain dynasty. There are two huge statues of 'Sri Gomateswara' or Bahubali, one built in 1432 measuring 13 m in height and the other built in 1604 to a height of 11 m. There are four ornate entrances to the shrine, known as 'Chathurmuka Basti'. These are the splendid works of the devout Jaini Kings. The other important monuments here include temples and bastis and St. Lawrence church. The Ananthasayana Temple and Venkataramana Temple both dedicated to Lord Vishnu also attract a large number of devotees.

About 29 km from Karkala is the Sivarakamabada Basti which is the biggest Jain Shrine in Karnataka, situated at the place called Mudabidri. This was raised by the merchants of the town in 1429-30. The unique feature of this shrine is that it has metallic images. There are about 18 Bastis in Mudabidri. The sacred vestiges of an ancient temple dedicated to Lord Siva built in 1604 can be seen at Vinur which is about 22 km from Mudabidri.

Udupi: About 58 km from Mangalore, this sacred place is where the famous ancient temple dedicated to Lord Sri Gopalakrishna, stands. Sri Madhvacharya who propounded the Dvaita philosophy was the founder of the temple and the Acharya's icon can also be seen in the temple. Sri Madhvacharya also established 8 Mutts to perform Pooja, in turns, to Lord Krishna, who is an incarnation of Lord Vishnu. The grand biennial festival known as the Paryaya held in the month of January marks the change-over of the turns.

The legend has it that 'Kanakadasa' was turned away when he sought to enter the temple since he belonged to lower caste. Pained at this and driven by ardent devotion he peeped through a hole to have the Darshan of the Lord. And the ever so merciful Lord turned from east to west in order to fulfil the desire of His devotee. Then Kanakadesa became famous. He was one of the great composers during the Bakthi Movement. His works are venerated even today and sung in several places of worship. The hole through which Kanakadasa had the amazing Darshan can be seen even today. It is now known as 'Kanakakindi', named after him.

The ancient structure of the temple has seen some recent developments by which the walls depict scenes from the great epic 'The Mahabharatha'. Sri Vidyamanya Thirtha Swamiji has recently donated a grand chariot made out of teak wood by the dextrous hands of the craftsmen of Poompuhar in Tamil Nadu. The chariot has been plated with 25 kg of gold alloyed with copper. The temple also has a tank in which the elegantly swimming fish entertain the visitors.

There are also other famous temples in Udupi (viz) Ambalapadi Shakthi Temple, Kadiyali Durga Temple, Venkateswara Temple and the Holy Mutt of Sri Raghavendra, a prominent saint in the hierarchical order of Sri Madhvacharya.

The 'Malpe' port near Manipal offers a fine beach resort. The Vadabhandeswara Temple dedicated to Lord Balarama is very famous. Manipal is also noted as an important centre of education.

The cuisines of Udupi, the wonderful coastal town, are popular. The titillating delicacies are much sought-after. Udupi, the city situated on a national highway has easy road access from Mangalore, and Karkala which is just 32 km away. The city offers good accommodation facilities.

Agumbe: About 50 km from Udupi this is the ideal spot for sunset watchers. The best season here to have a glorious view of the red sun disappearing in the west is between November and December.

Dharmasthala: About 75 km from Mangalore, the beautiful sacred island formed by the resplendent river Netravathi is famous for the ancient Manjunatha Temple and the Modern Sri Gomateswara Statue. This grand statue was carved out of a single stone to a height of 14 m in the year 1973. 'Annadhana' or 'free meals' is one of the salient features here. The pilgrims are also offered accommodation free of charge.

Kollur: About 147 km from Mangalore, nestled in vast verdant woods, Kollur is famous for its temple dedicated to Goddess Mookambika, the Goddess of arts and learning. This region is characterised by high green clad mountains and the ravishing rivulet Sowparnika. And this beautiful temple is situated on the scenic hill called Kodachadri. Even the trek up hill is considered sacred and believed to confer prosperity, health and fame. Thousands of devotees come here and worship the Goddess. An annual festival marked by devotional pomp and attended by scores of devotees from far and wide is celebrated between October and November.

Accommodation

Mangalore

- **Ganesh Prasad Lodging** K.S. Rao Road, Mangalore-1 ✆: 2440418
- **Hotel Indraprasta** L.H.H. Road, Mangalore-3. ✆: 2425750
- **Hotel Manorama** K.S. Rao Road, Mangalore-1. ✆: 2440306
- **Hotel Manoranjan** Old Port Road, Mangalore-1 ✆: 2420420
- **Hotel Navaratna** K.S. Rao Road, Mangalore-1 ✆: 2440520
- **Hotel Navaratna Complex** K.S. Rao Road, Mangalore-1 ✆: 2441104
- **Hotel New Swagath** Balmatta Road, Mangalore-2 ✆: 2439752
- **Hotel Panchami** Opp. KSRTC Bus Stand, Bejai, Mangalore-4 ✆: 2411214
- **Hotel Pentagon** Pumpwell Circle, Kankanady, Mangalore-2 ✆: 2439203
- **Hotel Poonja International** K.S. Rao Road, Poonja Arcade, Mangalore-1 ✆: 0824-2440171-186 (16 lines)
- **Hotel Roopa** Balmatta Road, Mangalore-1 ✆: 2421271
- **Hotel Shaan Plaza** K.S. Rao Road, Mangalore-1 ✆: 2440312
- **Hotel Srinivas** G.H.S. Road, Mangalore-1 ✆: 0824-2440061 (10 lines) Fax: 0824-2423302 Email: asrao@bg1.vsnl.net.in
- **Hotel Woodside** K.S. Rao Road, Mangalore-1. ✆: 2440296
- **Manjarun Hotel** Old Port Road, Bunder Mangalore - 1. ✆: 2420420 Fax: 0824-2420585 Email: manjarun.mangalore@ tajhotels
- **Moti Mahal** Falnir Road, Mangalore-1 ✆: 0824-2441411 (10 lines) Fax: 0824-2441011 Email: ocommotimahal@ cjfoundation.net.in
- **Saptagiri International** Aiport Road, Kavoor, Mangalore-15. ✆: 2481672

Manipal

- **Hotel Green Park** Main Road, Manipal-576119 ✆: 08252-270561-62, 270178-79 271389, 270851

Puttur

- **Hotel Rama** Main Road, Puttur-574 201 ✆: 08251-221660/61/62

Udupi

- **Hotel Janardhan** Service Bus Stand, Udupi - 1. ✆: 223880
- **Hotel Kediyoor** Bus Stand, Shiribeedu, Udupi. ✆: 222381
- **Hotel Mallika** K.M. Marg, Udupi. ✆: 221121.
- **Hotel Natraj** Fields Side Bldg., Maruthi Veethika, Udupi - 1. ✆: 220205
- **Hotel Ramakrishna** Geethanjali Road, Udupi - 1. ✆: 223189
- **Hotel Shaan** Mosque Road, Udupi - 1. ✆: 223901
- **Hotel Sindhu Palace** Udupi - 1. ✆: 220791
- **Hotel Tourist** Udupi - 1. ✆: 220641
- **Kalpana Residency**, Upendra Baug, Udupi - 1. ✆: 08252-220440, 222790, 222792, 222794

Chikmagalur

This district has a profusion of mountains and occupies an area of 7,201 sq. km. with 10,17,283 people as reported by 2001 Census. The name Chikmagalur is shared by both the district and its headquarters which is situated about 251 km from Bangalore with the enchanting Chandradrona Parvatha or Bababudan Hills providing a picturesque backdrop. These hills form part of the unrelenting range of the mighty western ghats. The highest peak in Chikmagalur reaches an altitude of 1829 m above sea level. This district has the honour of being the site of first ever coffee plantation in India - thanks to the efforts of the Islamic clergy, Bababudan who sowed the coffee seedlings brought all the way from Mecca, the holy Islamic centre of worship, in the 17th century. It can be seen that the hills has been named in his memory. This picturesque range of mountains brandishes some enthralling waterfalls.

There is also a number of pilgrim spots. The beauty of the Hoysala architecture has permeated through the district. The famous Trikuta Temple is situated in Belvadi in this district. Belvadi also has other wonderful temples. Sringeri is another sacred place. It has one of the four Mutts or Monasteries founded by 'Jagathguru Sri Adisankara'. The 'Rasikambas' or the 12 'Zodiac Pillars' at the Vidyasankara Temple testifies the deep astronomical knowledge the ancient people had. There are also other wonderful temples in the district.

The Kalahasthi and the Hebbe waterfalls make excellent picnic spots. These spots are endowed with copious natural beauty. The vast Bhadra Wildlife Sanctuary spreading its charms partly over Shimoga, also attracts a large number of visitors.

Belavadi: About 29 km from Chikmagalur city, the legendary place Belavadi is where the famous temple known as Trikuta is situated. The temple has three sanctorums one each for Lord Veeranarayana, Lord Venugopala, one of the various names of Lord Krishna and Lord Yoganarasimha, the Lord with a lion's head and a human body absorbed in deep meditation, the first being one of the various forms or divine manifestations and the latter two being two of the ten 'Avathars' or divine incarnations of Lord Vishnu, the protector of the universe. It is believed that Belavadi was known as Ekachakranagara in the Mahabharatha days.

The astounding architecture of the temple belongs to the Hoysalas. The structure is adorned with ornate carvings and splendid sculpture. There is also another temple in the proximity, called the Hatuda Ganapathi Temple. It is dedicated to Lord Ganesa, the principal deity of all Hindu endeavours.

Sringeri: This sacred place, on the banks of the holy river 'Tungabadra' is famous for the 'Mutt', one of the four, founded by 'Jagathguru Sri Adisankara', the Hindu religious leader who propounded the philosophy of 'Advaita'. This Mutt is known as the 'Sringeri Saradha Peetam' and obviously there is also an ancient temple dedicated to Goddess Saradha or Goddess Saraswathi, the Goddess of Arts and Learning. This temple is also believed to have been established by Sri Adisankara. The other Mutts or Monasteries are situated at Joshimath, Puri and Dwaraka.

This Mutt at Sringeri has enjoyed the patronage of Vijayanagar rulers. Tipu Sultan's liberal donation to the mutt deserves special mention. The religious leader Adisankara, after traversing the length and breadth of India on foot, performing noble deeds all the way along, settled at Kancheepuram of Tamil Nadu where there is a Sankara Mutt as well. All these mutts follow the hierarchical system of appointing the successive leaders, as established by Sri Adi Sankara. Apart from religious activities which are performed with profound alacrity, these Mutts also carry on service to the humanity.

Sringeri also has another ancient temple. The presiding deity of this one is Lord Chenna Kesava Perumal, one of the variations of Lord Vishnu. The temple structure, an excellent monument of captivating architecture remains incomplete even after 80 long years of work. A beautiful Jain monument 'Paraswanatha Basti' can also be seen here.

Another temple on the beautiful banks of the sacred Tungabadra, built in the 14th century is the Vidyasankara Temple. The architecture of this temple is astounding. There are 12 pillars called the 'Rasikambas' or Zodiac Pillars which have been so ingeniously positioned that the Sun's rays fall on the specific pillar or 'Rasikamba' during each solar month. These pillars get us an idea of the extraordinary knowledge, the people of yore possessed in astronomy.

Good accommodation facilities are available at Sringeri. There are 'Travellers Bungalow' and private hotels. The Sringeri Mutt also has a Guest House and a Choultry to shelter the pilgrims. It can be reached by bus from Chikmagalur, Hassan, Shimoga and Birur. It is about 334 km from Bangalore.

Amriteswara Temple: Situated in Amritapura, about 247 km from Bangalore, this temple known as Amriteswara Temple was built in the 12th century by Amrita Dandanayaka. The entire temple structure reflects the grand architectural style of the Hoysalas and the ground plan is star shaped, another exclusive feature of this architecture. This temple replete with splendid sculpture also has a wonderful image of Goddess Saraswathi, the Goddess of Arts and Learning, in a sitting posture. This temple is also noted as one of the masterpieces of the Hoysala architecture.

Kalahasthi Waterfalls: This enchanting waterfalls is nestled in the picturesque sylvan region of Kemmanangudi which is about 36 km from Tarikere and 48 km from Chikmagalur. This enthralling hill resort on the Chandradrona Parvatha or Bababudan Hills is gifted with a variety of flora and fauna. About 8 km from this falls is yet another roaring falls known as the Hebbe falls. The waters here cascade elegantly in two stages making a thunderous dive of about 250 feet in each stage. The higher of these two is called the Doddahebbe meaning 'Bigger Hebbe' and the lower, 'Chikkahebbe' meaning 'Smaller Hebbe'. About 30 km on this far-reaching range is the holy Dattatreya Peeta, a famous pilgrim spot which combines both the Hindu and Islamic faiths.

The Bababudan Hills is so named because it was here the Islamic clergy of the 17th century brought seedlings of coffee from 'Mecca' the sacred Islamic centre, and started the first ever coffee plantation in India. Hence the hills commemorate the Saint Bababudan.

Bhadra Wildlife Sanctuary: About 75 km from Chikmagalur city via Tarikere, this 492 sq. km. expanse of picturesque landscape shared by the adjoining district Shimoga, shelters a wide variety of fascinating flora and fauna. The visitors are greeted by mighty elephants, captivating deers, wild bears and the big cats like the panthers, tigers etc. It is also the asylum of a wide spectrum of reptiles. A large number of exciting birds which belong to various species in classification can also be seen here. This sanctuary can also be reached from Kemmanangudi which is 60 km away.

Accommodation

- **Taj Garden Retreat,** Opp. Pavithra Vana, K.M. Road, Jyothi Nagar, Chikmagalur-577 102. ✆: 220202 Fax: 08262-220222 Email: tgrgim.chk@ tajhotels.com

Shimoga

The city of Shimoga is the head quarters of the district known by the same name. The district spreads over an area of 8,465 sq. km. and the population according to 2001 Census is 14,52,259. The city, 274 km from the state capital Bangalore, is situated on the banks of the sacred river Tungabadra. It was very famous during the days of Keladi Nayakas.

As a district, Shimoga has a very interesting landscape punctuated by historic monuments. The temple at Badravathi where the presiding deity is Lord Lakshminarayana is again a testimony to the architectural excellence of the Hoysalas. Besides, the city also has a number of industries. Sagar the city noted for its ivory and sandalwood industries also attracts quite a few tourists who have a passion for these exquisite articles. The factories redolent of the exotic sandalwood fragrance and those suffused with the coveted ivory are open to visitors who would like to have a browse through. There are about 4 ancient temples in and around Ikkeri which also has a museum.

While the district caters to the wishes of various visitors with diverse interests, with its architectural temples and wonderful industries, there is yet another enchanting picnic spot which cannot evade the all pervading eyes of the curious travellers. It is the Jog Falls which stands out as the highest waterfalls of the Nation. With its enthralling natural settings it appears as though a figment of one's imagination has been brought into reality. The Mahatma Gandhi Hydro-Electric Power Station which has been made possible by the benevolent waters of the mighty river which gives rise to this fabulous falls is also worth a visit.

Badravathi: About 256 km from Bangalore, this popular industrial town formerly known as 'Benkipura' is sanctified by the ancient temple dedicated to Lord Lakshminarayana, a variation of Lord Vishnu. This temple with rich architectural workmanship was built by the Hoysalas in the 13th century. The beautiful river Bhadra flows along the north contiguous to the city. And along the banks of this river is situated, a number of industries such as the iron and steel industry, the cement and the paper factories.

Sagar: It is about 340 km from Mysore. The sandalwood and Ivory industries which produce fascinating articles earn fame to the city. The visitors are ushered through the various departments of these precious ivory and fragrant sandalwood factories. Purchases can also be made here.

Ikkeri: It is situated near Sagar. The 16th century Aghoreswara Temple is situated here and nearby there is a temple dedicated to Goddess Parvathy. The presiding deity of the former temple is a variation of Lord Siva while that of the latter is His divine consort. Two more ancient temples known as the Rameswara and the Veerabadra Temples can be seen at Keladi. Keladi also has a Museum.

Jog Falls: This ebullient water falls at an altitude about 1500 ft. above sea level nestled amidst gorgeous mountains blanketed by thick verdant forests with an enthralling sylvan setting which conjures up a fascinating image is noted as the highest in India. The reverberating waters of the glorious river Sharavathi which takes its birth at Ambuthirtha thunder down giving rise to this vociferous waterfalls, through a height of 253 mts in four magnificent branches named as Raja, Rowa, Rocket, and Rani. The gorgeous cloud formed by sizzling tiny droplets of water rising elegantly to a reasonable height from the foot of the fall, partially obscuring the objects behind and reflecting at certain convenient angles the lively spectrum of the rainbow colours, is a bewitching beauty to behold. The fabulous scenery of the fall against the backdrop of mighty mountains with picturesque environs seems to take one's imagination to unexplored dimensions.

The benign waters of the mighty river, which proffer sumptuous feast to the hungry eyes and copious calmness to the mind also go on to serve people by generating electric-power through the 'Hydro-Electric Power Station' named after the Father of the Nation 'Mahatma Gandhi' and situated about 1 km away. The Sharavathy Valley Project here has the credit of being the first and so far the largest of its kind in entire Southeast Asia. The beautiful Linghamaki Dam and its serene reservoir and Power House are situated about 12 km away. A journey through the lovely valley is entertaining.

Jog Falls is situated about 88 km from Shimoga and 378 km from Bangalore. Accommodation is available here.

Accommodation

- **Jewel Rock Hotel** Durgigudi, Shimoga - 577201. ©: 08182-223051 (10 lines)

Chitradurga

This district which sprawls over 8,388 sq. km. has as its headquarters the city of Chitradurga which is about 202 km from Bangalore on the Pune-Bangalore Road. The 2001 census reports the population of the district as 13,12,717. This city Chitradurga, a historic one, has a massive hill fort built by Hyder Ali and fortified by his son Tipu Sultan. This citadel has magnificent bastions, sturdy doors and seven rounds of ramparts. A spellbinding view of the ravine, 2 km away, known as Chandravalli Valley where ancient Roman coins have been discovered, can also be had from the fort.

The important monuments here are the temples of 1) Lord Sampige Siddeswara, 2) Lord Hidimbeswara 3) Lord Gopala Krishna, 4) Goddess Eknathamma, 5) Goddess Obeladevi, 6) Lord Chennakesava, 7) Lord Anjaneya, 8) Lord Venkataramana and 9) Goddess Uchhangiyamma and there are picnic spots such as Obbavva's cleft and Vanivilas Sagar (reservoir).

Devanagere: It is situated about 267 km from Bangalore on the way to Pune. The city derives its name from the name of a tank around which it developed. The name of the tank, 'Devanikere' means 'Cattle Rope Tank'. 'Devani' means 'tether'. Appaji Ram, one of the officers of Hyder Ali was instrumental in the development of this place as an important commercial centre. Devanagere has recently been recognised as a separate district.

Today, the textile industry is a thriving one here. The place has seen some tremendous development over the years. With the establishment of an

Engineering and a Medical College, it has also become an important centre of education. The Eswara Temple of Anekonda is famous here.

Harihara: On the Pune-Bangalore Road about 227 km from the latter, the rivulet Haridra gave the place its former name'Kudalur' by joining it here. However, after the 'Harihara' Temple was built here in 1223, the place came to be known as Harihara. This wonderful temple built by Polalva Dandanayaka under the rule of Hoysala Narasimha is dedicated to Lord Hari or Lord Vishnu and Lord Hara or Lord Siva. The temple structure is a product of artistic excellence. There are also other ancient temples dedicated to Lord Dattatreya, Lord Iswara and Lord Srirama. Harihara is also a notable place for industries, trade and commerce.

Accommodation

Chitradurga

- **Hotel Prakash** B.D. Road, Chitradurga. ✆: 08194-222958
- **Maruthi Inn Deluxe Lodge** M.H. Road, Chitradurga. ✆: 08194-223474
- **Maurya Deluxe Lodge** Santhe Bagilu, Chitradurga ✆: 08194-224448
- **Roopavani Restaurant** Roopavani Road, Chitradurga. ✆: 08194-223450
- **Union Lodge** B.D. Road, Chitradurga. ✆: 08194-223314

Devanagere

- **Hotel Shanti Park** No.216, Ashoka Road, Davangere-577 002. ✆: 253046, 253209 Fax: 08192-257672

Dharwad

This district spreads over an area of 4,230 sq. km. and has a population of 13,74,895 (2001 census). The city of Dharwad, about 437 km from Bangalore on the Pune-Bangalore Road was made the headquarters of the district way back in 1818 under the British rule. The University of Karnataka is situated here and Dharwad is the venue of a number of cultural and educational activities. Hubli is just 16 km from the city.

The important monuments are:

Temples: 1) Venkataramana, 2) Ulavi Basavanna, 3) Nandikola, 4) Basavanna and 4) Muruga Mutt.

Churches: 1) Bassel Mission Church, 2) Catholics' Church.

General: 1) Karnataka University, 2) Sanskrit College, 3) Agricultural University

Hubli: This is a famous industrial town on the Bangalore-Pune Road, about 408 km from Bangalore. It is noted for its handloom textile unit. This historic town was known in the olden days as Raya Hubli and also as Elaya Puravada Halli. This city metamorphosed into an important commercial centre for trade in cotton and iron under the Vijayanagara rulers.

The important monuments at Hubli are:

Temples: 1) Bhavanishankar, 2) Chaturlinga, 3) Kalameswara, 4) Siddharudha Swamy Mutt, 5) Moorusavira Mutt, 6) Hanneradu Mutt, 7) Rudrakshi Mutt and 8) Jain Bastis.

Churches: 1) The Church of Ascension, 2) St. Joseph's Church, 3) St. Andrews Church and 4) The Church of Holy Name.

Mosques: 1) Mahdi Mosque, 2) Mastan Sofa Mosque and 3) Dargah of Sayyed Fateh Shah Wali.

General: 1) Govt. Medical and Engineering Colleges, 2) Indira Gandhi Memorial Glass House and 3) Nripatunga Park.

Dharwad Fort: This fort was built by the Vijayanagar rulers. All that remains of this once magnificent fort is only the door frames. The other important monuments here are the temples, the churches and the mosques. There is an ancient temple near the fort, dedicated to Goddess Durgadevi.

Mailara Linga Temple: This ancient monument of the Chalukyas has an interesting history of transformations. This wonderful temple dedicated to Lord Siva had attracted the invading Muslim rulers so much that they converted it into a mosque. The Bijapur army was responsible for this conversion. However, it was reconverted into a temple by the Peshwas. This temple is situated at Vidyagiri.

Bankapura: Situated about 80 km from Dharwad, this place derives its name from its founder Bankeya, a commander of Amoghavarsha Nrupatunga. The Chalukyas raised a number of architectural temples in the city. The wonderful Nageswara Temple in the fort is also a sacred product of the marvellous Chalukyan architecture. A mosque can also be seen in the fort. The Siddeswara Temple is yet another masterpiece of the Chalukyas. The beautiful 'Pancharabhavi' with a swimming pool structure is worth a visit. The Kilari cow and rabbit breeding centre of Bankapura, whose office is located inside the fort, is very famous.

Dambal: The ancient inscriptions refers to this place about 21 km from Gadag, as Dharmapolal. The ancient Doddabasappa Temple here has a polygonal Garbhagriha or 'Sanctum Sanctorum' shaped like a star. The friezes bear fantastic workmanship. The highlight of the stupendous sculpture is the huge image of 'Lord Nandi', the sacred bull mount of Lord Siva. An ancient temple dedicated to Lord Someswara can also be seen at Dambal. Besides, a small shrine with a mammoth image of Lord Ganapathi near a 400 year old sacred tank and the Siddhalingeswara Mutt are among the important monuments.

Kittur: On the way to Belgaum, about 33 km from Dharwad, this place Kittur was in the olden days the headquarters of a minor principality known as Desagati. A Wada or a bastion known as Desai Wada stands in ruins here. The State Government Museum houses many a relic of this Desai Wada.

The other important monuments at Kittur are the Kalameswara Temple, Veerashaiva Mutts also known as Chauki Mutts and the Hira Mutts.

Degon: About 5 km from Kittur. Degon is where the famous temple dedicated to Lord Kamala Narayana stands. This temple adorned with the rich Chalukyan architecture was built in the 12th century by the Goa Kadambas. The temple structure is rife with intricate carvings. Captivating art work can be seen all over the sacred structure.

Lakshmeshwar: An ancient Jain centre known as Hugligere or Puligere came to be known as Lakshmeshwar, 72 km from Dharwad after the construction of the Lakshmeshwara Temple. The Somanatha Temple is also very famous here. There is also a mosque called the Kali Masjid built by the Bijapur Commander Ankush Khan. Over 50 stone inscriptions reveal the cultural importance of the place.

Lakkundi: This place is famous for a number of ancient and architecturally rich temples. The later Chalukyas, who had the place as their capital, were responsible for the construction of these wonderful centres of worship. The Kasivisweswara Temple dedicated to Lord Siva, the largest of the temples found here has two sanctorums, one on the east and the other on the west, with the latter bigger than the former. The sculpture in the temple is extra-ordinary. There are also some tranquil Jain temples here.

Accommodation

- **Hotel Ayodhya** (Deluxe) Opp. Central Bus Stand, Pune-Bangalore Road, Hubli - 29. ✆: 0836-2351951, 2354981
- **Hotel Naveen** Pune-Bangalore Road, Hubli-25. ✆: 0836-2372283, 2372126, 2374418, 2373401, 2373264, 2373215
- **The Ashoka Towers Hotel** Lamington Road, Near Railway Terminus, Hubli-20. ✆: 0836-2362271-73, 298440
- **The Hans Hotel** Pune-Bangalore Road, Vidyanagar, Hubli-31. ✆: 0836-2374770 (8 lines) Email:hans@hublicity.com

Uttara Kannada

Uttara Kannada or 'North Kannada' headquartered at Karwar lies along the sumptuous shores of the Arabian Sea with an expanse of 10,291 sq. km. The population of the district as reported by the 2001 census is 12,20,260. The district is marked by undulating lands. The headquarters has regions of presentable beauty. The ruins of an ancient fort can also be seen here. Around the place, there are important centres of worship. Gokarna, in this district is an important pilgrim centre. The temple dedicated to Lord Siva here attracts hoards of devotees. Ankola has a temple dedicated to Lord Venkateswara. The place Sonda is famous for more than one reason - the presence of the Jain Temples and the Hindu Temples. Ulvi presents the tranquillity of its cave Mutts. Banavasi has a Siva Temple. Magodh waterfalls and Dhandeli Wildlife Sanctuary are also among the crowd pullers.

Karwar: The headquarters of Uttara Kannada, Karwar approaches after a thrilling journey through 160 km long road meandering gaily through the scenic sylvan settings, from Hubli. This undulating stretch of road is graced by wild animals which inhabit the region galore. This area is characterised by beautiful hills and valleys.

Situated on the shores of Arabian Sea, Karwar also has an enchanting beach with the fir tree groves providing a cool canopy. The beautiful waters are sporadically scattered upon with placid islets, known as the Oyster Rocks about 11 km from the city of Karwar. A light house can also be seen here. These islets play a considerable role in maritime activities and a number of domestic and foreign ships can be seen here, moored around them most of the times.

The ravishing river Kali adds to the charms of the valley. The ruins of Shivaji's Fort known as Sadashivagarh stands on a bridge across this river. Exhilarating launches are conducted on the river to make the visit all the more memorable.

The important monuments here are the Durga Temple at Sadashivagarh and the Darga of Peer Kamruddin. There is also a modern Caustic Soda Factory at Binaga.

Gokarna: This popular pilgrim centre on the Arabian Sea shore, situated about 56 km from Karwar and 252 km from Mangalore is where stands the famous Mahabaleshwar Temple which is revered almost on par with the Siva Temple at Varanasi. This tranquil temple is reckoned as a heaven on Earth and attracts a large number of pilgrims from far and near. The Sivarathri Festival during which the devotees fast and forgo sleep singing the praise of Lord Siva, is a grand affair here.

There are buses to Gokarna from important places like Bangalore, Mangalore and Mysore. Accommodation is available at the Hotel run by KTDC and also at Dharmashala.

Ankola: An ancient temple dedicated to Lord Venkataramana with two grand chariots made marvellously out of wood, recounting Puranic stories from 'Ramayana', is situated here. Ankola which reminisces Sarpamalika, the king who ruled in the 15th century also has a small beach for a delightful dawdle. This place is near Gokarna.

Sonda: Situated about 35 km from Sirsi in the Sirsi taluk, Sonda, which was a popular Jain centre hosts the 'Samadhi' of the great scholar Bhattakalanka.

There is also a monastery here called the Swarnavalli Mutt. The 'Smartha' tradition is practised here. Two ancient temples are dedicated to Lord Trivikrama and Lord Sankaranarayana, the former a variation of Lord Vishnu and the latter a combination of Lord Shiva and Lord Vishnu.

About 5 km from here is an enchanting waterfalls known as the Shivaganga falls created by a 91 m fall of zapping waters of the ravishing river Shalmala.

Ulvi: Situated about 32 km from Yellapur, this place is noted for the serene Gavi Mutt which consists of a series of caves filled with an air of calmness. The Sharanas are said to have dwelled in these caves. One of the caves is named after Akka Nagamma. The remains of a ruined fort can also be seen here.

Banavasi: Banavasi has an ancient temple dedicated to Lord Mudhukeswara, a variation of Lord Siva.

Situated on the banks of river Varada, this place had for quite some time been the capital of the Kadamba rulers. Overlooking the river lie the vestiges of a once magnificent fortress.

Magodh Waterfalls: About 19 km from Yellapur is this wonderful waterfalls cradled in the verdant beauty of the mighty western ghats. The vivacious waters of the resplendent river Gangavathi clamour down through 600 ft giving rise to this ravishing waterfalls.The visitors come here and get besotted by the sumptuous natural embellishments. Accommodation can be availed at the Tourist Home run by the KTDC.

Dhandeli Wildlife Sanctuary: It is situated about 40 km from Karwar, 76 km from Dharwad and 104 km from Belgaum. This sanctuary which spreads over 128 sq. km. with a profusion of teak and bamboo plantations is located at an altitude varying between 375 and 685 m above sea level. A good number of elephants, bisons and sambars and the fierce big cats such as the tigers and cheetahs grace the sanctuary. Come summer, come birds! A variety of fascinating birds can be seen flocking around merrily during the migratory season. There are also a couple of watch towers wherefrom one can have a convenient view of the magnificent creatures in the wilderness. The sanctuary is nourished by the ravishing rivers Kali and Kaneri.

Buses are operated from Belgaum and Bangalore to Dhandeli which can also be reached by train from Alnawar. The Belgaum airport, the nearest one, is about 152 km from here. Private accommodations are available apart from the four bungalows belonging to the Forest Department, which are situated at Kulagi about 11 km away.

Accommodation

- Subhadra Hotel Katga Road, Mallapur Township North Kanara, Karwar Mallapur - 581 400. ✆: 08382-234882-84

Belgaum

Belgaum was known in the ancient times as 'Venugrama' which means **'Bamboo Village'**. The district headquarters whose name represents the entire district is situated on the Bangalore-Pune Road about 502 km from the former. Belgaum occupies an area of 13,415 sq. km. and the population according to 2001 census is 35,84,000. This historic city is noted as the capital of the Rattas during the 12th and the 13th century. The Rattas were the chieftains of Saundatti which is a popular pilgrim destination marked by sylvan region. This place Saundatti is one in which age-old conventions and traditions are still much in vogue. In Belgaum there is a 16th century mosque known as the Saba Mosque and two Jain shrines.

The moated fort at Belgaum arouses the painful memories of the travails of the fight for freedom as the Father of the Nation was gaoled here. However, the structure has attractive features. The Gokak falls is a frequent haunt of picnic makers from far and near. At the place called Halari, there are architectural temples and Jain Bastis built by the Kadamba rulers.

Belgaum Fort: Situated near the bus terminus at Belgaum is this massive fort which shoots the limelight of the freedom struggle as Mahatma Gandhi was once locked up here by the British. The famous 'Kamalabasti' inside the fort was built by Birchiraja, a Ratta officer, in 1204. As the name implies there is an attractive lotus carving jutting from the roof. Typical of the ancient forts, there is a moat running around this one as well.

Gokak Falls: An off-shoot of the road from Belgaum to Miraj, known as the Gokak road, which is 53 km from Belgaum, leads through its 8 km long stretch to the Ghataprabha station where the rail tourists alight to visit the vivacious waterfalls.

The glorious river Ghataprabha makes this gorgeous ghat section a pleasant picnic spot with its splendid waters making a marvellous dive of 52 m and thereby creating this smashing waterfalls.

Saundatti: This popular pilgrim destination is situated at the foot of the scenic hills known as Sidhachal or Ramagiri overlooking the beautiful river Malaprabha which enhances the richness of the region. This wonderful sylvan region is about 112 km from Belgaum. However Dharwad and Hubli are nearer, at a distance of 38 km and 58 km respectively.

A temple dedicated to Goddess Yellamma also known as Goddess Renuka, the consort of the mythical sage Sri Jamadagni and mother of Lord Parasurama, an incarnation of Lord Vishnu, forms the sacred crown of the beautiful hill, about 8 km from Saundatti. It is learnt from the legends that a part of the corpse of Sati fell here when it was severed by the Chakra or the 'Holy Wheel' of Lord Vishnu.

By a strange sacred convention, the devotees young and old, men and women bathe naked in the holy waters of the Kunda or tank known as 'Yogarbavi Satyamma Kunda' at the lower part of the hill as part of a sequence of rites and rituals during a festival, before donning new clothes and proceeding to the temple for worship which is marked by, among other features. 'Nimmana' which is the custom of performing clockwise reverential circumambulation in the Sathyamma Temple carefully holding sacred neem leaves in their mouths.

Another convention known as the 'Devadasi Custom' by which girls are given in marriage to none other than the Almighty God is also prevalent here. 'Deva' stands for God and 'Dasi' for 'Servant Maid' and thus 'Devadasis' means women who have dedicated themselves out and out to the service of God. It is also believed that the parents who give their daughters in marriage to God take another step towards the ultimate salvation.

The Goddess has a preponderance of devotees in western India who congregate here during the festivals of Devipaksha, Navarathri and Mughi Purnima. Behind the temple, there are three sacred tanks known as Kumkum Kundam, Yoni Kundam and Arishan Kundam where devotees take holy dips and perform, 'Pooja'. The holy waters of Yoni Kundam is sold in sealed containers. 'Jogal Bhavi' is a sacred well nearby whose holy waters are believed to cure skin diseases. Adjacent to the temple lie the sacred ground known as the 'Parasurama Kshetra', meaning 'The Place of Parasurama' where Lord Parasurama is said to have meditated.

Saundatti, the present taluk headquarters of Belgaum was in the olden days the capital of the chieftains called the Rattas. An 18th century fort built by Sirasangi Desai can also be seen here. Besides, there are also other wonderful monuments in Saundatti. The beautifully sculptured, sacred reliefs of Lord Ankeswara, Lord Venkateswara, Lord Mallikarjuna, Lord Puradeswara and Lord Veerabhadra are to name a few. Two small Jain Bastis of the Ratta era can also be seen. The river Malaprabha graces the outskirts of the city. About 2 km from Saundatti stands a wonderful hill fort which was expanded by 'Chatrapathi Shivaji'.

Halasi: About 14 km from Khanapur Railway Station, this historic place Halasi amidst the verdant sylvan region of the western ghats hosts the Jain Basti built by the early Kadamba rulers who were devout patrons of Jainism.

The ancient temple known as the Bhuvaraha Narasimha Temple built by the Goa Kadambas in the 12th century is also situated here. The temple structure replete with exquisite carvings gets us an awesome glimpse of the richness of the 12th century Kadamba architecture. The sculptural excellence is evident from the huge images of Lord Varaha, Lord Narasimha, Lord Narayana, Lord Surya and so on. The other important monuments here are the ancient temples dedicated to Lord Gokarneswara, Lord Kapileswara, Lord Swarneswara and Lord Hatakeswara.

Accommodation

- **Hotel Milan** Club Road, Belgaum - 1. ✆: 0831-2425555 (8 lines)

Bijapur

The City of Victory is what Vijaypur, the olden name of Bijapur during the days of Chalukyas, means. Situated about 579 km from the present state capital Bangalore, it was the capital of the Adilshahis between 1489 and 1586. Bijapur, one of the five sovereign states born after the fall of the Bamini Empire, was founded by Yusuf Adil Khan. And it is noted as one of the centres of Indo-Saracenic Art suffused with extravagant architecture. This city has inside its safe walls some exciting elements such as the beautiful lakes and the wonderful gardens. It was also an important commercial centre in the past and was called the 'Queen of Deccan'. There are magnificent edifices predominant of which is the 'Gol Gumbaz' which holds the tomb of Mohammad Adhil Shah the 7th of the Adilshahi rulers during whose reign the Islamic glory of the region reached its pinnacle. Besides, there is a number of monuments of Indo-Saracenic architecture.

Bijapur district occupies an area of 10,475 sq. km. with a population of 15,33,448 (2001 census). Around the headquarters, there are places of tourists' interests. The Basaveswara at Basavanawadi is a holy structure of excellent Chalukyan architecture. The place also hosts other important monuments: 'Badami' a place of legendary importance was the archaic city of 'Vatapi' which is associated with the mythical sage 'Agasthya'. This place was also the venue of some important historic events. There are tranquil temples here. A 7th century Jain Temple can also be seen.

Gol Gumbaz: Situated on the east of the city this mammoth rotunda with a base diameter of 126 ft and the biggest dome in India, came into existence in 1659. Four seven-storeyed minarets stand majestically around the capacious hall which measures 38 m, 66 m and 1704 sq. m. in circumference, height and area respectively. Circumferencewise it is second only to St. Peters at the Vatican City, which is 42 m. This grand edifice encapsulates the tomb of Mohammed Adil Shah, the 7th ruler of the dynasty and also that of his daughter, grandson, his lady-adviser Rambha and two of his wives after whom he was enamoured. The huge hall is surprisingly bereft of propping pillars.

The 'Whispering Gallery', a prime attraction of about 3 m width is an astounding feature which has been so ingeniously designed that even a feeble whisper made here is amplified 10 times and echoed several times, however the intensity waning with each echo. This acoustically engineered gallery which is above a case of 100 steps also offers a spellbinding view of the town-scape.

Besides, there is also a mosque, a dharmasala and quarters for servants.

Nagarkhana: Facing the grand Gol Gumbaz, Nagarkhana has an archaeological museum which houses some interesting artefacts. The tremor of the earthquake which hit the region in 1993 has left cracks in the dome of this structure.

Jami Masjid: This grand holy structure of 10,804 sq.m. built by Adil Shah I was later ameliorated by Aurangzeb with two minarets and a gateway. This mosque which can hold upto 2500 devotees in its various blocks stands out in its architecture. The array of astounding arches, the gorgeous terrace gardens, the placid lake and a fountain present a picture of serene beauty.

Ibrahim Rouza: Ibrahim Adil Shah II who ruled from 1580 to 1626 and his family are laid to rest here. There are beautiful gardens and tall minarets. The paintings and stone work also deserve mention. The dome is refulgent with the holy Quran inscribed on gold. The tomb of Ali Rouza is also situated near here. Ibrahim Rouza lies on the western part of the town.

Jorha Masjid: This is a war memorial of Khan Mohammed, the general of the Adilshahi ruler who fought Aurangzeb, and his son Khawas Khan who were executed charged with treason as they aided in the victory of Aurangzeb, who later raised the tomb where the father and son were buried. This masjid inside which women are not allowed is situated near the bus terminus.

Asar-I-Sharif: Situated in the heart of the city this grand edifice of high court was built by Mohammed Adil Shah in the year 1646. The vivacious frescoes depicting figurine of men and women with beautiful blossoms and leaves are gradually losing lusture. It was here that the two sacred strands of the beard of Prophet Mohammed had been preserved until 1700 which was when they were taken to Hazratbal in Srinagar.

Malik-I-Maiden: This ground on which stands the huge cannon with the massive dimensions of 1.5 m circumference and 4.45 m length, is situated near Asar-I-Sharif. A seething lion's head forms the mouth of the long barrel of this cannon which was made out of an alloy of copper, iron and tin by Mohammed Bin Hasan Rumi of Turkey in 1549. About 10 elephants, 400 bulls and more than 100 men were used in transporting this 55 tonne weapon from Bijapur to Ahmednagar. And today, it is looked upon as a granter of wish as it is believed that by touching the cannon with a wish in mind one can get it realised.

Nagardurg: The beautiful conference hall known as 'Durbar Hall' in this city fort was built by Adil Shah I in 1561. The fort has seven massive gates and a separate enclosure for royal women, called the Ananda Mahal. The tall watchtower or 'Pramod Mahal' nearby is a grand seven-storeyed structure wherefrom the guards kept vigil, day in and day out. A 'Lake Palace' known as the 'Jala Manjil' is situated in front of the fort. There is also a mosque which is patterned on, and hence named after the Mecca Mosque. A Jain shrine here which has been transformed into a mosque can also be seen. The 'Mehtar Mahal' is a masterpiece of the Indo-Saracenic architecture with splendid sculptures and captivating gardens.

A mausoleum which houses the tomb of Ali Adil Shah is situated near Gandhi Chowk. This mausoleum, though rich in architecture with a dozen arches bowing beautifully to add to the grandeur remains incomplete.

Upali Buruj: The observation tower built by Haridar Khan in 1585 rises to about 24 m in height. A panorama of the townscape and its surroundings can be had from the top of the tower to which there are as many as 70 steps. Olden arms and ammunitions are stored here.

Basavana Begewadi: The taluk headquarters which is also the birth place of Saint Basaveswara is about 43 km from Bijapur. The ancient Basaveswara Temple which in the archives is referred to as Sangamanatha Temple brandishes the grand architecture of the Chalukyas. The other important monuments here are the 'Samadis' or the 'Holy Tombs' of the saints Siddharameswara and Gurupadeswara of the Inchegeri School of Spiritual Pursuits.

Badami: This place of versatile importance, situated about 113 km from Bijapur and 500 km from Bangalore was known as 'Vathapi', the place associated with the sage Agasthya of the mythical era. This legendary place is marked by a number of sacred and historic monuments. The Chalukyas made Badami their capital and constructed some important monuments. In 640, Narasingha Varman, the Pallava King conquered the region. But again, the Chalukya rule was restored by Vikramaditya in 653. Then, a series of conquests placed the region under the rule of Kalchuris,

Yadavas the Vijayanagar rulers, other Bijapur rulers and Marathas.

Cave Temples: The tranquil cave temples carved out of mammoth rocks, as many as 5 of them with one being a natural cave are located on the inspiring incline of a scenic hill. The first of these caves is the temple dedicated to 'Lord Nataraja' or Lord Siva dancing in divine ecstasy. The image of the Lord has 18 mighty and protecting hands. The lord portrays 81 'Natya Mudhras' or 'Stamps' of dance. The splendid sculpture includes among others two icons of Lord Ganesa, the principal deity, one of Mahishasuramardhini, the Goddess who killed the demon Mahishasura and Ardhanariswara the deity constituted on the right half by Lord Siva and on the left by His consort Goddess Parvathi. The second cave is dedicated to Lord Vishnu. The Lord can be seen in the reposing posture and also in His various 'Avatars' or incarnations. There are also images of Lord Siva, Lord Brahma and the 'Ashtadikpalakas' or the presiding deities of the 8 directions.The third one which gives a hint of the Buddhist influence is a natural cave. The fourth cave, larger than the others, contains beautifully sculpted sacred images of Lord Siva and Lord Vishnu. The cave is also adorned with marvellous murals but these are gradually fading away. The last but certainly not the least of the caves, is a Jain shrine contemporary to the 7th century Ajantha Caves. The sculpture here is a replica of those at Ajanta.

A 'Holy Tank' called the 'Agasthya Theertha' situated at the foot of the hill tenders some good news to lepers. The sacred waters of this tank with amazing curative powers are believed to cure leprosy. There are also two wonderful temples dedicated to Lord Siva, known as Mahakutteswar and Maligetti Temples on the tank side. A little away is the ancient temple dedicated to 'Lord Boothanatha' one of the forms of Lord Siva. The sacred reliefs of Lord Ganesa, Lord Varaha, Lord Narasimha the reposing Lord Vishnu and Goddess Durga and a host of others mark the grandeur of the sculpture. The courtyard and the vestibule of the temple are replete with ethereal artwork.

The flight of rockcut stairs leading to the cave temples is about 1 km from Badami bus terminus and 5 km from the railway station.

Badami Fort: This citadel houses Tipu's cannon. A further treck up the hill from the cave temples leads to this massive fort.

Archaeological Museum: This museum which houses several interesting archaeological specimen is situated on the north of the tank 'Agasthya Theertham'. It remains closed on Fridays and can be visited on all other days between 09:00 and 17:00 hours.

Pattadakal: This historic place which has seen the coronation of kings, situated on the banks of the river Malaprabha was also the second capital of Chalukyas. Pattadakal abounds in ancient temples. There are about 10 predominant temples and many more. All the temples are adorned with ornate carvings. The superb architecture and sculpture of the Chalukyas has been at one of its best in the temples here. The famous temple of Pattadakal is the one dedicated to Lord Siva. The Papanas Temple built in 680, with its grand architecture is identical to the Kailash of Ellora. Scenes from the great epics are depicted on the walls as also are other figurines and friezes. The pillars are rife with artfully carved images of deities.

The ancient Virupaksha Temple built by queen Lok Mahadevi as an act of thanks-giving to the Lord after her victory over the Pallavas testifies the grandeur of the Dravidian architecture. The vast ceiling of the huge hall is propped up by 16 mighty and ornate pillars, all monoliths which schematise the social setup of the olden times. Events from the great epics can be seen on the walls. A 'Nandi' the sacred bull mount of Lord Siva can also be seen in front of the Sanctorum. This temple was formerly known as Lokeswar Temple.

The Mallikarjuna Temple built by queen Trailokya Mahadevi bears a close resemblance to the Virupaksha Temple. The sculpture and architecture are excellent. An image of Goddess Mahishasuramardini can also be seen here. The ceiling is engraved with the images of Lord Siva, His consort Goddess Parvathi and Goddess Gajalakshmi, a variation of Goddess Lakshmi the consort of Lord Vishnu. The holy 'Bhagavat Gita' is depicted through several puranic stories on the pillars.

The Sangameswara Temple is the most ancient of the group of temples here. It was built by the King Vijayaditya who ruled between 696 and 733 AD.

Pattadakal is situated about 29 km from Badami on the way to Aihole.

Aihole: This sacred place abounds in temples. About 125 ancient architectural temples dedicated to various deities are located in tight proximity to one another. These temples have been built over a span of about 250 years from 450 AD to 700 AD, the oldest being the Siva temple built in 450 AD. There are wonderful rock cut caves, and a unique temple dedicated to Lord Vishnu. The exquisite artwork of this temple is a fusion of Hindu and Buddhist styles. The architecture and sculpture of these temples take the observer to new heights of sheer astonishment. There is also a museum which houses sculptural specimens, in front of the Durga Temple. It can be visited between 10.00 and 17.00 hrs.

Aihole or 'Ayyavvole' according to the ancient stone inscriptions, is situated at an altitude of 593 m, and 17, 46 and 129 kms from Pattadakal, Badami and Bijapur respectively.

Accommodation

Bijapur

- **Hotel Mayura Adil Shah,** (KSTDC), Anand Mahal Road, Bijapur. ✆: 08352-220934

Badami

- **Hotel Badami Court** 17/3, Station Road, Badami - 587 201. ✆: 08357-265230-33 Email: rafiqmht@bir.vsnl.net.in

Gulbarga

The city of Gulbarga is the head quarters of the district which spreads over 16,224 sq. km. with a population of 25,82,169 as reported by the 2001 census. Situated about 62 km from the present state capital Bangalore, Gulbarga which was known as Kallubarige was the ancient capital of the Bhamini Sultans between 1347 AD and 1428 AD.The name of the city underwent a transformation under the Muslim rulers, and came to be known by the present name. The city has Raichur on its south and there are quite a few things to interest the tourists. The Chaya Bhagavathi Temple, the Fort, the Mosques and the Gulshan Gardens proffer copious enchantment. Gulbarga University is located here and the State Archaeological Museum is worth a visit. Besides, there are many modern temples here. Gulbarga lies enroute to Hyderabad of Andhra Pradesh from Bijapur, with the former being, 222 km and the latter 159 km away.

Hence buses plying between these two places also go to Gulbarga. There are busses from Raichur too. However, it is linked with all the three places by rail.

Chaya Bhagavathi Temple: This wonderful temple situated on the banks of the holy river Krishna, in Surpur taluk is dedicated to Goddess Chaya Bhagavathi the second consort of Sun God.

Fort: This massive fort here was built by Raja Gulchand. There are about 15 bastions to the fort. Spreads over an area of 38,000 sq. ft. stands the huge Jami Mosque inside the fort, built in the 14th century. This mosque is modeled on the famous mosque of Cardova in Spain.

The grand Moorish style is reflected in its construction. There are about 75 domes, and four more, larger than these in four corners, and one central dome, the largest. Several conference halls can be seen in the fort which also encapsulates the tombs of Bhamini Sultans and also those of the great Sufi Saint 'Bandi Nawaz' and Sharana Basappa. There are also other mosques to be seen.

Devala Gangapura: It is situated in Afzalpur Taluk, about 651 km from Bangalore. This place became famous after the Saint Sri Narasimha Saraswathi who miraculously cured the Bhamini Sultan of an incurable serious boil, at a hand's turn. This Saint was then reckoned as an 'Avtar' or incarnation of Lord Dattatreya. This sacred place is always busy with teeming devotees from Karnataka and Maharashtra.

Accommodation

- **Hotel Southern Star** Near Super Market, S.B. Temple Road, Gulbarga - 585 101. ✆: 08472-224093, 233385, 232934

Raichur

The city of Raichur is a repository of age-old relics and artefacts. In the past it had been a rolling possession of the Kakatiyas, the Bhaminis and the rulers of Vijayanagara and Bijapur. The ancient monuments are the fort built in 1294, the Mosques and Tombs. The important temples are those of Lord Manikprabhu and Lord Ramalingeswara. However, these are of present age. The district spreads over 5,559 sq. km. and has a population of 13,51,809 people (2001 census).

Situated about 415 km from Bangalore, 223 km from Gulbarga and 122 km from Guntakal. Raichur can be reached both by bus and by train.

The Fort: Just about 2 km from Raichur Railway Station, stands this monumental fort built by the Kakatiya rulers in 1294. A prime attraction here is the huge stone slab which extends to 41 ft in length, situated near the bus stand at Raichur. This slab depicts a record in Telugu and also the awe- inspiring scenes of the huge slabs being hauled up the hill with the help of buffallo driven carts.

The Ekminar Mosque: It was built during the days of Mohammed Shah Bhamini. The Jami Masjid, however is the largest Mosque of the place.

Itagi: Situated about 40 km from Gadag, Itagi is where the ancient temple with visibly the best of Kalyani Chalukya architecture is situated. Built by Mahadeva Dhandanayaka, this temple is noted for its intricately carved ingress. The ethereal sculpture makes a lasting impression. The architecture has drawn historic comparisons with that of the temples at Halebid.

'Saraswathi Mutt', the students' residence is yet another important monument here. About 10 km from here, at Kukanur stands the famous temple complex of 'Navalinga' obviously dedicated to Lord Siva. This is a fine architectural endeavour of the Rashtrakutas. There are also temples built during the rule of Kalyani Chalukyas. These are the ancient temples dedicated to Lord Mahamaya, Lord Kaleswara and Lord Mallikarjuna.

Koppal: Koppal is a modified nomenclature of the ancient 'Kopana'. Koppal was the capital of the provincial Kingdom of Shilaharas, a feudatory to the Kalyani Chalukyas. This place has a magnificent citadel.

It is also a holy place of Jains. At Palligundu, there is an ancient Siva Temple known as the Male Malleswara Temple. The inscriptions of Ashoka are also found at Palligundu and Govimatha. There is also a belief that it was this place Palligundu, referred to as Indrakila Parvatha in the great epic 'The Ramayana'. And Kinhal about 13 km from Koppal is famous for its traditional colourful lacquerware.

Hutti: This place is famous for its gold mines. It is about 18 km from Lingasugar.

Accommodation

• **Hotel Nrupatunga** Station Road, Raichur - 584101. ✆: 08532-220931/32, 240816

Bellary

This district is endowed with some minerally rich regions. Iron and manganese ores are found in Sandur. This place marked by gregarious hills is also noted for its temples. Hampi the capital of the Vijayanagar rulers hosts ruined monuments which recount the tale of ravaging war. Hampi abounds in architectural and tranquil temples. The monuments here is a mixture of ruined, partially ruined and still intact structures. The Vittala Temple here has been listed among the elite list of World Heritage Monuments. There have also been excavations which have yielded interesting artefacts throwing light upon the events of the past. The place Kishkindhya which has references in the great epic Ramayana, forms a bridge between the 'Puranic' and the modern days. There is also a temple dedicated to Lord Rama.

Areawise, this district with an expanse of 8,419 sq. km. is the 9th largest in Karnataka. The population according to 2001 census is 16,56,000.

The headquarters of this district, also called Bellary is situated about 306 km on the northwest of Bangalore. Two rocky hills are found in the outskirts of the city and one of them called Balahari has a temple on it. The city also offers other interesting sights. There is a magnificent fort encompassing a hill, built by the Vijayanagar rulers. Among the places of worship, a temple dedicated to Goddess Durgamma and two huge Mosques can be seen. There is also a Government Medical College.

Sandur: This scenic hill fringed region in a sumptuous valley has natural riches of iron and manganese ores. There is a massive fort which nestles a marvellous palace. This fort is a fabulous monument left behind by the famous Maratha rulers.

The gregarious hill range is graced by wonderful temple twins dedicated to Lord Kumaraswamy and Goddess Parvathi. Ideally located in serene surroundings these tranquil temples contain awesome elements of art and sculpture. Captivating rose gardens form part of the temple environs.

The Post-Graduate centre of the Gulbarga University is situated on the picturesque Nandi hills. About 16 km from Sandur is Ramanadurga or Ramgad.

There is a wonderful temple here, dedicated to Lord Rama, on the cosy hill resort. This temple commemorates the historic personality Kumara Rama who fought till death, against the sultans of Delhi.

Hampi: Situated at an altitude of 467 m above sea level, founded by Harihara I also known as Hukka, and Bukka the Telugu princes. Hampi was the capital of the historically largest Hindu empire - 'The Vijayanagar Empire'.'Vijayanagar' literally means 'The City of Victory'. The reign of the famous ruler Krishnadevaraya in the early 16th century is noted as the golden era. During this period, the empire extended from the south of the mighty rivers Krishna and Tungabadra to the Bay of Bengal in the east and the Arabian Sea in the west. There was marked growth in the fields of literature, arts, architecture and also military warfare. However, this glorious empire was ravaged by the combined army of five rulers of Bidar, Bijapur, Golconda, Ahmednagar and Berar in the later-middle part. of the same century. Priceless monuments of the hard-built city were crushed and the entire kingdom was thrown to ruins. But certain vestiges of the wonderful historic monuments, which have stood the foray do exist even today. And now, the city stands as a reliquary of the prestigious remnants of the great Vijayanagar empire.

Pattabhirama Temple: This temple on the south of the sacred river Tungabadra, located in scenic hilly surroundings is the largest among the ruins. It was built between 1530 and 1542. This wonderful temple is noted for its largeness. There is a capacious hall in front of the temple.

Dussehra Dibba (or) Vijaya Bhavani: This architecturally wonderful temple was raised by the distinguished ruler of Vijayanagar, Krishnadevaraya, as an act of thanksgiving to the ultimate Supreme Being, after his conquest of Orissa. The temple structure is decorated with exquisite carvings. There is also an embellished dais on which festivals like the Dussehra were celebrated. The remarkable reliefs depict gutfully marching soldiers, beautiful damsels in various dancing postures, horses and elephants. From the top section of the temple, the ruins of the once-magnificent palace can be seen.

Virupaksha Temple: Also known as the 'Temple of Pasupati' the construction of this temple is shrouded in uncertainty. According to a belief, it was built in 1509 to commemorate the coronation of Krishnadevaraya. Contradictory to this, another belief says it was built by Krishnadevaraya to commemorate his triumph over the Bijapur and Gajapathy rulers. The huge holy image of Lord Siva in the Sanctum Sanctorum is a sacred monolithic structure. The lord is worshipped as Lord Virupaksha here and hence the name of the temple. The temple also has beautifully sculpted images of various other deities.The huge Mandapa or 'Hall' consists of marvellous monolithic pillars with intricate and ethereal artwork. The temple tower called the Bhistappayyana Gopura became the model for all the South Indian Vijayanagar Temple Towers. These are also known as Rajagopuras.

Vittala Temple: Situated on the banks of the holy river Tungabadra, this temple dedicated to Lord Vishnu is one of the extant holy monument of the Vijayanagar empire, though the temple tower is dilapidated. This architecturally rich temple was built by Krishnadevaraya in the early part of the 16th century. The temple stands on a rectangular courtyard of 152 m × 94 m. There are as many as 56 sturdy pillars replete with fine artwork. Another spellbinding feature is the huge temple chariot made out of stone. The exquisite 'Musical Pillars' which emit musical notes when tapped offer melodious enchantment. A noteworthy point is that the temple has rightfully entered the list of 'World Heritage Monuments'.

About 2 km from here, is an enormous holy statue of Lord Ganesa, on the river bank.

Patal Lingeswar: This temple was unearthed during one of the excavations carried out by the British. It is believed that Lord Siva was the presiding deity of the temple which now has no deity. Facing the temple are the scattered remains of a ruined royal guest house. There is another temple in the proximity, dedicated to Lord Siva.

Hazara Ramaswamy Temple: The presiding deity of this temple, Lord Rama was worshipped by the generations of the royal family.The ancient temple is adorned with wonderful carvings which recount the great epics and the pillars depict various incarnations of Lord Vishnu. Besides, the ornate friezes include images of sacred animals.

Lotus Mahal: This grand edifice which is now an archaeological museum was the resting place of the kings in the past. This museum houses a good number of artefacts which have been unearthed from the excavations which started in 1976 and going on even today. Among the excavated articles, ancient Chinese coins can also be seen. The KSTDC runs a restaurant at the entrance. There is also another archaeological museum at Kamalapuram.

Kishkindha: The epic-fame Kishkindha seems to turn the timescale back to the Puranic era. It is said that the region on the sumptuous banks of the holy river Tungabhadra was the place called Kishkindha mentioned in the great epic 'The Ramayana'. Kishkindha was the realm of the Anthropoid King Vali in the great epic. The Purana (the epic) asserts that Lord Rama killed the erring and heedless king Vali to do justice to his (Vali's) brother Sughriva, who sought the help of the Lord through Lord Anjaneya. The awesome hills Hrishyamuk, Malyabanta and Matanga found here are referred to in 'The Ramayana'. There is also a mound where the king Vali is said to have been laid to rest. And obviously there is a temple dedicated to 'Lord Rama', the divine Hero of 'The Ramayana' and an incarnation of Lord Vishnu.

Twin Temple: This Twin Temple portrays exquisite artwork of the Chalukyas on the exterior walls. There are 59 polished and gleaming pillars. The 'Sikharas' are of a unique style. Another important monument here is the temple complex known as Kalleswara mentioned in an inscription of 1013 AD. The Archaeological Survey of India has set up a sculpture shed near here.

Tungabhadra Dam: Situated about 7 km from Hospet and 20 km from Hampi, the beautiful dam which rises to a height of 49 m and runs to a length of 500 m across the ravishing river Tungabhadra, with its conscientiously laid Japanese style gardens and a captivating horticultural farm makes an enchanting picnic spot. Here, the alluring blossoms refulgent with a spectrum of hues beckon to the curious visitors. Besides, a tower, a net factory and a steel project can also be seen.

The serene reservoir created by the dam spreads over 387 sq. m. The benevolent waters of the river not only irrigate over 2 million acres of arable land but also help generate electricity through the hydro-electric power project here. This site can also be visited on a special permission.

Accommodation

Bellary

- **Hotel Pola Paradise** New Trunk Road, Bellary - 583 104. ✆: 08392-242101,242302-242304 Email:hotelpola@hotmail.com

Hospet

- **Hotel Karthik** S.P. Road, Patel Nagar, Hospet - 1. ✆: 224938
- **Hotel Priyadarshini** Station Road, Hospet - 1. ✆: 228838
- **Hotel Sandarshan** Station Road, Hospet - 1. ✆: 228574
- **Hotel Shalini** Station Road, Hospet - 1. ✆: 228910
- **Hotel Vishwa** Opp. KSRTC Bus Stand, Station Road, Hospet - 1. ✆: 228910
- **Malligi Tourist Home** 6/143, J.N. Road, Off. Hampi Road, Hospet-1. ✆: 228101 (16 lines)
- **Sree Krishna Tourist Home** T.B. Dam Road, Opp. New Govt. Hospital, Hospet - 1. ✆: 228156
- **Sree Ramakrishna Lodge** Side Road of Andhra Bank, Hospet - 1. ✆: 227114

Bidar

With an area of 5,448 sq. km. Bidar forms the eighth smallest district of Karnataka and population according to 2001 census is 12,56,000. Located at the northern tip of Karnataka, Bidar has Andhra Pradesh on its east and Maharashtra on its west. This district is bordered on the south by Gulbarga.

The district headquarters Bidar is situated about 740 km from Bangalore. At an altitude of 664 m above sea level, Bidar offers a pleasant cool climate. This historic place was also the capital of Bahmini and Barid Shahi rulers.

Tranquil cave temples dedicated to Lord Narasimha, the Fort, Khwaja Mohammed Gawan's Madrasa, and the Tombs of the Bahmini and the Baridi rulers are the important monuments here. Bidar has road access to Gulbarga and rail access to Hyderabad.

The Fort: This magnificent fort built by the Islamic rulers contains a mosque known as the Solakamb Mosque and three palatial mansions known as the Ranjou Mahal, Chini Mahal and Turkis Mahal. Decorative wood work and mosaic add to the interior charms. The fort also has exquisite door ways and massive bastions.

'Bari Tope' or the huge cannon is one of the chief attractions. There is also a museum with a good collection of interesting artifacts. Facing this is the mosque behind which is the Dewani Aam and the Gagan Mahal.

Gawan's Madrasa: Gawan's Madrasa or the college of Mohammed Gawan is an elegant edifice of the Indo-Saracenic architecture.

Tombs of Bahmini Sultans: These tall tombs are situated at Ashtor near Bidar. These are imposing but devoid of paintings.

Nanak Jhora Gurudwara: Situated less than a couple of kilometers from Bidar this serene Jain shrine has been raised to commemorate the sojourn of Guru Nanak at this place.

The legend has it that this region was once hit by a severe drought and the hapless people bursting for water turned to Guru Nanak who happened to visit the place as part of His nation-wide mission. Moved by the entreats of the water deprived people, the ever so merciful 'Guru', created, out of His supernatural powers, a vivacious spring by pressing the top of a hill with His sacred foot. The legend also adds that by promising an iron bangle at the shrine here one can get one's wishes granted. Of course, it is a prerogative to meet out the promise.

There is a tank here whose steps are laid with beautiful white marble stones. Nearby, there is a larger enclosure of serene waters where a dip is believed to confer merit and cure diseases.

Basava Kalyana: Situated about 65 km from Bidar Basava Kalyana, the Taluk Headquarters of Bidar, is a city of historic importance. It was the capital of Chalukyas. This is also the place where the famous Saint Basaveswara lived. The Lingayat community owes its origin to this saint. The ancient fort here has been refurbished by the Bahminis. There is also an interesting museum of archaeological artifacts in the fort. There are also other important monuments to be seen (viz.) the modern temple dedicated to Lord Basaveswara, Prabhudevara Gadduge, Tipuranta Keswara Temple, Nagamma's cave and Madivala Machiah's Pond.

Accommodation

- **Hotel Mayura Barid Shahi,** Main Road, Bidar

Tumkur

Spreading over an area of 10,598 sq. km. with a population of 23,06,000 (2001 census). This is also one of the districts which share their names with their headquarters. Tumkur is situated about 70 km north of Bangalore. The records of the 10th century reveal that this place was known as 'Tummugere'. The temple dedicated to Lord Lakshminarayana, built in 1560 is the oldest temple here.

The Veerashaiva Mutt situated at Siddhaganga is noted for its yeomen service to education and religious activities. Another laudable feature of this noble mutt which runs many educational institutions including an engineering college is the charitable hostel which feeds as many as 5000 students absolutely free of cost. This place Siddhaganga is also where the Samadhi or the 'Holy Tomb' of Saint Siddhalingeswara, the prominent Veerashaiva Saint, is located. There is also a serene natural spring here, known as Siddhaganga.

Madhugiri: About 43 km from Tumkur, Madhugiri known in the olden days as 'Maddagiri', has wonderful temples dedicated to Lord Venkataramana and Lord Malleswara, built by the Vijayanagara rulers. The famous Mallinatha Basti is also situated here. There is also a citadel with imposing gateways called Diddibagilu, Mysore Gate, Antaralada Bagilu etc. About 19 km from here, at the place called Midigeshi, there is another majestic hill fort.

Sira: Sira, the taluk headquarters, is about 52 km away from Tumkur. The Khan Bhag Garden, the Jumma Masjid and Malik Rihan's Tomb are the interesting monuments found here. Sira was once the centre of Mughal Fauzdari and Kasim Khan was the first Fauzdar.

Seebi: This place known as Sibburu in the olden days, about 24 km south of Sira, is sanctified by the 18th century temple dedicated to 'Lord Narasimha' the incarnation of Lord Vishnu, with the head of a Lion and the body of a man. This tranquil temple was built by an officer under Hyder Ali, by name Nallappa who authored the famous treatise in Kannada on the ruler Hyder Ali, famous as 'Haider name'. This architectural temple is embellished with murals which schematise the themes of Ramayana, Mahabharatha and Dasaavathara.

Yediyur: Situated about 30 km from Kunigal, Yediyur is famous for two Veerashaiva Mutts and a temple dedicated to Lord Varadaraja, one of the forms of Lord Vishnu. One of the Mutts, known as Samadhi Mutt of the 16th century Saint Tontada Siddhalingeswara Yati has a wonderful wooden chariot with some interesting sculptures.

Accommodation

- **Hotel Sri Nanjundeswara** B.H. Road, Tumkur-572 101. ✆: 0816-2272373, 2272877

Kolar

About 72 km from Bangalore, on the national highway which links Bangalore with Chennai, the district headquarters Kolar is the place known in the olden times as Kuvalalapura. This historic city was the first capital of the Gangas. The Kambilis, as are called the beautiful blankets of Kolar, have a wide acclaim. The district spreads over an area of 8,223 sq. km. with a population of 22,17,000 (2001 census).

'Goddess Mahishasuramardini' who killed the demon Mahishasura, is worshipped in the name of Goddess Kolaramma in the famous temple known as the Kolaramma Temple. The Goddess is considered as one of the seven mothers installed here. There are also other wonderful temples dedicated to Lord Someswara, Lord Anjaneya, Lord Nanjundes-wara, Lord Kodhandarama and Lord Venkataramana.

Some of Hyder Ali's relatives were laid to rest at Makbara. About 3 km from Kolar, there is a sacred spot called Antaragange, on the scenic Kolar hill. There is a holy stream emerging gloriously from the mouth of a Nandi or the sacred bull of Lord Siva. This wonderful stream overwhelms the devotees with divine rapture.

Avani: Situated about 12 km from Mulabagal this sacred place is famous as the 'Gaya of the South'. The legend has it that the Ashram of Sage Valmiki, where the divine twins Lava and Kusa were born was located here.

The important temples here are those of Lord Ekanatha, Lord Ramaswamy, Lord Rameswara, Lord Lakshmaneswara, Lord Bharatheswara, Lord Shatrugneswara, Goddess Sita and Lord Subrahmanya. Atop a sacred hill here, there is a holy tank called 'Agni Tirtha'.

Accommodation

- **Woody's The Nagarjuna Hotel** N.H.4, Tamaka, Kolar-563 101. ✆: 08152-224466

Andhra Pradesh

Add 2 with all BSNL phone numbers wherever necessary in Andhra Pradesh.

Facts and Figures

Capital	: **Hyderabad**
Principal Languages	: Telugu and Urdu
Area	: 2,75,045 sq. km.
Population	: 7,57,27,541 (2001 census)
Density (People in Sq. Km.) •	: 275
Districts	: 23
Lok Sabha Seats	: 42
Rajya Sabha Seats	: 18
State Assembly Seats	: 295
Females to Males ratio	: 978 : 1000 (2001 census)
Literacy Rate	: 61.1 (2001 survey)
Birth Rate (per 1000)	: 20.6
Death Rate (per 1000)	: 5.7
Natural Growth Rate (per 1000)	: 15.0
Summer	: 20^{0} C - 40^{0} C March to May
Winter	: 13^{0} C - 32^{0} C January to February
Monsoon	: Hot to sultry June to December
Tourist Season	: November to February (varies with places)
Crops	: Cotton, Forest produce, Millet, Oilseeds Pulses, Rice, Sugarcane and Tobacco
Minerals	: Asbestos, Barytes, Bauxite, Coal, Copper, Iron ore, Graphite, Mica, Limestone, Manganese ore and Silica.
Industries	: Asbestos, Cement, Tobacco, Electronics, Paper, Engineering, Fertilizers, Handicrafts, Pharmaceuticals, Shipbuilding, Sugar, Textiles and Vegetable Oils.

ANDHRA - AT A GLANCE

Andhra, one of the southern states of India has a medley of lavish landscape, rich traditional and cultural heritage, a series of exciting events which emblazon the pages of history and a variety of scintillating stuff, to sport. The entire state with its delighting domains had been too enticing to prevent historic inventions and counter inventions which placed one or more parts of it under the reign of various dynasties in turns. The chronicles of the region project a number of

Charminar, Hyderabad *- The magnum opus of Qutb Shahi style of architecture was commissioned by Mohamd. Quli Qutb Shah and completed in 1591 AD. This materpiece is a sight to behold and perhaps is the first thing to come to mind when one thinks of Hyderabad.*

Nagarjunakonda *- Named after the 2nd century* ***Mahayana Buddhist Sage*** *Nagarjunacharya, Nagarjunakonda is an island museum where you will see the reassembled Buddhist sites as they were found at the time of extensive excavations carried out in the area. The museum also has on display numerous objects recovered from these sites.*

Alampur temples *- The origin of the Kadamba-Chalukya style of architecture can be traced to the typical conical shaped roofs of houses found in the North coastal districts of Andhra Pradesh which are often lashed by cyclones. The adaptation of this shape for temples is only more refined and lends these temples a unique and distinct profile.*

emperors of the long list of dynasties who are still survived by their bravery, benevolence, passion for architecture, patronage of arts and culture and things like that. The monuments, the flowery compositions, the literary works of the poets and scholars of yore provide an exhilarating vista of the well organised life style, culture, various forms of arts, occupation, recreation etc. of the people of the past.

HISTORY OF ANDHRA

As long back as about 230 BC, the region under the influence of Emperor Ashoka, who made peace his way of life, nourished the prevalence of Buddhism. 'Satavahanas', then usurped the remarkable region and kept it under their valuable possession until they conceded to the invading Chalukyas in the 7th century. Then in the 14th century, the Cholas, one of the three great Tamil dynasties, conquered the coveted region. Later, a series of war broke out until the vast empire of Aurangzeb permeated over Andhra in 1713.

GEOGRAPHICAL LOCATION

The entire state is at an interesting geographical location. The Deccan plateau forms most part of the state. The sizzling rivers of Andhra, some seasonal and some perennial, make up to over 34 in number. The ravishing rivers Krishna and Godavari not only quench the thirst of a multitude of populace, but lend fertility too, to a vast land along their long course. About 70% of the people of Andhra are engaged in agriculture and among the produce of the state are essentials like rice, maize, millets, pulses and cash crops like tobacco, groundnut, sugarcane, cotton etc.

FOREST WEALTH, AGRICULTURE, INDUSTRIES

The extensive forest region which contributes to about 23% of the entire land area of the state, plays a vital role in determining monsoon and the fiscal echelon of the state since it is invariably the land of high yields of teak, eucalyptus, cashew, bamboo, softwood and other forest products. It also helps in the conservation of wildlife. It is no wonder that with its sumptuous rice production, Andhra is reckoned as the '**Granary of South**'. The state is also wayward in industries. The industries of Andhra, with their state-of-the-art technologies and latest technical know-how, bring out a variety of products which go through a series of stringent scrutiny of quality assurance and quality control before running into customers. Nature has bestowed upon the state, potentially abundant regions of copper ore, manganese, mica, coal, limestone, etc. The handloom and handicraft industry has also not lost its lustre. The lacquer toys, Anakapathi articles, exclusive pottery, black metal triklets, palm products, Dharmavaram silk and Pochampalli silk sarees which have earned an indisputable repute, etc., all bear testimony to the 'sleight of hand' behind their making.

ARCHITECTURE

The ancient temples and other historic monuments of all state bring to the fore the grand architecture, traditions and conventions, faith and belief, arts and culture and suchlike interests of the glorious people of the bygone days. The architecture, sculpture and the intricate construction patterns unique to several royal dynasties are reflected in various temples of the state. The ancient temple at Thirupathi dedicated to Lord Venkateswara, one of the various forms of Lord Vishnu, situated on the peak of one of the marvellous mountains of a glorious range suffused with dense forests ranks first among worship centres or second at times to Roman Catholic Church, in its income by way of pecuniary offerings and votive oblations by the millions of devotees who throng the sacred dominion of the Lord, which is also called 'Ezhumalai' or 'Seven Mountains'. The 'Thirumala Thirupathi Devasthanam' is responsible for the maintenance of this temple and certain others as well. There are 'Temple Tanks' in almost all the temples here, a characteristic feature of the South Indian Temples.

***The Golden Shrine, Thirupati** - The Tirumala temple is the richest shrine in the country. An architectural masterpiece with exquisite carvings, the Vimanam over the sanctorum is covered with gold and is known as the Ananda Nilayam (Abode of Bliss).*

***Lord Anjaneya, Alipiri** - This huge statue of Hanuman, stands guard at Alipiri, the starting point of the journey up the hills to Tirumala. Inspiring pilgrims who choose to trek or take the winding road up the hills.*

There are also ancient Mosques and Churches, aplenty. The capital city, Hyderabad has a deep-felt influence of Hinduism and Islamism. The state has patronised a variety of cultures and religion during different periods in history.

ARTS, CRAFTS & CULTURE

The state as a whole, has a rich and varied heritage of arts and culture. Fine arts and traditional arts have been revered and treasured from a very long past. During the hierarchical era, classical art performances were coveted with passion. And the zest has been passed on generations after generations and the 'classics' are of pristine flair among even the people of today. The art forms are indeed of a wide range.

'Saint Thyagaraja', an ardent devotee of Lord Sri Rama, has produced innumerable and invaluable compositions in Telugu, the regional language of the state. His composi-

*The uncrowned prince of Carnatic music is **Tyagaraja** (1767-1847). His kritis on Lord Sri Rama have been immortalized due to their inherent lyrical beauty and tender feelings. Training in Carnatic music is never complete without learning his kritis.*

tions are of eternal reverence as they have been sung and resung over the years and form the predominant source of 'bread and butter' to a number of artistes even today. They are an indispensable part of repertoire in any musical concert. There were also other composers whose works carry perpetual value. Even today many a big name in Carnatic music belongs to Andhra. Thus, the state has been repeatedly producing great personalities in different branches of Carnatic music.

When it comes to dance, Andhra has as many as nine distinct varieties unique to its culture. Each of these varieties (viz) Veeranatyam, Butta Bommalu, Dappu, Chindu Bhagawatham, Thappetta Gullu, Lambadi, Bonalu, Dhimsa and Kuchipudi, recounts an impressive legend or a conventional belief behind its evolution. However, all of them are aimed at devotion to God and experiencing the eternal bliss.

Taking a look at the expressions, gestures and other customary movements involved in the art performances of the region, one gets a picture of the meticulous care and prudent thought that has gone into their invention or evolution. Every bit of the dance portrays one or more events or episodes from the Holy Puranas or the great epics, aptly supported by folk, traditional or classical music, coupled with pertinent, profound percussion beats and holds the audience in rapt attention.

'**Veeranatyam**' a wonderful form of dance, very famous at Draksharamam which is where Lord Siva, according to a legend, created Lord Veerabadra out of a hair from His Jata Jhuta, the Holy lock of hair on His head, brings out the outrage of Lord Siva at the humiliation meted out to Goddess Sati Devi, His divine consort, by 'Daksha' who was the father of the Goddess during Her human sojourn. This seething dance form was first rendered by Lord Veerabadra and practised by the community known as 'Veeramusti' which is supposed to be the descendent of Lord Veerabadra.

'**Butta Bommalu**' is a dance with a touch of folk charm. Hidden in the masks lavishly made out of wood-husk, straw, and cowdung are deft performers who fill the air with the charms of folk lore. A literal translation of 'Butta Bommalu' is 'Basket Toys' and that explains the masquerading of the dancers like gigantic toys.

'**Dappu**', a percussion instrument rightly enhances the spirit of the dancers and the audience alike. It is an indispensable part of many a festival, wedding and dance.

'**Chindu Bhagawatham**' originates from the Nizamabad district. Bright colours and beautiful costumes flash as the dancers display mythological themes with meticulous movements. Musical instruments like Cymbals, Tabla and Harmonium have a vital role to play.

'**Thappetta Gullu**', a dance that showers grace with its typical folklore to please 'Varuna' the 'Rain God' and receive showers from the Heavens, is famous in Srikakulam and Vijayanagaram districts.

'**Lambadi**', the dance that must have seen most places since it is the art form of the nomads, enunciates the agrarian chores. Glossy glass beads, tiny square and circular mirrors, ornate jewellery, ivory bangles and brass ankles emblazon the costumes of the dancers.

'**Bonalu**', the folk dance which involves the knack of balancing pots on the head while performing unrestricted movements is an inspiring sight at 'Mahakali' temples. The female performers, colourfully clad, dance their way to the temple followed by men dancers with entwined Margosa leaves tied around their waists. Men lash long whips while making rhythmic movements, according to the reverberating percussion beats.

'**Dhimsa**' is a dance of the 'Hill Tribes'. This dance is performed by women clad in typical tribal costumes. Instruments like Mori, Thudumba and Dappu add music and rhythm to the delightful sylvan dance.

'**Kuchipudi**', the famous traditional dance which originated in the village of 'Kuchelapau' or 'Kuchelapuram' is an ancient classical art which can be traced back to the 3rd century BC. Since its origin, this treasured art has apparently undergone quite a few modifications at the creative hands of several patrons all over the centuries and today it is presented as a dance drama with many characters. There is a unique way of introducing the characters. 'Daru' a short, introductory sequence of music and dance is first performed by the dancers to reveal their part. One of the spectacular features of this dance is that the dancers balancing a pot full of water on their heads, fix their feet on the rim of a brass plate and make awesome, intricate, movements pressing one foot down and rising the other in turns, swirling and bending all but without letting a drop of water out of the pot.

*The renowned **Kuchipudi dance couple**, Raja and Radha Reddy have travelled widely and brought recognition and fame to Kuchipudi dance from around the world.*

Now, Kuchipudi is being taught in many institutions and music colleges. There is a Government- run dance school proliferating the divine art among the multitude of dedicated aspirants, at the place Kuchipudi, 60 km from Vijayawada.

A Temple at Warangal.

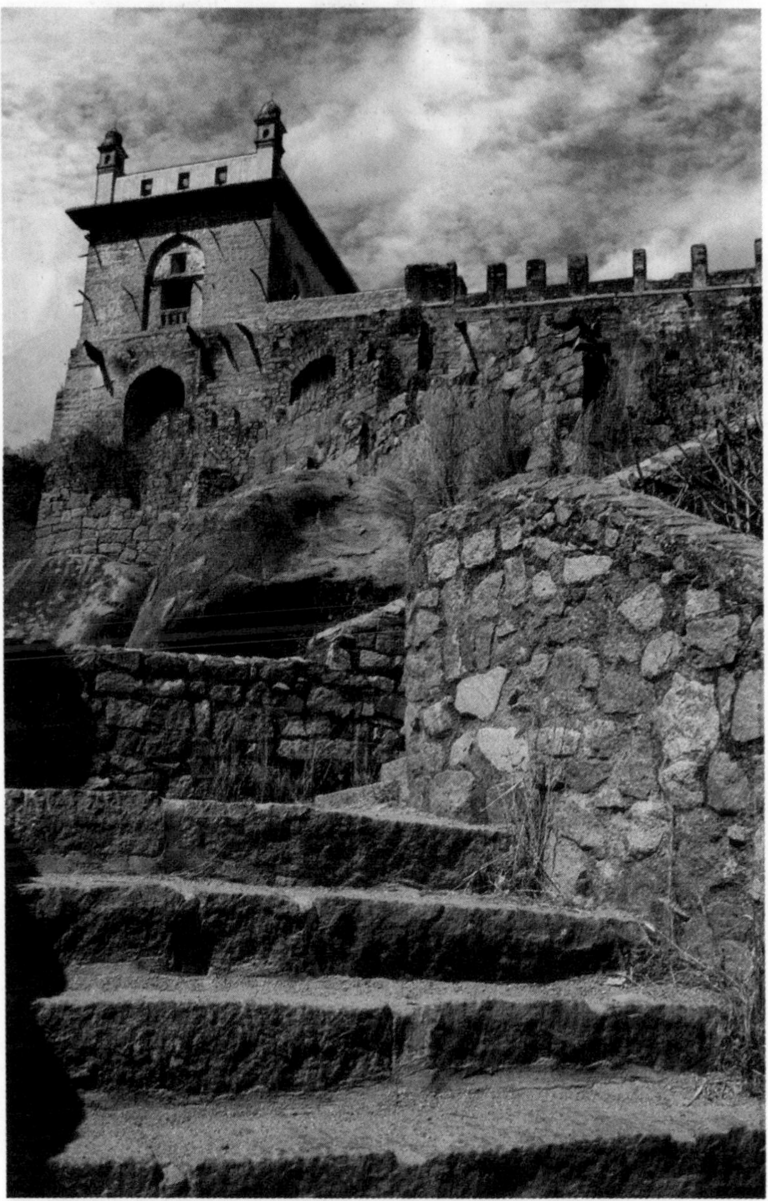

Golconda Fort, built by the Kakatiya rulers of Warangal in the 13th century. It was once famous for its flourishing trade in diamonds.

Narayanpet Sarees are very popular as traditional wedding sarees. It is known for its mixed or shot colours, which are predominantly purple with pink or maroon with mustard.

If the arts of Andhra are astonishing, the crafts are captivating. The crafts with a distinct lustre have been around for centuries. The ancient rulers have doted on the articles and have been the patrons, the crafts which produced them. Many of these crafts are still much in vogue today in the form of cottage industry. The crafty hands behind every creation is lucid.

The toys, dolls and puppets made out of wood decorate the shelves of many homes. Birds, animals, mythological characters, fruits, vegetables, etc., are among the wonderful creations. The puppets find use in shadow-shows in several festivals and children shows and they seem to do justice to themselves by conveying a sublime moral from mythical events, to a lot of fascinated young eyes.

'**Sculpture**', the art of giving life to lifeless rocks has reached great heights in the state since a long past. The ancient temples and palaces bear testimony to this fact. The astounding stone images are sculpted with meticulous care given to every minute detail. Sculpture and architecture has been cherished by a number of rulers of various dynasties, the evidence of which can be seen all over the state.

'**Folk Painting**' is another craft which has been handed down to generations after generations. It is believed to have originated from the divine architect Viswakarma who out of His mercy proffered the craft to the artists on Earth. The themes painted and also the forms are mostly mythological. Wall hangers carrying these paintings decorate many homes.

'**Nirmal Painting**' finds a predominant place in the series of crafts particularly in Adilabad district. This painting, generally depicts scenes from the great epics 'The Ramayana' and 'The Mahabharatha', however, birds, animals and also fictitious figures are no exceptions. The Moghuls have practiced the craft too. Moghul miniatures on Ponkiki wood are famous.

'**Bidri**', the handicraft which conflates silver on black metal articles has been relished by great emperors. Intricate patterns of breathtaking beauty are drawn on the black articles with shiny silver. The craft had influenced the Moghul rulers to the extent that they had all articles decorated by this craft. It is still a famous and a thriving cottage industry.

'**Bronze castings**' has also been one of the specialities of the splendid crafts of Andhra. Icons of various God-forms are made to an impeccable precision and beauty. Lord Nataraja, the dancing form of Lord Siva is one of the masterpieces of this craft.

Thus, the state has varied interests and rich heritage. A panoramic view of the state may baffle the onlooker with every part of it trying to make its rival null and void in every aspect of composure. Hence, tourism is a brisk activity in Andhra Pradesh.

FESTIVALS

Andhra has no paucity of festivals. Hindu festivals like Dasara, Deepavali, Sri Rama Navami, Sri Krishna Jayanthi, Maha Sivarathri, Vinayaka Chathurthi etc., are celebrated with a fabulous festive fervour. There are also certain festivals exclusive to certain temples and regions like the festival '*Bathkamma*' which is celebrated in 'Telangana'. Among the Muslim festivals are *Ramadan*, *Bakrid* and *Id-ul-Fitr* which are celebrated with much gaiety. The Christians have their share of the 'festive cake' during *Christmas*, *Easter* and of course the *New Year* which is in fact relished by everyone throughout the world irrespective of caste, creed, religion or nationality.

Sankaranthi and *Ugadi* are two regional festivals which bring about bountiful mirth upon people, the former in January and the latter in March or April. Sankaranthi, an agrarian Hindu festival is marked by the worship of Sun God and Ugadi marks the beginning of New Year in the Telugu aboriginal calendar.

Lumbini festival is reminiscent of Buddhism having flourished in the region in a distant past.

Hyderabad

This is the capital of Andhra Pradesh and the fifth largest city in India. This cosmopolitan city has rail and road links with Chennai-Delhi, Chennai-Calcutta and Chennai-Mumbai railway lines. It can also be reached by air. Hyderabad and Secunderabad separated by not more than a mile in between, are rightly known as **twin cities**. The beautiful city with all its modern structures and facilities has not failed to retain its old charm. There are ancient monuments of historic importance. There are enough specimen to evince the influence of Medieval Indian, Saracenic Mughal and later the colonial English architecture.

The city also has ancient Mosques, palacial forts, magnificent palaces, placid lakes and picnic spots. The art galleries and public garden draw thousands of tourists. In Hyderabad, the Hindu, Islamic and Saracenic architecture fuse together to bring out a secular structure.

The mean temperature in summer is around 22°C while it soars up to a maximum of 40°C at times. The winter temperature hovers beween a minimum of 12°C and a maximum of 22°C.

'**Bidri**' and '**Kinkhab**', the traditional handicrafts are still cherished in Hyderabad. '*Bidri*' is the art which adorns black metal articles with silver designs which leads to striking comparisons with a dark night sky being ripped apart by sparkling streaks of lightning. The Bidri style of decorations found on Moghuls' weapons evince how much they doted on the art. *Kinkhab* is an equally intricate art which decorates silk garments with gold and silver embroidery.

In and Around Hyderabad

Charminar: This marvellous edifice was built in 1591 by Muhammad Quli Qutub Shah and is located in the heart of the old city. The visitors here simply get carried away by the splendid architecture and grand construction. The roof supports a small Mosque. '*Charminar*', with its four famous minarets is the favourite subject of many portraits and wall hangers.

Mahavir Harin Vanashali: About 9 km on the Hyderabad- Vijayawada route, this exciting wildlife sanctuary and the deer park attract a number of visitors.

Hussain Sagar Lake: This beautiful lake dates back to the days of Qutub Shahi. Along the bund of the lake, stand 33 life-size statues of eminent personalities, which were erected as part of Buddha Poornima Project and on the 'Rock of Gibraltar' in the middle of the beautiful lake, a gigantic statue of the Lord Buddha, a massive monolithic structure of 18 m height and 350 tonne weight has also been erected.

Birla Mandir: Overseeing the placid waters of the scenic lake

Hussain Sagar, this wonderful structure of worship has been raised with the impeccable white marbles of Rajasthan. This shrine dedicated to Lord Venkateswara, the presiding deity of the temple at Thirumala-Thirupathi has in its construction an inspiring combination of the traditional architecture of the north and south. The beautiful carvings, splendid sculpture and the ornate workmanship are par excellence. There are also idols of other deities, all made of marvellous marble in the lush green gardens with capricious blossoms caressed by gentle breeze. When illuminated at night it is an amazing sight. As it is situated atop a picturesque hill, it offers an overwhelming panoramic view of the twin cities of Hyderabad and Secunderabad.

Visiting Hours: 07:00 - 12:00 hrs & 15:00 - 21:00 hrs.

Ghandipet: '*Osmansagar Dam*', here, built across the beautiful river 'Musi' about 55 years ago with excellent gardens and serene waters is an ideal picnic spot situated about 18 km from Hyderabad. The gardens carefully laid with alluring lawns, plants bearing bright, beautiful flowers and comfortable rest houses to relax promise tourists of a delightful time. The children in particular, have a lot to relish. The placid reservoir created by the beautiful dam is the source of drinking water to the twin cities of Hyderabad and Secunderabad which are about 18 to 20 km away.

Azakhana - E - Zohra, which is visible from the north bank of the river Musi, in a beautiful white building with green tombs built in the year 1930 by the last Nizam. It is also known as Madre-E-Deccan or Mother of Deccan Ashurkhana. The ceilings and inner walls are enamel coated.

Nizamsagar: About 144 km on the north-west of Hyderabad, the resplendent reservoir, Nizamsagar formed by the magnificent dam across the ravishing river 'Manjira' which is one of the tributaries of the glorious river Godavari, makes it a sought-after picnic spot. The road across the huge dam is 14 ft in width and offers an exhilarating view of the sumptuous surroundings. Comfortable accommodation facilities are available at the site.

Basar: The temple here is one of the two famous ones dedicated to Goddess Saraswathi, the Goddess for 'Arts and Learning' and the consort of Lord Brahma, the creator of the Universe. The other Saraswathi Temple can be seen in Kashmir.

The legend has it that the Sage Vyasa used to collect three handfuls of the river sand after his usual bath in the sacred river Godavari as part of his everyday routine. The sand thus accumulated turned into the images of Goddess Saraswathi, Goddess Lakshmi and Goddess Kali. 'Brahmapuranam' puts forth that 'Adikavi Valmiki' installed the presiding deity here and it was here, he wrote the great epic 'The Ramayana'.

The image of the Sage Valmiki and his 'Samadhi' can be seen near the temple which according to a belief is one of the three temples built by the Rashtrakutas near the confluence of the sacred rivers Manjira and Godavari. Contrary to this, another belief exists, by which this temple had been built by a Karnataka King by name 'Bijialudu' who ruled the province of Nandagiri with Nanded as his capital. In the Sanctum Sanctorum, the image of Goddess Lakshmi can be seen besides Goddess Saraswathi.

Since this place is graced by Goddess Saraswathi, the Goddess for Arts and Learning, Goddess Lakshmi, the Goddess for Wealth and Goddess Kali, the Goddess for Bravery, Basar is revered as the Holy abode of divine Trinity where the devotees are blessed with all the three vital traits.

Amber Khana: This is a huge granary built in the year 1642. Sufficient stocks of foodgrains were stored here to feed the people inside the safe walls of the fort during the siege laid by the Moghuls. It is situated near Ramdas Jail.

Ashurkhana: 'Ashurkhana', the mourning house used during Moharrum, with its middle section destroyed and the surrounding rooms and corridors with carved stone trays which evince the ancient glory of the whole structure, stands facing the Safa Mosque. It also houses beautiful wooden incense stands and some other artifacts.

Badshahi Ashurkhana: This complex comprises wide halls *ad hoc* for the 'Shia' sect of Muslims, where they assemble during Moharrum and mourn in reverence to the martyrdom of Hazrat Imam Hussain who played an important role in the Karbala battle. This structure, the oldest of its kind in Hyderabad, dates back to 1596. The inner wall was built by Muhammad Quli Qutub Shah and the outer hall by Asif Jah II. The building was beautified during the rule of Sultan Muhammad with some beautiful enamel tiles. This building remains open only on Thursdays.

Accommodation

Hyderabad (STD Code : 040)

- **Ayodhya** 11-5-427, Lakdi-Ka-Pool, Hyderabad - 500 004 ✆: 3393420
- **Badam Balakrishna** 6-1-1081, Lakdi-Ka-Pool, Hyderabad - 500 004 ✆: 3221652
- **Comfort Inn Wood Bridge** AC Guards, Lakdi-Ka-Pool, Hyderabad - 500 034. ✆: 3395441
- **Minerva** 3-6-199/1, Himayatnagar, Hyderabad - 500 029. ✆: 3220448
- **Sri Brindavan** Nampalli Station Road, Hyderabad - 500 001. ✆: 3203970
- **Pearl Regency** 11-5-431, Red Hills, Lakdi-Ka-Pool, Hyderabad - 500 004. ✆: 6666555.
- **Suprabhat** Opp. Venkataramana Theatre, 3-3-50, Kachiguda, Hyderabad. ✆: 4652011
- **Hotel Amrutha Castle Best Western**, (4 Star), 5-9-16, Opp. Secretariat, Saifabad, Hyderabad-63. ✆: 55633888 Fax: 55828222
- **Taj Residency**, Road No. 1, Banjara hills, Hyderabad-34. ✆: 3393939 Fax: 3392684 Email: trhbcentre.hyd@tajhotels.com
- **The Royal** 5-8-225, Nampalli, Hyderabad - 500001. ✆: 3201020
- **The Krishna Oberoi (5 Star)** Road No. 1, Banjara Hills, Hyderabad - 500 034. ✆: 3392323, Fax: 3393079
- **Welcomgroup Grand Kakatiya Hotel & Towers (5 Star)** 6-3-1187, Begumpet, Hyderabad - 500016. ✆: 3300132, Fax: 3401045 E-mail: kakatiya@ welcomegroup.com
- **Holiday Inn Krishna (5 Star)** Road No. 1, Banjara Hills, Hyderabad - 500 034. ✆: 3393939, Fax: 3392684 E-mail: hilk@hyd@rml. sprintrpg.ems.vsnl.net.in
- **Taj Banjara (5 Star)** Road No. 1, Banjara Hills, Hyderabad - 500 034. ✆: 3399999, Fax: 3392218 E-mail: tbhresv.hyd@tajhotels.com
- **Hotel Bhaskar Palace (4 Star)** 6-3-248/2, Road No. 1, Banjara Hills, Hyderabad - 500 034. ✆: 3301523, Fax: 3304036
- **Ramada Hotel Manohar (5 Star)** Adjacent to Airport Exit Road, Begumpet, Hyderabad-500016. ✆: 7903333, Fax: 7902222
- **Green Park (4 Star)** Greenlands, Begumpet, Hyderabad - 500 016. ✆: 3757575 Fax: 3757677 E-mail: hyd@hotelgreenpark.com
- **Hotel Ashoka (3 Star)** 6-1-70, Lakdi-Ka-Pool Hyderabad - 500 004. ✆: 230105, Fax: 230105
- **Hotel Golkonda (3 Star)** 10-1-124, Masab Tank, Near Banjara Hills, Hyderabad - 500 028. ✆: 3320202, Fax: 3320404 E-mail: golkonda@ nettlinx.com
- **Ohri's Cuisine Court (3 Star)** 5-9-30/16 to 20, Basheerbagh, Hyderabad - 500 029. ✆: 3298811 E-mail: baseraa@hd2.vsnl. net.in
- **The Central Court Hotel (3 Star)** 6-1-71, Lakdi-Ka-Pool, Hyderabad - 500 004. ✆: 3233262, Fax: 3232737 E-mail: cencourt@hd2.dot.net.in
- **The Residency (3 Star)** 5-8-231/2, Public Garden Road, Hyderabad - 500 001. ✆: 3204060 (18 lines) Fax: 3204040 E-mail: tres.hot@gmyd. tres.globalet.ems.vsnl.net.in

• **Hotel Nagarjuna** 3-6-356/358, Basheer Bagh, Hyderabad - 500 029. ✆: 3220204 (6 lines) Fax: 3372427 E-mail: redd_y@satyam.net.in

• **Hotel Dwaraka Palace** Raj Bhavan Road, Lakdi-Ka-Pool, Hyderabad - 500 004. ✆: 3237921 (10 lines) Fax: 3211900

• **Hotel Jaya International** P.O. Box 264, Abids, Hyderabad - 500 001. ✆: 4752929, 4757484 Fax: 4753919

• **Hotel Krystal** 5-9-24/82, Lake Hills Road, Near New M.L.A. QMS, Hyderabad - 500 463. ✆: 3229874, Fax: 3227877

• **Hotel Sarovar** 5-9-22, Secretariat Road, Hyderabad-500063. ✆: 237299/638/640-42/648

• **Kamat Lingapur Hotel**, 1-10-44/2, Chikoti Gardens, Begumpet, Hyderabad-16. ✆: 7764242 Fax: 040-7765151 Email: kamat_lingapur@hotmail.com

• **Quality Inn Residency**, 5-8-231/262, Public Garden Road, Nampally, Hyderabad-1. ✆: 6514060, 3204060, 3204080 Fax: 040-3204040 Email: reservations@theresidency-hyd.com; pliple@giasdl01.vsnl.net.in

• **Tajmahal Hotel**, 4-1-1000, Kingkothi Road, Hyderabad-500 001. ✆: 4758221 Fax: 040-4760068

• **Hotel Rajmata** 5-8-230, Nampally, Hyderabad - 500 001. ✆: 3201000, 3203222 Fax: 3204133

• **Blue Moon Hotel** 6-3-1186/A, Rajbhavan Road, Begumpet, Hyderabad - 500 016. ✆: 3312815 Fax: 3321700

• **Hotel Rajdhani** 15-1-503, Siddiamber Bazaar, Hyderabad - 500 012. ✆: 4740650 (11 lines)

• **Hotel Sangeetha International** Panjagutta "x" Roads, Above Shanbagh Hotel, Hyderabad - 500482. ✆: 6622142

• **Hotel Dwaraka Deluxe** Lakdi-Ka-Pool, Hyderabad - 500 004. ✆: 3297392, 242444 E-mail:dwaraka@hotmail.com

• **Neo Hotel Haridwar** 4-6-465, Esamiya Bazaar, Hyderabad - 500 027. ✆: 4656711/18 Fax: 4732780

• **Shree Venkateswara Lodge** 6-1-74, Lakdi-Ka-Pool, Hyderabad - 500 004. ✆: 3236871 (15 lines) Fax: 235914

• **The Royal Hotel** 5-8-225, Opp. Nampally Railway Station, Hyderabad-1. ✆: 3201020, 3201021

• **Viceroy** Opp. Hussain Sagar Lake, Tankbund Road, Hyderabad-80. ✆: 7538383 Fax: 7538797 E-mail: viceroy@hdl.vsnl.net.in

Secunderabad

This city is situated about 10 km on the east of its 'twin' city Hyderabad. The road on the bund of the beautiful Hussain Sagar lake connects the two cities. The vast parade ground, race course and polo ground signify the importance the city has enjoyed in the past. The British had one of their largest military establishments here. An observatory and the Saifabad Palace are situated on the east of Hussain Sagar lake. The Rashtrapathi Nilayam at Bolarum serves as the living quarters of the President whenever the president visits the place.

There is a number of historic monuments around the city, far and near. The famous Osmania University with a number of cottages in its campus, near here, produces a number of brain-thrusts every year.

In and Around Secunderabad

Mecca Masjid: Not longer than just a 100 yards of the ever-charming charminar there is yet another structure of grandness and beauty. As the name suggests, this Masjid resembles the grand one at Mecca. The sacred hall measures 67 m and 54 m in length and breadth and 23 m in height. One and a quarter dozen beautiful arches which support the roof, a massive wall, the two huge octagonal columns made out of a single granite piece, the beautiful gallery under a dome and the interior and exterior designs add elegance to the spacious grand Mosque which can hold upto ten thousand devotees at a time and which is considered to be one of the largest Mosques in India.

Golconda Fort: This marvellous monument, which is situated about 11 km from the city, has been left behind by the 'Kakatiyas' of the 13th century. Golconda was also the capital of the Qutub Shahis of the 16th century. The place has emerged over the years as a popular centre of diamond trade.

On the south-east of the fort, 'Musa Burj' is where stands the huge historic cannon, known as the *Azhdaha Paikar* cannon. It was among the ammunitions of the emperor Aurangzeb who made an effective use of it during the siege of Golconda way back in 1687. This cannon identical to the one known as the Fateh Rahbar cannon, on the north-west of Golconda Fort was capable of firing shots of 40 kgs in weight.

Qutub Shahi Tombs: About a kilometer from the fort, these beautiful tombs of Qutub Shahi rulers reflect the third and final stage of the 17th century architecture. These tombs are dome topped and have a square base surrounded by pointed arches. There are galleries of one storey and two stories in these tombs. The domes were originally overlaid with blue and green tiles of which only a few seem to have survived the test of time.

Visiting Hours: 09:30 - 16:30 hrs. (Closed on Fridays)

Salarjung Museum: This exciting Museum is named after the Prime Minister of the erstwhile Nizams, Salarjung III who constructed it. A number of ancient articles of arts and paintings of different parts of the world can be seen here. An exquisite room displays the paraphernalia of historic emperors like Aurangzeb, Tipu Sultan, Shah Jahan, Asaf Jahis, etc.

Visiting Hours: 10:00 - 17:00 hrs. (Closed on Fridays)

Paigah Tombs: Located at Santhosh Nagar, these tombs are made out of lime and mortar with beautiful inlaid marble carvings. These tombs are 200 years old.

Asman Garh Palace: This grand palace, named after its builder Sir Asman Jah, a noble from the Paigah family, who was also the Prime Minister of Hyderabad state, is located on a beautiful hillock. Granite structures and arched windows mark the grand structure.

Osmania University: The elegant arches and the foyers with Ellora paintings, the Damascus patterned huge gateway, the long corridors all add to the excellence of the edifice. Various colleges which contribute in leaps and bounds to the brain-thrust of the nation amidst tranquil gardens and a modern auditorium are situated within the campus.

Lumbini Park: This is a relatively new park in a historically old city. It offers excellent amusement crowned by a fascinating fountain show in which waters dance to the music.

Visiting Hours: 9:00 - 21:00 hrs. (Closed on Mondays)

Fountain Show: 18:30 - 20:00 hrs.

Falaknuma Palace: Italian architecture is reflected in this beautiful palace built by Sir Vikar Ul Umra. Nizam IV bought this wonderful palace in 1897. The palace has won international acclaim for its grandeur. This magnificent palace with its huge hall studded with precious stones, stands on a beautiful hill. Situated about 5 km from Charminar, this palace houses some rare treasures collected by the Nizam but it is not open to visitors.

Purani Haveli: This palace, situated in the old city, was the abode of sixth Nizam, 'Purani Haveli' stands for 'Old Mansion'. This palace is of 18th century European style in architecture. Certain old Western style furniture can be seen here. The marvellous wardrobe made of wood built by Mir Mahboob Ali is probably the longest of its kind in the world. It measures to 240 ft in length. Nawab Mukkaram Jah Bahadur donated this palace to Mukkaram Jah Trust in 1971 for educational purposes.

Raymond's Tomb: This tomb of Michael Raymond, a French mercenary who served as a commander in the military of the second Nizam, is situated at Saroornagar in East Hyderabad.

Nehru Zoological Park: Named after the first Prime Minister of India, Pandit Sri Jawaharlal Nehru, this fascinating area spreads over 300 acres and is rated among the largest ones in Asia. A wide variety of captivating bird and animal species, over 300 at a rough estimate, roam about in the park. The lion safari which offers the opportunity to the eager tourists to come face to face with the majestic kings of the jungle, is a special attraction.

The 'nocturnal zoo' an exclusive entity which minds the upkeep of those creatures which are naturally adapted to remain active at nights and retire during the daytime, is one of the salient features here. A special lighting system which simulates a bright moon enables the visitors to catch a glimpse of the exciting nocturnal creatures in the day. Rare and interesting creatures can be seen in the 'Natural History Museum'.

Large parks with exhilarating recreation facilities, beautiful gardens, pleasure rides on mini-train all enhance the fun and cheer.

Visiting Hours: 09:00 - 17:00 hrs. (Closed on Mondays)

Public Gardens: Situated in the city-centre and formerly known as Bagh-e-aam; the public gardens is a conscientiously carved verdant area with some important buildings like the State Legislature, Assembly, the Jubilee Hall, the Jawahar Bal Bhavan, the open-air theatre known as 'Lalita Kala Toranam', the archaeological Museum and the Health Museum.

The 'State Museum' here houses rare artefacts, sculptures, ancient inscriptions, old age coins, a host of armoury and traditional crafts such as Bidri articles, old Chinaware and textiles.

The offices of two Hindu nobles who served under Tanah Shah can be seen above the guard lines. Two huge iron weights in these buildings sprout from the sand. The purpose they served, whether they were intended to remain exactly in the way they are and things like that continue to be an enigma.

B.M. Birla Planetarium/Science Museum: This exciting Planetarium equipped with most advanced technologies takes the visitors to new heights of amusement and amazement. It offers the viewers a considerable part of the mysterious universe in a 'nutshell'. It opens up vistas in Astronomy. The show glues the spellbound viewers to their seats.

The 'Science Museum' displays various fathomless facets of science. It inculcates a flair for science in young minds. And it inspires the young and old alike.

Visiting Hours:

Planetarium: 10:30 - 15:00 hrs. (Closed on the last Thursday of every month)

Science Museum: 10:30 - 20:15 hrs. (Closed on the last Thursday of every month)

Accommodation

Secunderabad (STD Code : 040)

- **Hotel Heritage** 116, Chenoy Trade Centre, Park Lane, Secunderabad - 500 003. ✆: 7845020, Fax: 7841455 E-mail: tauras@hd1.vsnl.net.in
- **Asrani International Hotel (3 Star)** 1-7-179, M. G. Road, Secunderabad - 500 003. ✆: 7842267/68, 7846401 Fax: 7846903
- **Belsons Tajmahal Hotel,** 82, Mainguard Road, Secunderabad - 500 003. ✆: 7810810 (8 lines) Fax: 040-7810817
- **Hotel Baseraa (3 Star)** 9-1-167/168, S.D. Road, Secunderabad-500 003. ✆:7703200, Fax: 7704745
- **Silver Plate Hotel,** 1-7-194/195, S.D. Road, Secunderabad - 500 016. ✆: 7840019
- **Hotel Dwarka Heritage,** 116, Chenoy Trade Centre, Park Lane, Secunderabad - 500 003. ✆: 7845020 Fax: 7841455
- **Hotel Deccan Continental (3 Star),** Minister Road, Secunderabad - 500 003. ✆: 7845020 (9 lines) Fax: 7841455
- **Hotel Parklane** 115, Park Lane, Secunderabad - 500 003. ✆: 7840466
- **Hotel Ambassador** 1-7-27, S.D. Road, Secunderabad-500 003. ✆ 7843760 Fax: 7899095
- **Hotel Karan** 1-2-261/1, S.D. Road, Secunderabad-500 003. ✆: 7840191 (10 lines) Fax: 7848343

Chittoor

This district abounds in ancient temples with astounding architecture and hence has a number of pilgrim centres. The famous 'Sri Venkateswara Temple' here, attracts millions of devotees all through the year from far and wide. This temple receives the maximum pecuniary offerings, of all the worship centres in the world. The origin of this ancient temple is still a moot point among archaeologists and the religious heads. The Lord here has been worshipped by a number of rulers, saints and monks in the long past. The vast environs of the temple and the 'Seven Hills' of sublime beauty are considered sacred. There are also countless number of ancient temples in and around Thirupathi. At 'Alamelu-mangapuram', a marvellous temple is dedicated to Goddess Padmavathi, the consort of 'Lord Venkateswara'. The Siva temple at Kalahasthi, also an ancient one, is one of the five exclusive group of Temples known as the 'Panchaboothakshethra'. Nagalapuram and Narayanavanam have ancient temples too and interesting legends. The antique temples at Ramagiri, set in a scenic sylvan location recount interesting legends. The temple tank here is watered by a perennial spring which caters to drinking water and agrarian needs.

The Vijayanagar influence is largely felt in the district. The massive fort at Chandragiri believed to have been built in 1000 AD has been renovated by the later Vijanagar rulers.

There are also exciting picnic spots. The Kalyani Dam, one such spot, located about 18 km from Thirupathi regulates the drinking water supply to the town of Thirupathi. Horsley Hills is a cool resort in the hot seasons. Graced by benevolent ambience and picturesque scenery of this hill forms part of the mighty 'Eastern Ghats'. This place has been in the focus of tourism ever since it was discovered in 1870 and named after its discoverer W.D. Horsley. The Gurrumkonda Hills is also an enchanting hill resort.

Sri Venkateswara Swamy Temple: This famous ancient temple dedicated to 'Lord Venkateswara' also faithfully adored by other names as 'Venkatesa', Balaji', 'Venkataramana', 'Govinda', 'Srinivasa' and so on is ideally situated on the top of a cluster of seven sacred hills reverentially personified as the seven mammoth hoods of the mythical serpent 'Adisesha' whose numerous coils represent the limitless 'Time' as a cosmic concept. 'Lord Venkateswara,' the presiding deity here is one of the various forms of 'Lord Vishnu', the protector of the Universe, who reposes on the body of 'Adisesha'.

The exact date of the construction of the ancient temple is yet to be discerned. However, history cites the town of Thirupathi to have come into existence in the 12th century. The temple with excellent architecture has been worshipped by several heroes of the Pallava, Chola, Pandya and Vijayanagar dynasties and later by the rulers of Mysore. The Vimanam or the dome over the Sanctum-Sanctorum and the Dwajasthambam are completely gold plated. The temple at an altitude of about 853 m above sea level with its picturesque environs and tranquil ambience is indisputably a Heaven on Earth. The temple can be reached both by vehicle and on foot from Thirupathi. The foot path is 15 km long with a flight of rock cut steps.

This Holy place has repeatedly been visited by a number of saints, monks, religious reformers and the like in the long history.

There are references to this temple in the ancient literary works of Tamil.

Anointing the deity with camphor and the devotees having their head tonsured are two important traditional customs here. The Brahmotsavam is a grand annual festival marked by a series of poojas and rites and the arrival of 'Thirupathi Kodai' or the 'Sacred Umbrella' from numerous temples hundreds of kilometers away.

Another ancient temple dedicated to 'Lord Varahaswamy' who is again a variation of 'Lord Vishnu', is situated along the 'Temple Tank' called 'Pushkarani'. Legend has it that the entire region of Thirupathi is owned by Lord Varahaswami who at the request of Lord Venkateswara had accommodated him in the place. Hence, the 'Neivedyam', the customary feeding of the Lord, is performed at this temple first as also a few other rites, before being performed at the Venkateswaraswamy temple. A belief rules that all devotees willing to worship Lord Venkateswara ought to worship Lord Varahaswamy first since it had been so arranged between the deities in the Mythical era.

The 'Thirumala Thirupathi Devasthanam' which is responsible for the maintenance of this temple and a lot others offers 'Prasada' or free meals at their canteen here. TTD also has a branch at Venkatanarayana Road, T.Nagar, Chennai where an idol of Venkateswaraswamy resembling the one at Thirumala has been installed. The 'Laddu Prasadam', a sweet at the Thirumala Temple is much sought-after.

It is a very popular pilgrim centre and the number of devotees taking on a pilgrimage on foot from various spots, miles and miles away, with strict austerity, is constantly on the rise.

There are also other interesting places in the proximity. The ravishing waterfalls at Papanasam is just 8 km away. The beautiful park about 4 km from the temple is a favourite hang-out to many.

Alamelumangapuram Temple: This ancient temple is situated about 10 km from Thirupathi. The presiding deity here, Goddess Alamelumanga is the consort of Lord Venkateswara. This temple holds a grand architecture.

Govindaraja Perumal Temple: This temple dedicated to Lord Govindaraja who is a variation of 'Lord Vishnu' is situated right in the heart of the city.

This huge temple is rich in ancient architecture.

Kapila Theertham: Situated about 2 km from 'Alipiri', the point where the flight of steps to Thirumala starts, this is a sacred Tank beneath an elevated rock on which stands a temple dedicated to Lord Siva.

Chandragiri: It is situated about 11 km from Thirupathi and rose to prominence in the twilight days of the Vijayanagar Empire. The fort here is believed to have been built in 1000 AD and modified by the later Vijayanagar kings. This magnificent fort stands on a massive rock which is about 182 m above its surroundings.

The fort encompasses the remains of age-old palaces and temples which had once been the royal abode of kings and places of regular worship. The two huge buildings known as 'Mahals' near the fort were of multiple use to the royal family.

Kalahasthi: Situated about 40 km from Thirupathi this ancient wonderful temple is one of the five exclusive group of temples known as 'Panchaboothakshethra' dedicated to Lord Siva. 'Panchabootha' means 'The Five Elements of Nature' and 'Kshetra' means 'Place' and hence each of the five exclusive temples signify one of the 'Five Elements of Nature' (Viz) Earth, Space, Wind, Fire and Water. As this temple is the 'Vayukshetra', the place of wind, Lord Siva manifests as the 'God of Wind'.

It is believed, the Siva Linga here was worshipped by a spider by spinning a web over it, a snake by placing upon the Lingam a gem as an offering and an elephant by bathing the Lingam with water from its trunk. And worshipping the Lord here relieves people of difficulties during the periods of the Zodiac Aquarius and Pisces.

Narayanavanam: About 43 km from Thirupathi, this ancient temple where the presiding deity Lord Kalyana Venkateswara is again one of the variations of Lord Vishnu is situated in the region where the divine marriage of Lord Venkateswara, the presiding deity of the Thirumala temple with 'Goddess Padmavathi', the presiding deity of the Alamelumangapuram temple is believed to have taken place.

Nagalapuram: It is situated about 65 km from Thirupathi. The ancient temple here built by Krishna Devaraya and his mother Nagamba is dedicated to 'Lord Vedanarayana', one of the variations of Lord Vishnu. The temple bears testimony to the wayward development of a grand architecture in the olden days, since, apart from other wonderful features, it has been designed in such a way that Sun's rays fall on the Holy feet, navel and the forehead of the deity in turns as the day progresses during the day and only on the day of 'Surya Pooja', the famous grand annual festival.

Ramagiri: This beautiful place about 5 km from Nagalapuram and roughly the same distance from Pichattoor has a long and interesting legend associated with it. Picturesque mountains and sylvan scenery add beauty to the place while two ancient temples, one at the foot and the other on the top of a scenic hillock add sanctity to it. This sacred place is also known as 'Bhairava Kshethra', the 'Abode of Bhairava' as the presiding deity of the hill-foot temple is 'Lord Kalabhairava', one of the various forms of 'Lord Siva' in which the Lord assumes the role of commander of

The hill-top temple is dedicated to 'Lord Muruga', the son of the divine couple Lord Siva and Goddess Parvathi and the brother of 'Lord Ganesa', the principal deity in the Elephant- head and Human-body form.

The legend has it that while Lord Anjaneya on an errand bid by Lord Rama was making His way by air to Rameswaram with a Siva Linga taken from Kasi to be installed there carefully placed on His mighty shoulders. He was surprisingly confronted by strange and dry weather with the Sun scorching like never before and the wind blowing against and trying to emulate the air-borne Lord. But this was after all premeditated and perfectly organised by Lord Kalabhairava, the Lord of the land who wanted the Linga to be installed right here at His place. Unaware of this and driven by thirst, Lord Anjaneya went on screening the whole area for water until finally a beautiful calm cool pond caught His sight. As the Linga was not to be placed anywhere before Rameswaram, He looked for someone to keep the Linga while He drank water. 'Lord Kalabhairava', in the form of a small boy, at the request of 'Lord Anjaneya' consented to hold the Linga but only for a short length of time, inconspicuously intended to be shorter than the time in which Lord Anjaneya could get back.

Not a wink later than the stipulated time elapsed did the boy place the Linga down and was no show any longer. Anguished at the boy's carelessness, Lord Anjaneya rushed back and tried to lift the Linga but in vain. After several futile attempts He coiled the Linga with His mighty tail and pulled as hard as he could to which the Linga responded with nothing more than a slight inclination. Then Lord Kalabhairava appeared and expounded to Lord Anjaneya the realities behind the screen.

The Linga here can be seen slightly inclined with horizontal marks around, left by the tail of Lord Anjaneya. The temple tank here with curative powers is watered by a perennial sweet water spring which has fount oblivious in the mountains above. The waters flow into the sacred tank through the mouth of the Holy Bull-mount of Lord Siva, 'Nandi' sculpted beautifully on the side wall of the tank about a foot above the water level which is maintained a constant by the continuous inflow and outflow of the spring waters which replenish the tank with outbreak. The spring water is used for drinking and the water flowing out of the tank is used for irrigation in and around the place.

There are busses to Ramagiri from Uthukottai and Pichattoor which are enroute to Thirupathi from Chennai.

Suruttappalli: About 2 km from Uthukottai, near the Andhra Pradesh-Tamil Nadu border and 12 km from Nagalapuram, the ancient temple on the banks of the sizzling Arani river, dedicated to Lord Siva, has a unique feature.

In almost all South Indian temples dedicated to Lord Siva, the Lord is seen in His usual Linga form whereas here at Suruttappalli He manifests in a majestic human form in a reposing posture in His right, mighty, merciful palm. A crown is also seen on His head. Goddess Parvathi, the consort of Lord Siva and other deities are also seen in the 'Sanctum-Sanctorum'.

The legend states that Lord Siva here, took a brief rest after consuming the deluge of deadly poison that emerged from the ocean while it was churned for Amurdha, in order to save the living beings on the whole of Earth, who would otherwise have been killed by the poison.

It is said that this is the only temple all over India where Lord Siva can be seen in this form and in this posture. This historic unique temple is also rich in architecture and comes under the maintenance of the 'Thirumala Thirupathi Devasthanam'.

Kalyani Dam: About 18 km from Thirupathi, this beautiful dam regulates the outflow of sizzling waters from the resplendent reservoir which takes care of the drinking water supply of the town Thirupathi.

Kailasanadhakona: About 43 km from Thirupathi, an off-shoot from the main road between Puthur and Vadamalpet leads to this picturesque section of the magnificent Nagiri hills, with a ravishing waterfalls which courses along the huge mountains inheriting all the wholesome goodness of minerals and enrichments the mighty mountains offer. Hence, this water is believed to have curative properties. This place is rapidly developing into a picnic spot.

Horsley Hills: If some one visiting Thirupathi in the hot season is looking for a respite from the scorching sun, here is one. This beautiful summer resort which had been camouflaged until W.D. Horsley discovered it in 1870 is situated along the mighty ranges of eastern ghats, about 150 km from Thirupathi by road via Madanapalle. The last stretch of 10 km, making a difference of 746 m in height between the point and the base, gives an idea of how steep it is, even before one gets there. The beautiful hills reaching about 1265 m above sea level form the most elevated table land is south Andhra Pradesh. Here, in this resort, the houses constructed by its discoverer W.D. Horsley, a European civil servant, have stood the test of time for more than a hundred years now.

The mighty hills and the sylvan surroundings here are full of calm and charm. Cool mountain wind graces the region. The groves of teak, red sandalwood, eucalyptus, gulmohar and many other precious produces of the mountains spread gleefully over vast areas of the region. Huge rocks spring up sporadically amidst vast verdant expanse of vegetation. One might probably forget to wink, while looking at the hills in their changing hues and the large fantastically shapped boulder perching precariously on their sides. The summit gives a grand view of the low country around. The climate is delightful and bracing, the temperature being 18°C cooler than the plains below. As the evenings are quite chill, it would be a wise idea to carry warm garments along.

There is also an interesting legend associated with the place. This hill was originally called Enugu Mallamma Konda since a saintly lady called Mallamma who was protected and fed by an Elephant lived on the hill. 'Enugu' stands for 'elephant' and hence the name to the place.

Tourists can also visit Horsley's Bungalow and a nearby eucalyptus tree, believed to be more than 100 years old.

There are two vantage points to view the beauties of the landscape lying below. There is also a sericulture centre with numerous birds and a variety of blossoms and three small but sumptuous gardens to add to the mirth.

The nearest railway station Madanapalle is about 40 km and the town is 27 km away. However, this hill resort has road links with Bangalore, Madanapalle, Chennai and Thirupathi. The nearest airport is at Thirupathi while some prefer the Bangalore airport for convenience.

The Rishi Valley School: In the extensive surroundings of the exciting Horsley Hills, about 16 km from Madanapalle, this school is run by American Management on public school lines.

Madanapalle: This place is known for its sublime climate all through the year. This has been an educational and cultural centre since the days of the ever remembered Dr. Annie Besant. The Government Hospital, M.L.L. Hospital and Rajkumari Amrut Kaur, T.B. Research Centre, here carry on with their untiring services to the people.

Gurramkonda: About 17 km from the exciting Horsley Hills and 32 km from Madanapalle on way to Cuddapah, this, yet another historic hill is often confused with Horsley Hills. The English for 'Gurram' is Horse and 'Konda' is Hill and hence 'Gurram Konda' a Telugu nomenclature can be literally put as 'Horse Hill' and not 'Horsley Hill'. A wonderful fort atop the hill offers fascinating views of the low lying area. The 'Rangini Mahal' here was the headquarters of the Governor of 'Tipu Sultan' whose name is perpetuated in history, among a number of traits, for his undaunted resistance to the British.

Sompalle: About 37 km from Horsley hills and 50 km from Madanapalle, this beautiful place and its importance can be traced back to the historic Vijayanagar period. The temple here is one of those ancient ones where the grandeur of the Vijayanagar architecture is unfolded. Another temple in the proximity abounds in excellent rock carvings. A soaring monolithic pillar in front of the temple measures upto 46 m in height. The Kalyanamandapam carved out of stone is another attraction.

Arogyavanam: The Union Mission T.B. Sanatorium here is noted for its yeoman service to the suffering lot. It is an asylum to the T.B. struck patients who walk in down-cast and walk out up and about. A 'Post-Graduate Diploma' course in T.B. is also conducted here.

Kanipakkam: About 10 km north of Chittoor, this place is sanctified by a number of ancient temples. The temples reveal the grandeur of the elegant Chola architecture. The temple dedicated to Lord Vinayaka who is always worshipped as the primary deity in all religious rituals and festivals of the Hindus, celebrates a grand festival for seven days before and after 'Vinayakachathurthi Festival'.

The rulers of the Vijayanagar dynasty and the later ones have also made additions to the number of temples of the region.

Accommodation

Tirupathi (STD Code : 08574)

- **Hotel Sindoori Park**, 14-2-118/119, T.P. Area, Thirupathi-517 501. ✆: 256430 (18 lines) Fax: 256438
- **Hotel Bliss (3 Star)** Near Railway Overbridge, Renigunta Road, Tirupathi - 517 501. ✆: 237770, Fax: 237774 E-mail: blisspt@vsnl.com
- **Hotel Guestline Days (3 Star)** 14-37, Karakambadi Road, P.O. Box No. 9, Tirupathi - 517 507. ✆: 280800 Fax: 281774
- **Hotel Mayura (3 Star)** 209, T.P. Area, Tirupathi - 517 501. ✆: 225925 Fax: 225911
- **Bhimas Deluxe Hotel** 34-38, G. Car Street, Near Railway Station, Tirupathi - 517 501. ✆: 225521 Fax: 225471
- **Hotel Bhimas Paradise** 33-37, Renigunta Road, Tirupathi - 517 501. ✆: 237271 Fax: 237277

Godavari

This beautiful district derives its name from the marvellous river Godavari which nourishes many parts of the state with its benevolent waters. This river originates on the Western Ghats at Thriyambakam near Nasik in Maharashtra and takes a long course of 1450 km before meeting its destination, the Bay of Bengal.

The district has a number of places to suit a variety of interests. The serene lakes like the ones at Kolleru, Pakhal and Laknavaram in picturesque surroundings form ideal spots for picnics. These lakes are thickly populated by fish. Otters and alligators are also found. Some of these lakes had fascinated some historic travellers to the extent that they have left behind an alluring description full of encomiums.

There are also numerous ancient temples where grand architectural styles unique to certain region or dynasty and a fusion of the styles of two or more regions or dynasties are unfolded. The sculptures of these temples are of genuine excellence. The stone carvings and rock edicts on the walls of the temples recount a number of awesome events, conventions, customs, practices and legends. A number of royal dynasties have bequeathed in the form of architecture and sculptures myriad monuments of perpetual wonder. These ancient monuments have been revered and treasured generations after generations. The temples make very popular pilgrim destinations. The regions or the city around the temples assume festive colour when thousands of devotees congregate during the periodical festivals.

Thus tourism is a brisk activity in the region.

Kolleru Lake: This enchanting expanse of serene waters which caters to the drinking water requirements of the region has long since been an irresistable invitation to the rare pelican birds and the humans alike. These fascinating birds have made this place an ideal ground for them to nest and procreate. This exotic flock of birds in a picturesque environ is obviously greeted by flocks and flocks of tourists. Mention to this fascinating lake can be found in the writings of the famous Bernier who visited the court of the Mughal emperor, Shahjahan and also toured the entire country including the Golconda Kingdom.

Pakhal Lake: Another beautiful sheet of placid waters, spreading over 12 sq. miles, situated about 50 km from Hanamkonda, the Pakhal lake is surrounded by picturesque sylvan region on three sides and a bund on the other which in fact is responsible for the formation of the lake itself from a beautiful river. This river coursing over an outcrop of the magnificent Vindhya mountains confronts the bund and thereby forms this enchanting enclosure of water. The lake is suffused with fish and also contains otters and alligators.

Laknavaram Lake: About 70 km from Hanamkonda, this lake is contemporary to the Ramappa lake. Three short bunds across three narrow valleys give rise to this beautiful lake. This artificial lake which looks more natural like the Ramappa lake surrounded by the breathtaking beauties of nature leaves a lasting picture in the minds of the visitors.

Rajahmundry: About 581 km by rail from Chennai, on the way to Calcutta, this historic place is of religious importance. Rajahmundry ideally falls on the beautiful banks of the resplendent river Godavari. Overseeing the river are the ancient temples dedicated to Lords Markandeya and Kotilingeswara. This is a famous pilgrim spot.

Legend has it that 'Markandeya' was born to a devout couple after long pleading prayers to Lord Siva who made an offer to them to choose between a sagacious son with a short span of life and a nitwit with of course a long life while they wisely enough settled for the former. Then the Lord granted them their wish and Markandeya who was supposed to live only for 16 years was born. Markandeya as a child was absorbed in his devotion to Lord Siva. The Lord was pleased with his impeccable austerity. When the time came after 16 years, 'Lord Yama', the God responsible for death appeared before Markandeya to take away his life. Frightened, the boy embraced the 'Sivalinga' in unshakable faith when 'Lord Yama' threw one end of His 'fatal' rope with the other end in His firm grip as it always is, in an attempt to encircle the boy while rope fell around Markandeya and the Sivalinga. Anguished, the Lord blazed in before Yama kicking Him away with His Holy foot. Then Lord Siva was pacified when Lord Yama pleaded He was trying to do just what He was supposed to do. Lord Siva, then, not only pardoned Lord Yama but also declared that the benedicted child Markandeya will remain 16 years of age forever. Thus Markandeya became an immortal.

Rajamundry is also a centre for the manufacture of carpets and sandalwood articles.

Badrachalam: Situated about 161 km from Rajahmundry and 300 km from Hyderabad, this holy place has many prehistoric and historic references. The famous ancient temple here dedicated to Sri Seetha Ramachandraswamy is situated on the beautiful banks of the wonderful river Godavari. This popular pilgrim spot is where an estimated three lakh devotees congregate to witness the holy 'Kalyana Mahotsava,' a grand annual festival which is indeed the marriage anniversary of Lord Rama and His consort Goddess Sita. It is believed that Badrachalam was the venue of the divine marriage in the 'Puranic era'.

The legend recounts, Lord Rama manifested here long after He had shed mortal coils, to save a devotee by name 'Badhra Maharishi' and conferred upon him the 'Eternal Bliss', the 'Moksha' and the place came to be known after the Maharishi, as Badrachalam. There is also an allusion that Lord Rama once appeared in the dream of a woman called 'Pokala Damakka' and enlightened her of the existence of the idols of the present temple on the Badragiri hills. Taken by a pleasant surprise on witnessing the idols of the deity on the exact spot as she saw in her dream, she raised a modest structure. This was the origin of this temple.

Later, during the rule of Abdul Hassan Tanashah, in the 17th century, the tahsildar renovated the temple in a grand manner. But as the tahsildar, by name Gopanna, more popular as Ramdas used the revenue money of 6 lakh rupees for the renovation, he was arrested and put behind bars. After about 12 years, Lord Rama appeared in the dream of the king and produced a receipt denoting the due amount in the form of gold coins known as 'Ramamada'. The next morning the Sultan personally rushed to the cell to which Ramdas was confined and set him free. Astonished as he was, the Sultan presented to Ramdas a number of gifts and also his position again as the tahsildar. Stopping not there, the Sultan also declared several grants to the temple which carried on even under the Nizam rule. Some of the jewels presented to the deities here by the ardent devotee Ramdas, which include Kalikiturai Pachala Pathakam, Chintaku Pathakam can be seen in the temple even today.

The temple is situated on a hill top surrounded by 24 smaller shrines. The tranquil temple and its splendid environs make sublime impressions. 48 forms of idols of Lord Vishnu can be seen here. 'Sri Rama Navami', the birth anniversary of Lord Rama and 'Kalyana Mahotsavam' the wedding anniversary of Lord Rama with Goddess Sita are two main festivals here.

Draksharamam: This sacred place situated 17 km from Kakinada and 40 km from Rajahmundry has an ancient tranquil temple dedicated to Lord Siva. 'Sapta Godavari Kundam' or 'Seven Godavari Tank' is the sacred temple tank situated near the temple. The legend has an interesting event as to the naming of the tank.

The magnificent river Godavari known as the Akhanda Godavari or 'unbranched Godavari' was divided into seven smaller rivers here by the 'Sapta Maharishis' or 'Seven Sages' in order to attain the objective of their severe penance. Three of those seven divisions, the Bharadhwaja, the Viswamithra and the Jamadagni are submerged underground.

According to another legend, a king by name Daksha Prajapathi who had been bestowed upon with the coveted divine honour of being the father-in-law of the Almighty Lord Siva, as the Lord had married the King's daughter Dakshayani who was indeed none but a human incarnation of Goddess Parvathi, disdained out of vanity to invite his son-in-law to the 'Mahayagna' a religious ritual which he performed extending cordial invitations to all others. While Goddess Parvathi attended the Yagna though without invitation, in an attempt to straighten up the strained relationship between the father-in-law and the son-in-law, She too was ill-treated. Unable to bear the insult, She subjected herself to self-immolation. Thus the place came to be known as 'Daksha Vatika' which in due course of time transformed into 'Dhraksharamam' which is the present name.

The grand architecture and sculpture in the temple is the result of Chalukya and Chola styles a number of ancient 'Sasanas' or edicts can be seen engraved on the walls. The famous Telugu poet Srinatha who lived in the 4th century is said to have written the famous Bhimakhanada, an epic on this Holy place.

It is also believed that sage Vyasa performed a penance here and called the place 'Dakshina Kasi' or 'Southern Banares'. Pilgrims from far and wide throng the temple during the Sivarathri festival.

The art form 'Veeranatyam' is very famous here. It is believed this place is where Lord Veerabadra was created by Lord Siva out of His Jata-Jhuta, Holy hair.

Ryali: About 25 km from Rajahmundry, this wonderful temple where the presiding deity is Sri Jaganmohinikesava Swamy, unravels excellent sculptures, marvellous architecture and rare iconographs.

Guntupalli: About 44 km from Eluru and 85 km from Vijayawada,

Guntupalli in the western parts of the Godavari district reveals the Buddhist monuments of the olden days. The rock cut caves in the awesome hills, the placid environs and the ancient images of Buddha, Stupas and Viharas render tranquility.

Accommodation

Rajahmundry (STD Code : 0883)

- **Anand Regency (3 Star)** 26-3-7, Jampeta, Rajahmundry, East Godavari (Dist), Rajahmundry - 533 103. ✆: 461201 (4 lines), 465401 (6 lines) Fax: 461204
- **Dwaraka Hotel** Dwaraka Hotel Fort Gate, Rajahmundry - 533 105. ✆: 471851-53.

Krishna

This is another magnificent river, the other one being Godavari, by the name of which a district is known. Krishna has its founts in the robust ranges of the mighty Western Ghats, Mahabaleshwar in the state of Maharashtra. It has a beautiful long course of 1290 km and mingles with the Bay of Bengal. The main tributary of this resplendent river is the ravishing river Tungabadra. Obviously both the rivers are revered as sacred as all rivers and waterways in the nation. All along the benign banks of this beautiful path of serene waters are situated lush green fertile landscape and many ancient cities which retain their pristine beauty even with the foray of modernisation.

The beautiful, ancient and important city of Vijayawada with its scenic hills, historic monuments and sacred pilgrim centres is ideally situated on the beautiful banks of Krishna. The temples and hills have historic and Puranic references. The legends allude the regions here had been the stage of many mythical happenings. There is also a monument built after Mahatma Gandhi.

Kuchipudi in this district is where the gorgeous dance form originated and permeated to every nook and corner of the nation. This dance finds a warm welcome in many a festival, cultural meet, public function and marriage. The place Kuchipudi continues to play patron to the sought-after dance form through its Government run institution.

It is 60 km from Vijayawada. 'Siddendra Yogi', a forerunner who has contributed in leaps and bounds to this divine dance was born here.

'Natyacharya' which offers a five year dance course leading to a degree. Aspirants with a keen bent of mind for the fine art are taught and trained and shaped into wonderful dancers, here.

Kondapalle is where the inspiring toys, dolls and puppets made out of wood originate. It is chiefly a cottage industry practiced by a particular community which migrated from Rajasthan. These articles replete with splendid workmanship adorn the interiors of several homes. The sleightful hands behind their making are worth a million felicitations.

The gorgeous variety of the dolls includes mythical figures, humans, animals, birds, plants, fruits, temples, houses, carts and a host of fictitious figures. This place is about 20 km from Vijayawada.

In and Around Vijayawada

Kanaka Durga Temple: This ancient temple in the beautiful city adds divine significance to the picturesque hill the 'Indrakila'. Goddess 'Kanaka Durga', the presiding deity here manifests in a four foot tall idol with eight mighty arms all holding frightening weapons to destroy the evil. Mahishasura, the demon king can be seen under the Holy feet of the Goddess with Her 'Trident' ripping apart his heart. The Goddess who ravages the demon turns benign and benevolent to the innumerable devotees who have reposed unshakable faith in Her. Every bit of the rich precious jewellery and the beautiful fragrant flowers and festoons seems to emulate one another in adoring the all merciful Goddess.

The temple management has earmarked three points for devotees to have 'Darshan'. The first one is inside the Sanctum-Sanctorum in close quarters to the deity, the second one just outside the Sanctum-Sanctorum and the third, a little further away. 'Lakshakumkum' Archana, a special ritual is part of every day activities. The chanting of 'Manthras', the phrases praising the Goddess and the divine music buoy up the devotees to the higher realms of spirituality.

Legend has it that it was on this Holy hill 'Indrakila', Arjuna, the invincible archer of the great epic 'The Mahabharatha' performed a severe penance and obtained the sacred 'Pasupathasthra' from Lord Siva who appeared in the form of a hunter to test Arjuna's bravery and commitment to the cause and after He was pleased, bestowed upon Arjuna the wish he sought. Hence, this hill also has a temple in which Lord Siva manifests as a hunter.

Visiting Hours: 4:30 - 22:30 (Kanaka Durga Temple)

Archana Hours: 4:30 hrs, 8:00 hrs, 14:00 hrs and 18:00 hrs

The Gandhi Hill: In the heart of the city of Vijayawada, this is a fabulous monument dedicated to the 'Father of the Nation'. A memorial library and a seminar hall can be seen here. Various figures representing cottage industries which the Mahatma had laid repeated emphasis upon, are beautifully reflected on the crimson marbles. Identical images of his house at his birth place Porbandar, his Phoenix Ashram in South Africa, Sabarmathi Ashram at Ahmedabad all along the lavish incline of the hill are vociferous of the austere life style of the Mahatma.

A modest planetarium can also be found here. The observatory here has a telescope and a camera through which the curious visitors peep into the wonders of the firmament.

Maginapudi Beach: About 11 km from Machilipatnam, this beautiful beach which offers copious enchantment to the visitors has also the pride of being part of a historic city. Maginapudi has apparently served more than one purpose in the olden days. Not only as an important commercial centre but as the point of dispersal to various other points of India too, was the city of Maginapudi known for. The beach has a natural bay, comparatively shallow and hence safe waters. To compliment the natural beauty, there are man- made fountains in a conscientiously laid park.

Accommodation is avialable at Machilipatnam. The nearest railway station, Machilipatnam is about 15 km away. The nearest airport which is about 85 km away is at Vijayawada. Maginapudi can also be reached by road from Vijayawada after a 85 km drive.

Mypad Beach: 25 km from Nellore this beautiful beach facing a verdant expanse of vegetation and golden grains of abundant sand attracts a large number of visitors. Mypad has road and rail links with Nellore. The nearest airports are at Thirupathi and Chennai which are about 130 km and 200 km respectively.

Ghantasala: About 21 km west of Machilipatnam and 280 km from Hyderabad, Ghantasala, the excavation site has yielded evidence to reckon it as one of the places where Buddhism flourished. The Buddhist stupa unearthed here has a unique design. 12 constellations of zodiac can be seen engraved on the brick cube set in the centre. Ghantasala can be reached from places like Srikakulam, Vijayawada and Visakhapatnam by Government run busses. Accommodations are available at Vijayawada.

Accommodation

Vijayawada (STD Code : 0866)

- **Krishna Residency,** Rajagopalachari Road, Governorpet, Vijayawada- 520 002. ✆: 575301/ 302, 573197/170, 571571, 572709 (EPABX) Fax: 0866-574373
- **Hotel Ilapuram (3 Star)** Besant Road, Gandhi Nagar, Vijayawada - 520 003. ✆: 571282 (10 lines) Fax: 575251 E-mail: ilapuram@hotmail.com
- **Hotel Kandhari International (3 Star)** M.G. Road, Labbipet, Vijayawada - 520 010. ✆: 471310 (10 lines) Fax: 0866-473962
- **Hotel Mamata (3 Star)** Eluru Road, Vijayawada - 500 002. ✆: 571251, Fax: 574373
- **Hotel Manorama (3 Star)** 27-38-61, M.G. Road, Vijayawada - 520 002. ✆: 572626, 577221 Fax: 575619
- **Hotel Raj Towers (3 Star)** Congress Office Road, Governorpet, Vijayawada - 520 002. ✆: 571311 (10 lines) Fax:571317
- **Quality Inn Dv Manor (4 Star)** M.G. Road, Vijayawada - 520 010. ✆: 474455, Fax: 483170 E-mail: dvmanor@hotmail.com
- **Sree Lakshmi Vilas Modern Cafe** Besant Road, Governorpet, Vijayawada - 520 002. ✆: 572525 (5 lines)

Ananthapur

This district of Andhra Pradesh en capsulates many historic monuments, pilgrim spots and also several modern developments. The ancient forts and temples speak volumes of the splendid architecture and wonderful sculpture. Most of the citadels and forts unravel the grandness and intricacies of the Vijayanagar Empire. These forts encapsulate a number of forts with in and have been built to be self-consistent. Water sources can also be found in some forts. The rugged fort walls have protected the inmates against many fierce battles for long periods. However, in the late part of history some of them have been conquered, saboteured and the treasures inside, ravaged by the invaders.

The Prasanthinilayam at Puttaparthi, the Holy abode of Bhagavan Sri Sathya Sai Baba, is a Heaven on Earth. A number of devotees from all over the world throng the tranquil place. The trust run by Bhagavan Sri Sathya Sai Baba is actively engaged in a number of services to the cause of humanity. The trust run hospital, equipped with state-of-the-art technologies renders free medical service to the deserving and the desolate. The drinking water project put up by the trust quenches the thirst of the entire district including the dry areas which would otherwise be drought-hit most often. The educational institutions which have attained varsity status, moulds young minds and sparks the creative thinking ability of the brain.

The district also has a place to flaunt, which has entered the coveted 'Guinness Book of World Records'. It was in 1989 that the 550 year old tree 'Thimmama Marrimanu' ambled into the record book for being the biggest and oldest of its kind. The ancient tree also commands religious reverence.

Ananthapur is thus a region of diverse importance. There are places and monuments which recount historic and prehistoric events. The architecture and sculpture has reached great heights. The beautiful idols at Hemavathi Temple, made out of translucent stones produce musical chime when dabbed. Tourists of varied tastes find interests to suit their own.

Puttaparthi: This place about 30 km from Dharmavaram and 250 km from Bangalore is sanctified by Bhagavan Sri Sathya Sai Baba. Born in Puttaparthi, Sri Sai Baba is believed to be the reincarnation of Shirdi Sri Sai Baba. Even as a child, Sri Sai Baba displayed sagacity and profound wisdom and amused His playmates with His paranormal powers. As days rolled into weeks and weeks into months and months into years, His power of aura wafted over a very wide region spreading His fame all over the nation and abroad. Devotees flocked to Him in millions and in just a hand's turn he relieved them of their unsurmountable woes. The number of His followers is constantly on the rise. His devotees make a broad variety right from the meek to the opulent. A weekly 'Bhajan' which is the group recital of devotional songs, hymns and verses in praise of Bhagavan Sri Sathya Sai and all other forms of God is customary among His devotees.

'Prasanthinilayam', as it is called, His abode is one of the sacred places where tranquility prevails. The name literally means 'abode of peace'. The tranquility, serene atmosphere, subtle silence are all too compelling for any one to leave the place. In short, it is a Heaven on Earth.

The 'Sathya Sai Baba Trust' whose principal philosophy is 'Service to Humanity is Service to Divinity' renders untiring services to the very cause of humanity through a variety of its institutions, hospitals and projects. The entire Ananthapur district owes innumerable thanks to the trust for its drinking water project which caters to the sweet-water needs of its people. Even the dry belt areas of the district are supplied with sufficient water. The hospital run by the trust has specialist doctors, experts, famous surgeons and also advanced medical equipments which incorporate state-of-the-art technology. What is indeed touching about the hospital is that it offers free service to the desolate and the deserving regardless of religion, caste or creed.

The educational institution here has attained varsity status. It has a unique curriculum which includes special subjects in spirituality, meditation, discipline and impeccable character are imparted as a way of life here. The education received here opens up new creative arenas in the exploring brains of the inquisitive individuals.

The museum on a nearby hillock has models of the Golden Temple of Amritsar, the Holy Mosque at Mecca, etc. The models of these monuments which are the places of worship of people of varied religions corroborate the unity of human race above all diversities.

The planetarium within the premises of the Holy Prasanthinilayam is yet another addition to the attractions here. The planetarium virtually rockets the viewers to the unknown parameters of the mysterious universe.

Lepakshi: Located in between Hindupur and Kodikonda checkpost, about 16 km from the railway station at Hindupur, the beautiful small village Lepakshi has an ancient temple dedicated to Lord Siva. The murals of this temple recount episodes from the life of devotees and Saints. Diverse forms of God can also be seen. Every inch of the temple is an architectural splendour. The grand Vijayanagar style is vivid on the ornate workmanship.

There are references to this temple in 'Skandapuranam' which puts it as one of the 108 exclusive temples dedicated to Lord Siva. Sri Virupanna who was the treasurer at the Penukonda fort of the Vijayanagar empire was instrumental in raising this temple where Lord Siva manifests in the form of Lord Veerabadra.

An astounding feature in this temple is the 'Antarikshastambham' which is indeed a hanging pillar suspended from the roof. The sculptures, pictures and paintings command felicitations to their makers. A gigantic monolithic 'Nandi', the Holy Bull-mount of Lord Siva, measuring 6 ft in height and 8 ft in length, is the biggest of its kind.

The sacred place is obviously an active pilgrim centre. Asvayujamasam, a 10-day long annual festival highlighted by the temple chariot celebrations draws scores of devotees from far and wide. This occurs in the month of February every year. Comfortable accommodations are available for the tourists.

Penukonda Fort: This magnificent fort in the backdrop of a mighty hill which raises to a height of 914 m has been the target of many a historic foray. The ancient inscriptions refer to this fort as 'Ghangari'. The fort today encapsulates the remains of an awesome number of ancient precious monuments some of which have been partly and others completely destroyed by a number of attacks. It is said that there were as many as 365 temples inside the fort. These places of worship and other monuments were ravaged and plundered by the invading Muslim rulers. The remains of these ancient treasures are vociferous of the pain caused by the ruthless destruction meted out to them.

Thimmamma Marrimanu: A place which strikes a strange triangular significance, as a place of religious importance, as a place of picnic and also as a place which has quite justifiably occupied the pages of Guinness Book of World Records is Thimmamma Marrimanu.

It is believed that the huge tree here is named after 'Thimmamma' a saintly woman who was aptly deified by the local populace. The belief also holds that if childless couple worship 'Thimmamma' they would immediately be blessed with a child. The big 'Jatara' conducted during 'Sivarathri' festival attracts thousands of devotees.

Even picnic makers cannot help fancying the spot for its sheer beauty and the grandness of the huge tree whose age is estimated around 550 years.

This ancient living biological treasure entered the coveted book of Guinness World Records in the year 1989 as the biggest tree with 1100 prop roots. It is about 35 km from Kadiri.

Gooty Fort: It is one of the oldest citadels of Andhra. Situated at the mandal headquarters of Gooty, about 45 km from Ananthapur this ancient fort has been in place right from the period of Ashoka to the later British, changing numerous hands in the meanwhile. This mammoth fort resembles a shell in its composure and has 15 parts with 15 gates. A prudent master-plan behind its construction is explicit from the way it has been designed to be self-dependent in all respects including sources of water.

Rayadurg Fort: This is yet another masterpiece of the Vijayanagar empire. The fort ideally located at an altitude of 2727 ft above sea level has many interior forts. The layout and design of these magnificent structures have been so skilfully planned to keep the enemies at bay. There is also a wonderful temple known as 'Dasabhuja Ganapathi Temple' dedicated to Lord Ganapathi.

Here, the principal deity in all Hindu endeavours, Lord Ganapathi manifests with 10 shoulders which is discernable from the name 'Dasabhuja' which means '10 Shoulders'. The Holy image, about 4 m in height, has been sculpted out of single stone.

This fort, about 90 km from Ananthapur, very much in Andhra, is in fact closer to Bellary of the adjacent state Karnataka, which is only 25 km away.

Hemavathi: About 10 km from Amarapuram and 25 km from Madakasira and with Kodikonda on the east, this historic village which was prominent between the 8th and the 10th century AD under the Nolamba Pallavas is where stands the ancient Siva temple where Lord Siva manifests in the form of 'Lord Doddeswara'. The town known as 'Henjeri' during the Pallava reign was later rechristened as Hemavathi. The temple structure is a standing evidence of an ancient architectural excellence. It leaves one in sheer astonishment if one purports to fathom out the hard, meticulous and ethereal workmanship the sculptors of yore should have summoned to bring out such extraordinary sculptures. Amazing more, is the fact that nature had endowed them with such exotic, hard-found rocks, for the idols here are stunningly transparent and produce pleasant metal-like sound when dabbed. 'Rajendra Chola' had probably been so fascinated by the massive pillars with intricate carvings that he had removed as many as 44 of them to adorn the temple at Thiruvedi, which is evident from the inscriptions.

Captivating carvings can be found on the low roof made out of a large stone. A gigantic 'Nandi', the holy bull-mount of Lord Siva, at the ingress measures 8 ft in length and 4 ft in height. The temple wall reflects exquisitely carved human figures while the ornate carvings on the pillars in the enclosed porch depict events from the two great epics 'The Ramayana' and 'The Mahabaratha'. The 'Lingam', the usual form of Lord Siva, in the Sanctum- Sanctorum is a good 6 ft tall.

In another temple here dedicated to Lord Siddeswara, a variation of Lord Siva, the Lord manifests not in the usual Lingam form but in a sitting posture absorbed in deep meditation or 'Thapas'.

The Archaeological Department has established a museum which preserves the ancient idols, sculptures and carvings.

Accommodation

Puttaparthi (STD Code : 08555)

- **Sri Sai Sadan (Meda's Guest House),** Near Venugopalaswamy Temple, Puttaparthi - 515 134. ✆: 87507, 87891, 87892 Fax: 87508 Email: narasimhulu_meda@yahoo.com
- **Hotel Sai Renaissance** Bypass Road, Puttaparthi - 515 134. ✆: 87591-94 Fax: 87324
- **Sri Sathya Sai Towers,** 3/604, Main Road, Post Box No. 2, Prasanthi Nilayam - 515 134. ✆: 87270, 87327, 87368, 87329 Fax: 87302 E-mail: ssthpl@hd2.dot.net.in

Warangal

This district of Andhra is glutted with ancient temples, historic monuments and massive forts. Archaeologists find a bounty here while the layman is awestruck. Historians have a lot to take note of. The archive of the district appeals to historians while the monuments attract archaeologists. The Kakatiya rulers have contributed in leaps and bounds to the glory of the region. The Warangal Fort built by the Kakatiya ruler Ganapathi Deva is a fine example of construction in ingenuity as beyond the forbidding moat all along the outer periphery. There are two walls, the outer one built of mud whereas the inner one composed of rugged stone.

The temple of 'thousand pillars' where each one of them is embellished with conscientious carvings is an ancient specimen of architectural excellence. The Badrakali Temple atop a picturesque hill again reflects the grandeur of Chalukya architecture. The Ramappa Temple reveals what a great connoisseur of art and architecture its constructor had been. Konalupaka had been under the regime of Chalukyas and Cholas as evidenced from the chronicles. A Jain temple here is believed to have been built 2000 years ago.

Since the entire region had been in the middle of many historic events, which is learnt from the monuments and read from the inscriptions, the State Department of Archaeology and Museums has carefully collected these ancient treasures in and around Konalupaka and preserved them in a museum in a chronological order. The museum is open to visitors.

In and Around Warangal

Warangal Fort: This massive fort built by the Kakatiya ruler Ganapathi Deva and his daughter Rudramma is one of the masterpieces of the 13th century. The fort consists of two walls, the sturdy inner one built of stone and the outer one of mud. The fort is also surrounded by moat to offer additional protection. Excellent sculpture and exquisite carvings adorn the remains of the four magnificent gateways built of stone. The ruins provide an insight into the grand workmanship of a marvellous structure.

Thousand Pillar Temple: This ancient temple which stands in ruins now is a telling example of the grandeur of the Kakatiya architecture of the Chalukya rulers. Built in 1163 by Rudra Deva this star-shaped temple comprises 3 shrines, dedicated to Lord Siva, Lord Vishnu and Lord Surya, the 'Sun God'. The temple has a thousand ornately carved pillars. Marvellous sculpture marks the temple all over. The black basalt 'Nandhi', the Holy Bull-mount of Lord Siva is a monolith with a glossy finish. It is a baffling thought that the whole structure with every bit of it intact would look like when even the remnants are so astonishing.

Badhrakali Temple: Atop a scenic hill between Hanamkonda and the city of Warangal, this ancient temple again an outcome of the splendid Chalukyan architecture, is dedicated to Goddess 'Badhrakali', the Goddess of Bravery. Here the Goddess manifests with eight mighty arms all holding threatening weapons to fight evil and protect the noble.

Ramappa Temple: About 70 km from Warangal, this ancient temple known as Ramappa temple or Ramalingeswara temple dates back to 1213 AD. The presiding deity of this magnificent temple which proclaims the greatness and glory of the Kakatiya architecture through every inch of its massive structure is Lord Siva. An inscription in the temple holds that this Holy monument of architectural excellence was built by Rudra Swami on behalf of the then ruler Kakati Ganapathy Deva under whom he was the chief commander. It also conveys, the region was called Ranakude which is now in Atukaru Province and there were temples of Kateswara, Kameswara and Rudreswara, all the three dedicated to Lord Siva.

The pillars with ornamental workmanship and ornate ceilings display scenes from the two great epics 'The Ramayana' and 'The Mahabaratha'. The icons of several forms of God and Goddess, figures of warriors, acrobats and images of beautiful maiden in various dancing postures are the highlight of the sumptuous sculpture found here. The figures made of black basalt carved to a glossy finish are captivating. Every single specimen of the myriad items found here unravels the kind of connoisseur and patron of art the ruler 'Ganapathi Deva' was.

The serene Ramappa lake which offers pleasant excitement is just one kilometre away.

Vemulawada: About 35 km from Karimnagar, this ancient temple is dedicated to Lord Raja Rajeswara, a variation of Lord Siva. The sacred lake here known as Dharma Gundam is believed to have curative properties. The festivals celebrated are Maha Sivarathri and Kalyanotsavam.

Kolanupaka: This historic place was an active religious centre of Jains and the second capital of Kalyani Chalukyas during the 11th century AD. Historic battles kept the village rolling from the hands of Chalukyas to Cholas and then to Kakatiyas. Owing to a number of reasons, the place lost its charm and the Kakatiyas moved their capital to Orugallu near here after developing the place into one fit for the purpose. Now the region abounds in historic monuments, ancient temples, sculptures and paintings of the 10th and the 11th century AD. Kolanupaka is 80 km from Hyderabad.

Jain Temple: The Jain temple here in Kolanupaka contains beautiful images of Thirthankaras. This ancient temple of Saint Mahaveera stands here for 2000 years now. The impressive image of St. Mahaveera is carved entirely out of precious jade.

Sri Veeranarayana Temple: Chalukyan style is reflated on this wonderful temple built around 1104 AD whose countenance allude that it was originally a Jain temple and later converted to the present one dedicated to Lord Vishnu. This is situated in Kolanupaka.

Someswara Temple: This temple at Kolanupaka was constructed by the Kalyani Chalukya emperor Someswara III. Typical Chalukya architecture decorate the structure and the sculpture is a real splendour.

Kolanupaka Site Museum: More than 100 images of the ancient sculptural excellence collected in and around Kolanupaka are displayed in the Museum with a particular emphasis on the grand architecture of the Someswara Temple complex. These monuments recount a great deal from the Chalukyan and the Kakatiyan periods.

Visiting Hours: 10:30 - 17:00 hrs. (No entrance fees)

Kurnool

This district of Andhra Pradesh is also known for its famous ancient temples and pilgrim centres. '**Manthralayam**' which is popular worldwide is situated here. Saint Sri Raghavendra whose 'Brindavan' is at Manthralayam has devotees in every corner of the world. Tungabadra, the tributary of river Krishna flows by the place. The Brindavan of Sri Raghavendra has been established also in several other parts of India.

Ahobilam is where a cluster of three ancient temples can be seen. One of them is dedicated to 'Lord Narasimha', an incarnation of 'Lord Vishnu' who assumes the unique form of Narasimha with a lion's head and a human body. Here all the nine forms of Lord Narasimha are worshipped. The place is also marked by picturesque hills and scenic surroundings.

The Nallamalai forests with a captivating landscape punctuated by hills and replete with typical sylvan flora and fauna also covers historic and pilgrim spots like Srisailam, Mahanandi, etc. Srisailam apart from being the centre of one of the 12 'Jothirlingas' of Lord Siva is also the place of a fascinating wildlife sanctuary.

The unique 'Nava Brahma Temple' is situated at Alamapuram, the place which abounds in legends - Kurnool has everything to appeal to every visitor of every taste and liking.

In and Around Kurnool

Manthralayam: This sacred place is situated on the sumptuous banks of the splendid river Tungabadra which is a tributary of the magnificent river Krishna. This tranquil place is where Saint Raghavendra, a prominent saint in the holy hierarchical order of 'Sri Madhvacharya', shed His mortal coils. The 'Brindavan' here entombs the mortal remains of the saint. The air is filled with divine serenity here. It is believed that the saint exists in His Holy subtle form after he had relinquished the material world and that He will continue to dwell in this form till the point of time which marks the completion of 700 years from the time he attained 'Jeeva Samathi'.

Saint Sri Raghavendra took the 'Dwaita' philosophy promulgated by Sri Madhvacharya to places beyond horizons. 'Dwaita' the philosophy upheld by the Madhva School of thought is one of the three great philosophies, the other two being 'Advaita' and 'Visishtadvaita' promulgated by the Saivaite Saint Sri Adisankara and the Vaishnavite Saint Sri Ramanuja respectively. Saint Sri Raghavendra is believed to be the reincarnation of 'Prahlada', the divine prodigy who as an ardent devotee of Lord Vishnu even in His childhood displayed extraordinary wisdom, impeccable sagacity and untarnished courage against all odds imposed by his demon father Hiranya whom the all merciful Lord killed assuming the Lion-head and human-body form to rid Prahlada of the turmoils He was faced with.

Sri Raghavendra has a lot of devotees belonging to various castes and creeds far and wide as a result of which a number of 'Brindavans' have been established all over the country. These centres of worship follow the tradition unique to Madhva culture. 'Annadhana' or free meals is provided to the devotees every day at Manthralayam and also at certain other 'Brindavans'.

Manthralayam has road links with all major cities. The nearest railway station 'Manthralayam Road' is 15 km away.

Srisailam: About 232 km south of Hyderabad, on the gorgeous banks of the mighty river Krishna, the ancient city Srisailam has fascinating features.

The Bhramaramba Mallikarjunaswamy Temple, dedicated to Lord Siva stands on a picturesque hill amidst the verdant expanse of Nallamalai forest. This ancient temple is enclosed by mighty and tall fort walls. The 'Linga' here is one of the 12 'Jothirlingas' or the 'Lingas of Fire (Light)' in India.

The temple is also the seat of Mahakali in the form of Bhramaramba. The legend has it that Lord Siva and his consort Goddess Parvathi manifested to 'Lord Nandhi' the sacred bull who performed a penance.

There is a lot more to relish. Within the premises there are other antique shrines which include the Sahasra Linga Temple, the Pancha Pandava Temple and the Vatavriksha Temple. The most appealing feature is that the devotees are not prevented from touching the age-old icons and the Holy Feet, an act which they seem to revere as part of worship. Devotees of all caste and creed follow the custom of touching the Holy Feet. The Srikhareswara Swamy Temple is also dedicated to Lord Siva while there is also a temple dedicated to 'Lord Ganesa'.

The Srisailam wildlife sanctuary, part of which falls in Guntur district provides asylum to a large number of rare species. The sylvan region graced by the nonchalantly beautiful creatures attracts visitors from far and wide.

Ahobilam: About 74 km from Nandhyal and 360 km from Hyderabad, the place also known as 'Singavel Kundram' has an ancient temple dedicated to 'Lord Narasimha', one of the incarnations of 'Lord Vishnu' in which the Lord manifests in the form with the head of a Lion and the body of a man to kill the demon-king Hiranya. The interesting feature of this temple is that all the nine forms of Lord Narasimha known as 'Nava Narasimha' are worshipped. The lower Ahobilam is replete with sumptuous sculptures depicting scenes from the ageless epics.

There are also three more shrines not too far-away from one another. One of them forms the sacred crown of the scenic hill while another is situated at the foot of the hill and the third, about 6 km away.

Mahanandi: Situated 320 km from Hyderabad and 16 km from Nandhyal, Mahanandi the divine Bull-mount of Lord Siva is one of the nine exclusive Nandis known as the 'Nava Nandi'. It is ideally nestled in the vast ranges of the scenic Nallamalai hills. The presiding deity here is 'Mahanandeeswara', a manifestation of Lord Siva in the usual 'Lingam' form.

The temple tank is watered by five natural sweet water springs which are astoundingly perennial. The incessant waters from the springs suffice to irrigate 1000 acres of banana plantations.

Alamapuram: The 'Nava Brahma' Temple located at the awesome confluence of the sacred and splendid rivers Tungabadra and Krishna where the former veers as if impatient to meet the mighty Krishna, is one of the grand structures of worship raised by the Chalukyas. The gorgeous architecture and the stupendous sculpture hold the peering eyes fixed upon them.

'Nava Brahma' also draws a different explanation that, according to the legend, these are the names of the medicinal herbs put forth by Rasa Siddhas.

Accommodation

Kurnool (STD Code : 08518)

- **Hotel Raja Vihar Delux (3 Star)** Bellary Road, Kurnool - 518 001. ✆: 20702 (10 lines) Fax: 25097
- **The Mourya Inn (3 Star)** 40/304, Bhagyanagar, Kurnool - 518 004. ✆: 24999 Fax: 48990 E-mail: cyber_cafemourya@hotmail.com

Guntur

Guntur is one of the districts of Andhra where Buddhism flourished. Numerous Buddhist Stupas and Viharas bear testimony to this. The historic cities of the district has been the stage of a number of religious activities of the Buddhism and sequel to this are the ancient monuments and relics which form a weir to the past. The Mahastupa at Amaravathi has massive dimensions. The archaeological museum displays tremendous articles of the profound Buddhist faith. Nagarjunasagar and Nagarjunakonda interest people of varied tastes. The beautiful dam across the mighty river Krishna makes use of its benevolent waters in as many ways as possible probably well aware that Guntur is one of the fortunate districts nourished by the serene waters. This region has some real and touching tales to tell since the region known as Vijayapuri in the antiquity was consumed by the earth beneath. As deciphered from the ancient inscriptions, Buddhism was predominant here and the Mahayana form of Buddhism emerged here and was promulgated by the saint Nagarjunacharya. The beautiful island in the middle of an artificial lake at Nagarjunakonda has a museum which preserves the ancient treasures.

The undulating landscape of the region has also provided homes to a number of widlife species.at the sanctuary in Nagarjunasagar. The verdant expanse of the land and a placid lake on the way to Srisailam promise enchantment.

The ancient temple dedicated to Lord Siva on the river banks, with its grand architecture has an interesting legend associated with it, which says that the Linga was installed by none other than the King of Devas, 'Devendra'.

Vaikuntapuram, as the name alludes, has a temple dedicated to Lord Venkateswara, one of the variations of Lord Vishnu. This cave temple atop a hill offers a pleasant, placid experience.

In and Around Guntur

Amaravathi: About 35 km west of Guntur, this historical place Amaravathi situated on the sumptuous banks of the splendid river Krishna, contiguous to Dhanyakataka, the ancient capital of the mighty Satavahana rulers is replete with evidence to show that it was once one of the platforms of the wide-spread Buddhism. Over two thousand years ago, a Holy Buddhist Stupa stood here overlooking the magnificent river Krishna on its north, measuring about 36.5 ft across and about 29 m in height. The stupa built of special bricks baked in kiln, faced with glossy slabs made of marbles brandishes enviable carvings displaying events from the sublime life of Buddha along the crown of its rotunda and either sides of the railing. Amaravathi is hence, a famous pilgrim centre of the Buddhists.

Amaravathi can be reached by road from Guntur, Vijayawada or Hyderabad which are about 35, 82 and 350 kms respectively. The railway stations at Guntur and Vijayawada are 36 and 82 kms away. The Vijayawada airport is 65 km from Amaravathi. Excellent accommodations are available at Guntur and Vijayawada.

Sri Amareswara Swamy Temple: This ancient temple dedicated to Lord Siva stands on the extensive banks of the enchanting river Krishna. Legend has it that the 'Linga' the usual form of Lord Siva was installed by 'Lord Devendra' the head of 'Devas', at the end of 'Dwaparayugam' one of the four cyclic periods of time, in the order of millions of years.

Archaeological Museum: The fascinating museum at Amaravathi houses extraordinary sculptures. Among the treasured ancient sculptures are the lotus medallions, lotus-carved crossbars of railings, panels depicting Jataka tales, the revered 'Bodhi' tree and devotees in front of it in the act of worship, Dharmachakras and numerous other figures. These relief medallions are fine examples of the gorgeous Indian art. These splendid sculptures span over a long period of time from 200 BC to 250 AD. The Amaravathi School of Art whose products have been taken to Sri Lanka and parts of South-east Asia is marked with a distinction like the Mathura and Gandhara arts.

Vaikuntapuram: About 5 km from Amaravathi, a tranquil cave-temple on a beautiful hill is dedicated to Lord Venkateswara, the presiding deity of the temple at Thirumala Thirupathi in Chittoor district. The legends say that Lord Venkateswara manifested here. 'Vaikuntam' is the Holy abode of the Lord who is a variation of Lord Vishnu and hence the place came to be known as 'Vaikuntapuram'. Recital of Rosary and performance of Pujas is carried out everyday.

Nagarjunasagar / Nagarjunakonda: 'Nagarjunasagar' a beautiful dam across the mighty river Krishna set in picturesque environs serves more purpose than one. This enchanting dam site is the favourite resort of scores of tourists.

'Vijayapuri', the ancient name of the place, the old capital of Ikshvaku Empire nurtured a grand Buddhist civilization as long back as the 3rd century AD. Natural calamities had then buried them alive underground. The initial excavations carried out in 1926 led to more and more as fascinating relics, Mahachaita, the sacred Buddhist stupa, the ramshackle remains of a once sturdy university, vihara, Buddhist Monasteries which had been the sacred abode of many a Monk, 'Aswamedha' the sacred altar on which oblations were offered, exciting prehistoric tools which corroborate ancient ingenuity and the reticent ruins of a number of grand ancient monuments were unearthed. A Brahmi inscription states that the Mahachaita, the sacred stupa encapsulates the holy relics of Lord Buddha.

Nagarjunakonda, a serene island amidst the placid waters of a beautiful artificial lake preserved in a museum, these excavated ageless treasures. It is also learnt that the ancient town was the seat of Mahayana Buddhism, one of the two forms of Buddhism in which Buddha is deified as God the other being. Hinayana Buddhism in which Buddha is regarded as the religious leader or preacher. The Mahayana Buddhism was promulgated by the Saint Nagarjunacharya in the second century AD. A model of the now-submerged valley and its picturesque surroundings can also be seen in the museum.

Nagarjunasagar Srisailam Wildlife Sanctuary: This sumptuous sanctuary, home to a number of fascinating wildlife species spreads over an undulating sylvan landscape ranging between 200 and 900 meters in altitude is surrounded by Mahaboobnagar, Kurnool, Prakasam, Guntur and Nalakonda districts. A scenic lake is also to view on way to Srisailam from Nagarjunasagar.

By road Nagarjunasagar is about 22 km from Macherla, 150 km from Hyderabad and 180 km from Vijayawada. There are regular busses beween Macherla and here. The nearest railway station is at Macherla and the nearest airport is at Hyderabad.

Bottiprolu: This is yet another ancient sacred Buddhist spot of Andhra, situated in the Repalle Taluk, about 320 km from Hyderabad. The 'Mahastupa' here, as holds one of the ancient inscriptions, has yielded several sacred relics of the Buddha. The huge dome of the massive stupa measures to 40 m in diameter. The 2.4 m drum with oblong stone slab panelling, juxtaposed with pilasters is a captivating sight. A fascinating find of the excavation is the three stone receptacles replete with inscriptions, one of which brandished a number of awesome articles such as the blackstone casket, copper beads, precious pearls and ornate jewellery, glittering flowers made of gold, two thin pieces of gold with three pieces of bones, and other jewellery.

Ettipothala Waterfalls: About 6 km northwest of Macherla, this gorgeous waterfalls is created by the mighty river Krishna and the sizzling rivulet Chandravanka which has its captivating confluence with Krishna at a point before the ravishing falls where the turbulent waters fall from a height of 21 metres.

Undavalli: This beautiful location is on the vast banks of the wonderful river Krishna. The enthralling caves of the sumptuous sylvan region with their excellent architecture and sculpture draw a comparison with those of the world famous Ajanta caves. The Vishnukundin rulers of 420 AD are believed to have been closely involved with these magnificent caves.

Pedapulivarru: This place is where the beautiful temple dedicated to Lord Narendreswara Swamy, who is one of the various forms of Lord Siva, is situated. The temple structure has been so ingeniously engineered that the sun's rays fall directly on 'Lingam' at sunrise every Sankranthi day. The temple also has a huge bronze image of Lord Nataraja.

Accommodation

Guntur (STD Code : 0863)

- **Hotel Vijayakrishna International (3 Star)**
Collectorate Road, Guntur - 522 004. ✆: 222221
Fax: 225628

Medak

Medak, again a district known by the name of its headquarters which is about 70 km from Hyderabad on the way to Mumbai has places of varied interests. The church popularly known as Medak Church situated in a scenic region whose construction took 10 long years has an interesting legend associated with it. This massive church which can hold upto 5000 people at a time has wonderful glass windows and splendid paintings illustrating events from the 'Holy Bible'.

This district cannot evade the foraging eyes of archaeologists since a number of antique articles have been unearthed at the excavation site at Kondapur. These articles take one back to 3000 BC.

The 'Bison Range' at Popikondalu is replete with picturesque regions of nature's bounty. The beautiful river Godavari courses elegantly along the valley of the mountains giving rise to serene lakes.This region offers exciting scenery to stand and admire.

Medak comes under the meteorological subdivision Telangana which experiences a pleasant climate from November to February.

In and Around Medak

Medak Church: Medak had once been graced with the glorious Buddhist culture as deciphered from the archaeological excavations here. The captivating region of sylvan beauty is sanctified by the marvellous church built of exclusive white granite in the grand Gothic architectural style. According to a legend, this church with its fabulous stained glass windows was the outcome of the faithful gratitude of a large number of people who had been wailing in a seemingly unsurmountable famine which had its malicious spell for three long years during the World War - I.

The forlorn people took recourse to the Reverend Charles Walker Posnett, a British Missionary. Then, as the Almighty God, pleased by the prayers, provided them food, the Reverend proposed building the church. The proposal was spontaneously hailed and the church thus came into existence, with the conscientious hands of thankful hearts. Started in the year 1914, it was consecrated in 1924 during Christmas.

The roomy church which can hold upto 5000 people at a time has a lot of exciting features. The spiral bell tower rises to a height of 175 ft. The inspiring paintings in the church which had taken the British artist 40 years at his London Studio, recount holy events from the Bible. These pictures with a touch of sheen have been admired over the years by a number of visitors. The window in the north depicts the ascension of Lord Jesus to Heaven and it also forms a canopy to the Altar while the windows on the east and west display various events right from the birth to the crucifixion of the Lord.

Kondapur: About 90 km on the west of Hyderabad, Kondapur is the archaeological site of excavations which has yielded some antique treasures dating back to 3000 BC. Among the articles unearthed were, copper, silver and gold coins and relics of Buddhist, Roman and Satavahana Eras and also limestone sculptures and megalithic graves. Visitors come here to get lost in antiquity.

Popikondalu: The 'Bison Range' here flaunts some bewitching sights. It, in this range, the splendid waters of the magnificent river Godavari join the two districts, Medak and Godavari. The picturesque hills soar at places to a height of 2,280 m above sea level aptly punctuated by gorgeous gorges in between. The benevolent expanse of the verdant forests provides land to vast plantations of teak and bamboo. The mighty mountains contiguous to the ravishing river, open out and close in to form enclosures which give rise to placid little lakes. The delirious scenery leaves a lasting picture of awesome delight in the minds of the visitors.

Medak Fort: About 75 km from Hyderabad, this magnificent fort with five sturdy cascading walls, on a scenic hillock is said to have been built by the Kakatiyas. The hill is encircled by two of the five massive walls. Bastions can be seen at the entrance of each gateway. A flight of steps has been cut on the rocks for access in and out of the fort.

The fort also encompasses, a beautiful grand Mosque built in the 17th

century, a gorgeous palace known as the Mubark-Mahal, granaries where sumptuous heaps of grains were stored and beautiful stone houses which were the residences of the olden military commanders. The gracious incline of the hill is embellished with Hindu-temple carvings. The carving of Kakatiyan emblem 'Gandabherunda', a double-headed eagle can also be seen.

Vishakapatnam

This district owes its name to its headquarters Vishakapatnam which is noted for its importance ever since the historic days. The port city is known for its natural harbour. It is also the centre of a number of maritime activities. The Hindustan Shipyard, India's major shipbuilding and repair yard is situated here.

There are also ancient temples in the district located in picturesque regions. The temple at Simhachalam dedicated to Lord Narasimha was built in the 11th century. A temple dedicated to 'Lord Sathyanarayana' is situated at Annavaram. Scores of devotees undertake a special 'Vow' and perform 'Pooja' here. 'Sathyanarayana Pooja' is performed also at a number of places throughout the nation. 'Ekadasi' festivals and 'Kalyanotsavam' are very famous at Annavaram. The district has nurtured Buddhism in the past, which is overt from the grand monolithic stupas, ancient edifices and rock-cut caves at Sankara. These monuments date back to the 7th century AD. The district thus draws pilgrims to a number of parts.

Picnic makers also have a lot to relish in Vishakapatnam district. The benign Bheemunipatnam Beach which embraces the beauty of the estuary of the ravishing Gosthani river along with the ramshackle fort of 17th century giving a vivid account of ancient Dutch settlement, invites swimming hobbyists with its safe shallow waters. Even the undulating road to the beach makes the journey exciting. The 'Rishikonda Beach' with its vivacious environs attracts skiers, surfers and swimmers.

As the blue waters of Vishakapatnam are enchanting, so are the mountains and valleys. The 'Araku Valley and Borra Caves' draws comparison with the best ghat regions of the world. The gorges here combine the charms of scenic mountains and sizzling rivulets which during showers, gurgling with deluge, seem to play 'hide and seek' in between tunnels. There are also vast coffee plantations. A journey through the sumptuous sylvan region is ever to be relished with fun and frolic.

In and Around Vishakapatnam

Simhachalam: Simhachalam the mighty hill lies about 16 km north of Vishakapatnam. This hill, 244 m above sea level has a temple dedicated to 'Lord Narasimha', the Lion-and-Human-form of 'Lord Vishnu'. The temple rich in architecture belongs to the 11th century in construction. The stone inscriptions hold many important historic events. The deity here is always inundated with fragrant sandalwood paste and has the appearance of a 'Sivalinga'. The 'Chandanayatra' which is a grand festival in March-April is the time to see the deity in 'Narasimha' form.

Government busses ply between here and Vishakapatnam. The nearest railway station and airport are also at Vishakapatnam, 16 km away.

Annavaram: About 72 km from Rajahmundry, 124 km from

Vishakapatnam and 498 km from Hyderabad, the ancient temple here forms the crown of the beautiful hill known as 'Ratnagiri' on the banks of the serene river Pampa. This temple is dedicated to Lord 'Veeravenkata Sathyanarayana Swamy' one of the various forms of 'Lord Vishnu'. By a traditional convention devotees undertake a special vow and perform regular poojas in praise of the Lord here and get their wishes granted.

At an estimated average, about one lakh devotees undertake vow and offer 'Poojas' every year, most of whom are couples. This temple is much opted by many for conducting marriages and the Holy thread ceremony of the Brahmin community. The important annual festivals are Bhishma Ekadasi and Kalyanotsavam in January- February and Vysakha Ekadasi in April-May.

Bheemunipatnam Beach: About 24 km from Vishakapatnam, this fabulous beach is beautified by the enchanting estuary of the ravishing river Gosthani. The entire region of scenic beauty also has the ruins of a 17th century Dutch Fort, which evinces the place was one of the strongholds of the Dutch. An ancient Dutch cemetery can also be seen. This beach is a little different from the other beaches along the east coast in that the sharks which frequent the coastline are not seen here and the waters near shore are relatively shallow, safe for swimming.

Even the travel from Vishakapatnam to this beach would be quite enchanting as the road is undulating all along.

Rishikonda Beach: This is an exciting beach about just 8 km from Vishakhapatnam. This beach has lovely settings and interests swimmers, water skiers, wind surfers and layman alike.

Sankara: About 3 km from Anakapally and 40 km from Vishakhapatnam, this historic place 'Sankara' interests archaeologists and amazes the common man. The grand Buddhist stupas of this place are monolithic. The ancient edifices and the serene rock-cut caves are reminiscent of a splendid architecture of a bygone era. The brick clad main stupa here was first carved out of rock. These monuments date back to the 7th century AD.

Araku Valley and Borra Caves: This fascinating valley lies about 127 km from Vishakapatnam. The undulating ghat road here rises to a height of 1168 m above sea level and climbs down flanked by mighty mountains and fabulous scenery to Araku Valley which is itself about 975 m above the sea level. This vast expanse of sylvan beauty is inhabited by tribal community.

About 90 km from Vishakapatnam this beautiful village Borra offers a sumptuous feast to the eyes. A ravishing rivulet here becomes a deluge during heavy downpour and disappears into the limestone caves only to emerge again about 100 m below in a gorgeous gorge. This game of 'Hide and Seek' played by the sumptuous Nature obsesses the mind with delight. A large congregation of the locals can be seen on the festival day of 'Sivarathri'. The journey from Borra to Araku valley is exhilarating, which is 30 km of sheer pleasure. The entire region is rich in flora and fauna and also in fertile and pasture lands. The Anantagiri slopes near here are redolent of its rich coffee plantations.

Accommodation

Vishakapatnam (STD Code : 0891)

- **Taj Residency (5 Star)**, Beach Road, Vishakhapatnam - 530 002. ✆: 2567756, Fax: 2564370 E-mail: trhgm.viz@tajhotels.com
- **The Park (5 Star)** Beach Road, Vishakhapatnam - 530 023. ✆: 754488, 755185 Fax: 754181 Email: resv.viz@theparkhotels.com
- **Dolphin Hotels Limited (4 Star)**, Daba Gardens, Vishakhapatnam - 530 020. ✆: 567000 (27 lines) Fax: 567555
- **Daspalla Hotels Limited (3 Star)**, 28/2/48, Surya Bagh, Vishakhapatnam - 530 020. ✆: 2564825 Fax: 2562043 E-mail: daspalla@andhranet.net
- **Daspalla Executive Court**, 10-50-1/C, Waltair Main Raod, Visakhapatnam - 530 002. ✆: 2717300 Fax: 2717444 Email: decvizag1@rediffmail.com
- **Raj Residency**, 9-1-227, C.B.M. Compound, Opp. Rama Talkies, Vishakhapatnam - 530 003. ✆: 566666, 755797 Fax: 501136
- **SaipriyaResorts**, Beach Road, Rushikonda, Vishakhapatnam - 530 045. ✆: 815584/815284/816345/816282 Fax:815344 Email: prasaddrk@rediffmail.com
- **Green Park (3 Star)**, Waltair Main Road, Vishakhapatnam - 530 002. ✆: 564444, Fax: 563763 E-mail: vizag@greenpark.com
- **Hotel Meghalaya (3 Star)**, Asilmetta Junction, Vishakhapatnam - 530 003. ✆: 755141-145 Fax: 755824
- **Welcomgroup Grand Bay Sheraton (3 Star)**, 15-1-44, Nowroji Road, Maharanipeta, Vishakhapatnam - 530 002. ✆: 560101, Fax: 550691
- **Welcomgroup Grand Bay (3 Star)**, Beach Road, Visakhapatnam - 530 023. ✆: 560101 Fax: 550691
- **Hotel Prince**, 30-12-16/17, Ranga Street, Daba Gardens, Vishakhapatnam - 530 020. ✆: 747675-79 Fax: 747674
- **Hotel Prasanth Balaji Soudha**, Poorna Buildings, Main Road, Vishakhapatnam. ✆: 526948
- **Hotel Jyothi Swaroopa** 47-11-2, Dwarakanagar, Vishakhapatnam - 530 016. ✆: 748871/75, Fax: 741040
- **Palm Beach Hotel**, Beach Road, Waltair Uplands, Vishakhapatnam - 530 001. ✆: 754026/27

Mahbubnagar

Alampur: This historic place on the banks of the beautiful river Tungabhadra is replete with ancient monuments particularly with those of the Chalukyan era. The temples are rich in excellent architecture and sculpture. The beautiful Sikaras of these temples are of a curvilinear form inundated with astounding architectural workmanship. The miniature pillars, niches, windows, and amlakas deserve a special mention. The layout, architecture and the stone carvings bear a close resemblance to those of the Buddhist and Brahmanical caves of Western India. APTDC offers accommodation. Mahbubnagar district is adjacent to Hyderabad.

Nellore

Udayagiri: Udayagiri, in Nellore district which is an integral part of coastal Andhra, was formerly a fortified town. The once magnificent fort which had about 13 distinct strongholds stands now in ruins. The tantalising hill with its elegant cliffs, which at places are 305 m high, present a beautiful sight. In the 14th century, this place saw the birth of a new kingdom founded by Langula Gajapathy who made it the capital. The hill is topped by an ancient Mosque whose construction, according to the Persian inscriptions inside, was in 1660.

Pulicat Lake: This is a saltwater lake in a beautiful bird sanctuary which spreads over an area of 461 sq. km near Tada, Nellore district. This sanctuary is the seasonal hangout of about 75 species of birds.

Accommodation

(STD Code : 0861)

- **D.R. Utthama Days Inn**, 23/976, Dhandayudha Puram, Nellore - 524 003 ✆: 317777 (10 lines) Fax: 317813 Email: daysinn@pol.net.in
- **Hotel Murali Krishna (3 Star)** Beside Leela Mahal, V.R.C. Centre, Nellore - 524 001. ✆: 309030-37 (4 lines) Fax: 321137
- **Hotel Shivam International (3 Star)** 18/1, Achari Street, Nellore - 524 001. ✆: 320320 Fax : 348999
- **Hotel Simhapuri (3 Star)** Railway Station Road, Nellore - 524 001. ✆: 327040-45

Nalgonda

Yadagirigutta: Nalgonda district, about 70 km from Hyderabad, like Medak, falls in the Telengana region in the meteorological classification, where pleasant climate can be experienced between November and February while April and May, the peak of summer, are scorching. Humidity is high from July to September.

Yadagirigutta, the famous pilgrim centre is beautifully nestled among numerous blue hills. The temple here is dedicated to 'Lord Lakshminarayana', a variation of Lord Vishnu.

Legend has it that Gandaberunda, Yogananda and Jwala, three of the nine aspects of Lord Vishnu are manifested here. An oil lamp burns eternally to mark the manifestation of Jwala or Light. It is also believed that worshipping the Lord at this shrine is the panacea to cure all malicious diseases.

Prakasam

Chandavaram: Located in Prakasam district, Chandavaram, about 50 km from Vijayawada is also one of the historic places where ancient Buddhist monuments can be seen. This beautiful place is also an excavation site where over 30 exquisitely carved limestone panels were unearthed. These panels were once the ornate decorations over the dome of a 'Stupa'. The unique stupa on a picturesque hillock known as the 'Sinkarakonda' which literally means 'beautiful hill' overlooking the ravishing rivulet 'Gundlakaa' has two terraces and draws comparison with the famous Dhararajaka Stupa at Taxila. There are also several other smaller stupas and a Monastery complex in the proximity.

Government buses ply between here and Vijayawada where accommodations are available.

Accommodation

- **Sri Venkateswara Hotel** Ongole Road, Giddalur, Prakasam - 523 394. ©: 42100
- **Sid & Dip Beach Resort** Vadarevu, Prakasam - 523 394. ©: 08594-48222